M...
of Glasgow in 1948, the youngest and only girl
of three child... Thereafter she lived in the
Blackhill... **...RE COUNCIL**
ci... ...e last date stamped below.

...
...
...

th...
Service O...
to live on a Scottish island ...ame an adoptive
and a foster parent. Over the years she had 'kept
her hand in' by writing the occasional newspaper
article and when she gave up fostering she decided
to write full-time. She now lives with her husband
on the East Coast of Scotland.

Finding Peggy:
A Glasgow Childhood

Meg Henderson

CORGI BOOKS

TRANSWORLD PUBLISHERS
61–63 Uxbridge Road, London W5 5SA
A Random House Group Company
www.rbooks.co.uk

FINDING PEGGY
A CORGI BOOK : 9780552141857

First publication in Great Britain
Corgi edition published 1994

A CIP catalogue record for this book
is available from the British Library.

Addresses for Random House Group Ltd companies outside the UK
can be found at: www.randomhouse.co.uk
The Random House Group Ltd Reg. No. 954009

The Random House Group Limited supports The Forest Stewardship
Council (FSC), the leading international forest certification organisation.
All our titles that are printed on Greenpeace approved FSC certified paper
carry the FSC logo. Our paper procurement policy can be found at:
www.rbooks.co.uk/environment.

Typeset in Linotype Plantin 11/12pt by
Hewer Text Composition Services, Edinburgh.
Printed in the UK by CPI Cox & Wyman, Reading, RG1 8EX.

14 16 18 20 19 17 15

FOR

Nan, Peggy and George Clark,
Peggy's children and grandchildren,
and
The Clarks and the O'Briens

Also for my husband Rab, who knows why,
and our children,
Euan, Lisa and Debbie.

Acknowledgements

Willie McIlvanney
for years of encouragement and arguments.

Lynne Reid Banks
for years of encouragement and nagging.

John Saddler
for recognising the story before I did.

also

Bill Black, Radio Clyde
Dr A. Cameron MacDonald
Sean Damer
Tony Martin
The School of Scottish Studies,
Edinburgh University
Marion Zelukin
and my cousins:
Anne Caldwell
Vicky Clark
James Kelly
Nessie Robertson

Prologue

My life has been shaped by two women, who, in my childhood, instilled in me the values I still live by: my mother, Nan, and her sister, my Aunt Peggy. Although these days I earn my living as a journalist and TV documentary maker, working and mixing with media high-fliers and household names, I was born and brought up in the poorest and toughest areas of Glasgow. As I was growing up I wasn't aware of how much Nan and Peggy had influenced me, but the truth is that I bear their stamp, and the older I get the clearer this becomes and the more grateful I am for it.

We were three sides of one tightly-bound triangle from the day I was born, so that it was impossible to think of one without the other; prick one and we all bled. Nan and Peggy were bright, vivacious, vital women, always on the verge of laughter or tears and usually both. They lived on their emotions and acted on instinct, they knew no other way. When I think of them today I picture them laughing helplessly and holding on to each other for support, their faces awash with tears as they struggled to remember why they had been laughing in the first place. Somehow I always picture them laughing.

Nan and Peggy Clark were strong women in that they believed in things, they had ideals and shared a dream of how life should be. This dream was entirely non-political, but it was in essence what started the Labour Party, though I'm sure they would not recognize what has evolved as the Labour Party today as anything to do with them. They believed completely that people were good and honourable and that everyone was of equal worth; indeed it never occurred to them that this wasn't universally accepted. Looking back there was something naive about that, and given the hard lives they had

9

it is difficult to understand how they could have sustained such a belief. But there is something heroic and admirable about it too, painfully so, as my story reveals.

Peggy's sudden death at the age of thirty-six brought an end to the family as it had been; unable to deal with what had happened the Clarks simply fell apart. My mother became a recluse within months and my childhood ended abruptly as I had to take care of her. I never knew the exact details of how Peggy had died, except that there had been something especially awful about it, and the family found it too painful to explain.

It seemed that Peggy, so long an intregal part of me, had simply vanished without trace and even mentioning her name was frowned upon by the Clarks. Losing her devastated and scarred my life and with my mother's withdrawal I was suddenly alone for the first time, one fragile side of the triangle that had existed for ever. Within a short time Peggy's children went into care, and added to the confusion and the grief was guilt. We all felt it but were unable to express it because none of the Clarks connected anymore.

Much of my adult life has been spent fostering and adopting sometimes very damaged children and I can now see why I did that. When asked I would give what I truly believed were my reasons and I would use all the correct sociological jargon to explain. But the truth lies in the events of my childhood and in the guilt about Peggy's children. I was trying to reclaim her children over and over again.

All through my life I kept Peggy in my mind and in my heart. Though I knew she was dead, the Clarks' reaction had blocked the normal processes of grieving and healing. No one had ever explained her death to the child I was then, so how could I truly believe it? That was why in some secret place inside me I kept alive the fantasy that one day I'd look up and she'd be there beside me again, as she had been when I was a child. As time passed and I married and settled down, I realized that I would never find peace until I knew what had happened to her and why, and though more than twenty years had passed I managed to piece the story together. What I found out was shocking and tragic and terrible, not just because it happened to Peggy and my family, but because it could have happened to anyone. I understood for the first time how vulnerable working-class women were, and still are.

The other side of the experience, however, was that I also appreciated for the first time the extraordinary worth of the ordinary people I grew up among, especially the women, like Nan and Peggy. They are part of the unacknowledged history of working-class women. They didn't make speeches or form trade unions, they just kept their families alive against all the odds, they survived and ensured our survival.

All through my childhood I watched my mother fight highly effective campaigns to right wrongs, and to that end she valued education and knowledge. Education and knowledge equalled power, power to right more wrongs for those unable to do so themselves, power to change the way she and Peggy had been raised. Nan was the doer, the articulate, literate one, and Peggy, shyer and quieter, provided the back-up. Together they were a strong team, unable to accept that there was an alternative to what was Right, unable to refuse help to those who had been wronged. But caring exposes you to all sorts of hazards, and for the two sisters the cost, inevitably, was high.

Above all they provided me with a blanket of love and caring that has touched every corner of my life and covers me still. I didn't realize how important they had been in life, because like most people I simply accepted what I had grown up with. Until, that is, a conversation I had with a film producer I was working with. I mentioned that I had grown up in Blackhill and Drumchapel in Glasgow, two of the city's black spots and regarded by those who know nothing about life in either place as the far end of the moon. 'Well,' he said, clearly shocked, 'You've left that well behind!'

When our condemned tenement in the centre of Glasgow collapsed in 1952, three generations of my family were rehoused in Blackhill, a council estate three miles to the east of the city. It had a reputation for deprivation and violence that follows it to this day, and those sent to live there knew in advance that there was little likelihood that they would ever get out again. Blackhill wasn't so much an attempt at rehousing slum-dwellers as a judgement that they didn't matter; Blackhill was a life sentence.

With my mother, father and two brothers, I did get out though; as part of the inner city clearances in the 1950s, we moved to Drumchapel, a new estate five miles to the west. It was happening all over the country after the Second World War, vast housing estates, or schemes, were built and were optimistically regarded by the people who were sent to live in them as the first step to the good life. Extended families like ours, who had lived within doors of each other for several generations, were split up and sent to different estates, in the expectation of a bright new future. For my mother too, always chasing her dream, the move to Drumchapel heralded a better life for her children.

But Glasgow seized the opportunity to show the rest of the country how not to do it. The heart was torn out of the city as ghettoes were built to replace ghettoes; devoid of any amenities to make decent life sustainable, the new estates quickly became as rundown as the old. For the people who lived in them the situation was compounded by the loss of the support network provided by their extended families, by the loss of their roots.

My film producer meant it as a compliment that I had left Blackhill and Drumchapel well behind, but as I thought it over I saw that he was wrong. It made me think about my childhood and examine what and who had shaped it, who had enabled me to work with, and shock, film producers.

The people of Blackhill and Drumchapel remain a part of me and I of them; I have no need to leave them behind. To deny them would be to deny the two women who raised me. For now I see that without them I wouldn't be where I am today or be who I am. This then is the story of the family I grew up in and the tragedy that almost destroyed it. It's the story of my search for the truth of Peggy's death, of how I lost her and found her again. Much more than that though, it's about Nan and Peggy. Despite everything that happened they weren't destroyed; their values, their ideals have survived. And that I suppose is why when I think of them it's not sadness, sorrow or bitterness that come instantly to mind, it's that joyous picture of them laughing. They won in the end.

Chapter One

On the day I was born, so the story goes, there was a storm, so someone, somewhere, must have had an inkling. It was May 1948, I was part of the post-War baby boom and as my father was fond of relating, on that particular day, the 10th, Winston Churchill was given a medal by the Germans. I analyzed that thought countless times over the years but I never did find the connection. He was fond of linking unlikely events though, and often told me that his mother had died on his sixteenth birthday. All my life I was fascinated by that fact; even for the O'Brien clan, my father's family, it seemed a somewhat bizarre gesture for her to have made. He also liked it to be known that he had been born on the Feast of the Holy Innocents, a coincidence that was more apposite than he ever realized.

His name was Laurence Thomas O'Brien and he was called after a friend of his father's, a Frenchman who had ended up in a lunatic asylum. He would relate this with relish, then cackle madly to himself. We called my father's family 'the O'Briens', as though they were a thing apart, an alien entity to be categorized as a collective but separate genus, which they were. My father, the youngest in his family, was known to the O'Briens as 'oor Laurence', and to my mother as Laurie, to annoy the O'Briens, but to the rest of the world he was Skipper, or Skip. He had once proclaimed himself to be the Skipper of the good ship O'Brien, and the name had stuck.

My mother's name was Joan Henderson Clark, but she was known as Nan, and reluctantly as Mrs O'Brien. She wasn't exactly honoured to be part of 'they mad Irish pigs', as she called her in-laws. At this term of endearment Skip always gave another insane cackle, as though to prove her point.

Though Nan stood a fraction over five feet tall I weighed in at 10lb. 3oz., which must have been a considerable relief to her because six years earlier my brother Laurie had weighed 14lb. 6oz. Five years before that, as our brother, Mickey, liked to say of himself, the daintiest of the O'Briens had been born, a mere stripling of 9lb. 8oz.

I was blue when I arrived, which was put down to my being cold, so I was placed in a drawer and put beside the fire. It was years before I discovered that in fact I had been suffering from a fairly common condition where the closing of a flap of skin over a normal opening in the feotal heart is delayed. But I suppose the extra heat did me no harm on a cold, windy day. Though my mother said I was born on a Monday, it was in fact a Thursday, not that she ever accepted this. She had her own thing about dates. For instance, she was inordinately proud of her fertility and was happy to tell anyone who would listen that she had been married on 17 July and had Mickey on 20 July. In an era when such things mattered, she omitted to say that her marriage and the birth of her first born had been separated by a year. My father would just smile with sly humour and never once corrected her.

She was eighteen years old when she had Mickey, after walking out of the maternity hospital at Glasgow's Rottenrow because no one was bothering with her. She walked the mile back to our house at 21 Balmano Street and had him and, in later years, Laurie Junior and me, at home among her family. Her mother, my grandmother, called Maw Clark by everyone, was at my birth, as she was at my brothers' and all my cousins' births too.

I was called Margaret Anne O'Brien. Anne was Maw Clark's name and every female child had it bestowed upon them like an indelible stamp of ownership. Call 'Anne!' at a family gathering and a stampede started, but I was lucky, it was only my middle name. I was named Margaret in honour of my mother's younger sister, but it was her 'Sunday best' name; she was known all her life as Peggy.

To save a stampede of two I was called Rita by the family. Though I tried to get an explanation of why Peggy and I had the same name but were called something else, I never got it. Whenever I asked, my mother would immediately be engulfed in a disabling spasm of laughter that would then infect Peggy, so that the two of them would cling to each other for support while furiously mopping their eyes.

Skip had wanted me called after his mother, Mary Ann O'Brien, but Nan, in another fit of logic, pronounced it 'too Irish'. The truth was that her sons had been called after the O'Briens and she was damned if her daughter would be too. Naming me was one of the small victories she delighted in winning over my father's family.

We lived at 21 Balmano Street which stood at the top of Balmano Brae, so the street was known simply as the Brae. It towered above the city centre, on top of the steepest hill in Glasgow, a grey-stone tenement four storeys high. Underneath it ran old mineshafts and train tunnels leading into Queen Street Station. Each of the eight houses was the same: a room and kitchen, with a toilet outside on a landing down a flight of stairs that was used by two families. There were no bathrooms and no hot water; kids, and sometimes adults, too, washed in front of the fire, standing in a tin bath filled laboriously with water boiled on the kitchen range. A proper bath could only be had by using the public baths a couple of miles away.

The kitchen also served as a dining-room / sitting-room and it was where my parents slept. Along one wall was a set-in bed which was covered during the day by a curtain, and there was a further bedroom where my brother Laurie and I slept and where Mickey would have slept too if he hadn't spent years in hospital. He had TB in his knee-cap and since before I was born he had been in Mearnskirk, a hospital set in the open countryside, fifteen inaccessible miles to the south of Glasgow city centre. I grew up with him only as a name. Mickey was something or someone my parents and the rest of the family visited, but no-one ever explained who or what Mickey was, let alone that he was my brother. As far as I was concerned I had Laurie, who was six years older than me, and all my cousins, that was all.

There were seven families in 21 and the Clarks lived on the top storey until the children left to get married. By the time I was born only Peggy lived in the family home with Maw Clark. Next door to them my mother's widowed sister Mary lived with her son David; and my parents, two brothers and I had a house on the first. I have very few memories of the Brae, just feelings and impressions. First of all there was the closeness; I felt that all the families who lived there, the McCreadies, the Fitzgeralds, the Turnbulls and the rest, were my family too, because I knew them equally well. So when Nan and Skip visited Mickey in hospital, Laurie and I were cared for by everyone in the Brae. And there is an impression of the old buildings crowded around 21, the winding, narrow, covered lanes, or closes, of Townhead and Rottenrow that led to cramped, dark houses with several generations of families living in them. I had aunts, uncles and cousins living all around, because news of empty houses was passed by word of mouth by families who preferred living near to each other. So we could safely walk into any house in the area, because if it didn't belong to a relative it belonged to a friend. Skip's family had stayed near by in Tarbet Street, so we lived in an area of Glasgow where both sides of our family had been for two generations. It was our own enclosed little world.

I wasn't aware of the Brae's crumbling stonework or any other negative aspect, to me it was just home. But the living conditions were unhealthy and the tenants had been waging a long campaign, led by Nan, to be rehoused. Apart from the obvious overcrowding, with most families having three or more children, there was a constant battle against the bugs that were taking over the delapidated building. In October 1950 Glasgow Corporation had shored the tenement up on one side in an attempt to arrest gradual subsidence and the tenants of 21 were told to be ready to move out at any time. To the inhabitants of the Brae this clearly meant that they would move into a better tenement *en masse*, that they would remain together wherever they moved to, which was what they wanted. They wouldn't, however, be considered for new homes, they were told in a classic example of bureaucratic speak, until they were actually homeless. As a very small child I was unaware of all this, my reality was that I lived happily in a large family that took in all the streets around the Brae.

But of course all was not harmony, no family ever is, and as I grew I became aware of the divisions and sub-divisions that made up mine. I was nearer in every way to Nan's family, the Clarks, and gradually I absorbed the rules that governed Clark life. They were a close family and outsiders were never aware, to my knowledge, of the two 'sides'. There were the 'Fair Yins', those like Maw Clark who had fair hair and blue eyes, and the 'Dark Yins', who had the dark hair, eyes and skin of Da Clark, my grandfather. The 'Fair Yins' stuck together on all counts and were favoured by Maw Clark, and the 'Dark Yins' kept to their group and had the special affection of Da Clark. Yet there was no animosity between my grandparents, in fact Maw spoke of her husband with nothing but affection; still the two groups grew into adulthood regarding each other with deep suspicion. No 'Fair Yin' ever sided with a 'Dark Yin' or vice versa in inter-family matters. Much plotting went on, discussions about the motives and actions of the others and plans to subvert them were food and drink to the Clark factions.

And they were very different in character too. For instance, Vicky, Mary and Willie, the 'Fair Yins', loved to have a good time, something they shared with Maw. They went dancing, were known to drink alcohol and smoke cigarettes; Vicky and Mary even had their ears pierced. Nan, Peggy and George came from the other side and were altogether more circumspect. The 'Dark Yins' had very definite ideas of how to behave, which meant with decorum at all times – good manners were high on their list of priorities. The most damning comment my mother could ever make of anyone was to pronounce them common, and she could encapsulate every

17

possible shade and nuance of disapproval in to that one word.

Maw Clark was a strong personality and she cunningly ruled her children by keeping them divided. She would complain to one group of some supposed neglect or snub by the other and they would rush around competing to do things for her. If that didn't work, she had the ability to bring herself to death's door at will, which never failed to bring the entire family to her bedside. Once she had their full attention she would stage yet another miraculous recovery and my childhood was studded with her death-defying performances. There was a feeling that the 'Dark Yins' were constantly striving for her approval, which they never did get, and in the process they became do-gooders, ever ready to take the side of the underdog and to do the right thing. It was as though they felt they were out of favour because they had disappointed Maw and had to make up for it in whatever way they could.

They had a high regard for education and were always keen for their children to do well at school. They wanted a better life for the next generation, not in strictly financial terms, but in terms of status too. A good job wasn't one on an assembly line making a lot of money, it was one that allowed you to get on, to contribute something, to be somebody and to win respect by helping other people. This was directly at odds with the philosophy of the 'Fair Yins', who regarded their siblings as getting above themselves; that kind of thing wasn't for the likes of them.

The exception to the family rivalry was Willie, who outwardly qualified as a 'Fair Yin' but who had dreams for his kids too and wanted them to be bright. Despite his looks, a dark gene had inadvertently sneaked in at Willie's conception, rendering him loved but distrusted by both sides. Willie was everybody's friend, eternally stuck in the middle, though he'd go with his own group when the chips were down, always hoping not to be told any secrets because he knew he couldn't keep them. 'Don't say anythin' in front o' yer Uncle Wullie, hen,' Nan would tell me, 'It's no' his fault, bit thu'll get it oota him.'

18

As Nan's child I was counted as a 'Dark Yin' too. This meant that I absorbed the need to always be on my guard with the 'Fair Yins', to be careful what I told them, and that extended to their children too. It was assumed by each side that the other's children were attempting to extract information and we would be debriefed after every family gathering about what had or hadn't been said. It's a conditioning that exists still, when we're all old enough to know better, and to this day I'm more at ease with my 'Dark Yin' cousins.

As I grew the other differences became clearer too. The Clarks were Protestant and the O'Briens Catholic, that was the biggest, all-encompassing difference. Maw Clark was known to be a bitter Orange woman with an illogical hatred of Catholics, so what it must have done to her psyche that more than half of her grandchildren were Catholics can only be imagined. Of her children, Nan, George and Vicky had married Catholics, which of course meant they had to agree to their children being raised as Catholics too. I had no idea that I was a Catholic and wouldn't have understood had I been informed anyway, but from as early as I can remember I felt a tension in the family that went beyond being the child of a 'Dark Yin'.

All small children stick closely to their mothers during the first few years; fathers are optional extras, which is probably why I have no memories of Skip then. He was working as a bus conductor for Glasgow Corporation Transport Department when I was born and I vaguely remember playing with his badge. My mother and Peggy are the the ones I recall best. Their faces often merge into one as I look back, so I suppose that's how they seemed when I was little. They looked so alike anyway that outsiders were often unsure which was which, though they knew they were different people. So Nan would answer when called Peggy and Peggy would answer when called Nan, it was easier than explaining. To me they were beautiful women – whenever I hear the word 'bonnie' I think of them. They were in constant touch through what I suppose was telepathy and

I clearly remember them finishing each other's sentences or answering questions that hadn't been asked aloud. To me it was perfectly acceptable because it was there all my life. If they went out shopping alone they invariably returned with identical items and if they went out together they swapped whatever they bought anyway. This produced the characteristic Clark laughter, a helpless, almost soundless shaking accompanied by lashings of tears. They would hold on to each other and stumble about creaking with laughter, mopping uselessly at their streaming eyes. They told me endless stories of their family, the tales dissolving into the Clark laughter at the funny parts, or into tears of sorrow at the sad parts.

They had been particularly fond of their father, Da Clark, as he had been of them, and it was one of their greatest sorrows that he died before I was born. I think because we three were so close, it seemed 'no' right' to them somehow that we had no shared memories of him. Somewhere in the telling of the current story one of them would look at me, sigh and say, 'Oh, bit Da widda loved you!' and then the two of them would burst into tears. After a few minutes of communal grief one or other of them would say, 'Whit a daft perra buggers we ur! Look at the state o' us!' And they would then start laughing. This of course produced more tears and as they clung to each other one of them would say, 'Noo whit wur we laughin' at?' As though finding the cause would help them eradicate the effect. 'Look at that poor wean! She disnae know whit's gaun' oan!' But I did. I would watch them enthralled, a show in themselves that I never tired of seeing. Their performances were so memorable that Da Clark was ever-present in my life, he was real and alive to me because they kept him so.

Da Clark was the son of a Borders farmer and had run away from home when the farm horses he had cared for all his life were sold to the Glasgow Police. He was found sleeping in the hay beside the horses in the police stables in Bell Street and was promptly thrown out. For much of his teenage years he survived as and where he could, and in the process acquired 'a bad chest'. His family made one attempt to bring him home by sending one of his brothers to find him. Once released from the farm, the brother decided to remain in Glasgow too, and neither of them ever went home again. The brother worked in the Camp Coffee Factory, and though I have no memory of ever seeing him, I do recall that Camp Coffee was ever-present in all Clark cupboards.

Da Clark became a docker; I remember once seeing a photo of him at work, a tiny man with a huge black moustache, the inevitable bunnet, or flat cap, on his head and his shirt-sleeves rolled up; he hardly looked strong enough for the hard lifting that dockers had to do in those days. My mother used to tell stories of his breathing troubles, of how in summer he had to sit upright all night beside the window, trying to catch a decent breath, but still he went to work every morning. By all accounts he was a kind, if strict, father who worked hard and was fonder of his 'Dark Yins'. He fought incessantly with Willie, who being Willie never fought back, but just laughed in his good-natured way and merrily agreed that he was a waster who would never achieve anything.

The story goes that during the Second World War Da Clark lay unconscious and dying in Duke Street Hospital, with George, his eldest, still missing presumed dead. In the middle of the night the heavy tramp of army boots echoed through the hospital, coming ever nearer to the ward where the females of the family sat vigil by Da's bed. He opened his eyes, shouted 'George!' with great joy, and died before Willie walked in, dressed in his Highland Light Infantry uniform, having somehow managed to get home on leave. Strange that the one who caused Da the greatest annoyance should have been the one to let him die happy, but every time I heard this story as a child I wondered how Willie really felt about this crushing story against him.

After the war, with George safe and sound, it was Willie who took the badge and followed Da Clark into the docks. Da was fifty-five when he died, which seemed incredibly ancient to me as I listened to these stories in my childhood, but of course it was very young – and seems more so to me the nearer I get to it myself.

*   *   *

Another character who figured large in the lives of the Clark children was Granda Johnston, Maw's father. Old William Johnston came from Belfast, where he had been a bacon curer, but he was highly intelligent, a man of good taste and some education. He drove the less academic of the Clark children to distraction by waiting outside school to drag them to libraries and museums. He learned Scots Gaelic, for instance, and read music and became determined to teach his grandchildren whatever current interest he had, thudding them on the skull if they didn't perform well. My mother was the clever one of the family, the dux of Glasgow High School for Girls, as she never tired of reminding us. Nan at least showed some promise and he liked her but poor old Willie, at the other end of the scale, had to climb over the back wall of his school to escape from the self-appointed dominie.

From Da the 'Dark Yins' got their demeanour and sense of themselves, but it was perhaps from Granda Johnston that they got their appreciation that the way out was through learning and with that their determination that their children would be educated. Though quite why the message got through chiefly to them I cannot say.

Granda Johnston stole everything he could lay hands on as he got older and the family turned a blind eye to it. His favourite time was during the blackout, when everything walked under cover of darkness, but he didn't confine himself to it by any means. He would set out on a mass visit of the family and ask to wash his hands in each house, slipping the soap into his pocket when he was finished. Another trick was to pretend to be asleep, then when attentions were elsewhere, he would sneak whatever was on the table into a paper bag and resume his 'snooze'.

My only memory of him is of an occasion after the War when he hadn't noticed my brother Laurie in the room, lying in wait for him. As the old lad pocketed a bag of sugar, Laurie's voice rang out, 'Mammy! Granda Johnston's stealin' oor sugar again!' As he died in 1950, when I was two years old, I'm not sure if I was really there, or if I've heard the story so often that I just think I was.

Granda Johnston was a passionate Orangeman and a Past Master of an Orange Lodge, so it was partly from him that the dichotomy of my upbringing stemmed. Unlike his daughter, Maw Clark, he wasn't bitter, he was, as Nan and Peggy told me, a gentleman. By all accounts he was also a proud Scot despite being an Ulsterman. He used to sing 'MacGregor's Gathering' at family get-togethers with eyes blazing in stern defiance, ending the war song of the outlaw Rob Roy MacGregor with a rousing 'MacGreegor despite them, will flourish F-O-R-E-V-E-R!' He never seemed to notice, in his patriotic fervour, that my father and Willie were fencing around him and between his legs and arms with pokers from the fire, for the entertainment of the others.

It was Willie, naturally, who was given the job of staying with the old lad as he became increasingly confused with age, and he returned to find him dead one day. He got my father to help him lift the body and tidy the house up. All day they tripped over a box in the middle of the floor, and instead of moving it they kicked it out of the way and cursed it as they worked. They found countless sugar packets stuffed with half-crowns and when the coal had been removed from the bath, envelopes full of cash were discovered underneath. In his years of thieving from the family Granda Johnston had managed to put away a tidy sum. Then someone picked up the box from the middle of the floor, or as Willie said, 'Sumbody *honest*' and inside was a fortune in banknotes. Skip and Willie were heartbroken. If they had found it they would naturally have purloined the treasure and not been seen again for some time, instead they had kicked and cursed it all day long.

My father's family, the O'Briens, lived in Tarbet Street, behind the Brae. My grandmother, Mary Ann McCue, had been born in Scotland but her family came from the town of Carlow in County Carlow, to Dundee, where Mary Ann was a weaver. There Mary Ann met Tom O'Brien, whose family came originally from New Ross, in County Wexford. In

Dundee, Tom's family had run a guest-house and were quite well-to-do, and Tom was well-educated and well brought up. He was apparently destined for the priesthood, but in the parlance of the day, he got Mary Ann into trouble and had to marry her. Once married they moved to Glasgow, probably to escape Mary Ann's father, and quickly set about founding a dynasty.

Granda Tom was a studious, aesthetic soul and quite unsuited to married or family life, especially with the family he sired. I remember him as a distant, quiet little man with a permanent look of confusion on his face. He was a lithographic printer but gave this up to work as a janitor in St Aloysius in Garnethill, a Jesuit school for Roman Catholic boys. He did so for the simple reason that he wanted to be near the Jesuits, which demonstrates an astonishing lack of responsibility to his wife and the large family he was supposed to provide for.

He loved literature, art and the theatre and to escape from his family he buried himself in these pursuits and in the Roman Catholic Church. He was a devout Catholic, partly I suspect to provide some sort of order in his life. Marriage to Marry Ann was clearly not the life he would have chosen for himself and he was quite incapable of adapting to it. He was highly respected in the community and his growing brood regarded him in much the same light, mixed perhaps with a little pity. He was not like them in any way and they mostly realized this without blaming him. The exception was his son Tommy, who saw Mary Ann's health decline over her many pregnancies and blamed his father for doing nothing to help her. 'He hid nae interest,' Uncle Tommy would say bitterly, 'except when bedtime came.'

Granda Tom's devotion to the Catholic church extended to all his money, and countless black babies in Africa doubtless became good Catholics thanks to his donations. But Mary Ann suffered a slow, painful death from womb cancer when there was no pain relief available except alcohol. She was ill all during my father's childhood, and died, as he said, on his sixteenth birthday in December 1927. Her children suffered from rickets, caused by a lack of calcium in the diet, which was the scourge of working-class children at the turn of the century. Indeed my father couldn't walk until he was four years old because of rickets, and all his life he walked with a characteristic rolling gait. Uncle Tommy never forgave the Catholic Church any more than he forgave his father. 'It wis a' there if they'd looked,' he'd say darkly, 'bit they wurnae ony merr interested than him. They jist took his money an' turned thur faces in the oappisite direction.'

Granda Tom kept his distance from the entire family, and I didn't know him when I was a child, though I recognized him in the street as he hurried by with a curt nod. It probably wasn't that he was a cold man, he just had perfectly understandable reservations. He knew who my father was after all. Granda looked so like Wilfrid Hyde-White, that when I was a child and saw the actor in a film I was convinced he was Granda Tom and accepted his presence on screen without surprise; after all they were both far-removed from my life. He always wore a black suit, tie, topcoat and bowler hat and an immaculate white shirt, though my mother discovered that he wiped his hands on the shirt sleeves after stoking the St Aloysius boiler, so underneath they were as black as his suit.

He didn't have much luck with any of our family, including my brother Laurie, who failed to utter his first word to anyone for years. Once Granda Tom made a rare appearance at a family function and gave Mickey sixpence. 'And you, young man,' he said to Laurie, 'Will only get thruppence, because you won't speak to me.' Laurie was four years old and chose that moment to say his first ever words. 'Stick yer thruppence up yer arse, ya auld bastard!' Granda Tom was helped out, his saintly expression extremely compromised, and he doubtless headed for the nearest chapel to fill up again on piety. But at least it proved that the child wasn't deaf or dumb; he just didn't have anything important to say until that moment . . .

In his later years Granda Tom took to wandering the streets of Glasgow with his rosary in his hands, reciting his prayers aloud. There are parts of the city where this is not advisable, and it was obvious that something had to be done. Even in an age when caring for elderly parents was the norm, he was too far removed from his family for any of them to take him in, but none of them would take responsibility for putting him in a home either. In the end an adult grandson took matters into his own hands and placed the old lad in an old folks' home run by nuns, where he lived happily, rosary safely in hand, to the age of eighty-four. The O'Briens were very relieved to have that responsibility taken off their hands but they still roundly castigated the grandson who had put Granda Tom into the home; he had done the shameful deed, they hadn't.

Granda Tom died in 1952, when I was four years old, and I remember his funeral vividly. It was held in St Aloysius in Garnethill, and as befitted a Knight of St Columba he got the full works. Men in cloaks with scarlet crosses on the shoulders carried the coffin, and they wore large, plumed hats. One of the hats lay on the coffin too, and all around thousands of candles burned, the choir sang, the organ boomed and funny-smelling smoke made me cough. I thought I was at a pantomime and I loved every minute of it.

No one had consulted me on whether or not I wanted to be a Catholic, and as I grew up reluctantly and resentfully within the fold, I realized I had been right. It was all indeed a pantomime.

Chapter Two

By all accounts the O'Brien madness came from the McCue side, in particular from Mary Ann's father, old Hughie McCue. Skip, the youngest of ten, used to tell me tales of visits from his grandfather, visits Mary Ann would bring to an abrupt end. As soon as old Hughie arrived at the house, Skip would be commanded to escort him down to Queen Street Station and put him on the first train back to Dundee, but he never managed it. Old Hughie would go down one set of stairs to the underground men's toilet in High Street and come up the other side. Next time he would do it the other way round, so that his confused grandson could never be sure where he was. He would then bolt into the bars of the city and have a hooley, arriving back on Mary Ann's doorstep whenever it ended naturally or sometimes in the company of the police. 'Every time Ah saw him,' my father would say, 'Ah knew he wid get away frae me an' Ah wis in fur a dunt oan the heid frae ma mither by the end o' the day.'

The Tarbet Street house was more the O'Brien domain than a mere house and it was the setting for many of their ploys. They were bright, witty and inventive and none of them ever really grew up. Throughout their lives they waged a form of psychological warfare against the rest of the world, and each other in particular. It was called the Game, though family members didn't need to call it anything, it was in the blood. In the Game, points were awarded, but only when the players were family. Outsiders hadn't a hope of competing on level terms since they didn't know that the Game existed. Yet they still became its victims, even though no points were awarded for a score against a non-O'Brien.

An insurance man used to call at the house, and when he

was counting out Granny O'Brien's change he had a habit of saying "ere noo' with some regularity. 'One, two, 'ere noo, three, four, 'ere noo,' an opportunity for amusement that the family could not pass up. One day as he counted out the money, voices came from all over the house, high voices, low voices, unearthly voices, "Ere noo,' "Ere noo,' "Ere noo,' as he counted out each penny. The little man stared at Granny, who gave no indication that she had noticed anything. Everytime he came to the house after that the house rang to the sound of "Ere noos' up and down the musical scale, and still Granny's expression did not change, though apparently she beat the hell out of those she could catch afterwards. This, of course, meant that she had forfeited the points by reacting.

"Ere noo' became a family password, almost a means of identification, and it was written on Christmas cards instead of the more conventional 'From all the family'. Once, many years later, I put it on a telegram from abroad at the end of a message saying when I would arrive home. My father was delighted; all the other words had been put in a numeral code above the written message, but the bemused international operator had been unable to find a numeral that covered it, and there it was, "Ere noo' twice.

On another Tarbet Street occasion years ago that my father loved to tell us about, a travelling salesman's luck ran out. Skip was never sure where the salesman had come from, but he was black, wore a turban and arrived with a full caseload of clothes to sell on a day when the O'Briens were obviously bored and in need of amusement. The salesman was graciously invited in. There his case was emptied, and every one of the family decked out in the contents, layer upon layer, including his turban, which was arranged decorously atop the head of Norah, my father's older sister, who had a passion for hats. Then they sat down in all their finery and took tea together, pinkies stuck out, conversing in terribly polite voices, as though the unfortunate salesman didn't exist, until there was a knock at the door and he grabbed his chance to escape. They later found his coat outside, it had been caught in the door and rather than knock again and risk recapture, he had taken it off and fled, leaving it and all his merchandise behind. The O'Briens were shocked, they had only wanted a bit of fun and hadn't planned to steal the clothes. 'Poor auld bugger,' Skip would say everytime he told the story, 'He wis likely poorer thin us tae. An' he never came back either . . .', and he would shake his head in puzzlement at the strange ways of mankind.

In the basement of Tarbet Street my father in his youth had constructed a full-size boxing ring, and one of the family's favourite leisure activities was to con people into boxing in it. It didn't matter who they were or why they were there, they would be encouraged into the ring to perform. There was also a home-made still for making hooch and they tried every possible concoction of rotgut, none of which ever had a chance of reaching maturity. It would start with the necessity to 'check oan it', and when the checker didn't return another would set off in search of him. Then another, and another, until they were all out cold beside the empty still.

I didn't realize that the O'Briens were odd and wondered why the rest of the population was so boring. The oddest, and to me the most beloved, was Uncle Hughie, very aptly named after Mary Ann's father. At the age of four Hughie was knocked down by a horse-drawn tram and his right leg was severed above the knee, except for a 'sliver o' skin'. While a pair of scissors was located to deal with the sliver, his sister, Norah, (she of the hat fetish), took up a collection from the crowd of onlookers. Norah was an accomplished actress and her tears and sobs could fool the most cynical observer. The amount of performance money raised from this joint venture remained a subject of contention between her and Hughie for the rest of their days. Whenever life was dull Hughie would resurrect the argument and aver that he had been cheated, that Norah had kept more than she had given him when as the star of the show he should have received cash that reflected his leading role. After all, he had sacrificed an entire leg in the venture.

This vile accusation always produced one of Norah's

finest virtuoso performances as the wronged woman, with much sobbing and fainting, though strictly around well-placed chairs – Norah was nobody's fool.

As the drama unfolded Hughie would accuse Norah of wilfully defrauding a one-legged man, her own brother. This was a doubly heinous crime apparently, though in ordinary circumstances it would be regarded as entirely legitimate. Norah would throw herself on the mercy of the assembled audience asking for justice, but it depended who she had cheated last whether she got justice or not on each occasion. It was a highly entertaining show that I watched many times over the years and always with great enjoyment. Norah doubtless did cheat Hughie though, just as he would have cheated her had it been the other way round. But Fate had dealt him the lying down role, and he never quite got over the unfairness of it.

Uncle Hughie grew up with one leg and one wooden crutch, and he regarded that arrangement as the norm. Two legs was, well, deformed somehow. Over the years he was fitted with numerous artificial legs by well-meaning medical people, but he never used them for their intended purpose. One he arranged on the inside of his door, dressed up in a coat, trousers and hat. This, he told everybody, was his twin brother Louis, pronounced Looey to rhyme with Hughie. They had been born with two legs between them, so Hughie had taken the left one and Louis the right. Hughie and Louis lived amicably like that all of Hughie's life, and Louis was accepted by the family and greeted as they entered Hughie's abode.

The other legs meanwhile served more mundane, though perhaps more bizarre functions. For instance, one was used as a rubbish bin. Others were filled with ashes from Hughie's fire and thrown into the River Clyde. Yet another he kept solely for visits from well-meaning social workers, in those days called almoners, who naturally came from non-working-class backgrounds. Hughie had a special leg clad in a black fishnet stocking, which he positioned just sticking out of the side of his set-in bed whenever an almoner called to offer unwanted assistance. Throughout the conversation, which was conducted by Hughie in ultra-polite mode, the protruding leg and the temptress who was supposedly attached to it, was never mentioned, though the almoner couldn't drag her gaze from it.

Hughie could move at an incredible speed with the old wooden crutch and regularly raced two-legged unfortunates for money, winning every time. He once had a fight in George Street with another one-legged man, though no one can remember what it was about. They each balanced on their one good leg and bashed each other with their wooden crutches, while a huge crowd gathered laying bets and cheering on their champion. The contest lasted for hours apparently, with rest periods provided between rounds, and as far as I know Hughie won, though how anyone could tell is a mystery. It's a mental picture that can bring a smile to my face in my darkest moments, a scene so surreal that it could only have Hughie as its author.

A day spent with Uncle Hughie was an honour and to this day I remember every one. As my brother Laurie and I walked along the road with him we had to trot to keep up, and he would lodge the crutch on an electricity junction box or a handy windowsill and suddenly pole vault into the air. He would land with a cry of 'Alley-oop!', and then continue as though nothing had happened. I can still recall the feeling of pride at being related to someone who could accomplish such public feats of silliness and was daft enough to want to. He is clear in my memory still, a small man bent over the old crutch, with the ubiquitous Glasgow bunnet, under which were two bright grey eyes that sparkled and shone with the ever-present promise of mischief, of adventure waiting to begin. I never saw him without the bunnet, and even today when I see someone wearing one I remember him and I can't help smiling.

Uncle Hughie would take us on repeated tours of old Glasgow, each time pointing out the very spot where he had lost his leg all those years ago. All the while he would be giving a gripping running commentary on the events of that day. It didn't take us long to realize that he took us to a different place every time and that he gave many, many versions of how the 'sliver o' skin' had been dealt with, each one more convincing than the last.

As well as various venues throughout Glasgow, he lost that leg in the Crimea, at Waterloo, in the Boer War and in the First World War, according to Hughie. Laurie and I fervently believed all the stories at once because Hughie did. To prove his more heroic claims he had his photo taken wearing every available military uniform. Every one was one hundred per cent genuine, after all, unlike Hughie, the camera never lied.

Hughie was the first of the family to marry, but every day he returned to Tarbet Street. As part of their ongoing psychological warfare, the others would decide that he was 'It', and his knocks on the door and face at the window would be ignored. Eventually he would be allowed in, only to be given his tea in the mug that Granda Tom used to soak his false teeth. The full points were awarded to Hughie, who would drink up the tea with apparent relish and win a dubious victory.

Hughie had newly moved into a little house on a hillside, and, so the story goes, he was touched at the offer by his brothers to decorate it for him. 'A nice Regency stripe,' he ordered, and he left them to it. When he returned they had applied the striped paper horizontally, at the same angle as the hill outside. The pictures on the walls had been papered over, as had every door, which was then carefully cut around for easy access – no one could ever accuse them of being downright *silly*. Once again, though, it was Hughie who won the points by professing himself delighted and he lived with the wallpaper unchanged for years. To this day any home decorating, be it painting or wallpapering, is known within the family as 'A nice Regency stripe', though it's possible that some far-removed relatives might have no idea where it originated.

Despite all the hilarity in Hughie's life, his wife, Maggie, died young after giving birth to five children in very quick succession. Only two made it past babyhood, the others all died from the TB that killed Maggie. Granny O'Brien was still alive at the time and she placed the two surviving girls in convent homes. One died after a fall, aged fourteen, while cleaning windows in the convent, and the other was knocked down and killed by a bus after leaving the convent when she was sixteen. I didn't know any of this when I was a child. In the mythical O'Brien world of fun, sadness was not allowed, I simply regarded Uncle Hughie with adoring affection for the magical creature that he was. It was only in later years that I realized what a sad life he must have had, though he never once showed it. He brought constant joy with his belief that growing up wasn't obligatory, despite what the rest of humanity might think.

As Granny O'Brien had made the supreme sacrifice in honour of my father's sixteenth birthday, I never knew her, but she left a legacy that's still around today. She had a very potent curse, called the Curse of Cromwell, that has to be used with caution. Once put on it cannot be removed, and if it hasn't been used for a while it can become rusty; this is not a curse with a built-in margin for error, it demands exact coordinates. As Skip used to explain, 'It kin get the wan tae the side or jist behind the wan ye waant. So ye need tae be careful.' And the strange thing is that it seems to work. I have had few occasions in my life so serious that Cromwell had to be called into action, but each time he has, some catastrophe has befallen the recipient of the curse. I use it very, very rarely these days, it's too powerful to unleash on an ill-prepared world . . .

Chapter Three

My mother first set eyes on my father when she was ten years old and he was seventeen. She was playing with a piece of chalk, writing names on the pavement. She asked him what his name was and then wrote 'Lawrence O'Brien', which he changed to 'Laurence'; they married seven years later. At first she was prepared to 'turn' with my father and took instruction in the Catholic faith. It didn't last long though; she pronounced it 'A loada noansense', and walked out never to return.

They were married at the start of the traditional Glasgow holiday fortnight, on Fair Friday, 17 July 1936, in St Andrew's Cathedral in Clyde Street, beside the river at the Broomielaw. As a result of Nan's refusal to accept 'the one true faith' the ceremony was carried out at a side altar, while a real Catholic couple had pride of place at the front altar. As a child this slight to my mother made me simmer with rage, and I never understood why my father accepted it for her, after all, he at least knew it to be an insult. My mother thought it was an hilariously funny example of how infantile the whole thing was, and I learned from her that you can only accept an insult if you have some respect for whoever gives it: she hadn't.

After the ceremony they visited Granda Tom at St Aloysius. It was a mark of how isolated he was from his family that he hadn't been at the wedding, but he was due their respect, hence the visit. He wasn't even close enough to have been displeased at his son marrying a non-Catholic, it wasn't anything that concerned him. He was stoking the school boiler and that was when she discovered the secret of his dirty shirt-sleeves. It was my mother's first meeting with her father-in-law and she said he was very nice to them,

34

wished them luck and gave them one-and-sixpence, which they spent on a wedding picture. She looks so young in it that it makes you want to cry 'Foul!'

Laurie Jnr was the most vulnerable of our family. He was born during the war, six months after my father had gone overseas with the Royal Artillery. Skip's letters home showed clearly that he wanted a daughter, and wartime communications were so bad that he didn't find out he had a second son until Laurie was six months old. The only visible proof Laurie had that his father existed was a picture of him taken in dress uniform, which made him look tall, brave and handsome. The reality arrived in the early hours of one morning at the end of the War when Laurie awakened to find a five-foot-tall and perfectly unimpressive Glaswegian in his home. Laurie then went to school to tell the teacher his mother was in bed with a strange man. When told it was his father, he replied, 'Naw it's no'! Ma Daddy's a *big* man!' Laurie never quite recovered from the disappointment and he and Skip never did hit it off. Then to complete Laurie's unhappiness, I arrived soon afterwards, the longed-for daughter, not that I ever fulfilled my parents' dearest dreams in that department. The epitome of feminine charm I never was.

When my father arrived home that night to disappoint Laurie, he had noticed banners all over the street, but it was dark and he didn't stop to read them. Next morning he was borne shoulder high through the neighbourhood and saw that the banners bore the message, WELCOME HOME OUR HERO. Uncle Hughie had spread the story that his younger brother had been awarded the George Cross. He'd even told the local newspapers. My mother, who regarded anything that the O'Briens did to each other as none of her concern, hadn't warned the returning 'hero' and my father had to endure a lavish street party, complete with speeches by minor functionaries. Of course Hughie was nowhere to be seen, though it was my father's firm belief that 'he wis jist roond the coarner, watchin' and laughin'.' The points were shared though, because my father carried it off and never, ever mentioned it to Hughie.

Always missing from our family as we listened to these stories was my brother Mickey. He had been in Mearnskirk Hospital when I was born. As Laurie and I grew up, every available penny went to Mickey's needs, he was after all Nan and Skip's first born and that is always special. It was natural and understandable that in their frustration at being unable to help him, they tried to make sure that he had whatever he wanted. So they spent long hours on public transport going to and from Mearnskirk to deliver little luxuries to Mickey, and because money was tight it was inevitable that Laurie and I got less. It wasn't Mickey's fault and neither was it Nan and Skip's, it was simply one of those things. I had no experience of any other life, but Laurie had. He was deprived of Nan's attention by virtue of Skip's return, Mickey's illness and by my arrival. Laurie had needs too and they were undoubtedly overlooked.

Laurie and I spent a great deal of time together as children during our parents' absences visiting Mickey. I have no particular memory of anything we did, I just know that Laurie was always there. Neither have I any clear memory of our house in Balmano Street, except that it always seemed full of visitors. Gradually I came to realize that this was because of my mother. She was like a magnet to those in trouble, and wherever we lived there would always be a steady stream of people at our door looking for her. It would start with a knock and a voice saying 'Is Nan in?', and in they would come, usually bearing a letter of the official and intimidating kind. This heralded the start of one of her crusades, as she read the letter to the bearer and then discussed the facts. The next thing was to compose a reply, though if she thought the situation merited it she would beard the letter-writer in his den, wherever that might be.

After the War the stock of houses in Glasgow, as in all cities, was low. Throughout the War years no new house-building had taken place and money that should have be spent on repairing those that existed went instead to the War effort. Through Nan's campaigning 21 Balmano Street had been condemned and to stop it falling down it had been shored up on one side, still there was no possibility of a new home. In truth, what the inhabitants of 21 really wanted was a replica with one or two mod cons to sprout up beside the decaying building so that they could go on living together for ever. Even with improvements the housing would hardly have been ideal, but they had no experience of anything better, except for my mother, who had worked as a maid in 'big hooses' in the city when she left school at fourteen. It was always her dream that her children would live in similar 'big hooses', but the reality was Balmano Street which was like an extended family and none of the tenants seriously contemplated life apart. But time was running out as the building continued to rot.

The final collapse came one June night in 1951, after weeks of dry weather gave way to a prolonged and heavy thunderstorm. Sand had been trickling through ceilings all day, then a neighbour asked Nan to come down to her ground-floor home. The woman's sink was disappearing into the kitchen floor, and Nan suddenly realized what was happening. Just then there was a roar like an enormous clap of thunder, and the building started to collapse. Nan ran through 21 shouting at people to get out, knocking on doors and pushing her neighbours to safety. And that is my only clear, sure memory of the Brae, of being outside in the dark with the rain falling and of being in Laurie's arms, a blanket over our heads. Inside the little cave I remember feeling no fear, though all around there was panic, with people shouting and running and the ringing bells of the fire engines, police cars and brown ambulances.

In the middle of this I have a picture of Laurie, who was only a little lad of about eight or nine. He looked totally lost, as though whatever was happening was targeted at him personally. I remember it so well because it was a look I was to see often as we grew up; the night the building collapsed was the first time I registered it. He was a beautiful child, with hair so fair it was silver and big brown eyes, but always that look, as though life had dealt him a massive, unfair and irreversible blow that the rest of us had somehow escaped.

Then Peggy appeared and took me from him, and all was well because she was there. She had been out dancing and had felt that something was wrong, so she had rushed home just in time to see my father coax her mother across an open space four floors up, where their floor had once been. The gable end had fallen into the street below and a yawning chasm had appeared between one half of the building and the other. My father had eased a plank of wood across the divide and managed to get Maw Clark halfway across before it gave way. He caught Maw as she fell, then went next door and did the same with Mary, Nan's sister, and her son David, before the fire brigade arrived.

Meanwhile, as the newspapers reported next day, my mother had got all the other inhabitants of 21 out safely, no-one was even injured. While my mother had been saving neighbours though, Laurie and I had to be rescued by firemen. She had forgotten about us, and we used that against her for years. Of course Skip had forgotten us too, but by the time we were old enough to joke about it, my father's lack of concern for his family was past a joke.

The inhabitants of the building were taken to the Poorhouse at Foresthall by bus that night, but of course Nan refused to go. Instead we stayed with her sister Vicky, the leading 'Fair Yin'; it was a family issue after all, not an inter-family one. I remember press camera lights popping and all night a clock chiming every quarter of an hour, with my parents' voices talking on into the morning light. We didn't know it then, but we had spent our last night with the neighbours of 21, it was the end of the Brae era.

Chapter Four

Blackhill. The name filled Nan with horror. She wanted her children to go up in the world, to have a bright future, to one day live in 'big hooses'. Instead, it would be Blackhill, legendary home of rogues, thieves and murderers. Nan was told by the housing officials that it was only temporary, but she wisely didn't believe them. The Blackhill council estate, or scheme, was started in 1933 as a result of the Housing (Scotland) Acts of 1930/35, with the first tenants moving in, in April 1935. Incongruously, it was built on the site of the Glasgow Golf Club, much to the annoyance of the many senior Glasgow Corporation officials who were members.

For such a prestigous site the surrounding area was surprisingly unattractive. To the south was the Monklands Canal, to the west the Corporation's Provan gas-plant and its railway link. Beside the gas-plant stood the chemical works and nearby, across two tracks, was the White Horse Whisky distillery, known locally as the Bondie. The 872 houses that made up Blackhill were carefully secreted within these borders, to hide it and its residents, who were renowned for their violence and degradation.

The people living in Blackhill were those with no choice, no hope and no power; they were simply deposited there and abandoned. They were drawn chiefly from manual labourers, which meant they were either Irish Catholics or of Irish descent, Irish being synonymous with Catholic to the Glasgow of the time. There had long been a strong anti-Catholic bias in Glasgow, and for many years Catholics were not allowed to be tradesmen. Notices would appear beside job adverts, stating that no Catholics need apply, and even without the actual words, a silent prejudice applied – despite the claims of the PR men it often still does.

Even in the fifties, time-served tradesmen were predominantly Protestant, and of course they earned more and had better job security, so it followed that they also had better homes. So there was a tradition of Catholics being slum-dwellers, and as those slums were replaced by estates like Blackhill, it was logical that Catholic manual workers would form the majority of residents. As with all generalizations of course, others were lumped in who didn't belong. There were Protestants with Irish surnames for instance, or mixed marriages, like that of my parents, or those with nowhere else to go. For Nan that was three-out-of-three, and there was certainly ample evidence to base her fears on, like *the* story about Blackhill: the poisonings of 1949.

It was New Year 1948–9, a time when there was little alcohol available, and a party was in progress, until the booze ran out. A local lad, Terry Donnelly, who worked in the nearby chemical works, led a group of friends to a vat of methyl alcohol in the factory, on the basis that alcohol was alcohol. Bottles were filled and taken back to the house where the party was being held, but methyl alcohol is a poisonous industrial substance used in the manufacture of paint. Those who drank it that Hogmanay, neat or mixed with lemonade or wine, quickly became ill. The lucky ones were blinded for life, but ten men died slow, agonizing deaths.

The incident entered into the folklore of Glasgow, and the media played its shock-horror part, so that Glasgow came to accept that it was typical of the depraved monsters of Blackhill to behave in such a way. There was no sympathy, it simply reinforced the opinions of those who regarded Blackhill as a hell-hole for the hopeless and undeserving.

Terry Donnelly was given thirty days in prison for the theft of the methyl alcohol, a sentence that was regarded as harsh and unnecessary by the people of Blackhill. Though he had ended up unintentionally hurting his own, there was nothing malicious about it, he had meant no harm and had suffered enough by the outcome, and that is still the strong opinion of those who were alive at the time. But, of course, it became the one incident that characterized the place in the minds of many, and though it happened before we moved there, that notoriety was partly responsible for Nan's fears for her family.

Once in, there was little chance of escape, because no one would willingly exchange hell for a house in Blackhill, and wanting a better life and future for your kids added no points on the housing list. After all her years of campaigning to have Balmano Street condemned, the letters written, councillors ambushed and MPs coerced, the collapse of the building had played a sick joke on Nan and we were landed in Blackhill.

No buses or trams ran through it, there was no police station, only one or two shops, no social facilities of any kind and no employment within it. In the Fifties few sociologists had identified these problems and it was generally acknowledged by those outside that those inside were a bad lot and by keeping them together the better areas of the city would be that much safer. Nowadays I look at the South African townships, the ghettoes for the black or Indian people in America and the Aborigines of Australia; places that are no more than reservations to keep them in one place and contain them for whatever the authorities may wish to inflict on them, and Blackhill springs easily to mind. It was our punishment for the crime of being poor.

There were three distinct areas of the development: Blackhill Rehousing (a coy name for slum clearance), Blackhill Extension and Blackhill Intermediate. The first two were built along the lines of the traditional tenements and each housed the same kind of tenants, while the Intermediate were four-in-a-block houses of very much superior quality, and reputation. The Intermediate area was intended for the respectable poor rather than the disreputable poor. Those who lived in the Intermediate part referred to it as High Riddrie, in an attempt to disassociate themselves from the rest of Blackhill.

We moved into the rehousing part of Blackhill, though if anyone we didn't know asked where we came from, Nan always said Riddrie. This wasn't out of snobbery, but out of self-defence. The stigma of Blackhill was indelibly and irrevocably applied to all, and its residents were routinely

41

subjected to abuse. Indeed it wasn't unusual for children who ventured the few miles to the park in Alexandra Parade, in the respectable Riddrie/Dennistoun area, to be stopped by the police and questioned, before being sent back 'tae fuck where ye belang.' So if we saw the police we ran, though we had done nothing wrong.

There was no area for children to play in, a common cry heard in every council housing scheme to this day, but the children of Blackhill wouldn't have agreed. For a start there was the canal. The last words every child, including Laurie and I, heard going out to play were, 'See an'keep away frae that canal!' This of course ensured that we headed straight for it, because it had two elements that made it irresistible: parental disapproval and the sure knowledge that water is provided on earth to be played with and in by children. We never told Nan that we played there though, we knew it would only worry her.

In those days the attractions of the Monklands Canal ran to clear water, water birds, and live fish just waiting to be caught, not to mention all manner of flotsam and jetsam that challenged us to make them into rafts. Drownings were common and were accepted by the local kids almost as an occupational hazard. After each one a petition would do the rounds of Blackhill asking for the canal to be filled in, which the children of the area regarded as a gross infringement of their rights. There was nothing to worry about though, no one with the power to do so took any notice of petitions from Blackhill, and the canal remained there to tempt the local children until it was filled in to make way for the construction of the M8 motorway. The City Fathers had their priorities after all, the safety of the local kids counted for nothing. And when they did fill in the canal it was ironic, to put it kindly, that one form of environmental pollution was simply exchanged for another, the exhaust fumes of cars, buses and lorries. In the fifties the canal was part of our daily lives, something we lived with, and we never really considered it to be the danger that our parents did, though of course it was.

The railway lines ran behind the tenements at the lower

half of Acrehill Street, and there was also one, big triangle of grass. Bordered along the top of Royston Road, it had the gasworks, chemical plant and a railway track on one side, and the whisky bond and another track on the other. In those days no one had heard of the hazards of industrial pollution and, even if they had, in the eyes of our 'betters' it would have been regarded as good enough for our kind of people. Anyway, where else was there for us to go to if we didn't like where we lived? There was a lot of sickness, mainly eye trouble, and chest infections that settled into chronic bronchitis over the years. From the whisky distillery, the Bondie, ran a small stream carrying the effluent of whatever mysterious processes took place inside, but to the children it was a burn and, therefore, like the canal a legitimate place to play. We were disappointed, though, that no fish swam there.

Trains coming from the distillery-end met up at the point with those coming from the gasworks and chemical factory track, so to get to the grassy area in the middle we had to cross the line. Sometimes a railway man would descend from his signal box and attempt to chase us off. But until he did I would lie on my back, lost in the long grass, staring at the sky above, overcome at the immensity of it and wondering where it ended, as the other kids fought and played around me. It was the first feeling I had of being able to stretch my eyes, and the awakening of an awareness that there was existence beyond the streets and houses where I lived.

We lived at 34 Acrehill Street, a long, curved street of drab, grey-stone tenements like all the others, built in rows throughout Blackhill. Nan's sister Mary, and her son David, who had lived beside us at the Brae, were at 43. Maw Clark and Peggy had a house in Moodiesburn Street, towards the better Riddrie/Provanmill end.

Like all tenements there was an entrance, the close, which connected all the houses from the bottom storey to the top, and through to the backcourt, but in Glasgow it means more than a passageway. A close is a place in its own right, it's a meeting place, a talking shop, and tenement dwellers feel a strong sense of ownership over their closes. The close at

34, leading up to our first-floor home, had a distinctive atmosphere, just as every other one did to its owners. This time we had two bedrooms, a kitchen, sitting/dining-room and an inside toilet, so the house itself was luxury compared to Balmano Street. Just inside the kitchen, on the left, was the coal-bunker, and at the top, on the right beside the sink, stood the gas boiler. It was about the size of a large oil drum, with a gas ring below, and this was where the family washing was done. Mondays were boring days, because Nan had to boil the clothes up, then rub them with Fairy soap over the corrugations of the washing board, and put them through a mangle into the sink. Then she had to rinse them and mangle them again, and sometimes again. All this took a great deal of time, and on Nan's part a greater deal of effort, and I'd hear her puffing and panting while trying to keep singing, as she always did about the house. Until the washing was safely on the line, though, we couldn't go out and I had to hang around, bored and impatient to see Peggy.

The houses of the other Brae refugees were strung out between ours and Peggy's, and whenever we passed, old neighbours would rush out for a reunion. They clung to each other like prisoners in a foreign land, which indeed they were, with Nan the only point of safety, and they could never let her pass their doors.

Before long 34 became established as the place to go when in trouble, and the familar, steady stream of worried women, clutching letters and looking for Nan became the norm. Once again I didn't realize it at the time, but I was witnessing the much-denied link between wealth – or the lack of it – and education. Most of the people who brought their problems to my mother did so because they could neither read nor write. They weren't stupid and they weren't illiterate through choice, it simply went with their abject poverty and lack of power over their own lives. It came with the territory of deprivation.

Nan would read the proffered letter or listen to the story and we would hear her say, 'Noo, that's no' right . . . ,' the words that signified the start of another campaign. As in the Brae, if the matter was relatively simple she would compose and write a reply to the hapless sender of the offending letter, but if the situation was dire she would be instantly off in search of the miscreant, to sort it out face-to-face. People, she fervently believed, were basically good, and no one meant harm to another. There was only Right, and once any minor misunderstandings were explained, Right would be universally accepted and sweetness and light would prevail. It was her mission in life to do the explaining, for the simple reason that she could.

Skip maintained that the initials, HC, in the middle of her name, were born of the panic Nan induced in Council Officials. 'They see hur comin,' he would say, 'an' shout "Joan – Holy Christ! – O'Brien!" Then they a' run away hame.' She was anybody's idea of an earth mother, plump and maternal, with soft, concerned brown eyes that betrayed every emotion, dark brown hair caught up in a bun from which it was forever threatening to escape, and she always had a child by the hand. In her battles with officialdom she used this to its fullest advantage of course, knowing exactly what kind of Blackhill representative her adversaries were expecting. The best clothes were brought out and freshly pressed, stocking seams checked for ramrod straightness, hair carefully brushed and me (the 'wean') scrubbed clean. It caught 'them' off guard to be confronted with a well turned-out, articulate and polite matron instead of the stereotype they expected from the badlands of Blackhill. She then hit them with an impassioned honesty that could melt the heart of the hardest bureaucrat, and she usually emerged victorious, with respect and dignity preserved on both sides. As the youngest of her three children I was a pre-school accomplice on her missions, and I was trained to sit quietly without interrupting and to be well-mannered when spoken to. Nan didn't miss a trick when her heart was in the fray.

Years after my mother had died, I was in Glasgow City Chambers for what I thought was the first time. It is an extremely ornate building with extravagant use made of different kinds of marble and much opulent gilding of the lily; once seen never forgotten, even if you try hard. Halfway up a landing I turned left into an instantly recognizable place:

45

at the top of the next flight of stairs Nan had stood shaking hands with a tall, white-haired man at the end of a meeting, and he had given me the unheard of sum of half-a-crown, which my mother had immediately confiscated and handed back to him, declaring it to be 'too much'. My father at that time would have been earning something in the region of two pounds per week, and I had been handed the huge sum of an eighth of one pound! I remembered vividly how difficult it had sometimes been to be quiet and well-mannered, especially when my mother lost me the untold wealth of a half-crown. The memory was so clear that I could almost locate the three figures in mid-air as I followed the voices in my mind, but the reason for our being there was lost, if indeed I ever knew it. Undoubtedly though it had started with that knock at the door and an anxious voice asking, 'Is Nan in?'

This was the Teddy Boy era, intensified in Glasgow by the Catholic/Protestant divide, and there were running street fights every night, so Nan enforced a curfew after dark. I grew up hearing my father trying to calm her down as the sounds of battle ripped through the darkened streets, but being used to it I fell asleep quickly; it was just another familiar part of normal life. One night, though, Maw Clark had been taken to the Royal Infirmary with one of her terminal illnesses, and by the time the family had been reassured that she would live to con them another day, it was night time.

Arriving at our close we found a fight in progress, with four Teds against one. Skip, being a street-wise Glaswegian with a well-developed instinct for survival, turned and walked back out. Nan instinctively waded in though, wielding the ever-present message bag that served as both handbag and shopping-bag for working-class women. She had made it herself at a craft class at a local school, but never had she envisaged using it as a weapon. She brought it down on whatever head was nearest, and grabbed handfuls of hair, the knives and razors flashing around her. 'Bit Missus O'Brien,' shouted one of the men, 'He's a Proddy!' not knowing that so was Mrs O'Brien, not that it mattered.

She saw them off then took the victim into our house and cleaned him up, all the while lecturing him on how his mother must feel with him mixed up in knife fights. 'Missus O'Brien,' he said wearily, 'Ah huvnae seen ma mammy since Ah wis a wean o'three.' Listening at the door I wondered what this could mean. Life was simple; fathers went to work if they had it, mothers stayed at home to look after the house and the children. So why hadn't he seen his mother for such a long time? When he'd gone I asked Nan about it and she told me with a frown that the boy's mother had run away from home leaving him behind. This made me wonder even more; what terrible thing could he have done to make his mother run away from him?

Gradually, and to her great embarrassment, Nan became known as 'a guid wumman', and our home became a haven for neglected children whose mothers were away from home, either temporarily or permanently. If a mother couldn't find her child she came to our house, knowing that the child would be there, safe, fed and cared for. Children waited outside our close for her during the day happy to walk along the long road with her to the bus-stop, where the local gangs stepped aside to let her on first, though she tried not to notice. I only really became aware that Nan was different once I started school, and realized that the other kids tumbled out at going home time and fought to have her tie their laces. 'Kin ye still no' tie yur ain laces?' she would ask in mock disapproval, and the kids would grin back at her, 'Ah don't know whit kinda school that kin be!' With an exaggerated sigh she would put down the ubiquitous message bag. 'A'right then,' she'd say, 'Gimme yur fit oan ma knee.' It had always happened, but there was one day that I looked at the scene from the outside for the first time and wondered: why Nan? I wasn't bothered by it and neither was I particularly impressed, I simply noticed it consciously for the first time. By taking up a few minutes of her time the kids weren't depriving me of anything. They only wanted to bask in a little of her warmth, and she always had more than enough of it to go round.

Chapter Five

We were always aware that our friends' brothers, uncles and fathers disappeared into Glasgow's notorious Barlinnie Prison. It was known locally as the Bar-L, or more confusingly given Nan's ambitions for us, the Big Hoose. One day our cousin David boasted that he knew where Barlinnie was and Laurie dared him to take us there. We walked along the canal bank and stopped opposite a café on Cumbernauld Road called the Golfer's Rest, reputed to be a meeting place for the Teds. The stark, raw brutality of Barlinnie rose before us over the trees, and even though I was only about four years old, I felt a shiver run through me; the place was so patently what it was. As we stood there, engrossed in recounting the horror stories we had heard about the place, we became aware of three men standing behind us. One was Billy Fullarton, the leading Protestant baddie, and the other two we knew by sight as his henchmen and bodyguards. 'Walk!' said Fullarton, pointing back in the direction we had come from, and with a feeling of dumb terror we were trailed all the way home by them in total silence. I felt like a puppet with slack strings, nothing in my entire body was coordinated and I was cold all over. I was only a child, but I really believed that I was about to die.

At the foot of Acrehill Street, Fullarton leaned down and stared into the deepest recesses of our young souls. 'Yer mammy's a decent wee wumman,' he said, 'She'd no' like ye gaun near that place. It's a bad, bad place. So don't go near it again, or Ah'll see tae ye. Unnerstaun'?' He then released us to walk home alone in a state of shock; we were like hostages who had expected to be shot only to be inexplicably released instead. With every step there was an urge to turn around and see if he was still there, but we resisted it rather than be killed by one more glance from Fullarton's cold, hard eyes. When Nan opened the door it was like walking into a different world, like Dorothy opening the door after the storm to reveal the brilliant technicolour of the Land of Oz. I could smell gooseberry pie which was one of her specialities and up till then had always been one of my favourites. To this day I only have to see a gooseberry yoghurt to feel Fullarton's gaze on me and the terror I felt that day rushes back.

It took me a long time to work out why he had let us walk those last awful yards home alone. Nan would have been horrified if someone like him had arrived on her doorstep and obviously Fullarton knew this, so he had simply saved her the embarrassment. He knew the difference between Them and Us and he had acknowledged it that day in deference to Nan, who was 'a decent wee wumman'.

After that, whenever our paths crossed, he would stare at us coldly as he exhaled a long, slow stream of cigarette smoke, and we knew that he knew that we would never forget. Some time later I was on my way to the dentist and was wearing a scarf around my mouth, the traditional badge of the toothache sufferer. Waiting at the bus-stop with Nan I was aware of Fullarton and his two henchmen there too. To my horror, and doubtless even more to Nan's, I saw him approach us. He put his hand in his pocket, brought out a half-crown and put it into my hand. 'Ye kin get sweeties efter,' he said, and walked back to his friends. Nan took it from me and threw it away later. 'Ye don't know who he carved up tae get his hauns on that,' she told me, 'It's tainted hen.' It was a relief to get rid of it, after all it had belonged to Billy Fullarton, but even so, I wondered if I'd ever get to keep a half-crown while Nan was around.

Fullarton's intrusion into the civilian ranks had been exceptional, because the gangs were identifiable armies and though they lived among us they never truly lived with us. There was a subtle code that we picked up, like never establishing eye contact and never, ever talking to them. I wasn't aware of being told this, it was part of a collective sixth sense that we absorbed and was as natural and essential to Blackhill children as breathing. As a result we never felt that we would be harmed and neither were we. If a fight broke out when children were around we would simply move quickly out of the way or be moved by the adults present, so that the distance between the civilians and the fighting men was always maintained. Nan though, without that instinct born of childhood experience, saw danger everywhere and was unable to distinguish between real trouble and the imaginary kind. To her every minute we lived in Blackhill was filled with potential danger, and every second that passed safely was a bonus.

Laurie, David and I once dug up a gun wrapped in oilcloth in the backcourt, a hand-gun just like the ones we saw in the cowboy films. We fought over it all day, taking turns at pretending to fire it at each other, until we reached impasse on who should get to keep it. Just like everybody else, we took our dispute to Nan for mediation. She went totally to pieces when she saw the gun. The curtains were drawn, the door locked and for some illogical reason our prize was put into the coal-bunker. When Skip came home he took the gun back to where we had found it and re-buried it, and as far as he was concerned that was the end of it. Not for Nan though; it was weeks before she slept properly again, and whenever she saw a gang member she went through the closed curtains, locked door routine all over again, convinced that we would all be murdered in our beds for finding the gun. Laurie, David and I watched over our buried treasure from various close-mouths for a while to see who might come back for it. When no one did we remembered better things to do and gave up, so we never did find out who had left it there, and for all I know it could be there still.

The hard men of the gangs made their livings outside their home areas and not by robbing or cheating their own neighbours, so they kept on the right side of them. No-one in Blackhill would have grassed on any of the gangs, and not entirely through self-interest, but also because they took care to give us little to complain about. Besides, the police were our common enemy, so there was no one to grass to.

There was a convention that men didn't swear in front of women and children, so the first time I ever heard the phrase 'Fenian bastards' was from the police. Having an ear for words I of course repeated it perfectly to Nan, keen to know what it meant. Once she recovered she explained that it meant a Catholic who didn't have a father. ''Cos he's in the Bar L?' I asked. 'Aye hen,' she replied in a distracted kind of way, 'Sumthin' like that, bit don't you say it tae thum, they might no' like it.' Later, when she thought I was out of earshot, I heard her telling Peggy, as she told Peggy everything, and the two of them laughed till they cried. Then they looked at me, and I looked at them and they laughed again, till we were all three clinging together giggling. I was laughing because I was delighted to have caused them such happiness, if only I could work out why and how I'd done it . . .

The gangs survived materially by turning over factories, shops and businesses in other parts of the city, and their only money-spinners within Blackhill were protection rackets involving the pubs and illegal bookies. There was a little money-lending, but to fellow rogues, not to the ordinary punters, and of course there was dealing in stolen property. Most of the trouble that did break out that wasn't purely sectarian, was because one lot had moved in on another's territory, or someone hadn't paid up on a deal, and in that way the violence was contained within the 'armies'.

Nan's constant fear was a thing of puzzlement to me, because living in Blackhill gave me a feeling of security and safety that I have never regained and as a child I was supremely happy there. Peggy was near enough to visit every day, and *en route* we also saw the other refugees from Balmano Street. Yet from the day we moved into the house at 34 Nan was trying to get out. She would send letters to all the council officials she had approached countless times on behalf of other people, and make endless visits to meet councillors and MPs. None of it worked of course, there were no houses anywhere except those that no one else wanted, which meant houses in the worst areas, like Blackhill. Though her affection for and empathy with the ordinary people was to grow over the years, Nan never came to terms with living there and never lost her fear of the hard men.

One of the local characters who made Nan nervous lived at the top of of our street. From a ground floor house, a man leaned on his window-sill all day, every day. He talked to all the children going to and from school and gave us thruppenny bits for the ice-cream van that stopped outside his house. Skip always spent time talking to the man, but though Nan tried she seemed uneasy. When I mentioned this to Skip, he said with a laugh, 'Yer ma's mair genteel than the rest o' us.' Years later I learned that the man had married 'a bad yin', and had come home one day to find his kids locked out in the rain and his wife locked in with another man. In the fight that followed he had killed her, but he must have been convicted of culpable homicide (manslaughter) to have escaped the noose in those days.

When I knew him he was an old man and had served whatever sentence he had been given. He had never seen his kids again, so he lived through the lives of the neighbourhood kids for thruppence a time, a gentle soul who gave out no feeling of threat or danger, except to Nan, who was 'mair genteel'. It was part of her inability to judge Blackhill accurately that she couldn't relate one hundred per cent to him, though he was the kind of underdog that she would normally do battle for. Whenever the capital punishment debate resurfaces and I hear murderers described as monsters and perverts, somehow I can't help thinking about him; just an ordinary man who had lost everything, and regretted it everytime he saw a child.

Further down the long, crescent-shaped street, round about where it curved, was a different kind of man altogether. He was the father of a mentally handicapped boy of about ten, called Bobby. I never knew exactly what was wrong with Bobby, he was just 'no 'right'; he used to watch all the other kids out of his window but he wasn't allowed to join us and he didn't go to school. For long spells we never saw him, then he'd reappear again, watching from his window. One day Nan had a deputation of women at the door to report that Bobby had been heard being beaten up by his father and was badly bruised on the side of his face. Some of the women had gone to see Bobby's father and had been sent away with screams of abuse ringing in their ears, and poor Bobby got it again. Nan went to see the local health visitor, called the Green Lady because of the colour of her uniform, but she got short shrift too, and no one thought of involving the police because we knew better than to trust them. To the police, who came from outside, everyone in Blackhill was scum, fit only to be raided and thrown into the back of Black Marias en route for the Bar L, and it was accepted that we took care of our own problems without involving them. In fact, the unspoken rule about not looking directly at the hard men and not trying to engage them in conversation also held good where the police were concerned, and however bad a villain might be, no one would ever have helped the police to take him away.

Across the street from Bobby lived a woman called Mrs Logan. Her home was like a palace, everything spick and span and displaying riches beyond our experience. While we were lucky to have lino on all our floors, Mrs Logan had fitted carpets, and a taxi picked her up whenever she ventured outside, one of the few times we saw a car in Blackhill. It was said that Mrs Logan was Billy Fullarton's aunt. So Nan and I went to see her, which was an unbelievable treat for me, because Mrs Logan seemed to have an endless supply of biscuits and cakes. When we went back next day I really thought my boat had come in, but sitting there were Billy Fullarton and his two friends and suddenly I couldn't force down a crumb of the feast Mrs Logan had laid before us.

Nan hadn't acknowledged Fullarton's presence and he hadn't addressed a word to her either. Avoiding his eyes, Nan seemed to tell Bobby's story to no one in particular. Fullarton listened, his face taut and expressionless and those hard, icy eyes staring at her. When she had finished he still said nothing. As we were leaving he put a hand on my head and I drew back instinctively. 'It's a'right wee yin,' he said with what passed for a smile, 'Ah don't hurt weans. Except fur bad weans mibbe. Ur you a bad wean?' Then he laughed, which was just as well because I couldn't have thought of a reply. Afterwards, as we walked along past the two closes between Mrs Logan's house and ours Nan was shaking, and when she got inside she locked the door and made cup after cup of tea.

A couple of nights later there was a commotion in Bobby's close which we took as part of normal life at the time, but next day we saw Bobby's father badly bruised and cut about the face. He never touched the boy again, in fact whenever Nan stopped to talk to Bobby, his father was positively deferential. After all, she had Billy Fullarton at her beck and call, though she never admitted having any part in what had occurred.

To my great chagrin we never went near Mrs Logan and her Aladdin's Cave of goodies again, in fact my mother would take long detours to avoid passing the house. Sometimes in her attempts to avoid Mrs Logan Nan would get lost in the maze of backcourts and closes, and being more familiar with them I would guide her safely home. This meant clambering over middens, the three-sided, concrete structures with sloping roofs where the rubbish bins were kept. I discovered that Nan was no good at dealing with middens, and, if anything, worse at climbing or squeezing through the iron railings that separated the tenement back-courts. I remember feeling mildly embarrassed by her lack of aptitude in such ordinary skills.

Whenever we did pass her house, Mrs Logan would shout down to us to come up, but Nan always had an excuse. All those cakes and biscuits, all that luxury, was lost to me for ever. There were times when I just couldn't understand my mother; she wanted the good life for us, but whenever we got close to it she threw it away.

I can only recall actually witnessing one warrant sale in Blackhill, though I knew one was probably taking place if I saw a car. We only saw cars if a doctor, the police or the sheriff officers, or bailiffs, came calling. Warrant sales took place when someone couldn't pay a debt, and their possessions were sold off to make it up. Given the level of poverty of some families, or maybe because of it, there were fewer sales than might have been expected, because sheriff officers were reluctant to venture into Blackhill to enforce the warrant. There was never any actual violence that I remember, but the reputation of the place worked in our favour in a way and certainly the women used it to its full advantage to create an atmosphere of menace.

The goods being sold off, few as they were, often went to the sheriff officers themselves at knock-down prices, so the local women pooled whatever money they could lay hands on and bought everything up, then returned it to the victim. I didn't regard this as heroic at the time any more than the women themselves did. They knew that if their turn came next the same rescue operation would be mounted for them. It was part of the way things were to me as a small child, but looking back now from an era where nobody cares much about anyone else, and especially knowing how tight money was in those days, I admire their strength and decency in a way I feel but can't adequately explain.

On that particular day I was off school with tonsillitis, a constant complaint throughout my childhood, and I was hanging onto the handles of Nan's message bag as she and the other women made their way to the home of the hapless debtor. The sheriff officers had taken the precaution of bringing police protection with them, a move that amused the women and made their loathing of both stronger. After all, what kind of men could they be, to be afraid to face a bunch of women without bringing the police for protection? The sheriff officers and the police saw it as a demonstration of strength, but the women regarded it as an admission of fear. Nothing much happened, the goods were snapped up by the women but I can remember the tension as they stood in ranks so close that the intruders could barely move. When the sale ended the weeping woman once more took possession of her bits and pieces. As the sheriff officers were leaving the close Nan couldn't contain herself any longer.

'Excuse me!' she called after a bowler-hatted sheriff

officer, 'Ah wis wonderin' aboot yer mother. Is she still alive?' He stopped for a moment, puzzled, and stuttered that his mother was dead.

'Likely died o' shame,' Nan replied, as the other women gathered around. 'Hur wean growin' up tae dae this tae decent people.'

'I get no pleasure from this kind of thing,' the creature said, 'I am only doing my job.'

'Aye,' Nan said softly, 'Sumbody will've gied ye orders right enough. It's no' really your fault like.'

'Exactly!'

'Is that no' whit the Nazis said tae?' she asked.

'I don't need to take this from the likes of you! I fought in the War!'

'Bit oan whit side?' Nan retorted, 'Ah hope tae God it wisnae oors 'kis oor men wur surely *men*!' The other women formed a semicircle behind Nan as the police moved in to shepherd the sheriff officer towards his car. Nan reserved her fire until the car door was open and he had one foot off the ground ready to climb in.

'Ye don't seem sich a bad wee man,' she said kindly, 'Bit ur ye no' black affronted at earning yer livin' in this *durty* wey?'

He hesitated just long enough to register that her barb had gone straight home, before climbing into the car and being driven off. His chin rested on his hand and his face was turned away in an attempt to convey his complete lack of concern. But the women had witnessed that split second of hesitation as he got into the car and they knew better. Their derisive laughter rang out, and though I had no real understanding of what had happened, I knew we had won somehow; Nan had been taking lessons from the O'Briens. Yet much to my puzzlement, she hurried home, closed the door and burst into floods of tears. Then she made a cup of tea and got on with her housework, singing as she always did. I understand now, of course. She was crying tears of humiliation and rage, the tears of the helpless and powerless.

* * *

And yet despite the harshness of Blackhill life, it was for me filled with the magic of childhood. The summers were just as long and sunny, the winters as full of sparkling snow as anywhere else. Indeed, the only time I ever saw Santa Claus was in Blackhill. I slept in a bed cabinet in my parents' bedroom and on that Christmas morning I must have wakened just as Santa was leaving, because certainly I heard a noise that made me ignore my presents. I ran to the window and looked out – and there he was! He was just above ground level, guiding the sleigh through the air, laden with presents, giving instead of taking, and the sleigh was pulled by two long lines of reindeer. I tried to waken my parents but they didn't seem interested, so they probably missed their only chance to prove the existence of Father Christmas. I can still see in my mind's eye today what I saw that dark, early morning, and it really was Santa, it really, really was . . .

Chapter Six

Peggy was the only unmarried Clark, a gentle, vivacious woman with a lovely smile and quiet nature. My mother was regarded as the brains of the family, but together she and Peggy formed the core, even to the 'Fair Yins'. Peggy was less articulate than my mother, less intense, but they were two parts of one character. Nan was the doer, but only after discussing everything with her sister, including the approach to Fullarton through Mrs Logan. Peggy would never have had the courage to actually do it, but she would have agreed with the plan or Nan wouldn't have carried it out.

Nan and Peggy met every day, it would have been unthinkable not to because they needed each other, and I grew up the third part of a tight eternal triangle. Peggy's one ambition was to get married and have a family of her own, but there was a feeling about her of being one of nature's spinsters, a custom-made maiden aunt. If that was what fate had decreed, Peggy wasn't for accepting it though.

Weddings drew her like a magnet and she would stand for hours outside a church if she happened on a wedding, just for a glimpse of the happy couple, then she would smile for the rest of the day. If you saw a wedding when she wasn't there you had to recall it in great detail while her eyes misted over with the romance of it all. I used to dread being in town with her, because she would never go home until we had visited every wedding-dress shop for miles and admired every creation available. Having spent so much time in the company of Laurie I was a confirmed tomboy and very definitely not a lace and flounces child. Despite this Peggy's plan was that when she married I'd be her bridesmaid and so, she claimed, she *had* to window shop. I used to cringe at the frilly concoctions she dreamt up for me, but she never noticed, she was eternally lost in her dream.

Babies also left her dewy-eyed. Like my mother she had the unconscious ability to draw children to her, and Peggy hadn't my mother's experience of the reality to dampen her romanticism. Peggy wasn't interested in having a good time, she was interested only in settling down and starting a family. This naturally put men off, especially those who had returned from years of war-service and just wanted some fun.

Her taste in men was notoriously awful, and each one would be brought to my mother for approval. The waifs, the strays, the wasters, misfits and the undesirables, somehow they all found their way to Peggy and she convinced herself that each and every one was a god. Add to that list of catches the ones she fancied but never got near, all of them reprobates to a man, and Peggy's reputation as a magnet for disaster was safe for all time. I don't think she ever noticed my mother's grimaces, she was lost in her dream and adored each god who chanced along.

When each relationship failed my mother would heave a sigh of relief, until the next unsuitable match arrived on the horizon. Uncle George, the other 'Dark Yin', would seek out my mother and plead with her to put Peggy off whichever man she was seeing through her eternally rose-tinted gaze this time, and my mother would assure him it wouldn't last anyhow.

Peggy, much as they loved her, was a constant worry, she was too gentle for the world, too trusting and in need of protection. She had a heart of marshmallow and was easily moved to tears, which in turn moved my mother to tears. They'd stand there together, mopping their eyes, then the scene would strike them as silly and funny and they'd laugh, which in turn caused more tears. The vicious circle would continue until they were exhausted by it all and were rendered red-eyed and out of breath, unable to look at each other without suffering a massive relapse. Each blamed the other on these occasions, but in truth it was impossible to tell where one ended and the other began. They were equally to blame, though neither could ever explain why they were laughing or how it had all started. 'Wait a minute! Wait a minute! Whit wur we laughin' it?' one or other would demand breathlessly, which was more than enough to start it all up again. I used to watch them, holding their sides and groaning but unable to stem the laughter or the

59

tears, hanging onto each other for support and demanding that the other 'Stoap it noo!' No O'Brien could have or would have been able to abandon themself to such glorious, all-consuming emotion and mirth.

As part of her quest for marriage and motherhood, Peggy regularly enlisted the help of Norah, Skip's sister. Norah had a strong theatrical bent, as her performances with Hughie showed, and had decided that she could tell fortunes. This she did by reading teacups, and before each 'reading' she did for Peggy she would quiz me carefully about what was happening in Peggy's life. Thus was she able to come up with amazing details, almost as if someone had told her, and Peggy believed every word she uttered. *The* man was forecast several times and he never arrived, but that didn't put Peggy off. After all, look at the things Norah knew about her . . . There must be something in it . . .

Peggy was a highly skilled welder, a trade she had learned during the War. She made tabernacles for the Catholic church, the ornate little domes that house the Eucharist on church altars. Given the bitterness of Maw Clark's Orange leanings, this of course made Nan and Peggy laugh more than anything else did. Maw had an orange pin cushion, and embroidered on it was King William of Orange sitting on his white horse. Whenever Skip went into the Moodiesburn Street house he would insert pins in strategic parts of King Billy's anatomy, which would bring Maw screaming to remove them. This always puzzled me; what else could one do with a pin cushion but stick pins in it? Was it a dastardly plot invented by the Catholic church to manufacture the pin cushions and sell them to devotees of the Loyal Orange Order, so that pins *would* be stuck in King Billy? As with all running jokes, everyone, especially the children, joined in, so that King Billy was perpetually covered in pinholes. It wasn't because we were bigoted, we didn't understand any of it. All we knew was that it was a marvellous way to greatly upset Maw Clark.

★   ★   ★

The O'Briens were regarded by the Clarks with guarded affection, as honoured guests that they were lucky to have among them. The O'Briens of course accepted this as their due, with dignity and condescension and they put their usual ploys on hold, never subjecting the Clarks to any warfare. They were family, but family once removed after all and not up to the Game. There was no enjoyment in scoring points over an opponent who wasn't up to standard. Wisely the Clarks were never sure of them, though they loved to have them at family gatherings. It was like sin by proxy, as the O'Briens did and said the kind of things that the Clarks wanted to, but never dared.

Skip, Hughie and another brother, Pat, were famed for their sand-dance, shirt-tails out, trousers rolled up and pots on their heads. They scattered ashes on the floor from the fireplace of wherever they were, and performed their master-piece in total silence, and the sight of the five O'Brien legs sent the Clarks into their usual heaving, creaking laughter. For me the delight was in seeing the Clarks all holding onto each other, tears running down their faces, totally abandoned to their mirth. The sand-dance itself was common-place, after all I was an O'Brien and had seen it many times.

The O'Briens reserved their gentlest treatment for Peggy, who was shy with them and blushed as Hughie kissed her hand or sang her praises. There was something about her that brought out their sensitive side, and not many people could do that to the O'Briens. They would have fun with Nan by suggesting that Hughie and Peggy would make a good match, and Nan would scream with horror. 'Wan o' us bein' married intae this lot is bad enough!' she'd declare, 'Oor Peggy disnae deserve that!' She knew of course that they were having her on, but the enjoyment for them was that they knew Nan could never be entirely sure.

Clark family gatherings usually celebrated someone's birthday, Glasgow Fair holidays, Christmas or New Year, but they could just happen if enough people turned up at the house my grandmother and Peggy shared in Moodiesburn Street. A bottle would be spun and whoever it pointed to had to sing. I always sought a cave-like vantage point to view it from, usually under the table and waited for all the party pieces to be enacted. No gathering was complete without Peggy being persuaded to sing 'Mexicali Rose'. It was a maudlin country-and-western ditty about star-crossed lovers – what else would Peggy sing?

Mexicali Rose stop crying
I'll come back to you some sunny day
Every night you'll know that I'll be pining
Every hour a year while I'm away
Dry those big brown eyes and smile dear
Banish all those tears and please don't sigh
Kiss me once again and hold me
Mexicali Rose, Goodbye bye.

Mexicali Rose I'm leaving, don't feel blue
Mexicali Rose stop grieving, I love you
When the dove of love is winging through the blue
All the castles you've been building will come true.

The song might have been written for Peggy to sing, the sorrow for the lost love and the building of castles and as she sang, tears flowing from her big brown eyes, Skip and Willie would mime the song to the assembled company. They would swoon into each other's arms and sob sorely before riding off into the sunset around the table, as I watched their performance from underneath. By that time Peggy would have been forced to give up anyway, due to a combination of tears of sympathy for the unfortunate Rose and tears of laughter at the travesty of her sorrow being enacted. Then Uncle Willie would sing an army song about Quinn's Pub in the Springburn area of Glasgow, an establishment obviously held in great affection and built under a rocky outcrop that had been made into stairs. It was called 'Doon in the Wee House' and had to be sung whenever Willie was present, and if a do was on, Willie was there.

Doon in the wee hoose, underneath the stairs,
Everybody's happy, everybody's there.
We're a' gay and he'rty, each in his chair,
Doon in the wee hoose, underneath the stairs.

Noo Christopher Columbus sailed the ocean blue,
'Twas him that discovered America, if history books
    are true,
All honour tae Columbus, but honour I declare,
Tae the man that built the wee hoose, underneath
    the stair.

Noo when ye're feelin' lonely, when ye're feelin'
    blue,
Don't give way to sorrow, Ah'll tell ye what to do,
Jist take a tram tae Springburn, see if Quinn's is
    there,
He's the man that built the wee hoose, underneath
    the stair.

Noo when Ah'm feelin' weary, and ma bones are
    sair,
Ah won't get auld an' grumpy, like that auld
    bugger there.
Ah'll save up a' ma pennies tae buy a hurly-chair,
Jist tae tak' me tae the wee hoose underneath the
    stair.

When it came to the line, 'Ah won't get auld an' grumpy',
the entire company would rise as one, point an accusatory finger at Maw Clark and shout 'Like that auld bugger there!'

Skip's party piece, when the other three legs of the famous
sand-dance weren't present, was to begin singing an army
song that after a few lines threatened to descend into filth
but never did, because everyone jumped up shouting and
throwing things at him. It was what could be called a performance piece, with everyone else having to take part for full
effect, but watching from my cave under the table, it always
made me feel uncomfortable. I didn't quite understand what
it was about and of course no one would explain; it was one

of those adult jokes that make all children feel slightly uneasy for that very reason. Nan sang an odd little song, given the many others she knew.

Wance Ah hid a wee broon hen, it hid a wee broon
    tail,
Ah sent it fur an ounce o' snuff an' it never came
    back again,
Noo it's deid an' in it's grave fur many an' many a
    day,
God bless ma wee hen, it never came back again.

Ah'll hae a funeral fur ma wee hen,
Ah'll hae a funeral, fur ladies an' gentlemen,
Ladies an' gentlemen know ma wee hen,
God bless ma wee hen, it never came back again.

Everyone joined in with the chorus, as they did with every song apart from Skip's, because he never got that far, but it was a strange little song for my mother to sing. Despite the tragic end of the wee broon hen it was always sung with great gusto and greeted with much cheering and stamping of feet.

These happy family gatherings showed the great differences between the two families. The Clarks for instance lived on their feelings and lacked the emotional strength of the O'Briens, though that strength was the kind that children have, egotistical and selfish. To the O'Briens, showing what you really felt or thought gave others an unfair advantage over you, so emotions were kept tightly under control. Instead they performed a comical act that kept them safe from close emotional ties, ties that I think they were incapable of forming. They concealed their feelings behind a mask of knockabout humour and it was a matter of pride to them not to shed a tear, even under the most tragic circumstances. The O'Briens believed that control was strength, but the sentimental Clarks cared and that did make them vulnerable. As they would find out before long, caring costs.

Chapter Seven

I was a toddler when I first saw my brother Mickey. He was still in Mearnskirk Hospital and children weren't allowed to visit, so I was taken to look at him, or for him to look at me, through a fence. I had no idea what I was about to see or what I should do, but I remember feeling let down by the experience.

This creature called a Mickey had been so exotic and fabulous that my parents had spent every weekend and as many days or evenings as they could, going to see it. It was talked of incessantly, it was regularly bought gifts that were beyond the dreams of Laurie and me, therefore it had to be something wondrous to behold. At last I was being allowed to see it, to be in its presence. But it turned out that a Mickey was just a big boy supported by two wooden crutches. This confused me, because I thought only Uncle Hughie had a wooden crutch, yet here was Mickey with two. He looked physically like a 'Dark Yin', the only one of our family who had all of the Clark characteristics, dark skin, eyes and hair.

I have no idea if Mickey was as disappointed as I was by that meeting but I think he probably was. His whole attitude towards me was always impatience that I did not conform to his personal standard of what his sister should be like. So we both failed spectacularly to live up to the expectations of the other. If I wanted Mickey to be a magical creature, then he clearly wanted some ideal storybook sister he could be proud of on his terms. Not of course that we ever expressed any of this, because we never became close enough to talk of such things. We just settled into a mutual dislike that grew from the seeds of our seperate disappointments at that first meeting. It was little to do with actions or words and everything to do with unrealistic expectations that were bound to be dashed.

The only truly revealing thing Mickey ever told me was that when he was in hospital he thought he came from a rich family. Everything he wanted he got, and the best of it. Nan once saved money to buy him special soap for instance, because the hospital variety irritated his skin. It came as the biggest shock and disappointment of his life to discover that we were extremely poor. I often wondered if he made the next connection, that Laurie and I had done without to keep him in luxuries, but if he did he kept it to himself. It was something he had no control over anyway, he was, after all, a child at the time.

Mickey came out of hospital for a spell while we were in Blackhill, and because of his mistaken belief that we were rich, he hated it even more than Nan did. Apart from the feeling that he was unhappy, I have very little recollection of him then. He was after all eleven years older and therefore an adult compared to me, uninvolved in my life in the streets. Most of his time he spent studying to make up for the schooling he had missed. He was very bright and was interested in electronics and Nan was determined that he should get every chance. The only memories I have of his time with us is of his head bowed over a book and the caliper on his left leg. When he walked across the floor, which wasn't often because he spent most of his time in bed, the woman who lived below complained about the noise he made. I had no particular affection for Mickey, but the woman's insensitivity appalled whatever sense of justice Nan had instilled in me. Her name was Mrs Burrell, and to this day I dislike the name.

After years of operations Mickey's knee-cap had been removed and the joint locked, so that he could not bend it as he moved. Laurie and I were used to having a fully mobile Uncle Hughie about the place so Mickey's handicap didn't seem like one to us, but Nan cried a lot, though never when Mickey was around. I couldn't understand why; after all, she hadn't done it to him. Now that I'm a mother myself, of course, I understand only too well and I wish I could reach back through all those years and give her the cuddle I didn't understand enough to give her then.

I started school at Easter 1953, just before I was five years old, joining Laurie at St Philomena's Roman Catholic school in Royston Road, though being six years older than me he was in his last year at primary school. Nan had me kitted out in a frilly blouse, Royal Stewart tartan skirt and black-patent shoes with huge buckles, called kiltie shoes. All the children cried of course; it was the generation before play schools were invented to make the parting easier. Having gone the first day I could see no reason to go back again and had to be forced.

My teachers soon discovered that I could already read and I was instantly treated like a leper. Nan was summoned to be told how displeased they were and her protests that she hadn't taught me, that I had picked it up by myself, were treated with scorn. It wasn't until my own son was learning to read that I discovered how I had cracked the code. Apparently children begin to read by recognizing word shapes, and I have a clear recollection of picking out words with double letters in the middle; I liked words like 'good' and 'week' for instance. Knowing why I learned to read still doesn't explain how I knew what those words represented. That remains a mystery still.

Knowledge was the teachers' to give however, and if they didn't give it, it was not to be acquired. I was put at a desk apart from the other children and kept supplied with books, which I suppose was a form of punishment. If it was, then it backfired badly, because to this day I can think of no finer treat than to be left alone to read books endlessly. When the school inspectors arrived I would be trotted out to read to them, thereby proving the excellence of St Philomena's teaching abilities. I have often wondered since if the teachers were stupid for thinking the inspectors were taken in by this ploy, or if the inspectors *were* taken in and were therefore as stupid as the teachers believed them to be.

One of the more absurd features of life in Glasgow, then as now, was that schools were segregated by religion. Every morning we collected David at number 43 and together we walked to school, past the little man who had killed his wife to the end of Acrehill Street to where it met Craighead Avenue. There David had to veer off to the right and go to his school the long way. David, coming from my mother's side of the family went to the Protestant school, whereas Laurie and I went to the Catholic school because of Skip. In local parlance we were, without a hint of offence given or taken, Proddies or Papes. Despite the lack of animosity over names, had David passed our school he would have been attacked and severely beaten up, just as we would have been had we tried to pass his school.

Every lunchtime there were pre-arranged fights, with a gang of children from one school attempting to invade the other, and we stockpiled clods of earth for the battle. It would start in the ritual manner, with the day's aggressors standing outside chanting a song against the other side. We would shout 'Proddy dogs eat frogs!', which for some reason was regarded as a huge insult, and they would sing the few words they knew of 'The Sash My Father Wore'. We hadn't a clue why we should take offence at this either, we only knew that we had to or the battle couldn't commence and before long the air was heavy with clods of earth from both sides. The Proddies also sang a cheery little song that we all secretly joined in with, singing it under our breaths because we knew it was a sin:

> Hello, hello, we are the Billy Boys,
> Hello, hello, we are the Billy Boys,
> Up to the knees in Fenian blood,
> Surrender or you'll die,
> Hello, we are the Billy Boys!

Again neither side knew what any of it meant, it was just another adult insult handed down to children who sang it while happily throwing clods at each other.

At the end of the day, once out of sight of our respective schools, David, Laurie and I met up again at the corner of Craighead Avenue and Acrehill Street and headed home together. For us it was doubly bizarre, because David had been as close as a brother since our Brae days. Children just accept what they are brought up with and we never questioned it. That of course is the tragedy of it and how religious bigotry survives. Anyone who doubts this only has to look at the children taken to march in Orange marches, who haven't a clue what it's all about but will make their children march too when the time comes. So it was religion which drove a wedge between families and friends, and it's still happening today.

It was natural that David should want to continue playing with the children he had been playing with at school all day, and the same was true of us. Soon we were walking on opposite sides of the street, mouthing mindless obscenities at each other that we didn't understand, things we never heard or repeated within the family. We never made the connection between what was happening at school and King Billy on Maw Clark's pin-cushion, we didn't even realize it was all part of the same nonsense. Bigotry was a subject on the school curriculum, sticking pins in King Billy was a family joke, and it's very difficult to hate something that you laugh at.

Sometimes I look back to those days and I feel great anger at the way we were manipulated into expressing a hatred we didn't feel and even greater sadness for the innocent victims that we were.

The reality was that religion just wasn't for me, even at a very early age. It made no sense to me whatsoever and still doesn't. Skip took me to my first mass when I was about five years old and I found it unutterably, mind-crushingly boring. I was forced to attend mass chiefly by Nan, in a 'never let it be said that I stopped them being Catholics' way. Eventually I became impossible through desperation to escape, behaving so badly that they stopped making me go. Otherwise I might have become a serious arsonist.

Nan was delighted that I was bright at school, after all learning, education was all to her. It took her a long time to convince me that I would never be able to fly though, and I'm not sure even yet that she succeeded. Birds in the sky were like people flying to me and I simply assumed that one day I'd fly too; I was devastated when she insisted that I couldn't and wouldn't. Somewhere deep inside I think I'm still devastated. It must have induced fears in Nan that I had inherited too strong an O'Brien streak, because she forbade me from telling anyone, apart from Peggy of course, who wasn't just anyone. I wasn't hurt when Peggy laughed, she was after all a part of me, but I always felt that Uncle Hughie would have understood, so maybe Nan was right about my O'Brien streak. It was a good example of the difference between the two families: apart from Peggy's romantic castle-building, the Clarks dealt with reality and had their feet firmly on the ground, while the O'Briens dealt strictly in fantasy and understood the yearning to soar into the air.

Mickey was clever too, but Laurie couldn't read and he couldn't spell, and his writing was totally unintelligible. Letters were missing or back-to-front and always in the wrong order. He was dyslexic, but in the fifties no one in education knew anything about the condition. He had a calculator brain when it came to mathematics, but because of his dyslexia he was regarded as an idiot.

Naturally it brought out in Nan the lioness fighting for her cub, allied to her natural sympathy for the underdog, and she had another cause to fight. When he failed his qualifying test, the forerunner of the eleven-plus, he was consigned to a Junior Secondary School, where the idiots went. Nan would have none of it; she knew Laurie had a problem even if she didn't know what it was, but she also knew that with his ability with numbers he wasn't stupid. She lobbied the Education Department, harassed the school and won over a teacher to help her lobby the Education Department some more. Finally she won and six months after being consigned to the scrap-heap Laurie was sent to St Mungo's Academy instead. Once there though, with no more understanding of dyslexia than anywhere else at the time, Laurie's difficulties weren't addressed and he got no help. It was as if the authorities had relented and said, 'OK, you're in a Senior Secondary now. Be normal.' So Laurie continued to struggle, and because of the deficiencies of the system, he was made to feel responsible for his problem.

Every Saturday David, Laurie and I went to the pictures. This entailed walking the length of Acrehill Street, along Provan Road to the Rex or the Vogue in Alexandra Parade, a distance of perhaps two miles. It was an expedition that called for sustenance *en route* and for this we went to Galbraith's, a big shop near where Peggy and Maw lived, that sold chipped apples and broken biscuits. Sometimes the expedition took so long because of many detours to play along the way that we missed the film. On one of those occasions my brother Laurie gave me a black wine gum to eat that was really a slug. I ate it with relish, and he was sick; even when he did his brotherly duty by doing something nasty, Laurie was the one who suffered.

We used to sing 'The Black Hills of Dakota', as we walked along, a song we had first heard in a cowboy film. We would sing 'Take me back to the Black hills, the Black hills of Dakota', perfectly happy to accept that Dakota was the Apache name for Glasgow. Then Laurie developed a passion for toy knights in armour, and would occasionally purloin all our cinema cash to buy one for his collection. This naturally had to be kept from Nan, and to put in the necessary hours when we should have been cheering on the cowboys we went to the park or wandered the streets looking in the shop windows. To stop us spilling the beans Laurie let David and I play with the knights too. We weren't particularly gentle with them so he didn't make much out of his little scheme.

Laurie was eternally unhappy. He disliked Skip for coming between him and Nan, yet I always felt that what he wanted more than anything was Skip's approval. There was no natural meeting place between them though; Skip was unused to dealing with low self-esteem that didn't transform itself into eccentricity. Skip was an O'Brien, and that meant never admitting the possibility of being less than special. I think because Laurie wasn't like him my father regarded him as a bit of a wimp, a failure, though he never actually said so. He was not a man used to showing his feelings, if he had them, and he was embarrassed by the fact that Laurie did. I cannot recall my father ever making an encouraging or affectionate remark to his youngest son. Mickey he adored above all other human beings, and it was obvious without my father having to say so that Laurie wasn't in that league. Neither for that matter was I, but I had a different nature from Laurie, and anyway I had a close, warm relationship with Nan and Peggy.

Perhaps the seeds of my adult relationships with both of my brother were sown then. I was never close to Mickey and never thought of it as a possibility. All we now have in common is that we had the same parents and that sort of hold loosens considerably when the parents die. There's no particular bitterness, our paths simply don't cross often. As a child I was close to Laurie, but that stopped when he married and found himself a family of his own. When siblings are brought up to compete with each other they often make a sub-conscious decision to lead separate adult lives, indeed some cannot live in the same country. Looking back I think that was how we grew up, or Laurie and I at any rate, vying for attention and approval that my father could only give to one, his son Mickey. And the sad thing is, that I don't think Mickey gained anything from being the only one Skip cared for.

Chapter Eight

My father was a shoemaker – *not* a cobbler, but a time-served tradesman. Skip always made that distinction as strongly as possible, because of the anti-Catholic bias that had traditionally banned Catholics in Glasgow from being tradesmen. Uncle Hughie had been a shoemaker too and Skip had served his apprenticeship with him. There were attempts to get Skip away from the trade over the years. At the time when Balmano Street collapsed he was a bus conductor for instance, but he was what he was. Nan's official excuse for trying to convert him was to say that it was an unhealthy life, full of leather dust and noise and the wages were low; all true, but not her real objections.

He worked in a long, low, converted farm-building across the road from my school, and when lessons were finished for the day I would sometimes visit him. The farmland had been overtaken by the city, but some of the buildings still stood, and though they weren't used for their intended purposes they kept their original names. So Skip was a shoemaker in the byre and a shop beside him that sold no milk was called the dairy. His employer, Paddy Doyle, was rarely there, so Skip mainly worked alone.

I would take my books into the workshop and watch him at the various stages of mending or making shoes between reading my stories, growing drowsier in the warm, dust-laden atmosphere, lulled by the whirring machines until I fell fast asleep. He kept a yellow tin mug there for me that he had carried around the world during his sojourn with the 8th Army, and would prepare hot, sweet tea for 3 pm. He was a fine craftsman and I never tired of watching him work with the leather, selecting the quality he needed and cutting it to shape with the minimum of waste.

Then he would fill his mouth with nails and start repairing the shoes, placing each nail onto the new sole or heel and rhythmically tapping it into place.

Skip was very particular about the quality of leather he used, and if he ran out of the right kind he would set out on the rounds of the shoemaking fraternity in Glasgow, all Irish to a man. They were a close-knit group and borrowing materials from each other was common. Tools were immediately downed, wives and children called to the shop and every visit became a hooley. I used to go with him and loved the welcoming shoemakers and their families. At one time, had I found myself in trouble in any area of the city I could have gone to the nearest shoemaker and got help by announcing myself as the daughter of Laurie O'Brien.

Skip specialized in making surgical boots and shoes by hand and people were sent to him by other shoemakers. The trouble was that he couldn't bring himself to charge for the real price of the work because anyone handicapped enough to need special shoes was invariably poor, and besides, he had a boy of his own in the same position. The practical aspects of life were never Skip's strong points.

Behind the byre stood a tall, wooden building, the top half of which was the home of an Irish family called Kelly. The Kellys were a big family and countless redhaired, almost identical children tumbled from every crevice. It seemed that every day we were called upon to climb the rickety stairs to their house to admire yet another Kelly baby. The children were clean but never well-dressed and they were the happiest family I have ever seen, a living advert for large families. The railway line ran behind the Kelly house and beside it lay an old car that Nan was determined was full of rats. I could never see the connection between the car and rats, so I played in it for many happy hours with the Kelly clones. None of us had ever been in a real car, but the rat car took us to every exotic location we had ever heard of without once moving from beside the railway track.

I always wanted to walk home with Skip but he would never let me. He would send me on ahead, saying Nan would be waiting for me at home. I knew this wasn't true because

Nan knew exactly where I was, but I had no idea then why he sent me on ahead.

Although Blackhill was criss-crossed with railway lines there was no station anywhere near us. We treated the track like a road we had to cross, and as no buses ran through our streets people inevitably took short-cuts across the track. By getting off the bus at Royston Road, beside the chemical plant, you could cut across my triangle of grass and the track at the bottom end, thereby saving a very long walk. Occasionally someone got hit by a train, someone's man coming home from work or the pub, in the dark. It was how things were, so we accepted it. It never occurred to us that there should have been some sort of fence to keep us and the trains apart, but then we were used to being regarded as not worth the bother by anyone in authority. When someone was killed or injured, all that happened was that Nan and the local women organized a collection around the houses for the family and that was it till the next time.

Once, one of our friends was killed as we played together outside. He was a boy called Jamie Craig who was nearer to Laurie's age than mine. We were hurried away from the scene, but we had all seen enough to know what damage a train could do. His mother's greatest wish was that he should be buried wearing a suit, which we all knew was madness. We had seen him cut to bits, how could he wear a suit? Besides, a suit was an unbelievable luxury, something to aim for but rarely to achieve. Peggy, single and earning money, paid for the suit though, and as we watched the small white coffin being carried out of Jamie's close, we idly discussed the idiocy of adults with the callous logic that children have. There had been nothing left of Jamie to hang a suit on, and all around were live boys who would never have one. Soon the memory faded, as it always did, except for a vivid picture still in my mind today of Jamie's blood on the track.

The other dangers, from the gasworks and the chemical factory, were merely dark suspicions, based on the logical belief that fighting for breath was bad for you. In the fifties there was no concern for the environment and there were no filters fitted on the gasworks. Gas was made by baking coal and to make enough to cope with peak hours like lunch and tea-times, extra coal was baked for an hour or so before, with the by-products being discharged directly into the air over the houses. If washing was left out the smell of sulphur and tar clung to them, and if you were outside you nearly choked on the yellowish fumes. Everyone knew when the gasworks 'came out' and so it was routine to rush home beforehand and to close the windows until the discharge was over.

The gasworks and the chemical factory were suspected of causing the chronic health problems in Blackhill, but it didn't occur to anyone that something could be done about it. We had no idea what came out of the whisky bond either. Added to the industrial factors we couldn't prove, was the inherent dampness and poor insulation of the houses, built with the emphasis on quantity rather than quality. Glasgow Corporation was proud of the low cost of building Blackhill and we lived with the inevitable health risks that went with that priority. It was all part of what 'they' inflicted on us that 'they' wouldn't have inflicted on the richer areas of the city. But anything was good enough for those who lived in Blackhill . . .

Chapter Nine

I was about five years old when I first saw Uncle Jim, one of Skip's many brothers. In the Twenties he had been a bare-knuckle fighter of some repute, and legend had it that he kept a special pair of white kid gloves for his battles.

Jim was a tall man by Glasgow standards and that and his reputation as a fighter made him a target for every macho drunk. He was never a member of a gang and apart from one friend to watch his back he travelled alone. One night he and the friend were in a pub when the usual challenge was issued by a drunk, and the two men got up and left. The drunk followed them to another pub, and when Jim left again he trailed behind, shouting insults. When he still didn't respond the drunk dived at Jim's feet, and Jim kicked out, knocking him against the concrete base of a lamp post and killing him.

Jim was charged with murder, and Granda Tom arranged for one of his St Aloysius contacts, top criminal lawyer Laurence Dowdall, to defend him. Not only did Dowdall get him off, but the Judge praised Jim's restraint under severe provocation. He also ruled that the drunk had had an exceptionally thin skull and that this factor had contributed to his death. Not that this cut any ice with Nan, who wondered aloud what school the Judge had gone to.

Jim was the only O'Brien she actually disliked. She didn't trust him and she believed that he was no more than a thug. Skip when pressed would admit that Jim was 'a hard big man', a lacklustre defence that I took as proof that Nan knew what she was talking about. After the trial Jim went to London, saying that he would be a marked man in Glasgow, but Nan's opinion was that he knew other charges might be pending and was making a quick getaway. As she was an expert on the O'Brien psyche, she may very well have been right.

Nevertheless the myth was born of Uncle Jim, gentleman thief, and no one built myths like the childlike O'Briens, who wove mystery and romance around him in his absence. Jim, it was decided, was a master criminal in London, and every big robbery that hit the headlines was claimed in his name. Nan would give a snort of derision and say, 'Couldnae hiv bin Jim, naebody wis killed.'

Once, when he arrived unannounced and definitely uninvited at Acrehill Street, her words of welcome to him were, 'Sumbody efter ye in London?'. Jim smiled down at her with an easy charm that fooled her not a bit. He was laden down with gifts of jewellery and clothes, and I remember a beautiful dress that he brought me, even if it was six sizes too big. Once again Nan disposed of it all, saying we had no idea where and who it came from.

Like the rest of the family Jim was a born story-teller and I remember during this visit that he kept us entertained for hours with his tales, or as Nan maintained, 'lies'. He had worked as an embalmer – 'Cuttin' oot the middle man noo Jim?' – and he told us that the biggest problem was the rats. 'They'll do anything to get at the blood,' he said. 'Aye, well, ye'll know a' about that Jim,' said Nan tartly, 'Ye've hid yer ain difficulties in that direction.' Jim smiled back sweetly.

Whether Jim was an embalmer or not, the family latched onto it with gusto, never guilty of letting the damnedest lies stand in the way of a good yarn. It was decided that he embalmed only the top people, the richest, the heaviest in jewels and gems, items that of course they no longer needed, whereas Jim undoubtedly did. It fitted with the rest of the Jim myth that he never actually harmed anyone physically, though Nan of course had other ideas about that. He gave Skip two pairs of cuff-links; a gold hexagonal pair with a pattern in wine, black and white enamel, and a rectangular pair in silver, with a similar pattern in blue, black and white. They were quite beautiful and I now know that they were worth a fortune, so naturally the other O'Briens got to work on him. They laboured the point about stealing from corpses, which on this occasion was regarded as a dreadful crime, and being masters of their art they then left the thought to fester in Skip's soul, not to mention his fertile imagination.

Finally he could stand the guilt no longer and resolved to get rid of the cuff-links in a way that would bring him no gain; he must have felt very guilty indeed. He went to a Catholic church and tried to put them in the St Vincent de Paul collection box for the poor, but they wouldn't go in. He went to another church and found another box, but again the cuff-links wouldn't go through the slot, and in the next church it was the same.

Like the rest of his family Skip loved ghost stories and tales of the supernatural. His favourite was *The Monkey's Paw* by William Wymark Jacobs, where a talisman, the paw, is supposed to bring great fortune, but turns out to bring terror and tragedy instead. He felt the same about the cuff-links; in his fevered imagination they became the monkey's paw, and he was convinced that some awful fate awaited him if he didn't get rid of them. In a state of sweating fear and convinced that God himself had decided that he should be punished by having the cuff-links in his possession forever, he panicked finally and put them through the letter box of the priest's house.

In my experience, priests, despite their talk of poverty and charity, much prefer the good life. So I'm sure the recipient of Skip's largesse would have known quality when he saw it. The beautiful cuff-links would have gone no further than the priestly shirt cuffs and are doubtless an heirloom of his family today, if he isn't still living off the proceeds of their sale. Years later it emerged that they had in fact been given to Jim by a rich girlfriend, no doubt for services rendered, and that the rest of the family had known this all along. Obviously they couldn't claim the points unless Skip found this out, so they made sure that he did. But long, long after the beautiful cuff-links were irretrievably out of his reach.

Uncle Jim spent two weeks with us in Acrehill Street, during which he threw money around, mainly in the direction of the pub, and I doubt if Skip was sober for two minutes together the whole time. He never offered anything towards his keep though and Nan knew that the only way to get rid of him was to demand some cash. He left one day 'to cash a cheque' and we never saw him again.

That night the London train crashed and a few days later we got a letter from Jim telling us not to worry, that he was safe – not that this was of any consequence whatever to Nan. When he got home though, he continued, he had discovered in the turn-up of his trouser leg, a severed finger. Nan was not impressed.

'Ah'll bet ye anythin' it wisnae his finger cut off though,' she said cynically. Skip, knowing a good story when he heard it, thought that this was harsh and uncalled for and wondered how she could be so hard.

Jim had enclosed with the letter a photo of himself, dressed immaculately with gold tooth gleaming and fondling a kitten. Sensing another put-down Skip supplied the punchline before Nan could, 'Probably jist before he strangled it.'

We never heard from Jim again, but like Hughie he lives on in our imaginations. Everytime a spectacular robbery is pulled off we say with pride, 'Uncle Jim!', though he would be over a hundred years old by now. More recently however, we have had to put him into virtual retirement. Crime is so violent these days and we won't have Jim connected with anything sordid. There doesn't seem the demand anymore for skilful, classy criminals like Raffles Jim, but he's probably out there somewhere yet, still trying to cash that cheque . . .

Chapter Ten

In the early Fifties the Korean War was taking young men from Blackhill to fight in the jungle. Nan used to address us on the issues, which to her were inextricably linked to the Second World War.

After six years of a war we had won, the meat ration had actually been reduced in 1947, and clothes were rationed until 1949. Sweet and chocolate rationing had been abolished in March 1949, but the public had gone slightly crazy and it was reimposed in July of the same year and didn't end until February 1953.

On Saturdays we still went into town for the weekly shopping, going to the same shops we had used when we had lived at the Brae. We spent our sweets coupons at McLellan's in George Street, a little shop at the bottom of the Brae. George McLellan thought highly of Nan and it was said that he gave her extra sweets, and though naturally she denied it, she still took all of the Clark coupons to him. My weekly allocation was a tube of Smarties. Though it doesn't seem a lot, it was no real hardship as I had never known anything other than rationing. The business with coupons gave Nan the opportunity to complain again that not only did we still have rationing, but young lads were still being called up to fight in another war.

There were constant reminders of the war overseas. From a gap in the buildings at the top of Acrehill Street, we spent hours watching a blimp in the sky spilling out tiny parachutists as part of their training for Korea. It looked so near and we tried to find it many times but we never did. The blimp tantalized us and we argued endlessly about where it actually was but all our expeditions to find it failed. The boy Nan saved from the Catholic Teds came to say goodbye before he went to fight, I suppose she was the nearest thing to a mother he really had. She cried of course, then she told Peggy and Peggy cried too, then they cried together. This gave Nan another chance to deliver an impassioned lecture on the evils of war and rationing, getting so carried away that she and Peggy would collapse in tears once again.

Like the rest of my generation I grew up with the Second World War as an ever-present feature. It's almost like a race memory I remember it so well, though I wasn't born until it was over. The sound of an air-raid siren chills me to the bone only because it did the same to my mother. Though I never heard it sounded in anger I absorbed her anxiety and made it my own. Nan refused to leave Glasgow or to have Mickey and Laurie evacuated during the War, so the sound of the siren really did mean danger to her. I can still see the German planes flying over Balmano Brae on their way to bomb the River Clyde and the shipyards in Clydebank because she described it so often and so clearly that I felt I had been there too.

As for the lad Nan had saved for the jungles of Korea, we never saw him again. But every now and again I would think about him and hope he had survived. I'm sure she did too.

Some Sundays Skip took me for a walk along the canal bank. The canal was part of my everyday playground, but the weekly walk with Skip was somehow a special treat. Laurie never came; I don't know if he was ever asked, but if he had been I'm sure he would have refused, however much he wanted to come with us. I always wore the same dress, a charcoal and blue striped taffeta creation given to me by my godparents, Auntie Annie and Uncle George. To be truthful I only had one godparent, because Skip had taken Uncle George for a drink before the ceremony and they had disappeared, so Auntie Annie took me on her own to be christened in St Andrew's Cathedral, where my parents had been married at the side altar.

Uncle George had met her when he was twenty-three and boarding a troop train and she had been only ten years old. She and her parents were seeing her brother John off on the train and the two young soldiers had struck up a friendship on the platform that lasted forever. Her name coincidentally was O'Brien, but she came from a separate, more conventional and normal branch of O'Briens. After coming through the War together George and John O'Brien had remained close friends, and given the situation at home, where as a 'Dark Yin' George wasn't exactly a favourite, he spent more time with John's family.

Da Clark, who doted on George, Nan and Peggy, had died during the War, and the two sisters had formed their own mutual support group, so in a way George was finding his own with the normal O'Briens. As he and the grown-up Annie grew closer over the years, her father refused them permission to marry unless George became a Catholic. They split up for two months before George gave in, though he paid no more than lip service to his new religion. It was the price he paid to marry Annie, that was all. Like Nan though, he was forced to agree that their children would be raised as Catholics.

Naturally George took Annie to meet Nan before introducing her to the rest of the family, and having won Nan's support there was no problem with the rest. There were mutterings of course from the 'Fair Yins', who never missed a chance to have a go at a 'Dark Yin', that a real man wouldn't have given in, a real man wouldn't have turned. None of this was actually said to George. No Clark was ever that silly.

When I was born Annie was already pregnant with their first child and Nan won a twisted little victory over my christening. She needed Catholics as godparents, which logically pointed to the mad O'Briens but she didn't want them involved if she could help it, so Annie and George were chosen. They were a glamorous couple in my eyes; Uncle George was tall and darkly handsome, like a cross between Cary Grant and Gregory Peck, and wherever he went female heads turned. Annie wore glasses and used to wonder with a wry smile why George, who was so good-looking, had married her of all people. It was as though she was ugly, which she wasn't of course.

Annie had a beautiful figure and wore clothes well, so that

83

you always remembered a particular dress or outfit when you thought of her. She also had the nicest nature, and coming from a family of such extremes on both sides I was very impressed by this. She was genuine; when you talked to her you didn't have to work out the politics or the psychology of the situation first. Though this was refreshing when you got used to it, it was also a little confusing. She was an O'Brien after all, and O'Briens just weren't like that.

Because George was tall in a city of small men he had to keep his temper in check; a big man can do more damage than a small one. So there was always a feeling of tension about George. Like all the Clarks he had deep emotions, but somehow he couldn't risk letting them go for fear of who knows what. All through my life I can hear Annie's voice at moments of family tension. 'Watch George!' she'd shout, a warning that the big man was nearing the end of his tether. It was Annie who softened him and made him sociable, she was a gentle soul with a talent for smoothing out his awkwardness, and they were very obviously happy together. Whenever they came to visit I would wait for them at the bus stop, to bask in the glamour of walking beside them and showing them off as my relatives.

Peggy had a new boyfriend, or rather an old one for the second time. The family had breathed a sigh of relief the first time Jim McAvoy had disappeared off the scene. Now you could almost hear them collectively breathe it back in again. Soon she announced that she was marrying him, after a courtship that had tested the family's lung control and nerves to the limit.

If the Clarks didn't fit the public perception of Blackhill inhabitants, then the McAvoys did. They were, in the opinion of the family, a feckless bunch of lazy wasters who dabbled in petty crime, lacking the organisation or application for anything else, and Jim was the prime example. Like Nan, Peggy was a giver, and givers tend to marry takers. McAvoy was a charmless drinker and gambler who seldom worked, and he certainly wasn't what Peggy deserved. But at thirty-two she must have felt time running out; Fate was winning, and so she took what no one else wanted. 'She should dae better,' Nan told the family firmly, 'Bit she won't.' As the two of them sat stitching hats for the wedding, with me in between them, they discussed the family's antagonism endlessly.

'They'll never like him Peggy,' Nan said, 'If ye take him ye take him knowin' that.' And take him Peggy did, one cold March Saturday in 1953, with her favourite niece waiting outside St Paul's Church in Langdale Street, clutching a silver horseshoe and shivering in the chill wind. I couldn't go into the church because I was a Catholic, and it was a known fact that no Catholic could enter a Proddie church without suffering some unspecified but dire consequences.

Instead of the frills and lace she dreamed of, Peggy wore a grey suit with a pink blouse and hat, and she was solemn as I handed over the good luck charm, expecting a smile. McAvoy put his arm around me and I instinctively shrugged it off and clung to Peggy. The wedding reception had a desperate air of forced joy, as the Clarks tried to look as though they had wished for this dream match for years. I can see them yet, looking at Peggy with concern and sorrow when her attention was elsewhere, and smiling when she turned in their direction.

McAvoy didn't warrant the same consideration; he was already in no doubt about how they felt. From that day, to the anguish of the Clarks, whatever had lit Peggy from within grew dimmer, as though the deal she had made with Fate to escape from spinsterhood had required her to surrender the very brightness of her soul. Within a year she had given birth to a stillborn son. The umbilical cord had been around the baby's neck, and I heard Uncle George saying to Nan, 'Ah wish it hid been roon' McAvoy's neck instead.' 'Wheesht Geordie,' said my mother quietly, as though she was calming a distressed child, 'it disnae help son.'

We were still close though, because Peggy and McAvoy lived with my grandmother. Nan and I still saw Peggy at some time every day, and as Peggy opened the door my mother's first words were always, 'How is she the day?', meaning what kind of mood was Maw Clark in and how much trouble was she causing? Peggy's usual response was to raise her eyes heavenward; Maw Clark could give a new meaning to difficult without even trying. We would spend some time talking, catching up on the huge changes that must have taken place in the twenty-four hours or less since we had last met. Then I'd leave Nan and Peggy talking and go out to play.

My first task was to decide if I was yet up to jumping down the back stairs. There were eight of them outside Peggy's house, leading down to the backcourt, eight steep stairs, and jumping them was a test of honour for me and all my cousins and all the Moodiesburn Street kids. The back close, the rear exit to the tenement at the bottom of the stairs, was narrower than the stairs themselves, so a misjudged jump could take you straight into the wall. Even if you judged it right, the stairs were slippy and you could end up slamming into the wall anyway. Having thought it all through and chickened out once again, I'd run down through the backcourts, past the air raid shelters to the playpark beyond, with its slides – one long, one short – a roundabout, three swings and a maypole that had no ropes. Beyond that was a stretch of grass beloved of the local dogs and then the pond, where I could catch fish and watch the swans. A single track road with a pavement at one side separated the pond from St Philomena's, our school, but curiously we only associated the park and the pond with visits to Moodiesburn Street and rarely went near it at any other time.

Nan and I tried to pick a time of day for our visits when McAvoy would be out and we would leave again before he arrived, partly because Nan knew how the sight of the Clarks annoyed him and so Peggy suffered, and partly because we really didn't want to see him either. So life went on in Blackhill, and even if the horizon was clouded by the unwelcome arrival of McAvoy and the subtle change in Peggy, the essentials for existence were still comfortingly in place. Then came the night that started Nan's big push to get out of Blackhill once and for all.

During the War metal railings had been removed from all over the country to be used, it was said, to make munitions. We now know that after collection the metal was simply dumped. It was just a government propaganda scheme, designed to make those at home believe they were contributing something to the War effort apart from their menfolk, and even Blackhill was included. A nine-inch wall ran around every tenement, studded with the remains of the railings that had once stood there. They had been intended to enclose gardens, but, in fact, they only surrounded a muddy space between the pavement and the buildings.

One evening I was sitting on the wall with a friend, exchanging scraps. It was early evening, the safe time, because the Teds usually went into battle during the hours of darkness. Then someone ran down the street shouting, 'Thur's a man comin' wi' his heid in his hauns!', an interesting proposition, and I was fully expecting to see a ghostly figure with his head tucked underneath his arm. As he staggered into view we were all disappointed to recognize him as a very much alive Ted, his hands covering his face. Every few steps he would stop and bellow, 'Youse wimmen get they weans oota the wey!'

Adult hands grabbed children along the route and took them inside houses, and from behind someone's net curtains I watched him as he staggered past where I had been sitting, only feet away. His hands were holding his face together where the blades had slashed him repeatedly, and blood pouring from between his fingers ran onto his shoulders and chest and flicked onto the road. When it was obvious he wasn't being chased by whoever had carved him up, we were released, feeling cheated as we luridly examined the grotesque red paperchase he'd left behind. We were greatly put out that an event that had started with such high expectations had collapsed into the mundane.

For Nan it was the last straw and it reinforced her greatest fear that her own kids, especially Laurie, could be caught up in the violence. From then, her battle to get out moved up a gear. Getting a house somewhere else wasn't that simple of course, because of Blackhill's reputation. So there was an obstacle course set up: if you wanted a house in a better area you had to apply to the Council, and the Factor was asked to provide a reference. Without a Factor's reference you could give up any ideas above your station. The letting department sent a Housing Visitor to inspect your home as part of this procedure, and a form was filled in, giving the Housing Visitor's opinion of the general condition of your home, the state of your furniture and the 'type of person' you were. The scale ran from very good, through good and fair to poor, and Nan lived on her wits while this process was gone through.

Looking back it's hard to understand why we put up with such indignities. But the system was supported by the ruling Labour administration, and the Party of the People made sure it didn't stop there. There was also the constant threat of the 'Green Lady' health visitor, who had the power to knock on any door at anytime and inspect your home. At the first sight of a Green Lady in the vicinity the bush telegraph swung into action, sending all the women of Blackhill on a furious tidying spree, in case the Green Lady picked on their house and gave a bad report because something was out of place. The Green Ladies were forever trying to outsmart the women, because if you wanted to avoid a visit you took yourself off as soon as the bush telegraph sounded its warning. So the Green Ladies often came on a Monday, washing day, when they knew that the majority of women would be tied to the boiler, washing board and mangle for many hours. This made them doubly unpopular of course, the last thing any woman wanted or needed was an interruption on washing day.

Another good time was Friday afternoon, when the women were waiting for their men to come home with their weekly pay packets so that they could do some shopping. So again the last person they wanted was the Green Lady arriving to take up their time instead, and of course they couldn't refuse to let her in. There was a children's street song that we used to sing about not being able to find 'a bonnie laddie tae tak' me awa' ', the first line of which was 'Queen Mary, Queen Mary, my age is sixteen.' So powerful were the Green Ladies that I thought the line started with 'Green Lady, Green

Lady', and I sang those words for years without questioning them.

Then came the news that we had passed all three elements of the obstacle course, the Factor, the Home Visitor and the Green Lady, and after five years as temporary refugees in Blackhill we were told that we would get a house in Drumchapel. Nan was ecstatic; I was bereft.

Drumchapel was part of the City Fathers' destruction of Glasgow. Instead of renovating the old tenements in the heart of the city they decided to raze them to the ground. The tenements symbolized everything that was bad about Glasgow, except to the people who actually lived in them, but there has never been a politician who listened to the people anywhere. In the Fifties in Glasgow they bulldozed away our history and background, erecting high-rise monstrosities that the people neither wanted nor needed. They created council housing estates or 'schemes', that were no more than ghettoes to replace ghettoes. Two-thirds of Pollok, eight miles to the south-west of the city, was built after the War and then Easterhouse sprang up six miles to the east, Castlemilk, five miles to the south-east and Drumchapel six miles to the west.

Our move to Drumchapel was part of a mass, enforced exodus that was happening all over the UK after the war years, but in Glasgow it was undertaken with a vengeance. In some parts of the city there were 400 people to the acre and the need to rehouse them at minimal cost took precedence over what they wanted. People who had lived for generations in cramped conditions with outside toilets and no bathrooms needed better housing, but they didn't want to leave the areas where they had grown up and the close communities they lived in. It became a common sight to see sad little groups watching bleakly as their former homes, and those of their parents and grandparents were demolished. But the politicians still knew best.

It would be over twenty years before meaningful conservation of the old buildings began and the high-rise flats, once determinedly hailed as Utopia, were blown-up, to cheers from those who had been forced to live in them. The Glasgow experience undoubtedly helped other areas of the UK not to make the same mistakes on such a stupendous scale, but the cost to the ordinary people in the loss of identity and social cohesion was enormous, and the city has never recovered.

In the mid-fifties we knew none of this, but there was talk that soon we would have skyscrapers in Glasgow, just like the ones in America that we saw in the pictures at the Rex and the Vogue. It was a time when anything American was desirable and exciting, and I listened enthralled as Nan, Peggy and Maw Clark discussed high-rise living. I saw in it definite possibilities of a reprieve, because like the Balmano Brae inhabitants, I envisaged a skyscraper being built where I lived, which meant I wouldn't have to leave Blackhill. It was the perfect compromise; Nan would be far enough off the ground to be safe from the gangs, and yet I could still be at home.

'Ah saw it in a magazine, ye hivtae use a lift tae get up an' doon,' Peggy said authoritatively, 'An' thur's nae midden, ye use a kinda chute tae get ridda yur rubbish.'

I found it hard to envisage having no middens to jump, but a chute held delightful prospects of its own.

'Bit whit if this lift thing breks doon when ye're in it Peggy?' Nan demanded, 'Whit dae ye dae then?'

'Bit they'll huv thoaghta that, therr'll be sterrs or sumthin'.'

'So ye'll hiv this lift, an' ye'll still hivtae dae the sterrs!' Nan snorted, 'An' Ah suppose ye'd hiv tae take yur turn at waashin' the lift tae! An' talkin' aboot waashin', where wid ye hing it oot?'

'Tae hell wi' the waashin', jist think, ye'd be away up there!' Peggy persisted, 'Up in the sky wi' aeryplanes passin' yur windies! Ye could wave tae the pilots!'

'Ah widnae like that!' Nan decided, 'Ah'm no hivin' nae skyscraper thanks very much! Ah'll jist hiv a hoose!' And she and Peggy laughed. I was devastated; it had all been a diversion, they were winding each other up.

'Naw, me neither,' Peggy said, 'They're mibbe a' right fur the Yanks, bit Ah cannae see thum catching oan here.'

'Ah'll tell ye wan thing,' said Maw Clark, who had been listening as intently as I had, 'If any o' yese move tae wanna they big buildin's, it's the last ye'll see o' me! Ah'll no' be comin' tae see yese if Ah hivtae use a lift!'

The same thought passed through our minds simultaneously and I don't know yet how Nan, Peggy and I controlled ourselves. Peggy got up to make the tea, Nan went to help her and I followed, and when we reached the kitchen all three of us fell into a mutually supportive, creaking, crying, laughing huddle.

'Christ! It'd be worth it!' wheezed Peggy.

'Sshhh!' cried Nan, mopping her eyes, 'She'll hear ye!'

'Bit think o' it! Ye could be twinty stories high, an' she wid be doon below lookin' up at ye! Ye could drap things by accident like! Pails o' watter mibbe!'

'Bowls o' custard!' Nan supplied.

'Ye could even make a wee mistake an' miss the rubbish chute!' Peggy wailed, and Nan had to rush to the toilet, leaving Peggy and me to compose ourselves as best we could before we took the tea into Maw Clark. For the rest of the visit we avoided each other's eyes.

I can't pass a high-rise block to this day without seeing the phantom figure of Maw Clark, standing at the bottom looking up . . .

I put Drumchapel out of my mind for as long as possible, which was easy, because it was so impossible to believe. I kept hoping up to the last minute that the bad dream would go away, but the day came and there was the van loaded up with our furniture.

Children moving house usually have a fear that their beds will be left behind, but I hoped mine would be, so that I could stay in Blackhill. People came out of closes with presents for Nan, tins of food, biscuits, and sweeties and a few pennies for me. These were people who had very little themselves and of course Nan was so touched by this that she cried buckets; I don't think she realized till then how much a part of Blackhill she had become. Nan had started off being frightened and refusing to accept that the family had to live there, but she discovered that the women who made life bearable, even possible, who kept their families functioning against all the odds, were women just like her. Now she was leaving them behind.

The Balmano Brae refugees were in attendance too and they were almost as inconsolable as I was, but not quite. I cried uncontrollably, much to Nan's fury, partly I think because she was feeling unexpectedly fragile herself. I had never been outside the total security of Blackhill as far as I could remember, never more than five minutes away from Peggy, how was I supposed to survive hundreds of miles away?

As the bus left the city centre though, I began to glimpse another world, of trees, grass and wide roads. Along Great Western Road were huge, beautiful buildings that Nan told me were 'big hooses', not that I believed her of course. The council would hardly give one family a building big enough to house ten, and even if it did, what could one family possibly do in all those rooms?

Drumchapel was in its early stages in 1956, set in fields to one side of Drumry. Nan told me that she had come here on Sunday School picnics when she was a child, but it had been all open countryside then. Being a Catholic of course Sunday School picnics were an unknown world, a bit like the Proddie hymns we were banned from singing at school. We moved into 48 Halgreen Avenue, the top of four storeys built like an old-style tenement, but it was roomy, airy and white and it had an outside verandah, just the thing for the Scottish climate. Instead of two bedrooms it had three, so I had one to myself. I didn't think much of the deal.

It was too quiet at first; there were no gang fights and nowhere to play for a child used to second-guessing trains. I even missed the smell of the gasworks. I remember sitting on the steps at the close, unable to accept that I had to stay there, feeling totally lost and homesick for Blackhill and Peggy. I was on another continent, as far away as the people who were emigrating to Australia for ten pounds a throw. The newspapers were full of photos of them bidding tearful goodbyes to families they knew they would never see again, just as I would never see Peggy again. Part of me was missing without her; I couldn't believe that my own mother could have done such a thing to me.

I hadn't really been aware of trouble between my parents until we moved to Drumchapel, though I had a vague feeling of unease at times in Blackhill as I caught a tone of voice or a look. At family dos, as he capered and performed, the others would say, 'Leave him alane Nan, he's no' daein' ony herm,' and I used to wonder why she wanted to stop him having fun. Once we moved to Drumchapel though, like all the others who had been transported by the City Fathers and the planners, he had to travel back into Glasgow to work, adding at least two hours to his days. But he would come home later than that.

There were no pubs in Drumchapel, so he went to the nearest one before he came home, and that's when I remember the arguments starting, though there must have been others before that I wasn't aware of. Around the age of seven or so I began to realize that his drinking was different from the other men around me. Uncle Willie took a drink, Uncle George did sometimes too, though not often, but Skip drank all the time. Sometimes he came home without any wages, because his drinking money took precedence over everything else, food, clothes or paying the rent. In fact booze came before the need to breathe. As I grew older I would absorb the chronic anxiety about unpaid bills, though Nan always kept little stores of money all over the place to provide for the times he came home with little or none.

Gradually things became clearer. All those times I went to his workshop after school and he had sent me home alone, he had been going to the Provanmill Inn, the local pub beside where he worked. The times when Nan sent me with him around the other shoemakers, it was in the hope that he wouldn't get drunk with his little daughter to take care of, a forlorn hope born of her desperation. This was the start of another family myth, that Skip loved me so much that he took me with him wherever he went. To this day relatives still repeat to me this version of Nan's attempts to make him stay sober. It always ended the same, with Skip so drunk he couldn't see where he was going or stand up straight. As a child I often had to find our way home, sometimes at night, and it has left me with the ability to negotiate the city without knowing the names of places very well. In the dark I was frequently frightened, and even today I can catch sight of an alleyway in the centre of Glasgow as I pass by and it seems familiar, familiar enough to bring tears to my eyes, though I can't quite remember why.

The truth is that I didn't know Skip any other way but drunk, and as a very young child I had thought him great fun, which he was. But the other side of the amiable, life-and-soul of every party was a childish dictator, who would shout, argue and sulk, and for some inexplicable reason Nan couldn't handle these tactics. When he was late home there was never any doubt where he was or what state he would come home in, but she always feared he had fallen under a bus or been attacked. I would sit with her until we heard him falling up the stairs and trying to open the door, then I'd scamper off to bed and hide under the blankets until the inevitable row was over. I learned the art of diversion, of concentrating on something else to blot out the voices. Nan could handle the toughest bureaucrat, but she was helpless against her husband, and it always ended with her defeated and crying and him asleep in a drunken stupor; he always 'won'.

In truth, the shouting, distressing as it was, affected me less than the sight of my mother so totally vanquished each time. Everything had happened with Skip in no fit state to remember it, but Nan didn't drink and she remembered every word, as I did, and every word hurt. As the years passed I hoped rather than feared that he had fallen under a bus, and if anyone had attacked him, I wanted them to make a good job of it so that we could be free of him. The sound of his drunken falls on the stairs often reduced me to tears of rage and disappointment under my blankets. Skip was a survivor; he made it home every time.

Chapter Eleven

We went back to Blackhill every Saturday to see Peggy, the whole family assembled there and the excitement would build up all week until Saturday arrived. There was a kind of panic at first, a feeling that I would never see her again, a bit like losing a limb almost. Then Saturday would come at last and we'd set off to Blackhill.

After reassuring myself that Peggy was still there and hadn't forgotten me I would escape joyfully back to Acrehill Street to relive old times. As time passed though I found that I didn't belong any longer. I wasn't part of what was happening there every day and gradually I was losing touch with my old friends. The truth was that I had left the Acrehill Street kids behind; I wasn't one of them anymore, I was just a visitor.

So I began to stay more around Peggy's house in Moodiesburn Street, watching life go by from the top of the red-brick air raid shelter in the backcourt. I had suddenly realized that sights and sounds I'd taken for granted while living in Blackhill weren't part of my new home, and I missed them. Blackhill had a vigour and energy that made me yearn for the place even more.

In those days, before hygiene was a consideration, you could buy almost anything from a board carried around on someone's head. The baker sold cakes, buns and bread that way, shouting out as he came into the backcourt, and the fishman, the butcher and the man who sold coal brickettes too. I could earn the odd thru'penny bit by running upstairs with the goods and change to the women who had thrown down the payment from their windows. And there was Paddy the bleachman, who came around all the houses once a week selling bleach in big, green bottles shaped like whisky bottles. They cost a few pence each and were much cheaper than the kind in the shops. Every woman in Blackhill bought Paddy's bleach. Looking back, it seems incredible, given the outsider's view of Blackhill, that these people weren't attacked for the money or the goods they carried, but that wasn't a thought that occurred to anyone, and if it had happened the community would have sorted the situation out.

In the good weather a man called Ronnie McPhail came around the backcourts playing an accordion. The women would shout down requests and he'd play whatever they wanted then be rewarded with a few coins thrown from the windows. Whoever had requested the tune would start singing along, and other windows would fly open and their neighbours would join in or shout encouragement. I would lie on top of the air raid shelter, listening to the voices coming from the open windows high above, as women abandoned their housework to sing songs of grand passion or mournful romantic disappointment. When Ronnie McPhail moved on to the next street, they would be reluctant to give up the mood and a clabber, a backcourt concert, would take place.

Someone would bring down an old blanket and throw it over a washing line to form the backdrop to a stage, then the women would bring out chairs and sit like an audience at the theatre or the pictures. Everybody took their turn in front of the blanket stage, singing a song, sometimes in duos or trios, or doing a dance, and those watching from the windows joined in or sang from where they were. There was always a great deal of laughter as the women teased each other or sent themselves up, giggling at the songs of yearning romance they were singing. 'Fur coat an' nae knickers isnae in it!' they'd shout to each other, 'Ah jist look like Connie Francis, daen't Ah?', and they'd howl with laughter.

When it was coming near to tea-time, signalled by the stench from the gasworks, the clabber came to an end and the women would return to their chores, still laughing.

A clabber was a women's only do, the men had their own, quite separate pastimes, which mainly centred around the Provanmill Inn, which wasn't just a pub, but the male meeting place too. My favourite entertainment involved the drunks who took detours through the backcourts on their way home. They usually arrived after the pubs closed in the afternoon, or in the early evening if they'd been thrown out. Either way they were like lambs to the slaughter. They sang hoping for pennies, while insults and worse landed all around them. The O'Briens used to heat pennies before throwing them to drunks for the sheer pleasure of never giving a sucker an even break.

'Ah could gie ye "Ghost Riders in the Sky," ' the drunk would shout to the windows.

'Keep thum tae yersel', a' woman would shout back, 'Jist hop it Hopalong an' gie us peace!'

'Well how aboot "The Star O' Rabbie Burns?" ' the would-be entertainer would wheedle.

'Ye'll be seein' stars yersel' if ye don't get tae hell! How aboot jist buggerin' aff insteed?' would come the reply, closely followed by a pot of water or whatever unsavoury offering lay at hand. The drunk man would stagger around the backcourt, threats, oathes and missiles coming through the air at him from the windows above.

I never understood why the drunks did it, they earned nothing but a withering contempt that was always more entertaining than their singing, as the women cooperated in insulting them, shrieking with laughter at each other's attempts. I loved the drunks, not for themselves, but for the entertainment the women put on whenever they appeared.

Often though I would stay inside the house, because Peggy now had a baby son. I remember the day he was born because it was the first time I had ever been in a telephone box. The only public telephone around was in nearby Provanmill and Nan and I had squeezed into it to call the hospital. There was all the business with button A and button B, then Nan asking for the ward and for news of Mrs McAvoy. Outside we whooped and shouted with joy, Nan dabbing at her eyes with her hankie, then we rushed back to Moodiesburn Street to tell Maw Clark. We were in the house too a week later when Peggy came home with James Junior, and suddenly collapsed and was rushed back to hospital with a post-partum haemorrhage. It had happened with the stillborn child the year before and was to become the pattern everytime she gave birth. The new baby was a great novelty, of course, and Peggy seemed as relaxed as I could ever remember her. Mission accomplished: she was at last a mother.

A few months later, on Ash Wednesday, Nan and I had come through from Drumchapel to see Peggy and the baby, stopping at St Philomena's church first, so that I could have the ritual dab of ashes on my forehead. All Catholics knew that the ashes were sacred, to remove them was a great sin for which I knew I would be struck instantly dead.

Nan was shopping and I'd run on ahead because I wanted to see the baby. When I got to the house, one of Maw Clark's cronies was with her, a woman we knew as Auld Broon, and another strong supporter of the Orange Lodge. Peggy was changing the baby and suddenly Maw Clark leaned over, grabbed hold of me, snatched the dirty nappy and wiped it across my face, removing the ashes from my forehead. Then she and Auld Broon fell about cackling with delight.

Poor Peggy was embarrassed and took me into the kitchen, offering to replace the ashes with some from the fireplace, which was doubtless where the priest had got them from in the first place. But she didn't understand! The ashes were HOLY, they were BLESSED, and now I would be struck dead before finishing primary school as punishment for letting them be removed!

When Nan arrived Peggy motioned her into the kitchen and whispered what had happened, and the two of them entered into a conspiracy to calm me down by convincing me that the ashes put on my head by the priest had somehow survived. Then Nan went into the living-room and told Maw Clark off while Peggy kept me in the kitchen and gave me a special treat, some of the baby's National Orange Juice. I could still hear the raised voices in the living-room. 'It disnae maitter whit you think o' her being Catholic,' Nan was saying loudly, 'Ye've nae right tae take it oot oan the wean!' and my grandmother protesting that it had all been a joke. When we left, Nan was still angry enough to burst. I asked why Maw Clark had done it and Nan replied, 'Sometimes yer Maw's no' a very nice wumman hen, in fact maist o' the time she's no' a nice wumman! She's ma ain mother, bit she's common. Noo don't you go tellin' anybody that!'

'Dae they no' know?' I asked puzzled.

'Well yur Uncle George dis,' she replied, 'An' Peggy tae. Jist think aboot poor Peggy hivin' tae live wi' hur!'

Looking back at that incident all these years later, it was a rotten thing to do to any child, let alone your own grandchild. It taught me to keep my distance from my grandmother. Not only was I 'wan o' the Dark Yins', but I was also a Catholic, so I was learning that I was doubly at risk from her 'jokes'.

I used to hate arriving on those Saturday visits to find McAvoy there, and if he was in the house I would go out again until he had gone. I never mentioned it to anyone and never actually thought it out myself, but I just didn't like being around him. Somehow Peggy knew this and wasn't hurt by it. She would give me a cuddle and say with a smile, 'He'll soon be away oot, then it'll jist be us!'

While Nan talked to Maw Clark in the living-room I would stand beside Peggy as she made soup on the old kitchen range. These were the times I loved best, talking quietly to Peggy, just the two of us, and sharing secret spare ribs from the pot. We used to exchange little presents over the soup pot, too.

Peggy loved toffees and I remember buying her a tin for her birthday in August. There had been a choice of toffees in a tin with a battleship on the front, or some other sweets in a tin with flowers, so I made the woman in the shop empty out all the sweets and put the toffees in the flowered tin. Then Peggy and I had eaten them as the soup was made. Once she gave me a little square handbag that opened across into two triangles; I still have it somewhere. And I remember a red cardigan being handed over across the spare ribs, specially chosen to go with a black-and-white checked dress that she knew I hadn't been keen on. Eventually Nan would come in and demand in mock suspicion, 'Whit ur you two up tae then?' and Peggy and I would smile innocently and say 'Us? We're no' up tae anythin'!' through mouthfuls of spare ribs.

At the end of the evening Nan and I would take a trolley bus to High Street to meet up with Skip for the journey back to Drumchapel. Every Saturday he met old Eighth Army pals and they went drinking together, and I think Nan arranged that we met up so that she could be sure he was actually going to arrive home. She couldn't arrange what state he would be in though, and her anxiety ran through our precious hours with Peggy.

When we'd meet him Skip's moods would vary. He could be falling-down drunk and stupid, or nearly falling-down drunk and silly, and then again he could be rotten drunk and ready to fight, usually with my mother. There were pubs all along the way to John Street, the terminus for the Drumchapel buses, and it was just after throwing out time. There was a drunken fight at every pub door, so my heart was always in my throat. In Blackhill I had been protected from violence by the community and also by the men who caused it, but out in the open, in the dark, it threatened from all around.

It was always late when we travelled back to Drumchapel, arriving sometimes at nearly midnight. I hated those journeys because the bus was always full of drunks and there would be some kind of fight or someone being sick. I was terrified that my father would verbally join in a fight out of sheer cussedness, but usually he just slept. I was relieved when he did this, but disgusted too. Once we met him at High Street and he could hardly stand. We made the usual assumption, only to discover that he had stabbed himself accidentally with one of his knives at work that morning and had bled heavily; he wasn't just drunk, but weak from loss of blood. He didn't go to a doctor though. He didn't much believe in doctors.

There were no schools in Drumchapel when we moved

there. Laurie was at St Mungo's Academy by this time and had to travel as far as my father to get to and from school. Mickey was back in hospital, in Stonehouse this time, again, well outside the city. There had been no monitoring of his health after he had been discharged from Mearnskirk, despite the fact that the TB had already cost him the full use of his leg. Now the disease had moved to one of his kidneys.

Several months passed before the education department got organized. Then the Drumchapel children, including me, were bussed to and from the Marian School every day. The Marian had been founded in 1954 specifically for Catholic overspill children, as we were called. The Sisters of Notre Dame already had a fee-paying primary school in Dowanhill, and the Marian was set up alongside it. Nearby, the Sisters also ran Notre Dame High School for Girls, the top Catholic girls' secondary school in Glasgow. The bus ran through leafy avenues of quiet, 'big hooses', which seemed to confirm Nan's earnest belief that in moving to Drumchapel we had found Utopia. The Headmistress was Sister Frances Mary McNally, a quiet but imposing figure who regarded the Marian as her very own baby.

My teacher was Betty McGettigan, a marvellous woman who spoiled me for all other teachers, because she was what all other teachers like to think they are. While we worked in huge, high-ceilinged classrooms, in a class of forty-five children, Mrs McGettigan played Sibelius on an ancient gramophone. I had no idea what it was at the time or who wrote it, I only knew that quiet happiness existed in her classroom. Sibelius and Mrs McGettigan were ably abetted by the absence of boys, because the Marian was for girls only. The rooms and corridors of the school were panelled in wood just like the convent that adjoined it, and the smell of polish was the first thing you noticed when you entered. It was tranquil and orderly, and it was an extremely happy place to be in, chiefly I think because the nuns of Notre Dame genuinely liked children. It was the most civilized atmosphere to learn in and outside in the playground there were trees and grass and a cleanliness and freshness I had never known before. I discovered the existence of ladybirds in that playground one especially warm summer and I still have a fondness for the little beetles to this day, because seeing one takes me straight back to the Marian and Mrs McGettigan. However bad things were becoming at home, I had found an oasis of happiness and contentment at school in Glasgow's West End.

I was embarrassed by Mrs McGettigan's reaction when she found out that I read and wrote stories all the time. Just like flying, I assumed that everyone did these things. I read everything that was put in front of me or that I could lay hands on, and because I was busy doing so I hadn't noticed that other people didn't. It wasn't just that I enjoyed reading and writing, it all came so naturally that it was a part of me. So when Mrs McGettigan made a fuss over me it was like being praised for breathing. I thought she'd made a mistake and that when she realized this she'd be angry with me for misleading her.

She would give me a title and wait with barely concealed excitement until I had finished my latest masterpiece, then she would read it with unconcealed glee. Each time this happened I sighed with relief, then immediately started worrying about the next time, when she must surely find out. As far as I was concerned she was being extremely kind in letting me write a story, I was always grateful to be given a composition to do, so it was confusing to be treated as though I was doing her a favour.

Writing fulfilled a need. It gave me my happiest and most contented hours and made me feel really 'me', somehow. I suppose the seeds of being a loner were already taking root before I reached the Marian, perhaps in St Philomena's when I was given books to read and left on my own. Reading and writing marked me out as different throughout my schooldays. I was perfectly happy to be on my own, never needing or wanting close friends. Perhaps words were my escape from reality, just as Laurie's knights had been his. But what would I have done if I hadn't had words I wonder? How would I have coped then?

My complete incompetence with numbers saved me from

becoming really unpopular with the other children though, and I never understood why arithmetic was necessary or desirable in a civilized society; the truth is that I still don't. When it came to geometry and especially algebra I rebelled completely, refusing to accept that Y equalled anything just because someone arbitrarily said it did.

Betty McGettigan thankfully had a soft spot for creativity, and I was always aware that despite coming no higher than third in the class, and that only rarely, I was her favourite. She provided me with self-esteem at a time when I desperately needed it. I was coming to terms with the reality that I came way down my father's list of priorities, far lower than booze which came before everything else in the universe.

I made my First Communion while I was at the Marian, though not with as much gusto as the others in my class. While there were no schools in Drumchapel, lest the faithful had a chance to stray, the Catholic hierarchy built a church, called St Laurence's strangely enough. We practised making our first confessions at school for weeks, which must have been really riveting for some priest, and bravely swallowing bits of wafer in case we threw up the real thing on the day. Nan refused to spend money on a long dress, more to Peggy's disappointment than mine, so I was bought one that was short and very plain. Peggy, who naturally had tagged along on our shopping trip, was mortified; she didn't care about the occasion, she just wanted a few flounces and frills whatever it was all for. The veil was as short as possible and the head-dress plainer than the dress.

On the Saturday of the great event it was Nan who took me to St Laurence's, where all the other children were decorated like fairies on the tops of Christmas trees. They all clutched expensive rosaries in piously joined little hands and wore long, elaborate dresses under velvet capes trimmed with white fur, and they had walked proudly through the streets displaying their superb outfits. I had my coat on, buttoned up to the neck, the veil and head-dress stuffed in Nan's pocket. The only concession was a prayer book given to me by Auntie Norah, a special white one with a plastic cover made to look like marble and a little window on the front with a holy picture behind. At the last minute Peggy had given me a pair of white lace gloves, desperate for anything fancy to creep into the proceedings. When it was all over I was taken home again, my coat once again severely buttoned and my other knick-knacks concealed in various pockets.

It was left to my father to take me to a photographer for the ritual portrait, and it's no wonder I looked furtive, as though I was about to be grabbed and covered up again at any minute. Nan thought the whole thing was distinctly odd and was unable to hide it, and the cost of even a very plain rig-out must have taken a large chunk out of what little my father had handed her after his booze money had come out of it. I didn't feel cheated or upset, I never truly felt one of the faithful anyhow, but Nan was so annoyed at the whole business that it took her years to laugh at the strange little tableau we must have presented.

It was around this time, when I was about seven or eight, that Nan was diagnosed as having epilepsy, though there had been strange occurrences for a while that no one could explain. It had started a couple of years before, while we were still in Blackhill. I remember being on a bus with her one day, when she held up her hand, stared at her finger and earnestly inquired, 'Whit's that?' On other occasions, for a fleeting moment, she would seem not to recognize other familiar objects. Then very gradually she began to blank out completely for a few seconds, then for longer periods until just after we moved to Drumchapel she was having *grand mal* seizures.

During these she would collapse on to the floor, shaking and twitching all over and foaming at the mouth for several minutes, often biting her tongue or the inside of her mouth. Before the diagnosis was made she was having ten or more fits a day. Once she was put on various kinds of anti-convulsant drugs the frequency of the fits was reduced, but not completely controlled, mainly because she deeply resented having to take the tablets and would quietly cut them down or stop completely. She had very little warning of a fit, sometimes enough to call a name in a tone of voice we learned quickly to recognize, but after a time we could predict the kind of things that were likely to bring one on. If she was particularly upset, tired or excited we knew to expect a fit, which of course added another dimension to the rows about my father's drinking. There were times when I suspected him of deliberately upsetting her to bring on a fit so that he could meanwhile do what he liked without too much fuss. He was certainly childish enough to do it, but whether he was able to think up such a strategy in his befuddled state is something else.

Once, during a particularly bad argument he had raged on so much that she had had a fit. Next day, sitting in my class in the Marian, I was going over it all in my mind. Peggy was so far away and I couldn't talk to her till Saturday and my mother was at home by herself waiting for a repeat performance of the night before. I started to cry over my books and Mrs McGettigan noticed and tried to find out what was wrong. I had already learned the first rule for all families of alcoholics, that it was something to keep hidden, my own private shame, so I couldn't tell even nice Mrs McGettigan. Eventually it was decided by a process of elimination that I must be ill, and as we had no telephone at home my father was phoned at work to come and take me home. He was the last person I wanted to see, but at least he would be home sober for once. Mrs McGettigan spoke to him before we left. 'You know Mr O'Brien, Margaret is a very bright girl,' she told him, 'We expect her to take university in her stride, she's well capable of it.' He nodded and said, 'Oh aye, aye.' But even at that young age, I could see that she was trying to get something important through to him that he couldn't, or wouldn't, understand.

Because Nan's condition came on slowly over a period of two or three years, by the time she was having *grand mal* fits I had gradually learned to cope. It was simple, she had to be laid on her side for the few minutes the fit lasted and then she woke up. Afterwards she always had a splitting headache and temporary amnesia, but a couple of hours sleep would bring her back to normal. Her attitude to the condition settled into annoyance. She objected to having this nuisance thrust on her and was never reconciled to depending on the medication that eventually controlled the fits completely, but in reality it made little difference to her life. Taking my lead from her I took her epilepsy in my stride and it presented few problems.

The only reason she was ever given for her condition was possible oxygen deprivation at birth, which seemed at least possible. Like most city-dwellers at that time my grandmother undoubtedly suffered from rickets, which stunted skeletal growth, including that of the pelvis. So Maw would have endured a long, painful labour in those pre-NHS days, with no money for a doctor or the caesarian section she needed. It would have been entirely likely that at some stage the baby, my mother, was deprived of oxygen, and from the area of brain affected came her epilepsy. She refused to be called 'an epileptic', and became quite annoyed if anyone else used it as a description. 'Ah'm no' a disease!' she'd say defiantly, 'If sumbody his warts, ye don't call thum a wart, dae ye?'

Chapter Twelve

Drumchapel was beginning to grow on me. I discovered the Bluebell Woods, some distance from our house, carpeted during the spring and summer with the most wonderful blue flowers. I had never seen or smelt anything so beautiful and went on many expeditions to the woods with the other Halgreen kids, because Nan wouldn't let me go alone. Once there though I always wished I could be on my own in the beauty and the quiet. We pretended to ourselves that we were on an adventure by taking 'a picnic', which consisted of a slice of bread spread with jam and folded over. We used to take armfuls of flowers home with us, but bluebells are delicate creatures and they died quickly before we got there. We also discovered 'the Girnin' Gates', which were really no more than a large, arched stone gateway that was probably the remnant of a defunct estate. Once a rumour spread that the hands carved at the apex of the arch had been seen moving, and hoards of children gathered at the Girnin' Gates to watch for a repeat performance. It looked like the pictures we were shown of crowds at Lourdes waiting for another visitation, and just like Lourdes nothing more was seen, though those who wanted to believe still persisted in believing.

In front of 48 Halgreen Avenue was a deep valley that rose at the other side into another row of houses. On the floor of the valley ran a burn where we could catch sticklebacks, or baggominnows, called baggies for short, and on the other side of the slope stood massive trees that were just made for rope swings. Launching off from the side you would find yourself soaring hundreds of feet above the burn. It wasn't quite flying, but it was the nearest I had ever managed. No one was ever hurt seriously on the rope swing until Laurie took it a step further; Laurie always had something to prove.

He put the rope higher on the tree so that we could swing out even more, and inevitably someone fell off and broke an arm. That was the end of the rope swing. We tried leaving it till things had cooled down and then put the rope up again, but the adult bush telegraph was amazingly efficient and they quickly appeared to confiscate it.

In Blackhill I had discovered the joys of lying in the middle of the grass triangle and staring at the sky, and Drumchapel confirmed my preference for the countryside, because at first there was a lot of greenery around. Halgreen was bordered along one side by a farm complete with a field full of dairy cows. Sometimes an adventurous cow would escape into the street, even occasionally getting into a close, to the loud enjoyment of all the kids, most of whom had never seen a cow before moving to Drumchapel. It was great fun, of course, and we prolonged the entertainment by trying to return the bemused animal to the field again as slowly as possible. Because of the wandering cows, Halgreen became known as the Ponderosa, after the Cartwright ranch in the TV programme *Bonanza*.

On Sundays, Laurie and I would get up at 5 a.m. and meet up with one or two like-minded pals to go to the swimming baths in Clydebank. We had to walk about three miles in all, along part of Drumry Road, past the back of the graveyard and through bombed out ruins beside the railway line then onto Kilbowie Road. I liked playing in the ruins because the outlines of the rooms were still visible. I never thought about the people whose homes these had once been, I didn't know that the devastation had been caused by bombing because I was a Post-War child and had no experience of bombing apart from Nan's memories. The thing I noticed was that arum lilies grew all through the ruins; probably seeds had blown over from the nearby graveyard and taken root, and I remember them because I had never seen them before and they looked so exotic. Nan was none too pleased though when I took a bunch of them home to her. If poppies grew on the battlefields of the First World War it was perhaps fitting that arum lilies should grow on the scars of Clydebank, a small town that was as ravaged as any big city during the

War, because it stood on the banks of the Clyde and was the home of many famous shipyards.

We stayed in the swimming baths for hours and then walked home again, which took till lunchtime at least. Once I was thrown into the deep end by one of Laurie's pals and nearly drowned, but an off-duty policeman saved me. It was confusing to be grateful to a policeman; Blackhill had taught me that they came from a different planet and weren't to be trusted.

On Sunday afternoons my father took me to the Barras, the market place down by Gallowgate. Skip loved the bustle, the noise and particularly the bargaining. To him it was part of the Game to beat the stall-holders down, whether he really wanted something or not. Skip had a liking for bizarre china ornaments, but if some little curio caught his eye he didn't bid for it immediately – he would come back again, wearing his tattiest clothes, and try anything he thought might work to get it as cheaply as possible.

He once spotted a Satsuma-ware elephant teapot from Japan, and returned often to the stall, each time with a more pathetic performance. As the price went down so his clothes became poorer and his expression more downtrodden. Each time he sadly counted out the few coins in his pocket that were never quite enough to afford the elephant teapot. This went on for weeks, supplemented by heart-wrenching tales of some imaginary relative now breathing her last, whose dying wish for some peculiar reason, was to have just such a teapot. Eventually the stall-holder could stand it no more and practically gave it away to get rid of him, much to Skip's delight.

The main attraction for me was the possibility of seeing Uncle Hughie, whose house was within a street of the Barras. Skip would only visit him, though, if we happened to bump into him, because Hughie would undoubtedly assume points if his company was actively sought. I had absorbed all these insane, unwritten rules of the Game as I grew up, so I spent my time at the Barras constantly watching out for the figure of Hughie, hunched over the old wooden crutch, in the hope that he would happen by.

By this time he shared his house with his brother Pat, who provided the fourth and fifth legs of the famous sand-dance with Hughie and Skip. Pat was the least O'Brien-like of the family still around, and not quite up to the speed of mind their lunacy demanded. There had been a brother called John who had disappeared years before, who had been regarded almost as a changeling. He apparently hadn't a wit about him and had disapproved mightily of Hughie, so Hughie used to wait until he had fallen asleep and then paint John's bald head with black boot polish in vengeance. John eventually emigrated to Morecambe, where he married a hotel landlady, and who could blame him? He was never heard of again, so I was cheated of meeting the strange mortal who didn't like Hughie.

Pat wasn't quite as bad as John. He was at least aware of the Game but always made his move a beat or two behind the others. He was a lifelong bachelor who, it was rumoured, had had an unhappy experience at the hands of some female and therefore no longer trusted any of the species. So he had moved in with Hughie, and the two fought endlessly and happily for years. If things were dull Hughie would throw Pat out of the house on the grounds that it was after all *his* house, and Pat would then do the rounds of the family begging for their support. He would take the opportunity to go over each and every argument between himself and Hughie since the last time he had been evicted, much to the enjoyment of the others, then he would go home, by which time Hughie's mind would be on a different ploy. I always felt a bit sad about Uncle Pat because he wasn't quite like the others, but years later I heard a story from a cousin that he used to go up and down closes, removing doormats, mixing them up and putting them back at the wrong doors. So he may not have reached the heights of madness of his brothers and sisters, but I was pleased for him that he couldn't quite be called normal either.

Skip was so happy that I seemed to enjoy the Barras that he took me to his favourite place in all the world, Paddy's Market. As the name suggests, it started out as a place for the immigrant Irish to buy and sell whatever they had. It was situated in lanes and alleyways in the Saltmarket, one of the poorest areas of a very poor city at the turn of the century. I was appalled when I saw it, so shocked by a kind of poverty I had never suspected existed that I could hardly talk. The people were so poor that they were trying to sell the kind of things that others would throw away.

Skip loved it, he was at heart a street arab and he had some affinity with the people there, but I was one generation and some Clark dilution removed and I hated it. He saw it as a valid way of life while I could only see it as shameful, and my reaction was a very major disappointment to Skip. He had obviously thought at one stage that I was a *bona fide* O'Brien.

Paddy's Market is still there, in fact it has become a cult. I don't know if it's still as it was in the mid-Fifties, because I never went back. Indeed no one could persuade me or pay me enough to do so, and if I drive past it these days I steadfastly look in the other direction. Local colour it may be to those who have tried to reinvent Glasgow in recent years, but it's still shameful to me.

Drumchapel was the nearest Nan came to real happiness I think. The housing conditions and the general environment were better, at least by the standards of the late 1950s, so she had fewer problems to sort out for other people. She was still sought out by neighbours with family worries though, somehow she attracted the telling of deep personal secrets, but all she had to do was listen. She was particularly fond of the people next door, the Grimshaws, or as Skip called them, the Grimshanks. Alexa and Willie had two kids, Margaret and Alec. They were an eccentric family, but they didn't have the merest hint of malice or illwill towards any living soul. Alexa was a thin, friendly woman, always smoking, talking and rushing about, and always in the midst of some crisis that Nan had to be told about.

There was no heating in the Drumchapel houses, apart from a coal fire in the sitting-room, so if a natter was required it took place in the kitchen with the gas oven on and the door wide open to let out the heat. Nan was often summoned to the

Grimshanks' kitchen to hear the latest disaster, and always left laughing. The Grimshanks ate odd meals at odd hours and seemed to defy convention in an innocent, friendly way, if indeed they were aware of it. The house was full of all sorts of animals that Alexa had saved from all sorts of fates. Her husband worked in the Singer's sewing machine factory in Clydebank, and his hobby was collecting unusual musical instruments. He kept them in a bedroom, but he had no qualms about letting an unmusical and not very careful child spend hours torturing them.

I discovered the magic of the dulcimer in Willie Grimshank's music room, and also that I would never be a musician. We had a huge collection of old 78s, everything from Irish songs by John McCormack to opera by Caruso, and I used to spend hours singing along with them; Mario Lanza couldn't have reached those top notes without me. I then tried to pick out the tunes on Willie Grimshank's dulcimer and couldn't for the life of me understand what was wrong with the instrument that it couldn't do it.

Alexa's parents, the Dougans, spent a lot of time at Halgreen, and strangely enough they were a perfectly respectable and genteel old couple. They were as bemused by their daughter's lifestyle as everyone else was and it was hard to believe that they were related to Alexa. They never complained, but occasionally they'd catch your eye as if to check that it really was as odd as they suspected it was. Then they'd look heavenwards, shake their heads and smile slightly.

Once Alexa rescued a huge white rabbit that proved beyond any doubt that mental illness does indeed affect the animal kingdom. It went for anything that moved with fangs and claws bared, but it fitted easily into the Grimshanks' family life. All the family ran about avoiding vicious attacks from the demon rabbit, without giving any indication that they thought this was in any way odd. They would eat standing on chairs to keep out of its way, with other chairs strategically placed like stepping stones to other parts of the house. If anyone went into their house while it was loose, Alexa would shout 'The rabbit's oot!' and the visitor had to climb onto a chair too. If all the Grimshanks and the Dougans were in the house, visitors had to bring a chair from their own house, to climb on to, or wait until one became vacant or the rabbit was put back in its cage. It wasn't unusual to find the entire family watching TV or holding a conversation while standing on chairs, as though it were the most normal thing in the world, while the rabbit snarled and tried to get at them. But possibly the oddest of the Grimshanks was the son, Alec, a pleasant, cheerful boy a few years older than me, who even as a teenager took the cat to bed with him every night, dressed in a long robe. The cat that is, not Alec. It was that kind of household.

Chapter Thirteen

I was nine years old when Mickey came out of hospital again in 1957. At the age of twenty he walked with a strong limp because of the locked knee and he was now also minus a kidney, but the TB that had caused it was cured at last.

His final home-coming had been a focus for the family for so long that I was happy, but the reality didn't quite match up. It was like having another adult in the family to tell me what to do, one who had no particular affection for me as the other adults in my life had. How could he when he hadn't been around for most of my childhood? I resented his attitude and he resented the fact that I refused to accept his authority over me. Mickey was having his own problems adjusting to family life, especially poor family life, and all he did was complain and find fault with everything and everyone around him, chiefly me as I was lowest in the pecking order.

Peggy was the recipient of all my complaints about Mickey because my mother wouldn't hear a word against him. In our private chats over the Moodiesburn Street soup pot Peggy tried to get me to think about all my brother had missed and lost in his life, but I couldn't see that any of that was my fault. I thought he should think about what Laurie and I had lost because he had needed it, needed it and got it. It wasn't just the money that had been spent on him, it was also the lost time we might have spent with our parents if they hadn't been preoccupied with Mickey, spending long hours visiting him in remote hospitals. Sometimes Nan had been overcome with guilt about this and Laurie and I were subjected to 'treats' to make up. We would be taken somewhere for the day in the expectation that we would enjoy ourselves; I have clear recollections of a trip to

Edinburgh and another of a freezing day in Helensburgh, shivering in the sea to assuage Nan's needless guilt. None of this was Mickey's fault any more than it was Laurie's or mine of course, but it was a fair demonstration of the gulf between us, and not even Peggy's efforts could bridge it.

As Mickey came out of hospital Uncle Hughie went in. He was sixty-two and he had TB in his lungs, the disease that had killed his wife and three of his five children. He was in Robroyston Hospital and I wasn't allowed to see him though I never gave up trying. When the family went to visit he would take their gifts and exchange them before their eyes, so that they left with whatever the other had brought; he had an admirable way with insults.

To pass the time in hospital he declared himself to be a member of every religion that existed, and demanded to see a representative of each one. He then sent their holy pamphlets home to me; it was our joke, our way of keeping in touch, and I sent him notes and drawings via Skip.

Another gift he sent me was his prayer book, which had a crucifix inside the cover. The lower spar of the cross was loose, so that it swung under the Christ figure. I still have it; and everytime I look at it I swear I can hear him saying, 'Holy swinging Christ.'

He also used to engage the doctors in deep, meaningful discussions about the nature and cause of his illness, always ending by proclaiming, regardless of scientific fact, that 'That Mick Robés is tae blame. You find that Mick Robés an' soart the bugger oot!' No amount of detailed explanation could change his mind, and the unfortunate medics left his bedside in despair. Hughie meant microbes, but none of the learned and educated men of medicine could see that he was sending them up for his own amusement, they never cracked the Game.

About a year after he went into Robroyston, Hughie began to get worse. The report line was issued, calling all the family to his bedside to witness his impending demise. Skip was called from work and arrived with the others to find Hughie gone. Not dead, but gone. Somehow he had escaped from his deathbed and was found several hours later, sitting on the window-sill of the house he shared with Pat, as drunk as a monkey and singing 'Red Sails in the Sunset.' When Pat had arrived home to be greeted by this apparition, Hughie had demanded, 'Whaur's ma rent ya bugger?'

Still singing, he was escorted back to hospital, where the report line was hastily withdrawn. Over the months he managed a repeat performance six more times, and no one ever discovered how he had managed to cross the city with the trusty old wooden crutch safely locked up in the ward sister's office. Skip reckoned he must've bummed along . . .

Chapter Fourteen

Schools were soon built in Drumchapel, first the Proddie lot and then the Catholic ones. I watched mine go up literally in my own backyard, with no great enthusiasm I may add. It was called St Laurence the Martyr's, the same as the church where I had made my minimal first communion. The name had ironic connotations for our family of course, because Skip's standard act was that of the martyr, misunderstood by the world just for drinking all the booze money could buy until it either ran out or he passed out.

Finally the awful day came when the Marian closed its doors for the last time. The authorities came out with the same guff that they spout today, high-sounding twaddle about the good of the child and the importance of schools being situated within the community, but, as ever, the real consideration was money and damn the kids. Bussing was expensive. It was true that the Marian had only been intended to fill the gap until Catholic schools were built, but it was a good school, a happy school and that should have counted for something.

I sat at the back of the very last bus on the very last day, too blinded by tears to see the waving figures of the kindly nuns and Mrs McGettigan. Clutched in my hands was her parting gift, a book inscribed 'Special prize for composition, Margaret O'Brien', and earlier she had given a little speech as she made the surprise presentation. 'I know the rest of you will forgive me girls, when I say that my greatest joy has been reading Margaret O'Brien's stories. One day you will see her words in print and I hope you will remember that I told you so today.' I hadn't a clue what she meant.

Contained within the bright green covers of the book was

the proof that there was a happy land somewhere, and I held onto it like a thread through the labyrinth, leading home to Notre Dame. Once again adults had shattered my world, but I was determined that I would get it back together. I would hold fast to my thread and one day I would pass my eleven plus and find my way back to Notre Dame High School. That's what I'd do . . .

Meanwhile Peggy had given birth to a daughter, but there were problems. It had been a difficult birth and the child was handicapped, in fact she wasn't expected to live. A week after the birth Peggy came home without her baby and immediately collapsed with another post-partum haemorrhage. No one talked about the baby, not even Peggy, we all pretended she didn't exist. In later years I would recognize this strategy and despair of it, but it was the only one the family knew.

The child had been called Anne after my Grandmother, another appeasement. As the months passed Anne held on to whatever slim chance she had of life and her handicap slowly became clearer: she had cerebral palsy, but no one knew yet to what extent. Sometimes when we were alone I would quietly ask Peggy how the baby was – she was always 'the baby', never 'Anne' – and Peggy would whisper back 'She's a'right.' She must have visited the child in hospital but she never mentioned it, and because Nan never spoke of it at the time, it was many years before I discovered that my mother had gone with her.

If the child had died as she was expected to do, then her existence would have been kept very quietly between one or two. I suppose they thought this might save the rest of the family grief, but it didn't of course. Peggy's pain caused us all grief and perhaps if she had been able to talk freely about her baby we could have shared her pain. But the little girl survived against all the odds and came home aged ten months. Anne was an incredibly beautiful child, with fair skin, blue eyes and silvery blonde hair. She reminded me of Laurie before his hair had darkened to brown. Peggy barely left the cot for a second, her entire universe had become centred on the fragile little life that shouldn't have survived.

As Anne grew and her handicap began to unfold, Peggy would make me look into the cot. 'She's a'right, in't she?' she would ask earnestly, 'Ye don't think thur's anythin' wrang wi' hur, dae ye?' Young as I was I'd shake or nod my head as she wanted, sensing her desperate need for my lies. Over the months, as Anne made less progress than normal babies, Peggy insisted that she was 'jist a wee bit slow.' Mistaking their anguish for her only as rejection of Anne, Peggy vigorously defended the dribbling infant against the rest of the family.

As time passed too, McAvoy felt more and more intimidated by the Clarks, perhaps sensing their increasing hostility towards him and sympathy for their sister. After all, she now had a handicapped child *and* McAvoy. The Clarks 'think thur sum'dy,' he would declare defiantly, as long as there wasn't a Clark about. The family's attempts not to make their dislike of him too obvious, not to look down on him for Peggy's sake, were probably more damaging than outright contempt. Honest people, they simply made bad liars.

St Laurence's was a modern, bright, square-shaped construction, seemingly made of glass and plastic; it looked like a rather nasty warehouse. It couldn't compete with the wood-panelled Marian, set amid leafy avenues and genteel mansions, and the teachers were nothing like Mrs McGettigan and the nuns. It also had boys and a wider mix of abilities than I had been used to, a combination that brought me my first experience of the tawse.

One boy in my class of ten year olds was James Campbell, who was nicknamed Bramble, a huge boy more than two years older than the rest of us. Bramble had spent a year in a sanatorium with TB and had been placed in our class to catch up. He got no real help and in fact being with younger children reinforced his feelings of inferiority. He came from a very poor family too and the attitude of the teachers was easily detectable: he was riff-raff. Quite naturally Bramble reacted to his situation by disrupting the class whenever possible. Thus he was universally liked by the children and universally loathed by the teachers, who anyway were only really interested in the top ten or so pupils.

One day, having struggled with the mind-numbing convolutions of long-division and seen a glimmer of light, I was waiting in line to have my attempt marked. I found myself by Bramble's desk, where he sat as though on the outside looking in, making no attempt to work. 'Kin you dae this?' he asked, in a tone implying that a positive answer was tantamount to disloyalty. 'A bit Bramble,' I replied, and flushed with the zeal of having seen that glimmer, I asked 'Wull Ah show ye?' And that's where the teacher found me, doing what she couldn't or wouldn't do, trying to help Bramble break into the world of ticks. Three whacks on each hand she gave me, and as she sweated over her task I knew she was beating me with her own inadequacy and that it was a pitiful, if painful demonstration of might over right. I had the dubious benefit of a lifetime's exposure to the O'Brien view of life and though I may have had stinging hands, I knew I had won the points.

I was more popular with the boys at school than the girls. The boys involved me in their escapades and adventures and treated me as one of them, so the girls actually had little to be jealous of, not that this stopped them. To the girls any attention from the boys was welcome, be it rough horse-play or winks, because it all meant male attention. They were already conditioned to become future wives and mothers rather than people, so any male attention was important to them.

My compositions were still the talk of the place and the boys were always my supporters when marks were read out. The girls would try very hard to make their 'well dones' sound sincere, which made me laugh, because they so obviously weren't. There was a little clique of four or five girls who were always the top group academically and I was amongst them but not part of the clique. They came from the better-off families and already had fee-paying secondary schools earmarked for after the eleven plus and it annoyed them that I was bright yet uninterested in joining their gang. They were therefore delighted when a new boy, John Burgess, took over as top of the class and immediately went into competition with me for top of English, especially composition.

John was light years ahead of me in the dreaded Maths, but he could never beat me at composition and to my delight it irked him something fierce. He used up a great deal of time and energy trying, and each time he failed he showed his disappointment so openly that I almost felt embarrassed for him. Almost, but not quite. Once, to my immense satisfaction, he was unable to contain himself after losing again by just one mark and demanded to know why. Before the teacher could respond Bramble shouted ''Cos hur's is better, ya big shite!', to a spontaneous round of applause and laughter from the other boys. He received the teacher's staple punishment for any misdemeanour, three of the tawse on each hand, for which I somehow felt responsible and apologized to him. 'It wis worth it!' he said, dancing around, his hands tucked underneath his oxters, 'Did ye see his face?' Then he rolled around laughing and shouting 'Ouch!' at the same time.

Apart from Skip's drinking, Nan's belief in the magical qualities of Drumchapel persisted, she had even managed to get as near to a fitted carpet as didn't matter. It was a large square in blue, black and maroon, a colour scheme that went with nothing else, and though it lay in the middle of the living room with a linoleum border all around, she was delighted with it. A little man had come around the doors selling terrazzo doorsteps, instead of the council's nondescript wooden ones, and she had recklessly ordered one then had to scrimp and save to buy it. Halgreen may not have been the 'big hoose' of her dreams, but it was Nan's palace. She still planned a better life for her kids though, and her fantasy for me was that I'd become the private secretary to some rich managing-director then marry him. I treated this as I did Peggy's dream sequences about weddings, I winced and said nothing.

Laurie had struggled through school and left at fifteen to become an apprentice engineer in the Albion Works in Scotstoun. Nan was pleased that he'd have a trade and that he wouldn't become a shoemaker and therefore a drunk like Skip, something she had always dreaded. Mickey was working in Glasgow University, which gave Nan no end of pleasure and she tried to bring it into every conversation. Neither job brought in a lot of money, but at least Nan had the satisfaction that her sons were doing well. If that meant living with the chronic anxiety over unpaid bills, well that was something she had lived with all of her married life anyway.

Gradually the fields around Halgreen Avenue became built up with houses and the roads became the only places for children to play. The main problem with that was that the roads carried double decker buses and were barely wide enough for two to pass each other. Even the valley with the burn, the only piece of greenery left, was filled in and built on. There were few shops and no social facilities or employment within Drumchapel; it was just another ghetto, somewhere to dump those who couldn't afford anything better. The actual housing conditions had improved, but life in general hadn't, and like all the other Fifties estates it gradually went downhill. This gave the planners and the City Fathers the opportunity to wring their hands in woe; they had done their best for these people, given them inside toilets for heaven's sake, and still they weren't satisfied, still they didn't behave like model citizens! Therefore, it must be their own fault.

In the last years of the Fifties though, the worst faults of Drumchapel had yet to materialize, and Nan could see only blue skies ahead.

Once I came in from school to find her cuddling a little man, both of them in tears, and apart from the fact that I didn't know him even by sight, the scene didn't strike me as all that odd. I later discovered that he had come to fix our rented TV and Nan had been working about the house, singing, as she always did. Suddenly he had burst into tears and asked her to stop. He was a Polish Jew whose entire family had died in Hitler's concentration camps, and the tune my mother had been singing was a Yiddish lullaby he had known all his life. He was the first person I ever saw with the chilling tattooed number inside his left forearm, and for me he shrank the world and made fascism and the holocaust personal. He also became a fringe member of the family from then on, dropping in for chats and tea even when our telly wasn't on the blink.

So they came to her still, the people who needed whatever solace it was that Nan provided. Usually they found her doing her housework and singing, going from room to room carrying a shovel on which reposed a tortoise called Tormy, the last one we ever owned. Tormy was obviously a tortoise in distress because he worshipped Nan too, and he attempted to follow her on her rounds on his stumpy little legs. Despite her resistance to anything connected with O'Brien insanity, she grew fond of Tormy and felt sorry for him, but she couldn't bring herself to actually touch him. So instead of lifting him up she carted him around with her on a shovel, as he gazed up at her adoringly and gulped in that silly way that even the best-bred tortoises are apt to do. I don't think she ever stopped to consider what impression this eccentric apparition made on casual callers who didn't know us all that well, and that of course was exactly what made the rest of us smile.

We never had a pet that wasn't a tortoise; whenever we asked for a kitten or a puppy Skip appeared with yet another chelonian reptile. It was many years before I discovered why he was so fond of the little creatures. Apparently the O'Briens had two of them in Tarbet Street, and whenever Granda Tom arrived home after one of his sojourns with his aesthetic friends, Granny O'Brien belaboured him over the head with the tortoises. It doesn't take a great deal of psychological understanding to recognize the Freudian significance of Skip's fondness for tortoises, and it was the only adverse comment he ever made about his father that I know of. Tortoises of course do not fare well in the Scottish climate and none of ours lasted more than a few years. We buried them all beside the Tarbet Street originals, in the

Ramshorn Graveyard in Ingram Street, where the upper echelons of Victorian society lie at peace under metal cages to protect them from body-snatchers.

Some century in the future, archaeologists will dig up the site and conjecture about what the tortoise shells tell them about Glaswegian burial practices, little knowing it was confined to the O'Briens. One of my dearest wishes is that they should if possible be the same archaeologists who find Hughie's unwanted legs, filled with ashes at the bottom of the River Clyde – I would love to be around to hear their conclusions.

Chapter Fifteen

Peggy had given birth to another child, a healthy boy she called John, and apart from the usual post-partum haemorrhage all had gone well. She now had three children under four years of age though, one handicapped to a still uncertain degree, and Nan and George discussed the situation. After a further talk with the 'Fair Yins' it was decided that George, the eldest male in the family, should talk to McAvoy about the wisdom of avoiding any more pregnancies.

The first mistake that McAvoy made was to take George's deceptively quiet manner as uncertainty, and the second was in daring to compare himself with George. 'Ye've goat three weans yersel',' he swaggered, though George's children were each separated by more than nine months, unlike McAvoy's. His next mistake was to take George's silence for surrender instead of the gathering anger he struggled all his life to keep under control.

'An' Ah'll dae wi' ma wife whit Ah like!' the little man swaggered.

In reply George just picked him up and shook him like a rat. 'Listen wee man,' he hissed, 'You an' me ur no' the same! An' Peggy wull aye be ma sister, long efter she's your widda!' He had lifted McAvoy off the ground to get eye-to-eye contact and was holding him by the front of his jersey, which was slowly tightening around his neck. The rest was drowned out by shouts and screams, and I heard Auntie Annie's voice with the familiar warning, 'Watch Geordie!' and then my mother's saying, 'George! George son! Pit him doon! Ye don't waant tae swing fur the likes o' that insect!' I had taken refuge under the table as usual, and as George's grip was released finger-by-finger, I saw

McAvoy slowly sinking to the floor only inches from me. A long way above, Uncle George's face was ashen with rage, his hands still clenched with fury. As my eyes locked with McAvoy's I saw that he was shaking with terror, and I was glad that he knew I'd seen it.

Within months Peggy was pregnant again.

I was neither happy nor unhappy at St Laurence's; it was just somewhere to fill the time before I went back to Dowanhill and Notre Dame. I would have to sit an entrance exam and then there would be modest fees of around two-pounds per term. Skip was drinking more than ever and money was even tighter, but still I contrived not to pick up the coded messages that I might not get back to Notre Dame. I still harboured the certainty that it was only a matter of time.

I was still at St Laurence's when Uncle Hughie died in September 1958. Uncle Pat had been summoned from work by the hospital and had gone straight home to find the windowsill empty. But Hughie wasn't to be outdone; on his deathbed he informed the assembled family that if they made him die he'd get even, he'd haunt them forever. Who else but an O'Brien would believe that the O'Briens had the power of life over death?

Afterwards Skip, Pat and Norah went to St Alphonsus' down by the Barras, to arrange the funeral with the priest, who in a moment of madness left them alone in his study, along with a store of communion wine. When he returned he found Skip dressed in various vestments, marrying his sister to his brother. The 'groom' was handsomely dressed for the occasion in the priest's chasuble, the richly embroidered, sleeveless garment worn when giving communion. The 'bride', whose passion for hats was well-known, sported the black three-cornered biretta with the central pom-pom at a jaunty angle, and all three were clutching the last of many half-empty bottles of wine. The priest then sat down with this motley crew and arranged Hughie's funeral. Norah disgraced herself by falling asleep and snoring loudly throughout. The biretta slipped over her eyes, but miraculously her grip on the bottle remained strong. When the meeting was over, the three O'Briens stood up and silently divested themselves of the ritual garments, laying them neatly in a pile before leaving. The priest had said nothing throughout, which I found puzzling until Skip reminded me that he was Hughie's parish priest, so he would have been used to worse. 'Mind you,' he said disapprovingly, 'Norah ferr gave us a showin' up wi' hur snorin'.'

Skip, to whom tears were a sign of weakness, sat in George Square until he got enough control of himself to come home and tell us that Hughie had died, missing the ordinary buses and having to wait for the night service in the early hours of the morning. His eyes though were still red-rimmed and Nan spotted it instantly and maliciously accused him of crying. Skip hotly denied it of course, but the points went to Nan; she had caught him showing human emotion, crying for his dead brother, and it was one of the few victories she ever got over him.

'Did your uncle have the last rites?' asked my teacher, and I glumly nodded. Uncle Hughie had made a fetish out of having the last rites. Up till then he had celebrated each reprieve with a few choruses of 'Red Sails in the Sunset' and the odd bottle of plonk. 'Well that's all right then,' the silly woman replied, 'He'll be in heaven now.' It somehow failed to raise my spirits. I didn't want him in heaven; what had heaven done to deserve having him? I wanted him here to keep my world bright. Even though I hadn't seen him for over a year I knew he was still there and so the light of his lunacy had still illuminated the land. The last time I had seen him was just after Mickey had come out of hospital. He ruled the roost so much that neither Laurie nor I were happy to have him home. We were looking for ways to demonstrate our feelings, when we hit on the idea of joke soap to turn his face black. We had no money of course, so we had set off to find Uncle Hughie, who took us to his one-roomed home, his single-end in Bridgeton's Stevenston Street, listened to our story and gave us enough to buy the soap. Now he had truly gone and there was no adult left in the world who would understand the importance of spending money on black-face soap . . .

Hughie's funeral was preceded by a family conference to discuss his threats of long-term hauntings. To be on the safe side it was decided to have him buried without the trusty wooden crutch. As he had managed to find his way across the city on numerous occasions – and that while falling-down drunk – quite why they thought coming back from the next world without it would cause him any problems I have no idea. But then logic was never their strong point.

When the coffin, minus crutch, arrived at the church for the receiving service the day after Hughie's death, the O'Briens sat as far from each other as possible, because with very good reason they simply didn't trust one other. At the end of the service they all moved independently with one thought in mind, to touch the coffin in a last gesture of farewell, or as Skip insisted, to make sure the lid was on securely. There was a sharp intake of breath from the assembled congregation that always turns up uninvited at such events, as coincidentally the O'Briens reached the coffin at the same time. They surrounded it and each laid a hand on it, in a theatrical, almost cabalistic ritual. But the effect was nearly ruined when Tommy, who had no time for the Catholic church or the family's excesses, paused on his way out. 'Christ aye, that'll be right!' he said sarcastically from halfway up the aisle, 'Arise an' walk ya auld bastard!' Then turning to leave he obviously remembered the missing crutch and turned back. 'Or at least hop aboot a bit!' he added with relish.

Refusing to be put down by this interruption, the others were so taken with the effect their performance had created, that the 'laying on of the hands' became a tradition at every family funeral thereafter. A piece of genuine O'Brien folklore had been invented.

When Hughie died I was ten years old and beginning to show the effects of the dilution of the blood; some Clark sensitivity had crept in. At the wake I told Skip it was wrong that we should be having a good time while Hughie lay alone in the cold, dark church. Skip was aghast; no family member had ever mouthed such obscenities before in his hearing. 'Don't be daft!' he exclaimed, 'It's the first time in ma life that I've goat the better o' the auld bugger. An' if it'd been me insteed, him an' that crutch wid be up here the noo, dancin' aboot, as drunk as a monkey. An' besides,' he added, looking furtively about, 'How dae ye know he's no' here tae?'

Next day, the family, attired in their Sunday best, filed into the church for the final service before burial, and behind them extra mourners arrived unexpectedly. Every down-and-out and wino in the vicinity was there, and arriving last they left first after Hughie had been carried out to the waiting hearse. They took up position on foot immediately behind the hearse and along the route more joined in. This made it impossible for the posh cars provided for the family to take their rightful place of prominence because they were falling further and further behind. Eventually the cars were abandoned and the family had to follow the unofficial mourners, none of whom had been any too fastidious about their personal hygiene or attire.

'He's planned this!' I heard Skip mutter in delight, 'An' he's roon' the coarner noo, laughing at us!' The same thought seemed to strike the rest of the family and they all started laughing, which put a nice finish to a very odd funeral. I'm sure they were right too; no one had ever won the points from Hughie while he was alive, what possible difference could a little thing like death make?

'. 'Ah'm sorry aboot yer Uncle Hughie hen,' said Peggy softly, and cuddled me to her. Then she pointed to the sky, where shafts of sunlight pierced the clouds. 'See that?' she said, 'That's God sendin' doon pathways tae heaven fur people that's jist died, mebbe Hughie wull be oan wannae thaim.' Even at the age of ten I had to smile at Peggy and her hopeless, undying romanticism. If I knew Hughie he'd be selling spaces on God's pathway to those bound in the opposite direction . . .

Pat, now alone in Stevenston Street, was haunted by

Hughie's 'twin' behind the door, but he finally summoned up the courage to dismantle Louis and then tried to lose his leg, the last artificial leg in existence. Not for him the formal handing over of the leg to the relevant authorities though, instead he tried to burn it, but it wouldn't burn. He left it in a hospital waiting-room and it came back to him next day. He abandoned it on a bus and it was returned the same day. He put it out for the binmen and they left it propped against the door, so that when Pat opened it the leg fell across his feet. 'Ah'm tellin' ye!' he wailed to the others, who were enjoying the whole business hugely as his paranoia grew, 'It's him! He's efter me!' Finally he tried Hughie's own solution to the unwanted second leg problem, and it joined the rest, filled with ashes at the bottom of the Clyde.

The hauntings weren't finished though, because Norah reported doors and windows opening by themselves. The others, delighted at the opportunity to add to the family collection of myths, decided that they had noticed the very same phenomenon. Soon every and any odd happening came to be attributed to Hughie, and so generations who were never privileged and fortunate enough to have actually known him, look up as the breeze blows a door open, or when they lock themselves out, or if there's a power cut, and say 'It's Hughie again!' He managed it after all, not just gone and not forgotten, but gone and very much still here. And if that isn't immortality, I don't know what is.

Chapter Sixteen

In my entire school career I only got the tawse twice, both times at St Laurence's. The first was for trying to help Bramble do his sums, but it would be years before I understood why I got it the next time.

I went home every day for lunch, partly to satisfy myself that Nan was all right, and partly because we couldn't afford school lunches, and Nan would have died rather than apply for free meals. Free meals were a badge of poverty and the kids who qualified for them were told to stand to one side, just to reinforce the point that they should be both ashamed and grateful, and to let them know that everyone else knew of their crime.

At the end of one lunch-break Nan had a fit and by the time I had got her to bed, where I knew she would sleep soundly for a couple of hours and then be fine, I was late for school. Late comers had to report to the deputy head, who invariably beat the living daylights out of them, but this time I thought I had the perfect reason. 'My mother had an epileptic fit, Sir,' I explained, 'And I couldn't leave her until she had come out of it.'

'You evil-minded madam!' he yelled, and went at me with the tawse like a man possessed. I hadn't a clue what had happened to him and simply assumed that he had gone bananas, as we all knew teachers were wont to do from time to time.

Something else happened at school that wasn't cleared up until the first incident was solved too, which also involved Nan. I had gone home on another lunchtime to find the house covered in blood and Nan staggering about almost comatose, begging 'Help me, help me.' A few days earlier she had been given new tablets by the GP, Dr Fields, who had been reminded at the time that she was already on medication to control the epilepsy. He had become quite annoyed at this, 'I'm the doctor here,' he'd said, 'You're only the patient Mrs O'Brien.' When I found her that day she had fallen semi-conscious against furniture and walls and her face was badly injured. I knew immediately that the new tablets were to blame. Growing up with a condition like epilepsy you develop an instinct for pitfalls and learn to identify problems quickly, but I didn't know what to do about it. We had no phone and neither did any of the neighbours, so I had to leave her while I ran back to school to ask the headmaster to call a doctor. I put Nan to bed first, which in fact was probably the wrong thing to do, but had I left her out of bed she would certainly have hurt herself more.

The headmaster was very sympathetic when I told him my mother was ill and rushed along to the school office to phone a doctor, while I trotted at his heels telling him the full story. When he heard that Nan had epilepsy he stopped in his tracks and refused to make the call. So I had to run home again, take money from one of Nan's secret stores and find a phone-box to call Mickey at work, the only number I actually knew because it was at the top of a letterhead that Nan had kept. Mickey called Dr Fields and we sat by her bed all day waiting for him to arrive, which he never did, and it was, I'm sure, sheer luck that she recovered. Dr Fields arrived the next day and took the new tablets away, but he didn't make any comment and certainly he never admitted his part or apologized for it.

Over the years I would replay the incident in my mind and wonder what had happened. Had I explained it wrongly to the headmaster, had he somehow misunderstood? Why else would a learned, educated man react that way except if he had misunderstood? I was an adult before I learned that epilepsy was regarded by the general public as a sign of being possessed by the devil, that epilepsy sufferers were thought to be mad, unclean or given to excessive sexual appetites, and I could hardly stop laughing. Then another mystery from the past suddenly fitted into place.

One day we had been going to see Peggy. We were about

to get off a tram in Parliamentary Road when Nan had had a fit. I was nine or ten years old, and there I was trying to prevent her falling off the platform of the moving tram onto the road, and no one would help me. The conductor and passengers stood back watching, but not one of them would help, and when the tram stopped they all insisted I had to somehow get her off. This was a situation I could have handled blindfold within our own four walls, but she had never fitted outside before and it took me ages to persuade her to go home with me. She was so confused that she couldn't cooperate and I remember her saying over and over again, 'Ah don't know whit tae dae . . .'

She had brought me up to believe that her condition was a nuisance, nothing more; for her it meant inconvenient fits and the necessity, the indignity, of depending on tablets. For me it meant coping with the fits and trying to make sure she didn't cheat on her dosage. Beyond that it curtailed our lives not at all. But to the good people of Glasgow she wasn't safe to touch, to the deputy head it was an insult, and to the head, well God knows exactly what he thought. Strange to think that Nan had so respected learning and education, yet a man who represented it so ably was a bigoted idiot and not one hundredth the human being she was.

Chapter Seventeen

In the Winter of 1958 we had a family wedding. One of my cousins was getting married, the son of Nan's sister Vicky, the eldest Fair Yin. Vicky had 'turned' to marry a Catholic and so her son had been brought up in the religion. Now he was marrying in St Mungo's, and much to Peggy's delight it was to be a white wedding. Nan, Peggy and I went out to buy wedding finery for the two of them at a club store.

A little man called Arnold White had come to the entire Clark family for as long as I could remember. For an agreed weekly sum he would issue a line to buy clothes from one of two warehouses he dealt with. The prices were high and so was the interest paid, and it meant there was little choice of where to shop, but it was the only way we could ever afford anything for the wedding. Mr White had issued Nan and Peggy with lines for both warehouses and off we went. It was a good day, full of fun and laughter, even though Peggy was pregnant again. They tried on everything in one warehouse and then tried on everything in the other, just for the fun of it. Peggy wanted Nan to buy me a fancy dress too, because she knew one of my 'Fair' cousins had a new rig-out, there was 'Dark Yin' honour at stake. I'd been given a pink dress for my tenth birthday a few months before though, and Nan was having none of it. Feeling sorry for me, Peggy gave me a necklace to wear, a cheap plastic popper of pink flowers with a glittery rhinestone in the centre of each one. Nan eventually settled for a blue dress and Peggy for a pink one with an all-over pattern of pale blue flowers. In the centre of each blue flower on the bodice was a glittery rhinestone, just like the necklace.

When the wedding day came around they had swapped, as they always did; Peggy was wearing the blue dress and

Nan the pink. Being Proddies they hadn't a clue what to do during the wedding service, and tried to follow my knowledgeable movements, kneeling, sitting, standing and generally bobbing about. Eventually it became too much for them and they collapsed against each other, laughing so much that the tears ran down their faces and the familiar creaks of merriment echoed all the way through the ceremony. And the more they tried not to laugh the more they did. They were like two schoolgirls, and I remember reflecting that had I behaved like that I'd have had a severe dressing down. Once outside at the end they mopped their eyes and told each other what a hoot it had all been, which set them off again of course.

That night, at the reception, after the bride and groom had gone, I went upstairs and heard singing coming from the room where the bride had changed out of her white dress and veil. And there sat Peggy at a dressing table, the wedding head-dress and veil on top of her curly hair, staring into the mirror and singing 'Mexicali Rose' very quietly to herself, lost in her dream of being a white bride. Somehow I knew enough not to disturb her; I left her alone to enjoy her fantasy and crept downstairs again, but the picture became imprinted on my memory forever and I see it still all these years later. Peggy as the bride of her dreams . . .

Chapter Eighteen

It was 19th December 1958; I know this because it's recorded in my ten-year-old script on the back of a plastic calendar, the kind you keep in a wallet. We were watching TV at home; it was a nature programme, something about birds, and the wind was howling outside. There was a knock at the door, and when I answered it I found Alexa Grimshank standing there in her usual agitated state. 'Thur's a fire through the wa'!' she said, and returned to her own house.

I closed the door and sat down again. 'It wis Mrs Grimshank,' I said, 'She said thur's a fire through the wa'.' Everyone nodded; Alexa was known to fly the odd kite and we all knew not to accept what she said as gospel. Still, something made me get up and look out of the window, where there was a lot of debris flying about, then I ran out onto the verandah, Laurie close behind, and Alexa had been telling the truth.

The top floor flat in the next tenement, which adjoined the Grimshank house, was well ablaze. We did what anyone would do in similar circumstances, panicked a bit, tried to figure out what to save, came to the conclusion that there was very little, then grabbed our coats and left the house, knocking on all the other doors on the way down. We stood outside in the cold, night air, watching sixty foot flames shoot into the sky, waiting for the fire-engines to appear. It was *déja vu*, shades of Balmano Brae.

The house belonged to the Ramsays, a family of shy, attractive children, two boys and a girl. They were a quiet, respectable family and both parents worked, so the grandmother, who lived with them, looked after the children. That night, it was thought that the youngest boy, who was about five years old, had been playing with matches in bed and had set the house on fire. The two boys and the grandmother were safe, but there was no sign of the middle child, Ella, who was the same age as me. Ella rarely played with the other children in the street. A pretty child, with blue eyes, short, curly blonde hair and a shy smile, she was always well dressed and we thought her mother wouldn't let her out to play for fear of getting her nice clothes dirty. We felt sorry for her because she was a pleasant girl and we all thought she would have liked to play with us more often.

The adults were knocking on doors up and down the street and in the facing block of tenements, trying to find her, while the rest of us huddled in the cold, watching the firemen being raised on turntable ladders with hoses going full-bore into the flames. A *Daily Record* reporter took Laurie and I into his car and gave Laurie a slug of whisky to heat him up, and from there I saw Alexa Grimshank. She had her hair in rollers and was wearing her fur coat over her nightie. On her feet she had an ancient pair of slippers over ankle-socks, and looped over her arm was a handbag containing all her money. In one hand she carried a budgie in a cage and clutched a dog on a leash, and in the other was the killer rabbit in another cage, plus the inevitable cigarette sticking out between two fingers. I wondered where she had secreted all the other animals, the cats with sore paws and the birds with broken wings, for I had no doubt that she had them with her too. It was the sum total of everything Alexa held dear enough to rescue from the flames, the clearest statement imaginable of what made her tick, and despite the drama being played out in front of me that night, the sight of her made me laugh.

The Ramsay parents arrived home within an hour or so and had to be held back from rushing into the burning building. I remember Mrs Ramsay's voice clear against the noise of the fire-engines, the crackling of the flames and the howling of the wind, screaming 'Ma weans! Ma weans!'

It was nearly 4 a.m. before the fire was out and the people in our part of the building were able to go back to their houses, but still Nan and the others looked for Ella. Then the firemen lowered a black box by rope from what was left of the Ramsay house. 'Whit's that?' Nan asked a fireman, 'It's the wean,' he replied, 'We found the wee lassie in her bed.' On the ground below the windows lay the Christmas presents the Ramsay children would have got in less than a week and I remember a doll lying there, grotesquely twisted from the flames and matted with mud.

The smell of burning was everywhere, a characteristic smell that lingers in the memory still, different from any other kind of smoke. Our house wasn't damaged but Alexa's house was. The room where I tortured the dulcimer was a blackened shell and water had penetrated the places that the flames had missed. The chimney was unsafe and part of the roof between us was open to the sky, so the firemen covered the hole with a tarpaulin and sat up for what was left of the night making the chimney safe so that the families below could go to bed. That night was the start of my admiration for firemen. During my working life I would have cause to admire them over and over again. They remain to me the finest human beings ever to draw breath.

Nan couldn't sleep and spent the night making soup and tea for the firemen. By the first light of morning she was on first name terms with them and when they finally left it was like losing friends we had known for years. I was allowed to sleep on into the day after the fire, which annoyed me, because I had badly wanted to go to school to tell everyone about it. As it was a Friday I wouldn't be able to tell them now until after the weekend. Being me, though, I had to write it down. I used the plastic calendar, the first thing I could find, to record the event in very small script.

Next day the basic details were on the front pages of every Glasgow newspaper and I was concerned that Peggy might think we had been hurt. After all, it was reported that an unnamed girl of my age had died in a fire at Halgreen Avenue, and maybe Peggy would think it was me. When we saw her as usual the next day, though, she said she hadn't been worried.

'Ah knew it wisnae you,' she said, 'Ah knew ye wur a' a'right.'

'How?' I asked.

'Ah jist knew hen, that's a',' she replied with a shy smile.

Later I asked Nan how Peggy could have been so sure.

'She tellt ye hen, she jist knew,' she said, smiling the exact same smile.

We never saw the Ramsays again, they were moved to another part of Drumchapel and never returned to Halgreen Avenue. Occasionally a neighbour would report bumping into Mrs Ramsay and that she had walked past them, and I found that very odd. With hindsight though, I can see that she just couldn't take any more reminders of what had happened on that December night.

Chapter Nineteen

Christmas and New Year 1958 passed in the usual mixture of family celebrations and drunken arguments with Skip. But I remember it particularly because of an incident that will remain with me for ever.

A few days after New Year Skip took me with him to see an uncle and his family. They lived with his wife's parents, because her mother had been an invalid for years and was totally bedridden. I liked going to sit with the old woman because the stories of her childhood were like history to me and I loved to hear them.

That night I left her bedroom and walked down the long, dark corridor towards the living-room, where the rest of the family were talking and laughing. Suddenly the old lady's husband stepped out of the darkness and grabbed me. He had obviously been waiting for me and pulled me against him, his wet mouth all over me, the smell of stale booze and cigarettes making me feel sick. One hand held me tightly while the other one was fumbling about in my pants and I could feel something hard pressing against my stomach. I froze completely. The living-room was inches away but I was so shocked and confused that I couldn't summon up the fight to get away from the old man to safety. What shocked me most was that I had known him all my life. He was an old drinking pal of Skip's and my cousins' grandfather. I couldn't believe he was doing this to me. Then the door handle turned and he pushed me away.

We both went into the living-room, where the party was in full swing. I felt physically sick and disorientated; everyone had been enjoying themselves without the slightest suspicion that inches away, on the other side of the door, the old man had been sexually assaulting me. When we were leaving he tried to give me money and I put it on the table and left it there. When he asked for a kiss I refused and Skip was annoyed, so once we were outside I told him what the old man had done to me.

Skip's response was a mixture of anger and annoyance, as though I had broken some unwritten social code by mentioning it. It wasn't that he didn't believe me, it was that he didn't want to know. It was as though these things happened, but they shouldn't be mentioned and he was ashamed of me for not adhering to that social nicety. His ten-year-old daughter had been sexually assaulted by someone she should have been safe with, but it would upset his life to acknowledge it or do anything about it.

I felt ashamed, dirty, unclean, and Skip's reaction had reinforced all of it. It must have been my fault, something to do with how I behaved or looked, or else Skip would have done something . . . wouldn't he . . . ? I didn't tell another soul, not my mother and not Peggy, who anyway, was now out of bounds. Peggy was expecting a baby in early May, my mother had told me, and I knew how sick Peggy got, so I mustn't annoy or upset her. So I kept my dirty, nasty, guilty little secret to myself. It had been all my fault, and even if I could have told someone I don't think I would have, I was just too ashamed of myself.

Every excuse was dragged out to explain why I couldn't sit the entrance exam for Notre Dame. Skip wanted me to go to Garnethill Convent near St Aloysius, because Granda Tom had had close connections with the school. Suddenly it seemed we were to honour the name of dear, departed Granda Tom, whose name hadn't been mentioned in years because no one cared anything for him. Couldn't I just try the exam? There was no point, I was told, even if I passed I wouldn't be going there, 'family duty' meant I had to go to Garnethill.

So the little clique of top girls at St Laurence's went to sit the entrance exam and returned with the papers. They had all passed. The teacher read out the questions and I was the only one, including the clique, who got all of them right.

And I'd have walked the composition too. I didn't think it was possible to be so unhappy, but I was only a child then; time would teach me that there are troughs and depths of unhappiness not even hinted at in the worst nightmares of a disappointed, almost eleven-year-old . . .

By this time Mickey had found a way of escaping from weekends in Drumchapel. Working at the University he had met up with a crowd of people who went to the hills instead of spending their weekends in the city. Being Mickey he soon amassed the equipment he needed to go with them and every Friday he would disappear and every Sunday night he would reappear. All of this was welcome in a way, because I now heartily loathed the sight or thought of him; the gulf between us had never lessened. He just wasn't one of us yet he controlled all of us. Nan still adored him unconditionally, I think she felt guilty about all those years he had spent in hospital, as though somehow she had been to blame.

Workmen had dug a deep hole in the road leading to Halgreen. Skip had been warned to watch out for it as he left for work that Friday morning, warned several times. 'Ye'd think Ah wis a drunk!' he protested indignantly. That night, coming home drunk as usual, he fell down the hole and couldn't get out for hours. Nan sat up waiting for him, but I had a feeling he was down that hole. He managed to scramble out in the early hours and we heard the familiar sound of him crawling up the stairs. He had broken his nose and his face was covered in blood mixed with the sandy-red soil, but he was in playful mood. As we tried to clean him up he would slip under the table and shout 'Peeka boo!' When we turned our backs he hid in a cupboard and shouted 'Ye cannae find me!' Next morning after his 'anaesthetic' had worn off he suffered. Apart from the broken nose he was covered in bruises from the fall and from falling back again everytime he had tried to clamber out.

It was one of the few occasions when he didn't win the points. But Nan did, she went around smiling for days!

Chapter Twenty

It was around this time that Skip became a businessman. Looking back, it had all the elements of farce that were as necessary to his daily life as booze. Somehow he managed to rent a shop near Gallowgate and set up his own shoe repair business. He had no capital and of course had done nothing to find out whether such a business was needed or wanted in the area.

Every Monday and Tuesday evening Laurie and I would be sent around the doors of countless houses throughout Drumchapel, asking the occupants if they had any shoes to be mended. These would be carted home, often very late at night, and next day Skip in turn would cart them to his shop for repair. On Friday, pay night, we repeated the process, only this time returning the mended shoes and collecting the money. Again it would be very late by the time we got home and carrying the money laid us open to all sorts of dangers. There were times when we were scared, and one night we were certainly followed by two men. There were police houses nearby, so we sat in one of the closes for half an hour, knowing that if the men did intend to rob us they wouldn't do so anywhere near the police. When we came out the men had gone and we ran home. We never told Nan anything of this, she already disapproved of the arrangement but had been won over by Skip's assurances that all would be well, and it was only for a little while until business picked up. And anyway, the kids liked it.

Luckily for Laurie and I, the experiment into big business was headed for failure after only a few months. Skip had taken on someone to help him mend the shoes, but from what was coming in he could only pay one wage and that went to the other man. Together they would drink that, plus anything more that Skip might have, and soon he was back working for someone else again. All his life he insisted that if he had had another twenty-five pounds he could have made the business pay, but in truth it was like all of his fads, doomed to failure through short-lived enthusiasm and lack of thought.

Peggy wanted a home delivery. With her obstetrics history of difficult labours and haemorrhages, Nan had been sure that she wouldn't get it. The GP would tell her that it would be best if she went into hospital to have the baby, and Peggy would follow that advice. So it was a shock when he agreed to Peggy's request. It seemed impossible. Peggy was looking after Maw Clark, running the house, caring for three children under the age of five, one of them handicapped, and coping with McAvoy. Peggy was worried about leaving her children, so the other Clarks offered to care for them while she was in hospital. But McAvoy refused to let my mother, or any of the Clarks for that matter, take the children, either singly or together. Nan tried talking to him, and then arguing that Peggy needed to be in hospital, that she always had a bad time, and that she also needed rest. But the little man decreed that he would look after his own family.

When Nan told the rest of the Clarks they glanced knowingly at each other. 'When did he come up wi' this idea?' Uncle George asked sarcastically, 'He's never bothered aboot lookin' efter thum afore.'

'Leave it,' Peggy pleaded, 'Jist leave it. Don't annoy him, ye know whit he's like.' Anything for a quiet life, that's what she meant, she had to live with him and it was easier if he wasn't upset. And besides, the last baby, John, had arrived without any fuss or trouble, this one would too. Anything to keep the peace . . . It became another reason to despise McAvoy, as though another reason were needed.

George and Nan talked about how to deal with the situation, but they knew there was nothing to be done. McAvoy should've been thinking of his wife instead of using her to get one up on the family, they said, but

My Auntie Peggy in 1943, aged 21.

(Above Left) My father Laurie (Skip) O'Brien Snr in 1942. This photo made Laurie Jnr think his daddy was 'a big man'.

(Above Right) My mother, Joan Henderson Clark, shortened to Nan for some reason. Taken in 1943.

(Right) My parents' wedding day, 17th July 1936. Skip was 24, Nan was only 17 and looks so young you want to shout 'foul'.

... then the gable went

TOP FLOOR—CLARKS

SECOND FLOOR—TURNBULLS

FIRST FLOOR—McCREADIES

GROUND FLOOR—FITZGERALDS

(Above) Balmano Brae after the collapse in June 1951.

(Left) My cousins James and John Kelly, sons of Vic the 'Fair Yin' head, at Balmano Brae shortly before the collapse.

(Above) Peggy's wedding 27th March 1953. From left to right:
Uncle George Clark, Maw, Uncle Harry Clark, Mrs Brown (Auld Broon),
Uncle Willie Clark, Auntie Vic Kelly and Skip.

(Above) My maternal grandmother, Annie (Maw)
Clark, in 1943, looking deceptively angelic.

(Right) My paternal grandfather, Tom O'Brien,
ringing the bell at St Aloysius' College.

(Above clockwise from left) Uncle George Clark, Auntie Annie and their youngest child Anne at Loch Lomond. Uncle Tommy O'Brien and a friend (Tommy is the one standing). The photo Uncle Jim O'Brien sent of himself with a kitten, which caused my father to joke that it was taken 'Probably jist before he strangled it'. Uncle Willie Clark in the uniform of the Highland Light Infantry.

(Above) Me and my parents.

(Right) Me and Nan.

(Below) Me and my brother,
Laurie Jnr. –
*All taken in Edinburgh on
one of Nan's 'Guilt Trips'.*

(Right) Me and Nan in the early 60s.

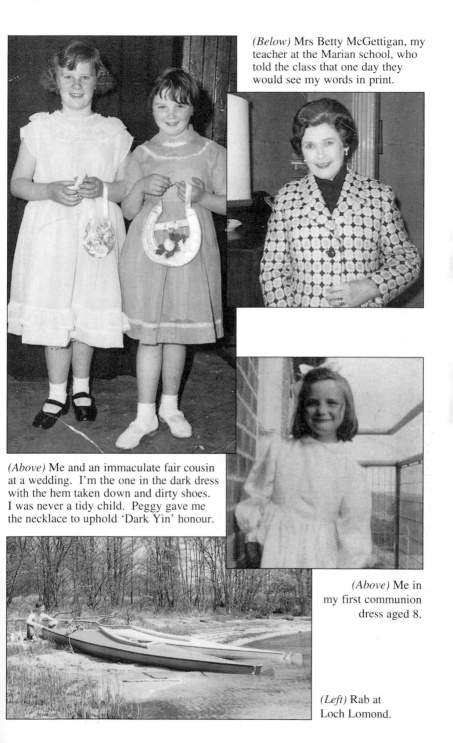

(Below) Mrs Betty McGettigan, my teacher at the Marian school, who told the class that one day they would see my words in print.

(Above) Me and an immaculate fair cousin at a wedding. I'm the one in the dark dress with the hem taken down and dirty shoes. I was never a tidy child. Peggy gave me the necklace to uphold 'Dark Yin' honour.

(Above) Me in my first communion dress aged 8.

(Left) Rab at Loch Lomond.

My family.
From left to right: Rab, Debbie, Euan, Lisa and me.

their hands were tied. 'Ah'll tell ye wan thing,' George said darkly, 'This is the last wean. She shouldnae be hivin' this wan, bit it'll be the last yin!'

Something was wrong with Nan. It seemed as though one minute we were all talking, thinking and worrying about Peggy, and then without anyone noticing, Nan became ill. There were sobs and screams every night and often we would find her re-doing housework in the early hours, afraid to sleep and face whatever demons lay in wait for her. There was about her a frantic cheerfulness, a tendency to be jovial and talk too much, but never to meet your eyes. Then she would lapse into a deep silence, as if the pretence of communication was over, and having concealed whatever it was that she was hiding from everyone else, she could now brood on it alone. Dark circles appeared under her eyes, her skin took on a yellowish tinge and she aged rapidly, yet she refused to see a doctor. Every nightmare was explained away next day and became transformed in the telling into a funny story. It was as though she had surrounded herself with a protective wall of false laughter to deflect those who knew her and were close to her, a kind of emotional radar jammer.

'Ah hid this dream,' she told us one day, 'Aboot oor Peggy. She wis wearin' a long, white dress, an' cairryin' a big bouquet. Pink they wur, big pink roses. An' you wur therr,' she told me excitedly, 'An' ye wur fussin' roond aboot hur. Ah tried tae talk tae hur bit she jist stared straight aheed, widnae take any notice, it wis like it wis jist the two o' ye and yese wurnae botherin' wi' anybody else! Then she drapped her flooers and ye picked thum up, and she took wan o' the flooers oot o' the bouquet and gied it tae ye!'

Having lived all of my life with Peggy's wedding fixation, I was keen to tell her. 'She'll like that story!' I enthused, and was stung by the immediate change of mood. 'Ye'll no' tell Peggy! Ye'll jist leave Peggy alane!'

These spells of dark, brooding silence were followed by others of scaring hyperactivity, and she would hustle and bustle around, organizing, directing and then abandoning whatever she had been so engrossed in. She alternated between snapping viciously and greeting with over-enthusiasm anyone she met, and all the time there was that haunted, driven expression in her eyes.

There was no balance in her life or in her behaviour. Although I was about to sit my eleven-plus exams she would suddenly decide to keep me off school and we would set off together to visit Peggy, usually on the day of her ante-natal appointments with the McAvoy family doctor. For some reason Nan waited for the results of these appointments in a state of tension, but often after setting out on the journey to Blackhill we would turn back and return home instead, once only yards from 6 Moodiesburn Street, without seeing Peggy. There was never any explanation, probably because she didn't have one. I was barred from 'annoying' Peggy, now in the last three months of her pregnancy, so Uncle George was the only one I could turn to. 'She'll be worried aboot Peggy hen,' he told me, 'Ye know whit hur an' Peggy ur like. It'll be a' right when Peggy's better again.' Despite all this Skip didn't seem to notice anything wrong.

Easter Monday fell on 30 March in 1959, and at nearly eleven I could easily find my way alone from Drumchapel to Blackhill, so I had gone on my own to see Peggy. She was pale and quiet. The warm times, the funny times had gradually faded away during her pregnancy, but we still had our own private times together.

She decided we would walk to Hogganfield Loch, a mile or so away. I'd been there often with Laurie and David. We used to go on the pleasure boats or feed the ducks and swans, and we'd collect wild rhubarb for Nan to make pies or give us to suck raw with sugar.

It was overcast and chilly that Easter Monday, as Peggy struggled to fasten her coat over her growing belly before we set off. It was a green coat that had belonged to Nan, only Nan had become convinced that green was an unlucky colour, just as she was equally sure that keeping a lock of baby's hair would bring bad luck. Although she was by no means certain that the bad luck wouldn't follow the coat, reluctantly Nan had let Peggy have it.

Peggy was unusually quiet, in fact she didn't say a word as we walked along. I picked up a stick and started hitting stones along the ground and she made me stop. At the Loch I practised skiting stones; I was never any good at it, two bounces across the surface of the water was a major achievement for me, and I needed all the practice I could get. She stopped me doing that too. We had brought along some bread for the birds, but she wouldn't let me feed them. I began to wonder why she had wanted to come. On the way back she wouldn't even let me collect any rhubarb; it was as though she needed me to be there with her, not to talk, to play or pass the time, just to be there. It was something I nearly understood at the time, but not quite, like so much of what was going on. It was a time of restlessness, of waiting, without knowing what was being waited upon, somehow.

I was just reflecting on what a washout the day had been, when she did something truly puzzling. Our way home took us by Riddrie Cemetery, and she knew I was scared of it. Nan and I had to pass it on Saturday nights after our visits to Peggy, to catch a bus into the city centre, and to tease me, Peggy would laugh and make ghostly noises at me as we left her house. It was a place I would walk miles out of my way to avoid, and if I had no choice I'd hurry along with my eyes averted, breathing a huge sigh of relief when I was safely past. But on that Easter Monday, Peggy went inside, and I felt the hair on my neck bristle.

'Ah'll meet ye at the other gate Auntie Peggy,' I said, and made to hurry along the road.

'Naw hen,' she replied, 'C'moan in wi' me,' and with that she put an arm around my shoulders and propelled me into the graveyard. I was horrified. She knew I was scared of the place and I couldn't understand why she was doing this to me. I fixed my eyes on the the wall that separated the cemetery from the road and tried to calculate how quickly I could get over it, but again Peggy had other ideas.

As I hurried on, she dawdled, stopping to read the headstones on the way, and all the time I was struggling to keep my nerve and not bolt for home. I was torn; I knew I had to take care of her and go slowly because she was pregnant, yet every fibre of my being was screaming at me to run. I was angry with her, and the longer she took the angrier I became. She looked up at me as though she had heard my panic and laughed softly, then she put her arm about my shoulder again and hugged me to her. I was almost crying with the confusing mixture of emotions, fear, anger, hurt – feelings I wasn't used to having about Peggy, all mixed up with the closeness, the oneness, I always felt with her. Then to my huge relief, we left by another gate, and without a word of explanation from Peggy, we made our way back to the house. McAvoy was there when we returned. He looked at me. 'His she no' goat a hoose o' her ain?' he asked Peggy, 'She's aye here.' Peggy glanced at him and replied, 'You kin talk when it's *your* hoose she's in! She's merr right here than you!' I was amazed; I had never heard her answer him back, but she'd been tetchy all day.

Later, back home in Halgreen again, I told Nan about Peggy's detour through the cemetery, and she was as puzzled as I was. There was no one buried there that Peggy had known, she hadn't after all been raised in the area, there were no schoolfriends in it and no family either.

'Wis she wearin' that green coat?' Nan demanded, narrowing her eyes suspiciously, and I nodded. 'Ah shoulda burned that green coat!' she said with conviction, as though this explained everything, and Skip laughed.

'Did that green coat shove Peggy in the gates?' he asked in exactly the same suspicious tone of voice that Nan had used, 'That green coat's a bad bugger, a sneaky bugger! It aye goes lookin' in graveyairds so it dis!' He had narrowed his eyes too and was squinting about theatrically. Nan tried not to laugh but she couldn't help it.

'Ah jist don't like green!' she protested.

'Christ aye, we a' know that!' Skip laughed, 'Yur a' the same you Proddies, ye'd like the grass better if it wis blue, or orange mibbe!'

'Ye know whit Ah mean!' Nan was chuckling, but still trying to stand her corner.

'Aye,' replied Skip, 'Ye jist don't like green! Ye *tellt* us!' In the cold light of Drumchapel, it seemed funny and we all laughed.

Skip's greatest, and, perhaps, only talent was laughter and he could convert almost any situation into hilarious fun. This was a perspective the Clarks lacked; because they cared more deeply, they often took the world more seriously than was good for them.

Nan's superstition was already the subject of one of Skip's favourite jokes against her. Once his sister Norah, the family's self-appointed psychic, dragged Nan off to a spiritualist meeting. Nan wasn't happy as it was, but her discomfort had been increased when the medium had approached and told her she had an aura. Giving a detailed description of Da Clark, he urged Nan to come back to receive a warning message from her father. Nan was petrified and came home white as a sheet, but Skip was merciless and Nan's aura became a fixture. 'How's yer aura the day?' quickly became one of his sayings, 'Watch oot noo,' he'd say as she went downstairs, 'Don't fa' an' break yer aura!' In company he'd suddenly announce 'Did ye know ma wife's goat an aura?' He'd then go on to describe it, 'It's a wee thing, aboot so high,' he'd say solemnly, holding his hand a couple of feet off the ground, 'It's orange of coorse, wi' six legs an' it's covered in blue fur. It disnae bark or growl, it sings "The Sash". Bit it's a pedigree aura ye understaun', nae rubbish . . .' Given his way with Nan's aura, her thing about green was mincemeat.

Nan's dreams went on, and curiously, the more manic her behaviour became, the quieter Peggy grew. We saw her not only on a Saturday but also whenever the mood moved Nan, and although the two of them talked they didn't seem to communicate. I would watch these two women, who together had raised me, looking from one to the other as they spoke without connecting, trying to put my finger on what was wrong. Sometimes it seemed I nearly understood, then it would slip away from me before I could grasp it. In turn I would feel Peggy watching me, and smiling quietly;

as if she knew that we were all three of us part of the same restless, waiting, waking dream.

The 10th of May 1959 was my eleventh birthday and Peggy's pregnancy continued. She was now a week overdue and and as the month wore on she suffered the traditional remarks of, 'Ye still here yersel'?' 'No' better yit?' with her usual quiet, good humour. Nobody in those days referred directly to the baby or to childbirth; pregnancy was regarded as an illness that was cured by the totally unexpected appearance of a baby, and even that much was talked of in hushed tones. Children were left to understand by osmosis that the baby was inside in the growing stomach of a pregnant woman, and if this was actually mentioned by a child it was treated with great embarrassment. So hidden was the whole subject that I can remember wondering where babies did come from, because by the reactions of the adults around me, they obviously couldn't come from where they obviously did. If that wasn't the baby inside Peggy, I wondered, what was it and where then was the baby?

Monday the 25th of May was a public holiday and Nan had decided we were going into town together. Then she changed her mind and we ended up in Peggy's house. It was unusually hot that May and Peggy was sitting by the window, her folded arms resting on a small table in front of her. The sun was streaming through the window, putting her face in shade and lighting the outline of her curly hair in a fuzzy halo as she turned towards us. She was very quiet, becalmed in the final days of a long pregnancy that had tired and drained her even without the hot weather to help. So she didn't see us out, and we stood by the living-room door, winding up the conversation before we left.

'See ye oan Saturday,' Nan said, 'If yur still here that is!'

Everyone laughed.

'Cheerio Auntie Peggy,' I said. There was about her an air of fragility, of vulnerability and reacting to it I impulsively ran across the room to hug her. Everybody laughed again.

'Cheerio hen,' she smiled, holding me so that our two cheeks were crushed together, 'Ah'll be seein' ye!'

I rejoined Nan at the door and together we looked at Peggy, not seeing her smile because of the sunlight, but feeling it. Walking down the road to the bus stop I saw tears running down Nan's cheeks. I didn't say anything; I was by now used to all sorts of bizarre behaviour. Over that week her nightmares continued unabated and the weather remained too hot for comfort.

The following Saturday my mother suddenly decided that Peggy's baby was arriving, and much earlier than usual I was rushed along the road to begin the journey to Blackhill. Nan was very bright, her eyes shining.

'How dae ye know?' I asked, because we had no phone, few people did in those days.

'Ah jist know!' she replied cheerfully, and caught up in her excitement I could hardly sit still on the bus.

As we went in Peggy's door we were met by an aunt, one of the 'Fair Yins'.

'It's Peggy,' she said.

Nan and I looked at the closed bedroom door.

'His she hid it yit?' Nan asked, 'Is she a' right?'

As Nan sank slowly to the floor I was already moving away, our different movements in unison, triggered by the same knowledge. The aunt's arms closed around me, holding me so tightly that I could hardly breathe. I felt a terrible force rushing towards me, something was going to happen and she wouldn't let me go. So I punched and kicked, trying to get to the outside door, desperate to escape before it found me. I didn't hear the words, I felt them coming at me from a long, long distance before they were actually said, if indeed they were. In that split second I knew that Nan knew, had known all along, and I felt totally betrayed by her.

Out the door and leap down the eight back stairs to the backcourt. My ankles hurt with the jarring impact, but run on. *Run!* Across to the midden and dive behind the dustbins, lie flat among the garbage. Stop now to listen for them coming after me, only I couldn't hear anything because there was a thudding in my ears, drowning everything out. I turned my head to left and right then back again, but I could still hear only the pounding. Through a gap in the concrete I could see an illegal bookie paying out in the corner close, his minder at his side. The crowd milling around him seemed to be miming; heads thrown back laughing, arms waving, all normal except no sound apart from this thudding in my ears. The demons of hell were after me, the same demons that had pursued Nan all these months and I had to escape. Had to!

I crept out, zig-zagged between the air raid shelters and into a close to the left and sat down till the noise in my ears cleared and my chest stopped hurting. Think. *Think!* It was Saturday. Everybody came to the house on Saturday, so Uncle George would be here later. All I had to do until then was find somewhere safe to wait, somewhere the demons wouldn't think to look for me; so that ruled out the playpark and the pond.

Beside the bus-stop was an old ruined house that the local kids knew was haunted, we used to dare each other to go inside. The crisis had exorcised the ghosts, so I made my way there. I didn't think about anything, only waiting for Uncle George, that was all, not why. Hours must have passed, I was cold but it didn't matter; it was growing dark and he still hadn't come off any of the buses. Then I saw him, standing on the platform of an approaching 102 trolley-bus. I ran to meet him.

'Hullo wee yin,' he smiled, jumping off before the bus had stopped, 'Whit ye up tae?'

'Jist muckin' aboot,' I told him. I kept my eyes from his; if he read my eyes it would give him a clue and that might make it come true.

He looked at the grazes and the dirt on my clothes. 'Hiv ye been fightin' or sumthin'?'

I shook my head. He put out a hand and touched a long scrape down my arm. 'Christ hen, ye're freezin' cauld!'

'Ah'm a' right Uncle George.'

'Ye comin' in wi' me?' he asked softly, beckoning with

his head towards the house. I shook my head again, still looking down.

'Well, don't stey oot here too long eh?' He stood looking at me, puzzled. 'See ye then,' he began to move off, his cigarette half-raised to his lips.

'Don't go in there Uncle George,' I said.

'How no' hen?'

'Thur sayin' daft things,' I replied, still looking at the ground.

'Daft things? Who ur? Whit kinna daft things hen?' He stared at me for what seemed like hours, then his face seemed to freeze. 'Is it Peggy hen? Oh Jesus Christ! Is it aboot Peggy hen?'

The cigarette fell from his hand and he was running towards the house, the words still hanging in the air where he'd been. Later, as I watched from my cold sanctuary, I saw him set off to look for Skip, who was drinking somewhere. Uncle George was a 'Dark Yin', he had always looked like my mother; now he looked like the shadow she had become over the last few months. He had become part of the nightmare. Maybe it was true then . . .

Hours passed and he came back alone; Skip always knew how not to be found when engaged in his favourite pastime. We met up with him again as usual in High Street on our way back to Drumchapel. The 'Fair' aunt had come too because my mother was in such a state, which enabled me to sit well away from them on the bus, untouched by what had happened. I don't know what words they had used to tell Skip, I had walked away to look in a shop window, but my mother had collapsed again.

It was then decided to take her to the aunt's house for the night, because it was nearer and she couldn't have made the long journey to Drumchapel. At this news I threw an uncharacteristic tantrum. I hated staying in other people's houses; no matter what I always had to get home and especially on that night, to reclaim some kind of normality. So though I knew I couldn't win, I cried and screamed in protest. Nan was mortified that I should create such a scene, but I didn't care. I felt totally detached from everyone in the world and couldn't have cared less about Nan especially. She had known this was going to happen, had known it for months and had pretended she didn't. Well the nightmare was of her making and she could have it, I'd take no part in it.

Next day I sat as far away from my parents as possible on the bus home to Drumchapel and concentrated on the 'big hooses' I had first seen the day we had moved. As usual I gazed down the road that led to Notre Dame, trying to see as far along as possible before the bus passed and it was out of sight. At the Drumry Road bus stop I ran ahead of Nan and Skip and up into my bedroom. Laurie came in to ask why we hadn't come home last night and I ignored him. Later I heard Skip's voice in the room next door that Laurie shared with Mickey; it was muffled through the wall, but I knew what he was telling them by the tone. I climbed into bed and hid under the blankets, imagining myself somewhere else until it was over.

That Sunday morning we quickly changed our clothes and then returned to Peggy's house, where I eavesdropped as snippets of information were passed in whispers from one shattered relative to another. I wasn't being chased anymore I decided, the demons had after all accomplished their work, but if I kept my eyes down I discovered that I became invisible. That way I could hear without being told and could thereby not know if I chose not to. Only if I lifted my eyes would someone reach out to me, only then would I become part of their awful reality.

Peggy had apparently gone into labour on Saturday morning and the doctor had been called, but he wasn't there and a locum had come instead. In fact 'he wisnae a real doacter', and Peggy had screamed all day. The doctor had locked the bedroom door and only opened it to demand more towels and sheets. Maw Clark had to knock on neighbours' doors and ask for any they had when her own had been used up. I overheard her telling someone that 'the screamin' stoaped aboot four,' and she had gone out into the street and stopped two passing policemen.

The doctor who 'wisnae a real doacter' had refused to unlock the bedroom door, so the two policemen had broken it down, and when they saw what was happening inside they had sent for an ambulance. Peggy was barely alive by that time; the towels and sheets had been used to soak up a massive haemorrhage. At the Royal Maternity Hospital at Rottenrow she was taken straight to theatre in an attempt to save her unborn baby, but it was found to be already dead. Fifteen minutes later, so was Peggy. She was two months short of thirty-seven years old.

It was easy to avoid my mother over the next couple of days. She was locked in her own private world, but her eyes were docile now instead of frantic and her voice flat calm. It was like the end of a storm. Family activity centred on Peggy's home, now oddly quiet and empty, despite the rooms overflowing with people, and to my great relief they had little time for me. Now that Peggy was about to return once again to the room where she had suffered and died, the mirrors in the house were covered in keeping with tradition. This was to prevent her spirit seeing its own reflection and deciding to remain in the house. The white sheets covering the windows were a symbol of cleansing against the pollution of her death. It added to the unreality of the situation and helped me reject all of it. Nothing made any sense.

I spent most of my time on top of the old red-brick air raid shelter in the backcourt, out of reach of anyone, twelve feet above the ground. I lay on my back on that Sunday, determinedly concentrating on the clouds that were bringing an end to the hot spell. Some people see castles and things in clouds, but I never did; clouds were fine enough illusions in themselves. As I lay there, bright shafts of sunlight broke through, Peggy's 'pathways to heaven' and I told God what to do with them in no uncertain terms, and what I thought of Him just as candidly. I used every 'bad word' I had ever heard. 'Bastard!' I yelled, 'Swine! Git! Shite! Pig!', and then to make sure He knew I meant business, the ultimate insult, 'DRUNKEN IRISH PIG!' There was a sudden commotion and the door to Peggy's house burst open. Uncle Willie bounded down the stairs and was noisily sick in the backcourt, then he sank to his knees and wept, his forehead against the grey stone of the tenement. On top of my refuge I calmly turned my head away and my attention back to the sky; whatever was happening was part of the adults' world. None of it had anything to do with me and I didn't want to know . . .

On the Monday I had to endure a visit to a shop to buy shoes for an event I had no intention of attending. I still hated Nan and wouldn't talk to her or make her lot any easier if I could possibly help it. She tried coaxing me into conversation, but all I wanted was to be left alone forever. And I didn't want her rotten shoes either.

'There's a nice perra black patent yins,' she said, 'Try thaim. Ye *know* ye like patent yins,' hinting at the famous shoe quest when she had sent me with Peggy, who had been warned to buy only good, serviceable school shoes for me. 'Don't let hur talk ye intae anythin' fancy,' Nan had ordered, and Peggy had nodded firmly, full of resolve. We came back with a pair of bright-red patent shoes with ankle straps that fastened at the front with a single red button, and they made a clicking noise as I danced along the pavement. Sitting on the trolley bus on the way home to Blackhill I had kept my feet stretched out in front of me in case someone stood on my beautiful, magical shoes. As I stared at them in wonder Peggy laughed and kept repeating, 'Yur ma wull kill us, ye know! She'll kill the baith o' us stone deid when she sees thum!'

If Hughie was the only adult who understood about black-face soap, Peggy was the only one who understood that just once in every girl's life she needed bright-red, patent shoes that clicked when you walked. I became Ginger Rogers; for the duration of the red shoes I danced along the streets, the shoes didn't allow walking.

I wore the red shoes long after they fitted comfortably, and one day the local priest stopped me as I tapped along the pavement.

'These are awful red shoes ye have,' he said in his soft

Irish brogue. I wondered what he meant; awful red, or just awful?

'I suppose your Proddy mother let you have such vain things?' I hadn't a clue what he meant; they were red not vain, whatever that was.

'Naw,' I answered proudly, 'Ma Auntie Peggy, bit she's a Proddy tae!'

The priests always had a go at my Proddy relatives, who they knew for a fact were hellbent on destroying my good, pure, Catholic, eternal soul. Well, eternal as long as my Proddy relatives didn't win that was.

'Jist try thum,' Nan pleaded, holding the black patent shoes.

'Naw! *Naw!*' I shouted at her. I was behaving in a way that I had never dreamed I was capable of, but there were no boundaries any longer. Normal life had been suspended. Nan bought the patent shoes anyway, no doubt hoping to win me round. Next day, as I climbed the midden and jumped up onto the air raid shelter, I deliberately scraped the toes of the new shoes along the bricks. Then I lay down to concentrate on the sky, which was thankfully dull and overcast; God had taken the hint, not a pathway of sunlight to be seen. From there I could keep an eye on the comings and goings at Peggy's door, mainly callers in Brogan's vans delivering flowers. I remembered the Brogan's van that was always parked in Frankfield Street, on the route between Acrehill Street and Moodiesburn Street when we still lived in Blackhill. It had a huge basket of flowers painted on one side, and I used to run over, 'pick' the flowers and present them to Peggy when we reached her house. To tease her sometimes I pretended to forget and she would say, 'Where's ma floors then?' Then I would hand them over; it was our private game, our little bit of nonsense that no one else knew about, except Nan of course. Now Brogan's vans were bringing Peggy flowers that she would never see . . .

From the door I heard a cousin being dispatched by an aunt to find me.

'Yer waantit,' a voice said from below.

'Beat it!' I growled.

'Ye'd better come doon ur yur fur it!'

I jumped down from all of twelve feet, landed on my cousin and thumped him about the head.

'Noo beat it!' I snarled, and climbed back up on the shelter. He lay below crying, 'Yur daft you!' he shouted, 'Yur daft! Everybody knows it tae! Ma mammy says ye don't care aboot Auntie Peggy, yur jist oot here playin' a' the time because ye don't care!' I made to jump down again and he got up quickly and ran.

'Your mammy's a "Fair Yin",' I told him, 'So whit dis she know aboot anythin'? You go back in an' say ye cannae find me ur Ah'll get ye later!'

As I lay back down on the shelter roof I could hear him in the distance, obediently reporting that I was nowhere to be found.

Later I made another invisible sortie into the house to keep tabs on the situation. The 'fair' aunt pounced on me.

'They'll be takin' yer Auntie Peggy away soon hen,' she said, 'Dae ye waant tae see hur?'

'Naw.'

'It's a' right hen, it's no' frightenin' nor nothin'. It's jist like she's sleepin'.'

'SHUTUP! NAW!'

Her hands were coming towards me as I backed off in panic, making for the door and pushing past Uncle George as I ran, my aunt's voice protesting behind me.

'It's no' right! That lassie meant a lot tae Peggy! She should be made tae pey her respects insteeda playin' ootside a' the time!'

'Leave the wean alane!' Uncle George's voice was low and angry.

'An' she tellt me tae shutup tae!'

'Ah said leave the wean alane, ya stupid bitch!'

Chapter Twenty-One

From the top of my shelter fortress I could see movement out of the corner of my eye. Cars had arrived at the front of the house, and with a growing sense of panic I felt reality closing in. I wasn't ready for this; I'd thought I could keep it at bay by ignoring it, but it was happening anyway.

Still trying to maintain my cloak of invisibility, I slipped off the shelter and ran through a close at the side. A crowd had gathered outside Peggy's house, blocking the whole of Moodiesburn Street. Keeping my eyes down I found a way through and suddenly came upon my uncles and McAvoy carrying the coffin out of the close-mouth.

My instinct was to turn and run, but before I could I realized that though I was only inches away from them, they couldn't see me. I was totally detached, watching as though I had no more part in this than the huge throng of onlookers all around us. The muscles of Uncle George's pale, drawn face were working furiously, the way they did when he was trying to keep his temper. He stared at the ground, the coffin resting on his right shoulder, his eyes wet. Skip was in front of him opposite McAvoy, and behind was Uncle Willie, always the most emotional one, sobbing noisily, his face awash with tears. Keeping in step, I followed behind and watched them slide the coffin into the waiting hearse, the only sound Willie's crying.

An eternity seemed to pass and from inside the house I could hear Nan wailing as I watched the men pile flowers around the coffin. Suddenly aware that time was running out I instinctively put one hand on the coffin, the O'Brien farewell, just to say 'Peggy, it's me!' As I did so a bouquet fell off into my arms and as I put it back hands gently guided me onto the pavement again. I put my hand against the cool glass of the side window, and as the hearse moved away I felt it slowly slip across my palm. The car behind was filled with flowers, tributes from people all over Blackhill that they could ill afford. The whole community had turned out, many of the women crying softly, and with quiet dignity they saw Peggy off on her last journey.

The cortege didn't go into the nearby Riddrie Cemetery, it was bound for some place I didn't know. I stood on tip-toes to keep it in sight as long as possible, and as it finally faded from view, I felt something in my other hand. It was a single pink rose from the bouquet that had fallen from Peggy's coffin. Later, when I showed it to Nan she said the bouquet had been from me. She had ordered flowers from herself and had asked the florist to send something from me to Peggy. For some reason a bouquet of pink roses arrived. 'An' know whit?' she said, her voice flat and defeated, 'Peggy wis wearin' a long, white dress tae.'

I found that I no longer hated my mother, I realized that deep down I had known all along too; how could I not? And Peggy, watching me as I in turn watched the awful, unstoppable tragedy being played out between the three of us those last months, deep down did she know too? How could she not?

I remembered that Easter Monday, only two short months ago, when Peggy and I had gone on our odd walk to Hogganfield Loch. She had been wearing Nan's unlucky green coat tightly stretched across her stomach, and on the way back she had made me walk through Riddrie Cemetery with her. What had she been doing, I wondered, laying ghosts for me? If she knew then that soon I would only be able to visit her in a cemetery, did she also know it would take me more than thirty years to bring myself to do so? I took all those years to discover what had really happened to her on Saturday, 30 May 1959. I didn't find her again until I was an adult, older than she lived to be, standing by her grave with a bunch of pink roses, saying once again 'Peggy, it's me!'

While the men were at the cemetery the women removed the covers from the mirrors and the white sheets from the windows and prepared a meal. I was safely back on top of my shelter again, and hours after the men arrived back another car drew up outside the house. A tall, dark-haired young man got out and I watched him knock on the door and then walk in. There was a wild roar of raw animal rage from inside the house and Skip emerged, pulling the young man behind him. He pushed him into the car and shouted, 'Git oota here son, ur sure as hell ye'll git killt!' Later I heard that the young man was the 'doacter' who had been with Peggy. He had wanted to apologize, but Uncle George had come within a few feet of killing him.

The day after Peggy's funeral I went back to school. Nan had written a note for my teacher explaining my absence; I didn't read it as I normally would have because I didn't want to know what it said.

'Your aunt died in childbirth,' the teacher said, 'That means she would go straight to heaven.'

'She's a Proddy,' I stated, defiantly.

'That doesn't matter. If she died having a baby she would go straight to heaven.' I thought she was the stupidest person I had ever come across.

'Would you like us to say a prayer for her?'

'Naw.' Like every other child in Scotland I usually spoke Lowland Scots outside and 'proper English' at school, but none of that mattered anymore and 'proper English' could go hang itself, along with this silly woman and her prayers. First I was supposed to be grateful that Hughie had gone to her heaven and now Peggy; if I ever came across this heaven I'd blast it to hell with the biggest gun I could find. Later it was noticed that I was withdrawn and quiet and the Parish Priest, Father Sheridan, was called in, the same one who gave me my First Communion.

'We're going to say a prayer for Margaret O'Brien's aunt and her wee baby who died last Saturday and are now in heaven watching over us,' he announced to the children, and I walked out of the class and out of the school. It was the only time in my life that I 'plunked' school.

*　　*　　*

With the eleven-plus over we were assembled in class and handed out notes with the name of our next school. I knew mine said Garnethill Convent; it was the alternative to Notre Dame for those who weren't quite good enough or rich enough. For a moment the thought surfaced that I'd tell Peggy on Saturday, then I remembered that I couldn't. There was a deep, black emptiness that stretched as far as I could see and feel and imagine . . .

Chapter Twenty-Two

The months after Peggy died passed somehow and are etched on my memory like an endless tunnel of pain that left the Clarks unable to think or act coherently. There was no conversation save for the occasional reluctant syllable when there was no alternative, and everyone seemed locked in their own distracted silence that didn't connect to any other.

There was no fatal accident inquiry into the circumstances of the death, as there undoubtedly should have been. Though the family were aware that there were questions to be asked, they were unable to summon up the strength to ask them. George, who had struggled with his emotions all of his life, now descended deeper into a preoccupied anger that he never truly emerged from, and Nan floated without direction, lost without Peggy.

At first we still visited Moodiesburn Street every Saturday, where McAvoy and the children continued to live with Maw Clark. There was no plan, we went because that was the pattern of our lives. Saturdays meant returning to Blackhill, it was that simple. I hated those visits and stayed outside the house as much as possible because there just wasn't any reason to go there any longer. Within a few weeks we stopped.

There was no way through the huge, awful void that Peggy had left, and the paralysis spread to everyone so that they simply could not function normally. There would be no recovery because the injury was too massive and life would never, ever be the same again.

On what was to be our last visit to Moodiesburn Street, though we didn't know it at the time, Maw Clark gave me the decoration that had stood on the top tier of Peggy's wedding cake. In 1953 I had waited outside the Proddy church and handed over a silver horseshoe to Peggy. To that small extent I had taken part in Peggy's wedding. I was also Peggy's favourite; perhaps Maw considered the cake decoration to be an appropriate memento. In the years since, it had stood at the top of the living-room press, the cupboard where the special china was kept, on the little triangular shelf formed by the way the press was built across the corner.

It had started out as a sugar bride and groom on top of a latticework dais, but Skip had made a cardboard horseshoe to stand behind the bridal couple, and painted it white and silver. It's an O'Brien trait to gild the lily, but it fitted in with Peggy's liking for all things extra-fancy, and she had been delighted.

I took it home to Drumchapel and examined it in my room. It had lost its sharpness over the years, the little figures seemed to have melted when you saw them close to. I didn't want it; it was a symbol of how, when and why Peggy's life had become a nightmare, so I smashed it to bits then threw the bits in the fire. I never, ever wanted any reminder of Peggy's disastrous marriage. To this day, whenever I see a decoration on top of a wedding cake, I can't help thinking of that one and what it signified. When I married, I decided, there would be no wedding cake.

Nan gradually withdrew after giving up the pretence of the Saturday visits, and by Peggy's birthday in August she had become a recluse. There were no more family gatherings; no decision was taken, it just happened. It was as though the heart and soul of the Clark family had been ripped out by Peggy's death and Nan's withdrawal, and the rest of them then withdrew in turn into their respective families. The pain of losing Peggy was intensified by being together without her, and it was simply more than they could bear.

Peggy's name was never used again, except as a means of fixing time. In the same way as people talked of events happening before or after the War, the Clarks talked of events before or after Peggy died, but she herself became a closed subject. Her laughter, her kindness, her gentle good humour and her hopeless romanticism, and by association the loss of these, became banned by an unspoken, mutual agreement. Better, they decided, to pretend that she had never existed than to accept her death, and Nan's self-imposed exile handed them another brick with which to build a wall around their collective pain.

It became accepted that 'Nan isnae well,' and therefore wasn't to be upset. They would cite this as a reason not to see her, because she did become upset at seeing them, as they did at seeing each other. Grieving together would have been the healthy way to deal with the pain, but it hurt too much. In that manner they contrived not to face it, and so it would remain a raw wound within them forever.

Nan, at barely forty years old became a shadow of herself, nervous of people, afraid to go out and cut off from her family, and so it would remain for the the rest of her life until her death at sixty-one. Nowadays her symptoms would be recognized as the grief of bereavement, but in the late fifties and early Sixties there was no diagnosis for what she was going through and therefore no treatment.

Skip was incapable of understanding what had happened to her because it was so foreign to his own nature. He was also incapable of getting help, even if he'd thought of it. Nan was the help-getter and always had been. Worn out with years of coping with the effects of Skip's drinking, she was now hit by the biggest blow she had ever faced. There was no one to turn to. Peggy had been her solace and support all of their lives, and Peggy had gone forever.

Had I been older I might have helped, but I was only eleven. With my brothers so much older and starting independent lives of their own, I was left to run the house, look after myself and my mother. I remember waiting for Skip to take over, but he never did. His life in fact was easier; he could stay out as long and as often as he liked, drink as much as he pleased and come home or not as he chose. Nan's attempts to bring order to his way of life had imposed some boundaries in the past, however weak. Now these were gone and he had a daughter to step in as housekeeper. He wasn't a bad man, he was a child and children think only of their own needs. Just as I had, till then . . .

Chapter Twenty-Three

Garnethill Convent came as a shock. Instead of the leafy, genteel avenues of the West End where Notre Dame was situated, Garnethill was a seedy, red-light area in the centre of the city, deprived in ways that Blackhill would have been ashamed to stoop to. Leaving the bus from Drumchapel at the main road, there was no alternative to the uncomfortable walk through the Garnethill streets to get to the school. There were in the city two shops that sold porn magazines, and I would walk miles to avoid passing them. There was something about the men who hung about outside that made me feel a kind of sick fear, and if I had to pass them I dreaded it all the way there and felt incredibly relieved when it was over. Walking through Garnethill gave me the same feeling; I never became accustomed to it and had to steel myself for that walk to and from school every day. If the nuns had come here to convert sinners I decided, then they had failed dismally.

The nuns were called the Sisters of Mercy and there again they failed dismally to live up to that description. One, Sister Annunciatta, carved her way through the children by lashing out at bare legs with the long, leather strap that hung from a belt around the nuns' waists. You could always tell where she had been from the weals on the children's legs, her own peculiar version of 'Excuse me please.' It always made me laugh to see the outsized rosaries falling from around the sisters' waists, accompanied by the thick leather strap, the sole intention of which was to beat the hell out of children: the perfect picture of their Christian values, suffer little children to come unto me, and by God you'll know you've arrived!

The headmistress was Sister Aquinas, a pale, skinny

Irishwoman of indeterminate age, with the palest blue eyes and thin lips which I never once saw break into anything resembling a normal, human smile. She had chosen to teach, and her starting point was the belief that all children were intrinsically wicked, evil, wily and permanently engaged in finding ways to sin. Her philosophy for dealing with her unfortunate charges, therefore, was simple: always be suspicious, always believe the worst regardless of evidence to the contrary, and always punish hard, whether warranted or not. I had her for English for one very long, hard year. While other teachers tried to draw from me any hint of imagination Sister Aquinas did her best to bludgeon to death any spark of creativity I had. Anything I produced was returned blue-pencilled to death and accompanied by detailed critiques in her tiny, pinched script, informing me that all my ideas and thoughts were 'sinful'.

'Kindly remember,' she wrote on one of my compositions, 'that your body is a temple created by God and must be treated accordingly and not defiled.' I didn't have a clue what she meant then and I still don't; I can only imagine she had been secretly reading *Lady Chatterley's Lover* and somehow got it mixed up with my innocent meanderings.

Eventually I worked out the kind of thing she wanted and wrote a morally uplifting piece of candy-floss about a straying Catholic returning to the fold. She loved it; it was the nearest I ever saw those martyred features and that thin, bloodless mouth get to a genuine smile. Having satisfied myself on her level of literary appreciation, I never descended to it again, and thereafter she should have bought shares in whatever company specialized in blue pencil production. She couldn't understand what had happened, kept saying I had shown that I could do good work, so why did I persist in producing such offensive material? For one so versed in the evil workings of children's minds it always surprised me that she never realized my sole intention was to offend her.

Another of Sister Aquinas' great obsessions was the monarchy. It was, she said, the Catholic church's last bastion against communism and we all had a duty to support it. This was an amazingly generous endorsement, given the prohibition on Catholics succeeding to the throne, a fact I loved to point out to her whenever she had worked herself up to her usual emotional frenzy when giving her anti-communism lecture. In her bid to keep the monarch dear to our hearts she kept a large, regal portrait of Her Majesty outside her office, and had the task of turning it right-side-out or wiping a moustache off it, depending on which mood I had been in when I passed by. Once I managed to hide it under the school altar in the main assembly hall. There, addressing the entire school, but looking directly at me, in her truly Christian fashion she called down God's curse on whoever had taken the portrait, and all the while it was no more than three feet away from her. What she didn't know of course was that God and his curses held little fear for me. He had done all he possibly could to me already and I had survived. After a fashion at any rate.

She also set herself up as a censor, telling us what books not to read and thereby ensuring a rush on them. DH Lawrence was right out, the man being morally depraved. Robert Burns was a fornicator and a Proddy, and James Joyce was even worse. Not only was he a Catholic, an *Irish* Catholic, but he was filth personified, though it was never quite clear where she stood on this issue. She could never make her mind up if being an ordinary Proddy was worse or better than being a filthy Catholic, so she did the ecumenically correct thing and heartily hated and despised them all, which managed to take in most of humanity. She seemed to me the opposite of the Irish people I had grown up among, a joyless, life-hating mutant, an O'Brien gone warped, and I couldn't resist taking her on.

'Have you read any of these books?' I would ask, 'And are you, a bride of Christ, now corrupted?' Her rage was a delight to behold.

'So Hitler was right?' I asked on another occasion when she was in mid-tirade against some other literary transgressor.

'Yes he was!' she spluttered. She was, without doubt, the

maddest, saddest, most repressed creature I have ever met, and she used to say that she had to be especially hard on me because I reminded her of herself at the same age. Apart from being a gross slander on me, this was, on reflection, a pitiful declaration of self-loathing, and the poor woman clearly needed more help than she would ever get in the convent, or from me.

Every now and again, when she could restrain herself no longer over one of my many indiscretions and was in danger of seriously attacking me, she would send for my father. After she had recovered HM's portrait and her world was thus safe once more from the influence of Marx, Lenin and Trotsky, he was summoned to listen to the details of my latest heinous crime. To my delight he put on his 'humble Irish Catholic' routine, which was almost as amusing as his sand-dancing.

'Bit Sister,' he said in deferential mitigation of my misdeeds, 'Hur mother's been ill recently.'

'My mother died when I was ten!' she raged, 'And I had to look after nine younger children!' This explained her hatred of children to my utter satisfaction.

'But Sister,' I said, 'You grew up to marry God, you're a saint, while I'm just a half-Proddy heretic.' Beside me I could hear my father trying not to laugh as Sister Aquinas performed spontaneous combustion.

'Your grandfather would be ashamed of you!' she seethed.

'Well that's OK,' I replied, 'I've always been pretty well ashamed of my grandfather as it happens. The Catholic one anyway.'

Later my father said reflectively, 'Ye mibbe went a wee bit too faur there.'

'She's aff hur heid,' I replied, 'She deserved it.'

'Aye,' he mused, 'Right anuff!' As I said, he wasn't a bad man, just a rotten father, but every now and again he got something right.

When school finished at four o'clock I would have to rush for the bus home and then immediately set off in search of the mobile grocery van that was prepared to give us tick. It had stopped outside our close earlier, but Nan wasn't able to get downstairs to it and anyway, she was so nervous of people that her speech wouldn't have made any sense to them.

Finding the van was pretty hit and miss, because I only had the vaguest idea where it would be at any given time, and there was always the fear that I wouldn't find it. If I didn't, then we didn't eat unless Nan had managed to keep a little cash back, which in those days was unusual. If there was money I would have to walk to the nearest shops some two or three miles away, join in the long queue and then walk back. At that time Nan could still manage to work around the house and to cook, but slowly she stopped doing even that. I found that I had little time or energy left for homework, and though I started out in an 'A' class at Garnethill, before long I had slipped down the 'B's.

Nan's withdrawal meant, of course, that she couldn't buy clothes for herself or anyone else, so I took that over too. The only way we could afford anything was with a Provident check, which was made out for a set sum, five pounds perhaps or ten pounds, with weekly payments plus interest, paid to an agent who called every Friday – pay night. The week's debts to the mobile van were settled then too, so though Friday night felt like money night, it wasn't by the time everyone was paid off.

Only certain shops accepted Provy checks and the goods in these shops were inferior and more expensive than elsewhere. So I found out early on how the poor are kept poor and felt the shame creeping over me if a shop didn't display its Provy sticker and I had to ask. If the assistant said 'no' then I felt even more ashamed to have revealed our poverty.

I was very young and at an age when I needed a mother to guide me and look after me, but instead I was looking after my mother. Nan took no part in buying my first bra for instance, in fact by that time I was buying hers, and no part in the agonies of puberty. She never asked about my periods and when they arrived out of the blue I was terrified but knew I couldn't confide in her. And of course there was no one else any longer for me to go to, so I learned from other girls at school, trying all the while desperately to put two-and-two together from the usual playground half-truths, and pretending I knew it all already so as not to look a fool. Looking back, it was the most confusing and dismal time of my life, more so than it usually is for any girl. I used to wonder why it was all happening and if it happened to others, and if it did, how come they coped so well?

Chapter Twenty-Four

We called Mickey's new friends the Crowd. They were
part of a working-class movement to get into the hills
and countryside during the depression of the 1920s and
1930s, when most were unemployed and penniless. Until
then the outdoors had been the preserve of the gentry.
With cheap transport and short working hours for those
who had it, even shorter for those who didn't, and nothing
to fill the endless days, the countryside became accessible
to all. For the natives of Clydebank, the Old Kilpatrick
Hills were the starting point, then the 'Bankies as they were
known gradually moved further afield, forming the core of
the movement.

Laurie had followed Mickey's escape route out of Drumchapel and our weekend hell to join the Crowd by the hills
and the lochs. As soon as he had served his time as an
engineering apprentice, Laurie had joined the Merchant
Navy. Shortly afterwards Mickey had married at twenty-
four. He had spent very little time with our family and had
got out as soon as he could, marrying one of the Crowd. I
was thirteen at the time and that's my first clear memory
of Rab, my future husband, though I had been vaguely
aware of his existence before that through stories I'd heard.
Mickey and Rowena had married in a Registry Office and
then had a ceilidh at her house afterwards instead of a
wedding reception. My grandmother had been invited, but
luckily she didn't stay long, because if she wasn't the centre
of attraction she didn't hang about. If she had staged one
of her dying swan acts in front of the Crowd they would
have stepped over her and continued with the ceilidh. We
had songs and chat, and sleeping-bags were put down in a
separate room for sleeping off the effects.

It was 1961 and I had shopped for new clothes then managed with great difficulty to get my mother out of our house and settled down at the ceilidh. As the crowd assembled and the festivities started, she wanted to know one thing, 'Which wan's Rab?' I pointed to him standing against a wall, whisky glass in hand, and at that moment he slowly slid down onto the floor, one of the things he was most famous for. It was odd to think of my mother sitting there being entertained as I wondered how we could keep her calm among all the people. A few years before she would have run this show and revelled in it, she and – no, that era was all finished.

At five o'clock the next morning I was trying to persuade someone out of a sleeping-bag so that I could get in, when a voice said, 'Take mine.' It was Rab, the master of sliding down walls, and I gratefully accepted his offer. 'Fool!' I thought, as I snuggled down in the warmth he'd left behind and leaving him shivering on a couch I fell instantly asleep.

I had my first taste of how good weekends could be after that. Until then the Crowd were just names that I heard occasionally, but Laurie was home on leave for the wedding and he bought me my first pair of hiking boots. From somewhere I acquired a cast-off rucksack and an old sleeping-bag, and one Friday in late September we took a bus together from Buchanan Street to Drymen. From there we caught another to Balmaha on Loch Lomondside then walked the seven miles to Rowardennan, where the boatshed stood.

The shed was owned by the Scottish Youth Hostels Association and had as its commodore a little man called Freddy. He was English and looked it, with his long khaki shorts and knitted bobble hat, and he was unfortunately unable to pronounce his 'r's. So Fweddy he was to one and all, including himself. There was a strict rule banning sleeping in the boatshed, a rule made to be ignored, as indeed it was. So sleeping-bags were laid out on the floor between the canoes every weekend when the Crowd were in residence. Many a snap inspection was carried out by

Fweddy to make sure no one was sleeping in the boatshed, which of course they were. He never seemed to figure out what to do about this blatant flouting of the rules, so basically he did nothing and he therefore was held in some esteem by everyone, even if his authority was totally ignored.

That first Saturday morning we paddled up the loch to join another party who were camped halfway up, at the Major's Land. Then later we all paddled to Ptarmigan's Point at the head of the loch and camped there. I remember I was in the front of a double canoe, the first time I had been in a canoe in my life, as Laurie steered from behind. I was wearing one of his sweaters and the water that flicked off his paddles had soaked the arms, making them trail in the water. I was wet through, my arms and hips ached from the unaccustomed exercise of paddling and I was more tired than I had ever been in my entire life. While Laurie put the tent up I sat by the camp-fire with Ronnie, who had grown up with the wall-sliding Rab in Clydebank, as he made up a curry. I had never had a curry before either, and even if I had it wouldn't have been anything like this one. He just threw everything he had into a pot and tossed in an eye-watering amount of curry powder. I was tired, sore, wet, cold and hungry and I wolfed the curry down gratefully. I remember Ronnie watching me from behind his thick glasses and shrugging as I devoured his concoction, as though no one had ever done so before. Later I discovered that no one had . . . and why.

The deer were rutting and the night air was full of the throaty barks of stags; it was late to be at the loch. I think Nan had agreed to my going in the expectation that I would hate it, but if that was her plan it back-fired. I was captivated. It wasn't just getting away from the especially awful weekend drinking bouts of my father, it was the silence of the loch early in the morning that hooked me, a silence so loud I could hear it, and it was the Crowd. Pyschologists say that if you have bad family experiences it is possible to offset the damage through a substitute family group – and that's what the Crowd was. I was the youngest by some years and was therefore treated as a younger sister, but one who was accepted and quietly protected, much more than I had been with my natural family.

The only problem for me was my brother Mickey. I was always on trial with him, over-conscious of what I said, did or looked like. He was forever on the lookout for something to criticize about me, and his sarcasm could be stinging. He even had Skip's frown of impatience, and whenever I made a mistake there it was. The others in the Crowd often stuck up for me when he zoomed in on one of my many imperfections, laughing and telling him to leave me alone. It was as though I only existed in Mickey's eyes as a reflection of himself, and he saw me as a constant embarrassment.

It was many years before I saw that he acted as he did because of his own insecurities, but even if I had realized it at the time I could have done nothing about it because of my own. Behind me was the great, yawning wound that Nan had disappeared into and all I had to do was look out of the corner of my eye to see it clearly. My life had become a constant struggle not to be swallowed up too, yet no one else seemed aware of this and, therefore, of the effect it was still having on my life. I suspect that it would anyhow have come under the heading of 'pull yourself together', whether I could or not.

Chapter Twenty-Five

Laurie married six months after Mickey, only his wedding to Ellen, also one of the Crowd, took place in a Catholic church. It seemed to me again to be an attempt to win Skip's approval, at least in part, though I'm still not sure if Laurie realized it at the time. I found weddings a drag, I was never a creature made for ceremony and protocol, and a Catholic service provides lashings of both. The Crowd assembled afterwards at what was a fairly traditional wedding reception, and Skip maintained tradition too, by disappearing to the nearest pub so that he could drink at his own speed.

For Nan the very long day had held more terrors than the more homely, relaxed wedding ceilidh that Mickey and Rowena had chosen. She regarded Laurie as her weakest cub, the one who had to be given extra care and consideration, so she was already more on edge. None of this deterred Skip from abandoning her among strangers though, which made me so angry that I went to the pub to drag him out again to support his wife. It was raining when I found the place and even my resolve and anger were held in check by the convention that females, particularly young females, did not enter pubs. Then I heard Rab's voice.

'Where ur ye gaun?'

'Ah'm gaun' tae drag that auld swine oota there!' I replied, 'He's left ma mother sittin' at the reception by herself!'

'Leave it,' he said quietly, 'Ah'll get him oot.'

He went into the pub and then came out again, saying that one of the Crowd would bring Skip back to the hall. Then he took his jacket off and put it around my shoulders and walked with me up the road in the rain. I didn't know how to react to this. Giving me his sleeping-bag at Mickey's wedding was one thing, but his latest gallantry puzzled me. What puzzled me even more was my own reaction of no reaction. I was used by now to having to rely on myself. After thirteen years of living with the reality of Skip, there were no fairy-tales in my mind about men and chivalry. To say that I could be prickly if patronized would be an understatement, yet I accepted Rab's protection and I couldn't have explained why, not even to myself.

After his marriage Laurie took to his in-laws with a vengeance, they were the best people who had ever drawn breath apparently, and we saw considerably less of him. It was understandable, of course, he had escaped and now he had a fresh start with a new family where he had never been hurt or found wanting. We all do what we must to survive.

Garnethill Convent was suddenly interested in world politics. The reason was simple; in 1960 John F Kennedy was elected and in 1961 he had been sworn in as President of the United States. JFK was a Roman Catholic!

I was in Art class when news of the election result was conveyed to the entire school by a specially selected messenger who ran round every room. I sniggered and the Art teacher assumed I was smiling with pleasure. 'Yes,' she said, 'Isn't it wonderful? A Catholic President!'

In fact I was quite taken with JFK but like most of America I had to overcome anti-Catholic prejudice to keep supporting him. Here was a politician who seemed to listen to what young people said and thought, who rehabilitated idealism while the older, supposedly wiser lot shook their greying heads and told us we'd grow out of it eventually.

None of this mattered to Garnethill though. To them he was simply a Catholic and could therefore do no wrong. During the 1960 campaign, while old Joe Kennedy wisely trusted in securer methods like buying votes, Garnethill was offering daily prayers for JFK's success, and on that cold January day in 1961, when he was sworn in, the whole school was allowed home early.

*　　*　　*

My favourite teacher at Garnethill was Miss Johnstone. She taught Geography but had been forced to teach English as well, a subject at which she did not shine. We all grew up caught in the dichotomy of language, speaking standard English to teachers and the Glasgow version of Lowland Scots to each other and at home. Miss Johnstone though had failed to absorb the particular rules governing this and spoke her own peculiar pidgin version that strangely encompassed the two. 'I'm giving oot forms about the school trip,' she would announce, 'And I waant youse to take them home, fur tae be signed. Youse'll see that the train has a buffet,' which she pronounced as in 'tuffet'. To emphasise her little local dialect difficulty we of course spoke to her only in the best BBC English.

Miss Johnstone was a tiny, bird-like soul of about sixty, with badly dyed blond locks and thick glasses. The glasses put her at a disadvantage when it came to applying make-up and nothing ended up where the fashion magazines recommended. Lipstick was applied lop-sided, halfway up one nostril on one side and nearly to her chin on the other. Eye-shadow was always a disaster, landing anywhere between her forehead and nose, and we avoided a lot of work by helping her sort it out. There was about her a disorganized, distracted air, as though she was permanently in a rush to be somewhere else, and her black academic gown invariably hung off one shoulder and trailed on the ground. She would come in determined to work very hard, after a lesson the day before had deteriorated into a beauty session instead, then someone would produce a new eye-liner. 'Noo, put that away,' she would say, full of resolve, 'We huv goat to work today!' 'But it would suit you Miss Johnstone,' the devious one would say, 'I bought it specially for you!' 'Oh well,' she'd say, her eyes by now glued to the item, 'Mibbe jist a little look, and then we must git back tae the lesson!' We could have sent Miss Johnstone out into the world like a painted hussy, but the truth was that we were fond of her, and though we frequently distracted and teased her, we wouldn't have hurt her.

Another ploy we used was to muse out loud about

the number of unmarried teachers we seemed to have at Garnethill. 'Funny how all our teachers ended up old maids,' someone would say with a theatrical sigh, 'I'm *sure* it wasn't because nobody fancied them,' another would chime in, 'I mean some of them are still quite passable . . .' Miss Johnstone knew what we were up to, but she could only take so much before launching into a spirited defence of her feminine attributes. 'Ah've hud my chances!' she would shout, 'Don't you worry hen! I have hud them lining up oot there! A twinty-inch waist I had, and a perra – a figure like an oor-glass!'

She married a farmer when she was in her sixties, the widower of a friend, which provided us with unlimited entertainment. 'Did you always fancy him Miss Johnstone – sorry, Mrs Crane? Did your friend know, or did you keep it secret?' She would get herself into all manner of predicaments trying to explain that love had blossomed amid the pong of manure only after her friend had shuffled off, and were we suggesting that there had been something going on while her friend was still alive? No, no, we'd say, we just hoped it wasn't on the rebound for him in that case, and it was a pity she had to settle for someone second-hand, that was all . . . she had had all those suitors waiting in line, unused so to speak, a bit of a come down . . . And was she having any, you know, difficulties adjusting to married life? 'Like whit?' she would demand, eyeing us suspiciously. Well, it must be difficult adapting to certain things at her age, doing certain things that she hadn't done before, or that we *presumed* she hadn't done before when she was *Miss* Johnstone, especially as Farmer Giles had been used to having certain services for so long . . . 'Whit do youse mean?' Well, cooking for more than one, for instance, washing smelly socks; why, what had she thought we meant, what else *could* we have meant? Next day she would deliver a little sermon before work started; she was having no distractions today, she knew exactly what we were up to and she was having no more of it. 'You're looking tired this morning Miss John – sorry, Mrs Crane,' someone would remark, 'I don't know *what* you've been up to, but look at those shadows under your eyes!' 'Noo, I'm no' having that!' she would smile slyly, thinking she was right on top of the situation, 'I know whit youse is up tae . . . shadows ye say?' A make-up bag would immediately be produced and the rest of the lesson would be spent repairing her ravaged countenance. It never failed.

At home life continued. Nan became more settled in her isolation and Skip, more entrenched in his drinking. I went away every weekend possible, after Nan said she didn't mind. It was of course exactly what I wanted to hear, and I'm ashamed when I look back now and imagine what her weekends were like. She would be alone with the TV while Skip was out drinking, with no one to talk to and nothing to do, and when he came in he would be in whichever mood the booze had produced. That was how she would spend the days and nights when I was away enjoying my freedom, enjoying missing what she was forced to endure. If I felt guilty at the time I can't recall it, being away was like breathing fresh air for the first time.

Skip's family was dying out now and more than once I was required to attend the funeral of someone on the O'Brien side that I had never met because of one of their many feuds. O'Brien funerals were fun though, totally unlike the other one I had gone to in 1959, the one we never talked about. Then Uncle Pat died. Inevitably, after all the years he and Hughie had lived and fought together, he too had contracted and died of TB.

Their sister Norah was there in a flash, laying claim to everything in the house, each item being apparently tailor-made for some niche or other in her own home. In fact, if she wasn't very much mistaken, this or that, and probably both items had been long-promised to her. The remaining O'Briens exchanged disapproving glances but said nothing; there was more than one way to sort Norah out after all, and they knew them all.

Uncle Tommy arranged the funeral, and after what was known in O'Brien talk as the creamy-tartar and to other mortals as the cremation, he assembled the survivors to go over the financial details. At the end of the discussion he slapped a half-pound slab of lard on the table in front of his sister.

'An' that's fur you Norah,' he said.

'Me Tommy? Whit fur?'

'Well Norah,' he said with relish, 'Ye claimed everythin' else, so we thought ye might as well hiv whit wis left when we burned him tae!'

After the laughter and jollity of the funeral, something happened that was to scar my relationship with Skip forever. Coming back later that night with a long-lost cousin, Skip walked with him into the Crystal Bells pub, a favourite O'Brien haunt in the Gallowgate, leaving me outside. There was no warning, so I had no chance to protest. It wasn't the safest area to leave a thirteen-year-old girl to stand alone and it was getting dark. I was already feeling scared and humiliated, when a man suddenly came out of the pub and tried to talk to me. I ignored him, my heart thumping, and to my great relief he walked off, but then turned again to watch me from a short distance away. I was desperately watching the pub door, hoping Skip would come out, willing him to come out, but even when the man came nearer again I had absolute certainty in my mind that nothing would happen. He wasn't watching me, I was imagining the whole thing. Only, I wasn't.

He grabbed me from behind, his forearm across my throat, and dragged me backwards through a close and into a derelict tenement. I have heard of women fighting bravely to protect their honour, but with me it was blind panic, not a thought-out response. As I fought against him, some mad desire to keep my dignity stopped me from screaming. Some Clark point of decorum told me I had to get out of this not just alive and as unharmed as possible, but without drawing attention to myself. The only reason I got away from the man was because he was drunk and that had made him less coordinated than a panic-stricken, teetotal girl.

I immediately ran into the pub, unheard of behaviour for a female of any age at that time. Everyone turned and stared in sudden silence as I entered. The cousin had gone and Skip was drinking alone. He looked up, calmly drained the remains of his whisky into his beer, drank it and walked out with me. As I told him what had happened he said impatiently, 'Ye know no' tae go intae a pub, yur auld anuff tae know better than that!'

I tried again to explain what had happened, but I was wasting my time. He had no intention of listening or of going after the man. Instead he kept walking towards John Street, where the Drumchapel buses left from, all the time keeping up a perfectly normal, but one-sided conversation with me. He went over the events of the day, laughed at the jokes and insults, made comments of his own, and carefully edited out any reference to the minor fact that his daughter had been attacked and assaulted while in his care.

I couldn't think of anything to say. My mind whirled with the twin shocks of what had happened to me and Skip's surreal reaction to it. Then gradually I felt the physical things, like the bruises and gashes. My clothes were ripped and torn and my hands were stiffening up because the skin across my knuckles had been scraped off; my knees were grazed and the hardened, dried blood stood out like shiny rivers down my legs. There was blood running down my throat from my nose, and over my chin from my split lips, and one eye was so swollen that it was closed. As Skip ignored it all and fell asleep on the bus, I could see my reflection in the window and could well understand why the other passengers looked at me curiously. My obviously distressed appearance also explained the sudden silence when I ran into the pub earlier. As we got off the bus to walk the short distance to Halgreen Avenue, Skip made his only reference to the incident, then or ever. 'Ye'd better tidy yersel' up,' he said disapprovingly, with that characteristic frown expressing his distaste, 'An' we'll tell yer Ma that ye fell doon the stairs oan the bus. Nae point in upsettin' hur, is thur?' No; no point at all really . . .

Just as in the earlier incident with his old drinking pal, my uncle's father-in-law, I felt ashamed, but not this time of myself. I was ashamed that this man was my father. Curiously, all his life he liked to pretend that there was a special bond between us, but if there was, it was a bond of shame forged during those terrifying incidents. I found it impossible to meet his eyes after that time, because I had such contempt for him. For the rest of his life, whenever we talked about anything, I always thought of the assaults with a kind of furious wonder that he had managed to wipe them from his memory.

Adult perspective later brought some understanding, though I have to say no forgiveness. To have taken the incidents seriously he would have had to address the cause, which was his drinking, and to have done that would have threatened the man's very existence. He was an addict, he needed booze to live, and everything else came after that. This included the health and well-being of his wife, the care of his family and the protection of his child. Somewhere in his soul I think he knew this, and he didn't have to see the contempt in my eyes to know that it was there, because I'm sure he held himself in the same contempt.

Like any child I had a right to better. The world may not have owed me a living, but Skip owed me care and protection, and I never got it. Though all my life I have tried to be logical and place the blame where it belongs, my self-esteem has remained dented by those assaults and the fact that Skip didn't care for me as much as he cared for the bottle. No matter what happened later, regardless of what I achieved or what others may have come to think of me, the shame and the guilt of being so debased and worthless in the eyes of the first man in my life, somehow linger on.

Chapter Twenty-Six

Garnethill had its share of sexual incidents too. The area around the school was frequented by prostitutes of both sexes and the ugliest, least convincing transvestites I have ever encountered. Because of this there was a constant police presence and we were encouraged by the Sisters to report any suspicious characters we saw hanging around. Unfortunately, when we did so they invariably turned out to be undercover policemen, and we then embarked on games of 'spot the polis' instead. This prompted a request from the police that leering convent schoolgirls should desist from sidling up to their officers and offering them a good time.

The Sisters had a curious mixture of attitudes towards us. On one hand we were pure, innocent, vulnerable Catholic maidens who had to be protected from men at all costs, because men were evil. On the other hand we were scheming madams, who given half a chance would tear off our chastity belts and fornicate in the middle of the street whilst wearing a school tie. Regardless of which was true we had to be kept away from any temptation of the male persuasion and convinced that men were the enemy. The image they tried to create for us was of men as sexual time-bombs, ready, willing and able to explode into sexual activity at any moment and without much encouragement. We were therefore advised not to make eye contact with any male, anywhere at anytime, and not to wear patent shoes, lest the creatures caught sight of the reflection of our knickers and be inflamed beyond control. It was little wonder really that Convent schoolgirls had the reputation of being sexually active at the earliest opportunity and promiscuous with it, there being no fruit so sweet as that which is forbidden. And there was another embargo that I have never understood, on whistling, which for some reason made the Virgin Mary cry . . .

On one occasion, the Sisters seemed to be proved right about our 'wickedness'. There was a flasher in the cobbled lane between the school and the convent who was somewhat surprised, it must be said, to attract an avid audience shouting, 'Show us yer willie!', 'Fling it ower yer shooder!', 'Is that the best ye kin come up wi'?', and other such maidenly encouragements. Out came the Sisters of Mercy, whipping everyone in sight with their belts, including the unfortunate star turn, who was attacked with such ferocity by these paragons of virtue that he would certainly have been rendered unable to raise as much as a smile for some considerable time, if ever. They beat the holy bejezus out of the poor creature and he limped off, bent double and with grounds for charging the Sisters with GBH at the very least. This incident gave Sister Aquinas a most welcome, and some might say a Godsent, opportunity to become quite flushed of face and hoarse of voice from denouncing the lustful, sinful nature of the male of the species, and it was noticeable that she did so with unnecessary frequency. I never did discover if she had personal experience of the male transgressions that she spoke of with such eloquence, though it was not for the want of asking. Taking deep offence she would then send for Skip, to remonstrate with him about the sexual nature of my questions, which from every point of view was a bit like taking coals to Newcastle. Apart from his contribution to my knowledge of the subject, wasn't he, as a representative of the lustful, sinful crew the wrong person to stop such questions?

I was as much a puzzle to the other girls at school as they were to me. It was the swinging sixties after all and they spent all week talking about boyfriends, pop music and fashions while waiting for the weekends to get to discos. I went through my weeks waiting for the weekends too, to get out of the city and off with the Crowd. Every Friday I took my hiking gear into school and come four o'clock I changed in the toilet into trousers, boots, anorak and rucksack and dashed down to Buchanan Street to catch the bus. My schoolmates considered this to be bizarre in the extreme and never shrank from telling me so. Needless to say I found their preoccupations every bit as bizarre, but then, I had been too well brought up to say so.

During the summer months we headed for Loch Lomond and the eight mile walk to where the boatshed stood. Inside, the canoes lay in tiers along both sides of the long shed, supported by wooden struts. At the top was the stove, that roared so loudly that from the outside the boatshed looked and sounded like an enraged, wheel-less, abandoned steam train. Inside there were two tables covered in leftover paint from numerous canoes, and painted on them in bright blue were the words, 'WUR TABLE' and 'PEASANTS' TABLE'. We still laid our sleeping bags on the floor between the serried ranks of canoes, except for Ronnie, who slung his hammock from two beams above.

We went away for the peace and to act the fool where civilisation couldn't protest. My favourite time at Loch Lomond was very early in the morning, when the silence and the light had a special quality that seemed to extend the senses. I would creep over the sleeping figures, like giant, snoring maggots, and make my way to a rock beside the water and there I would sit until sounds of life came from the boatshed. A maggot would shuffle and hop onto the pebbly shore and collapse again, having been kicked enough times to make it move out of the way, or needing to escape the smell of cooking.

Once Rab, the wall-slider, who was a shipyard worker in 'real life', lost his way in the forest. In his befuddled state all the man knew was that he had to keep going upwards, because the loch could become suddenly and dangerously deep in parts and he was a non-swimmer. He was discovered next morning, twenty feet up a Caledonian Pine, fast asleep across a bough, and an animated discussion took place underneath about how the best use could be made of this diversion. Some suggested yelling loudly in unison so that he would fall out in shock before he realized where he was, and though this plan held undoubted attractions it was decided to leave him alone, after taking photos, of course. There wasn't the slightest chance that anyone would climb the tree to save him, in fact the possibility wasn't even raised. When he finally made his way down no one mentioned where he had spent the night and neither did he, until the photos were developed.

Rab's main contribution to the Crowd was to cause furious anger and severe irritation whenever possible. Every topic was debated around the camp-fire for however long it took, and the disagreements were bitter and noisy. Rab would start out with a belief that was guaranteed to be at odds with the majority and at the end of several hours of serious discussion he would say with a grin, 'Ah don't care, Ah still think the same!' He did this even when his argument had been comprehensively demolished and proven invalid hours before. He had never been known to change his mind on anything, so he was a constant challenge that the others couldn't resist. Invariably the night would end with frustrated oaths being screamed into Rab's impossibly smiling face, as we all crawled into sleeping bags at 4 a.m. There was no doubt about it, the man understood about scoring points and he won every time. I went away every weekend hoping he would be there and would be disappointed when he wasn't. I felt this about other favourites, but though I thought nothing of expressing my hopes or regrets about them, I kept quiet about Rab.

Chapter Twenty-Seven

Just after New Year's Day 1962 Uncle Willie turned up in Drumchapel; I opened the door and there he stood. It seemed a lifetime since I had seen him – but then it was. We greeted him with delight and settled down to a night of laughter and jokes. Skip put a record on our ancient radiogram, an old 78, and Willie said, 'Ah like that!' Skip said 'Dae ye Wullie?' removed the record from the turntable and smashed it over his head. Willie smashed one over Skip's head, and so the evening continued until we had a heap of black jagged shards on the floor and Willie was laughing and mopping up the tears. Sheer vandalism, in fact, and we lost a lot of the records I had learned to sing to. Hours of my childhood I had spent by that old radiogram, duetting with Mario Lanza in 'The Drinking Song' from *The Student Prince*, John McCormack singing 'Danny Boy' and of course, 'Red Sails in the Sunset'. Now they were all gone in one mad evening.

It all ended in tears, of course, because it reminded us too clearly and poignantly of similar occasions in years gone by. When the bottle had been spun and the party-pieces trotted out, the thought in each head was of the song that wouldn't be sung, that night or ever. 'Mexicali Rose' would never be heard again, but it hung there more strongly than those that were. We always recognized that the sentimental words had fitted Peggy perfectly, but since her death they had taken on a deeper significance. 'Mexicali Rose, I'm leaving . . . Mexicali Rose stop grieving.' They echoed through every heart and mind, so that we each withdrew deeper into our separate shells with our memories.

During the evening I heard Skip complain to Willie in a serious tone that I wasn't up to scratch as a housewife, that I didn't devote myself entirely to scrubbing floors for instance. 'It's a' fits an' starts,' he said, in the tone of a man sure of getting support for his complaints. 'Fur Christ's sake Laurie,' said Willie angrily, 'She's only a wean, she shouldnae be daein' hoosework at a'!'

At the end of the evening he and Nan clung to each other and wept. It had been an all too painful, bitter-sweet reminder of life once upon a time and it wouldn't be repeated.

Sometimes, however, my godmother, Auntie Annie, came to see us and occasionally there would be a spur-of-the-moment visit from a group of three or four of the family, in a desperate attempt to recapture what they had lost. She stood there between them all though, the one who would never be there again, and no matter how exciting and happy the reunion had been, there was a sadness, a shared poignancy at the end, and no words were needed to explain why. Once my brother Laurie's wife asked who Peggy was. 'I keep hearing about before she died or after she died, but who was she?' To my amazement I found myself giving her the Clark treatment, by behaving as though she had made an unfortunate social gaffe. From Nan there was icy silence as she turned her head, staring into the distance, and I had to force myself to reply, 'She was an aunt, Nan's younger sister. She died young.' It answered the question she had asked, but it didn't begin to explain the raw, painful world that we had been trapped in since. Somehow there were no words for that.

Shortly afterwards we heard that McAvoy had placed Peggy's children in care. The two boys went to Quarrier's Homes at Bridge of Weir and the girl to Eastpark Home in Maryhill because of her handicap. It was the final twist of the blade. The only person who could have coped with the three children and would once have fought McAvoy for the right to do so was Nan, and Nan was no more. She knew this too and I watched her wilt further into herself at that time. It was to be a guilt Uncle George would carry for the rest of his life too, that he hadn't taken Peggy's children as his own. But he shouldn't have blamed himself. He and Annie already had three children all closer in age than Mickey, Laurie and I, and he was just an ordinary working man with an ordinary pay packet. Quite apart from that, McAvoy was the only one with the right to make that decision and he would never have let any of the Clarks have the children. Rather than do so he chose to place them in institutions for their entire childhoods.

For myself, at thirteen and too young to be able to affect what was happening, I could only feel that I had let Peggy down by accepting what was being done to her children. Nothing had gone right for her in life and it seemed that even in death she wasn't getting a fair deal. Something took hold in me then, a determination to get the kids out of the institutions McAvoy had sent them to, a resolve to put things right some day.

At Garnethill I was struggling. Looking after the house, Nan and myself obviously took its toll on my schoolwork, but I never told my teachers why I wasn't coping with work I was really perfectly capable of doing. Keeping secrets is normal life for the families of alcoholics and this was just one more. To the Sisters of Mercy I was simply a non-trier, except in English, History and Art, the subjects I liked.

Stressed in every aspect of my life I had subconsciously decided to rely on the things I found easy, rather than struggle with the ones I found harder or less interesting. In a twisted way, too, I began to accept my position as fair payment for the years of being feted as 'one of the bright ones'. I had always felt acutely embarrassed by the glory I received for excelling at what came naturally, when I knew from my sufferings in Maths that it was possible to work hard for little or no result.

By the third year I had gone down to a 'C' class, much to the annoyance of my English teachers (apart from Sister Aquinas) who knew I read books voraciously and scored consistently high marks in their classes.

My classmates had all been in 'C' classes from the start and had been learning shorthand and typing from the first year, regarded as only fitting for the lowest form of academic life, while I had been learning Latin. Sister Aquinas had reeled with shock and horror when I explained in first year that I wanted to learn shorthand and typing too because I wanted to be a journalist and a writer. My request was denied with all the disgust she could muster, and the good Sister could muster a lot. Two years on, those regarded as natural low-achievers were thus better off than I, and as I dropped Science, Latin and French, I had the gaps filled with more English and Art. It seemed that just like Granda Tom, I was escaping from my home life by immersing myself in Literature and Art, and I became so good at design and screen printing that the Art Teachers and School Inspectors bought my work. Endless discussions then ensued about whether my work was mine to sell, the school's or the Education Department's. Not that it really mattered, because characteristically I lost all interest in the finished article and gave it away to whoever wanted it.

'I don't understand you!' I remember one of my Art teachers saying, 'You have this talent and so many people recognize it, but you don't seem to care!' I didn't understand it either, but now I do. It was low self-esteem; whatever I achieved wasn't up to much, because I wasn't up to much in my eyes. If it was mine, it had no value. It was that simple. For similar reasons I was doing what Laurie did with his Maths ability, making it mean nothing because it was my skill.

My excellence in a few subjects was enough to make me top of the class, which understandably irked the others, because I didn't compete at all in the subjects they were good at. Looking back, it should have been obvious that this was a bright child in some sort of trouble, but the Sisters' minds didn't work like that. I was different from the others and that was as far as their insight reached. The aim of the other girls was right on target, to get married as soon as possible to a good Catholic boy and to start a good Catholic family with all due haste. This wasn't my ambition and I resented the constant attempts to force it on me; I resented the relentless religious bias of the school in a way that the Sisters and the good Catholic girls understandably objected to.

One week out of every year was dedicated to Nun Recruitment. We would be subjected to non-stop propaganda about what an exciting life lay ahead of us in a convent, a career second only to giving birth to hordes more of the faithful. We had talks in which we were urged to search the deepest recesses of our souls for the merest shred of a vocation, and endlessly shown films of nuns taking their vows at different stages of the process. While the others found the wedding ceremony, complete with wedding attire and gold bands, but minus a groom, a thing of beauty, I could barely contain my astonishment.

Missionary Nuns would arrive to tell us of their good works among natives of various descriptions, and how these people had been made into good Catholics as a result. Couldn't the good works be done without conversions, I wondered; was it strictly necessary to be a Catholic in order to be saved from starvation? Soon they were warned to accept no questions from the unbeliever, so that avenue of discussion was cut off. I was only trying to cause trouble, I was told, which suited the situation perfectly: for discussion read trouble. For the hell of it I would seek out Sister Aquinas and express an earnest belief in a vocation. She would glare at me, as she had done the previous year, and the one before that, and tell me that mockery was a sin, for which God would surely punish me. I thought He had already done so in advance, by sending me to Garnethill.

Newly ordained priests were regularly sent to us to get used to being adored, but in reality it was a baptism of fire. The idea was that we would anonymously submit questions and receive replies wise beyond reason, and these sad young lads would stand before us in their new outfits, which were always several sizes too big, trying to look confident, paternal and pious. It never worked. The girls saw them as the nearest thing they would ever get to human sacrifices and the *double entendres* flew. They were only lads and the girls knew it, so they would flutter their eyelashes, lick their lips, suck their pencils, wink – anything to put the new priest completely off his stride.

I, on the other hand, had to take them on in earnest, which spoiled the fun for the others. If the Pope was against the Pill for destroying human life, why didn't he join CND, to stop mankind being wiped out by nuclear war? By the time I got on to the holocaust and the blind eye turned by Pope Pius XII, the fledgling had usually flown to Sister Aquinas for protection against the anti-Christ. My classmates were quite rightly furious, because they had every right to their fun and I always cut it short, which was my fun. Then I would be hauled before Sister Aquinas and castigated for questioning The Will of God, which in turn led me to question the existence of her God, leading to the old argument about communism and the monarchy.

She beat me on the young priests, too, eventually, first of all by censoring the written questions in advance to eliminate the O'Brien ones, and then by banning me entirely from attending the sessions. So instead of talking seriously about serious issues, the young priests reverted to being the sexual playthings of the *good* Catholic girls, the girls enjoyed themselves again and all was right with the world. Me? I went to Art or the library, which were of course enormous punishments to fit my terrible crimes, and I suffered mightily.

Though Nan had no time for any religion, all of my pagan thoughts were of course put down to my having a Proddy mother, and prayers were frequently sent heavenwards, entreating some saint or other to arrange for Nan's immediate conversation to The One True Faith. Only then would my good, pure, eternal Catholic soul be saved.

The Catholic faith permeated every subject and minute of school life. Indeed it was the Maths teacher who was most devout in her entreaties for Nan's conversion, more so than in the teaching of Maths. Her method of enlightening us into the mysteries of her subject was to write some obscure formula on the blackboard and have us copy it down. If she was asked to explain she would exclaim, 'I've just written it on the board!' Little wonder really that she never succeeded in having Nan turn into even a nominal Catholic. I'd go home and tell Nan that any minute now her entire life would change, that the divine power of St Someone-or-other was about to strike, and she'd laugh uproariously.

At least twice a week the entire school would be marched down to St. Aloysius church, where Granda Tom had received his pantomime send-off, for whatever religious service was in season. It became clear well before I reached third year however, that if forced to attend I could, and would, put on such a convincing performance of choking from the pungent smell of incense, that I might well expire from over-acting. A tacit agreement was therefore reached that I could instead make my way to the nearby Art College to watch the screen printing in progress. This left both the school and myself to our own individual acts of worship, but it really did annoy Sister Aquinas. Had she been a different kind of Irish she would have understood the Game and not let her annoyance show. There was no real satisfaction in beating someone who didn't know about scoring points, but I was so dismally unhappy at Garnethill that I'm ashamed to say I took what little was available.

Chapter Twenty-Eight

JFK was killed in November 1963. Garnethill went into mourning for a martyred prince of the church, cut down in his prime. With hindsight there were elements of farce and irony about the Sisters' reaction, because had they but known it, JFK was an especially fine example of the lustful male whose sexual appetites were out of control, the kind of male they spent so much of their time protecting us from.

I was inconsolable; it felt like the end of the world, and as I watched events unfolding on TV I identified with them so much that I felt I was actually there. Even all these years later and with Camelot uncovered as Shamelot, the memory of those events still affects me. That JFK was just the same as every other politician I have no doubt, in fact I now think he was worse. A generation's ideals and the glimmer of hope that JFK represented, that those ideals could be made to count for something died that day on Dealey Plaza. I get that same lump in my throat when I hear the old pacifist folk song, 'The Strangest Dream', because it represents the same age of innocence as JFK did to us then.

Everything that we know now about JFK wasn't of course common knowledge at the time. He was a young, handsome hero who had been cruelly murdered in front of the world's appalled gaze. We were given time off school to watch the funeral, of course, but Garnethill's reasons for mourning JFK were not mine. I wrote a great deal of very bad poetry about it, and won new respect from Mrs Crane, neé Johnstone. It was so excruciatingly bad that she thought it was good and at first refused to believe I'd written it. Thereafter she regarded me with deference as a genius and often asked me to read and explain the significance of poems by real poets, as though I had something in common with them. I got away with a lot, because she was not a good English teacher and had very little understanding of words, spoken or written. So I used to make up ludicrous explanations that made a travesty of great works and she agreed with every one.

It was a valuable lesson to me of how easily fools can be made to look like sages. Since then of course I've seen it happen many times. You only have to look at any area of public life, especially the House of Commons, to see living examples of that particular phenomenon.

I had my only serious illness in 1963. It started up at Loch Lomond and at first it seemed like sunstroke. My head ached all Sunday, but when I got home it eased off and then on Monday it got worse again. Within hours I was vomiting and light hurt my eyes. The GP arrived and asked me to touch my toes, which hurt my back, but I told him that it was the strain after a weekend in the canoe. Luckily he listened to his own instincts rather than me and diagnosed meningitis, and almost before I knew it I was taken by ambulance to Ruchill Hospital.

The Clark attention to dignity won out even in this situation and I refused to be carried on a stretcher. Before the ambulance arrived I struggled upright, washed and dressed, and when the crew knocked on the door I walked past them to the ambulance, leaving them in the house looking for this seriously ill patient. Nan looked desperate, but still she couldn't summon up the strength to leave the house, so Skip went to hospital with me. Despite my bravado I felt really ill in the ambulance, but Skip typically turned away from me as we drove to the hospital, unable to handle any human attempt at communication.

In the hospital meningitis was quickly confirmed, which struck fear into Nan's heart. One of my cousins had had it when he was a child and had been treated with the new wonder drug, Streptomycin. In those early days the dosage of the drug wasn't certain, and he got too much, destroying his hearing and leaving him completely deaf for the rest of his life. I only had the viral strain of the illness, but it was bad enough. Within a week I was home again, but weaker than I would have believed possible. I wasted what energy I had getting angry because I had so little of it. During my week in hospital Skip had been run off his feet doing all the chores I usually did, and despite my weakness he instantly and gladly handed them all back to me.

I went back to Garnethill for my fourth year to take my O levels. The Education Department had given me a grant in the form of a cheque to buy a uniform, and as we didn't have a bank account Skip took the cheque to one of his pubs to have it cashed; naturally that was the last we ever saw of it.

I have no idea why Garnethill put up with me in what was to be my final year. Skip had decided that as I would just get married anyway there was no point in staying on any longer. What he meant was that if I was earning he would have more to spend on drink, but my mother, who once would have fought such a nonsense, was no longer able to do so. I remember looking at her for some sort of reaction as he announced his decision, the three of us knowing what he was really saying, but all she could do was lower her eyes. Though she had long ceased to function as the woman and the mother I had known, sometimes I still had expectations and so was often disappointed. It was illogical of course; like expecting her to live without a beating heart. All of the problems she had were symptoms and without diagnosing the source she would never get well again, but facing the cause would be too painful. What if she died from the cure?

At lunchtime one day one of the Crowd passed my school on his motorbike and stopped to chat. I was aware of one of the Sisters watching us, and assumed she was ready to attack him if he turned out to be easily inflamed and exploded into a sexual frenzy. Later I was told to report to Sister Aquinas, who wanted to know who he was. She couldn't handle the fact that he was a friend; males couldn't be friends, they were sexual time-bombs or they were nothing. No other kind of male existed.

'You were seen touching him!' she seethed. I hadn't a clue what she was talking about, but then that wasn't an unusual experience, as far as I was concerned she spoke Sanskrit with a Russian accent most of the time.

'Touched him?' I asked, wondering if his masculine powers stretched to hypnosis of a maiden in order to make her unwittingly commit obscene acts in front of a nun.

'You put your hand on his arm!' she stuttered, 'Don't deny it! You were seen!'

I could think of nothing to do but laugh, in fact I didn't even think, I fell about in front of the wizened old crone and shook with mirth. She didn't know it of course, but the weekend previously, and many more before, I had slept beside him and numerous more males, our sleeping bags actually touching for hours on end! She didn't know how to handle laughter, so she stomped up and down her study, delivering a lecture on morality, then she ordered me to go to confession. I'd had enough of her over the past four years. 'Get burnt,' I replied, and walked out, fully expecting, indeed hoping, that she would expel me this time and let me out of the madhouse for good. But she didn't; I have no idea to this day why not. Maybe I was her challenge, sent by her God to test her, maybe she just liked touching fire by associating with my extreme brand of evil. But it wouldn't be long before she was rid of me and I of her. As soon as I took my O Levels in English, History and Art, the only subjects I now studied, I left Garnethill forever.

Chapter Twenty-Nine

I didn't fight Skip's decision that I should leave school after my fourth year because I hated Garnethill so much, so I can't lay all the blame on him. Having said that though, I know perfectly well now, as I did then, that any protest would have failed.

Before I left I saw Sister Aquinas for the last time, by accident on my part at least. She wanted me to consider something: that those who are the strongest rebels often have the strongest vocations and are trying to fight their destiny. The shallowness of the woman's understanding still surprises me and I'm more than old enough now to know better. It was one of those occasions when I actually did have the right reply instead of thinking of it later and wishing I'd said it. 'See you in hell,' I said as I walked out.

The sad, not to say tragic, thing, was that a fair proportion of my schoolmates did become nuns, most joining the Sisters of Mercy, brainwashed by the false glamour that the nuns deliberately projected. Most of them left later, once years of their lives had been wasted in discovering that there was no such thing as the much-vaunted vocation that we heard so much about during the annual recruitment week. In my opinion it was no better than the kind of indoctrination tactics used by the Moonies, tactics the good Sisters would rightly have condemned. Together with the nuns' silliness, their insensitivity and dislike of humanity in general, the wasted years of those young girls remains my lasting memory of the unhappiness I associate with Garnethill Convent.

Many of the girls who didn't become nuns married quickly as soon as they left; one, a bubbly, vital girl called Anne-Marie, married the following week. All through our school years she had come in with gifts and enormous cards from her boyfriend, for her birthday, Easter, Valentine's Day, Christmas or whatever. I met her a few years later, pushing a baby in a pram and holding a toddler by the hand. She was nineteen-years-old. She appeared happy, but all I felt for her was profound pity, and anger at those who pushed Catholic motherhood as a gift from God and a duty to Him.

There was yet another group who had always seemed so much more worldly-wise than the rest of us. Their zest for living had been held in check so long that any fool could see the danger that it might one day burst forth with unknown consequences. Girls like Jan, who had been at every school with me since the days of the Marian, a slim, pretty girl who knew it all. Her group were the ones whose skirts were just that bit shorter and who wore make-up so discreetly that it was undetectable, even to the nuns who had a sixth sense for anything on their banned list. While the majority of the girls lived for discos and dates, Jan's little group of sophisticates had gone further along the path to adulthood and had left such childish things well behind many years before.

I used to envy Jan and her little group their knowledge of life, their easy acceptance of all the things that made me feel awkward. They didn't experience puberty, their bodies simply caught up with their existing mental maturity without any apparent trauma or effort. They had no problems with males, in fact they had mastered the art of manipulating men very early on and had a confidence years beyond mine, and certainly light years beyond anything the Sisters could have dreamt up in their worst nightmares. For that little group marriage and kids had never been an option, but unlike me they hadn't made it a battle-ground; they had simply served their time as quietly as possible until they could leave it all behind them and start their adult lives.

As soon as they left school they disappeared into the upper reaches of city life without any discernable pause in the transition from the schoolgirl stage. Jan went to London and became a model, and every so often I'd see that pretty face with the secretly knowing expression smile at me from the pages of magazines. Garnethill had done nothing for Jan except contain her till the age of sixteen, but at least she had survived it, she had made a successful life for herself and done what she wanted. I had never been close to Jan, she had always been too mature for me, even when we were both eight-year-olds in Mrs McGettigan's class, but I always envied and liked her and I was secretly pleased that she at least hadn't fallen for the lies and become a nun or a breeding machine. I had this mental picture of Jan in my head for years; she was wearing black patent shoes, staring men straight in the eye, and I could almost hear her whistling!

In the Summer of 1964 I left school at the age of sixteen, and we also moved away from Drumchapel, one of the worst decisions for my mother. At 48 Halgreen Avenue she had neighbours who, if not quite in the Balmano Brae class, were as near it as possible. On the bottom flat lived Mrs Boyce, who regarded the entire close as her own property and dashed out to shoo away anyone who lingered on the stairs for longer than she found acceptable. Across from her were the Hannahs. Mr Hannah, as everyone knew, was hen-pecked. He was a tall, thin man with steel-grey hair and a quiet, long-suffering manner. Everytime he entered his own home he had to take his shoes off at the outside door, and we were all used to his wife's screams if he actually touched anything inside. Then one day he disappeared and we discovered that for years he had enjoyed a secret romance with a much younger, and richer woman, and they had now left together for a new life in Spain.

Mrs Hannah, now left on her own, showed no outward sign of grief and continued in her houseproud ways, refusing as ever to admit anyone into her shrine. No one noticed very much that she hadn't been around for a while because no one saw her normally. Then the smell alerted the other inhabitants of 48 something was wrong. When the police broke down the door they discovered that Mrs Hannah had been dead for a couple of months at least.

On the first floor lived the Williams family. Mr Williams

was severely disabled but he still managed to father seven daughters and only stopped when Mrs Williams' reproductive life did. Next door were the Wilsons, who mysteriously changed their name to Connor, which did nothing to improve the life of Mrs Wilson/Connor, who was a slim, beautiful woman of incredible sadness. Below us lived the Baillies, another family of girls, three this time, all vivacious, dark females, one of whom was addicted to Elvis Presley and for some reason Rennies antacid tablets, which she chewed like sweets. I don't know which aberration amazed me most, though these days I certainly rank curing heartburn above listening to Elvis.

Beneath Alexa Grimshank, on the third floor, lived the Rankins, and it was Mrs Rankin's proud boast that her husband had not been allowed his conjugal rights since the conception of their fourth child fourteen years before. Sexual relations were regarded by her as indecent, and any respectable woman would be morally bound to bring them to an end as soon as possible. She disappeared too, under a huge coat that covered her from head to foot, before she tearfully confessed to Nan that at the age of fifty she was about to produce Rankin offspring number five. Mrs Rankin never came to terms with being caught out as a lying fornicator, much to the amusement of the other women in 48, and made up all sorts of stories to cover what she maintained had been her only lapse in fourteen years of unblemished purity. There were dark hints that she had been ravished, which gave us all a new perspective on Mr Rankin, a quiet, unassuming electrician in Singer's sewing machine factory, who didn't remotely resemble Rudolph Valentino.

So 48 was a place where people still knew other people to varying degrees, and when Nan became unable to leave the house the other women continued to come to see her and bring her up to date with the news. With both Laurie and Mickey now married, the house was one bedroom too big, but I don't know whose idea it was to move out of Drumchapel. After eight years, the conviction took root that we lived too far away from the centre of

Glasgow and were too isolated. If we lived within the city, or so the argument went, the family on both sides would visit more; Skip's argument I'm sure. My mother had a different agenda of course, she hoped that by moving to the city again Skip would come home more often. Nan was still looking for Utopia. Both hopes were unrealistic of course. After she heard that we were moving, Alexa Grimshank sobbed every time she saw Nan, and on the day we moved out of Halgreen she took herself off to her mother's at the crack of dawn so that she wouldn't have to see us go.

A few miles north-west of the city centre a new housing estate had been built on the site of Maryhill Barracks. It was a mixture of high rise and of the traditional tenement blocks that existed in Drumchapel and elsewhere. The boundary wall of the Barracks had been retained, which proved that whatever lack of judgement and imagination governed the design of homes for people to live in, someone, somewhere, must have suspected there were things from the past worth keeping. Part of the old barracks' wall ran along Wyndford Road, so in a ludicrous attempt to give the estate an upmarket image, it was called Wyndford Estate, though to everyone in the area and all who came to live in it, it was known simply as The Barracks.

Twenty-four families lived in our block of one and two bedroomed flats in Kirkhill Place, and we never came into direct contact unless we met in the lift. There were no young families, indeed most of the new tenants were OAPs, so there was little life about the place, and none that could penetrate the vast number of doors separating the flats. It was like a maze.

The days of washing greens had long gone, but the memory lingered on in the token provision of a small area on the roof that could be used for drying clothes. It seemed so unnatural, though, that no one ever used it, and it was troublesome too because it meant going through the inevitable labyrinth of doors, up in the lift and then unlocking the door leading to the drying area. The flats were heated by electricity that was too expensive to use for long, and there was a large, heated airing-cupboard, like a huge tumble-dryer without the tumble, that was equally costly. If they didn't have washing-machines and tumble-dryers of their own most people went to a laundrette. Comparative affluence, it seemed, was bringing a breakdown in social contact in the city, but the collective folk memory remained somehow, and the laundrette served as a meeting place for those reluctant to give up that contact.

For Nan the move to Kirkhill Place was nothing short of disastrous, because for a start Maryhill was an area of the city we knew nothing about, it was as foreign to us as Drumchapel had been but without the attractions Drumchapel had at first. She knew no one and because of the way the flats were laid out she got to know no one. She saw no other soul and spent all of her time staring out of the kitchen window as traffic and life passed her by two floors below. When I went out her face was at that window, and regardless of when I came in again, it was still there. There were many pubs in the area, too many for Skip to contemplate passing, so his drinking habits didn't change significantly. He'd come out of work, head for a pub, hop on a bus home and head for another pub. He usually slept some of it off for a couple of hours before heading out for the pub again in the evening. In some ways his frequent non-appearances while we lived in Drumchapel had been a blessing, because now he was just as drunk but he was around more, and it was impossible even to think of bringing anyone home. This of course bit deeper into Nan's isolation; I at least met people during the day when I went out.

I often asked my mother why she had married Skip and she'd reply, 'Ach . . .', and turn her head away; I don't think she understood why herself. He had been looking for a mother I think, and who better than Nan Clark, a famed earth-mother? He was just another sad, lost child who had found his way to Nan but unfortunately no one had arrived to claim him back again. And how was she to judge? She was seventeen when they married and had no other relationship because he had always been there, waiting, needing to be mothered. She hadn't a chance.

The world it seemed wasn't wide open to receive a sixteen-year-old journalist/writer with O Levels in English, History and Art, even if I threw in Mrs McGettigan's special prize for composition into my application. It was all I wanted to do, although my Art teachers had been keen for me to go on to Glasgow School of Art to study textile design. This would have meant staying on at school to take more exams, which had already been ruled out, of course. In any case, no matter how much I enjoyed Art, it was never in the same league as writing. It was more 'something to do' when not writing. A pastime, not an instinct.

By this time Mickey had built up a good career in medical electronics and he mentioned that jobs were going in the Eastern Infirmary. I had absolutely no hankering to do hospital work, but it could bring in a few pennies while I waited for my great literary skills to be discovered, something even I had to concede might take a while. Meantime I had to find money to live on, cash for the necessities of life, like a tent, a groundsheet and some climbing socks. When I turned up for the interview I hadn't a clue what I was being interviewed for and cared considerably less. If I got it that would be fine for a little while, if not then something equally temporary would do.

The Consultant Cardiologist interviewed me with the Hospital Secretary, who it was clear didn't matter greatly in the proceedings.

'I see you went to a convent school,' said Dr Alexander Cunningham, 'Presumably this means that you are of the Catholic faith?'

'Does it hell!' I replied, 'It means that my father is. I had no choice in the matter of where I went to school but I see no reason why I should take his religion any more than his politics. It's bad enough that I'm lumbered with his Irish Catholic name without an intelligent man like yourself making objectionable assumptions!'

He smiled politely. 'And the assumption that you are a Catholic is objectionable, is it?'

'In other circumstances you might well have been invited outside to settle the insult with claymores drawn!'

Just as well I didn't care about the job I thought. As I left I had a mental picture of the two of them immediately dropping to their knees, rosaries in hand, to offer up hundreds of Hail Marys to cleanse them from listening to my blasphemous outpourings. Next day a letter arrived asking me to start within a week. Dr Cunningham, it transpired, was a mite anti-Catholic, and he was to turn out to be the nicest, least prejudiced bigot I have ever met. I wasn't remotely qualified for the job, I had no Maths or Science qualifications and would have to study at night school just to get what I should have started with. I'd have to go to college to take the standard technician's course, all while working in the hospital. Because of my anti-Catholic remarks Dr Cunningham decided I could do it, while I didn't really care, because long before I had to do it I'd be a famous writer . . .

Sandy Cunningham was a very shy man and a brilliant doctor; a man of deep passions and even deeper moods. He had fallen foul of the medical mafia that ran the health service in Glasgow and had therefore been denied both power and influence. His brilliance remained, but he regretted that he had never mastered the art of dirty dealings and in-fighting essential for a successful career in medicine. Had he learned to be as unscrupulous as the rest he would have advanced further and as he saw it, could have achieved more, 'got things done', as a result. He was a very humane man though and could no sooner have fought dirty than applauded a goal scored by Celtic Football Club; it simply wasn't in him, he was too decent.

To get him through board meetings, where he was inevitably in a rebel minority of one – doctors forget loyalty to friends when it means being looked upon with disfavour by those above – he took the odd tipple. This of course only gave the mafia another weapon to use against him. 'Blown it again!' he'd mutter, 'I've blown it again!

What a bloody fool I am!', and he really didn't object
if you agreed with him. Then he'd brood in his room
for however long it took for the mood to pass, until the
next time.

Chapter Thirty

On my first day as a Student Cardiological Technician, I was taken by an experienced technician to 'Thor's ward'. As we entered the huge swing doors, Marie let them go again ever so quietly, and tiptoed around the ward. 'It's OK darlings,' said a voice, 'The old bastard isn't here yet, you're perfectly safe!' Marie sighed with relief. 'Thanks Dr Patel!' she smiled, and as we walked on down the ward she whispered, 'His name's Patel, but we all call him Petal. He's a bit, well, you'll find out!'

We stopped at the bedside of a man in his sixties and Marie rubbed a gel on his ankles and wrists, then fixed rubber bands around, and screwed wires to the small, hooked metal plates holding the bands together. The wires ran to an ECG machine, and when the dial was flipped, various different tracings spewed out of the machine. They made no sense to me, but Marie explained that the patient had suffered a heart attack a few days before and the leads recorded the electrical activity in different parts of his heart. By comparing the tracings taken over the last few days it was possible to chart the rate of damage, recovery or otherwise. Then another lead attached to a small suction device was moved to different positions across the patient's chest and more tracings spewed out.

When we had finished we removed all of the equipment, placed it back in the drawer under the machine, re-made the bed, and then just as we were about to pull back the screens we heard an army of footsteps marching across the long ward. Marie winced, put a finger to her mouth to silence me and then very carefully, like mime artists, we crept out of the ward, pushing the ECG machine in front of us. I let the door go behind us with as much care as

Marie had when we went in, but from inside the ward a voice bellowed after us, 'Who's that crashing through my ward? Who is it? I know there's someone there! Come out you bugger!'

Marie grabbed my arm, propelled me and the machine down the corridor, turned right down another and through a doorway. Behind us feet crashed along in pursuit as the voice continued to yell demands and threats, but whoever it was hadn't been quick enough to see us go in the door. With great aplomb Marie walked out again, humming gently and going very slowly in the direction we had just come from at high speed. We passed the owner of the voice, a very tall, thin man with thick, steel grey hair and a hawklike face. He was striding along the corridor with several other white-coated males in tow, going in the opposite direction to us.

'Good morning Dr Murray,' Marie said smoothly.

'Good morning, Miss . . . er . . . Did you by any chance pass some blighter coming from the direction of my ward?'

'Why no,' she replied, all calm innocence, 'I don't think so. Did you notice anyone Meg?'

I shook my head dumbly, wondering what in hell was going on.

'Are you sure they didn't use the other lift Dr Murray?' she offered helpfully, 'The one beside your ward?'

'I . . . um . . . don't think so, Miss . . . um . . . But then again . . .'

'I think it's disgraceful,' Marie continued, 'Disturbing you like that Dr Murray. I'd never go into your ward during rounds!'

'And I appreciate your consideration,' the voice boomed, 'Not everyone in this hospital is as professional and considerate as yourself, Miss . . . um . . .'

With that he barked us another good morning and we made our way to the lift 'the blighter' might have used, passing Dr Patel on the way. He wrapped his white coat around him, folded his arms theatrically across his chest and said, 'Nice performance darlings, your secret is safe with me!' He was the campest act I'd ever seen, as he disappeared down the corridor, half-heartedly 'searching' for whoever had upset Dr Murray.

'Now you know why we call him Petal,' Marie sighed, 'And it breaks my heart, he's so gorgeous and he's out of reach, unless you're six-foot-four, have a beard and happen to be a bloke!'

'Who . . . What was that all about?' I asked.

'Oh *that*?' she said, 'That's Thor, he's the chief of this unit and he hates people being in his ward. In fact he hates people, to be honest. No one is allowed to *think* loudly when he's doing his rounds, but if we don't have an up-to-date ECG to show him he blows up.'

'Well what are we supposed to do?' I asked, 'How do we get tracings for his ward rounds if we can't go into his ward?'

'Well we do go in silly!' she replied, 'Then we get out while his back's turned of course! Haven't I just shown you how to do it? Don't you think Petal's gorgeous? I'd give my all for him, if only he'd take it!'

'Why is he called Thor?'

'Oh him. Well his name is James Thor Murray. He was born nine months after his parents' marriage and honeymoon in Iceland. They met this good-looking young man there, called Thor, became friends, and when the monster arrived he was called James after his father and Thor after this good-looking friend.' Marie laughed, 'Well that's the story Thor tells, because that's the story his mother told his father and him, but we all think the original Thor was probably much more than a good friend, and mummy gave him both names to cover all options. It would certainly prove what we all know to be the truth anyway.'

'Which is?'

'That he's a complete bastard of course!' She continued humming as we walked into the lift and pressed the button to close the doors.

'D'you think it'd be possible to turn him?' she asked, her mind still on the unattainable Dr Patel, 'I mean, surely if Petal experienced the love of a good *woman*, someone just like me? Of course I'd have to get him drunk first and talk in a deep voice. What do you think?'

Nan had been delighted that I was going to work in a hospital, it was so respectable, so learned, so close to all those single young doctors who came from 'big hooses'. If only she knew, I thought, if only she knew . . .

It was in the hospital that I was first called Meg. There were already two other Margarets in the department, a third would cause too many problems, it was decided.

'We'll have to call you something else,' said Sandy Cunningham, and I kept quiet about being called Rita, because I hated it. 'How about Peggy?' he asked.

'NO!' I almost shouted.

'OK, keep your hair on! It's a perfectly decent name, but if you don't like it we'll think of something else!'

'It's not that I don't like it . . . it's just . . . I'd rather not . . .'

'OK, OK! Meg then, how about Meg?'

And Meg it's been ever since.

Going to and from work at the hospital every day I passed Eastpark Home, where Peggy's handicapped daughter had been sent five years before. The sign on the main road outside, with breathtaking tact announced 'Eastpark Home for Infirm Children', and though I loathed cigarette smoke I always went upstairs on the bus so that I could look through the windows. I don't know what I expected to see, a small cousin, perhaps, holding a placard proudly proclaiming our family link. It was on my mind constantly as the months passed, then one day I got off the bus at the Home and went in.

I explained to a nurse that I was Anne McAvoy's cousin, that I'd only recently moved to the area and could I see her please? Anne was ten years old by then, and she slept in a long dormitory. There was a locker by each bed, and in hers she had every birthday, Christmas and postcard that she had ever received. She had on display every present and every postal-order – uncashed – that she had ever been sent, a gesture of reassurance to her that she existed, that she mattered. I found her bright and cheerful, showing off her visitor to the other kids without the slightest suspicion that her visitor felt ashamed of being accorded the honour.

Seeing her was incredibly painful on all sorts of levels. Firstly there was shame that I hadn't been to see her before. She was, after all, Peggy's child. There was also the awful frustration that she simply shouldn't be there. This thought, of course, skirted the edges of the reason, the unspeakable reason that we still hadn't faced, the loss so unacknowledged that we couldn't mourn it. I still hadn't shed one tear over the events of 1959.

She was still there you see. Peggy. As a way of coping the family had unconsciously decided that she hadn't lived, therefore she couldn't have died. Their logic may have been tortuously faulty, but it was understandable. *I* knew that she had lived though. Peggy and Nan had made me what I was; I was the living proof of her existence. So I had secretly kept her alive somewhere deep in my soul, suspended in an emotional infinity. She was just as I last saw her on that Monday in May, and every now and again I would check that she was still there, smiling at me, her hair lit by the sunlight behind her. I suppose I must have known by some kind of instinct that we all had to let her go some day, and we could only do that by mourning. Sometimes, without planning it, I would push against the edge of the wound until it became too painful, then I would back off, returning her to where I kept her, until the next time.

This was to be the only time I saw Peggy's child. When I went back to the home McAvoy had been told about my first visit and had banned any more. The Eastpark staff were embarrassed but I was relieved, though it still makes me ashamed to admit it. However much the visit may have meant to the child the awfulness of the Home and of the situation had paralysed any good intentions I may have had. I was no better than the Clarks, my latest push had reached the painful area and it was just too much.

But the scenario stayed etched in my mind no matter how I tried to flush it away. Peggy's child shouldn't have been raised like that, not Peggy's child, not any child. When the children had been placed in Homes I had decided that one day I'd get them out again, but reluctantly I accepted now that I never would. I amended my list of things to be done in the future though: one day I'd find out the truth about Peggy's death, and added to that aim was a determination to get children out of institutions. All children in Homes became Peggy's children to me and though I never mentioned the items on my list to anyone, they lived quietly in my mind. They weren't ambitions or exciting goals to reach, but certainties that would happen, one day.

Though I had drifted into medicine, I found to my astonishment that I worked well with sick people and coped in a stressful world where crises were routine. I didn't have as many Saturdays free to go away with the Crowd, but that turned into a minor irritation rather than a disaster. Besides, the others had started to pair off and get married, so those of us still single met in the couples' houses. I saw Rab in Laurie's house sometimes and he was one of the few it was safe to allow into my own house. He would arrive out of the blue and whether I was there or not he would stay, making Nan laugh. She admired his clear, blue eyes, saying for some reason that they were 'sailor's eyes.' 'Naw thur no',' Rab would reply, 'Thur mine!' and Nan would giggle like a girl.

What kept me in the hospital was Glasgow, or rather its citizens. Like every Glaswegian I had always been of the opinion that it was the finest city in the universe; it didn't matter if the universe didn't agree, we took no offence, we were that sure of ourselves. It was only when I worked in the 'Eastern', as it was known locally, that I saw why Glaswegians were so special though. They will lay before complete strangers the most intimate details of their lives; if they feel a story coming upon them, then a story you will hear. Out-patients that I would see at a clinic for perhaps ten minutes of their lifetime, treated me like a member of the family, privy to all aspects of their personal lives.

One woman in her late forties came in for a routine ECG, and as I was explaining the procedure to her she said, 'Stockport! Whit dae ye think o' that? Stockport!'

I knew better than to make any comment at this early stage. She undressed and lay on the couch, and as I started to attach the electrodes she got down to the tale.

'Ma man's goat hissel' a joab in Stockport! Stockport! Whit dae ye think o' that then hen?'

I made a non-commital noise; I had no idea yet where this story was going.

'That's oota Glesca, in fact oota Scotland!' I marvelled at the breadth of her vision; Glaswegians rarely acknowledge that their city is actually a part of any land, even Scotland.

'Naw, naw,' she stated, 'Nae Stockport fur me, he kin go if he waants, Ah'm steyin' whaur Ah belang! Mibbe that'll pit an end tae a' these weans!' I had a fleeting vision of hundreds of xenophobic children clinging to every inch of her, all of them refusing to go to Stockport.

'Ah've goat wanna twinty-five,' she continued, as my little machine churned out her paper heartbeat, 'Wanna twinty-three an' wanna five! Terrible intit?' She was overcome by a spasm of laughter that destroyed the ECG, so I waited till she had recovered and then tried again. 'Y'know,' she continued thoughtfully, 'Ah've oaften thoaght, if Ah'd hid some Kit Kats in the hoose that day he'd probably have settled fur a cuppa tea instead! That'll teach me tae forget the biscuits, eh hen?' I could see a whole new Glasgow advertising campaign on family planning, with hoardings throughout the city proclaiming, 'Gie's a brek – hiv a Kit Kat.' With that she put her clothes on again, said 'Ta ta hen!' and disappeared forever, leaving me still wondering after all these years, what became of her and her Stockport-bound spouse. Her ECG incidentally, was clear.

If Glaswegians are communicative at the best of times, I discovered that illness rendered them positively verbose. Being sick stripped them to their raw best and characteristics I had been aware of became somehow enhanced, making me look at them again, surprised that I had passed over them so lightly before. Working with ordinary Glaswegians, if there is such a thing as an ordinary Glaswegian, took me back to Blackhill, and in a way that made sense, because the people of Blackhill had been fighting for their survival too.

A large part of my working day was taken up with acute heart attacks and we drew many of our patients from the Clydeside shipyards and the heavy industrial works in our part of the city. I was constantly surprised by them and surprised at being surprised too. A welder from Browns turned out to be an expert on Spanish poetry, a riveter from Fairfields was an authority on Renaissance Art, and Charlie, a shipyard electrician, knew everything about the works of Robert Burns.

He was in his fifties and his face was grey with pain. The ECG showed a massive heart attack, yet apart from his pallor he was showing no real signs of discomfort.

'Are you OK Mr Thomson?' I asked, always a silly question but it opens the score sheet.

'Ca' me Charlie hen,' he grinned, 'Mr Thomson wis ma faither!'

'OK Charlie; how's the pain?'

'Bloody awful hen, bit Ah've goat ma ain wey tae deal wi' the bugger.'

'Eh?'

'Well, ye know thaim wimmen that concentrate oan sumthin' else when thur havin' weans? Ah'm gaun ower in ma heid everythin' Rabbie ever wrote. Mind you, it's gettin' a bit cheeky oan it noo, Ah wish Rabbie hid wrote a bit mair!'

'We'll give you something for the pain then, give Rabbie a rest.'

Over the next few days I got to know Charlie and learned more about Burns in the process. Charlie's knowledge was immense, because he loved every line the Bard had written. I used to try to trip him up, regarding myself as a more than passable Burns buff, but he came through every time. 'Ye'll never beat the champ!' he'd grin, and I never did. If he had some pain he'd call to the nurses, 'Wee, sleekit, cowerin', tim'rous beastie!' and as the pethidine hit home he'd serenade them with 'My love is like a red, red rose.'

A week after the first heart attack he had another and we could do nothing for him; there was too little left of his heart muscle. He died reciting 'A Man's a Man for a' That.' As we worked on him, knowing it was utterly hopeless but having nothing more than effort to offer, his voice trailed away, '. . . the man's the gowd for a' that . . .' From a poetic point of view, and doubtless also from Charlie's, it was a fine way to go, but I never got over the feeling that we lost something special everytime someone like him died. Yet a few weeks before we would have passed each other in the street without a second glance.

They were the kind of people I had grown up with and the more I knew about them the more I respected them. I was always the last to give up on cardiac arrests. 'Christ Meg!' the rest of the team would argue each time, 'You *have* to accept it, we've lost this one!', but I always wanted to keep trying and afterwards I would analyse the whole event for something we could have done that we hadn't.

The doctors were representatives of the monied classes, everything about their backgrounds kept them far removed from the people they dealt with. As a rule, unlike the vast majority of their patients, they had gone to fee-paying schools, had lived all of their lives in wealthy, high-amenity areas and they spoke differently. Living on a different level they often missed the true worth and richness of the people that Charlie represented, while I was one of them and so I knew exactly what was being lost. Maybe that was why I hated giving up and why I fought harder each time; it was after all what I had been brought up to do, to fight for those who couldn't fight for themselves.

Chapter Thirty-One

At this time the Crowd would meet up every Thursday night to decide where we were going the following weekend. For years our meetings took place at the Continental Café in Sauchiehall Street, until it was raided and we discovered that it was a notorious centre for drug dealing. We'd never noticed what had been happening around us as we argued over who was paying for the espresso.

Every August the diverse strands of our weekend life met up at the Cowal Highland Games in Dunoon. Even if we had gone in very separate directions throughout the rest of the year, we always met up at Cowal. The main attraction was the rolling ceilidh from the camp-sites through every pub and hotel in the town, taking in the famous march-past of hundreds of pipers after the Games. For the tourists the march-past was the climax of the day, but for us it was all just beginning.

The Crowd would swell as we walked about the streets picking up people we hadn't seen since the previous year. We didn't even actually have to see each other. Once, walking past the George Hotel we heard the strains of 'Morag's Faerie Glen' sung in a fine tenor voice. We knew that only one man sang that song and in that voice, so he was collected and on we went. We ended up that year at a ceilidh given by the Rose Fletcher Women's Pipe Band from Dagenham. It was held in the Innellan Village Hall, a few miles outside Dunoon and I have clear recollections of several of the Crowd being up on the stage singing, and the usual 'lasting friendships' being struck between strangers destined to remain so.

In the early hours of the morning we were to be found making our unsteady way back on foot and in the rain to the camp-site some miles away. Inevitably we lost some along the way, who had 'decided' to sleep it off in ditches or wherever, but the triumphant band who were able to continue suddenly remembered as they approached the camp-site that it was inconveniently situated on top of a hill. As we struggled upwards to the comfort of the tents, singing raucously and dragging the more moribund behind us, a voice shouted 'HALT! WHO GOES THERE? GIVE THE PASSWORD!' High above us, silhouetted against the skyline, were four Highlanders, Pringle's Nightwatch.

Nobody knew much about Wullie Pringle, though it was rumoured that he was a failed welder from Govan. Nobody knew either how he and his followers got from A to B; they just appeared then disappeared. There was a theory that they were the result of a failed 'Brigadoon' experiment, that they had once been perfectly ordinary half-wits but had wandered along just as the button was pressed to start the process. They were thus trapped in time, condemned to roam the earth for all time, dressed like Highland clansmen and transformed into tartan half-wits.

Wullie believed himself to be the reincarnation of Bonnie Prince Charlie and therefore always dressed in full Highland regalia. More curiously, his band of followers also believed his claim to the throne and they gathered around him, all dressed in heavy caped coats over kilts, with long feathers attached by silver clan crests and pinned to the glengarries they wore on their noble heads. Wherever Wullie went they arranged themselves around him, long cromaks at the ready, *sgiann dhus* sharpened, prepared to protect the royal personage from any insult or injury.

Not only did these retainers cook his meals, but they tasted them too, presumably in case they had inadvertently spiked them with arsenic. Before the Prince entered a pub, two of his senior followers would check it out for the presence of enemies, and once inside they would stand around him, eyeing the company suspiciously, just in case. At night they mounted a guard around his tent as he slept, four men at a time for four hours each, through wind, rain, hail and snow. Needless to say they were a bizarre bunch, and they wore their very warm clothing all year round. For some reason on that Cowal weekend, they had honoured us by pitching camp next door while we were having a jolly time in Innellan with Rose and her girls.

'FRIEND OR FOE?'

'Whit the f—?' somebody demanded of Wullie's protectors.

'STATE THE PASSWORD OR DIE!' boomed the caped half-wits, cromaks in one hand, drawn *sgiann dhus* in the other.

'Away tae buggery!' suggested a half-asleep, wholly inebriated voice, and above us the spiritual remnants of the '45 still barred the way to our tents. In the darkness it was difficult to judge with any accuracy what happened next. There was a claim later that it had all been a ghastly accident, but I know that I heard giggling in our ranks first. Someone, or two, certainly grabbed Wullie's guards by the ankles and pulled them down on top of us. Naturally this had a domino effect, and we all rolled back down the sodden hill we had only just managed to climb up, landing at the bottom in a large heap. There was a great deal of laughter, several of the company being in that peculiar stage of intoxication where everything seems funny, even rolling down a hill in the rain and dark, with large sticks and *sgiann dhus* about.

'Wait a minute!' shouted a voice, 'Wanna Pringle's mob is wearin' Y-fronts under the garb! That's no' right!'

'Yer lucky!' yelled another, 'Ah've goat a big bare arse stuck in ma face!'

A bloodcurling scream rent the air as the said big bare arse was soundly bitten. It took some time to sort the situation out, because everytime we climbed up the hill the memory of what had happened the last time overcame us and we all ended up laughing and falling down again. Meantime, of course, the Prince was unprotected in his tent.

Next morning, or whenever we awoke, the Young Pretender and his following pretenders had slunk off in disgrace as we slept. Whenever we spotted them again after that embarrassing contretemps, we never mentioned their defeat at the hands and teeth of a bunch of drunks and a teetotal girl; that would have been unnecessarily cruel, and possibly treasonous. Perhaps the humiliation had some effect though, because not long afterwards Wullie emigrated to Australia, leaving his stunned henchmen to mourn for their 'Prince across the Water'. They wandered about, still in full theatrical garb, lost and lonely, looking for someone to follow, like extras in search of a Scottish Tourist Board film.

Some time after Wullie's emigration, on a sweltering hot day, one of the Crowd, Calum Young, happened upon Tam the Druid, on the walk to Rowardennan. Tam, a devoted member of Wullie's entourage, was in his twenties and had a serious heart complaint. As a matter of honour he refused ever to remove his caped coat, which was a warm item to cart around on top of a kilt, especially in the middle of summer. Normally pale to the point of translucence, Tam the Druid had the extremely disconcerting habit of coughing and turning blue. To be fair to him this was hardly his fault, but it could be frightening for bystanders, especially as Tam's honour also prevented him from resting. He may have had no Prince to protect anymore, but that wouldn't stop him dropping dead for the cause, whatever it was. And that was exactly the performance he seemed about to visit upon poor Young that Saturday when Tam the Druid suffered a harsh fit of coughing.

With sweat running down his blue face and presumably the rest of his anatomy as well, Tam refuted Young's suggestion that he remove the topcoat. 'I never take off my coat!' he stated, staring enigmatically towards the horizon, as heroes are wont to do, then he collapsed in another coughing bout. Young had had enough; the last thing he could have coped with was a dead Druid, so he jumped over a wall and found an alternative, solo route to the boatshed.

Tam survived that episode, but the last we heard of him and his fellow abandoned Pringle-ites was that they were trying to raise money to bring the Prince back from the Antipodes, where, it was said, he had become incapacitated by homesickness. Apart from being barking mad that is.

Chapter Thirty-Two

Youth Hostels weren't quite our scene, except for the 'Den', where one of our own, Jack Savage, was Warden. Jack kept 'K' Dorm for our exclusive use, something the average hostelite resented but could do nothing about. If Jack said 'K' Dorm was fully booked, then 'K' Dorm was fully booked. Apart from this justified and perfectly understandable little foible, Jack was the most honest man ever to draw breath. Every forgotten item, no matter how small, insignificant or useless, was carefully logged and kept in the store in case the owner came back to reclaim it someday. Even discarded bottles were collected and the deposit of a few pence redeemed, the money joining the rest of the lost booty in the store. We all nagged him about this – and then came victory day.

In the store lay an old pair of disreputable white sandshoes that had been left behind years before; anyone else would have assumed they had been thrown away, not forgotten. Anyone except Jack. The day came when Jack needed a pair of 'sannies' and the shops were miles away. 'Dae ye honestly believe the bloke's gonnae come back fur thum?' we nagged, 'Be serious Jack, a tramp wid refuse tae wear thum. Ye take these things tae the pointa fetish Jack!' We condemned his elitism, his determined show that he was more honest than the common man, knowing that this would really hurt, because Jack was the purest communist ever born. Eventually, under attack from all sides, he caved in and proved us wrong by donning the old white sannies. Two days later a bloke turned up, 'Ah left an auld perra white sannies here a coupla years ago,' he said, 'Ye don't still huv thum by any chance?' Jack, his toes curling up with shame inside the stolen sannies, had to deny that he had ever

221

seen them, and he never got over the guilt. Especially as we used to ask after his white sannies for years afterwards and mutter, 'A thief *and* a liar, tut, tut. Ye used tae be such an honest man Jack. Whit happened tae ye?'

It was a normal day in the hospital. There was a general examination room just inside the main entrance, where patients were examined and then dispatched to whichever department their ills demanded. It was a barn of a place with curtained off cubicles, and behind one a surgical houseman was faced with a problem posed by two homosexual gentlemen. They had 'married' each other and then become too hooked on the symbolism by placing the gold band on a very original extremity.

'It was all right at first,' suffering one wailed, 'But when it began to swell the ring got stuck, now it's *very* sore!'

'We'll have to cut it off I'm afraid,' said the bemused houseman, and the bridal pair screeched as one. 'Well we can't leave it on!' said the houseman in exasperation, 'Gangrene could set in very quickly!'

A terrible howling was heard this time, then the houseman realized what was wrong.

'I mean the ring you idiot, the *ring*! Not his dangly bits!' He left a nurse spraying the be-ringed appendage with cold water to reduce the swelling and sent for someone with pincers. Outside he wrote up the case notes, 'Months I've been qualified,' he muttered, 'And I haven't met one yet! Where are they?'

'Who?' I asked.

'The normal patients!'

'This is as normal as it comes!'

Behind another curtain the medical houseman was struggling with a gentleman who had collapsed on a train. He was refusing to remove his city uniform of pinstripe suit and bowler hat to be examined.

'Let me talk to him,' I suggested, 'I know what's wrong.'

'Now you mustn't be embarrassed,' I cajoled, 'I know what the problem is and I promise you no one will say anything about it.'

'You won't laugh at a silly old man?' he asked, clipped military moustache quivering and his arms tightly crossing his chest.

'Of course not! Now you must let us do a couple of tests and then you can most probably go home.'

He then removed his shirt to expose a lovely little red silk bra trimmed with black lace; it was too small for him, no wonder he'd passed out on the hot, crowded train. They always wore such exquisite things, far nicer than most women thought practical and more expensive than most could afford. No doubt he had the full matching set of panties and suspender belt underneath too.

'How did you know?' asked the houseman.

'I didn't for sure,' I replied, 'It could've been chains, or rubber.'

Sometimes I wondered at the wisdom of letting these young lads loose, straight after their Finals, when they had no experience of the big, bad world; it didn't seem fair on them somehow, or on the rest of us. Outside another cubicle a more Glasgow-wise Senior House Officer was explaining to another puzzled houseman why his patient kept worrying about her brown kittens instead of helping him with her symptoms.

'I ask her what's wrong and she just goes on about these damned brown kittens! I keep telling her someone will look after her cats, but it's all she'll say to me!'

'Well son,' said the SHO, 'She *is* telling you what's wrong with her. It is her considered opinion that she is suffering from bronchitis. "The Broon Kittens" is Glasgow slang for bronchitis. By the sound of her cough she's probably right. It's your task my boy to apply your mighty stethoscope to her rib cage and confirm it. Go to it!' Two years ago someone had probably given him the same teach-in. A normal day, and into this normal day came a porter pushing a trolley.

'Joe's fainted,' he said to no one in particular, 'So Ah've jist pit 'im in cubicle four till he comes 'roond.'

From around the assembled medics there came a collective growl.

'You can put him in the incinerator for all we care!'

someone said, and there was a bitter laugh of agreement all round.

Joe was the car park attendant for the main forecourt and he kept his forecourt for 'those and such as those'. Senior consultants were assured parking spaces and all others were pounced upon and threatened if they as much as stopped to let a passenger out. He even resented the ambulances stopping in their own bay to bring patients in. Our main point of contention was that the forecourt was the quickest way into the hospital, and it made more sense for genuine workers to get inside fast, rather than consultants who were hardly on the front line.

People like the infamous Dr Thor Murray for instance, who drove a beautiful white vintage Lagonda that would have financed the building of a new hospital, were waited on with due and sickening deference by Joe. Thor had his own reserved space that Joe shepherded him into every day, with much bowing and his own weird combination of a salute and a tug of the forelock. Thor would then sweep off to his luxurious suite deep inside the hospital, where he would see his private patients, using every NHS facility available. This was against the rules, but Thor was stuck way back around 1920, and the board turned a blind eye. This was most appropriate, because the board were all Thor's private patients. Most of them were non-medics and mistook show for substance; they had no way of knowing that Thor had ignored every piece of medical progress after 1920 as well as all other aspects of normal life. So the resentment we all felt for Thor and his like applied to Joe, who fawned over him and them, and tales of Joe's treatment of generations of ordinary, mortal hospital staff regularly did the rounds. Now here he was, snoozing in the examination room.

'I don't like the colour of him,' said another tech, looking behind the curtain.

'I hate every one of his rotten cells,' said someone else, 'So what's new?'

'He looks a bit blue.'

'Let us know when he turns black!' Everyone laughed.

'He's arrested!' shouted the tech, feeling for a non-existent pulse. Everyone laughed again. 'Next you'll be saying that Santa does exist and that there really is a tooth fairy!'

Then we realized that she was serious, dropped what we were doing and the resuscitation routine took over. All the way through voices could be heard muttering, 'I can't believe I'm doing this!' and 'We'll never live this down even if he doesn't make it!'

Sod's law really is an odd thing. You can work on patients deperately for hours, with everything going for you and nothing going wrong, and still you lose them. Joe we got back. He was lying on the floor, pink and breathing again amid much cursing from the assembled company. The SHO glared at the tech who'd looked behind the curtain and said, 'There is no hope for you, you understand that, don't you? For a start everyone in this room will never forgive you, but the rest of us must all swear a blood oath here and now. We must all promise to deny any involvement in this obscene act and any knowledge of who took part, even under torture, OK? If the rest of the hospital hears about this we're all done for!'

Just then the door opened and in thundered Thor. 'The porters told me the car park Johnny was here!' he yelled, and catching sight of Joe lying on the floor with tubes and wires attached all over his body, he bellowed, 'Is that him? Where's his hat? Don't know him without his hat! Hey you! Car park Johnny! Get up! Some bugger's taken my space! I want his arse kicked out *now*! Get up! D'you hear me? I want you to get up!'

'It's a little tricky at the moment Dr Murray,' said the SHO very smoothly, 'Five minutes ago he was dead. You see we've only just resuscitated him.'

Thor stopped mid-roar and took in the scene around Joe for the first time, then said with utter contempt and distaste, 'My God, will you people stop at nothing? Why don't you let people die in peace?' With that he swept out and off to his suite, leaving the Lagonda parked in the ambulance bay.

A couple of months later I was helping to get a patient out

of an ambulance as Joe watched in disgust. The SHO was there too, and as we turned towards the hospital together, the white Lagonda swept past in style. We watched Joe go through his usual odd salute-forelock tug routine and as Thor disappeared inside Joe approached us.

'That Dr Murray,' he said, 'He saved ma life y'know.'

'Really?' said the SHO with total uninterest.

'Aye, sure enough,' said Joe, his horrible little eyes shining with tears of admiration, 'Ah hid this bad turn, nearly died so Ah did, an' he saved me. Ah heard this voice an' opened ma eyes, and there he wus, telling me Ah hid tae get up! Saved ma life he did, a wunnerful man!' Overcome with emotion he sniffed loudly and hirpled over to assault some innocent soul who was trying to find somewhere to park. The SHO shook his head. 'I'd rather that old bastard Thor took the blame than us,' he said, 'But ain't life an absolute bitch sometimes?'

Chapter Thirty-Three

One day I was walking through my own unit's female ward when I spotted a familiar face. I looked at the ward list, and it was, it really was. It was Jan.

'What's wrong with her?' I asked the houseman.

'Do you know her?'

'I went to school with her.'

'Really? That might be helpful actually, she won't say a word. Maybe she'll talk to you. We got her in last night, an overdose, and she nearly managed it too. We want her to see the shrink, but she won't even tell us to bugger off.'

'She was working as a model the last I heard of her a couple of years ago, I always thought she'd got it made.'

'Well she won't work as a model again,' he said, 'She's only held together with chewing gum and pills these days.'

I walked towards her bed, noticing how thin she was, the dark shadows under her eyes and the pale, almost transparent skin; it was Jan, but it wasn't the Jan I had known.

'Hello Jan,' I said, and she looked up at me with total indifference.

'You probably don't remember me,' I continued, 'We went to school together.'

'It's Margaret,' she said, pointing at me and smiling, 'Margaret O'Brien! What are you doing here?'

'That's my line! What are *you* doing here?'

She shrugged. 'I took an overdose.'

'Why?'

'Because I want to end it all.' She wasn't upset and she didn't even seem sad; it was a statement of fact. I sat beside her bed.

'But Jan, you had it all stitched up while the rest of us were still playing with dolls, what went wrong?'

'Me? I had it all stitched up? Me? Are you kidding? You were the one who knew all the moves!'

'Are you sure you *do* remember me?' I asked.

'God! Do I remember you!' She was laughing now, a good sign I supposed, but I hadn't a clue what she meant.

'How you handled all those mad nuns,' she said, 'You drove them even crazier than they were! Do you remember the time that second year got pregnant and had to leave the school, and they were lecturing us about it? And you said she should just say an angel had appeared announcing a virgin birth and before she knew it she'd have her own flock of nuns! I thought Sister Aquinas was going to explode in flames!'

'I don't remember that,' I said, 'But it sounds like me.'

'And the time you told her Jesus Christ was just a local politician who had offended the establishment, and before she could get up from the floor you said in fact he was probably a communist!'

Yes, it was definitely me she remembered, that was certainly one of mine.

'I used to envy you!' she said, 'You knew just how to get them going! Where did you get all that stuff?'

'From books,' I replied, 'Where else?'

'That's right,' she laughed, 'You always had a book in your hand. I always thought you'd be a writer, how come you're wearing a white coat?'

'I wish I knew,' I replied, 'I still write, but just for myself. But what happened to you? I used to feel so smug knowing this famous face on the front pages of magazines.'

'I couldn't handle it,' she said, 'You have to be really in control in that game, and I wasn't. Seems to me I've spent my entire life trying to get control of it. I ended up taking pills to keep me awake, pills to make me sleep, pills to keep me thin. And men! Around me like flies they were, and I always chose the wasp!'

She was on the brink of tears now, lying against her pillows, staring at the ceiling.

'Jan, it might help to talk to someone.'

'A psychiatrist? Forget it Margaret, it's too late now. Besides, do you think I haven't talked to them before?'

I decided to leave it till another time, so I changed the subject to the one thing that had made her smile before, our schooldays. As I left she said, 'I always admired you Margaret, you were always so confident, so sure. You didn't need a group around you, you were always yourself and you said what you thought. I never had that courage, but every time you scored a point against the nuns I felt like cheering!'

Funny the impressions we make on other people. All through my childhood I'd been a loner, keeping the awful secret of my father's drinking and the shame of how poor we were from the rest of the world. Since 1959 my mind had been constantly in turmoil and I'd looked at Jan and her little group, thinking they were sophisticated and so worldly-wise compared to me. Yet there was Jan trying to end her life at the age of twenty, having tasted success, messed around with drugs and been involved with who knows how many men. What had I done? I had wanted to write, it was the only thing I had ever shown any aptitude for, yet here I was, in a demanding job to be sure, but given that I could do it, it was as safe as houses.

As far as the swinging Sixties and the drug culture were concerned, they might as well have not been happening. I avoided going out with men on a one-to-one basis, and those I had dated lasted one date; I couldn't bring myself to get involved with anyone. Part of that was a natural reluctance given the one marriage I had any close knowledge of, but it was also partly because the earlier assaults had left me with a dislike of being touched. I used to think this dated from the time of Peggy's death, when one of my aunts had held onto me as I tried to escape hearing the actual words, but that incident had only compounded the dislike. It was really rooted in the first assault just beforehand, and the later incident outside the pub.

There was another reason though that lurked at the back of my mind, one I hardly dared think about because it was so impossible. That reason was Rab. I realized even then that anyone I dated reminded me of him in some way, a similar way of laughing perhaps, or 'sailor's eyes', but they weren't him. At the time I didn't admit any of this, even to myself, but whenever I saw him I felt more alive than at any other time. Our meetings were no more than verbal duels as we slagged each other off with insults; he was at least ten or twelve years older than me, well out of my reach and I knew it. He hadn't shown the slightest interest nor had there ever been the merest hint that he might regard me as anything other than the kid of the Crowd. The possibility of romance had never been considered. Rab was completely unattainable, but while he was there I couldn't sustain interest in anyone else.

Sod's Law, which had dogged me all of my life, even operated here. There were plenty of girls dashing around looking for Mr Right and bemoaning the fact that their relationships never came to anything. I, on the other hand, wanted only friendship, so naturally I attracted the kind of men who wanted to settle down and raise families. I never saw the warning signs. I'd have some perfectly nice chap I considered a friend proferring a diamond ring and I wouldn't have a clue how or why the situation had sneaked up on me without my having any inkling of it. I then reacted badly, out of embarrassment and confusion, hurting them in the process without actually meaning to. There were the others, whose only crime was to remind me of my father in some way so that I had to get rid of them as brutally as possible. There was nothing wrong with them, it was nothing they had done, and looking back I still cringe at how I treated them. If Jan thought I had all the answers, I was obviously a better actress than I had given myself credit for.

Next day, when I went to the ward Jan had gone. She had signed herself out and disappeared. I couldn't shake off what she had said though. Why was I here when I should have been writing? Had I drifted into the safe haven that the NHS was in those days and settled for that safety? In thirty years time would I end up as a long-serving chief technician, wishing I had struck out and at least tried to write instead of playing safe all my life? That thought joined all the other uncertainties and confusions in my head, rumbling around and crashing into each other but never coming to the surface or to the remotest prospect of a conclusion.

Chapter Thirty-Four

My father's main preoccupation, apart from drinking, was his Eighth Army connection. He had spent six years away from home as a gunner in the Royal Artillery and every Saturday he still met one or two of his old comrades in a pub in the centre of Glasgow. The outcome was entirely predictable of course, he came home barely able to stand, but then he spent a lot of his time like that. Every year there would be a reunion in London, and off he would go in his black blazer with the gold buttons and the Eighth Army badge on the breast pocket. The badge was a yellow silk cross on white, all outlined with real gold wire; no expense was spared if it was something for himself. Those weekends when he boarded the coach to London were heaven for Nan and me. He would leave on Friday, drink himself senseless for three days and arrive back on Sunday night. But we had the sheer bliss of knowing that he wouldn't come falling through the door at any moment, so we didn't waste time and nervous energy waiting for the sound of the key missing the lock that usually heralded his arrival. The trouble was that we never knew what kind of mood he'd be in, screaming abuse, fighting mad or hysterically funny, at least to himself. So when he went to London we spent a relaxed and happy weekend together, and I used to say to her that if only she had left him years before it could be like this all the time. If only.

Of course by this time Nan wasn't physically or mentally capable of making a fresh start. Anyone meeting her for the first time would never have believed the kind of woman she had been, I had trouble myself relating her to the crusading earth-mother I had known as a child. There were odd flashes of the old Nan, when she read a newspaper item that described some kind of injustice perhaps and she would become quite articulate with anger about it. She had a healthy dislike of all politicians and would roundly berate them whenever they appeared pontificating on TV, regardless of what party they represented. But it was all from her armchair, she never showed any interest in re-entering life again.

Sometimes I would try to persuade her to see a doctor, but she really didn't want to; her life, the one she wanted, had gone with Peggy, and she didn't want what was on offer without her. What I didn't know at that time was the manner of Peggy's death and how it had destroyed all Nan's belief in justice, natural or otherwise – it nullified the code of honour she had lived by. There was a feeling of marking time, of waiting for the day she could go too. She had grandchildren by then from both Mickey and Laurie, but there was no rebirth through them. There was a distance, a preoccupation about her, as she sat in her armchair and simply waited.

It was a holiday Monday and things were slack. Our prospective patients either kept their crises for ordinary times or else they took them on holiday and visited them on resort hospitals. Either way we had little to do. I was summoned by one of the three housemen our unit employed and found two of them waiting for me. They manhandled me into a prepared bath of cold water, partly to pass the time and partly in response to what I had done to them, which was doubtless payment for something they had done to me first. A few weeks before, I had got revenge on one by pouring a jug of cold custard down the back of his trousers while he was doing a ward round with various professors. I then put the other one's name on all the coupon applications in every magazine I could find and his few free hours had thus been filled with calls and visits from double-glazing salesmen and kitchen installers. As I emerged soaked to the skin I ran into the other houseman, the one who had admitted Jan.

'Oh Meggie, I was meaning to talk to you. We got your

friend in again last night, whatsername, Janet Wotsit? No go I'm afraid.'

'She still won't see the shrink? I'll talk to her again if you like, but I'm not sure it'll help.'

'Well it won't as a matter of fact; what I meant was she was dead on arrival. Sorry.'

I was used to death by now and I knew that overdoses far outstripped all other admissions to medical wards. It was considered a cry for help, though we knew there were many more we never received, they were DOAs – they had finished crying, they meant it. But still I felt stunned: twenty years old, the same age as me, and so sick of her existence that she had made the calm, considered decision to die. It gave me a few more questions to add to those already rattling around inside my head. If there was a lesson from Jan's life and death, what was it? Was it to go for it at all costs, to at least try, or was it to play safe and keep whatever you had? In the back of my mind too was a thought that I kept to myself, the thought that my mother was doing exactly the same as Jan had done, only more slowly and painfully. As some guru once said when all other words were superfluous, ain't life a bitch sometimes?

Chapter Thirty-Five

One evening I was in someone's house, one of the Crowd. In the back of my mind was the chance that Rab might be there, a small chance, but it was better than nothing. He wasn't. It was a good night though, we talked about what had happened since we had last met, then someone said,

'Oh guess what? Rab's gone to work in New York!'

'Has he?' a voice said calmly, 'Good for him!' It was my voice.

My mind whirled and my stomach churned as I fought the blankness for some means of keeping the conversation flowing. The world had just collapsed, the moon had disappeared and the sun had fallen from its orbit, and all I could think of was how I could keep talking as though everything was normal. The conversation turned to something else and somehow I managed to keep up with it. It was all thanks to the NHS training that I could act normally in the deepest of disasters, and at that moment I thanked all manner of non-existent gods for it.

Later I escaped to the toilet to lean my forehead against the cool tiles of the wall and make myself take deep, even breaths. I remembered the arguments between my mother and father when I was a child and how I had learned to divert my attention from the mayhem that was all around me. I would lie under my blankets and mentally transport myself somewhere else to drown out the voices, and I told myself that that was what I had to do now. I had to concentrate all my attention on appearing my usual self, and keep talking normally until I could leave. Then and only then, could I scream and sob, when there was no one to see me or hear me. All I wanted to do was get under those blankets and never come out again. Later, on my way home, feeling

235

empty and hollow inside, I caught sight of my reflection in a shop window and I couldn't believe how ordinary I looked. Anyone seeing me would have thought everything was fine, that the world hadn't stopped turning, that I wasn't falling apart. God, but I was good!

There was no way I could ask anyone when or why or for how long Rab had gone to America, at least not without arousing the suspicion that perhaps I gave a damn. I decided that I couldn't risk hearing the answer anyhow, so I avoided the Crowd for a while. I could admit to myself that he had gone for good, but I wasn't sure I could hear it actually said by someone else without throwing myself on the ground and howling like a kicked dog. I tried to rationalize it, to bring down the inflammation. It didn't really matter did it? Even if he had stayed at home forever he wasn't interested in me, so what possible difference could it make that he had gone thousands of miles away? He had been no more attainable at home, had he? No, but at least I could see him sometimes, talk to him. Then the awful thought occurred that he might have gone away with some woman and that the next thing I'd hear was that he was married. Well, said that infuriatingly calm, medic's voice, that was always on the cards, here or in America, so what was the fuss about? He hadn't even told me he was going, that was how important I was to him. Face facts. He had told the important members of the Crowd and hadn't given any particular thought to the kid; didn't that tell me something, if not everything? But what if I never saw him again? Well what was different, asked the voice. Everything. *Everything!*

After he'd gone I concentrated on my exams and work. The Crowd was virtually finished for me now and weekends at the loch were a thing of the past. I still occasionally saw my brothers and the others and sometimes someone would produce the latest letter from Rab and read it aloud as I tried to appear uninterested. I sneaked a look at the address on one and copied it down, calling myself every kind of fool under the sun. Even as I picked the postcard, wrote it out and then sent it off to him, I knew I was being as stupid as it was possible to be. He didn't reply, but some weeks later he mentioned in a letter to Laurie that 'Your sister sent me a postcard.' That was all. The medic's voice was growing weary of going over old ground; how many ways did the man have to spell it out? Get lost was get lost! I headed for the refuge of my blankets again and tried to transport myself somewhere else, somewhere it didn't hurt. But everywhere did . . .

I had to do something with my life I decided. It was the beginning of 1969, I was nearly twenty-one years old and I could see no future. I was stuck in the mould of the dutiful daughter and as far as my father was concerned, I was a ready-made housekeeper. At work I was a Senior Technician and had passed all my exams; I could do everything on automatic pilot. If I decided to stay I could indeed be here in thirty years time, having gone nowhere, done nothing and had no life of my own. There was marriage and motherhood of course, but that would mean settling for second best and I had never done that, never would. I had no idea what I wanted, I only knew I didn't want what I had.

The idea of going abroad started gradually. I had nowhere particular in mind, but I didn't want to go to America. And what of Nan? How could I leave her? I wrestled with the questions constantly, trying to come up with answers and not succeeding very well. There were sisters-in-law now, wasn't I due some time off, a life of my own? I knew that Nan as she had been would not have tolerated her daughter sacrificing her life, but she wasn't as she had been, she was as she was and I felt I was abandoning her. But still the feelings of frustration, of suffocation nagged at me. America was where the money was, but America was where Rab was too, and I knew myself well enough to know that if I went there I'd try to find him. That way lay humiliation and tears. Besides, I was Nan's daughter; if I went abroad I couldn't go for the money, I had to go on a crusade. I thought about Voluntary Service Overseas and wrote off without telling anyone, that way if I was rejected or decided not to go ahead with it, who would know? Then I relaxed and put it out of my mind.

Chapter Thirty-Six

Allan Forsyth was a brilliant surgeon; he was dashing, handsome and he had that gleam of danger in his sparkling eyes. He was the stuff of heroes, a devilishly dark man made to be a swashbuckling pirate, and every other doctor in the hospital hated him. He existed on research grants, an uncertain way to earn a living and one that most doctors wouldn't touch, especially one of his ability. His team wandered around the hospital dressed casually in open-necked shirts, slacks and desert boots, not for them the obligatory old school tie, the pinstriped suit and the well-polished black-leather shoes with the regulation three laceholes. They laughed a lot and showed no signs of respect and this added to the reasons why Allan Forsyth and his mob were so disliked by the ultra-conservative medical profession. Needless to say, anyone who didn't quite fit the conventional mould admired the Forsyth team, the man cried out for renegades to join him, and we cried out to sign up; it was, naturally, one of my dreams to work with him.

One wintry lunchtime I was sent to a disused theatre recovery room on the second floor and told to report to Mr Forsyth. I was walking on air, I was one of the chosen, and I longed to tell everyone I met along the way. I'd say very casually, and with a sigh that denoted a blasé manner, 'Allan Forsyth's just asked me to come along,' – if anyone asked that was, which no one did. The patient was a down-and-out who had been brought in with hypothermia and he was in cardiac arrest. It was my own unit's receiving day, so Forsyth must have been asked to take this one over, and I was in dreamland, because I was part of it.

His entire team of bright young things had been assembled and my job was to record tracings at various times and monitor the effects of what was being done to bring the patient back. There was a heat bath over the man, a metal cage lined with light bulbs to warm the body, because the heart couldn't be restarted below a certain temperature. Forsyth had opened the sternum from throat to navel and was pouring warm saline over the exposed heart; it was exciting stuff and it was happening before my star-struck young eyes. The brilliant members of his disreputable pack were doing things with fancy equipment, buzzing around the patient like so many industrious bees around a particularly luscious flower, and the room was full of people watching or helping.

A blood technician leaned across to take a sample from the patient and the man's arm pushed her, though of course he was dead. She looked up at Forsyth, who smiled below his mask so that those dangerous eyes crinkled and sparkled above. 'It's just a muscle spasm,' he laughed, and we all laughed too at the tech's reaction. Then I tried to replace an electrode that someone had moved and the patient pushed me too.

Unlike the blood technician I was used to handling arrested and newly-dead bodies and I knew this wasn't a muscle spasm; the man *had* pushed me. I remembered a paper that Dr Cunningham had insisted we all read, about a doctor who had arrested in his own hospital and afterwards was able to recount everything that had happened and what had been said by whom. The theory was that if the brain was well enough supplied with oxygen during a resus attempt, then it remained aware of events, even though the patient was unconscious and clinically dead. The black humour that we needed during life-and-death situations could, it was suggested, be heard and understood by the unfortunate patient, and Sandy Cunningham wanted us to think about that in future. In the instant that the man on the table pushed me I remembered this and I looked up at Allan Forsyth. He held my gaze for a moment and then he looked away; he didn't try to laugh and reassure me. But still, we were trying to save this man's life, weren't we? Even if we had to do unpleasant things to save him, it was worth it.

Hours passed, countless samples and readings were taken, and then suddenly Allan Forsyth called a halt, thanked everybody and swept out with his motley crew, all laden down with equipment and bits of paper. He stopped briefly by my machine, took all of my tracings, muttered his thanks and gave me one of those heartmelting smiles. I was totally bemused. What about the patient?

'Why aren't we going on?' I asked a houseman attached to Forsyth's team, and he shrugged.

'He's got all he needs,' he replied.

'What do you mean?'

'Well Allan is doing research into hypothermia at the moment . . .' he said, and left the light to penetrate my grey-matter without any further help. I had worked for hours in the hope of saving the patient, and all that time Allan Forsyth had been collecting data for his latest research project. Once the glamour of the event had cleared I realized that the patient's chances of survival had been almost neglible to start with, so Allan Forsyth had used him for his own purposes and when those had been satisfied he'd let the man die. I felt sick. I remembered the man pushing me away, and I felt sicker still. Later I discovered that the patient was being taken by a houseman and a porter to my own unit when Forsyth had come across him in the lift as he went to lunch. So he had simply pulled rank and stolen a live lump of research material, who being a down-and-out, just happened to have no interested relatives who might have asked questions. It was ideal; how could he have passed up such a gift from hell?

A few weeks later, engaged on another research project, Forsyth passed the word that he was looking for stroke victims in medical wards, the terminal, deeply unconscious cases, preferably without any troublesome relatives. Obviously impressed by my work, not to mention my devotion to him, I was one of those chosen to inform him of appropriate cases I came across. One of the old consultants, one of the less academically minded sort who simply made patients better, approached me. My admiration of Allan Forsyth was well known and the old boy didn't beat around the bush. 'You're not going to do this awful thing?' he demanded, 'You're not going to help that terrible young man are you?'

Remembering the man in the recovery room I replied that I had absolutely no intention of helping Forsyth.

'Good Meggie,' he replied, 'I know he's attractive to females, though God knows why, but he isn't at all a nice man.' He patted my shoulder and started to move off, then he stopped and said, 'And another thing, I wish you wouldn't wear trousers in the ward you know. It quite makes my day to see the odd inch of black lace under a white uniform as you bend over a bed!'

A few days later he caught me in the ward again.

'Has Forsyth been in touch with you?' he asked.

'No.'

'Well he spoke to me and I told him I wasn't taking part in his gruesome experiments and neither were you,' he said angrily, 'And d'you know what the jumped-up little bastard said to me? Said we were holding medical research back for decades!'

The thing was, he was undoubtedly correct, we were. But I still feel sick when I remember the patient who pushed me away when he was dead. Not surprisingly there was no longer any possibility of my joining Allan Forsyth's team after that, they had changed from free-wheeling swashbucklers to tacky, cynical quacks in my mind. It added to my growing disenchantment about everything around me and strengthened my need to get away.

Funnily enough, I saw Allan Forsyth on TV recently. He's Sir Allan now of course, an important, influential man, and how could anyone ever have doubted he would be some day? The dark hair is edged with grey now and he is possibly more handsome than he was as a young man, and that gleam in his eyes that I once found so irresistible, remains strong and bright. He has a long list of letters after his name now and an even longer list of achievements and is universally admired and feted. Gone are the days when he had to steal patients or ask for favours. And I wouldn't dream of letting him near any of my family.

★ ★ ★

The letter from VSO invited me to an interview in Edinburgh in March. All I knew about the organization was that it had been set up to provide help for the Third World by providing professionals who would train people to work in their own countries. It pre-dated the Peace Corps, which being American naturally got all the publicity. For spending one or two years on a specific project the payment was board and lodging and the local equivalent of £3 per week. Sounded just my thing. Other people with my qualifications could clean up financially in the developed world as well as the Third World, but if there wasn't a whiff of doing good and *not* making big money about it, I couldn't be interested, could I?

The day before the interview, which I hadn't mentioned to anyone, I got a cardiac arrest call from one of the operating theatres. The average surgical response to any and everything is to grab a scalpel and cut, and so it had always been in surgical arrests. Patients who could have been brought back using external cardiac massage were invariably opened up, the heart grabbed and manually pumped and the whole unfortunate episode complicated by the introduction of major surgery. There had even been cases of patients dying from the unnecessary surgery rather than whatever had ailed them, and we dreaded a call from a surgical unit, because it inevitably meant they had done the damage and had now run out of ideas.

Usually we would arrive to find the patient in the latter stages of rigor mortis, having been subjected to perhaps an hour of surgical 'help' and so dead that Jesus on a good day couldn't raise him. The surgeons would then say that calling the medical cardiac arrest team was a waste of time, they'd called them the other day and they were useless. So I was very pleasantly surprised this time to find the patient lying on the table, untouched by surgical hand, having gone just as the anaesthetist put him under. I ran through a series of tests and found the heart beating normally, so as befits a medic in the position of putting down the surgeons, I hammed it up. The odd breathing problem isn't unheard of as a patient goes under, together with a slight disturbance in heart rhythm, and usually the anaesthetist stops for a minute, puts in some oxygen until the patient stabilizes and then the operation can continue. In this case though the anaesthetist had played it cautiously. Perhaps he didn't really want to do the op I mused, maybe he had a date to play golf and was calling foul to make sure he got there in time.

'Well there you are chaps, a perfectly normal heartbeat,' I said grandly, 'Don't blame yourselves, could happen to anyone, and you *are* just surgeons after all. How could you be expected to know anything about a difficult subject like whether or not the patient was alive? This is medicine after all, not some knife and fork job!' It was standard procedure for us to put the surgeons down as it was for them to put medics down. All the same, they were being very submissive about it, you could usually count on some opposition, some vengeance at least. I had taken the electrodes off and was heading for the door.

'And don't hesitate to call if you're ever in difficulty again,' I said, 'You know we don't mind helping you lads out, even if it is a waste of our valuable time.' I always had to gild the lily.

'Mmm, Meggie,' said the anaesthetist, 'I'm very worried about this patient.' He looked it, as he leaned against the tiled wall, idly reading his paper. 'I think if you don't mind, I'd prefer you to stay for the operation. In case he goes again, and we can't handle it.'

The two surgeons sniggered. It was my own fault, entirely my own fault. I should have quit while I was ahead, several sarcastic insults ago.

It was an exploratory stomach operation and the finding was gangrenous colon. The smell of gangrenous colon is beyond anything dreamed up by the Hammer House of Horror. There is nothing I can think of that even approaches the stench. It clings to you, smears itself over your respiratory system and hooks into every crevice; it is so thick and strong that you can almost see it and feel it. So bad was it that one surgeon worked for fifteen minutes alone, while the other one had fifteen minutes outside, breathing real, beautiful air. The anaesthetist suggested the same arrangement with me and we tried it once, but the shock of coming back in again convinced me to stay put throughout. Sixteen feet of reddish-purple intestine, together with its putrefying contents, was removed, but I still hadn't suffered enough. The theatre orderly put it in a plastic basin which he then took great pleasure in placing on top of my machine. It lay there, inches from my nose, glistening horribly with slime, the fumes rising from it.

'There y'are Meg,' he said, 'Some link sausages for your tea!'

Medical honour, as well as my own, was at stake. I swirled a finger in the awful brew and said casually, 'No thanks, I prefer the sliced variety myself!' Everybody laughed. Slowly I dismantled my equipment from the patient, whose heart and breathing hadn't faltered throughout, and took my time over labelling the tracings. Then I sauntered out of the theatre, singing to myself as I went. 'Oh Meggie!' came the anaesthetist's voice as I left, 'You handled that so well that we'll be sure to call you whenever we have trouble again!'

'Anytime chaps!' I replied, 'I know how often surgeons get into trouble. It's so refreshing to meet the odd one or two prepared to admit it!' They all laughed again.

Down the long corridor to the lift I went, pushing my machine ahead of me, still singing – you never knew what deceitful surgeons might still be watching. Into the lift and down to my own department. Still singing. As soon as the door closed I grabbed a large bottle of Lysol and scrubbed the finger that had swirled so nonchalantly through the feet of revolting colon, then I scrubbed the entire hand and then the arm. Finally I went upstairs, had a shower, brushed my teeth, sprayed myself with enough perfume to give a tart's boudoir a bad name and finally changed my clothes before I felt clean. It was standard procedure to keep a change of clothes in your locker, because you never knew what would happen, from a patient being sick over you to being thrown into a bath of cold water by some idiot houseman, but I had never been so glad of it as I was then.

At the VSO interview next day I was faced with a panel of three people, an elderly man, a middle-aged woman and a tanned young man. I have always liked interviews and never feel nervous, which probably says a great deal about me that doesn't bear closer investigation. This one was par for the course. I didn't desperately need them to accept me and to be honest I was finding out as much about them as they were about me; it was entirely possible that I could turn them down and go looking for the big money instead. Then the tanned young man put his foot in it.

'I wonder if you have any idea of the kind of smells you can get in an African hospital,' he said in a very superior tone of voice. He was a VSO himself and obviously knew it all. 'I mean they do differ considerably from the antiseptic smells you are used to, I just wonder if you could take it.'

'Listen chum,' I said, 'Have you ever been inches away from a gangrenous colon?' He shook his head.

'Have you had any experience whatsoever of gangrenous colon, even from a very great distance?' He shook his head again.

'Well until you have, don't bother me with your African hospital smells, because I can guarantee that they just don't begin to compete!' That showed the little twerp! I seemed to have this way with interview panels, I thought as I went out, I kind of grabbed them by the scruff of the neck and threw them around my head a bit. Oh well, nothing lost really.

A week later the letter arrived saying if my references checked out I would be accepted and would then undergo courses in tropical medicine. I really was going abroad. Now all I had to do was tell Sandy Cunningham that he was giving me a reference.

And Nan of course, I had to tell Nan . . .

Chapter Thirty-Seven

Norah was the only one of my father's family still alive. She was a tiny lady, certainly under five-feet tall, and by now into her seventies, but she kept in touch, visiting the Barracks on the odd Sunday. She sometimes came with her husband, Uncle Harry, a tall, quiet, straightforward soul whom she'd run rings around for nearly fifty years. The hats for which she was famous were still very much in evidence, and the deceit for which she was infamous was still there too. Behind the latest millinery creation lurked a mind sharp enough to cut unsuspecting victims to the bone, not that this let those of us with well-founded suspicions off the hook.

I had at that time a collection of blouses in every material, colour and design, and much of her efforts were directed at getting her hands on as many as possible. This one was for a very sick friend, that one would suit her daughter so well, the daughter who'd had such a bad time lately. Not that her daughter knew she was being used for the pitch nor would she ever set eyes on the blouse – other than on Norah's back. She never came empty-handed of course, I was always offered a pair of shoes that didn't fit, suit or interest me, or some awful pair of earrings she had doubtless conned out of some other defenceless individual.

Hughie, her main adversary was dead and gone, in the flesh at least. Doors and windows still opened but it was difficult to compete for points unless he actually made an appearance, and so far he had decided to win his points while invisible – cheating though it undoubtedly was. Jim was off looking for good, honest, non-violent crime to commit, on one side of the great divide or another, though Norah, the great mystic of seances and teacups, always insisted that she 'felt' Jim was still alive. While he was otherwise engaged he wasn't around to provide her with entertainment, so the nonsense with the blouses was mostly a diversion for her. I at least knew the basic rules of the Game, and even if we both knew I could never seriously hope to win the points, the tantalizing prospect of a lucky draw forever hung in the air between us to amuse her. Her acting talents were still prodigious, so I was never really sure if she'd had the three heart attacks she laid claim to, chiefly when negotiations for the latest blouse were going against her. A hand would go to her chest and a pained expression would take up residence across her features, together with an earnest entreaty 'No' tae worry aboot me hen . . .'

Then one Sunday she seemed to be in real pain that didn't even respond to the lashings of brandy that usually did the trick. My mistake was to take this seriously, because once I had she lost all sense of reality and the theatrical performance took over. I phoned the hospital, arranged for the receiving physician to see her and took her, Uncle Harry and my father down by taxi. By this time she was in danger of having a heart attack from the fear of having a heart attack, so I ran the tests myself; her latest hat remained firmly on her head throughout. Her heart was as strong as an extremely robust ox, there wasn't the slightest sign of any of the three previous attacks, and all that ailed her was indigestion. She carried this news off beautifully by simply ignoring it, and informing one and all that this attack had been every bit as severe as her other three. The medicine given to her by the doctor, a common antacid available over the chemist shop counter, she hailed as a wonder drug, and that was that.

While we were waiting for a taxi to take her and her husband home, I opened up the cardiology department and made them coffee. I wasn't aware of having created any impression until I realized that Norah and Uncle Harry were looking at me with a certain awe. Then I saw what they were seeing: their niece with all this clout, having access to this impressive looking world of technology, being on first name terms with the godlike doctors – it far surpassed any interest my latest blouse might have aroused a few hours earlier. Then I looked at my father, who sat sipping his coffee beside them. He was completely unaware of all the things that had impressed his sister, and the contrast was startling. The thought popped into my mind that perhaps he should have been more impressed than Norah, and that if I had been Mickey instead he would have been beside himself with pride. I wasn't aware of competing with Mickey, but I did have a sudden insight into how difficult it must all have been for Laurie, who was in the same category as myself; the one marked 'Not Mickey'. We would never match up: no matter what we achieved we would forever remain in the 'Not Mickey' section. The thought made me smile to myself, but it also made me feel sadder for Laurie than I had ever felt; he was a male after all and throughout his life he had tried in all sorts of ways to matter to my father. In that moment I knew it had all been useless and always would be, yet I also knew it wouldn't stop Laurie from trying. Laurie was like one of the Clark 'Dark Yins', forever trying to win affection from a parent incapable of giving it and without realizing that it wasn't worth much even if it had been forthcoming. Laurie was always much more of a Clark; if only he could see the true value in that.

The following week Norah turned up again and brought me a pair of nylons. By this time every female I knew was wearing tights, but I appreciated the trouble she had gone to and wondered who had been conned out of the stockings for my benefit. She left with my best blouse. Well, what could I do? She had now suffered four heart attacks and I thought a little kindness was in order. It was the nearest I ever came to that lucky draw with her and I didn't have the heart to go for it. That's what distinguishes the truly great Game players from the second leaguers like me; being able to go for the kill!

Sandy Cunningham was sitting behind his desk when I went in.

'Chief,' I said, 'I need a reference.'

'What for? Are you leaving?' He said it as though an

affirmative answer would book me straight into a psychiatric appointment. Leave the Eastern Infirmary? Could this be the action of someone who claimed a passing acquaintance with sanity?

'I'm going abroad,' I replied.

'Where? America?'

'No, to one of the developing countries, Africa probably.'

His expression suggested that I was already speaking Swahili and his eyebrows were having problems disentangling themselves from his hairline.

'I'm going with VSO, Voluntary Service Overseas.'

'Aren't they the lot who do it for nothing? I mean you don't get any cash?'

'Well you get some, but it's voluntary, yes.'

He sat staring at me.

'There's a man in this somewhere isn't there?' he demanded, with the conviction of one who believes he's hit on the truth.

'No,' I said, 'I've just got to get out of here.'

'I knew it! There *is* a man involved! It's not that large houseman upstairs is it?' His face wrinkled with disapproval.

'There's no man, and the chap upstairs is just a pal.'

'That's not what everyone else says,' he said, 'Everybody knows he's keen. I'd hate it to be him, can't stand these religious maniacs, can't stand him!'

'You know what this place is like for rumours,' I smiled, 'It's nothing to do with the religious maniac houseman upstairs. I shouldn't be here though, I don't really belong in medicine, it just sort of happened.'

'But you're good at your job!'

'I know that,' I replied, modest as ever, 'But all I ever wanted to do was write, it's my only talent, and if I stay around here much longer I'll end up trapped for life. I've got to get away somewhere to think about what I really want to do.'

He smiled a fatherly smile. 'Oh Meggie, we all want to write when we're young! It passes! We all grow up! I could show you reams of poetry I wrote when I was still a normal human being, that would do my reputation as a bastard no good at all!'

'I'm going,' I said, 'And you must give me a decent reference.'

'OK,' he said, 'But I still say there's a man involved in this and I intend to give the religious maniac a bloody hard time on principle.'

'Another thing Chief, could you keep it very quiet? I don't know where or when I'm going yet, I don't want to talk about it to everybody for months and months.'

'You know me,' he smiled his determined smile, 'The soul of discretion! Not a word!'

As I was leaving he called me back and pointed to a calendar on the wall. It was the kind the drugs companies put out, filthy or funny for the younger doctors, pseudo-arty for the older ones like Sandy Cunningham.

'Is that the Pope?' he asked.

I looked at the title underneath. 'It says the Doge.'

'Yes, but is it really the Pope?'

'Why would it say the Doge if it was the Pope?' I demanded, 'And why are you asking me anyway? I wouldn't recognize the Pope if I fell over him in Casualty!'

'Yes, but you'd recognize a Pope-ish look, wouldn't you? I can't bear it, the eyes follow me everywhere. If it is the Pope he could be putting the evil eye on me, don't you think?'

'It's the Doge!' I said, 'It says it's the Doge, so it's the Doge!'

'OK. Right. Fine.' He looked at it with an uncertain smile on his face then reached forward and tore off the picture. 'But just in case, I'll get rid of the ugly bugger anyway!' he said, catapulting himself a month forward. 'You see how I depend on you? Who else could help me with problems like this? You are very selfish, just going off into the wide blue yonder like this without a thought of the effect on others!'

Next was Nan. She was sitting in her usual chair by the fireside, and I started by saying that I had the chance to work abroad for a year, maybe two.

'Ye hivtae go,' she said firmly, 'Ye hivtae say ye'll go.'

'But what about you Mum? How will you manage with him? You'll be losing my money too.'

'Look hen, Ah married him,' she said, 'You didnae. A' these years Ah've been worried sick that ye'd gie up yer life tae look efter him. Ye've made somethin' o' yersel' wi' nae help frae him and no' much frae me since, since . . . Ye've no' tae throw a' that away.'

She sounded like my mother, as though the clock had been turned back years. Any minute now Peggy might walk in. I didn't know what to say.

'Ah always waantit ma weans tae see the world,' she said proudly, 'Ah waanted ye a' tae make a decent life fur yersels and no' tae grow up tae be like him. So ye've tae go hen. Don't stey away mind, come back hame sometimes, but get as faur away frae him as ye kin. If ye don't it'll a' hiv been fur nothin'. See?'

It was a conversation I was to go over in my mind all of my life, so often in fact that I memorized it. After she had retired from the world in 1959 there were times when I had blamed her for deserting me at the very age when girls need their mothers most. Yet she seemed to be saying that she had lived these last ten years to make sure that I didn't end up trapped by duty to my father as she was. It hadn't occurred to her that I might feel a sense of duty towards her, that I might stay at home because she needed me. If I hadn't been there, if she'd had no reason to go on, she might not have survived Peggy's death. Only then did I really appreciate how severe that blow had been, but there had to be more than I knew, and my resolve to find out one day was underlined in my mental notebook.

Devastating as the loss of Peggy was to all of us, and my mother in particular, there had to be another element to it that had destroyed her faith, her hopes and her belief in everything. It had shaken her to her very roots, but far from giving up, she had summoned the courage from somewhere to hang on until the moment when I decided to leave the nest. I remembered how upset I had been as a child when I realized that I would never fly like a bird; maybe that had prepared her for the day when I would spread my wings in one way or another. I'd been dreading telling her, but she was quite delighted; it had made her effort worthwhile.

The entire hospital knew; everywhere I went someone wanted to talk to me about going abroad. Sandy Cunningham had obviously thought the whole thing over and decided that my going reflected some sort of glory on him, and he made a point of touring the hospital and telling staff and patients alike. It was quite a let down when I told them I had no idea when I was going and no idea where. Then slowly and thankfully life returned to normal.

In July 1969 Neil Armstrong became the first man to set foot on the moon. I watched it live on TV in the early hours of the morning, wrapped in a sleeping-bag, with chicken sandwiches and a flask of coffee beside me, as Armstrong took his giant leap for mankind. At the same time Rab was doubtless watching it in New York and when the tickertape parade was held to welcome the astronauts home, he would probably be in the crowd. Rab was rarely mentioned these days, the Crowd had become used to the fact that he'd gone, and I couldn't ask.

Hospital life was full of ordinary days that were jam-packed with tedium. To the patients we were admitting, every day was a personal crisis, but even crises can be handled on automatic pilot; I needed something to do. One day the cardiac arrest bleeper sounded and announced 'Cardiac Arrest, Orthopaedic Theatre,' and all over the hospital, crash team members wondered if it was April 1st, then yelled into their bleepers 'Are you sure?'

The Ortho Theatre and wards were only yards along the corridor from our department, but we rarely saw the Orthopods. They just got on with whatever it was they did with bones and things and left the rest of us to get on with real medicine. We passed them in the corridors or in the canteen, friendly, smiling faces that we didn't know well because we had never worked with them. As we hadn't worked with them we therefore hadn't fought with them, so they remained friendly, smiling faces. The

Orthopods were so far removed from mainstream hospital life that they weren't quoted on the gossip hotline.

The theatre block housed identical operating theatres on every floor, one directly above the other, and so the Ortho one wasn't really different, it just felt different because we had never been in it before. And there were the friendly, smiling Orthopods, standing back from the patient on the table to let us get at him. Usually there were so many hands eager to help and getting in the way that harsh words had to be spoken, but the good old Orthopods weren't to know that. And the patient was cooperative too. Our success rate was very low; the real world wasn't a bit like those impressive TV soaps where with one dramatic shock the patient immediately gets up and starts raising money for hospital equipment. But this chap had obviously watched enough of those to know what was expected of him; one such dramatic shock and he was back in normal rhythm. It made us look so good, and we were all acting a shade smug, but then it was nice to be able to put on a slick show in front of the surgeons, and the Orthopods *were* surgeons, of a sort anyway. I got quite carried away and decided to run a completely unnecessary series of tracings that could have waited a couple of hours. It would look impressive in the case notes, so professional and efficient, quite unlike the usual chaos on these occasions. Then the tracing went off. It was the theatre orderly, he was fiddling with the electrodes. I had seen the old chap around and I'd often thought how typical it was of the Orthopods to keep him on at his age, but then nothing much happened in the backwaters. Still, he must have been about a hundred and of limited use to anyone else. How kind the Orthopods were not to throw the old boy on the scrap heap.

'Do you mind,' I smiled, still flushed with success, 'If you touch the electrodes the tracing goes off.'

'Sorry, I didn't realize.'

'It's OK, no problem,' I replied. Who could be angry on a day such as this? I flicked the dial back and started again, and once again the tracing went off, because Methuselah was fiddling again.

'Whatever you're doing,' I said, 'Could it wait just a few minutes please, until I get this done?' I asked, going back to zero again.

'Oops! I really am sorry!'

'No, no, not at all, don't give it another thought.' Regular members of the crash team were by now standing back in amazement; under this amount of provocation bodies had been forcibly removed in the past. But this was different, this was me under the glow of success. Then the tracing went again, and I sighed heavily and swore loudly.

'Dear me,' said the old orderly, 'I've done it again haven't I? I really am sorry!'

'You said!' I replied through gritted teeth, but before I could start once more he was at it again. The time had come for those harsh words. I leaned over the patient on the table, grabbed the orderly by the lapel of his white coat and pulled him down to my eye level.

'Listen chum,' I snarled slowly and patiently into his face, 'Your friends here made a muck-up of this patient, and we had to come in to sort it out. Now until we hand him back so that you can trim his toenails or what-ever it is you pass your time doing in this dump, we are in charge, and what I'm doing is infinitely more important than whatever the hell you think you're doing. So if you even think of touching those electrodes again there will be two small, spherical objects bouncing around on the floor, and you'll be singing falsetto! Do I make myself clear?'

There was a sharp intake of breath all round the theatre. They were such a pleasant bunch the Orthopods, they had probably never heard harsh words spoken before; they didn't live in the real world like we did.

'Yes, oh yes,' the orderly said, 'Crystal-clear!' and then he did the decent thing and left.

An hour later, with our cooperatively alive patient safely installed in coronary care, I wandered back to the depart-ment to be told that Dr Cunningham wanted to see me. Congratulations coming my way!

'Come in Meg,' he grinned, 'There's someone here you

should meet.' It was the Ortho orderly, no doubt sent over by his chief to apologize.

'No need for apologies,' I told him grandly, 'Just remember to keep out of the way in an emergency in future.'

'Meet,' said my Sandy Cunningham, 'The Professor of Orthopaedics.' Orthopaedics *had* a Professor? Well they said that attack was the best method of defence, I only hoped 'they' were right.

'In that case he *should* apologize!' I said, 'Even a Professor of Orthopaedics should know that when you call in the pros you stand back and let them get on with it instead of getting in the way!' I'd just seen the film 'M*A*S*H', and I'd lifted the dialogue straight from Trapper John. They looked remarkably like fish, sitting there with their mouths hanging open as I headed smartly for the door.

Then I went to the toilet, switched out the light and did some serious cringeing in the dark for half an hour. How was I to know? Who would ever have dreamed that there was an Orthopod Professor? And he did mess around with the electrodes, didn't he? And for all he knew he could've been doing some serious damage, couldn't he? So it was all his own fault, wasn't it? He thoroughly deserved to be totally humiliated . . . in front of his entire staff . . . by someone young enough to be his grand-daughter . . . didn't he . . . ?

Later I saw Dr Cunningham again. 'I suppose the silly old sod is going to have me shot?' I asked.

'No,' he replied, 'What he actually said, and I quote, was "God, if I were only fifty years younger I'd bed that wild young thing! What a woman!" The silly old sod is in love, and you live a charmed life if I may say so.'

Whenever I saw the Orthopod Professor after that he leered at me, licked his lips and blew kisses, loudly exhorting his team to prove they were real men by bedding 'that wild young thing' and telling everyone in earshot exactly what he would've done in his youth. 'You'd have the best sex of your life!' he'd roar, 'Trying to tame that one!' I blushed to the roots of my toenails at every encounter, and the rest of the hospital enjoyed themselves by whistling 'Wild Thing' whenever I was around. It followed me down corridors, in the lifts, the operating theatres and in the wards, and to this day, whenever I hear that song on the radio I hide my head and blush scarlet.

I never did find out if the Orthopod Professor meant it, or if he had some O'Brien blood coursing through his body and had found the perfect way of paying me back. But he succeeded in putting Orthopaedics on the gossip hotline for the first time in living memory and he certainly won all the points. No question.

Skip came home one Saturday afternoon, in his usual state, and announced that he was going to bed. He had met a friend who was coming later to collect him for another drinking session and naturally he wanted to be fresh for the event. The friend was Jim McAvoy. Nan and I exchanged looks of anger and disgust. It was as low as Skip could stoop; we knew he'd drink with anyone, but McAvoy wasn't counted as among the human race. He was actually expecting us to invite him into the house and be sociable to him!

Silly man. Whenever Skip slept off the booze he heard nothing, it was like a mini-coma, so he didn't hear McAvoy hammering on the door a few hours later. Nan and I walked past it, making no attempt to hide the fact that we heard him and were ignoring him; at one point he even looked through the letter-box and shouted to be let in. We ended up laughing so much that we could hardly stand, and clung to each other for support.

When Skip got up he fretted about McAvoy's non-appearance as we fought to keep straight faces, and eventually, with good drinking time passing, he went out again. He came back hours later freshly reinebriated and with McAvoy, but I got to the door in time to push his 'friend' out again and lock the door behind Skip. He drew himself up to his full five-foot-one-inches and tried to act out the master of the house routine. This was his house apparently and he'd say who came in, then he ruined it all by being too drunk to negotiate the opening of the door. Nan sat in her chair, weeping with laughter.

'Jim tellt me he looked through the letter boax an' ye baith ignored him!' he yelled, plainly aghast that such deceit could exist within his own family. McAvoy listened outside the door.

'He's bloody lucky we did ignore him! My Uncle George wouldn't have ignored him!' I replied for McAvoy's benefit, 'We remember the life he gave Peggy! Ask your wee pal if he remembers someone called Peggy. Dark-haired, attractive, a pleasant woman, too good for him! Ask him if that rings any bells.'

'Ah invited him as a guest! You apologize tae Jim!'

'He's a rat! And you only get in because you're married to my mother, otherwise the embargo would apply to you too!'

'Ye think yur sum'dy!' he screeched pathetically, falling back on the old insult that no doubt he and McAvoy had been discussing all night in whatever pub they had met up in. But it awakened something in Nan.

'Aye, ye're right,' she said savagely, 'Thur's mair Clark in hur than O'Brien, she *is* sum'dy!'

Eventually McAvoy gave up and went away and Skip yelled himself to sleep like the baby he was, but it was a kind of turning point. Instead of trying to placate him for the sake of peace we had laughed at him, and he hadn't known how to deal with that. It gave Nan some form of upper hand for the first time in many years and I began to believe that she could cope while I wasn't there. It was a new low for Skip in my eyes though, I was disgusted that he'd have anything to do with McAvoy and the thought that we'd have him in the house was beyond belief.

Later, out of the blue, Nan said quietly, 'Dae ye remember Peggy?' It must have been triggered by my jibe at McAvoy earlier. She really didn't think I had forgotten her, it was simply the only way she could manage to bring up Peggy's name after having avoided it for so long.

'Of course I remember her Mum!' I replied, 'It's like it was yesterday! I could never forget Peggy!'

'That's good,' she said, 'The three o' us wur good pals, wurn't we?'

'It was like we were one Mum, the three of us were so close.'

She nodded. 'It's no' the same withoot hur,' she said, 'Ah jist feel kinda . . .' The words ran out. It was the first time she had ever talked about Peggy and I held my breath, hoping she'd go on.

'Like a part of you is missing,' I said, 'And a part of me too.'

'Aye,' she said, 'That's it. Missin'. Dae you feel like that tae?'

'All the time. I've felt like that ever since. Sometimes I feel as if I'm still looking for her, though I know I won't find her.'

'Dae ye think there's another life efter this wan?'

'And we'll all meet up again? No, I wish it could be true. Sometimes I'd do anything to see her again, I can't believe she's really gone.'

'It's jist that sometimes Ah wake up in the middle o' the night, an' Ah'm sure Ah've heard hur sayin' ma name. Ah aye heard her sayin' "Nan" when sumthin' was happenin', it wis like that a' oor lives.'

'I remember,' I smiled, 'The two of you didn't need to talk.'

'A' they months while she wis expectin' the last wean, Ah kept hearin' her sayin' "Nan". An' a' that Seterday, Ah heard it tae, an' Ah knew she wis hivin' the wean. Then it stoaped, an' Ah knew . . . Bit noo I still think Ah hear hur, an' sometimes during the day Ah get this feelin' that she's there. Y'know, right there beside me. Dis that sound like Ah'm daft?'

'Of course you're not daft!' I said, 'You're just keeping her alive in your mind, same as I am. I can't really believe she's not there any longer either. Peggy was always there . . .'

My mind was working frantically, making sense of the memories of those months when Nan couldn't sleep. She was hearing Peggy calling for help, and that was normal for them, it worked both ways. Only when she rushed to Peggy's side there seemed to be nothing happening. But there was something happening, of course, and the prophetic dreams had tried to sound the warning that Nan didn't want to hear, so by morning she had converted them into funny stories.

But she hadn't fooled herself, and she hadn't fooled me, either. I had known something was wrong, even if I couldn't put my finger on it. While she spoke I was hoping Nan might say something about how Peggy had died, but I had a feeling that if I asked questions she wouldn't be able to carry on. Each word came out sounding fragile, as though the slightest pressure could blow them all away forever. There was a silence and then she said, 'Dae ye mind that seance Norah made me go tae? The wan where the man said Da Clark hid a warnin' for us? Ah've aye thoaght Ah shoulda went back tae see him.'

'You don't believe that do you?' I asked, 'If Da had a warning about Peggy he wouldn't have needed some stranger to pass it on, would he? And how would Da have known? We were the closest to Peggy, and we couldn't stop it happening, could we?'

'Ah wis wearin' that green coat that night,' she said, 'Ah couldnae wear it again efter. Ah shoulda burned that green coat . . .'

'No Mum,' I replied, 'We should've burned McAvoy! Or better still, we should've burned McAvoy's old man, just to make sure!' She laughed, but then she said sadly, 'Still, Ah shouldnae hiv let her hiv that green coat . . .' Ten years on and still all that longing and 'if onlys'. All that pain and misplaced guilt. She never spoke of the events leading up to Peggy's death again, and I never asked because I knew she couldn't tell me whatever was still hidden. I was convinced that there was more to the story though and one day I had to know it all.

The news came at the end of August; I wasn't going to Africa, I was going to India. The hospital I was being sent to was in the former French Protectorate of Pondicherry, just outside Madras in the south of the country. In the Sixties France had been trying to get rid of its empire and had built a huge complex in Pondicherry along the lines of an American campus. The hospital, called the Jawaharlal Institute of Post-Graduate Medical Education and Research, JIPMER for short, had its own staff accommodation, post office, school, shops and snake-catcher. What it didn't have was trained staff, and I was to train a technical team to run their own department. I had been expecting Africa probably because of the sun-tanned young man who had challenged my ability to cope with African hospital smells. India was more exciting, and I would leave on 30th November, St Andrew's Day.

The months between would be filled having vaccinations for smallpox, cholera and all manner of other nasties, and at least I didn't have to pay any doctor a professional fee for wielding the hypodermic; they were fighting each other for the chance. I also had to assemble a completely new all-cotton wardrobe for the different climate. I was going in the Indian winter, but compared with a blisteringly good Scottish summer it would still be tropical. Sandy Cunningham bustled around taking an interest in every detail, reading books on India and passing on information and generally taking charge whether I let him or not. Having come to the conclusion that my wonderful altruism was really a feather in his cap, he had ensured that not only the hospital but the entire medical world knew all about the great adventure too. He arranged for me to go to London, to watch advanced cardiac surgery at Guy's Hospital, where unfortunately neither patient made it off the table. Well at least it laid to rest the myth of London superiority.

Next were the farewell parties, which worked out about one a week at the hospital. At each one Sandy Cunningham got up and gave an emotional speech about how the Scots were seasoned globe-trotters, and how I was following in a great tradition. This took him, for some reason, onto the disproportionate number of island fishermen who had died during the last War protecting shipping convoys, men who were never recognized as the heroes they were. For that reason I should avoid Germans at all costs, and the English, which went without saying, even if he did say it anyway. Foreign travel was clearly a wonderful thing, as long as the foreigners were weeded out of the experience.

The Crowd had to have a ceilidh too, any excuse was seized on for a ceilidh now that most of them had settled down with wives, children and mortgages. The invitations were individually written in as near copperplate script as I managed to learn in the time available, and put in language meant to suggest the Raj.

'You haven't done one for Rab,' someone said, going over the list with me.

'I hardly think he'll come all the way back from America!'

'He's back. He only went over for a year.'

'OK, I'll do one for him,' I replied, in that calm, casual voice, though my heart was thumping like, well, like a wild thing.

The excitement was short-lived though, because that cold, analytical voice in my head quickly reminded me that even if he was back, he'd hardly gone out of his way to let me know. Nothing had changed. He went without bothering to tell me and he'd come back the same way; it remained a pointless business. But I could still see him sometimes, I thought. With his wife, probably, the voice suggested. That was something I really couldn't face. Imagine bumping into him and him saying 'This is my wife . . .' It would certainly happen sometime soon, if it hadn't happened already, and I didn't want to be around when it did. I wrote out another invitation and sent it off to him, because he was one of the Crowd and it would have looked odd if I hadn't.

Nan seemed to have a new lease of life. There was no miraculous transformation, but she was taking notice of everything that was happening, inspecting all the new clothes for the tropics and talking more than she had in years. I was playing it all down a bit though, I didn't want my leaving to be a great big event. I still had work to go to and time to fill before I left, so a fever pitch of excitement would have been hard to sustain.

The ceilidh was set for the Saturday before I left, to give those attending all of Sunday to recover. I opened the door to the first arrival; it was Rab. The medical report given by some nervous houseman would have been, 'Please Sir, the patient's heart leapt clean out of her thorax and it was last seen dancing on the ceiling, singing "Happy Days are Here Again" . . . I fear the patient's condition is hopeless.'

'Oh,' I said, 'It's you, the Yank.'

'An' it's you,' he replied, 'The ratbag. Ah need tae get some booze, ye'd better grab yer coat an' come wi' me an' show me the nearest boozer.'

It was the first time I'd been alone with the man in years, since the time he had taken his jacket off and walked with me through the rain when I was no more than a child. Now I was sitting across a pub table from him, drinking coke and fending off insults.

'Ah'm embarrassin' ye, go oan, admit it,' he grinned.

'I admit it,' I replied, 'It's like being with neanderthal man.'

'Good,' he winked, 'Ah've never met the bloke, but he must be a stoatir if he's like me. Ah love tae embarrass ratbags!'

When we got back the ceilidh was in full swing; the Crowd didn't stand on ceremony, it didn't matter to them that the hostess wasn't even there. Rab disappeared into the throng and I got caught up in a sing-song somewhere else. When the first wave retired to sleeping-bags on the floor upstairs, another wave arrived and took over, and so it went on all night. At one point Rab demanded that a woman be brought to him, to shouts of derision all round about who would take him. Well at least that proved there was no Mrs Rab on the horizon.

'I hear you're looking for a woman,' I said.

'But no' a ratbag,' he replied, and was once again lost in the Crowd. Arguments that had lain dormant since the last time we were all together were resurrected and re-argued, and songs were sung without the aid of a campfire, until the call was heard, 'Goodnight Rab!' Rab couldn't drink a lot of whisky, in fact after one glass his eyes gleamed and his banter scintillated for an hour or so and then he fell asleep. This was common knowledge and the Crowd waited for the moment at each gathering and yelled out in unison as he dropped off where he was or crept off in search of his sleeping-bag.

Slowly the night drew to a temporary lull and I lay down beside Denis, who also came from Drumchapel. He had a well-earned reputation for being a stud, but I had grown up knowing him and considered him to be nearly a brother. Much to my surprise, as I lay down beside him he grabbed me and instantly launched into a love scene from *The Thomas Crown Affair*, a film that was all the rage at the time. He had cast himself as Steve McQueen and I was Faye Dunaway apparently, or I would have been if I hadn't laughed. I got up and went upstairs, smiling wryly to myself. Sod's Law again. The only man I wanted had gone to America, which was at least partly responsible for my going to India. Only he had come back and I was still committed to going. The only man I wanted was lying snoring in a sleeping-bag in front of me, while one I didn't want was grabbing at me. I aimed a kick at the sleeping figure and muttered 'Sod you Rab!' He stirred mid-snore, turned onto his side and resumed snoring where he had left off. I lay down beside him; I wouldn't be able to say I had slept with him of course, but I figured it was as near as I was ever likely to get. Downstairs someone woke, started singing and the ceilidh swung into another phase. I stayed where I was.

The Crowd began to disperse around lunchtime. Rab didn't know where to get a bus home so I volunteered to show him; to my annoyance a few of the others came too, 'for a breath of air'. On the way nothing of note was discussed, and as Rab boarded his bus he said to me 'Well cheerio. Remember to write, and don't gobble too much rice!' If Humphrey Bogart had had that little to say to Ingrid Bergman, *Casablanca* wouldn't have been worth making; as romantic farewells went it didn't exactly rank way up there with the best. But then it wasn't a romantic farewell, was it?

Chapter Thirty-Eight

It was my last week in the hospital. While I had been at the ceilidh one of the surgical housemen had attempted to murder a patient; it was the talk of the place, and no one could talk about it without laughing, of course. It was not just any houseman, but John Alexander, one of the pleasantest, easiest to work with chaps in the history of the sub-species. I had known him as a medical student and as a medical houseman before he had gone on to do his six months with the surgeons, which admittedly could turn anyone into Frankenstein's monster.

John had been on casualty duty, the worst ordeal anyone can ever undergo, and apparently it had been a particularly bad go. His wife had given birth to their first child the day before and John hadn't managed to see her or their son yet. He had been awake for over twenty-four hours, then he had been presented with a Chinese cook whose brother had tapped him on the head with a knife in the family restaurant. The knife was sticking out of the cook's head and all he wanted to do was kill the brother who had put it there. The knife didn't seem to be bothering him, but the reason for the argument, that he kept a dirty kitchen, still did. So while John had been trying to deal with the kind of injury he had only encountered before in his worst nightmares, the injured man was trying to get at his brother. At one point he had succeeded and the two Chinamen were wrestling on the floor, and John could see his career disappearing before his very eyes. It wasn't every doctor who lost a patient by allowing him to scramble about the floor with a knife imbedded in his skull, after all.

He had just finished dealing with that when the next one arrived, a pleasant, calm little man in his late forties, with

264

a fireside poker sticking out of his chest. John's weary eyes watched in horror as the poker jumped in time with the man's heart-beat, and he listened as the history unfolded. The little man was a bachelor who lived with his mother, and as they had been watching TV together he had stirred the fire with the poker and then left it in the coals. When it was glowing red-hot, he had lifted it out and plunged it into his chest, so that as John could plainly see, it had come to rest against his heart. The patient was clearly feeling no pain and was polite and helpful. John then made the fatal mistake, he asked why he'd done it. The little man replied amiably, 'It seemed a good idea at the time.' No one could do anything other than sympathize with young Dr Alexander; it had been a tough year, a tough twenty-four hours in particular and of course there had been all the anxiety leading up to the birth of the son he had yet to see. The fates had clearly conspired to get at him and it was little wonder that he felt off form. The first the rest of the casualty staff knew that there was a problem was when they heard a kind of gurgling sound behind the screens, and when a curious nurse looked she found nice, pleasant John Alexander with his hands around his patient's throat. John had had enough, he had flipped and it took three of them to prise his fingers off the man's windpipe.

I saw the patient a few days later. He had inflicted a serious injury on himself, or rather, series of injuries. First of all he had a neat hole burned through his chest, through which you could watch his heart beating; that would clearly need a few goes of plastic surgery to close up. He had also inflicted a burn on the outer surface of his heart that would leave a scar similar to a heart attack, and there he sat in bed, courteous, smiling, grateful for whatever was done for him. Happily the slight bruising around his throat was fading. I was tempted to ask John Alexander's question – it seemed such a totally demented way to kill oneself – but I wasn't at all sure that I trusted myself to refrain from John's solution if the little man gave me the same reply; so I didn't.

If Indian medicine could top this, I'd be very surprised.

* * *

On my last day at the hospital I was asked to see a patient called McGettigan, a man in his early sixties. I knew little about him except that it was a routine check, there was nothing wrong with his heart. Was he, I wondered, any relation to a Betty McGettigan who was a teacher? Yes, she was his wife. Did she teach at the Marian school many years ago? Yes, she did. Before I left the ward I asked the houseman what was wrong with the patient.

'It's the nervous system,' he said, 'Incurable I'm afraid. We've just told the family.' He screwed up his face and shook his head, it was a rotten part of the job. Losing patients was bad enough, but telling their relatives we'd lost them was worse. As I left I saw them sitting outside the ward, Mrs McGettigan and her two daughters, their heads close together, deep in conversation. Her hair was as I remembered it, swept back with a deep wave on either side framing her face, and caught in a French roll at the back of her head. It was exactly the same, only now it was pure white. I stood at the lift watching her with her daughters, tempted to go up to her and talk, but there is a time and place and now wasn't the right one for a reunion with a former pupil. What could I have said anyway?

'Hello, I know you've just had devastating news about your husband, but guess who I am?' It seemed strange to be close to her and not to talk to her, but if I'm honest there was also a feeling of relief. I should be writing; she'd always said so. 'One day you'll see her words in print,' she'd told the others on the last day of the Marian school. Yes, I knew she needed time with her family right then, but another factor was that I really didn't want her to know I was working in medicine. If I had any nagging doubts about going away, seeing her settled them somewhat.

It was 30th November, 5 a.m., time to go. There were no emotional goodbyes as I left the house in the early morning darkness for Glasgow Airport. My father had got up for some reason to see me off and as I turned to go he made a movement that suggested he might be about to hug me. He couldn't do it though, it wasn't in the man to show emotion, if that was what he was thinking of. Instead he patted my shoulder, which made me smile; the truth was that I couldn't have taken a hug from him anyway, it was years too late for that. As I closed the front door I heard Nan's voice coming from her bedroom, 'Cheerio hen, hiv a good time.' I might have been going for a night out. I knew even then that I would regret for the rest of my life not telling her all those things we all leave unsaid until it is too late, but all I said was 'Bye Mum.'

Peter, Paul and Mary were singing 'I'm Leaving on a Jet Plane' as the shuttle took off for London; I made a mental note to one day find that record and jump up and down on it, for threatening my stiff upper lip.

Glasgow is a corruption of a Gaelic word meaning 'dear green place', and from the air a surprising amount of greenery was still visible. My mind was in turmoil as I watched it fall away below me, all my doubts had returned and they now seemed like sound sense. What was I doing? Was I running away from all the parts of my life that didn't work rather than sort them out? Rab was down there somewhere, unaware and uninterested, but that was a fact I would always have to live with, so how did going off to India help that? Nan was down there, and Peggy too, buried with all sorts of questions I wouldn't find the answers to in India. Just what did I think I was doing? Nan had spent her entire life, and mine, searching for Utopia; it was just over that far-off hill, just beyond the next house move. Perhaps I was doing the same, taking on Nan's quest without really thinking it through. Whose search was I going on and just what did I think I was doing?

I didn't realize it at the time, but as I flew off from Glasgow on my great adventure that St Andrew's Day I was already planning my return.

Utopia, after all, is where the heart is . . .

Epilogue: Voices, Dreams and Searches

Rab and I had been married for eight and a half years and lived with our three-year-old son, Euan, on an island off the West Coast of Scotland. It was 4th February 1980 and it had been snowing heavily most of the day. Nan was in hospital on the mainland. She had burned her leg, nothing serious, but the dressing needed changing three or four times a day. To save time for the district nurses she had gone into hospital for a few days.

I had arranged to visit her on the Wednesday, but I had taken a notion to go across instead that Monday. The blizzard struck as I was negotiating the farm-track with Euan in his buggy. The local postie stopped me at the road end and told me it was blocked further along, so I couldn't get to the ferry terminal. Reluctantly I turned back, annoyed at myself for being so stubborn. Wednesday was only two days away and Nan wasn't expecting me till then, so why this determination to get there today? I had a young child to consider after all, why subject him to howling winds and snow too thick to see through?

All that day Rab drove a snow plough in an attempt to keep the island's one road open. He came home briefly to refill his thermos and to grab a bite to eat, then dashed out again at 8 p.m. I was getting Euan ready for bed when I heard a voice say 'Rita'. Assuming Rab had forgotten something, I went to the front door, wondering as I opened it why he had called me Rita. He disliked the family name and like everyone else these days he called me Meg. When he wasn't at the front I went to the back-door, annoyed now that I had to leave the baby. Why couldn't Rab use his keys for heaven's sake? The snow plough had gone; there was no one there. Outside there was nothing but swirling snow.

Without thinking about it I went straight to the phone and called the hospital.

'Can you please tell my mother to call me?' I asked the staff nurse on Nan's ward.

'Have you spoken to anyone already?'

'Yes, I spoke to the ward sister the other day,' I replied, 'Tell my mother to reverse the charges and none of her nonsense. I'll worry about my own phone bill.'

'Have you spoken to anyone today?' she persisted, and for the first time on that freezing cold day I felt a chill.

'What's wrong staff?' I was aware that I was holding my breath and forced myself to let it out again, slowly and easily.

'She's had a relapse.'

'Look staff, I'm stuck on this island and I can't get off. I'm a medic, tell me in medical jargon what's happened and I'll understand.' There was a pause as she wondered whether she should tell me on the phone. I concentrated on my breathing.

'She's had a full systemic collapse. She has double pneumonia, septicaemia and renal failure. Five minutes ago she slipped into a coma.'

'She's dying,' I said, moving up a gear in crisis mode, 'How long?'

'I really can't say.'

'Come along staff!' I said in my most officious medical voice, 'My mother's dying and I can't get to her! Kindly stop playing with words and tell me the truth!'

'I shouldn't tell you this over the phone, but I'd say a couple of hours at the most.'

It was just after 8 p.m. I put Euan to bed and sat down, my mind totally concentrated on Nan. Exactly two hours later I called again and she had just died. I was perfectly calm, thanked the staff nurse for caring for Nan and for being honest with me. Then I sat down again to wait for morning. I couldn't be there with her, it was the nearest to a vigil by her side that I could manage.

To this day I have no explanation for the voice calling my name as Nan slipped into unconsciousness, all I know is that I heard it. It was neither male nor female, just a voice, but plain and clear. Neither do I know why I went straight to the phone, because I had made no conscious connection between the voice and Nan. And the thing that has haunted me ever since is that I had thought whatever bound us closely together had weakened and died after 1959. If she was calling me then it had still been there, and I hadn't even known. All those years when I had needed her and missed her, yet she had been there all along . . .

The dreams started in 1985. Night after night I would wake up covered in sweat and shaking with terror, and soon I was finding reasons to avoid sleeping. I was thirty-seven-years-old, happily married with three children; nothing was wrong. Yet out of a clear blue sky I was having nightmares. And they didn't fade in the cool light of day, they remained crystal clear afterwards, and still are today.

In one I was walking down a road with beautiful gardens on all sides, all filled with pink roses, nothing but pink roses. I kept looking around, in a desperate attempt to find some other flower, but everywhere there was nothing but pink roses. When I woke I couldn't understand why I should find pink roses so distressing, but soon I was watching for them wherever I went during the waking day, and hoping not to find them. And I couldn't understand why.

In another dream I was in a room I didn't recognize and Jim McAvoy was standing beside a closed door, looking down at the floor. I was facing the door, and the Clarks were behind me on all sides. There was something awful behind the door, but I had to open it and I knew somehow that the family didn't really want me to. I turned the handle and as the door swung open, there stood Peggy, her face solemn, almost reproachful, as I had never seen her. Her dark-brown hair was swept up in a sophisticated, smooth style that was all wrong; Peggy had a mass of curls. She was wearing a long dress of heavy, powder-blue satin, plain, simple and beautiful, but nothing like Peggy would have chosen. She loved pink, and nothing could be too fancy, no amount of lace and frills was ever enough, everything had to be a riot of over-the-top, cheerful nonsense, or she considered it plain. None of the Clarks spoke in the dream, but they seemed to be showing Peggy to me and telling me everything was fine. Only it wasn't Peggy, not the real Peggy, and nothing was fine, and the look on her face terrified me.

Then I was sitting in a booth in some fashionable restaurant. It was thick with tropical plants and music played softly in the background, some vaguely familar tune I couldn't quite place. I had a cup of coffee in front of me as I chatted to someone. I could, she was saying, get the information fairly easily, there was the new freedom of information legislation for instance, and I knew where to start, I knew the date in 1959, and I had enough medical contacts. The place to start, she was saying, was the Registrar's Office, which seemed logical to me and I was agreeing. Then as I turned to look at her I found it was Peggy, but before I could say anything she disappeared and I sped around the fancy restaurant desperately trying to find her. Then I noticed that the tropical plants had turned into pink roses and the music in the background was 'Mexicali Rose'.

Next I was walking along a familiar road near to the Eastern Infirmary and I saw someone I knew coming out of the flower shop carrying a bunch of flowers. She was wearing a beige wool coat and expensive black patent high-heeled shoes, and she carried a plain black clutch bag. Her jewellery was discreet, but quality, and her hair was beautifully swept back from her face. I touched her sleeve, and she turned towards me; it was Peggy. Once again she looked at me with that solemn, reproachful stare. Then wordlessly she handed me a single pink rose from the bunch she carried and disappeared before my eyes.

These dreams kept recurring and terrified me for no reason that I could understand. I had never been scared of Peggy in my life and if her ghost had appeared before me I would have been delighted. I had never truly known what had happened on 30th May 1959; whatever else the dreams might mean, they were reminders of how much I didn't know about a tragedy that had changed the entire course of my life. In my new, happy life I had attempted to put it all behind me, I had crammed it all into a mental compartment and put up a notice saying 'Finished. Do not open.' Only it wasn't finished and now it was leaking out, forcing itself into my life, and I couldn't get it to go back into the compartment again.

After a few sleepless months I gave in. There was only one thing I could do. I had to go back to 1959 and find out everything that had happened, I had to know why Peggy had died to understand what had become of us all afterwards. The dark, yawning abyss had to be filled in, no matter how painful it might be, or it would remain there, seething and furious for the rest of my life.

I planned it carefully. First of all, even if I did succeed in uncovering the events of that day after twenty-six years, I was so close to the story that I might misinterpret whatever I discovered. So I found Ian Cameron, a Consultant I had known in the Eastern who was also a psychotherapist, and one of the wisest men I had ever known. I told him the story and he agreed that the dreams were pushing me into investigating Peggy's death. 'Isn't that funny?' he said, 'When I was a medical student in the forties we had to do home deliveries, and Blackhill was my area.'

So the streets where I had played as a child in the fifties were the streets he had walked as a young man, delivering babies in the forties. Then I had grown up to work with him and later to involve him in my quest over an obstetrics death in those same streets. Dr Cameron agreed to help evaluate whatever information I turned up, he would be my thread through the labyrinth.

The first thing I did was to visit the Registrar's Office in Martha Street, Glasgow. This was the area where the Clarks and O'Briens had lived. Their births had been registered in this office, just as mine had been and Mickey's and Laurie's. Peggy's death had been too, and it was where Rab and I had married. In the next street was Rottenrow and the hospital where Peggy had died, and further along was the Brae. So all around were reminders of events in my life.

I asked the clerk for Peggy's death certificate and gave him the date. When he came back he took me into a side room. There had apparently been a change of cause of death. The first was signed by a Dr S A Collins at the hospital, citing 'Obstructed labour ¼ day. Rupture of uterus. Severe Haemorrhage.' Then there was a police post-mortem by a Dr W P Weir, and he'd changed the cause of death to 'Rupture of uterus and intra-peritoneal haemorrhage following forceps for foetal distress,' clearly blaming the use of forceps.

I paid for a copy of the certificate and wandered back down the road. W P Weir was Walter Weir, a well-known pathologist, and luckily someone I knew, albeit slightly. Another coincidence; like Ian Cameron I had known him professionally without suspecting that his shadow had crossed my life years ago. When I phoned him he told me he had just retired and I explained what I wanted to know. He had no difficulty in remembering Peggy, despite all the PMs he had carried out.

'It was a bad case,' he explained, 'I had seen very few like it, a real mess.' In my experience medics only remember the bad ones.

'You seemed to blame the forceps,' I said, 'And you dropped any mention of obstructed labour from your findings.'

'Yes, that's right. I was very clear about that. There was no obstruction, and the use of forceps would have been wrong anyway, an obstructed labour needs a Caesarian section. Whoever used the forceps that day killed the woman and the child. The haemorrhage was well-established, if I remember correctly there was very little blood left in her body, she had virtually bled to death before she reached Rottenrow. They wouldn't have been able to do anything for her by that time. I'll have a look, I might have my notes still, I'm sorting stuff out now that I've retired. Give me a call back and I'll see what I can find.'

I found Dr S A Collins through the medical mafia. Though he wasn't in the medical directory, the list of doctors in this country, I found his brother. Steven Collins was now a Professor of Obstetrics in Malaysia. I immediately wrote off to him and planned my next move. It had to be the family doctor, but I didn't even know his name, only McAvoy would know that. I picked up a Glasgow telephone directory and called up every McAvoy listed. The McAvoys were a large family and the GP had been their doctor, if I could find one of them I might be able to avoid actually talking to Jim McAvoy, if he were still alive.

It was surprisingly easy. I quickly found one of McAvoy's brothers, who told me the name of the GP, Dr James Hammond. McAvoy was apparently living with his – and Peggy's – youngest son in Glasgow. All attempts to find Dr Hammond then hit a brick wall. I tried the medical mafia and the word came back that Hammond was dead. I tried every medical organization and the reply was the same: there was no record of a Dr James Hammond. I discovered that he had had a partner in the sixties and I called that man's home to discover that he had been dead for years; his widow told me that Hammond had too. She gave me the number of the practice they had shared, but when I called I was told the same story. I don't know why I kept going down that road, perhaps it was just a natural cussedness, but somehow I didn't believe what I was being told about Hammond. I had a distinct feeling that he was alive. I went back to the Glasgow telephone directory once again and called every Hammond I could find. And there he was. I could hardly believe it, but his voice was on the other end of the line. I told him that I was writing a book and one of his former patients came into the story – totally untrue at the time, but I didn't want him to know Peggy and I were related, or he might clam up.

'Her name was McAvoy,' I said, 'I think she died around 1960, I wonder if you remember her?'

'Margaret McAvoy,' he said, 'Six Moodiesburn Street. 1959.'

Instantly I knew that what had happened was out of the ordinary; you only remember the bad ones. Twenty-six years later and Hammond could still remember Peggy's address; it must have been very bad. I had caught him off guard, so I asked him if I could see him rather than keep the conversation going on the phone and arouse any suspicions. In the flesh I'd be able to judge how honest he was being in his answers too, and it would be harder to throw me out than it would to hang up the phone. He agreed to see me in two days time and I hung up without leaving my number, so that if he thought better of it he wouldn't be able to contact me and cancel.

Over the next couple of days I tried to compile a list of questions and settle on some strategy for dealing with both Hammond and the situation. I was finding it very difficult sometimes to think about Peggy in a detached way. While I was talking to Walter Weir I had struggled to keep my mind from picturing the scene in the bedroom that day. Long-hidden memories kept intruding and putting themselves in context, making the picture more complete. The more I found out the more I had to feel emotional about and I couldn't afford that if I was going to get to the bottom of the story. So if the two days before I met Hammond were an eternity, they were also an opportunity to put some distance between the truth and my feelings.

Hammond lived in Newton Mearns, in the affluent south of the city, in 'a big hoose'; I smiled to myself as the daily woman let me in. His home was a typical Victorian mansion, with large airy rooms and high corniced ceilings. The decor was ultra conservative, antique furniture and a cream and beige colour scheme, the kind of house that gave the feeling of permanence. Nothing had moved from its allotted spot in a very long time here, a house where children had never lived to disturb the quiet gentility. There was only one picture of a baby and it had that indefinable look of having been taken many years ago.

Dr James Hammond was sitting by the fireside in an elegant armchair with curved, wooden legs. He was a small, portly figure with receding white hair that had once been sandy-red. Dressed immaculately but soberly, his cuff-links bearing the entwined initials of his name, he sat smiling. His clasped hands rested in his lap, and a gold tie-pin bearing the same monogram held his dark maroon tie. I thanked him for seeing me, and to put him at ease I told him of my medical background and we talked of doctors we had both known. He was delighted to have someone to swap gossip with and told me a little about his days as a GP during the setting up of the NHS. He'd had a single-handed practice for most of the time apparently, until the early sixties, in fact. I asked him how he had coped with the demands this must have made on him and he bristled with pride and said he simply sacrificed himself for his patients, not that they deserved it in the main of course, but it was the kind of man he was.

He'd been a widower these last five years and he often looked back now and regretted how much time he should have spent with his wife that he'd spent instead with his demanding patients. He took out a monogrammed handkerchief and blew his nose. Then I told him the story I had prepared, that I was writing something about Mrs McAvoy's sister, who had saved the lives of her neighbours when Balmano Brae had collapsed. He blew out his cheeks derisively.

'I should be very surprised if we're talking about the same family!' he laughed, 'Those people weren't capable of anything notable apart from prodigious breeding, believe me!'

'Really?' I said, 'I wouldn't know. I just stumbled across this story and felt I had to follow it through.'

'Well for a start they came from Blackhill,' he said, 'Now a young lady such as yourself wouldn't know anything about Blackhill. It was a hell-hole, a den of thieves and murderers, but as we used to say in those days, if we kept them all together, at least we knew where they were!' He laughed merrily at his little jest. 'Many of my patients came from there. They had to be looked after like children, told whether they were ill or not, and more often they weren't. Too much booze and too little solid food, that was their trouble in the main, give that sort money to feed themselves and their children and they followed a liquid diet if you know what I mean! I was the only person who could go into Blackhill in a car and not have the wheels stolen while it was still moving. I was strict with them you see, let them know who was boss!'

'Weren't there any decent people there?'

'Not a one my dear, decency wasn't something that counted in Blackhill. It must be very difficult for someone like you to understand, but those people were barely human, the absolute dregs of humanity at the most.'

'And Mrs McAvoy?'

'Oh she was just like the rest, a big, blowsy, coarse-spoken creature.' I wondered for a moment if he had actually known Peggy, if he'd ever set eyes on her.

'Didn't know her well, mind you,' he continued, 'I was the McAvoy's family doctor, only saw her after she married Jim McAvoy.'

'What was he like?'

'Pretty much par for the Blackhill course. Low intelligence, no education, but with a kind of animal cunning.'

'And did you see Mrs McAvoy throughout her pregnancy?'

'No, no, you didn't see that sort until they went into labour, then it was a knock at the door and "Please doacter'," he mimicked a Glasgow accent, and as I looked at him I remembered Peggy going to ante-natal appointments. Nan and I had waited for her in Moodiesburn Street once, on one of my mother's sudden desires to see her, and as Peggy came in she smoothed her cotton smock over her belly and said, 'If Ah'm no' away by Monday Ah've tae go back tae see him.' At that time she was already overdue and only weeks from death. This was Peggy, who had longed for motherhood, who adored babies even if she was having too many. Peggy kept her ante-natal appointments.

'And was she overdue?'

'Overdue? No, no; not that I remember.'

'And who was at the birth?'

'I was.'

'You were? That's lucky, you'll have all the details. I had been told that someone else attended that day.'

'No, it was me.' We were having no more amusing detours

into the backward ways of the Blackhill natives I noticed, he was too busy paying close attention now.

'And what happened?'

'Well McAvoy called me, I went to the house and the labour progressed.'

'But she died in hospital didn't she?'

'Yes.'

'Well how did that come about?'

'Oh, it was taking a long time and she was getting a bit tired so I decided to send her in.'

'Who else was there?'

'Nobody, just me.'

'No nurse?'

'No.'

'Who called the ambulance then?'

'I did.'

'But I understood that the nearest public phone was some distance away.' I knew exactly where it was. I had a clear recollection of being squashed in the phone box listening as my mother called the hospital to be told that Peggy had just delivered her first live child.

'I took my car.'

'So you had to leave the patient to do that?'

'Well she was OK. As I said, she was just a bit tired. There was no danger as such.'

'No sign of bleeding?'

'No . . .' He thought about it for a moment and said, 'Perhaps her pulse was a little fast.'

'But there was no outward sign of bleeding?'

'No.'

'Did you go with her in the ambulance?'

'No. If she had been in any danger then of course I would have, but she was just having a long labour and was tired.'

'So who went with her, if you didn't and there was no nurse present?'

'I think McAvoy went.'

'Was there anyone else in the house?'

'No.'

'But there were children weren't there? Who looked after the McAvoy children?'

'Well perhaps there was someone else there too, I can't quite remember, it's so long ago . . .'

'When did you hear that she'd died?'

'A couple of weeks later. McAvoy came and told me.'

'Didn't you call the hospital after sending her in?'

'Well I would have if I'd had any reason to be concerned of course, but it was all quite straight forward you see, so I didn't bother.'

'And when you heard she was dead?'

'Well I was shocked of course. I don't know what Rottenrow could have done to her, they must've made some sort of mistake.'

'Didn't the Fiscal contact you about a Fatal Accident Inquiry?'

'No.'

'And didn't you hear the cause of death?' He shook his head and I read both causes out to him.

'Well Rottenrow must've done that,' he replied, 'I didn't use forceps at all. She was tired, that was all.'

'I heard that you had treated McAvoy very kindly afterwards,' I said, testing a family suspicion that McAvoy had been paid for not causing a fuss, 'I heard that you had given him some financial assistance.' He was a little unsettled by this.

'Well I did feel sorry for him, rogue that he was, with his wife dead and three children to provide for, so I did give him a few pounds. When you've been a GP for so many years you find yourself giving more than medical care to these people sometimes. When I retired a few years ago my patients were in tears, begging me to stay on. They're not bright you see, it's like dealing with very dim children. McAvoy was like that, I just helped him out at a bad time and told him not to say anything to anybody.' He gave a conspiratorial laugh. 'The last thing I wanted was a line of Blackhill spongers at my door every day looking for booze money!' He had paid McAvoy off; the family had been right.

I wasn't going to get anything else from Dr James

Hammond. He was lying, I was convinced of that, but pushing him would be useless, so I steered the conversation back to mutual medical acquaintances and he visibly relaxed. I could see how nervous he had been just by the difference in him. He was obviously a lonely man and he was enjoying the conversation so much that he didn't want me to go.

'I'm sorry I couldn't help you more with the McAvoy case,' he said as I was leaving.

'Oh please, don't worry,' I smiled, 'I thought it was all a wild goose chase, at least you've confirmed that.'

We were at the outside door when he said it. He said it all.

'And besides, what difference would it have made if she had lived?' he asked, 'My wife only had the one, a girl who died of heart disease, and my wife was a lady, she would have made a wonderful mother. Those women, the Margaret McAvoy sort, they had them like shelling peas. If she had lived she would have gone on spawning them, year after year, more thieves and murderers from Blackhill to terrorize and pollute the city.' It was the bitterest, blackest, most chilling little speech I had ever heard. His voice seethed with distaste and venom. I wondered what kind of childhood he had had, what awful experiences in his life he could have suffered to fill him with such poisonous bile. I gave an involuntary shiver as I walked back down the road to the railway station.

Everything was jumbled up inside my head, all sorts of feelings and emotions jostling for position alongside the logical dissection of what I'd just witnessed. I felt like running away from Hammond and his 'big hoose', I had to get away as quickly as possible. I felt dirty in some way, tainted by hearing his putrid little speech. When there was no train due I almost panicked, I *couldn't* wait, I *had* to get away. I ran outside and stopped a taxi, not entirely sure where I wanted to go. I asked to be taken to the Royal Maternity at Rottenrow then sat back and tried to calm down. I felt as though I had been beaten up, I was aching all over and my insides felt as though a huge, long-taloned claw had reached within me and ripped me apart. I couldn't believe I had sat still and listened to such savagery against Peggy and my family, such blatant lies about them and about Hammond's part in our tragedy. A pure Clark couldn't have done so; my Uncle George would have hit him and Nan would have delivered an impassioned, articulate speech then wept for hours on Peggy's shoulder. Whatever else I had to thank the O'Briens for I now had to acknowledge that their policy of never showing their emotions, and their facility with the tactical lie, could be very useful skills. But the Clark emotions were churning around and I was feeling very fragile.

I walked around the maternity hospital, unable to explain to myself why I was there, then I decided to go to Blackhill, so I hailed another taxi. The driver was less than impressed by my destination.

'Blackhill hen?' he asked, 'Ur ye sure? Hiv ye no' made a mistake hen, Ah mean dae ye know whit Blackhill's like?'

'I don't want you to stop, I just want to drive past.'

'Well a'right hen, bit it's no' the kinda place where ye staun' aroon', understaun'? Ye really need sumb'dy tae ride shotgun fur ye!'

The chemical factory had gone, but the gasworks was still there, the two gasometers now painted a nice shade of blue, the Gas Board's attempt at improving its image. If you can't be 'green' then blue is nearly as valid in 'green' terms. There was no hint in the air of gas emissions though, filters had been fitted, so the gasworks no longer 'came out' in a solid lump of lung-stopping fumes. My old school had gone, so had Paddy Doyle's, where my happiest memories of my father were rooted. Even today the slightest whiff of leather can bring those early days back to me, and I see him again, a little figure hunched over his last, mending shoes as I sat beside him drinking hot, sweet tea from his old army mug. Happy memories of when I was too young to know what life was really like for my mother and so had no reason to suspect what it would become for all of us in time.

I directed the taxi driver from Royston Road to Craighead

Avenue which had bordered St Philomena's School. There used to be a high metal fence all the way along, over which the enemy Proddies threw clods of earth at us in our mutually satisfying lunchtime battles. Past the pond and right, to where Craigendmuir Street joined Acrehill Street. There we had met up with David and his pals at the end of the school day, and thrown insults at each other all the way home. Past the gap in the tenements where we had watched the paratroopers jumping from the blimp we never found, and the house of the little man who had murdered his wife.

David's house was there on the right, and a couple of closes further on was where Bobby, the mentally handicapped boy had lived. Between the next gap was where Jamie had been killed by the train, nearly in the backcourt of his own house. Across the road was Mrs Logan's house of plenty, courtesy of her gangster nephew, Billy Fullarton, and our close was two along. Only it wasn't there anymore. Instead, huge concrete pillars rose hundreds of feet above, carrying the M8 motorway. All those times I had driven over that exact spot, never suspecting it was the site of 34 Acrehill Street; over where Fullarton had made us walk home alone, and where Santa had rushed through the air one magic night on his way to deliver presents to other children. I asked the taxi driver to take me to Moodiesburn Street and he feigned ignorance, so I firmly directed him and made him wait outside number six.

'Dae you know who lives in that hoose ower the road?' he demanded, and I shook my head. 'Arthur Thomson!' he said, 'Arthur bloody Thomson, y'know, the Godfather o' Glesca crime! This isnae ony place tae linger hen!'

Thomson, Fullarton, names I had grown up with so they held no terrors for me, and I smiled at his nervousness. I went through the close and paused at Peggy's door. It felt the same as it had after her death, as though she was there, just beyond the corner of my eye, and if I turned my head quickly . . . Down the eight back stairs I went, half expecting to meet myself. I'd only managed to jump them once, on a Saturday in May long ago, with the demons of hell after me.

The air raid shelters had gone and the backcourt was a backgreen now, with real, green grass. The middens had vanished, given way to more modern means of disposing household rubbish. It all looked smaller, of course, shrunk by the years, but that apart it was as I remembered it. I went back to the taxi, where the driver was sweating with unease. When I asked him to head back to the city centre he became verbose with relief. Did I know this part of the city, how did I know the street names, was I looking for someone? But I didn't reply, I was deep in some rite of passage, taken beyond words by an instinct to touch base. I had known it all so well as a child, my footprints would be there somewhere, along with generations of others, indelible, invisible, but there. I just had to see it all one more time before I could put it away. We passed the cemetery where Peggy had made me walk with her only weeks before she died, helping me lay ghosts. It occurred to me that that was what I was doing on this day: that I was making my peace with the ghosts of my childhood.

During that night I thought through everything that Hammond had said about Peggy, my family and the people of Blackhill, and his awful, bitter outburst as I left him, and I was physically sick.

It took me a couple of weeks to settle down enough to think through Hammond's story. He hadn't been with Peggy that day. I remembered lying on top of my shelter after the men had come back from burying Peggy. Another car had drawn up and a young man had got out and gone into the house. He was the one who had been there, the doctor who 'wisnae a real doacter', a tall, dark-haired lad in his late teens or early twenties who had towered over the much older figure of my father as he hurried him away from George's rage. Hammond was barely five feet tall, the same as my father, he was in his seventies, which meant that in 1959 he would have been in his late forties, the same again as my father, and his hair had been sandy-red. Hammond hadn't been with Peggy.

I called Walter Weir again and repeated Hammond's version of Peggy's death.

'Hammond's lying,' he replied, 'He has a lot to lie about. I don't think he was the attending doctor that day.'

'Why?'

'Well what I saw wasn't the work of an experienced GP, and Hammond was certainly that. What I saw was the work of a complete novice, to put it kindly.'

'Don't put it kindly.'

'Then an apprentice butcher could have made a better job of it. Let's go back a bit. Firstly, there's a tendency towards bigger babies with each pregnancy, and this lady had sub-acute rickets. She didn't have the disease, but no doubt her mother did and Mrs McAvoy carried the marks of that. Most Glaswegians of that era were very small, like all poor city-dwellers her skeletal growth had been retarded. So her pelvis wasn't roomy; it could've coped with a smaller baby, but this one – it was a male foetus – was bigger, partly because it was also overdue. She was thirty-seven and she was getting tired. Any experienced GP would've sent her to hospital, she'd have had a section and all would have been well. Whoever was there that day didn't know what he was doing. Tiredness or obstructed labour, it doesn't matter, either should have meant a section, but instead he tried forceps, and he wasn't experienced with those either. The bad luck just piled up from there on. He probably applied the forceps just as a strong contraction struck, stretching the uterus paper-thin, and it all ruptured. Then she began to haemorrhage and he made the wrong choice again. Instead of sending for help he tried to stop it, and he had no chance of doing that. It all smacks of lack of experience and panic. You have to ask why he didn't try to get help when he was in such desperate trouble, and the likeliest explanation is that he couldn't.'

'Why? What do you mean?'

'My guess is that he wasn't a doctor, so he couldn't send her to hospital and risk being found out. Once she ruptured she needed to be in hospital pretty damn quick, and he still didn't send her. He tried to handle it all himself because to do otherwise would've risked discovery. And he couldn't contact Hammond because Hammond wasn't at home. So he panicked.'

'If he wasn't a doctor, what was he?'

'Probably a medical student who'd agreed to cover for the GP for less money than a fully-qualified locum would accept.'

'That's illegal isn't it?'

'Yes, then as now. The medical fraternity would swear on a stack of bibles that it couldn't and didn't ever happen, but you and I both know they'd swear to anything on a stack of bibles. It did happen.'

Ian Cameron listened as I told him the story. 'So how do you feel?' he asked.

'Overwhelmed, mixed up. Tell me, what kind of medical student would have put himself in that position do you think?'

'Most likely one who didn't have daddy's money to see him through. After the war we began to see more working-class boys coming into the profession, not many mind you, but the odd one. And I'd imagine that he probably thought nothing much could go wrong in one little day. If, as you say, Hammond was concerned about spending so little time with his wife and wanted a day off from his single-handed practice, he probably thought the same. He'd get cheap cover for the day and what could possibly go wrong? At least what could possibly go wrong that couldn't be covered up, anyway?'

'Nothing. That's just it. Nothing went wrong that wasn't covered up. Just the death of a young woman and her child and the destruction of an entire extended family.'

'And you have to remember that the NHS was still in its infancy in 1959. I used to deliver babies in Blackhill when I was a medical student only ten years or so before, the GP probably did the same. It wouldn't have taken much for him to persuade himself that all these new-fangled rules were nonsense, and more so if it saved him money.'

'Especially as the people of Blackhill were so worthless and undeserving of proper medical care.'

'Yes, awful, isn't it?'

'Do you know what would have happened if it had all come out at the time?'

'Well the guilty man was the GP, but I suspect if there had been an investigation he would've come out of it looking like a hero anyway. You must remember that in those days, even more than now, doctors were gods. If he couldn't be got out of it he would've been suspended on full pay for perhaps six months.'

'Is that all?' I asked incredulously.

''Fraid so. And the family would have had to fight bloody hard to get even that, bloody hard. It wouldn't have been seen as in the public interest to pursue anyone involved, the establishment would've covered all tracks.'

'Would the police have covered up for Hammond? Two of them broke down the door and sent for the ambulance.'

'It would've been out of their hands, they couldn't have questioned the "doctor's" professional qualifications and very likely they wouldn't even have entered the event in their notebooks. I would imagine sending for an ambulance wasn't exactly an uncommon occurrence for policemen in Blackhill.'

I wondered what had happened to the medical student, if he had gone on to qualify. If the lad who'd been with Peggy was around twenty years old when I was eleven, he would only be in his forties now. For all I knew I could've worked with him. I couldn't help feeling sorry for him. Everyone makes mistakes with patients, but his must have marked him for life. What had happened in the bedroom of 6 Moodiesburn Street was a nightmare for him too, and it must still be keeping him awake, wherever he was. The lad wasn't to blame, Hammond was.

I couldn't stop the picture of Peggy's dying. Awake or asleep it played in my mind like a film endlessly repeating itself, as I tried to change the ending.

'Well you must remember,' Ian Cameron explained, 'The eleven-year-old child you were, has been secretly keeping Peggy alive all these years in the hope that the ending could be changed.'

'But I'm an adult for God's sake!'

'An adult with a child inside, still running through the backcourts and hiding in the darkness, desperately trying to hold on to the fabric of her normal existence. Now she's been brought face-to-face with reality and it hurts. That's why the dreams scared you so much. In themselves there was nothing frightening about them, except the fear of facing up to the pain that had to come. There was no grieving for Peggy at the time and supressed grief will find a way out, someday, somehow.'

There was still something missing, the picture wasn't complete, and no matter how I tried to ignore it, it bothered me. I needed to know absolutely everything, to confirm it in every way that I could. I tried to get out of it by wondering if I was turning the knife, making it hurt more for some reason. The missing piece was McAvoy. The thought of seeing him again, of talking to him, made me feel angry, sick, a mixture of all sorts of feelings, none of them positive. But he *had* been there throughout. I put the idea into cold storage for a while then I got up one day, caught the morning boat to the mainland and went to see him.

McAvoy was living with his younger son, John, and his family in Johnstone, another housing estate with a bad name. He didn't know me at first, then I saw recognition dawn on him along with the horror. I don't suppose he ever thought he'd see one of us again, and clearly he wasn't anymore delighted at the prospect than I was at seeing him. He had faded with age, he looked as though he had melted in some way, his features were so indistinct. I thought of the groom on the wedding cake decoration, the one I had smashed after Peggy's death. The eyes were the same though, showing what Hammond called his animal cunning.

I told him I wanted to know about Peggy's last day and he looked as though he wanted to run out of the room. He couldn't remember. I said I remembered every second, so surely her husband must remember something, hadn't he been with her to the end? I had come a long way, both in miles and in emotion, I wasn't about to let him off the hook, so I stood my ground until he believed that I wouldn't go away until he talked. I asked him how he'd met Peggy and how long he had known her before they married. He told how they'd met at work five years before and because they lived near each other in Blackhill they'd travelled on the same bus. Another reason to curse the collapse of Balmano Brae. He couldn't remember the date of their marriage, Peggy's birthday, the date when she died or what sex the child had been. I was trying to keep the conversation neutral so that he would give me whatever information he had, but already I could feel my anger rising. Peggy had gone into labour around 8 a.m., he told me, and the doctor arrived soon after. It was Dr Hammond. 'I've talked to Hammond,' I said, 'He was on holiday that day so it couldn't have been him.' McAvoy looked uncomfortable.

'Oh aye, that's mibbe right anuff. Ah furgoat. Ah think sumbudy else came insteed.'

'When did she die?'

'Aboot five o'clock, hauf an 'oor efter we goat tae the hospital. Ah wis sittin' ootside an' the doacter came oot and tellt me.'

'And was there an Inquiry afterwards?'

'Aye. Ah went doon tae the court a while efter an' they tellt me tae wait ootside. Then they came an' tellt me tae go hame, that Ah wisnae needed.'

I remembered my mother saying that McAvoy had told the family to stay away, and they had been so destroyed by the months since May that they couldn't fight back. McAvoy was the only one able to function with any purpose, and he should've been the one most affected by her death, surely? I asked if he'd told the family any of this.

'Naw. It wis nane o' thur business! They hated me the Clarks, aye causin' trouble atween me an' Peggy,' he snivelled, 'Thoaght Ah wisnae good anuff fur hur, ye'd think she wis royalty ur sumthin'! They wur a' like that, thoaght they wur sum'dy!'

'They were somebody,' I said, 'And Peggy was better than royalty. She deserved a lot better than she got.'

He glared at me with his bright little eyes, but he was too intimidated to say more. There he was, a shrivelled little nothing, and there I was, young, healthy and a Clark.

Later my cousin John walked with me to the train station. I could hardly drag my eyes from him. Every expression on his face, every movement of his head, even his laugh, it was all my mother. It was like seeing a male version of her. He told me that he and his brother and sister had grown up in care, and that his father had always refused to talk about Peggy. In fact he had believed that his mother had died giving birth to him. But he'd been just over a year old when she died and he hadn't even one memory of her, neither did his brother or his sister. I tried to tell him what she had been like, but I was talking to a stranger about another stranger who meant much more to me than to him, much, much more. He gave his father a home, he said, because there was nowhere else for him to go and he had remained in some contact throughout the years he and his brother and sister had been in children's homes. Protecting his future meal tickets Nan had always said. John obviously had no idea that McAvoy had discouraged the Clarks from seeing them, and of course no idea of how Peggy's death had affected us all.

None of Peggy's children had any real curiosity about their mother, she might never have existed, and I found it very sad. Had she lived we would have been as close as brothers and sisters, because our mothers would have been joint mothers to us all, and instead we had nothing in common. Nothing, that was, except a noticeable physical resemblance to one another and in John's case a staggering likeness to my mother. Our life experiences had made us strangers, and I couldn't see any prospect of changing that. It would remain a major regret of my life that I would never know Peggy's children. There was no feeling there between us, and it would have been pointless to pretend that there was.

Looking back on my day I thought about the differences

between us. I had survived the trauma, I had found my way out of poor housing, bad job prospects and an unhappy life, but only because I had Nan, and even a subdued Nan had been enough. The motivation and drive towards education had come from Nan and Peggy, and my cousins had lost both and so they hadn't achieved what I had. The only real difference between us was that my mother had lived and so had her dreams for her children, while for my cousins, both had died.

The months of searching for the truth about Peggy's death had left me feeling angry, but had brought no relief, no peace. I was angry at McAvoy, because he couldn't remember anything about Peggy because he simply didn't care. He could at least have loved her a little bit . . .

And I was angry at Dr James Hammond on so many fronts that it was hard to separate them. Mainly because of his attitude to the people of Blackhill, who had provided him with his 'big hoose' and his standard of living and had doubtless given him respect over the years, respect that he didn't earn and didn't deserve. How could he have worked so closely with those people and have no understanding of them or their situation? And his attitude to Peggy made me seethe with rage. Peggy had died because she lived in Blackhill. She had no money and came from the poorest orders of the working class, therefore she wasn't worthy of Hammond's personal or professional care.

But it went further. In reality her fate was sealed before her own birth. She died as she did because of the family she was born into. Before I set out on my quest for the facts that possibility simply hadn't entered my mind, and now I wondered why it hadn't. How could someone of my background and experience fail to have spotted it? The more I thought about it the clearer it became. I had been brought up among the Clarks and the people of Blackhill. They were decent, honest people with a basic belief in what was right and just. Even though they were treated shabbily and unfairly by those in power over them, they *knew* that treatment to be wrong. Which had proved to be my handicap; I hadn't been taught to look for the indecent and dishonest, so I didn't. That had been the case all my life; it was doubtless why when I did find it I was so outraged, and it was that outrage that had made me a crusader like Nan.

Amongst all of this personal grief was anger that *any* woman should have died as Peggy did, that the medical and legal world could regard a woman's life to be of so little consequence that they so quietly and effortlessly covered up the circumstances. They should have been appalled, shocked, enraged, that in 1959 any woman should have been so mistreated. I learned that the Procurator Fiscal had informed the Crown Office of the death in September 1959, a month after McAvoy had gone to his office in the court building and been sent away without being interviewed. No information had been collected from the others involved either, and the story emerged of an unfortunate woman who had died in childbirth, so an FAI wasn't required.

Even without the information I had uncovered after twenty-six years, Walter Weir's report would have been enough to alert them that something wasn't right. But the last thing anyone wanted to do was to hand the working-classes a stick of injustice to beat the good guys with – though of course that would not have been how it was put. No, it would have been represented as in the best interests of the family, that they had already suffered enough, best not upset them further, simple souls that they were.

The truth was that Peggy was of no importance and neither was the family. They came from Blackhill after all, so what did they matter compared to the reputations and careers of upstanding, educated, professional men? Justice? What was that and what understanding did the Blackhill element have of it anyway? After all, it wasn't as if they felt the same about their families as the educated classes, was it?

So my dreams of Peggy were replaced by violent dreams of shootings and warfare, angry dreams that were every bit as disturbing. I often wondered how much my mother had known. I realized that subconsciously I had waited until after her death to do my sleuthing. Had Nan still been alive, how could I have told her all I had found out, and yet how could I not? Uncle George was still alive, though I hadn't had any contact with him in many years. I toyed with the idea of talking to him, dropped it, then toyed with it again.

When Auntie Annie answered the phone we went through a potted history of the years since we had seen each other, then I asked her if she thought Uncle George would talk to me about Peggy. She doubted it; he hadn't spoken to her about 1959 in any detail. She remembered the doctor who 'wisnae a real doacter' coming to the house after the funeral. 'Tall, young, dark-haired,' she said, 'He wis upset, wanted tae say he wis sorry how things turned oot. Geordie wis sitting by the fire facin' him an' this doacter wis by the door. An' Geordie jist went fur him, he wis acroass that fast, an' the roars o' him! If yer Da hidnae goat tae the doacter first Geordie widda killed him. Yer Da shoved him ootside and the rest o' us hung ontae Geordie tae he wis away.' All my life I remembered Auntie Annie's voice in any family crisis, 'Watch Geordie!', that familiar warning to everyone present that he was near boiling point. I spoke to Uncle George.

'Hullo therr wee yin,' he said, 'How ye daein'?'

'Fine Uncle George, but I need to talk to you. I need to talk about Peggy.' There was total silence at the other end. 'Uncle George, can I come to see you?'

'Aye, a'right hen,' he said quietly.

He was sitting in an armchair by the fire, his hands clamped on the arms, looking down. He was white-haired now, but still a striking man. I had a glimpse of how Nan and Peggy would have looked in old age, had they lived to see it. I told him what I had found out, and as he listened the muscles in his face kept tensing and relaxing.

'Ah know a' this hen,' he said quietly, still looking down.

'Then why did the rest of you let it go?' I asked, 'This wasn't just anybody, this was Peggy!' He was silent for a long time.

'Ye don't unnerstaun' hen,' he said, 'Ye don't know whit it wis like.' Another long silence, then the words came from him slowly, dragged out over twenty-six years. 'Fur Peggy Ah mean. Me and yer Da an' Wullie hid tae clear the room oot efter. Thur wurr piles o' sheets and towels everywhere, a' soaked wi' blood. It wis like a . . . like a slaughthoose.' The knuckles of his hands were white and he had the facial expression I remembered that told you George was having problems with his emotions. I thought of the three of them, all returned from war combat some ten years before, men who had seen terrible sights, cleaning out the bedroom after Peggy died. My mind went back to when I had been lying on my shelter and I had watched Uncle Willie rush out of the house and down the stairs where he was sick in the backcourt. Now I knew why.

'It wis oan the wa's tae,' he continued, 'An' the smell. Even years later Ah could smell it in the hoose, an' Ah coulda pointed tae where the marks hid been oan the wa's.'

'And the doctor, the one who came to the house after the funeral?'

'He wis jist a boay,' he said, 'Jist a big boay, nae mair than twinty. Ah cannae mind a lot aboot that, Ah kin jist remember everybody haudin' me doon . . .'

'But why did you let it go?' I persisted, 'You knew she hadn't died, she had been killed.' He sighed.

'We didnae waant people tae know,' he said, 'Me an' Nan, we talked aboot it, bit we didnae waant people tae know.'

'Know what Uncle George?' I asked puzzled.

'Whit it wis like fur her hen, fur Peggy.' He was looking at me, willing me to understand because he couldn't go on. Then slowly it sank in. Nothing could bring her back, but they had been trying to preserve some sort of dignity for Peggy. They didn't want outsiders idly conjuring up mental pictures of gentle Peggy's agony as she died in a welter of blood. It was the best they could manage. The story was that she had died in childbirth, end of story. A tragedy to be sure, but the less people knew the less they had to talk about. The 'dark yins'' sense of self, their dignity.

'How much did my mother know?' I asked.

'Nan knew it a',' he said, 'We didnae tell the rest everythin' an' Ah don't know whit they f'un oot fur thursels.'

I thought about Nan carrying it for all those years and never being able to tell anyone. All that poisonous knowledge locked up inside her and no one to share the horror with. That's what had come between us and opened up an unbridgeable gulf, the awful truth that she couldn't share. I had been convinced that whatever closeness we had died in 1959, until the voice calling my name before she died had made me wonder.

'Ah blame masel',' Uncle George said, 'Ah've thoaght a' these years that Ah coulda stoapped her marryin' McAvoy. He didnae gie a bugger fur her, Ah coulda pit him aff the idea mibbe. Thur wis wan time, afore she wis expectin' the last wean, Ah hid him by the throat an' Ah coulda squeezed a bit harder, Ah coulda ended it. Ah've sometimes wished Ah hid, an' Peggy wid still be alive. Ah widnae hiv minded gaun' tae jile, Ah shoulda done it while Ah hid the chance.'

'Uncle George, you couldn't have stopped Peggy,' I said, 'She was desperate to get married and anybody would've done but he was the only one around. Nan told her, I remember them talking and Nan telling her that the family would never accept him and if she took him she took him knowing that. Peggy had no illusions, she knew nobody approved, but she thought it was her last chance.' He nodded his head sadly.

'Bit ye aye wonder, dain't ye?' he said. 'Efter he pit Peggy's weans intae care Ah wis that angry that Ah went up tae Moodiesburn Street an' pit him oot, did ye know that? An' Ah thoaght tae masel', "By Christ! An' urn't you the Big Man? Ye shoulda did it afore!" It wis easy, he wis sich a wee weasel. Ah shoulda went up there while she was still alive and pit him oot.'

We had all gone our strange, separate ways after that awful day in 1959, yet we were thinking the same things, feeling the same guilt and desperately fantasizing a different ending. Nan never said it, but I felt her regretting that she hadn't tried to persuade Peggy into a hospital birth. And she could have done it, we both knew that, she more than anyone could have changed Peggy's mind. And Nan had always felt guilty about giving Peggy the unlucky green coat . . . that she hadn't heeded the medium who told her she must come back . . . that she hadn't acted on the dreams.

For myself, I had often day-dreamed about it. If some power had given me one chance to go back in time, what could I have done? I could have gone back as an adult to that morning when she had gone into labour, and passed myself off as Dr Henderson, Hammond's locum. It would have been easy to send the boy who 'wisnae a real doacter' away. I could have used some sort of disguise to cover the family resemblance, and anyway, Peggy wouldn't have known the adult me. Then I could tell her that she would have to go to hospital to have her baby and she would obey, because she respected and trusted doctors as people of learning. I knew enough about hospitals and doctors to have carried it off far better than the scared, panicky 'doacter'. And while she was being sectioned she could have been sterilized so that there would be no more pregnancies, no more threats to her life. Then I would have disappeared, mission accomplished and returned to the present time, having had all those changed years with Peggy, Nan and the family. It was the stuff of dreams. The other fantasy was that if only I had been older Peggy would have listened to me because I worked in a hospital, in her eyes I would have been someone of importance and so I could have influenced events. That was my illogical guilt, being too young to stop what was unfolding before me, the guilt of a powerless child.

After speaking to Uncle George I began to appreciate the depth of the blow to Nan. The loss of Peggy was terrible, but it went beyond that. All of her life she had believed people to be equal in worth and had thought it was a universal belief. The people who brought their problems and their letters to her weren't inferior in any way, through no fault of their own they just weren't able to solve their problems.

I remembered once complaining to her that she had sent

us out into the world armed with her beliefs but minus the knowledge that most of humanity didn't think the same way. She looked puzzled for a moment then said, 'Bit that's their problem, no' yours. They jist don't understaun', bit you know whit's Right.' There was only what was Right, that tangible, unshakeable and undeniable central pillar of all she lived by. But Peggy's death, and the manner of it, had shaken her beliefs to their foundations. Not only was it Not Right, but the educated people whom she had always respected and wanted her children to join, were exposed as frauds. An intelligent woman, she would have finally understood that Peggy had died because Hammond had regarded her as worthless, and that the legal establishment had covered it all up. 'The boys' had protected each other. Who knew better than Nan how much work it took to right a wrong, and that this one could never be righted? It was too big, too comprehensive, and at the end of the day she would still have been left without Peggy. For the first time in her life she had to accept that justice did not always prevail, and the best she could achieve was the protection of her sister's dignity in death.

Her final surrender had come that August, when it became clear that the Procurator Fiscal in Glasgow wasn't going out of his way to inquire. When that became clear, where was there for her to go but inside herself, demoralized, confused and wounded to the core of her spirit? The one duty she had left was to see me grown and on my way to independence, and looking back at those years when she had come so near yet never quite given in, I realized what an effort it had been for her to keep going. There was no one to confide in, no one to help her shoulder the burden. My father was incapable of that level of understanding, or if he did understand, his addiction to booze had long since rendered him incapable of acting upon it. My brothers hadn't shared the unique relationship she had with Peggy, and although I had, there was that old problem, I was too young. The world could ill afford to lose someone as good and gentle as Peggy, but it had also lost the wonderful, shining idealism and zeal of Nan, that was the real tragedy of 30th May 1959.

The light didn't completely die though, and perhaps she suspected that, or at least hoped for it. It's there still in me, and as I get older I see myself reacting as she did to situations and I hear myself using her words to explain to my children that Right is all. Peggy's death and the aftermath have made that belief stronger. It's why I'm a journalist after all, a small modern-day attempt to right wrongs. I happen to have a facility with words, so as Nan would have said, I do it because I can. I have often wished that my own children could have known Nan and Peggy, but now I realize that they do. Because of what they taught me, Nan and Peggy live still in me and so they will live in my children.

The letter with the foreign stamps on the outside arrived many months later, long after I had given up on Dr Steven Collins. Yes, he did remember Mrs McAvoy as it happened, she was his first fatality after leaving the army and taking up the Rottenrow obstetrics post. The GP hadn't been able to be there apparently, he had a single-handed practice and had taken the day off. Whoever had been left to cope wasn't as knowledgeable or experienced and had made rather a mess of it – he had never known who that was. They had no hope of saving Mrs McAvoy by the time she arrived, the haemorrhage had been too great, but they had hoped to save the child by performing an emergency Caesarian section. They didn't get that far though, the child's heartbeat had gone and it was obviously too late. Mrs McAvoy should have been brought in much sooner, the child had been in distress too long and Mrs McAvoy had died very shortly afterwards. The worst possible outcome to lose both, all very sad. The GP had turned up next day full of remorse that he hadn't been there himself, but no one pushed it because it seemed he was well thought of as a GP. No one blamed him, it was just one of those things. If you wanted to lay blame, lay it on inadequate medical care in the poorer areas of the city, the legacy of poor nutrition over generations, poor education . . .

It was only the simple piece of information that connected all the others, but the effect of Dr Collins' letter on me was like a barrier finally being breached. In whatever secret corner of my heart I had kept Peggy alive, the illusion began to crumble. Peggy was dead and it was now time to let her go. It was as if she had died that day, and I cried as though I had just been told. Adults don't cry, they leak tears, but children sob till the pain recedes and I was wracked by an eleven-year-old's grief. After a long, difficult search I had found her again, but in finding her I had also to lose her. Finally able to grieve for her, to acknowledge all the horror of her death, I found that the good memories had been released as well as the bad.

I remembered how she cried as she laughed, the way her eyes shone and the way she encircled you in her warmth as she spoke to you, giving you a feeling of total security. I remembered her wearing a full-skirted dress, white it was and covered in deep pink roses. She had looked so beautiful, the most beautiful creature I had ever seen. Whole conversations between Nan, Peggy and me came flooding back, I could hear her voice again in my head and I smiled at the sound. It took several months, but very gradually, the terrible event that had broken the Clarks as a family, that had destroyed Nan and decimated my childhood in one fell swoop, began to shrink in proportion. It became one terrible event, but it no longer threatened to destroy me. With the brake off, life could go on.

I wanted to talk again to Walter Weir, to thank him for his help and to tell him his analysis had proved correct. When I phoned his number his son answered and I discovered that he had died only months after I had first spoken to him. I also wanted to see Dr James Hammond again. I wanted to tell him who I was, and more importantly, who Peggy was, to make him understand the consequences of his brand of patient care and the fact that the ripples were still going on, two generations later. I didn't want revenge, there was no point in that, but perhaps Nan's belief in anything that went wrong being a misunderstanding that needed to be explained had taken stubborn root. At any event I wanted to state my relationship to Peggy as I couldn't when we talked, to let him know that I was proud of it. His dark, bitter tirade against Peggy, my family and the people of Blackhill had stayed with me and perhaps I wanted to see him again to help me come to terms with that, a kind of cleansing of the psyche. But he too had died, even before Walter Weir. If I had left my search much longer I wouldn't have found out anything.

When I told Ian Cameron all this he smiled his wisest smile.

'I don't believe there's such a thing as coincidence you know,' he said, 'I think we all carry some instinctive means of communicating on a universal timescale. You didn't know Walter had done the PM and you didn't know about Hammond, but something made you look for them at that precise time. And when everyone told you Hammond was dead already, some instinct told you he wasn't and that you would find him. There's only one thing left that you *have* to do. You know what that is, don't you?' I shook my head, but I was lying.

'You must find out where Peggy is buried and visit her.'

'I know where she's buried,' I said, 'Uncle George told me.'

'You must go, you'll find it very healing.'

'No,' I shook my head again, 'There's no point. It's not as if she'd be waiting for me there, it's just a piece of land after all.'

'You're making up excuses,' he smiled, 'You're sensitive and instinctive, you'll go when you're ready, but you *will* go.'

Granda Johnston had bought the plot from a John Dunning, who funnily enough had lived beside Uncle Hughie in Stevenston Street. For all I know the Dunnings could have been frequently treated to 'Red Sails in the Sunset' long before I was. The story was that the Dunnings had gone to find a new life in America, but maybe they were just moving out of earshot. A child was buried in the plot, twelve-year-old Christine Dunning, then the family had sold it to Granda Johnston and gone. It was very fitting I thought, that a lost child should be lying beside Peggy.

Next to be buried, in September 1916, was thirteen-month-old Catherine Clark, a well-kept family secret. No one had ever spoken of a dead child, so it was there from the start, this means of dealing with tragedies by pretending they hadn't happened. Catherine had died from 'catarrh of the bowel', which in a baby would have meant gastro-enteritis. She died when George was a month old, so she would have been weaned from the breast to let the new baby feed. In those days of poor hygiene such deaths were commonplace, as they are in the Third World today, and there would have been no money for a doctor or for the medicine that was available.

What, I wondered, if Catherine, the firstborn child of Annie and Henry Clark, had been fair and blue-eyed? George had been the first 'dark yin'. Was it possible that the death of that little one could be linked to Maw Clark's preference for 'fair yins'? Common though child deaths were at the time, there is no reason to suppose that she was any less affected by the loss of her baby than any mother would be today.

Next to be buried was Da Clark followed by Granda Johnston, then Peggy and her baby and finally Maw Clark. In 1985 I didn't want to go there, not ever. Then one day in October 1992 I went. People who don't know me think I'm impulsive, but I'm not that exciting. Before I do anything I have it fully mulled over in my mind from every direction but because I don't discuss my thoughts it looks like sudden impulse to outsiders.

It was a nice, autumn day and I took with me a big bunch of pink roses that I'd had to search for at that time of year. All the way there I thought that this was the route Peggy had been carried on all those years ago, this was where she came after I had watched the cars out of sight that day, her gift of a pink rose clutched in my hand. Along this same road she had gone, past these houses, turn left into the lane and through the gates. Turn left again and up a little hill, follow the path to the right and it was third from the roadside. I had been scared that it might be awful, that Peggy might be lying in some desolate, ugly place, but she wasn't. There was no headstone; to have erected one would have been to admit that she had gone, and besides, there had never been money in the family for that kind of thing. I decided that she would have one soon. It was well-tended and there was a weeping willow close by, its branches sweeping over where she lay. On either side there were headstones, one for a young man killed during the War. It wasn't at all traumatic, it was a very peaceful and an almost happy visit. I felt that I was with her again. I imagined the scene; my uncles and my father gathering around for the final service, and all those flowers, so many that an extra car had to be provided to carry them. In my mind I could see it as though I had been there. I laid the pink roses on the grass and said, 'Peggy, it's me. I love you.' And standing there beside her I started to laugh, it was not after all the kind of language one working class Glesca lassie uses to another, even if they are related. In my mind's eye I pictured her laughing with me, and Nan too, I could hear the three of us laughing together again. Ian Cameron had been right. It was a very healing experience.

This is a story of a working-class family in Glasgow, and the ordinariness that made them extraordinary, because if I have learned one thing about working-class Glaswegians it is that. But it is also the story of any poor family in any big city at that time. They all had their tragedies, it came with the poverty. It's also the story of those two strong women who were the most important influences in my life. Ironically, both perished, but it's still their story, their standards, that will be remembered, and looking back at my childhood Nan and Peggy stand out like brilliant stars. The hardness, the sadness and the suffering pale into insignificance as well as those who caused it, while Nan and Peggy remain clear and proud.

As I lay on top of the old red-brick air raid shelter that became my haven during those days that changed the course of my young life in 1959, I have a clear memory of deciding not to bother with what was unfolding behind the white-covered windows of Peggy's house. But I promised myself that one day I would find out everything, I'd tell our story . . .

None of the Clarks or the O'Briens were to become rich, famous or influential. They were better than that, they were ordinary and had to struggle to survive, so their story is more courageous and inspiring than anything the nobility ever achieved. Not all ordinary family stories are traced to source, nor all the heroes and heroines acknowledged and celebrated for the sheer guts they showed in surviving. But they should be.

THE END

ALONE
by Pip Granger

In 1950s London, a little girl is busy being brave.

The only daughter of alcoholic parents, Pip Granger spent much of her childhood on the margins of society; on the outside of life, looking in.

Drink was the factor behind the series of crises, the furious rows and life-threatening accidents Pip had to contend with. It also explained why her home life was so very different from that of most other people she knew.

Bullied at school, neglected by her parents, and cared for, at times, by complete strangers, Pip realized that there was only one way to turn her life around. One day she would have to cut loose from her family, and have the courage to build her own life – alone.

Set in a world when sheets and blankets were washed by hand, bananas were considered a luxury, and separation and divorce were shameful events, *Alone* is a brave, original and totally authentic book about a young girl's courage in a trouble-filled world.

9780552155366

A PIECE OF CAKE
A Memoir
by Cupcake Brown

The number one bestseller

From beloved daughter to abused foster child to crack addict, this is the heart-wrenching true story of a girl named Cupcake Brown.

Following her mother's death, Cupcake was just eleven years old when she entered the child welfare system. Moved from one disastrous placement to the next, like so many, she was neglected and sexually abused. She developed a massive appetite for drugs and alcohol – an appetite fed by hustling and turning tricks – and before long, stumbled headlong into the wild, notoriously dangerous world of the gangsta.

But ironically, it was Cupcake's rapid descent into the nightmare of crack cocaine addiction that finally saved her. After one crack binge she woke up behind a dumpster. Half dressed and more than half-dead, she finally knew she had to change her life or die.

Brutally frank, startlingly funny, *A Piece of Cake* is the remarkable true story of a resilient spirit who took on the worst of contemporary urban life and survived it. It is also the most genuinely affecting rollercoaster ride through hell and back that you will ever take.

'A story that is poetic in its simplicity. Beautifully stripped to the basics'
Washington Post

9780553818178

Can't
HELP
Falling

Center Point
Large Print

Also by Kara Isaac and available from
Center Point Large Print:

Close to You

**This Large Print Book carries the
Seal of Approval of N.A.V.H.**

Can't
HELP
Falling

Kara Isaac

CENTER POINT LARGE PRINT
THORNDIKE, MAINE

This Center Point Large Print edition is published
in the year 2016 by arrangement with Howard Books,
a divsion of Simon & Schuster, Inc.

The text of this Large Print edition is unabridged.
In other aspects, this book may vary
from the original edition.
Printed in the United States of America
on permanent paper.
Set in 16-point Times New Roman type.

ISBN: 978-1-68324-206-2

Library of Congress Cataloging-in-Publication Data

Names: Isaac, Kara, author.
Title: Can't help falling / Kara Isaac.
Description: Center Point Large Print edition. | Thorndike, Maine :
Center Point Large Print, 2016.
Identifiers: LCCN 2016043688 | ISBN 9781683242062
    (hardcover : alk. paper)
Subjects: LCSH: Large type books. | GSAFD: Love stories.
Classification: LCC PR9639.4.I83 C36 2016b | DDC 823/.92—dc23
LC record available at https://lccn.loc.gov/2016043688

For Melody
World's greatest sister,
longest suffering reader,
most honest critic,
and loudest cheerleader.
Thank you.

One

It was like being in jail. But worse, because Emelia Mason had paid for it. Nonrefundable. Nontransferable. Not that she hated anyone on the planet enough to try transferring this epic disaster in online booking to them.

Emelia turned around, taking in the full three hundred sixty degrees of the small, dark, cold room. Her breath wafted in front of her. Inside. At four in the afternoon. The space was pretty much bare, save for a rickety desk, an ancient mini-fridge, a few hangers on a metal stand, and a bed. She suppressed a shudder at the sight of the sagging mattress in the corner. Even from a good six feet away, Emelia could tell it would light up like the Rockefeller Center Christmas tree if a UV light ever came within a block of it.

Well, she'd wanted to reinvent herself. She'd certainly done that. Even if being one step up from homeless hadn't exactly been in the game plan. Though, after what she'd done, it was about what she deserved.

Stupid, stupid. Emelia still had no idea how she'd managed to book three weeks at the euphemistically named Magnolia Manor, instead of the Magnolia Inn. A mistake she'd discovered when she'd shown up at the latter, only to be told they had no record of her. A review of her furiously waved booking confirmation revealed her error.

Emelia stretched her arms above her head and lifted herself onto her toes. Her fingers scraped the ceiling, dust brushing against their tips.

Brilliant. No doubt in a few minutes she'd be sneezing like Earth's rotation depended on it.

"Do you need anything else?" The voice coming from behind her clearly said there was only one acceptable answer. Emelia turned around. She hadn't realized the dour manager had stayed in the doorway. Was watching her with gray, beady eyes.

"No." Emelia couldn't bring herself to say thank you. She felt ill just thinking about how much she'd paid to stay in this hole. She had no job. Minimal savings. And when she'd come through the front door, its paint flaking, the greasy-haired woman who had opened it had taken one look at her and pointed at the NO REFUNDS, NO EXCEPTIONS sign that hung on the wall.

Emelia bit the inside of her cheek to stop the tears she could feel welling. It was a room. With a roof. There were worse things in life. That's why she was here. Squaring her shoulders, she moved to the door and put her hand on the handle, clearly signaling her desire for the woman to leave her alone.

"I finish serving breakfast at eight on the dot." Even the woman's English accent was unappealing. Guttural and harsh.

8

If the room was any indication of the quality of the food, Emelia planned on never ever eating anything served under this roof for as long as she was stuck there. "Okay, thanks."

The woman finally got the hint and shuffled off down the dim corridor decorated with peeling wallpaper and brown shag carpet that had probably been passé in the seventies.

Emelia had to put her shoulder into getting the door to close properly. The wood finally smashed into the swollen frame.

She dropped her purse on the decrepit desk. The scarred top was graffitied with years' worth of contributions, most of which were R-rated. Emelia reached inside her bag for her gloves so she could strip the bed without risking contact with her skin. Tonight, she'd sleep in her clothes.

As she pulled out the leather set, a pale pink slip of paper fell out onto the desktop. Her stepmother's cursive handwriting swirled up at her. An envelope had arrived the day Emelia had left for Oxford. She'd been foolish enough to hope it contained something useful, like cash. But no, all it held was pages of Carolina's deluded social aspirations.

I really don't understand your reluctance about Harry. All the benefits of royalty without the responsibility of the crown. And Kate would be your sister-in-law. Just imagine!

9

Emelia suppressed a shudder as she crumpled the lavender-scented note and tossed it at the trash can in the corner of the room. The pink ball hit the rim and bounced to the floor, rolling across the worn carpet.

No offense to the duchess, who, from all appearances, seemed like a thoroughly decent human being. But given the events that had resulted in Emelia's transatlantic relocation, her stepmother's obsession with getting a foot in the door of the House of Windsor was about as appealing as the contents of Emelia's inherited minifridge. And she hadn't even opened it yet.

She took a swig from her water bottle as she assessed the disconcerting situation she'd found herself in.

This wasn't exactly the arrival at Oxford she'd imagined.

But then, her childhood dreams had also included visions of a full academic scholarship to study her literary idols. Living at one of the university colleges. Lectures and tutorials and being someplace where everyone spoke the same language as she did.

This. Was. Not. That.

Wiping her hands against her travel-worn jeans, she suddenly couldn't take the silence anymore.

She needed to get out of this grubby room.

She needed to find a wardrobe.

Two

Peter Carlisle had spent ten years hunting for the perfect birthday present for his mother. A saner man would have given up by now and settled for a sweater. But no. He had to go and develop an obsession with a teacup that was more elusive than the White Witch's sense of humor in *The Lion, the Witch and the Wardrobe*.

His feet slipped on the icy cobblestones of Oxford's Turl Street. He zipped his jacket up until it covered his chin and tugged his hat down to minimize exposure to the icy February sleet.

Dodging a slow taxi, he cut across the road, one of the few pedestrians crazy enough to be out ona night like this. He checked his watch. Quarter to six. He should make it just in time, even though it was a total long shot that Oxford Antiques would have the prized piece of bone china he was seeking. But he'd spent the last two hours scouring every antiques shop in town, hoping a miracle would happen at the last second. This was the final store.

It had seemed like a fun challenge ten years ago. He'd decided, at his mother's fiftieth birthday party, that by her sixtieth, he would have found the last four teacups for her vintage floral Aynsley collection. He'd thought it would

11

be easy. And he'd succeeded with the first three for her fifty-first, fifty-fourth, and fifty-seventh birthdays respectively. But the last one, a 1950s corset-shaped teacup with large pink roses, had proved determinedly elusive. Not even the disturbing development of an eBay obsession that saw him losing hours of his life on the site had come through.

So here he was. The day before his self-imposed deadline expired. About to fail. Which pretty much summed up the last twelve months of his life. At least this time only he would know about it. Wouldn't be subjected to the sympathetic inquiries of family and friends asking how he was doing.

Steeling himself against the inevitable disappointment he was about to be dealt, he turned the knob to the door of the antiques store, the bell above announcing his entrance.

The shop was almost the same temperature as the street. Reginald, the proprietor, didn't believe in heating. He proclaimed it better for his wares if customers shivered while they browsed. It certainly had the effect of weeding out anyone who wasn't a serious buyer.

Peter gave a nod to the elderly owner at his usual perch behind the cash register. And he meant *cash* register. The man must have been one of the only retailers still left who dealt in cash and only cash.

Peter ducked into the corner where Reginald stacked his mismatched assortment of vintage crockery. For the second before he saw what sat there, a hit of anticipation buzzed inside him. And left just as quickly. His gaze scanned the five teacups that sat arranged on a sideboard. All familiar. Only one Aynsley, already in his mother's collection.

His phone vibrated deep in his pocket. Probably one of the team wanting his take on how they'd done at training. The famous Oxford vs. Cambridge Boat Race was less than two months away and the provisional rowing crew for Oxford's Blue Boat had been selected. But the men who'd just missed out on the lineup and been consigned to a reserve boat were still putting up a fight. As the brutal sets of five-hundred-meter sprints earlier in the day on Dorney Lake had shown.

He pulled the phone out and glanced at the screen. *Victor* flashed up at him. He would've welcomed talking to anyone else. In the background, the bell rang above the door, signaling someone else doing some last-minute antiquing. He answered the call.

"Hi." His tone was curt.

"Bunny." His brother's voice held a familiar cadence. The one that indicated he was a few beers down but not yet obliterated. When Peter had left Victor a few hours before, he'd been drinking beer out of a fellow rower's shoe in the back of the team van. All class, his big brother. "So, whatcha doing?"

Peter almost didn't tell him. An uncharitable part of him hoped his brother had forgotten what the following day was. "Shopping for Mum's birthday present."

A pause was followed by a muffled curse. "Was it today?"

"Tomorrow." February 21. Same date every year, strangely enough.

"What are you getting her? Want to go in together?"

Ha. Not likely. "Don't know yet, so probably best if you sort yourself out." He stepped back to allow a girl with brown, wavy hair and a focused expression to brush past him, heading for the adjoining room. There was something in the tilt of her head, the determined stride of her legs, that pulled his gaze to follow her as she walked.

"Do you mind if I crash at your place for a couple of nights? Marissa's kicked me out." His brother's voice jerked his attention away from the woman and back to their conversation.

"Again?" Peter couldn't think of anything he'd like less. He already saw way more of his brother than he had any desire to.

"Says the guy who's had all of, what? One girlfriend in his entire life? How about we talk when you have some experience under your belt,

14

little bro." Peter couldn't have been less interested in the kind of experience Victor referred to, but his brother's jab still hurt.

Didn't matter what Peter said; his brother would have taken up residence on his foldout by the time Peter got home. "Two nights. Max."

"Gotcha."

No doubt Victor would be on the charm offensive tomorrow, wooing his way back into his on-again, off-again girlfriend's forgiveness for whatever his latest transgression was. And she'd relent, as she always did. For a smart girl, Marissa was mighty dumb when it came to his brother. Peter would have put money on Afghanistan's winning an Olympic rowing gold over his brother's backing up the promises that slipped off his lips like honey but always delivered vinegar.

"And pick up some milk and cereal on your way over. We're out." He ended the call before his brother could reply. If Victor managed one out of the two, Peter would count it as a win.

He'd spent his entire life covering his older brother's backside, and it had reached new heights in the last year. He was over it. Over being hauled out of bed at crazy hours to get him out of trouble. Over his flat being treated like a halfway house whenever it suited. Over helping Victor achieve the very dream that Peter had been robbed of. Over trying to help cover up the

15

gaping crevices in his brother's character. Yet he kept doing it because the alternative was worse.

He scanned the teacups one last time. As if one might have miraculously transformed in the last thirty seconds. Nope. Still nothing.

Jamming his phone back into his pocket, he turned to head back to the front door, then paused. Might as well keep looking around. Maybe the teacup was a bust, but something else might grab his eye. It wasn't like he'd been smart enough to come up with a Plan B on the present front.

Turning back, he pulled his hat off his head as he ducked under the archway into the next room, partly intrigued to see what it was the girl with the wavy hair had been so intent on reaching.

Stopping, he blinked, trying to work out what he was seeing. Or wasn't. There were no exits from the room except the one he was standing in. But the girl had disappeared.

Once Emelia had located the town center, it had been easy to find an antiques shop. Now she just hoped it held the one thing she was looking for. It had to. This was England. The first room hadn't yielded anything apart from a gentleman manning the register who looked like he predated most of his shop's contents and a tall guy on a phone.

Ducking through an archway, she stepped into another room packed with furniture. It was almost impossible to move between tables, chairs, side tables, and desks to get farther into the space.

But there it was, in the far corner: a tall, wide wardrobe flush against the wall. How she didn't see it as soon as she walked in, she had no idea. Imposing. Majestic. In the crowded room, there was space around it, a gap between it and the other pieces of furniture. As if even inanimate objects instinctively knew that this was something deserving of deference. Not to be crowded around like baked beans packed into a can.

Moving furniture out of the way as quietly as possible so as not to attract any attention, Emelia drew closer. Until she was close enough to touch it, to see her breath fog up the varnished mahogany.

Of course, the real one was made of apple-tree wood, but who really knew what that looked like?

It was deep, one of the deepest she'd ever seen. And tall. Towering above her, not even an inch between its top and the ceiling.

Lifting her left hand, she brushed the wood with her fingertips, then placed her palm flat against the cool surface.

Looking over her shoulder, she scanned the space. No one. The only sound was the low, muffled voice of the guy on the phone in the other room.

Biting her bottom lip, she let her fingers run along the side of the door. The wardrobe tugged at her, the way all wardrobes like this had since she was a little girl.

Wherever you are, Emmy, you will always find safety in here. And one day, one day, you and me? We'll find the wardrobe.

The words her mom had whispered to her tiptoed through her mind. Whispers of the past that haunted her every step.

The door swung open without even a squeak. Smoothly, on hinges that felt like they'd been oiled seconds ago, even though the cobwebs in the top corner told a different story.

She stuck her head in. Darkness met her like a warm embrace. For all the unfulfilled promises her mother had made, for some reason the one about always feeling safe in wardrobes had stuck. Along with the compulsion to continue her mother's lifelong mission to find *the one*.

There were rules, of course. No feeling for the back until you were inside. No playing it safe, keeping your feet on the outside and reaching out. You had to commit. Narnia would never be found by those who were uncertain or ambivalent.

Sitting on the bottom, she swung her legs inside, tucked them toward her chest, and pulled the door closed behind her until just a sliver of light remained. Her hand hit something small. In the darkness she couldn't see what. Picking it up, she held it right in front of her face. A floral teacup and saucer set. What was a teacup doing in a wardrobe? Though, to be fair, it was probably thinking the same thing about her. Her hand relocated it under her tented knees so she wouldn't accidentally break it.

She sat for a second. Felt her shoulders relax against the wood. Then realized she wasn't alone in this space. Something soft brushed against her head. Reaching up, she grasped a sleeve. Her pulse drummed in her throat. Maybe . . . She'd never really allowed herself to hope it might be true. Even though she couldn't deny her compulsion to climb inside every antique-looking, wooden wardrobe. The deep-seated kind that wouldn't allow her to walk away until she knew *for sure* it wasn't a portal.

But there had never been one filled with coats before.

Well, if this was it, she wasn't going to discover the mystical land sitting on her backside. Pushing herself up to standing, she faced the back of the wardrobe and reached out a hand in front, pre-paring for disappointment, yet half expecting to feel the soft whisper of a snowflake against her fingers.

Her hand hit wood. Solid, unmoving wood. Her whole body sagged. There was no portal here. She was crazy. Just like her mother.

Emelia battled the urge to sink to the floor. To curl herself up into a ball and cry. What was she doing here? In Oxford. In an antiques shop. In a wardrobe. It would have been funny, if it weren't so pathetic.

Turning around, she leaned her forehead against the frame of the door, trying to settle her thundering pulse and soothe the unreasonable disappointment that had blossomed inside.

Suddenly, light flooded in. Everything shifted and her body jolted, discombobulated by the sudden change.

"Argh . . ." Arms flailing, she plunged headlong into the space where the door had vanished faster than a Turkish delight within Edmund's reach.

"Oomph." The sound of air bursting from lungs registered about the same time as the sensation of arms grasping her waist, preventing her from hitting the floor.

A blur of navy blue and the scent of cinnamon were all she managed to distinguish from the chaos as her feet found the ground.

One thing she knew for sure: there was no chance this was the octogenarian who'd been holding down the fort when she'd walked in. A good thing, since she would have squashed him flat. Instead, she found herself staring up into the very surprised face of a green-eyed male with an unruly thatch of what could only be described as flaming ginger hair.

Relinquishing his hold, he grinned down at her. "So . . ." The accent told her he was as English as mushy peas and warm beer. "Are you a Susan or a Lucy?"

• • •

A Susan or a Lucy? Where did that come from? Victor was always the one with the lines, not him. Never him. Peter was the guy who could practice a line for days and be left dry mouthed and mute when it came time to deliver it. Let alone when someone who looked like a Narnian wood nymph fell on top of him.

The missing girl stared up at him. All wide blue-gray eyes and wavy hair the color of Cadbury milk chocolate. She was tall too, reaching his nose when most girls barely made it to his shoulders.

She was clearly a Lucy. Susan, ever the older sister, was way too practical to go climbing into wardrobes on a whim.

"Let me guess. You're Peter." Both her tone and her face were inscrutable. The only thing that gave anything away was the American accent.

He frowned, searching her face for anything that could trigger a memory of her. "Do I know you?"

Now she looked confused as she shook her head, hair bouncing across her shoulders. "No. Why?"

"Then how do you know my name?"

"Your name?"

This was the weirdest conversation ever. Not that, he supposed, much more could be expected when it began with someone falling out of a wardrobe onto you. "How did you know my name was Peter?"

Now she gave him the kind of look one gave someone extraordinarily thick. "I was being sarcastic. Peter. As in Peter and Edmund. Lucy and Susan's brothers. And no one ever wants to be Edmund, do they?"

Good one, clever clogs. For once in your life, you come up with a good line and you manage to blow it.

"Are you trying to say your name is actually Peter?"

"Guilty."

Awkward silence. She stared up at him, her face unreadable. "It's a bad line. It gives you away."

"As what?"

"That you're not a real Narnia fan."

"I'm not a real Narnia fan?" He almost laughed aloud at how wrong she was.

"A true Narnia fan would never ask a girl if they were a Susan or a Lucy."

And with that cryptic remark she somehow managed to cut past him, weave her way through the furniture-filled room, and disappear. Leaving Peter to stare after her with her final statement resounding in his ears. The sound of the bell ringing and then the front door slamming shut shook him from his daze. What had just happened?

He turned back to the wardrobe and its open door. He'd seen it in here before but never really paid it much attention. He stepped toward it. It looked deep. A few coats hung on old metal hangers. Reaching in, his fingers traversed past the rough woolen material before grazing the wooden back and then traveling down.

His hand brushed against something cool and smooth sitting on the floor as he leaned back. Crouching down, he looked into the depths, his breath snagging at what peered back at him. He blinked, then rubbed his eyes to check he wasn't dreaming.

A teacup. Slowly he reached for it, pinching the saucer between his fingers and pulling it toward him, not even daring to breathe.

Not just any teacup.

The elusive Aynsley 1950s corset-shaped teacup with pink roses he'd spent the last ten years looking for.

Three

"Five, four, three, two, one." Peter counted down the sprint as Max's seat on the rowing machine moved like a blur. At Peter's last count, the tall, muscular athlete let go of the handles and collapsed over his knees, shuddering and gulping in air.

"Good work." Peter uttered the useless words as he dropped to one knee. Max didn't even acknowledge them. It didn't matter what he said. The only thing that mattered was the numbers.

The athlete didn't even flinch when Peter drew blood. A tiny prick was nothing compared to the abuse every muscle in his body was giving to him.

Peter tagged the sample and read the numbered sticker out to Grant, so the cox could note it on the clipboard he held. The Boat Race may have been considered an amateur rowing race, but the teams had access to all the same training support as the professionals. The lactate levels in his blood would tell the coaching team far more about how Max's body was responding to the ever-increasing training load than anything else.

Peter looked at the time on the screen. Grant would note that too. Not incredible, but not bad, keeping him squarely in the middle of the pack. It was going to be a close call who the last oarsman would be for the Blue Boat. Peter was glad he was just the assistant coach—a token one at that—and the decision wasn't on him.

It had looked pretty cut-and-dried after the winter training in Spain, and then James had gone and gotten pneumonia, taking him out of the running and opening the field up again. The news had just come this morning that he wasn't going to be fit to return anytime soon. The guys contending for the now-open seat were throwing everything they had at the opportunity.

Peter clapped Max's sweat-covered shoulder as

he stumbled away to cool down. A year ago, he'd been that guy. Body sagging over his knees, lungs trying to grab oxygen with rapid short breaths. Now he was standing in a gym in Oxford, drawing blood and cross-checking paperwork. He'd only gotten the job because Sean had taken pity on him, scrounging up enough hours between working here and teaching some beginners' rowing courses at the Oxford Academicals Rowing Club to pay what he needed to barely scrape by.

"Ethan, you're up next." The big American ambled forward and set himself up on the erg. He'd lost a lot of the cockiness he'd rolled in with in September, used to being the big man on campus at Harvard with a string of impressive victories behind him.

It happened every year with the internationals, accustomed to being rowing superstars back home. They showed up at Oxford expecting to be a shoo-in for a seat in the coveted Blue Boat. Then the reality that there was a world of mind-breaking pain between the standard race distance of two thousand meters and the Boat Race distance of six thousand eight hundred set in.

Ethan rolled his shoulders and swung his arms a couple of times before gripping the handles.

"Whenever you're ready." Peter stepped away before the muscular rower could even start. The machine would do all the counting he needed.

Exiting the gym, he walked down the hall to drop the blood off with all the other samples that had been taken that morning.

He let his mind drift back to the excitement on his mum's face the night before when he'd presented her with her present. It had been more than worth the price tag, which would have him pretty much living on rice and cereal for the next few weeks.

Not even Victor, who had gone easy but expensive with some kind of day spa experience, had come close. And his brother's glower showed he knew it too. It was nice to be one up on the golden boy for once. Especially when said golden boy lied through his teeth to their parents about pretty much everything and dragged Peter along as an unwilling accomplice.

His mind flipped over to the girl, a thought not far from his mind during the last couple of days. It still all seemed like a surreal dream. Her falling out of the wardrobe onto him. The teacup being left behind. It was about as crazy as anything that had happened in Narnia. If he'd heard it from one of the guys, he'd have assumed someone had been consuming something that was definitely not approved by UK Anti-Doping.

"Who is she?"

"What?" He turned to where the burly president of the club was leaning against the doorframe. He hadn't even heard Tim approach.

"You have a weird smile on your face. You have a hot date last night?"

"If by 'hot date' you mean my mother's birthday, then yes."

"Huh." Tim didn't look convinced but let it drop. "How are the guys doing?"

Peter looked down at the clipboard Grant had handed to him. "Pretty good considering the brutal row yesterday. Max and Hayden are pretty much neck and neck, time-wise. Will be interesting to see what their bloods show."

Tim rubbed a hand across his forehead. "I hate this part. One of them is going to have his dreams come true, the other will miss out by the slimmest margin. And he'll know it."

"Yes, well. Anything can happen still." As he well knew. One second a rower on the Great Britain national team, a sure thing for Olympic selection, the next a has-been before he'd managed the has.

"Victor's been throwing some crazy-big numbers. Cambridge would stroke out if they could see them." Tim made the observation casually.

"Good for him." Peter managed to keep most of the bitterness out of his voice. It had been easy to excuse himself from any role in Victor's selection for the Blue Boat, not so much to try to hide the animosity that existed between the two of them.

27

His brother hadn't rowed a day in his life until Peter had gotten injured. Peter had almost lost his breakfast the day Victor had shown up at trials. There was a glint in his eye as he said he'd decided to "give it a go." Just his luck his brother had proven to be freakishly good at it. Like he was at pretty much everything he tried.

Tim's eyes narrowed. "How's the physio going?"

"Okay." He wasn't ready to admit aloud that his improvement had plateaued a month ago. That even Kevin, one of the country's best sports physiotherapists, seemed to be less optimistic with every session.

Peter rotated his left shoulder, checking for any pain or tension. Plateauing wasn't an option. The only option was total recovery. He had not come all this way to be permanently out of the game now. He was going to make a comeback if it killed him. He owed it to Anita.

"You'll get there." Tim gave him the same shoulder clap Peter had given Max a few minutes before. "You've got time until Tokyo."

It wasn't supposed to be Tokyo, it was supposed to be Rio, he wanted to shout. His entire life since he was fourteen had been oriented around being in the Team Great Britain boat in 2016. And he'd almost made it too. Then he'd had to try to be the good guy. And paid for it by losing the only thing he'd ever really wanted.

Four

Emelia sucked in a breath. Forced one out. Curling her fingers around the bottom of her rickety chair, she stared straight ahead at the notice board on the wall opposite. The flyers and pamphlets sat at all angles, pinned seemingly at random. Some proclaiming dates months old. Emelia's fingers itched to go over there and restore order to the poor overladen board. But no. She, more than anyone, knew the importance of first impressions.

Everything rested on now. She'd cut ties with LA. Changed her appearance. Booked a one-way ticket to England. Spent four nights in a hovel that deserved to be condemned. All for this. There was no Plan B.

For some reason, the green eyes and red hair of a certain Englishman floated into her mind. *"Are you a Susan or a Lucy?"* His half-laughing question had echoed there since he'd asked it. It was a great pickup line. She had to give him that. If she'd been a girl who had only seen the movies. Unfortunately for him, she was a true Narnia fan. She knew what had happened to Susan. Worse, she knew she *was* a Susan.

"Emelia Mason?" The words came from her right. Emelia loosened her death grip on the chair and stood. Next to her was a woman with an immaculate gray bob and a weary face. Her voice sounded tentative, even though Emelia was the only one there. She could only hope that meant there were few contenders for this job.

She pressed her palms to her skirt for a second, then held out her hand. "Hello, I'm Emelia."

The woman gave her a quick handshake but didn't quite look Emelia in the eye. Not a promising start. "Elizabeth Bradman. Thanks for coming in." The woman gestured toward a hallway and then led her through a door that sat ajar a short distance away.

They entered a cramped, utilitarian room. Along one wall stood a row of filing cabinets, in the middle a battered wooden desk. Facing the desk was one worn chair, stuffing poking through a couple of cracks in the brown leather cover. No one was ever going to accuse the charity of wasting donors' money on aesthetics, that was for sure.

The one incongruous thing was the top of the desk. Precisely positioned folders and papers surrounded a green blotter, on which sat one piece of paper at a ninety-degree angle to the edge of the blotter. A fountain pen sat to the side, parallel with the edge of the paper. Perfect order. It made Emelia feel happy just looking at it. A woman after her own heart.

"Take a seat." Elizabeth gestured to the chair

positioned facing the desk, again, right in the center.

Emelia's feet moved across the worn carpet, her breath shallow in case it happened to dislodge any of the papers.

She placed her purse on the floor and perched on the chair as the woman moved behind the desk and sat. Her posture remained as straight as a broomstick. "I'm the acting executive officer for SpringBoard. Please tell me, succinctly, why you applied for this job."

Clearly this was not a woman who believed in small talk. Or making potential employees comfortable, for that matter. Fortunately, Emelia had prepared for this question. "I have recently moved to Oxford. As you'll see from my résumé I've had a range of involvement with charities in Los Angeles. I've spent the last few years working as a journalist but am looking for a career change. This seemed like a role that would be a good fit for my skills."

Ms. Bradman tapped a tapered finger on the sheet of paper in front of her. "You have an American accent, yet your application states you have the right to work in the UK. Is that correct?"

"I'm a British citizen. My mother was British." The only thing her mom had left her that turned out to be any use. "I have my passport with me if you'd like to see it." She reached for her purse, but Ms. Bradman waved her hand.

"Why the sudden desire for a change from journalism?"

Because I was the type who made headlines out of other people's misery. Because somewhere in the last five years, I lost myself in pursuit of scandal. Because someone is dead because of me. Because this job is my one chance to make some kind of atonement.

The thoughts flashed through her mind, robbing her of breath for a second. She forced herself to push them back, to focus on the task at hand. Emelia framed her response carefully. "I enjoyed the work that I did with charities back home and when I read this job description it looked like a great fit for me."

SpringBoard focused on getting books to kids at poor schools. Not unlike thousands of other charities around the world. But their point of difference was they then connected every book they provided with experts who came in and talked to the classes, made them real. Academics, historians, archaeologists, even a few of the authors themselves were listed on the honor roll on the charity's website.

"I see." Ms. Bradman looked her up and down. Emelia was thankful she'd worn the most conservative outfit she owned. Black skirt and jacket, blue shirt. Finally, a sigh escaped. "I'm not going to lie. We are not in good shape here. The last executive officer quit without notice a few months ago. I'm filling in temporarily as a favor. The board has given us until the end of the year to turn things around. You seem like a perfectly nice young woman but I can't afford to make a hiring mistake. And the truth is that Americans and the English are very different. I'm not sure I can trust our one chance to someone who doesn't even know the English way." She started to push her chair back as if to signal the end of an interview that hadn't ever really begun.

A streak of desperation surged through Emelia. She was in Oxford for this job. She had burned her bridges, had nothing to go back to. It could not already be over after less than ten minutes in a closet-sized office. "I knew Anita." She just blurted out the words from between her lips, causing her chest to constrict.

Something crossed Ms. Bradman's face. She didn't say anything but paused, seeming to really look at Emelia for the first time.

Emelia scrambled to explain without lying. "We weren't close but I promise you, I will do everything in my power to get her charity back on its feet."

The woman's face softened at the mention of SpringBoard's founder. "So this is personal."

It couldn't get any more personal. "Very much so."

Ms. Bradman pursed her lips, tapped her capped fountain pen on the blotter in front of her. "You've seen the salary?"

Emelia could understand her hesitation. "Salary" was a generous term for the pittance they were offering. If she were still in LA it wouldn't have even covered her mortgage payments. "Yes, ma'am."

"When are you available from?"

"I just moved to Oxford. I can start as soon as you want." The desperation practically leached out of her pores.

"Okay." Ms. Bradman scribbled something on the piece of paper in front of her. "Tell me about your references."

"Ava Brownley is the event co-coordinator for LA Lit, which is a charity for inner-city children in LA. It has a number of similarities with SpringBoard's work. I worked on a number of fund-raising events for her. Kevin Wright is the chair of Outside the Box, which is a foundation that assists people with mental illness. I did some communications and PR work for them."

Not for the first time, she gave thanks that she'd kept her charity work and her real job completely separate. Neither Ava nor Kevin knew anything about Mia Caldwell, so there was no chance of their inadvertently dropping the name that would ruin everything.

"Okay. Assuming your references check out, let's go with starting on Monday. I'll take a copy of your passport and I'll be in touch tomorrow with what further information we require."

What? That was it? Emelia couldn't have been more surprised if the woman had offered to fly her to the moon. "Um, yes. That would be fine. Thank you." The woman didn't even look up from what she was writing. Right. Dismissed then.

Emelia crept out of the room, hardly daring to breathe until she was out the door lest the woman inside change her mind.

Once in the hallway, she sagged against the wall. She'd done it. Gotten the job that she'd thrown her whole life in for. Now she just had to work out how on earth to do the impossible.

Five

Peter walked in his front door and stifled a groan. Not again. From his entryway, he could see his brother's feet hanging off the end of his couch.

He was cold. He was soaked through from two hours in the freezing February rain. It had not been a good rowing session. The team had spent most of the time struggling to get into a good rhythm on the lake, all of them growing more frustrated when they failed. And now he knew, without a doubt, he would get into the shower and discover Victor had used up all the hot water.

He'd just seen Victor all of an hour ago at training. Funny how his brother hadn't thought to mention then he was planning to take up residency on his couch. Again. It had only been three days since his last stint. But then, Victor had always lived by the motto that it was easier to ask forgiveness than permission. Not that he ever bothered with the former either.

Stomping into his living room, Peter found his brother balancing a bag of potato crisps on his torso and a beer in his hand. Both of the Peter's. Because that was what his brother specialized in: taking.

And he was done.

"What did you do this time?" Peter picked up his brother's keys off the coffee table and started flipping through them. Finding his house key, he started twisting it off the ring.

"I— Hey! What are you doing?" Victor lifted his head to watch Peter extract his key and stuff it in his pocket.

"We're done with this being a halfway house. I have an actual flatmate. And both of us like having hot showers and not having our food eaten. So I don't care what kind of girlfriend troubles you have, I'm no longer your alternate for when she kicks you out."

"Wow, look at you, little bro. Gone and grown a backbone and everything." Victor cast him a sardonic smile as he reached for another handful of crisps. "And here I was just enjoying some of your moments of glory."

Peter looked toward the TV to find some kind

of sports highlights show on and saw his team, faces taut with agony, pulling back against the oars. The yellow Team Great Britain boat chasing Germany's green one.

In a split second, he was back in the previous June. Out on the water in Varese, Italy. With his guys. Lungs burning. Body screaming. Sun beating down. The longest five minutes and twenty-seven seconds of his life as they'd fought to take the lead and then hold it against the powerful Germans, who took the fight right to the end. A third of a second was all that separated them at the finish line.

It was one of his biggest victories. It was also the last time he'd raced. Little did that guy in the boat know he was only hours away from losing everything.

He steeled his face before he turned back to Victor, refusing to let him see how much it hurt. His brother would only go out of his way to pour more salt in the wound if he knew.

"I might need to stay a few days. Marissa and I, we're proper done this time."

Peter couldn't say he was sorry. The truth was Marissa was better off without his brother. The guy treated women like they were disposable. He just hoped she'd been the one to work it out and end things. There were already too many girls bearing the scars of Victor's charm-them-and-leave-them approach to life. Once he donned the blue jacket, the sign of having reached the highest sporting level at Oxford, he would be unbearable.

"You've got two days. I've got a friend crashing this weekend." Jackson was actually going to sleep in Tony's room, since his flatmate was going to be away, but there was no need for Victor to know that.

Victor took another slurp of his beer. "Okay, fine. Relax. I guess I can always go home. Tell Mum you kicked me out."

He'd forgotten for a few brave moments his parents thought he and Victor lived together. Victor had spun that tale a while back, and Peter had never found a way to break his mother's heart and tell her the truth—that her eldest son was actually shacked up with some girl she'd never met.

"Sure. Go for it."

They stared at each other. Despite all his brother's character flaws—and they made a long list—Victor did actually seem to care about their parents. As much as he cared about anyone.

Peter had long since stopped praying that they would ever be friends. There was too much between them. Had been since the day he dared to be born. The gap had just grown exponentially over the years. Something he was reminded of every time he looked at the scar marring his brother's face.

About the only thing that still held them together

was their uneasy truce to keep the depths of their antagonism from their parents. So Peter was going to take his chances that Victor wouldn't go out of his way to upset their mother.

"So, little brother, how much does it suck knowing you've already lived the greatest moment of your life?" Victor pointed at the TV screen as the two boats crossed the finish line, Team Great Britain just ahead. Peter's eyes locked on the sheer joy and exhilaration that radiated from his face. From the faces of his entire team.

Victor's taunting question was one that dogged his every waking moment. It was the reason that, no matter what the experts said, he couldn't accept he would never experience that again. He had to. There was no other option.

Six

Emelia stepped into the small office she'd been assigned at SpringBoard, dropping her bag on the top of her pristine desk. She didn't officially start for another forty-five minutes, but her latest strategy was to spend as little time in the hovel as possible.

Hopefully the alerts she'd put on roommate-search websites would yield something. So far she hadn't been able to find anything that fit her criteria. She didn't think she was being too picky.

Her standards had started off pretty high but slipped by the day as her desperation mounted. Now she was down to affordable, within cycling distance of the city center, not with weirdos, and in a building that didn't deserve to be condemned.

Sitting in her chair, Emelia ran her hand over the wooden desk. Four days since she'd started and there was no hint of anything personal. Nothing that would tell a passerby anything about her. Just stacks of paper and a plastic tray that held her stationery. The way she liked it. It was a habit she'd gained as a tabloid hack where the com-petition was as fierce between colleagues as it was between outlets. Anything personal hinted at a potential weakness. You didn't get to be the best in the cutthroat world of tabloid journalism by displaying your vulnerabilities.

Emelia logged in to her computer, pulling up all the websites she'd been searching, hoping that maybe, in the last twelve hours, someone had listed her dream situation. But as the minutes ticked by, her hopes deflated. She was paid up at the so-called Manor until next Wednesday. She would not be staying there for one night more. If she didn't have somewhere new to live by then, she'd dig into her meager savings. Stay in a hotel for a couple of nights. If even just to remind herself what it was like to be able to shower in bare feet again.

Closing down the sites, she pulled up the to-do

list that Elizabeth had emailed her the previous afternoon. With the staff down to a bare skeleton crew, everyone was pitching in to cover basic administration. She scanned the columns. Photocopying, envelope stuffing, a few phone calls to the few remaining donors to take their pulse. Not exactly a heavy intellectual load.

Picking up the stack of photocopying that had been left on top of the filing cabinet, she double-checked the instructions. Eighty copies each. That should keep the photocopier humming for a while.

Walking down the hall, she stepped into the photocopier/stationery cupboard. As she crossed the threshold she was met by a loud bang. Emelia jumped, a small scream slipping from her lips.

Startled, the petite redhead standing at the photocopier also let out a shriek.

They stared at each other for a second.

"Sorry. I didn't know anyone else was here." They spoke in unison, then paused.

Emelia glanced at the red flashing lights on the copier. "Do you need some help?"

The other girl looked at her with an expression of defeat. "Could you? It just keeps jamming and I can't work out why." She gestured to the floor by the machine, which was strewn with a collection of rumpled, half-torn pieces of paper. "I think it just hates me." The accent wasn't English. Australian, maybe?

Emelia placed her papers on a shelf and walked

over. "We've had a few battles this week. I make no guarantees, but I'll see what I can do."

She started opening doors and flicking knobs, pulling out crinkled pieces of paper as she went.

"I'm Allie, by the way."

Emelia glanced at the friendly green eyes and smattering of freckles. The woman's auburn hair was pulled back in a messy ponytail. She could have been anywhere between her midtwenties and midthirties. That was a contrast to the norm at the charity. All the other volunteers she'd met had decades on her.

"Emelia."

Reaching deep into the bowels of the machine, she reached for one of the last places she'd discovered paper could get caught and felt her fingers brush against the edge of a sheet.

"Are you new here?"

"Yes. I started on Monday. I'm the new fund-raising coordinator." She said it with far more confidence than she felt. What did she know about fund-raising? Yes, she'd helped Ava with some event-related stuff for LA Lit but the woman had been a seasoned veteran of the LA charity scene and made it all look easy.

"Thank goodness. I've only been volunteering here a few weeks but even I know we need you badly." There was no hint of a joke in Allie's expression. "Where are you from?"

"Boston." She didn't really think of herself as

from anywhere. But Boston was where she'd been happiest. When she'd had dreams of being an investigative reporter working for the *Post* or the *Times*. So that was what she claimed. "You?" Her fingers managed to grasp the corner of the paper and pull it free. She crumpled it up and dropped it to the floor to join its comrades.

"New Zealand. Have you been in England long?"

Emelia flicked knobs and switches, closing the copier doors as she went. "Almost a couple of weeks." Standing, she closed the final door. "That should hopefully do it. Let's give it a shot."

Allie loaded the feeder again, tapped "20" into the keypad, and hit the green button. They both watched as the machine whirred and then started spitting out copies.

"Fund-raising coordinator and photocopier miracle worker." Allie smiled. "Don't you dare go leaving anytime soon."

Emelia flushed. Why, she had no idea. Of all the praise she'd had in her life, it wasn't exactly near the top of the list. Fortunately, the sound of the machine spitting out sheets of paper covered the potentially awkward silence. "Glad I could help. It's the last turny thing. The one right at the back. Where the paper gets stuck. People don't usually think to look there." Now she was just blabbering like an idiot. She pivoted to collect her copying from the shelf.

"Emelia?"

She turned back. Allie was gathering up her set of papers. "If you're new in town, you probably haven't met many people yet. Our age, I mean. This place isn't exactly brimming with youth."

"Um, no. Not really. I've been trying to get settled."

"I'm having a house party on Saturday night. Just a small gathering. You should come. I mean, you don't have to. Obviously. But if you don't have anything better to do."

What did she say to a party invite from someone she'd known all of two minutes? This didn't happen in LA, where the people she crossed paths with specialized in the superficial.

Allie grabbed a pen and scribbled something on a Post-it. "Look. No pressure. But I just moved here in September so I know what it's like to be in a new city." She handed her the piece of paper. "This is my address. Anytime from seven thirty."

Emelia took the paper, folded it, and put it in her pocket. As far as things that she hated most, going to a party where she didn't know a single soul rated up there, but it might just beat any other option she had. Really, she only had one: another night hanging out in a used book shop she'd found that stayed open late. "Thanks."

Allie's machine spat out its last copy and stopped whirring. She gathered up the papers, placing them perpendicularly across the first. "Anyway, thanks so much for the help. I would've been stuck here all day if it wasn't for you." She made a face. "Showing up at my first school visit without the handouts wouldn't be great. I might see you Saturday?"

"Yeah, maybe." Emelia watched as Allie disappeared in a flurry of papers and swishing trench coat, a warm feeling expanding in her chest. For the first time since she'd arrived in Oxford, she felt like she wasn't alone.

Seven

The noise practically burst out of the small house, sounds of laughter and music. Through the windows, Emelia could see people already packed in and talking. What was she doing coming to a party hosted by someone she'd met for all of three minutes? She didn't even know Allie's last name.

Her fingers gripped tighter to the paper bag that contained the fancy-looking soda she'd brought. Maybe she could just walk in, put it down somewhere, and walk right out the back door.

Emelia didn't know what she was even doing here. A small gathering, Allie had said. If this was what they called a small gathering in New Zealand, she would have hated to see a large one.

She was bad with people. Especially strangers. The old her had been great with strangers. With anyone. But she wasn't professional schmoozer

Mia Caldwell anymore, with her blond hair and sassy smile. She didn't know who she was, but it wasn't her.

Emelia stopped on the front stoop. Frozen. Not able to knock on the door, but her feet refused to obey her instructions to turn around.

C'mon, Emelia.

Nothing could be worse than another night staring at the walls of her freezing room, listening to *Coronation Street* at full blast in the lounge directly below. The only other option she had was hiding out in the used book shop. That was where she'd spent the last few evenings, smuggling in a sandwich and hunkering down between the stacks. But the owner had started giving her looks of sympathy. Being the object of a stranger's pity grated. So here she was.

It's just people. They don't know you. That's why you're here. To reinvent yourself. To start again. To atone.

Blowing out a breath of icy air, she raised her hand, only for the door to fly open before she'd even touched the wood.

"Thank goodness. For a second there I thought you were going to turn around and leave." Allie greeted her with a cheery smile, like Emelia wasn't basically a stranger.

"I, uh . . ." Struggling for words, Emelia half shoved her brown paper bag at Allie. Like she was six years old and trying to bribe someone

46

to be friends with her by giving them cookies.

"Oh, thanks. Come in. Come in." Allie said the right words but didn't move at all. The only way Emelia was going anywhere would be if she shoved her out of the way. "I'm so glad you came."

"You going to actually let the poor girl in, hon?" a voice said from behind Allie.

"Yes, of course. Sorry." Allie stepped back into the entryway, allowing Emelia to step across the threshold. "This is Jackson." Allie gestured behind her to a tall guy with piercing blue eyes and a warm grin.

He reached around Allie and held out his hand. "You'll have to excuse her. This is the first house party she's hosted. She's a bit excited." Never had Emelia thought she'd be so glad to see another American. The familiarity of his accent was like a balm to her nerves.

"Emelia."

His hand enveloped hers as she shook it. A good firm handshake. "Nice to meet you." He planted a kiss on Allie's cheek. "I'll just go refill the snacks."

Allie closed the door and put the bottle Emelia had handed her on a table nearby. "Let me take your coat."

Emelia scanned the entryway quickly before she started unbuttoning it. She'd had no idea what to wear to something like this. Hadn't even thought to ask in the surprise of the invitation. So she'd played it safe with black pants and a tunic top. Not that she had much to work with given the minimal clothing she'd brought across the Atlantic with her. It was the first time since she'd left that she'd hankered for the extensive collection she'd had back home.

"Can I get you a drink?"

"Just a soda—um, fizzy drink, would be great." She was still trying to come to terms with what the English called things. Thankfully, with a large international student population in Oxford, when she fumbled and asked where to find a drugstore, people knew she meant a chemist, not a place to acquire illicit substances.

"Great. I'll just go grab you something." Allie gestured down the entryway to a room filled with people. "Go mingle. They're all friendly. There's a couple of other volunteers here. Lindsay. April. Elizabeth said she might drop by. I'll come find you."

And with that, she was gone.

The floorboards creaked as Emelia walked. Peering into the room, which turned out to be a combined kitchen and living area, she looked for Lindsay, a serious girl whom she'd met once. A PhD student, if she recalled correctly. They may not exactly have been kindred spirits, but she would take whatever she could get over walking into a room full of complete strangers.

No sign of the studious blonde.

"Excuse us." A couple of guys stood behind her, wanting to get past.

"Sorry." She stepped back, but even then she ended up pressed into the wall, personal space nonexistent.

What was she even doing here?

Everything whirled around her. All the conversations near her were academic debates. Dante and Hobbes. Something about quantum physics. People stood shoulder to shoulder in intense discussion. All of them way over her head. No room for a newcomer. She hadn't felt so out of place since her first day interning at the *Washington Herald*. The place that had taught her connec-tions mattered more than talent.

Her hands were clammy, her face hot. She didn't belong here. Turning around, she almost fell into a table filled with presents running along the entryway. A card on top of one seared her vision. *Happy Birthday.*

She had made a mistake coming. That much had been obvious before she'd even realized she'd crashed a birthday party. *Coronation Street* at full trumpet blast was definitely better than this.

"Here you go." Allie had appeared beside her like a mirage, a glass of light pink soda in her hand. "Hope you like pink grapefruit."

"Great, thanks." Her voice wavered a bit at the last word. Emelia tried to force her face into a neutral expression, but it was too late.

Allie peered up at her. "Are you okay?"

"I'm . . . I'm so sorry. I had no idea I was crashing your birthday party." She gestured at the table.

Allie looked around, as if surprised to see the presents. "Oh, you're not. You're totally not. It's not. My birthday was ages ago, I just never had a party and some crazy friends decided to use this as an excuse. Knowing them, they're probably all empty boxes." Allie tapped one with her knuckles. Sure enough, it sounded hollow. "You're new to the snowy spires of Oxford, right? You said you'd just arrived? Do you have family here?"

"Yes. Week before last. And no. No family." No anyone. Which had been part of the appeal, but now that she was here, she was realizing a life of splendid isolation wasn't all it was cracked up to be.

She'd expected to miss Lacey, her cousin, the only family member she was still close to. What she hadn't anticipated was that in the last few days, there'd even been the odd instance she'd have welcomed a conversation with Carolina. Which was saying a lot, given that the few times she'd seen her stepmother in the last couple of years, her social climbing and simpering had almost had Emelia reaching for the nearest blunt object.

Allie gave her a sympathetic look. "I get how

crazy moving to a new country can be. I've only been here five months too. But please, don't go. If you need some space, head on upstairs. Bathroom's up there. Take a few minutes. I have to go rescue some food in the oven, but I promise, when I'm done I'll introduce you to some great people. And if you're still not having fun in an hour, I will personally call you a cab. Deal?"

Emelia didn't have the heart to disappoint the hopeful face looking at her. She could always just hide in the bathroom for the next half an hour. She could hardly count on the party hostess to coddle her for the evening. "Deal."

As Allie disappeared back into the crowd, Emelia took a deep breath and wound her way to the staircase at the end of the hall. Climbing up it, she felt immediately calmer as she rose above the noise and crowd.

There were four doors leading off the upper landing. All closed. Turning to the one to her right, she knocked and pressed her ear to the door. Silence. Turning the handle, she pushed the door open and peered into the room.

Not a bathroom. A bedroom. Allie's, judging by the large photo of her and her boyfriend on the dresser. Emelia was about to retreat when her gaze drifted past the dresser and stopped on a large wardrobe nearly covering one wall.

Another Narnia wardrobe. Was Oxford full of them?

She turned, ready to pull the door closed behind her, but spun back around before she could.

Don't be crazy, Emelia.

You can't.

Her feet stepped into the room as her mind argued.

But she hadn't been able to resist the pull of finding Narnia her whole life. No matter the consequences.

Just like her mother. And for her the consequences had been fatal.

Peter wasn't a party guy. Especially when he had a training session early the next morning. Never when he had a session the next morning. Not even for Jackson and Allie, who seemed to have made friends with the entire city in the months they'd been in England.

So why was he breaking his rule tonight? There was zero explanation beyond the internal tugging he'd felt that he needed to be here. He could only hope the reason would become apparent sooner rather than later so he could go home to bed.

"Peter!"

Peter almost dropped the wrapped present cradled in his arm thanks to the trumpeting shout that erupted beside his left eardrum.

He looked down at the firecracker hostess standing beside him. "Thanks, Allie. I didn't need to hear out of that ear."

"Sorry." She didn't look sorry in the least.

"Happy not-birthday." He held out the large gift.

She looked with horror at the box. "Seriously? What am I supposed to do with all this stuff? You remember my contract is up in six months, right? No job, no England."

He seriously doubted there was any chance of that. From what he'd heard, Allie's Tolkien classes were so popular, there had almost been a few brawls between students trying to get seats.

She took the box, a smile quirking up at his amateur wrapping attempt before she placed it on a stack of other presents. His eyes widened at the height of the pile, and he suppressed a grin. When someone had suggested that everyone put their presents into the biggest boxes they could find, just to wind Allie up, he hadn't expected they'd do so well.

"I'm glad you're here. There's someone I want you to meet."

He sighed. "C'mon, Al. I know you're all flush with love, but I thought we'd agreed no more setups after the last one." Most excruciating blind date ever.

"How was I supposed to know she'd go all fan girl on you?"

It had been the longest two hours of his life, starting with the girl wanting to take selfies of them and then spending half the time tweeting or Instagramming or whatevering them to her friends. "Awkward" didn't even begin to describe it.

"I don't need to be set up, okay? Especially not with only weeks to go until the Boat Race. That's all I'm going to have time for." And after that, all he'd have time for was his coaching commitments to the local rowing club and training for his own comeback. Doing every-thing in his power to keep his promise.

Allie pulled a face. "Don't try and use that excuse with me. Do you forget some of your guys are in my classes? I've got plenty to keep them occupied the hours they're not rowing. It's not a setup, anyway. She's new in town. I just met her at church on Sunday."

Well, she'd come to the right place. Allie had the amazing ability to make people feel like they'd been friends since they were missing front teeth and drinking out of juice boxes.

"She's a rower too, so I'm sure she's not going to go all gaga on you like the last one." Allie studied him through critical eyes. "Though I'm not sure if I want her to meet you like this. You look like a total dork. What is with that sweater?"

He looked down at his green-, blue-, and red-covered torso. "Don't go knocking the jumper. My grandmother knitted this." And he was only wearing it because, between training, the horrible weather, and not having a dryer, he hadn't done laundry in weeks. It was the ugly jumper that only came out in times of desperation. Not that he'd ever admit it to Allie now.

"Is your grandmother coming to this party?" Allie made a show of looking around. "Because that is the only acceptable reason I can think of on God's green earth for you to be wearing that monstrosity."

He couldn't hold in his laugh. Jackson was never going to have a boring life with this girl, that was for sure.

"There she is." Allie waved at someone over his shoulder. "Stay right there, don't move." She ducked around him. Peter stayed where he was, as ordered. The room was so packed that even if he'd wanted to make an escape he wouldn't have been able to before Allie caught him.

She appeared beside him, a petite blonde trailing behind her. Peter's whole body tensed. It couldn't be. Surely not—

"Peter, this is Sabine. Sabine, this is Peter."

It was. His ex-girlfriend's blond hair hung around her face like a golden sheet, her blue eyes big. This was about to get as awkward as the blind date Allie had set him up on. "Sabine."

"Hi, Peter." She looked as weirded out as he felt. No surprises there. Months of no contact and the first time they saw each other was like this. "Look, I had no idea it was you. That you'd be here."

55

"You two already know each other?" Allie tucked a piece of hair behind her ear as she directed the question to Peter.

Peter fidgeted. Shoved his hands in his pockets. "Sabine and I used to date."

Allie raised her eyebrows while Sabine gave him a look he couldn't quite interpret. Then she turned to Allie. "For three years. Right, Seven?" She used his old nickname, after his rowing position. He hadn't heard it in months.

Allie glanced between the two of them as Peter tried to beg her with his gaze to save him somehow. Of all the things he'd come prepared for tonight, the second face-to-face post-breakup conversation with his ex was not one of them.

Allie either didn't see his plea or ignored it. "So, um, I'm just going to go and top up the snacks." Traitor. The girl moved faster than a speeding snowball as she turned and disappeared into the crowd.

The two of them studied each other for a second, both trying to find their bearings.

"Seriously, what are you doing here, Bine?" He switched to her nickname. As far as he knew, since their breakup, she'd stayed ensconced in London or wherever the women's rowing team was training. Both of them staying out of each other's turf. Her presence now in the middle of his was a clear breach of the unofficial settlement they'd drawn up. After three years together, a decent geographical distance between them seemed sensible.

Sabine shrugged a slender shoulder. "The team is on break for a couple of weeks so I came down to visit. Annabelle was coming to this and suggested I tag along."

He studied her feigned nonchalance, letting his eyes linger on her perfectly coiffed blond hair, immaculate makeup, and clothes that made the most of her figure without being ostentatious. He checked his emotions. Tried to work out what was tangled there. Was relieved to see that it didn't seem to be dormant attraction.

Certainly nothing compared to the girl who'd fallen out of the wardrobe, which was insane considering he had a long and complicated history with the girl standing in front of him and absolutely none with the one he'd met in the most unorthodox of ways.

"Since I ran into you, can we talk?" Sabine placed a hand on his arm.

"Bine, I don't think we have anything to talk about." He tried to say the words gently. It had been six months since their relationship had ended. It had been hard enough at the time, pain filling her face the day he'd broken it off. He didn't see what good could come from revisiting it.

"Peter, please." She looked up at him, hurt on her face. "Don't I deserve more than that after three years?"

Was he being too hasty? Was the reason he was here tonight to mend some kind of bridge with Sabine? He ran a hand through his hair. "You're right. I'm sorry. How are you?"

"I'm good." She looked up with the limpid gaze that had caused many a male rower twice her size to turn to jelly in her presence. "I've heard you're trying to save SpringBoard."

He was momentarily speechless. That wasn't what he'd expected her to say. "Yeah."

"I want to help."

"Sabine, I don't think that's a good idea." Working with his ex-girlfriend trying to save his dead cousin's charity? That had all sorts of shades of disaster painted around it.

"Anita was my friend too. This isn't about you. I can help."

She was right. He wasn't being fair. He still forgot he wasn't the only one who had loved Anita. He sighed. "Okay. I'll let you know—"

"Sorry to interrupt." Jackson didn't look sorry at all. Peter might've hugged the guy if his arms hadn't been laden with coats. "Do you mind taking these upstairs? We're out of room here. Al says there should be some space in her wardrobe. Otherwise just leave them on her bed. Her room's first on the right."

Peter took them. "Sure thing."

"I don't think we've met. Jackson Gregory." Jackson poured on the charm as he held out his

58

hand to Sabine. At which point Peter knew he'd been sent over by Allie with orders to extricate him. The guy was so besotted with his fiancée, he didn't give strange girls the time of day unless there was a good reason.

Sabine held out her hand. "Sabine Montclair."

"Not the Sabine Montclair nominated for sportswoman of the year?"

Peter did a double take halfway into his exit. He hadn't known about that. It had been one of her dreams for as long as he could remember. He tamped down the urge to give his ex-girlfriend a hug, but she deserved the accolade as much as anyone he knew. Sabine may not have been the girl for him, but he still wanted great things for her.

Sabine's eyes widened, and her jaw dropped a little. She clearly hadn't expected it either. Then a radiant smile spread across her face. "Yes. It was a huge surprise." Peter gave it about thirty seconds before Allie returned to stake her claim. It was now or never if he wanted to escape.

Stepping back, he squeezed through the crowd and headed for the stairs. Lifting the coats so they didn't drag on the floor and trip him up, he turned on the landing and walked to where the first door on the right stood open.

He dropped the coats on the bed, grabbed one of the hangers that Allie had left on the cover, and hooked a red wool coat over it.

Turning, he paused at the sight of a large, ornately carved wardrobe. A smile played on his lips. The last time he'd seen one of these, it had been under far more interesting conditions.

No doubt he'd never see the girl again. A pity since she'd intrigued him far more than he'd have liked to admit. Who climbed into a wardrobe in an antiques shop? And, the question that bugged him most, what had she meant with her comment about his not being a Narnia fan? And how did the teacup he'd been looking for for a decade fit into it all?

He'd almost prayed that they'd cross paths again but had stopped himself. It felt too trivial, too crazy. God had better things to be doing with His time than that. If He was going to do Peter any favors, he'd prefer it involved fixing his shoulder.

Swinging open the wardrobe door, Peter pushed a few hangers aside to make room for the coat, then shoved it in. It was a squeeze, but there might be room for a couple more.

He turned and walked back to the bed and picked up a designer-looking beige trench coat to go next. Settling it on a hanger, he turned. *"Argh!"*

The garment slipped from his hands and fell onto the floor like a sandcastle collapsing under a wave. He blinked. Once. Twice. Just to make sure he wasn't hallucinating.

There she sat. The Narnian wood nymph.

Perched on the edge of the wardrobe, boot-clad feet on the floor, clothing swinging around her head, like it was the most natural thing in the world.

Eight

The poor guy looked like he'd seen a ghost. Not that Emelia could blame him. Having someone fall out of a wardrobe once was strange. Finding them in a second one was just lunacy.

She'd held her breath when someone had first opened the door. Almost choked on it when she'd gotten a glimpse of his profile. The only reason Peter hadn't seen her was because he hadn't looked down. She'd hoped with all the desperation of Lucy trying to find Narnia a second time that there was only one coat. But when he hadn't closed the door, she'd known he'd be back and there was no chance he was going to miss a person folded into the bottom of the wardrobe again.

So she'd made a split-second decision to salvage what little dignity she had left and make herself known before she was found.

And so, here they were. She half in and half out of the wardrobe. And he staring at her, opening and closing his mouth like he'd lost the ability to speak.

Emelia took the advantage of surprise to study him a bit more. His hair was as flaming ginger as she remembered, his eyes as green, and his height still as imposing. So she cataloged the smattering of freckles across his face, his wide mouth, his athletic build, and his ugly sweater. Oh, his so-ugly sweater. Green with blue and red diamonds. It had better have some serious sentimental value, because there was no reason anyone should have been wearing it otherwise.

He had a nice face. Not one that would be called up for a *GQ* advertisement anytime soon, unlike Allie's guy, whose name she'd forgotten, but it was nice.

He still hadn't said anything. Instead, he'd kind of sagged onto the bed, still just staring.

Wow. Now this really was getting awkward. It looked as if the ball was in her court. "Hi. Um, sorry if I scared you." She pushed herself up as she spoke. Tried to subtly stretch her legs out.

"You're real." There was a kind of childlike wonder in his voice that wrapped around her heart. "I mean, of course you're real, I just . . ." He flapped one hand around. "Sorry. I'm just not used to finding cute girls in wardrobes."

She laughed as he pinched the bridge of his nose. "If it helps, I'm not used to being found in wardrobes either."

He seemed to regather himself at her words. Rising to his feet, he stood just under a head taller than her in her flat boots. Which would put him at about six foot three to her five foot nine. "I have a model of the *Dawn Treader*. I built it with my grandfather."

What? "Um, that's nice?"

He slid a smile at her that made her feel like she needed to sit back down for a few seconds. "It took us six months. It was like a gazillion pieces. You can't tell a guy who spent six months of his childhood building the *Dawn Treader* that he's not a Narnia fan."

Oh, that. "So you're practically Drinian." She threw out the name of the captain of the ship to test him. If he was such a fan, what was with the Susan/Lucy question? Only those whose knowledge of Narnia began at *The Lion, the Witch and the Wardrobe* and ended at *Prince Caspian* would ever want to be a Susan.

"I like to think I'm slightly less cynical than he was, but just as loyal." Peter tilted his head. "So, do I at least get to know the name of the girl who's almost given me two heart attacks?"

She wanted to offer her name, but something held her back. Once she gave him her name, it would be personal. She'd be more than the crazy wardrobe girl. She wasn't here to do personal. Well, not this kind of personal. She was here for atonement. That couldn't be derailed by some cute English guy, especially not one who had already been exposed to her particular brand of crazy twice and didn't seem to think she belonged in the closest psych ward.

The moment stalled.

"Great, you've found Emelia." Allie bustled into the room with another coat slung over her arm. She looked at Emelia. "Please don't judge him by the sweater. I promise he's cooler than he looks."

Emelia couldn't stop the grin that spread up her cheeks. "It would be hard not to be."

Peter looked back and forth between her and Allie. "She was lost?" She spent every day surrounded by accents, but for some reason, his tugged at something in her every time.

Allie shook her head. "Not lost. Just new. Emelia's recently moved to Oxford. I promised I'd introduce her to a few people."

He gave her a wink and held out his hand. "Well, I guess we should meet officially then. Peter Carlisle."

She held out her hand, aware of Allie watching their every move. "Emelia Mason."

His hand enveloped hers, and his gaze captured hers. Warm, secure. "Nice to meet you, Emelia Mason." Something about the way he smiled sent her heart beating in a way that a host of A-list celebrities with their million-watt grins hadn't managed.

It was nice to meet him too. Which made it a very big problem.

• • •

"Did he really spend six months building a model of the *Dawn Treader*?" Emelia directed her question to Allie, giving Peter a second to try to get some air. He had a name. And for some reason, his heart pounded like he'd just sprinted a mile.

"Oh, is that how long that took?" Allie didn't look in the slightest bit put out by the weird question as she grabbed a hanger out of the wardrobe and hooked the coat over it. "I don't know if that's true. But I can tell you he certainly has a model of the boat that he gets very anxious about if someone as much as breathes heavily near it."

"Hey now." That was an overexaggeration if there ever was one. Between the digs at his attire, the Sabine situation, and this, he was beginning to think Allie was more foe than friend.

"Who's your favorite character in the book?" Emelia was still studying him as if she was setting a test and waiting for him to fail.

"There was a boy called Eustace Clarence Scrubb, and he almost deserved it." Peter quoted the first line of *The Voyage of the Dawn Treader* without even thinking about it. Admittedly, the boy was a certified pain in the backside at the beginning, but he was also the character who underwent the biggest transformation over its pages.

"Huh. Interesting." Emelia pulled some kind of upside-down fish-mouth thing as she turned his answer over in her mind. Peter waited for an indication as to whether he had passed or failed whatever the test was, but she gave away nothing. Instead, she plucked another hanger out of the wardrobe and picked another coat off the bed, mirroring Allie's smooth movements.

"Who's yours?"

Emelia thought for a second, her head tilted. *"To defeat the darkness out there, you must defeat the darkness inside yourself."* She took a couple of steps and shoved the final coat into the already full wardrobe.

The words came from the magician Coriakin. Peter tucked away the knowledge that Emelia felt a kinship with the magician who had once been a star but had fallen from grace.

Allie turned from closing the wardrobe doors. "Okay, you two. Are we done trading lines or do we need a few more minutes to hide in here? Want me to bring up snacks and some drinks to tide you over a bit longer?"

Emelia looked startled. As he was sure he did too.

Allie looked at Emelia. "You're hiding from having to try to infiltrate a room full of strangers. Which is fair enough because I hate those as much as the next person, but that's going to change because I'm going to introduce you around now." Allie pointed her finger at Peter. "And he's hiding from his ex-girlfriend. Who I tried to set him up with. My bad. But I can't help him with that short of tying my sheets together so he can shimmy out my window. Which could be quite fun."

Peter blinked as Allie threw him under the bus. Hold on, she was the one who'd sent him up here with the coats . . .

"I'm quite good with tying knots," Emelia offered.

The three of them all stilled for a second as they processed her words.

"I mean . . ." The girl blushed to the tips of her hair as her words trailed off.

Peter's phone buzzed in his pocket. He pulled it out and looked at the screen. *Victor* flashed up at him. Silencing the call, he slid the phone back in his pocket. He was done being his brother's keeper for tonight. Victor would be turning twenty-nine this year. Time for him to get it together. He was the oldest in the rowing squad and still acted like some eighteen-year-old kid getting his first taste of freedom.

His phone started vibrating again.

"Looks like someone really wants to talk to you." Emelia tilted her head at him.

His finger itched to just turn his phone off, but he couldn't do it. He huffed out a breath. "I'm sorry. I should probably take it." Swiping to answer, he walked out into the hallway as he put his phone to his ear. "This had better be good."

"It'shh always good, little bro." His brother's slurred voice came over the line. Charming. Drunk before nine. "I just wanted to let you know, I took your carsh. But I'll bring it back tonight."

"You took my car?"

"Just for a couple of hours. I'll drive it back shoon. No problem."

Uh, yes problem. Very big problem. "Victor, you can't drive."

"I'm fine. Right as rain."

"Where are you?"

"Mazza's place."

Had they all lost their minds? They had training most of the day tomorrow. Starting at six. Not to mention a big five-kilometer erg test first thing on Monday.

Peter heard the sound of shuffling, then someone else on the line. "Coach?"

"Mitchell?" "Mazza" was what the rowing boys called him, but Peter stayed away from nicknames as much as he could. Tried to keep some sort of boundary between coach and team. Even if his brother made it his mission to make it almost impossible.

"Victor's pretty hammered, Coach." The seasoned international didn't sound impressed. Not that Peter could blame him. The guys took their rowing seriously. It probably killed them as much as it killed him that Victor had the superhuman ability to drink until hc was completely trollied and still somehow pull phenomenal times on the rowing machine the next morning.

"I'd let him stay here but honestly last time he did, he made a bit of a mess and my flatmates weren't very happy."

It was about a twenty-minute walk from Allie's to Mitchell's flat. As much as he'd have liked to tell the guy just to tip Victor out into the gutter and let him sleep it off, he couldn't. Especially since the sod had nicked his car, and Peter needed it in the morning to get to Wallingford for training. No doubt with his brother half passed out in the passenger seat. "Okay, I'll be there in about half an hour."

Turning, he walked back into Allie's room. "I'm sorry, I have to go." He tried to keep his gaze from Emelia. If he even looked at her, it would probably be written all over his face how much he didn't want to leave.

Allie gave him the stink eye but didn't say anything. She didn't need to. Her view that he should just leave Victor to fend for himself in situations like this was already well established.

"It was nice to meet you, Emelia." In trying to not give himself away, he came off disinterested. It was probably better that way. Meeting a girl who intrigued him was not in the cards for this year. There was no time to be distracted. The only thing that mattered was getting back in the game. He could never make up for how he'd failed Anita, but he was going to do everything he could not to break the final promise he'd made to her.

Nine

Week two. At the job that, if Emelia got it right, would be her atonement. Or some of it at least.

She'd spent the previous week learning about the charity and her way around the system. Now she was on her own. Emelia straightened the pad of paper on her desktop and picked up a ballpoint pen. Across the top of the page she scrawled *HOW TO SAVE SPRINGBOARD?* in large block letters and stared at the four words.

In nine months she'd have either answered that question or not. If it was the former, she could return to LA with some sense of closure. If not, Anita's legacy would be consigned to the same scrap heap as the many other charities that had tried and failed.

Peter did not feel very brave; indeed, he felt he was going to be sick. But that made no difference to what he had to do. The quote from *The Lion, the Witch and the Wardrobe* flashed through her head. That was basically how she felt about the rest of the year.

"Emelia?" Elizabeth stuck her head in the door. "Great, you're here. Can you drop by my office at nine thirty? I need to introduce you to the board member who's been given oversight of fundraising this year."

Great. Just what she needed. Some pompous middle-aged man breathing down her neck. Emelia summoned up a smile about as fake as the color of Pink's hair. "Sure. Who will I be meeting?"

"Of course, his—" The phone in Elizabeth's hand buzzed and she looked down at the screen. "Sorry, I need to take this." She put her phone to her ear and her gray head disappeared from view.

Oh, well, it couldn't be that hard to figure out. Emelia had done her research on the board before she'd interviewed for the role. There were three men on it. Pulling up the homepage, she refreshed herself on their details. One was a retired lawyer, one a semiretired teacher, and the last a has-been children's author from the nineties. Calling any of them middle-aged would have been generous. She sighed as she closed out of the page.

She doodled on her paper. No point trying to dream up any grand fund-raising plans until she had the measure of what she was going to have to work with. Or, more likely, work around.

Her phone buzzed in her purse. Picking the purse up off the floor, she placed it on the top of her desk and started rifling through it. Unable to locate her phone, she tipped the contents of her bag onto the surface, everything falling out into a messy pile. Her cousin's name lit up the screen of her phone.

"Hey, Lace." She wedged the phone between her ear and shoulder as she returned her wallet, change, and a handful of pens. A copy of *The Silver Chair* teetered on the edge of her desk. She reached for it but only succeeded in tipping it over the edge. It landed with a slap on the floor. She'd salvage it later.

"I still can't believe you managed to talk them into it." Though Lacey's opening line didn't show it, her cousin was a professional schmoozer who excelled at small talk. She just only used it when she had to.

"Clearly a case of desperate times, desperate measures." Emelia didn't mention that she'd gone out of her way to hide her connection to Mia Caldwell. She already knew what her cousin would think of that.

"So what's it like?"

Emelia cast her gaze over the industrial metal filing cabinet in the corner of her office, the old desk in front of her, and the faded wallpaper. "Let's just say no one is ever going to accuse them of wasting money on high-class office space." In her mind's eye she imagined Lacey's LA office with its large windows and sprawling view of the city. Her cousin's idea of slumming it would be Starbucks running out of hazelnut syrup for her latte.

"So what's up on today's agenda?"

Emelia let a groan rumble out of her throat. "Apparently I've got some board member who is going to be overseeing my work. I'm meeting him in"—she glanced at the clock—"seven minutes."

"Oooooooh." Her cousin was the type who saw romantic possibilities around every corner. Which was also part of the reason she went through men like water.

"You wouldn't be saying that if you'd seen the three options. Go have a look at the website." She waited a few seconds for her cousin to do just that. Lacey was perma-attached to multiple devices. For her, a high-speed Internet connection was a close second to oxygen.

She knew the instant her cousin had seen the page by the sound of the snort coming from the other end of the line, one Lacey tried to smother by clearing her throat. "Okay, maybe not. But you never know. New city, new possibilities."

"I'm not here for new possibilities, I'm here to save Anita's charity. That's it. The last thing I need is some British guy complicating things." She forced her mind away from a very specific British guy in particular. There was no way she could ever mention Peter to Lacey. What Emelia planned to write off as nothing more than a set of random and meaningless coincidences, Lacey would see as some kind of crazy cosmic intervention.

Whatever the phone call Saturday night was about, it had made him leave the party at full speed. She'd lasted another hour, the time simply a blur of names and faces as Allie had been on a mission to introduce her to people. Stupidly, she'd stayed that long hoping Peter would come back. Which was about as crazy as climbing into strangers' wardrobes.

"Are you sure you want to be doing this?" Her cousin's question jolted her back to the present.

"I have to do this."

"I worry about you, Meels. I worry about what will happen if this doesn't work out."

"Don't. It's going to work." It had to. She didn't know how she'd live with herself if it didn't. The clock on her screen changed to 9:27. Time to find out if she was being paired up with googly eyes, bad teeth, or rampant facial hair. "Gotta go, Lace. I'll talk to you later."

Closing out the call, she stood and smoothed down her navy knee-length wool skirt. *You can do this, Emelia.* She gave herself a pep talk as she exited her office and headed down the hall. *You have charmed the world's crankiest misogynistic men to get a story. And this is more important than any of those stories ever were.*

She approached Elizabeth's door, which stood ajar. From inside the office, a male voice came. Clipped, frustrated. Emelia's hand froze just before it knocked, as she registered what he was saying.

". . . an American? You know what they are like. Loud. In your face. Treading over everyone's toes. They offend people even when they don't mean to."

Loud? Offensive? Emelia felt her face flush.

"Well, it wasn't like I had much choice." Elizabeth's voice came back low and terse. "For what we were offering we're lucky we got any applicants at all. I grant you, it's not ideal, but at least she had some charity experience in LA. The one other applicant may have had the right accent but she was so witless she couldn't have organized a drink in a brewery. Anyway, it's done. She's been hired and will be here any minute now."

Googly eyes, or whichever he was, heaved a sigh. "I think we're making a big mistake. Americans seem to think everything can be solved with a GoFundMe page. Putting someone in charge of saving SpringBoard who doesn't even know how the English do things? I agreed to help out with supervising, not babysitting."

Babysitting? At that Emelia lost all sense of self-preservation and pushed the door open. Her gaze first landed on Elizabeth's startled face, before she pivoted to face her self-christened "babysitter." "I can promise you, I don't need any—"

Then she registered the agape mouth and green eyes staring at her. Oh. No. It couldn't be. "Peter?"

There was no way. There was absolutely no way. Except there was. The American he'd just been so vehemently deriding, who'd overheard presumably every word he'd spoken, was the same one he hadn't been able to stop thinking about since their first meeting.

"Do you two know each other?" Elizabeth tilted her head, scrutinizing him.

"Um, yes. We've met." Peter managed to force the words around a chest that felt like he'd just rowed 5K at full stroke.

Elizabeth's gaze bounced between the two of them. Peter had no doubt he'd turned as white as the snowflakes drifting from the sky outside. Emelia's blue-gray eyes were so large they dominated her face.

The only person in the room who was taking things in her stride was the calm executive officer. "I see. Is this going to be a problem?"

Peter opened his mouth to say no, but no matter how much he tried, he was unable to force the word out. Emelia seemed to be waiting for him to take the lead.

After a couple of seconds of silence, Elizabeth took control of the situation. "Emelia, can you give us a few minutes? I'll come and find you when we're done."

Emelia didn't say a word as she stepped backward and closed the door firmly behind her.

Elizabeth waited for the door to click before crossing her arms over her red cardigan as she leaned against her desk. "Care to tell me what that was about?" Even though he had a good foot and forty kilos on her, Peter felt like a six-year-old boy summoned into the headmistress's office to be told off.

Peter looked down at the résumé he held in his hand. Emelia's résumé. He hadn't even opened it. All he'd heard Elizabeth say was that she'd hired an American and he'd gone off. For no good reason. At least none that was related to the matter at hand.

"Do you mind if I sit down?" Without waiting for an answer he sagged into the seat behind him. It creaked under his weight, the arms pressing his legs together.

He sucked in a breath. *Pull it together, Peter.* Emelia, *Emelia,* of all people, was SpringBoard's new fund-raising coordinator.

"It's nothing, Elizabeth. Really." It still felt weird calling her Elizabeth. Since he'd been ten he'd known her as Greg's mum. "Mrs. Bradman" or "ma'am" whenever a designation beyond that was required.

She snorted. Loudly. He couldn't have been

more surprised if the ladylike, conservative Elizabeth Bradman had started dancing a jig. "Peter, whatever that was, it was not nothing. And I need to know exactly what it was. Is she an ex? A one-night stand? Some rowing groupie you took home once and now there's a voodoo doll with your face on it stabbed with a hundred pins sitting on her dresser?"

"What? *No!*"

"Well, then *what?*" Her fingernails tapped on the desk beside her.

"We just met at a party on Saturday night, that's all."

"Really."

What was he supposed to do? Tell Emelia's boss they'd met when she'd fallen out of a wardrobe onto him? That at the party she'd been hiding in another one? Mrs. Bradman had always seemed like a good sort but who knew how she'd take that. "Look, I think we were both surprised to see each other here. That's all."

Mrs. Bradman—Elizabeth—sighed. Gave him a look that said loud and clear she knew there was far more to it than that. "Peter, you aren't getting this. I have an employment issue here. I've hired Emelia. On her second week she has just over-heard one of the board members openly doubting her ability to do her role. And not just any board member, the one whom she is meant to be working with. Putting aside the fact that she's an

American, do you have any kind of knowledge, or evidence, that Emelia is not fit for this position?"

"No."

"Well then." She said the two words with a sense of finality.

Well then?

"You're going to be the one to step down."

Step down? His shock must have shown on his face because she quickly added, "Not from the board. But you can't be the member in charge of fund-raising. We'll have to ask one of the others to do it."

Peter cast his mind across the remaining three board members. All well-meaning, perfectly nice people, but totally ill-suited to the task at hand. That was the whole reason he'd joined the board. Because even from a distance it was obvious that the status quo was going to lead to Anita's dreams for the charity going up in smoke. And that couldn't happen.

He tried to speak calmly, rationally. "Elizabeth, you and I both know that none of them are up to the task." He attempted to ignore the little voice in his head suggesting that wasn't the only reason he didn't want to give the role up.

"What I know is that I can't have the two key people we need to give us a chance at saving this place at odds with each other. Or with some kind of unresolved tension, whatever that's about. That's a recipe for failure right from the beginning." She leaned forward and touched him briefly on the shoulder. The same lilac scent she'd had for years wafted with her. "Peter, I know this is personal. But you know I'm right. If this isn't going to be a viable partnership then we need to change it now."

"Let me go and talk to her." He put his hands on the chair's arms and stood, managing to unwedge his legs from their grip.

"I don't know if that's a good idea."

"Please. And, after that, if she says that she would prefer to work with another board member, I'll step down. No questions asked."

Elizabeth leaned back against her desk, considering for a few seconds. "Okay, but don't let me regret it."

He could only hope he wouldn't either.

Emelia sat ramrod straight in her chair. Hands clasped in her lap. Waiting for Elizabeth to walk in and try to fire her. "Try" being an important word because there was no way Emelia was letting this job go without a fight. Not when she'd crossed an ocean for it. She'd left her door open. Figured she might as well see it coming.

Peter Carlisle. The whole crazy scenario made working with googly eyes or bad teeth or rampant facial hair look like a costarring role with Brad Pitt in comparison.

Her fingers ached to pull up Google. All she

would need to do is type in his name and a few key words, and in seconds she'd at least have a clue what she was dealing with. Some kind of idea as to why, of all the charities in the world, he was on the board of this small, unglamorous, almost bankrupt one that couldn't even keep its website up to date.

She'd even typed in his first name before she'd remembered her vow to no longer snoop about people online and closed the browser, pried her fingers off the keyboard.

She'd almost called Lacey, but then she would've had to fill her cousin in on the whole backstory, and that really wasn't worth it with a girl whose guilty hobby was churning through Fabio-covered romance novels like they were Diet Coke.

So instead she sat, still as a statue, counting the seconds and waiting for the sound of Elizabeth's door opening.

Five hundred and eleven. That was how many she counted before the sound came, accompanied by heavy footsteps in the hall. Peter. She waited for his footsteps to head toward the exit, but instead they came toward her office.

For some insane reason she held her breath. Like it would—what? Cast some kind of invisible cloak around her?

The sound of his approach stalled as he got closer to her door. Emelia pictured him standing there, just out of sight. Well, she wasn't going to sit there like some kind of piece of prey. "So, are you planning to come in or just stay out there all day?"

Her voice was clipped, no-nonsense, betraying none of the break dancing her insides were performing.

After a second or two, Peter's head came around the corner, followed by the rest of him. Between his impressive height and muscular build, he took up the entire doorway. She took the opportunity to notice what she hadn't in her shocked stupor. The ugly sweater was gone, replaced by a dark jacket, V-neck T, and worn jeans. "I was wondering if you were going to throw something at me."

Tempting. And not just the throwing part. Emelia gestured around her empty desk and sparse office. "That would have been a distinct possibility, but as you can see, I don't actually have anything suitable."

Peter took a step into her office, his presence dwarfing her. She had to tilt her chin up just to see his face. "I, um, owe you an apology."

"Are you sorry that you said it or just that I overheard it?"

His green eyes widened. What? Had he expected her to go easy on him? Brush it under the carpet? Pretend it hadn't happened? If they were going to have to work together it wasn't going to start out with her acting like a doormat. Even if it was all very *American* of her.

"I just—" Peter pulled out the chair opposite her desk and squished his frame into it. Leaning forward, he placed his elbows on his knees and clasped his hands. He gave her a wry smile. "I'm definitely sorry that you overheard it. Elizabeth has just read me the riot act."

Emelia said nothing. Just looked at him. That was his apology? His red hair stuck up at all angles. It hadn't been like that in Elizabeth's office. She could almost see him running his hands through it in agitation as if she'd been there.

"Look, I'm sorry. I was rude. I'm sorry for how I said what I did."

Yeah, still not a real apology. "But you meant it."

Peter looked trapped. She waited. She could already tell he was a terrible liar, so it would be interesting to see if he tried to bluff his way through. He huffed out a breath, shoulders dropping. "Look, I'm sorry that I was rude, I'm sorry that you heard it, but I can't pretend that I don't have concerns about whether an American can do this job. English and Americans, we're just . . . different. And, as I'm sure you've worked out, SpringBoard is in trouble. We can't afford to make any mistakes." At least he had the guts to look her straight in the face as he said it. She had to give him that.

"You're new. On the board." He could read whatever he wanted into her leaving his half apology on the table.

He gave her a look of grudging respect. "Yes. Just a couple of months."

"How bad is it?" Her number one job for the week had been to try to put an exact dollar figure on what she needed to accomplish. She might as well take advantage of having a board member in her office to get the intel. And one who owed her. "How much do we need to raise between now and the end of the year to make it viable again?"

"One point one, give or take."

A million pounds was roughly 1.5 million US dollars. It was worse than she'd thought. Emelia schooled her expression into neutral. Unlike the guy sitting opposite her, she was a great poker player. If worst came to worst she might well need it to supplement her paltry wage from this place. "Okay."

"Okay?"

"I guess we've got our work cut out for us."

"So you'll work with me? Even after what I said." Peter ran his hand through his hair, sending the tufts in a different direction.

"If it's not you, then it's one of the other board members, right?"

Peter eased back in the chair. "Yup."

"Well then, I choose you." For some reason,

when the words came out, it felt like they had a lot more meaning than she'd intended them to.

She was here for atonement, not for anything else. And definitely not with some guy who was practically her boss.

Ten

Emelia walked into work on Wednesday morning, her brain hazy and body aching. This week was it. No matter what, she was getting out of the ghetto B and B with the cray-cray landlady.

The night before had been the final straw. The TV in the room below had blared infomercials until after four. Then this morning a new boarder had eyed her up and down like he'd just done a ten-year stretch and she was the first woman he'd seen on the outside. She was done. She had two days to come up with a plan that would let her prove herself to Peter and she couldn't do that when she was so tired she could barely think coherently.

"You okay?" Elizabeth looked over at her from where she sat at the front desk, sorting the mail. Her boss spent most of her time in that spot since SpringBoard could no longer afford a receptionist.

"I . . ." Emelia rubbed the back of her neck. She didn't really want to admit how bad her living situation was, but it was her own naivety that had gotten her into it. Maybe she'd have better luck if she got some local help. "I need a new place to live. The one I'm in isn't working out so well."

"Where are you at the moment?" Elizabeth took a sip from the porcelain teacup that always sat wherever she was working and was never empty. Its pretty floral pattern reminded Emelia of the one she'd found in the wardrobe the night she'd met Peter.

Emelia sighed. "The Magnolia Manor."

Phswew. Tea sprayed back into Elizabeth's cup. She looked like Emelia had just told her she was sleeping under a park bench.

Reaching for her linen napkin—yes, she kept one of those on hand too—Elizabeth dabbed at a tiny spot of tea that had landed on her gray skirt. "I think that would be a good idea. I've heard it's not the most salubrious of establishments."

The British. The epitome of understated.

"Any ideas?"

"I have to admit that I'm not exactly tapped into where the young folk find flatmates these days, but I'll ask around." Her boss ran the napkin over the sides of her cup.

"I've been keeping my eyes on a few web-sites, but nothing I'm interested in is available for a few more weeks, and I'd like to find a new place sooner rather than later." There was no chance she'd survive in the B and B for much longer without committing a felony.

Elizabeth scrunched her face up, then brightened. "Oh, I know. There's a bulletin board in the staff room. Occasionally, there's accommodation listings on that."

Emelia checked the clock. Still six minutes before she officially started work. "I think I'll go and take a quick look." Yes, she was that desperate.

Dropping her bag and coat in her office as she walked past, she made her way to the staff room. Which was a generous term to describe the small kitchenette with a sink, microwave, and minifridge. Above the counter hung a corkboard, a hodgepodge of notices stuck to it. Some were so faded and curled, Emelia was sure they'd been there since the last millennium.

Housemate wanted. Female. Town house within 30 minutes' walk of university. 150 pounds a week + expenses. Available immediately. See Dr. Allison Shire.

Emelia looked at the date in the right-hand corner. It had been posted a couple of weeks ago. She was probably already too late. And one fifty a week would take a hefty chunk out of her paycheck. But she'd happily pay it for a room where she could sleep at night. Even if it was with a seventy-year-old spinster academic.

She pulled the stiff card off the bulletin board and walked back to the front desk, the edges of the card poking into her hands. *Available imme-diately.* The magic words.

"Anything?" Elizabeth's gray bob swung as she looked up when Emelia returned.

"Maybe. A Dr. Shire is looking for a female housemate. Or was, anyway. Do you know if she still is?" Emelia held up the card in front of her.

"No. I haven't had much to do with her. She's a recent volunteer but seems lovely. Rave reviews from the first school we sent her to. The kids adored her. Unfortunately, she's just here until September. She's a guest lecturer at the university. Specialty is Tolkien."

Emelia almost choked. Was this some kind of joke? "Dr. Shire's specialty is Tolkien." She didn't quite manage to keep the incredulity out of her voice.

A smile tugged at Elizabeth's peach-colored lips. "I know."

"She's also kind of hobbit-sized." Emelia froze as a familiar female voice came from behind her along with a gust of cold air. She glanced over to Elizabeth to find she was studiously staring at her screen like it contained the solution to world peace.

Emelia turned to see Allie's green eyes and freckles. In a stylish beige overcoat and high-heeled brown leather boots, she looked about ten years older than she had battling the copier. Allie. Allie. Allison. *Oh.*

"Morning." Allie smiled as she pulled a gray knit cap off her head, shaking her copper hair free.

"Hi." Emelia's mind was still trying to wrap around the fact that the pretty young girl she'd taken for a student was actually a lecturer. Who'd just heard her mocking her name. Who'd been her one hope of escaping the ghetto anytime soon.

Oh, this was bad. She didn't need to feel the heat creeping up her cheeks to know she was turning as red as a blood moon.

Allie—Dr. Shire—shifted the pile of books she was holding in one arm. "Anyway, the answer is yes."

"Yes?"

"Yes, I'm still looking for a housemate. Are you interested?"

In living in Allie's cute town house. Was she serious? "Yes."

"The lease is only through September because that's when my contract currently finishes up. And you can hassle my name all you want as long as you don't make the mistake of calling me Australian. We New Zealanders are a bit precious about that."

"Have you been to Hobbiton?" The question was out before Emelia could stop it. Ever since she'd seen the movies, she'd wanted to visit. Allie probably got asked that all the time. Way to be original. She could've kicked herself.

"Many, many times. So rent is one fifty a week

and power, Internet, stuff like that usually adds up to another thirty. Excluding food. I hadn't really thought too much about that. I figure we can just buy our own breakfast and lunch stuff and see how we go for dinners."

Under two hundred pounds a week. She'd gladly have paid double that and lived on noodles. More so with every passing second. "Sounds fine."

"Um, what else . . ." Allie tilted her head and looked into space. "Oh, I should tell you about Jackson."

The name rang a bell.

"He's my fiancé. He's at Cambridge doing an MBA, so I'm up there every second weekend and he comes down here every other weekend."

Of course. The good-looking guy from the party who had stared at Allie with besotted eyes whenever they were in the same room. Responsible for the very large diamond on Allie's finger, which Emelia had just noticed. "I think I met him on Saturday."

Allie's face brightened. "Of course you did."

So she'd be the third wheel for three days out of every fourteen. And probably need to buy some earplugs. Sounded like a bargain price to pay. "When are you getting married?"

"We, uh, haven't set a date yet." Something in Allie's countenance shifted. Huh. Interesting. From what she'd observed they were practically the world's most smitten couple, yet they hadn't set a wedding date. Her journalistic radar pinged with the scent of a story but she ignored it.

Allie hurried on. "So, what do you think?"

Emelia's face must have been blank because Allie expanded on her question. "About moving in?"

That was it? A ninety-second quasi-interview? "Don't you want to know anything more about me?" Emelia regretted the question as soon as she'd asked it. What was wrong with her, inviting questions she might not be able to answer? She liked Allie. Didn't want to lie to her. But there was no chance Allie would have her as a roommate if she had any idea what Emelia had done. The pain she'd caused.

Allie scrunched up her forehead, then shook her head. "Not really. Peter likes you and Elizabeth hired you." Emelia looked to where her boss was watching the whole exchange with an amused look. "Between those two things, I know pretty much the most important stuff. And if you end up being one of those flatmates urban legends are made of, my name is the one on the lease, so I can just change the locks and leave your stuff on the stoop." She grinned.

Emelia's heart rate had escalated at the mention of Peter, but Allie moved on before she could dwell on the words "Peter likes you."

"When do you want to move in?"

It almost killed her to say it, but she didn't want to appear too eager. "How about this weekend?" Two more nights wouldn't kill her.

"Sure. Where are you staying at the moment?"

"The Magnolia Manor."

Allie's mouth almost dropped off her face at the same time as the top book slid off her pile and hit the floor with a bang. "The grotty place they parole inmates to?" She ignored the tome at her feet.

"They do?" Well, that explained a lot.

"I have a car. How about tonight?"

Eleven

Peter opened the door to SpringBoard's office and stepped inside, a blast of sleet accompanying him. Someone had forgotten to tell nature it was spring already. Slamming the inclement weather out, he pulled his hat off and ran his fingers through his damp hair.

After an hour standing on the riverbank, watching guys out on the water, frozen to the bone, bodies straining against the wind and rain, not even a shower with the hot water on full blast could get the chill out of his bones.

"Morning." Elizabeth looked up from her perch at the front desk.

"Morning. How's everything looking?" She was probably doing month-end. There was a board meeting coming up where Elizabeth would be giving the latest financial update.

She pulled her glasses off and pinched the bridge of her nose.

"That bad, huh?"

"We're going to need a miracle. You here to meet with Emelia?"

"Yeah." His pulse thrummed in his neck. It had been five days since she'd managed to see a way through his behaving like a donkey's behind and not replace him with another board member.

Elizabeth gave him a piercing look. "Emelia told me she's willing to work with you, but don't forget what I said. If there are any issues . . ."

He would be the one to go. "I know." There wouldn't be. He wouldn't allow it. Saving Spring-Board was way too important. He could do cordial-but-distant. Lord knew he'd had enough experience with some of the rowing groupies over the years. "We'll come up with a plan, Elizabeth. A good one." At least the board had given them until the April meeting to come back with some formal fund-raising proposals.

"Just do your best, that's all any of us can do." He hated that there was an air of defeat about the way that she said it as she turned her attention back to her computer screen. But then she was the one taking the calls from donors with every excuse under the sun as to why they were pulling their support.

Shrugging out of his coat, he hung it on the rack in the corner, adding his hat to another hook. Stalling for time. The twisting in his gut was a sensation from the past. It was reserved for the starting lines of big races. He hadn't been on one of those in nine months. It didn't belong in this dingy office, about to start a meeting with a girl he had to maintain a professional distance from.

He strode down the hall, the sound of his feet announcing his approach. Emelia looked up as he rounded her door. Her wavy hair was pulled back into a thick braid and she wore a fitted red sweater that did nothing to downplay her curves.

His confident stride stalled at the distinctly unprofessional, non-distant thought.

"Morning." She tilted her head. "Are you planning to come in?"

"Yes. Sorry." He took a couple of steps forward, sat down in the chair opposite her desk. It was different from the one he'd sat in last time.

"I traded it out. It looked pretty uncomfortable. Being wedged in the last one." She answered his question before he could even think it, the hint of a smile on her full lips.

"Thanks." Interesting. Emelia was very observant. He filed the piece of information away.

They sat in silence for a couple of seconds.

"So—" they both said at once.

"You go first—" And again. Then silence.

"How are you finding Oxford?" Peter grasped

94

at the first thing that came to mind. Good one. That wasn't lame at all.

Emelia leaned back in her chair. "Pretty good." She cast a glance up to her small window, where the sound of wind whipping around outside seeped through. "Can't say this is what I imagined when I pictured an English spring."

"Are you staying with family?" He tried to sound only politely interested. Hopefully she'd say she was living with her boyfriend. Some nerdy Harvard alumnus doing his PhD in biophysics. He was busy hibernating in a lab somewhere, which was why he hadn't been at the party. That would kill whatever this distracting chemistry was between them. Force him to focus on the task at hand. The one that mattered.

"I've, um, moved in with Allie."

Peter just stared at her. Had she just said she'd moved in with Allie? His Allie? Well, not *his* Allie, but . . .

"If it's going to create problems, I can find somewhere else." Emelia rushed in, seeming to take his silence as discontent. "I'm sorry. I didn't think about this. Us." Her hand gestured between the two of them. "I mean not us us. Obviously. I mean they're your friends. I get that it might be awkward. Or weird. Of course it is. I fall out of a wardrobe onto you. Then you find me in another one at a party. Then I'm working here. Now I've moved in with your friend. Wow. Now that I've

95

said it aloud it's very weird. I'll find somewhere else." Her words kind of tumbled out, falling over each other.

"No." He held his hand up to try to slow the tirade. "It's not weird."

Her brow rumpled. "It's not?"

"I mean, it's certainly an interesting lineup of events. I was just surprised." *In the kind of good way that should have alarm bells flashing.* "Look, Allie is great. And I know Jackson will be happy she's got a roommate. He worries about her living alone since he's in Cambridge." He flashed her a grin. "The *Lord of the Rings* and Narnia nerds together under one roof. Tolkien and Lewis would be thrilled."

Emelia laughed. "I'm pretty sure I have a long way to go before I'll come even close to Allie's level."

The sound of her laughter resonated inside him, resulting in a lighthearted feeling that he hadn't felt since Anita died. If his cousin were here right now, she'd probably have been giving him eyes, mouthing "I like her" at him.

But she wasn't. And it was all his fault.

If Lacey were here right now, she'd have been mentally designing her couture bridesmaid's dress. And part of Emelia wouldn't have blamed her. She hadn't had this kind of chemistry with anyone since . . . well, ever, if truth be told.

She'd walked in here this morning knowing exactly what she was doing. Guarded. After two nights of real sleep and hot showers she was back on her game. Playbook prepared and memorized. Two minutes of small talk, then down to business. Cordial but professional. Everything had changed now that Peter was her sort-of boss.

Then it had all unraveled the instant she had connected that moving in with Allie put them in not only the same professional circle but also the same personal one.

"So, um . . ." Peter cleared his throat. "We should probably talk about how we want to approach this. Working together."

Emelia tried to divert her gaze from the way his sweater stretched across his sculpted shoulders. Allie had mentioned he coached the Oxford rowing team and he was clearly a rower as well. Or had been. Even though she'd managed to find him a larger chair his powerful physique still dwarfed it like it was a piece of doll's furniture.

"Emelia?" Peter tilted his head and gave her a bemused look.

"Yes, of course." *Focus, Emelia. Guard up.* Her self-imposed Google exile still stood, so she couldn't research him online, but there was only one reason she could think of why a guy like Peter would be involved in a failing charity. There had to be some kind of personal connection.

Which meant that if he knew who she really was, he would hate her. Rightfully so. "I've drawn up a draft proposal for your consideration. Very high level." Picking up two copies of the plan she'd spent the day before sweating over, she pushed one copy across her desk toward him.

He reached forward, the movement doing absolutely nothing to hide his muscular physique. She forced her gaze to the page in front of her. The words swam out of focus but it didn't matter. She knew the whole thing back to front.

There were only three things that mattered: Saving Anita's charity. No one here finding out who she was. And keeping her wildly inappropriate attraction when it came to the man sitting opposite her firmly in check.

Peter scanned the pages. Emelia pretended to be looking over hers, while reading into every tap of his fingertips, twitch of his cheek, and furrow of his brow.

He hated it. Oh, he hated it. Maybe he was right. She didn't have any business being here. Her little stints of charity involvement back home had nothing on this.

Finally, he lowered the pages and leaned forward, looking directly at her. "Tell me about these three big events."

Emelia leaked out a breath. He hadn't shot her down outright. That was a start. "Given our size and resources"—*or lack thereof*—"I think that we're better placed to focus on three major fund-raising events. We can fit in smaller ones around them if it works but one of the big mistakes charities often make is spreading themselves too thinly across too many small activities that just don't offer a good return on investment."

Something flickered in his green eyes. Not quite approval, but maybe grudging acceptance. "What kind of things could they be?"

"It could be anything. Sporting. Cultural. Intellectual. We are in Oxford after all. I have a couple of ideas but I was hoping you could maybe give me some guidance." As much as it pained her to admit it, he was right. She did need someone who knew the "English way."

"You're thinking summer, autumn, and winter?"

"Yes, since we're already into spring. I was thinking everything should culminate in a big event toward the end of the year. That also gives us some time to . . ." She trailed off, not sure how to say what she needed to. But it had to be said if they were going to make any headway. Or they'd just be spitting into the wind.

"To?"

"Work on reputation repair." She said the words quietly, gaze focused at a spot just over his shoulder.

"You're referring to Anita." His shoulders tensed a little, but his gaze, his tone, remained neutral. Nothing to give her any hint as to how close their personal relationship was. Or even if they had one.

"Yes. I'm assuming that's part of why you've been losing donors."

Peter leaned back, looped his hands around his propped-up knee. "It would be fair to say that a number have given that as their reason for reconsidering their involvement with SpringBoard, yes. She was also our biggest fund-raising weapon. The board are well-meaning and dedicated to the cause but none of us have the hobnobbing skills that she did. SpringBoard's success was all down to her."

"I'm sorry." Emelia struggled to keep a hitch from her voice. She'd seen Anita out on the LA social circuit a few times. The girl was beautiful, vivacious, and intelligent. The type who could sell sand to Saudi Arabia. If it wasn't for who Anita had been engaged to, she'd still have been alive and Emelia would still have been in LA making a career off destroying people's lives. She couldn't change it. The one thing left was to ensure Anita's legacy didn't die along with her.

Peter turned his attention back to her as he finished the document. "So, tell me, what's your great idea?"

Under the intensity of his gaze she suddenly doubted herself. What if it wasn't a good idea at all? Not that she'd even claimed it was. "So Cambridge and Oxford are quite big rivals, right?"

Peter's mouth twitched. "Very."

"Could we use that somehow? Have some kind of Oxford-versus-Cambridge event? Or even a couple of them?"

"Go on."

"I was thinking you obviously have an in with the rowing team. What if after the Boat Race we set up some other kind of contest between the two teams? It wouldn't have to be rowing. It could be something more friendly." The famous annual rowing fixture between the two universities was only a few weeks away. The opportunity to leverage off it was too good not to explore.

Peter barked out a laugh. "You could have a knitting contest between the Oxford and Cambridge rowing teams and it wouldn't be friendly." He bit the bottom of his lip, thinking. "We'd have to get the go-ahead pretty fast. Once the Boat Race is over the guys are generally pretty jammed catching up with their studies and preparing for exams. Then they all disappear in July. And it wouldn't be an official Oxford-versus-Cambridge fixture."

"But even if it was something unofficial? With only some of the guys voluntarily participating? Would it still be enough to get people interested?"

She held her breath as he pondered her question across from her.

After a few seconds he grinned, a dimple she

hadn't noticed before appearing on his left cheek. "Probably. The rowing competition is so intense people would pay to watch them play tiddly-winks against each other. You might just have cracked something. I'm embarrassed I didn't think of it myself."

She couldn't stop herself from grinning back.

"I'll just need to talk to a few people. I'm sure I could get some of the Oxford guys on board easy enough. Give me a few days to sound out my Cambridge connections. I'll work out if it will be better to formally raise it before the race or after."

His moss-green gaze connected with hers across her desk and for a second neither of them looked away. "Right, so . . ." She trailed off, not having a plan for either his unbridled enthusiasm for her idea or whatever it was that was bouncing between them.

"The team leaves for London tomorrow. We train there the last few weeks before the race. Is it better for me to call or email when I've talked to a few people?" He quirked up a smile. "Actually, we'll be keeping some pretty weird hours, I'll just email."

"No!" They both jumped a little as she practically yelled. Why didn't she just write *call me* across her forehead? "I mean, phone is fine—"

A ringtone saved her from herself. Not hers. Peter fumbled for a second, then pulled his iPhone out of his pocket.

"Sorry. I need to take this." Swiping the screen, he put it to his ear. "Hi." The other person spoke for a couple of seconds. "You're joking." A few more words. "Okay, I'll be there as soon as I can." Stabbing the screen, Peter shoved the phone back into his pocket and blew out a huff of air. "I'm really sorry. I've got to go."

"Right. Sure." The sudden sense of loss left her disconcerted.

Peter was already out of his chair and halfway through her door. Then he paused and turned back. "Are you coming? To the Boat Race?"

"I, um . . ." She floundered. For all the hype around the city about the big annual showdown between the two universities, it hadn't occurred to her to go.

"You should. Jackson and Allie are coming. It's pretty amazing." He tilted his head, flashing the dimple. "I think you'd like it, Emelia Mason."

She couldn't have said no if she tried. "Okay."

"Okay, I'll see you there." And with that he was gone, leaving her as flushed and flustered as a dorky mathlete who'd just been invited to the prom by the star quarterback.

Emelia Mason. She replayed the way he'd said her name in her head. It had sounded nice. Respectable. Maybe even a little bit girl-next-door.

Everything she wasn't.

Twelve

Peter tried to clamp down on the churning inside of him as he ran, cutting across lanes and streets, almost slipping a few times on cobblestones. Puffing, he pulled up in front of his destination, sweat trickling between his shoulder blades despite the cold. He wished he could say it was the first time, but it wasn't. Far from it. The Saint Aldates police station sat in front of him, three imposing stories of beige stone. At least it was barely a couple of kilometers from the SpringBoard offices.

What had his brother done now? Peter trudged through the main door, pausing to let out a man who smelled like he hadn't taken a shower this side of Christmas. Walking inside, his feet tramped their way across the familiar peeling linoleum to the front desk. The bobby tending it offered up a flicker of recognition. "Can I help?"

"Peter Carlisle. I've had a call from Sergeant Grant."

The flicker of recognition turned into a mental connection. "Ah, you're the brother. I'll just get the sarge for you."

Peter drummed his fingers on the front desk as the constable disappeared through the door behind him. In a few seconds, he returned with

Sergeant Mark Grant behind him. His friend opened the partition off to the side and let him through. Mark looked weary, annoyed, which was to be expected.

No point wasting any time. "What was it this time?"

Mark strode ahead of him through the bowels of the station. "The usual. Drunk and disorderly. Urinating in a public place as a bonus."

Classy, his brother. Peter glanced at his watch. "It's barely lunchtime." He'd only last seen Victor a few hours ago at training. They still had the second session of the day this evening. What on earth was wrong with him?

"We picked him up at ten. I gave him a couple of hours to dry out before I even called."

A sigh escaped him. "Thanks, Mark. I really appreciate it."

His friend studied him with a somber face. "He's got to sort it out, Pete. And I mean soon. This is the third time this month. At this rate, it's only a matter of time before he's going to get charged with something. And when that happens, there's no special favors. He'll get exactly the same as anyone else."

Peter pinched the bridge of his nose. "I'll talk to him." Like Victor would listen. But what else could he do? His brother's wild ways were already breaking his parents' hearts, and they didn't even know the half of it.

"You ever think that you might be making it worse by constantly rescuing him?"

Well, it clearly wasn't making it any better. "What happens if I don't? If you call me and I don't come, then what?"

Mark shrugged. "Depends on the situation. But maybe it's time to let him find out."

And take the risk that the papers would get wind of the fact that the future Viscount Downley spent half his life sobering up in the slammer? No thanks.

Victor would be off the squad for sure if Sean had any idea what he got up to. Even if the race was only weeks away. The head coach had no tolerance for stuff like this and there were plenty of reserve rowers desperate for Victor's spot. Who wanted it more, deserved it more. Which would be a relief for Peter. Not having his brother rub it in his face every day that he was living his dream. So why did he keep on saving him? Most of the time he didn't even know.

"Think about it, okay?" Without waiting for Peter's response, Mark nodded to the copper at the entry to the cells and pulled out his keys as they went in. The stench of urine, vomit, and body odor hit Peter like a wall. Why anyone would put themselves on a path that led to getting locked in here more than once was beyond him.

In the end cell, his brother lay on the rudimentary bed, hands tucked under his head, staring up at the ceiling. He looked as relaxed as if he were enjoying an afternoon on a lounge chair in the Bahamas.

Mark gave the bars a shake. "Time to go, sunshine."

Victor rolled over, his expression revealing nothing when he saw the two of them. Pushing himself up, he stood and waited for Mark to unlock the door and swing it open. "Excellent hospitality as always, Sergeant. See you next time."

"There isn't going to be a next time." Peter quashed the desire to push his brother behind the bars and tell Mark to lock him back up.

Victor cocked an eyebrow at Peter. "Says who? The fun police?"

"You are such a pillock."

"Look, little brother. No one made you come here to get me. Lord knows I certainly didn't ask to see your smug, sanctimonious mug. If you want me to grovel with gratitude for your liberating me again, then like I've already told you, you're going to be waiting a long time."

"You've got five seconds to get out of my cells or I'll arrest you myself." Mark intervened before Peter lost his cool and did something that would put him where Victor had just been.

"Sorry, officer." Victor gave Mark a mock salute.

Striding out of the cells, past the station traffic,

Mark led them back out into the main entryway. And closed the gate behind them.

"No lecture this time?" Victor tossed the question at Mark.

The bobby crossed his arms over his broad chest. "I'm done lecturing. I've got better things to do with my time. Let's be clear, Victor. I don't care what our family connections are. I will arrest you if you keep on this track. That will give our mothers something to talk about at bridge."

For a second, Peter saw something flicker across Victor's face that cut through his insolent, smug expression. But then it was gone, and the usual mask fell back into place before he could work out what that expression even was.

"Oh, look at that." Victor checked his watch. "Perfect timing. I've got to check in with the professor at two. She's always happy to see me."

Only Victor could manage to be a full-time drunkard, genius scholar, and top-level rower. Peter should've just left him in jail. Let him see what it felt like to be on the losing side for once.

Thirteen

The day of the Boat Race. You'd have had to be deaf, dumb, and blind if you were within five miles of the Thames and didn't know about the famous rowing race.

Emelia tugged her Oxford-dark-blue sweater down and peered at her fitted jeans tucked into her brown leather boots. She'd spent a decent chunk of the morning trying to work out what one wore to a rowing race. In London. And had landed on this. Only to show up at the river's edge and discover that it really didn't matter. The entire spectrum was there, from men in suits to women in yoga gear.

"You cannot be serious!" Emelia turned to where Allie was pointing a finger at Jackson. Who, at some point, without either of them noticing, had draped his neck with a scarf in Cambridge light blue.

Jackson smirked at his fiancée as she tugged at her opposing dark blue scarf. "It's a win-win. No matter what happens, at least one of us will be victorious."

"If Cambridge wins, I'll choke you with it." Emelia raised an eyebrow. For someone who had been at Oxford all of six months, Allie had certainly drunk the Kool-Aid.

So much, in fact, that they had been there hours early to stake out a prime spot on the Thames bank by the finish line. At least England had finally gotten into the swing of spring and the skies were blue and the sun shining.

Emelia patted her phone in her pocket, confirming it was still there. Over the last couple of weeks she'd exchanged a few sporadic emails and phone calls with Peter about the fund-raising idea. All very professional and aboveboard. He was clearly very busy with the team and absorbed with race preparation. The distance had her half-convinced that she'd overblown the attraction that she'd felt between them.

Though not even that had prevented her stomach knotting itself up when she'd texted him an hour ago, wishing him luck, despite the talk she'd given herself about how he probably wasn't even near his phone. She probably wouldn't even see him today. He had much more important things to be doing than responding to her lame message, but she still couldn't help but check her screen every time a phone went off. Which was often, since she was surrounded by a crowd of people.

Emelia glanced over her shoulder to see that Allie had her grip on Jackson's scarf, holding on to its ends as she tugged him down for a kiss. That was what she got for agreeing to be the third wheel.

A helicopter buzzed overhead. The hum of the crowd seemed to get louder as the minutes counted down to the start. The women's race had already happened, followed by the men's reserve crews.

The banks of the river were awash with people in the two shades of blue. According to the news reports, they were expecting over two hundred and fifty thousand in the crowd along the course.

Another fifteen million would be watching it on TV. It was like the British version of the Rose Bowl. She'd had no idea this would be so huge. And to think that Peter was in the middle of it all.

Her phone buzzed in her pocket, and she pulled it out, her breath stalling as she saw his name on the screen.

Thanks. Thanks for being here.

She read the message once, twice.

"What are you smiling at?" Allie had curiosity written all over her face.

"Oh, nothing." She tried to slide her phone back into her pocket subtly, but her roommate's eyes missed nothing.

"If that was nothing, I'd love to see something."

Thankfully Emelia was saved from having to reply by another helicopter roaring right overhead.

It was stupid, whatever it was. She'd come to England to reinvent herself, to make amends for what she'd done. The last thing she needed was a relationship. Not with Peter. Especially not with Peter. Instinct told her that he wasn't a guy who went into something lightly. The idea of dating someone just for a bit of fun wouldn't even be on his radar.

Not that it was on hers, but it was all she had to offer.

Which made a text that made her wistful a big problem. As big as the strapping guy who'd sent it.

"They're coming down." Emelia craned her

neck to look at one of the big screens nearby. They'd been erected along the river's banks especially for the race. Sure enough, the cameras panned across the cox of the Oxford team leading the dark blues down to the water.

Emelia's heart thumped against her rib cage. She didn't know a single guy on either side, with the exception of one ginger-headed assistant coach, but suddenly she felt like she was as invested as anyone.

She craned her neck back up at the screen again. It showed the two teams maneuvering at the start line, both coxes' hands in the air to show the umpire they weren't ready to start.

The commentators droned on about each athlete in each boat, reeling off height, weight, and rowing lineage. Emelia stopped listening and focused on the boats bobbing in the current. The race was meant to start when both coxes' hands were down, signaling their boat was ready. But the two seemed to be playing some kind of game of rowing Ping-Pong, one dropping his hand, only for the other to shoot his up. A few more seconds passed, the crowds growing silent as they waited for the two boats to finally be ready.

The Cambridge cox dropped his hand but the Oxford one remained upright.

Finally, his hand dropped.

"Attention, go!" The umpire wasn't wasting any time.

Both boats surged forward, all sixteen men pulling their oars in perfect unison. Forward and back, forward and back. The boats leapt, accelerating swiftly.

Emelia was peering through her fingers without even realizing it. How was she going to survive this for another sixteen or so minutes? Oxford had a nose in front, then Cambridge. The slight coxes yelled instructions through their headsets, hands on the rudders. Oxford managed to get maybe a quarter of a boat length ahead.

"C'mon, Oxford!" Allie's yell ripped through Emelia's right eardrum. She sure had a lot of volume for such a small person.

Emelia watched, her heart trying to break out of her sternum, as the Cambridge crew drew back even. Then Oxford managed to get a slight lead back in the first bend.

She kept her eyes glued on the screen as the crews approached Hammersmith Bridge. The perfect synchronization of the oars, the bodies in motion. The crowd roared as the boats swept along the course, coxes screaming, the rowers' bodies flexing and straining. She'd never seen anything like it before.

The boys almost tumbled out of the boat as it pulled up to the riverbank. The buzz of adrenaline and euphoria saturated the air.

"Good work." Peter hugged crew member after

crew member, clapping backs, shaking hands, rubbing heads.

He should have been as euphoric as everyone else but it all felt a bit hollow. He pasted on a broad smile, forcing himself to pretend he wouldn't have given anything to be one of the guys in the boat, stroking their way to victory, instead of just a bystander, a glorified water boy.

It killed him even more that his brother had been in the boat. And he hated himself for having the fleeting thought, more than once, that if they lost it would be good that Victor would know what it felt like, for once, to taste defeat. Never mind the other seven rowers and cox in the boat, who would be utterly heartbroken.

"Great work, Grant." He clasped hands with their slight cox, towering over him.

"You too, Coach."

He hadn't done anything. This day had no more to do with him than if he'd been standing on the banks of the Thames as an average-joe spectator.

"Bunny!" His brother's voice boomed in his ear, one of his hands slapping him on his bad shoulder. Peter tried to cover up a grimace as pain radiated out from his brother's palm print.

Peter turned his head and braced himself for his brother's usual smug smirk. Victor's hair was wet from the combination of the Thames and the magnum of champagne that had already been sprayed over the team. His brother grinned at him, for once no hint of cynicism or loathing in his expression. Just unrestrained joy. Even his scar seemed to fade into the background.

"Congratulations. It was a great race. You earned it." Peter found himself actually meaning the words. Maybe this could be a turning point. Maybe they could finally leave the animosity between them in the past.

"Tough luck you'll never know what it feels like again." His brother gave him another whack on his shoulder, as if to underscore his point, and just like that the magic was gone.

Before Peter could even conjure up a response, some curvy brunette was hanging off his brother's arm, and Victor's attention had shifted.

Whatever joy he'd had in the win evaporated, and Peter left the boys to their celebrations. Busying himself supervising the removal of the boat from the water, he tried to ignore the press pack still swarming around, snapping photos from every conceivable angle.

He stayed as far away from them as possible. More than a few requests for interviews with him and Victor had come in since the Blue Boat lineup was named. All of them framing their story as some variation of a human-interest piece on "passing the torch" from the tragic injured Olympic hopeful to the rowing-prodigy brother who hadn't so much as picked up an oar in his life until he'd decided to try out for the team.

Uncharacteristically, Victor had been no more interested in the attention than Peter. Declining every single overture was the first and last thing they'd agreed on in years.

Exhaustion seeped through him. The Boat Race was over. The thing that had driven him to get out of bed every morning for the last six months was done. Tomorrow morning he'd wake up and there'd be no training to go to. No drills to oversee. No tactics to strategize. The boys would go back to what they were ostensibly here for—academics, prepping for exams—and he would be left with a few beginning rowing courses that he could teach with both hands tied behind his back. At least he still had the fund-raising for SpringBoard to keep him going while he waited to hear back on the latest scans of his shoulder.

"Did no one tell you you won?" Emelia's voice came from behind him. He turned to see her standing about six feet away. One of her hands held her hair off her face. She wore a navy sweater for Oxford.

"The boys won. Not me."

Emelia sized him up with a long look. "I may not know much about rowing, but even I know that Sean Bowden doesn't have anyone on his team out of charity."

How did she . . . ?

Emelia smiled at his look of confusion. "Allie loaned me *Blood over Water* when I said I was coming. I've only just started though, so don't expect too much."

Peter tried not to read anything into the fact that she was reading his favorite book, about two brothers who rowed on opposing teams in the Boat Race one year. She probably wouldn't even finish it now that the race was over.

Emelia pulled her hair into a pile on top of her head, took a hair tie from her wrist, and twisted it around the knot as she crossed the distance between them. "If you're this sad over their win, I would hate to see you if they lost."

He would never confess that there had been moments where he'd hoped for just that. So he wouldn't be the puddle of failure in a sea of victory.

He tried to summon a smile. "I was just thinking it's going to be weird waking up tomorrow. Without this." The beginners' courses he had lined up would keep the bills paid, but they weren't exactly all-consuming like the Boat Race had been.

But then the plan had been that by now his shoulder would be ready to get back into some serious training. So much for that.

"Well, you don't need to worry about that. I have plenty to keep you occupied."

"Is that right?"

"While you've been busy in London, I've been busy with the spreadsheets and planning. How do you feel about origami swans? One of the schools SpringBoard works in is having an origami contest. Could get us a good profile. Now that you've got some time on your hands I thought we could put them to good use folding."

Peter flexed his large hands, trying to imagine them transforming pieces of paper into birds. "Are you serious?"

She looked at him straight-faced, her head tilted, her hands tucked into the back pockets of her jeans. "It's not a real contest without origami swans."

He waited for her to give him some clue that she was joking, but she gave him nothing beyond big blue eyes and a Mona Lisa smile. It didn't even matter. There was something about this girl that made him want to learn to fold ridiculous shapes out of pieces of paper if it would make her happy.

"Peter!" One of the staff gestured at him. Almost time to go and claim the trophy.

"I've got to go. I'll see you tonight. To talk about the swans?"

Emelia sent him a smile that made him feel like he was trying to breathe underwater. "Wouldn't miss it for anything."

Fourteen

The rooms at the Hurlingham Club buzzed with a strange mix of euphoria and simmering disappointment. Emelia ran her palms down the front of the cocktail-length navy blue dress she'd picked up on sale the day before. As if smoothing her dress would somehow calm the butterflies flurrying up a hurricane in her stomach. It was only because Allie had somehow sourced a last-minute spare ticket that she was even there at all.

The rowers, rowing alumni, and other guests had been seated in two separate rooms for the meal, but now that dinner was over and the music had started, people were crossing between the rooms.

She sucked in a breath, trying to convince herself she'd dreamed up the chemistry that had arched between them on the riverbank. But the way her nerves were contorting themselves insisted differently.

"Go dance, you guys." She gave Allie and Jackson full props for not making her feel like the third wheel for most of the day, but the two of them didn't get enough time together as it was. She certainly didn't want them wasting any more of it babysitting her.

Allie laughed as she put her water glass down

on the tabletop. "I'm not sure my toes are up to being mangled quite yet." She slid a teasing look at Jackson.

"I'm pretty sure I specifically mentioned my lack of skill the first time we danced." Jackson's arm rested around his fiancée's shoulder, his fingers twisting a lock of hair that had fallen out of her chignon. The strands shimmered like spun copper under the lights.

"But not with enough conviction to make me realize it was really true." Allie giggled as Jackson nuzzled her hair. Right, time to leave.

Emelia pushed back her chair as the music changed to something slow. "I'm going to get another drink. Either of you want anything?" They both shook their heads. Despite Allie's protestations, Emelia was certain by the time she returned they'd be dancing, lead feet or not. You didn't put your fiancé in a tux, bring him to an event like this, and not get in at least one slow dance.

Dodging the limbs and elbows of people who had already imbibed a bit too much, she threaded her way to the bar. The lights had dimmed, turning people into moving shadows.

The crowd parted for a second, and her breath stuttered as she thought she saw a familiar profile. It wasn't possible. He couldn't be here. She stood on her tiptoes, scanning the room, heart threatening to break out of her rib cage.

She was seeing things. The room was filled with plenty of tall blond men in their twenties who thought they were God's gift to mankind. There was no reason for *him* to be here. Last time they'd crossed paths, he'd been well entrenched in the LA party scene, using his title to cultivate a harem of socialites and C-list TV stars. The entitled son of the Viscount Downley belonged here about as much as she did.

She forced herself to let her breath out as another scan of the room yielded a number of blond men but not him. Then, in the middle of the crowd, she felt her hand being grasped and tugged.

It was over. She'd been found out. Somehow she'd always known it was going to happen. It had been a nice time while it lasted.

Preparing herself for the worst, she turned, ready to see the person she had one horrible thing in common with: the same person's blood on their hands.

Peter.

If it hadn't been for the crowd, she might have hit the floor as a wave of relief weakened her legs.

Peter's brow furrowed. "You okay?"

Emelia placed her palm on her chest. "You scared me."

"Sorry." He bent down low, close to her ear. "Didn't want to risk losing you in the crowd."

The guy was like six foot three, and she stood

a good half a head above most of the women. There was no chance he would lose her in the crowd. Her insides warmed like the hand he was still holding.

"How was dinner?" It was the best she could manage as she processed that she still had her boring, normal English life. Her cover hadn't been blown.

He shrugged. "Fine. The boys are in great form. But considering I've spent the last six months with them, I'm glad to be done."

"So, how can I help?" She had to half yell the question to be heard over the background noise. The guy was easy on the eyes, she couldn't deny it, but for her own good she needed to maintain distance with her quasi-boss. Especially when just looking at him made her think inappropriately of slow dances against a certain broad chest.

"Do you have a second? I've had an idea."

"Sure."

He placed a hand on the small of her back. "Let's go outside, where we can hear ourselves think."

Cutting through the crowd, it took them a couple of minutes to work their way outside, where a few ball-goers stood around smoking and one ardent couple pressed up against a wall seemed to have forgotten they were still in public.

The sudden change from hot packed ballroom to cool spring night had Emelia suppressing a shiver. But Peter's eyes didn't miss anything. "Here, take this." He shrugged out of his jacket and draped it around her shoulders before she could protest.

"Thanks." Emelia tucked it around her torso and tried to ignore the scents of cedar and sandalwood enveloping her.

Of course he had good taste in cologne.

"So, tell me about this idea."

"We need something big for our final event, right? Something to make lots of money. Put the charity back in the black but also something high-profile."

"Yes. All of the above."

Peter gestured around him. "What about this?"

"This?"

"A ball. A big black-tie charity ball."

He looked so excited she didn't have the heart to tell him that she'd already considered it and nixed the idea. Balls cost a bomb. You could just as easily come out of them in the red as make lots of money. And there was no way the charity had the money to pay a lot of the up-front costs that would be required before tickets even went on sale.

She gripped the silky inside of his jacket. "Peter, balls are really, *really* expensive to put on. There would be a huge risk we wouldn't even make back what it cost to do one well."

"Look, I know that SpringBoard doesn't have

any money. But the one thing we do have is some connections. Between the board members we would know enough people to be able to make a real go of this."

How could she phrase this nicely? She didn't want to kill the guy's enthusiasm. Especially not when she was going to be stuck with him for the next eight months on whatever they did end up going with. "Look, I'm not doubting that the board knows a lot of people, but for a charity ball to be a success it's not enough to know people, you have to know *people*." She put the emphasis on the last word, hoping he would not ask her to spell out what she meant.

"I know." He studied her face, the moonlight making his freckles stand out. "You think I don't know what you mean?"

"Why don't you tell me who you're thinking of?" She hoped she was about to be surprised. She wasn't sure what she would do if he said he knew the local ancient county squire or something. Was that even still a thing in England?

He crossed his arms, stretching his white dress shirt across his back. "Well, before I injured my shoulder, I was on the Great Britain rowing team so I know quite a few Olympians."

Emelia knew that her mouth had sagged but she couldn't do anything to lift it. Peter was on the national team? How did she not know this? How had no one mentioned it? She stared at him, her mind spinning at warp speed through the Rolodex of opportunities she'd just been presented with. He was still talking but she'd missed the last couple of sentences until a name cut through.

"Anita had quite a few celebrity friends with good connections I'm sure we could tap as well."

"Okay, great." She tried to sound nonchalant. This changed everything.

Just then a couple of Oxford boys, easily identifiable in their blue jackets, stumbled toward them.

"Oh, brother." Peter muttered the words under his breath. "Sorry, those are mine. I need to make sure they get away okay. Should we pick this up next week? At the office."

"Sure. Great. Yes." She watched as Peter strode away, catching up to the boys in a few steps.

She turned, adrenaline suddenly buzzing through her system. She needed to go and tell Allie she was leaving, get back to the hotel they were staying at, and start working on some spreadsheets. She had a ball to start planning.

She half ran back toward the entrance. Coming around the front door, she barreled straight into someone with the height and width of a large tree.

"S—" Looking up, her apology cut out as the slate gray eyes of her worst nightmare drilled into her. *Speak, Emelia. Then move!* "Sorry, entirely my fault."

The heir to the Viscount Downley unraveled one of the smiles that had taken many a simpering starlet out at the knees. The jagged scar that ran down one cheek twitched. "My fault. I insist." Then he tilted his head and gave her a quizzical look. "You look familiar. Have we met?"

She shook her head, too fast, too desperate. "I don't think so." He couldn't. Her hair was a different color and style, her eyes no longer enhanced by colored contacts. She stepped to the side, trying to go around him, but was blocked by some people coming the other way.

"Excuse me." Someone brushed past her but she didn't even look at them.

He narrowed his gray eyes at her, then they widened and he dropped an expletive. "What are *you* doing *here?*"

Think fast, Emelia, think fast. Show no fear. Pulling herself up to her full height, which was not much compared to his, admittedly, she stared Victor straight in the eye. "I could ask you the same question. Daddy recall you back home after our last meeting?" She forced the words out in a cavalier way. If she gave any hint that he had the power to ruin her, everything she was here for would be destroyed.

He averted his gaze for a second. Good. It showed he had something to lose. Maybe not as much as she did, but something. And she'd grasp at any straw, no matter how thin. She took her chance. "Look. I don't know what you're doing here and I don't really care. London's a big city. So how about we just stay out of each other's way and let the past stay there?"

Victor was silent for a few seconds. Obviously weighing having no idea what she was doing in London and whether he had any leverage over her versus what she knew about him and what evidence might or might not exist to back it up. "I never saw you."

She tilted her head at him and shrugged, as if it didn't matter to her one way or the other. An Oscar-worthy farce if there ever was one. "Right back at you."

It was only after he'd stormed past her that she realized she was still shrouded in Peter's coat. And had wrapped it around herself so tightly it was practically a straitjacket.

Peter walked back toward the ball, having tipped his two drunken rowers into a taxi and dispatched them back to the house the team was staying in. He passed the spot where he'd spoken to Emelia and a smile tugged at his lips. A charity ball. He was sure they could pull it off. Between his connections and Emelia's tenacity— something about her made him think that when she decided to do something she was all in—it was the one real shot they had.

Victor stood outside, leaning against the wall, bow tie hanging askew.

"You all right?" The guy looked like he'd seen a ghost.

"Fine." His brother shook his head, his expression haunted. "Big day. Think I'm going to head back to base."

Hmmm . . . that wasn't like Victor at all. Usually he was the last one to leave a party. If he left at all, rather than being found the next day passed out somewhere.

"Okay." Peter didn't push it, too relieved that he wasn't going to have to spend the rest of his night trying to keep Victor out of trouble. "See you in the morning."

Striding back into the ball, he scanned the room. He was off the clock. All of the team were over eighteen and could look after themselves. Or not, as the morning might reveal, but none of them were his official responsibility. Not that it stopped him from keeping an eye out for them. He'd experienced what they were living. Could well remember what could happen when you were heady with victory and felt ten feet tall and bulletproof. His shoulder twinged and he rotated it, checking for pain. He wouldn't wish what he was going through on his worst enemy.

He smiled as he remembered Emelia's shocked expression when he'd told her he'd been on the GB rowing team. Her full, rosy lips making the kind of O he'd thought only happened in cartoons. It had been all he could do not to run his thumb across the lower one, to see if it was as soft as it looked.

He shook his head. He couldn't allow himself to think like that when he had to spend the next eight months working with her. He didn't know anything about Emelia. Not why she was in Oxford, her background, or, most importantly, her beliefs. And after having a front-row seat to his parents' difficult marriage, he had promised himself he would never make the same mistake. A couple of meetings that belonged in a rom-com movie did not happily-ever-after make.

"Fancy a dance, stranger?" It was a familiar woman's voice, but definitely not the one he'd been thinking of.

"Um, sure." Sabine's hand already rested on his arm, and he mechanically took her other hand, his movements awkward and stilted.

At five foot four, Sabine barely reached the top of his chest. Which made her perfect for the talented cox that she was, but not perfect for him. A thought he'd never had until meeting a certain brunette.

"For a guy whose team just won the Boat Race, you sure look glum."

He turned his attention to the intelligent eyes staring up at him. "What are you doing, Sabine?"

She moved smoothly through the crowded

dance floor, ignoring the fact that he was doing a lousy job at leading her. "I just wanted to say congratulations. Or is that not allowed?"

He sighed. "Of course it's allowed. Sorry. Thanks."

Sabine was a great girl. Any guy would have been lucky to have her. It wasn't like they had parted ways badly. It had just become obvious, after his injury, that their shared obsession with rowing had allowed them to ignore all the other problems in their relationship. Ones that became as obvious as the neon signs at Piccadilly Circus once it became clear it would be a long time before he rowed competitively again.

"I hear you're back in the boat." She leaned up on tiptoes and had to practically shout the words to be heard above the music and crowd.

Where had she heard that? He'd been keeping his occasional forays on the river in his scull pretty quiet. He shrugged and leaned down so she could hear his response. "Barely. Just for a bit of exercise. Nothing serious. The last set of scans, well, they weren't great." It felt good to be honest about it with someone. Sabine got what the dream meant.

She tilted her head, staring straight into his eyes. "I'm really sorry, Peter. But I know you can come back from this. You are a great rower. You're going to stand on that podium one day."

That was one of the best things about Sabine. She'd always believed in him. Even more than he believed in himself. Even still. After everything.

"By the way, what's happening with Spring-Board? How can I help?"

Peter blinked at the abrupt change in subject. "Actually, we're looking at setting up some kind of a friendly race between the Oxford and Cambridge rowing teams. I'm sure we could use you with that somehow." She would be perfect. If he failed at convincing some of the guys, there wouldn't be a rower on either team who would be able to turn her down.

Sabine laughed. "Like there would be anything friendly about that. Sounds like fun. Just let me know what I can do."

He shuffled them between a couple of pairs. "How about you? How are you doing?"

She shrugged a slender shoulder against his chest. "I'm thinking it might be time for me to retire soon."

"What are you talking about?" He could no more imagine Sabine voluntarily giving up rowing than he could the queen giving up the throne. She'd coxed her women's eight to the final in the London Olympics. There had been scuttlebutt about her maybe even coxing the men's team one day. She still had years left on her career. He might have had the potential to be great, but she actually was.

Sabine tilted her head so that she was looking right at him. "Maybe I need to move on. Look at what rowing's cost me."

"Like what?"

"Like you."

He stepped back, tried to subtly put a little more space between them. "Rowing didn't cost you me. If anything, it held us together for far longer than we would've lasted otherwise. You know that."

She stared up at him, her blue eyes full of consternation. "No, Peter. I don't know that. What I know is that after you got injured, you were angry, and frustrated, and hurt. You wanted an excuse to push me away and you used that. When I think the truth was that it hurt too much to see me still doing what you loved, and I don't blame you. You can't pretend there wasn't still something there that night we had coffee."

She was right. There had been a night soon after they'd split up that they'd run into each other at Paddington station. Both the victims of delayed trains. They'd had a drink. And there had been something still there. But he'd told himself that was natural after three years. And then Anita had died and everything changed. "We were together for a long time, Bine. Feelings don't die just because something didn't work out."

She shook her head, adamant. "It was more than that."

"What are you saying?"

She looked up at him, all big blue eyes and pleading expression. "I'm saying I think you made a big mistake breaking up with me, and I think I made one letting you. I'm saying being here, with you, feels like everything is finally right again after it being all wrong for months."

They'd stopped any attempt at dancing. Instead, they just shuffled along the edge of the dance floor as he stared at her.

What on earth was going on tonight? One second he'd been thinking about kissing Emelia, which would have been unwise at best. The next Sabine was making some kind of case . . . for what?

"Sabine, this is crazy talk. All of it. You don't have any time for a relationship right now. You are at the peak of your career. We both know that's all you have capacity for." Just like it was all he'd have had capacity for if his shoulder hadn't been shredded in a barroom brawl.

From the hope that sparked in her eyes, Peter saw he'd said the wrong thing. He should've just said a straight no instead of trying to soften the blow.

"I know. I'm not asking you to wait. I'm just asking you not to . . ." She trailed off, looked down for a second.

"Not to what?"

"Not to choose someone else." She scrutinized him. "Or am I too late already?"

"I don't know." *Emelia.* The luxurious wavy hair. The enigmatic smile. The intensity behind her gaze. The way that when she laughed it made him feel lighter. But when her heady presence left, all the reasons as to why pursuing something between them was crazy remained.

"Look, I don't want to be the villain ex-girlfriend here. I'm not jealous that you might have moved on. Well, maybe I am a little, but that isn't what this is about. I've been trying to get the nerve up for months and I'm kicking myself. I should've said something at Allie's party that night but you just disappeared."

The same night he'd properly met Emelia. In the second wardrobe. What might have happened if he'd never gone up those stairs? If Sabine had snagged him there for this conversation?

"If you can look me in the eye and tell me that it's her, not me, then I will walk away. I will. I don't want to make your life harder. In fact, I want you to be happy. I just believe that I can give you more than she can." She cast a sad smile. "Whoever she is."

His mouth opened, but nothing came out. Just the sound of silent panic.

"You don't have to decide right now. You just have to not decide." And with that, she stood on her tiptoes and dropped a kiss onto his left cheek while sliding her other hand down his right. "See you 'round, Seven." And with that, she turned and disappeared into the crowd, leaving him an island on the dance floor.

Fifteen

Emelia was early. Like an hour early. Between the fund-raising ideas bouncing around inside her head and her excitement over getting to see where C. S. Lewis and the Inklings used to meet, the afternoon had dragged on agonizingly slowly.

She'd suggested they meet somewhere other than the office given that you couldn't swing a cat in any of the rooms there, let alone spread papers out and plan. She'd meant the library or something similar but when Peter had suggested the Eagle and Child, Emelia hadn't been able to say yes fast enough.

She looked around the room, trying her best not to look like some wide-eyed tourist. The historic pub looked just like she'd imagined it would. Wood paneling, rich tones. The kind of decor that was somehow both ancient and timeless. It didn't take much imagination to see Lewis, Tolkien, and the other Inklings gathered around a table somewhere, engaged in debate or critiquing each other's work.

"What can I get for you?" A bored-sounding waitress materialized beside her.

"Um, can I just have a Coke, please?" She didn't even like Coke that much, but it was one of the few drinks that she didn't have to struggle to remember the British translation for.

"Would you like a menu?"

"Yes, please." The buzz of the busy room didn't bother her. She could happily sit here until Peter arrived and lose herself in Lewis. *The Magician's Nephew* perched inside her bag for this exact occasion. "Actually, no need. I'll have the fish and chips, please." She'd been intending to try some ever since she'd arrived.

"Garden peas or mushy?"

"Mushy." When in England, do as the English do. At least once. And she hadn't tried them yet.

Pulling out her battered paperback copy of the book that chronologically started Narnia, she flipped it open and reread the words that were engraved in her brain: *"This is a story about something that happened long ago . . ."*

Within a couple of sentences she was back with Digory, Polly, and crazy Uncle Andrew.

"Fish and chips are generally best hot." His voice cut into her world just as Digory struck the bell that awoke the slumbering world of Charn and brought about the White Witch's first appearance. It was one of her favorite parts in the whole series.

Slipping her bookmark between the pages, Emelia closed the paperback and placed it down on the tabletop. Craning her neck, she let her gaze travel up, landing on Peter's freckled face. "You're early."

He smiled as he slid across from her. "Not as early as you."

Touché. Along with Peter, her early supper had also arrived at some point and been placed in front of her.

"Sorry for interrupting. You looked very absorbed. But, honestly, cold fish and chips are nasty."

"This is the first time I've had them." For some reason, the presence of the muscular rower made her forget all notions she'd had of being happy sitting here reading alone.

Guard up, Emelia.

His face registered shock. "Really? How can you have never had fish and chips?"

She shrugged her shoulders. "They're just not really a thing where I come from."

He gestured to the plate. "Well, please don't let me stop you."

Now that she was looking at the food, the smell of its greasy goodness wafting up at her, she registered the hole her stomach had gnawed in her insides.

"You sure?" She didn't give him a chance to answer before she picked up a fry—which wasn't really a fry; it was much fatter—and popped it into her mouth. Grease and salt and potato all exploded into a hot bite of bliss. Two more followed in quick succession. "Want some?" She nudged the plate toward him, and he helped himself.

"Thanks."

She managed to find her manners long enough to use her cutlery to get a bite of fish. But she almost forgot about them when she bit into the flaky goodness. "Oh, wow."

"Good, huh?"

She nodded, her mouth too full with the next bite to reply.

The peas were next. She loaded her fork up with a pile of the bright green lumpy sludge that looked like baby food. Popping it into her mouth, she prepared herself to be overwhelmed by the new experience.

Which she was. In the worst way. Wrong, wrong, wrong. It was all wrong. The consistency. The taste. The . . . all of it. If she'd been by herself, she would've spat it into her napkin. Instead she forced herself to swallow the nasty things down.

"Not a fan, huh?" Peter's eyes crinkled as he smiled.

"What did those poor peas ever do to you? To this country?" She picked up another pile of the green sludge on her fork and studied it, trying to work out how it could taste so nasty. "Why would you do that to them?"

He laughed. "Ease up. They're a national treasure."

"If these are a national treasure, I'll—" She'd always been the kind of person who gestured when she talked. Which the poor guy discovered when the fork suddenly jumped in her hand and catapulted the pile of green at him.

It was like something from a slow-motion sequence. She watched the sludge fly through the air. At the last second, she closed her eyes, unable to bear seeing where it landed.

Knowing her luck it would be . . . she slid one eye open. Yup. It'd hit him right on the side of his face and was already starting to slide down his cheek. An avalanche of green.

Peter blinked and pointed at her napkin, which lay on the table. "May I?"

Only the British would be so polite after someone had just assaulted them with a vegetable. "Of course."

Picking it up, he swiped at the mess and caught a decent amount before it dropped off his jaw-line onto his sweater. Folding the napkin, he gave it a second attempt, leaving only a green smear across part of his cheek. "Got it all?"

Emelia shook her head. "There's just a little bit left about halfway down." He wiped. Missed. "Here." Plucking the napkin from his hand, she leaned over and blotted away the last bit. His moss-colored gaze caught hers as she did it, and he gave her the kind of smile that almost made her forget where she was, what she was doing.

"Well, Emelia Mason." The accent got her every time. The guy could have been about to insult her five ways to Christmas and she would have listened happily. "I have to say, it's never boring when I see you."

She stared at him. At a loss for words.

He didn't seem to notice. "Think I might order something as well. I won't have time to go home and eat before church."

She blinked at him. Replayed the sentence. Yes, he had definitely said "church." Huh. Apart from the occasional door-to-door types back home, she didn't know a single person her age who was religious. Though, now that she thought about it, she wouldn't have been surprised if that was where Allie went on Sunday mornings. She was always gone by the time Emelia woke up. She'd just assumed she and Jackson went out for brunch every time he was in town.

Peter smiled at her. "That bad, huh? You look like I just said I was on my way to rob a retirement village."

"No—I mean—"

"Would you like anything, sir?"

Thank goodness she was saved from herself by the waitress. She tuned out Peter ordering while she filed away this new piece of information about him, unsure what to make of it. Who even still went to church these days? And on a *Monday night?*

"How did you enjoy the rest of the ball?" Peter asked the question around one of her fries.

"Um, I left pretty soon after we spoke. I wanted to get back to the hotel to start planning."

"Planning?" He looked puzzled.

"The ball."

He stared at her for a couple of seconds, then started laughing, shoulders jumping like crickets.

She held up her hands. "I know, I know, I'm a total nerd."

He finally stopped laughing and swiped another fry, dragging it through the disgusting pea sludge. "Well, you certainly get points for commitment to the cause."

"Thanks. I think." She picked up another fry and crunched down.

"Why don't we talk about the other two. We should get started on planning those first since they'll be sooner. What do you think of a row-off and a cricket match?"

"You're going to have to explain the terminology."

"Well, a row-off is pretty much as it sounds. We'd hire a gym or some other similar large space. Chuck a few ergs on the floor and have all the rowers race over a set distance. I was thinking we could pair up the Oxford and Cambridge rowers by position. That will make it really competitive."

She was going to guess that "erg" was another name for a rowing machine. Didn't want to look dumb as a hammer asking. Especially not when she now knew an Olympic-level rower sat across from her.

Emelia pulled out her planner from the bag beside her and made a show of reading her notes. She knew them all by heart but it was a helpful distrac-tion from the unwavering gaze sitting across from her. "When we last talked about dates, we were thinking about the end of May for the first one, assuming the board approves it next week. Will that still work or is it getting too close to exams?"

"We might want to make it mid-May. I think exams are early June but I'll check with a few of the guys and get back to you. If we were going to try a second event it would probably need to be straight after exams end, before everyone leaves for summer." Peter snagged another fry.

Which would give them a month to get this row-off approved by the board, organized, and done, and then another month to arrange the cricket thing. Whatever that was. Hard but not impossible. Especially if they started soon and could capitalize on the post–Boat Race fever. "Have you got anyone willing to do it yet?"

"I've asked a few and have had good responses —depending on that date, of course. But if anyone says no to me they definitely won't say no to Sabine."

"Sabine?" Emelia tried to ask the question lightly, disconcerted at the spurt of jealousy that had shot through her at just the sound of his mentioning another girl's name.

"She used to row with Anita back in school and wants to help out. She's now the cox of the women's Olympic eights team. No guy rower will be able to turn her down." Including him, Emelia would have guessed by the way his gaze flickered as he talked about her. Peter drummed his fingers on the table, evading her gaze slightly. "In the interest of full disclosure, we used to date. We broke up about eight months ago. Is that okay?"

Emelia tried to untangle the question. Was what okay? That they broke up? That they used to date?

"That she helps, I mean." Peter's food had arrived and he speared a piece of fish.

"She's your ex-girlfriend. If it's okay with you, then it is more than okay with me. Sounds like she'll be a great asset." Emelia did her best to keep her tone neutral, hiding her expression by jotting some meaningless notes down on her pad.

Sabine was probably blond and gorgeous. To be a cox she was definitely going to be as petite as they came. And as far as Emelia was concerned there were only two reasons you offered to help out your ex-boyfriend with something like this. Sabine was either the nicest person on the face of the earth or she was on a mission to take the "ex" out of "ex-boyfriend."

Emelia would have placed some good money on which one it was.

Sixteen

"Someone has told you we're planning a ball, not a war, right?" A week later, Peter paused in the doorway of Allie's—Emelia's—living room and scanned it for somewhere to put down the pizza he was carrying. Every flat surface was stacked with reams of paper, magazines, brochures, or her computer.

"You're right. War would be way easier." Emelia barely even glanced up at him from where she sat hunched over her laptop and didn't seem the slightest bit surprised at his appearance. He'd happened to arrive just as Allie was heading out and let him in. Emelia's hair was bunched up in a bun on top of her head, a pencil shoved through the middle. She wore a baggy gray sweatshirt and black track pants. He felt overdressed in his jeans and jumper.

In the last seven days they'd gotten approval from the board for the row-off and the cricket match and agreement for Peter and Emelia to work up a more detailed proposal for a winter ball. He'd gone into the office to run a few things past her, only for Elizabeth to give a knowing smile at his clothes and say Emelia was working from home for most of the week.

"Can I get you a drink while I'm up?"

Emelia rolled her head across her shoulders. "A soda, please. There should be some in the fridge."

Walking into the kitchen, he grabbed a couple of chilled cans and headed back toward the bunker. "What are you working on?" He sat down on the couch next to her, maintaining appropriate distance.

"Our plan of attack. Look." Emelia turned her screen to face him, and he was hit by a haze of boxes and bright colors.

Had he stepped into some kind of time warp or something? Been frozen like a Narnian statue and brought back to life a few months later? How on earth had she managed to achieve all this in the few days since the board meeting? He blinked, the colors spinning in front of his eyes. "So, I got a phone call on the way here."

Emelia tilted her head. "About?"

"It was the eighties. They want their fluoro back."

"Oh, you're a comedian now, Drinian?" But \ she was unable to stop a grin from spreading across her face. It filled his chest with the kind of feeling usually reserved for winning big races.

"You make it too easy." Peter grinned back at her and something jumped between them that he'd never experienced in his life. He cleared his throat, turned his attention back to the spreadsheet. Right across the bottom there were even more marked tabs. Venues. Caterers. Florists. Rental places. The list went on.

Emelia clicked on the one marked *Venues*. Another color-coded screen. "So, I created a matrix listing all the material characteristics. Most important of which, obviously, is availability, but you can't get that off websites. But then I added in scoring based on criteria including location, cost, capacity, in-house catering or whether you can bring your own, indoor and outdoor options, those sorts of things. And I'm thinking we should probably talk to Elizabeth to run the weightings past her. I mean, availability is obviously critical, but after that would she rather be somewhere farther out but cheaper? Somewhere that you can bring your own caterers or somewhere that has a superior layout? Once they're all weighted and we've scored them, then the formula will practically make the choice for us."

Emelia leaned closer into him as she pointed at the screen. "We could also further distill the variables. And we'd probably have to allow a category for gut reaction as well. There's a lot to be said for instinct, don't you think?"

She blinked up at him, eyes shining, cheeks rosy.

Marry me. The words flashed through his head. That was the instinct that he had when faced with a woman who could probably have made organizing the Normandy invasion look easy. Except that when he mentioned going to church she'd looked at him like he'd sprouted an antenna and started talking in Klingon. He swallowed it back down. "Yes. Definitely. A lot to be said for instinct." His words came out husky and a little stilted. But she didn't seem to notice.

"I've done some short-listing."

"Of course you have."

Emelia raised an eyebrow at him. "Anyway, using the very rudimentary criteria I've already drawn up, I've got us fifteen places to go visit."

Peter almost choked on the gulp of soda he'd just taken. "I'm sorry. Did you say fifteen? As in one-five?"

"What were you thinking?"

Peter shrugged. "I don't know. Three." Seemed like a good number. More than two, less than five.

Emelia skewered him with her gaze. "*Three*. You have got to be joking. This is saving SpringBoard we're talking about here. We can't leave any stone unturned. Twelve. And that's me being generous."

"Ten." Peter uttered the word in desperation.

"Twelve." Emelia smiled with satisfaction, as if she knew she had him.

"We can't do twelve. When are we going to look at twelve venues?"

"This weekend. We need to get it done before it gets busy with the row-off. They're all scheduled." She flipped to another screen and there he saw it, his entire weekend laid out in Technicolor glory.

"Seven? We're seeing the first one at seven in the morning?"

"They have two weddings. It was the only time I could get. Besides . . ." She smiled sweetly. "Seven is luxuriously late for you, isn't it, rower boy?"

He couldn't have stopped himself from grinning if he tried. Lord help him, he liked this girl. More than was smart. Why? Why did she have to be so perfect in every way except the one that mattered most? More importantly, how on earth was he going to hold on to his self-control while spending the next seven months planning a ball with the one person he desperately wanted but couldn't have?

Seventeen

"Coffee?" Peter asked the question as they got back in the car after viewing venue possibility number four.

"You just had one before the last place."

He quirked an eyebrow at her. "Don't judge me. I thought all you Americans would consume the stuff intravenously if you could."

"I'm not judging you. I'm just . . ." Emelia trailed off before she could ask the guy if he had a bladder the size of a planet. When he'd arrived to pick her up at six forty, he had been clasping a venti-size coffee cup like it was his firstborn. Plus one for her, which she'd made it about a quarter of the way through.

Since then, he'd had another two. And no bathroom break. And not a single hint that he might need one in the future. She might've suspected he'd decided to answer the call of nature somewhere if not for the fact that the only time she'd left his side, for her own bathroom trip, he'd been in the care of the venue's events coordinator, who had been flirting up a storm with him.

It was totally ridiculous, since Peter had a good foot on the girl, so most of her eye-batting was directed straight at his armpit. Not to mention, the man himself was completely oblivious.

"Fine. I guess coffee can wait until after this one."

Emelia started, realizing she'd left the conversation hanging and he thought she was still thinking about his caffeine habit.

"Where to next?"

Emelia consulted her color-coded list. "Rhodes House."

Peter let out a low whistle. "Nice."

"Have you been?"

"Not personally, but I've heard of it. Didn't realize we had that kind of budget."

Emelia consulted her spreadsheet. Rental cost was eight hundred and forty pounds including tax, which put it midrange of all the places on her list. "It's pretty reasonable, actually."

Peter glanced at her but didn't say anything as he pulled out into the road. Emelia tried to look anywhere except out the windshield. Even after a couple of months, driving on the left still caused her blood pressure to climb like one of those never-ending stair climbers at the gym.

Time to find something to talk about. Anything. "So, is the team ready?" She blurted out the first safe thing that came to mind. Between all the ball organizing, she couldn't lose sight of the "friendly" row-off that was taking place in a few weeks' time. Its head-to-head nature was getting more press than she'd imagined. She could only hope the money would follow.

Peter kept his eyes on the road. "More than. They're all still feeling pretty cocky from the big win."

"Is it weird? Being on the other side?" She regretted the question almost as soon as she asked it. *Good one, Emelia. Nothing like reminding the guy of what he can't do.*

His fingers tightened as he changed down a gear. "Very."

She waited for more but realized after a few seconds it wasn't coming.

"How's your shoulder doing?"

"Not great." Another two-syllable answer. She'd interviewed rocks more talkative than this guy.

"I'm sorry."

Peter pulled in front of the gray mansion she'd seen in the website photos. In real life, it was even more impressive. And enormous. Four huge stone columns lined the front of the verandah, with another four behind them, guarding the black front door. The entryway of the house, covered with a dome-shaped roof, connected onto a Colonial-style building.

"Oh. Wow." For a second, Emelia was speechless and glad they'd both dressed up for the day in smart casual clothing, instead of the pair of jeans she'd been tempted to put on. But even in her knit dress, the towering building made her feel like she should apologize for not wearing designer cocktail attire.

Getting out of the car, they crossed the sidewalk and approached the doors, stepping up to the porch, whose ceiling was so high she had to tilt her head back to see the top.

"Good morning." A thickset man with slicked-back gray hair and fierce eyebrows opened the door before she had even knocked.

Emelia stared at him for a second. If Carson from *Downton Abbey* had a brother, this guy was it. "Good morning, I'm Emelia Mason. We have an appointment at ten o'clock to tour the venue." She pulled out her snootiest voice. The one she'd always used to get herself into parties she had no business being at.

The man inclined his head. "Miss Mason. My

name is Stuart Goldfinch. I will be showing you around Rhodes House today."

"Nice to meet you. This is Peter Carlisle."

The man's ramrod posture grew even straighter. "Mr. Carlisle. Of course." He was practically fawning as he held out his hand to Peter. "Welcome to Rhodes House. May I say, I was so sorry to hear about your retirement? But of course, such great luck for the Blue Boat to have you with them."

"Thank you for seeing us on such short notice."

Emelia stared at him. Apparently she wasn't the only one who could put on the posh accent. Peter suddenly sounded like he lived in a palace and regularly took tea with the Queen.

"It is our pleasure. Now please . . ." The portly man gestured into the mansion.

Emelia tried to take in the soaring walls of oak and stone, the huge windows giving a glimpse of extensive gardens. It had looked gorgeous on the website, but that didn't even come close to doing its grandeur justice. She barely listened as the man rattled off the selling points of the venue. Room sizes, layout options, they all flowed over her head. She hoped Peter was taking it in, because she was ready to sign on the dotted line.

This was it. She could feel it in her bones. She could see men in tuxes and women in gowns dancing. Tables set with silverware and huge arrangements. Waiters in white gloves with silver trays.

Before she got her hopes up, she knew she should double-check . . . "Now, as I said on the phone, the ball is going to be in early December. Is it correct you've still got a weekend available?"

"Yes. Generally, our weekend dates are booked far in advance. But it has just so happened that this weekend we've had a cancellation for the first Saturday. Fate, may I suggest?"

"Maybe."

"Now, you'll see in our brochure we have a number of excellent catering firms we partner with. I can guarantee you they all serve exquisite cuisine. Fit for royalty, one might even say, should any be joining you."

"I'm sure," Peter said evenly.

Emelia half listened to the exchange as she flipped open the brochure she'd been handed. A set of numbers seared her retinas. Oh. Wow. Oh. No. She read them again, hoping that maybe she was seeing things wrong. But no, that had been the first time. This venue wasn't the reasonable eight hundred and forty pounds she'd thought it was. Try adding a zero. Try eight thousand four hundred pounds.

"Emelia?" The way Peter was looking at her suggested it wasn't the first time he'd said her name.

"Yes?"

"Would you like to see the gardens?"

"Yes." Her voice sounded weak. "Some air would be excellent."

Emelia had realized her mistake. Peter had seen it the instant her pupils had dilated as she'd read the brochure and her face had gone a shade paler. He'd known there had to be an error the moment she'd called Rhodes House "reasonable." Sure, if she was secretly a multimillionaire heiress.

Maybe he should've asked more questions. But he couldn't bring himself to ruin the satisfaction she derived from her perfectly coded and mapped spreadsheet. And, he had to admit, there was a certain amount of fun in watching her discover something was ten times more expensive than she'd thought when she was making him suffer through twelve potential locations.

"You okay?" He bent his head toward hers, lowering his voice so their escort couldn't hear.

Emelia licked her lips. "There's . . . I seem to have . . ." She must have seen something in his expression because she promptly whacked him on the arm. "You knew!" She hissed the words under her breath.

"Ow." He rubbed the spot above his elbow. The girl packed some power.

"You've been having a great time, haven't you, Smirky McSmirkster. Watching me fall in love with a place, thinking I'd found the venue bargain of the century." Her words were sharp, but a touch of a smile hovered at the edge of her lips.

"I can neither confirm nor deny."

"As is no doubt evident, the gardens are award winning." Their tour guide spread his arms and gestured around him. Peter had to admit the garden was impressive. If he had almost ten grand to spare, they would've won him over.

"They have entertained many a distinguished guest." The man waggled his caterpillar eyebrows at Peter meaningfully. Peter wished he would stop. Emelia wasn't stupid. He didn't want to rouse her suspicions. Didn't want her knowing who he was until she needed to. Emelia was one of the few people he didn't have to worry about being a groupie. A rowing one or a peerage one. He preferred to keep it that way for as long as humanly possible.

"Well, that's that, then." Emelia slumped into the passenger seat after they left the twelfth, and final, venue for the day.

"What was wrong with that one?"

Never before had Peter imagined how hard it could possibly be to find a ball venue. Over the last twelve hours, Emelia had knocked off every place they'd visited. For reasons Peter would have never even thought to consider. This was why guys had as little as possible to do with planning things like this.

"I thought it was fine." It had been nice enough. A ballroom at one of the big hotels. Maybe not exactly unique, but nice, with staff who clearly did the big-event thing all the time.

"Fine isn't enough. To save SpringBoard we need spectacular." Emelia blinked rapidly.

Wait, was she . . . Peter stepped a bit closer. She was close to tears.

"Hey." He rested his hand lightly on hers. "It's okay. We'll find something."

Emelia blinked some more and swiped her hands across her eyes. "I know we will. I just thought . . . I just wish . . ."

"What?"

She was silent for a second, then she sucked in a breath.

"I just wish I'd never seen Rhodes House."

It was like a kick to his solar plexus. "I'm sorry. That was all my fault. I shouldn't have let us go there. I just didn't want to be the one to tell you your perfect spreadsheet had a critical error."

That got half a smile out of her. "No, it was mine. I don't know why I thought something so great would cost so little. I guess I just thought that maybe, if there was a God, this was His way of making some magic happen."

He'd thought it wasn't possible but at that, he felt even worse.

"I just saw it there, you know. We walked in and

I could imagine a huge ball. The kind that would get people writing the huge checks we need. I just felt like it was it. And I know I'm being super picky about all the other ones we've seen. It's just that once I saw that one, nothing else has measured up since."

Which pretty much summed up how he felt about her.

"I'm sorry." She ran her hands through her hair. "You have more important things to do than this. Look at you. You've been slammed with Boat Race stuff the last few months and now you've spent the day driving me around ball venues. Plus everything you've been doing for the row-off." She sucked in a breath and straightened her shoulders. "It's okay. We'll find something even better than Rhodes House. I just need to broaden the parameters. We can reconvene after the row-off. I need to focus on that now anyway."

The combination of disappointment and determination did him in. If he'd had eight and a half grand, he would have handed it over there and then.

So he offered up the only thing he did have. The one thing that was going to force him to reveal to her what he'd been avoiding. "I might know somewhere else we can look at."

Eighteen

"And Cambridge takes this one by four point seven seconds!" Emelia could barely hear the announcer's words over the sound of people yelling, clapping, and stomping. An hour into the row-off and her ears were ringing. Apparently the passing of the Boat Race had done nothing to dull the competitive spirit between the Oxford and Cambridge crews.

Peter had really been the one who had pulled off the event. Somehow between him and Sabine they'd managed to get almost every single crew member to agree to be part of the fund-raiser, as well as the two coxes. All Emelia had to do was organize ticketing and logistics.

Like Peter had suggested, the crew members from the same seat in the Boat Race were pitted against each other in a head-to-head battle over one mile. Not only had it meant all they'd had to do was relocate four ergs—two for racing and two for warm-up—onto the gymnasium floor, but with the big screens they'd put up, the place was packed full of spectators. Family members, friends, rowing groupies—they'd all somehow been convinced to part with twenty pounds each to watch.

And that was before Sabine had pulled a rabbit

out of her hat. She'd somehow gotten some BBC sports commentator—whom Emelia didn't know from a piece of pine but everyone else was giddy over—to commentate the event, with highlights screening on some sports show later in the week.

It still wouldn't be close to the kind of money they needed to be pulling in, but hopefully it would create momentum. And that was what the first event was about.

"This next one is going to be a dead heat. John and James are pretty much identical in height and weight." Sabine made the observation from where she stood a few feet away on the sidelines. Emelia had been exactly right about Peter's ex-girlfriend. Blond, petite, and gorgeous. She'd walked into the gym at six a.m. and immediately taken charge of all the things Emelia had no clue about and Peter hadn't thought of. The only thing she couldn't get her head around was whether Sabine was the coolest ex-girlfriend in the world or making a play to get her man back. If it was the second, she was one of the best players Emelia had ever seen. Not so much as a hint of neediness or desperation.

Even in a pair of jeans and T-shirt, there was no hiding Sabine was a top-class athlete. From her perfect posture, to the muscles that rippled under the denim, to the determined set of her jaw, it oozed from her. It wasn't difficult to see why she was an elite-level cox. Or why Peter had once dated her. Or that pretty much any other guy in the room would have jumped at the chance. Emelia felt like a pudgy Amazon next to her. "I understand you're a cox for the Olympic team. That's impressive."

"Thanks." Sabine kept her eyes on the two rowers next up as they finished their warm-up. The roar in the room had dulled to the buzz of conversation as people waited for the next race.

"Thanks so much for your help. I'm sure it's obvious I'm way out of my depth when it comes to anything to do with rowing." For some reason Emelia felt the need to fill the conversational void.

"If you don't know rowing, you can never know Peter. Not really." Sabine didn't so much as glance Emelia's way.

Her pointed delivery hit Emelia like a barb in the side. Left her breathless for a moment. "I think you underestimate him. He's more than rowing." She delivered her own sting back.

Sabine swung around, ponytail bouncing. "Of course he is. But what have the last ten years of his life been about? Rowing. It's what he ate, slept, and breathed. It was what he dreamed about. It was why he trained twelve times a week for years. It's what he would still be doing if he hadn't been sidelined by injury. The fact that he can't is what breaks him every day. Have you even Googled him? Do you have the faintest clue how great he was? How far he could've gone?"

Emelia just stared at her.

"No. Well, let me enlighten you. He was a shoo-in Team GB for the eight. He would've been competing at Rio. And I would have bet everything I had that the question wasn't if he got his team to the podium, it was just where. He was *that* good."

"But he's not." Emelia wasn't even sure what she was doing. It wasn't like she and Peter were dating. It wasn't like they were *anything*. So what was she fighting for exactly? "I may not know much about his injury, but I'm guessing that it's bad to have taken him out of rowing this long. Maybe he will never row at that level again. That's reality. No matter how much any of us may want it to be different, it's just not. So you're right. I haven't lived in your little rowing bubble. I don't get it all. But he doesn't live there anymore either."

Sabine jammed her hands in her pockets and sucked in a breath. "Look, I'm sure you're very nice. You have a cute accent and you seem smart enough. I'm sure you're very refreshing with your naivety about rowing because he's hurting. At some point, when he starts his comeback, the fact that you don't know anything about what he loves isn't going to be cute, it's going to be irritating. The fact that you have no insight into what drives someone to train that brutally for so long will mean you can never really get him.

So I have nothing against you, but you are not right for him."

Emelia tried to keep her face impassive, not let Sabine see how much her words were shaking her. "And you are?"

Sabine summoned up a regret-filled smile. "I was."

They watched as the next two rowers slid their feet into the footplates on the ergs and adjusted the straps.

"Look, I made a mistake when he was injured. I let him push me away. I thought that maybe space was what he needed. It was the wrong move. And I'm sorry that I'm the inconvenient ex-girlfriend showing up and throwing a spanner in your little fledgling romance, or whatever it is. But I've never quit on something I've wanted in my entire life, and until the day he can look me in the eyes and tell me there's no hope for us, I'm not going to quit on him."

"Sounds like you already did."

Sabine flinched like Emelia had struck her.

"I'm sorry. I . . ." Emelia floundered for words. "Look, we're not even dating. So it's not like I'm in your way. He's free for the taking."

Sabine studied her for a second, her gaze softening. "I know competition when I see it. I'm not sneaky. I fight fair. I just want you to know that I'm in this."

In what? Emelia ran her hands through her hair.

This was an insane conversation. "Fine. Thanks for the heads-up. Notice received."

Someone called Sabine's name from across the room and she gave them a wave as she turned toward them. Allie appeared on Emelia's other side, watching Sabine as she stalked away. "She doesn't look happy. What was that about?"

"I think it was the English version of throwing down the gauntlet."

Allie raised her eyebrows. "For Peter?"

"For Peter."

Allie gave her a look that Emelia couldn't quite decipher. "I didn't know there was a gauntlet for Peter."

"You and me both." Emelia had only spoken to the guy in passing all day. She had no idea what it was Sabine had seen that had made her think they were in some kind of competition for him. Time to change the subject. "Speaking of gauntlets, have you guys set a date yet?" Emelia regretted the question as soon as she asked it. Something crossed Allie's face that wasn't the smile most brides-to-be seemed unable to restrain. Which made no sense given Emelia's observation that their relationship was one of the most functional she'd ever seen.

"No."

Hadn't they been engaged for like seven months? Not that she could talk. She avoided relationships like someone with a peanut allergy avoided a Snickers. "I'm sorry. It's none of my business."

Her roommate let out a sigh. "It's complicated." Allie dropped to the bench behind them, pulled her legs up to her chest, and wrapped her arms around them.

"Visa stuff?" Emelia settled in beside her, keeping her gaze on the guys in front of them taking a few warm-up rows. Through the| windows tree leaves were a lush green. Summer was definitely in the air.

"Sort of. I'm from New Zealand. He's from America. We live in England. But only temporarily. I might get an offer to stay at Oxford. I might not. It's all just uncertain."

Emelia shifted her focus to her roommate. "Is that the real reason?" It was only a guess, but Emelia had a strong suspicion that there had to be more than that to it. The couple she knew wouldn't let something like a little uncertainty stop them from getting hitched. People from different countries faced the same thing all the time.

"Yes . . . no." Allie ran her hands through her hair and blinked rapidly. Allie sucked in a breath, looking like she was trying to get her emotions under control. "I guess I thought the fear would go away. I'm thirty-two years old and I foolishly believed when we got engaged that everything would magically be okay. How stupid is that?"

This was definitely a side of her bubbly, confident friend she hadn't met. "What are you afraid of?"

"Getting married."

"As in . . ." Emelia was clearly missing a connection here, but she wasn't sure what it was.

"The wedding." Allie's fingers were twisting over themselves. Again and again. Emelia wanted to reach out and make them stop. "Every time I think about it, I freak out. I walk into a dress shop and start hyperventilating just looking at them. We start talking about where and when and I just feel this vise in my chest. The last time I got married was the worst day of my life. I just didn't know it. And now when I think about getting married that's all I remember. I don't get excited. I want to throw up."

Wow. Emelia never would have guessed that underneath Allie's bubbly exterior sat all this angst. Or that she'd been married before. "So elope. Go stand in front of a judge, or whatever it is here, and just get married." Emelia shoved aside the selfish thought that Allie's marriage would leave her homeless. No way was she living with newlyweds.

Allie looked at her, eyes wet. "I can't do that to Jackson. He wants the real wedding. He deserves a proper one. His family, they're amazing, and he's the only son. I can't take that away from them. Not because of my stupid mistakes. I know that once I'm walking down the aisle and he's waiting for me, I'll be fine. I just don't know how to get there."

"Does Jackson know this?" She raised her voice as the announcer started counting down to the beginning of the next race.

"Some of it. I don't want to hurt him. And every time I mention Derek, he gets this set in his jaw like he wants to go and hunt him down and beat him." A wry smile played on Allie's lips as she traced something on the wooden bench with her pointer finger.

"Have you tried . . ." Emelia couldn't believe the words that were about to come out of her mouth. "Praying about it?" That was what church people did, right? Prayed about stuff? If there was a God, surely He would listen to Allie. She studied the big screen for a few seconds. The guys had started rowing; the crowd's roar was low but it would grow exponentially over the next few minutes.

"All the time." Allie shrugged. "But God's not like a magical fairy up there waving a magical wand that will—poof!—make everything all better. I need to take responsibility for dealing with my own stuff. And it's hard. And it wrecks me that Jackson has to deal with it too. That he has a fiancée who turns into a mess every time we try to talk about what should be one of the best days of our lives. That I'm dreading it, instead of excited about it." She heaved a sigh and ran her hands through her hair. "Maybe we should actually have an engagement party first. See if that helps."

Emelia turned to her. "You haven't had an engagement party?"

Allie shrugged. "When we got engaged, I'd only been in England a couple of months and Jackson even less. We hadn't made a lot of friends, and with him in Cambridge and me here and our families on two different continents, it just hasn't happened."

"Okay. So have an engagement party. Start with that."

Allie sighed. "The only problem is even that will probably be over my mother's dead body."

Two hours later, Emelia closed the gym door behind her and breathed in a lungful of fresh air. It had come down to the two coxes, Cambridge winning with five rowers winning to Oxford's three and a margin of three seconds. The way they'd whooped and danced you would've thought it was the real thing. The part of her that cheered for the underdog had smiled on the inside, careful not to let any of the Oxford team see.

Allie unlocked her car and they both opened their doors. Emelia's backside had almost hit the seat when she remembered. "I left my water bottle in there."

They'd been almost the last to leave too. Knowing her luck, the facilities manager had locked the door behind her.

Allie stuck the key in the ignition. "Run back. I'm sure someone will still be there. I'll wait."

Emelia climbed out of the car and jogged toward the gym. She could picture exactly where she'd left it. Against the wall behind the ergometer she'd tried out rowing before the crowds had showed up. And after a thousand meters of feeling like she was about to pass out, she'd decided it was definitely not the sport for her.

The door swung open easily, and she took the stairs two at a time. Allie had some kind of guest-lecture thing tonight. She didn't want to make her late.

Turning the corner at the top, she could hear the whirring of an erg. The rowing club was going to collect them the following morning. She rounded the corner, then stopped. Peter sat on one of the rowing machines, his back to her. Even from meters away, she could see the sweat beads rolling down his neck, his shoulders and arms rippling as he pulled the handle with such power, it wouldn't have surprised her if the tether broke.

His left shoulder had some strapping tape across it. One large strip came out from under his sleeve-less top. Not that from the way his arms and quads rippled as he rowed you'd have had any idea he'd been injured.

She inched forward, trying to get a glimpse of the numbers on the display screen. Her jaw almost unhinged as she caught sight of them flashing up over his shoulder. Her average split of two minutes ten over five hundred meters had made her feel like she was about to lose everything she'd eaten in the last week. Peter was pulling a minute thirty-five and, judging by the determined set of his profile, had no intention of slowing down anytime soon. And this was him injured.

This guy wasn't good—he was superhuman. Her confrontation with his ex still rang in her ears. Sabine was right, Emelia was never going to be able to understand what this sport meant to him.

Her gaze shifted from Peter to her water bottle, sitting right where she'd left it. Tiptoeing over, she picked it up silently and moved back toward the exit, allowing herself one last glimpse at the pure athleticism in motion. What had happened to him? Maybe it was time to break her self-imposed Google exile to find out. It wouldn't be prying, exactly. It wasn't like it wouldn't be public knowledge.

So why don't you just ask him yourself then? The question followed her as she walked away. Emelia was almost at the top of the stairs when a roar followed by a smacking sound made her spin and sprint back into the room.

Peter was on the mat beside his erg, knees curled up to his chest, one hand gripping the opposite shoulder. By his head, the seat still slid up and down on the rail, the fan still spinning.

Emelia sprang over the three ergs that were between them and dropped to her knees beside him. His eyes were clenched shut, face tinged with gray under the sheen of sweat.

"Peter. Peter!"

His eyes opened enough to become slits. "Emelia?"

"What do you need?"

"My bag. Pills." He huffed the words out as though it took extreme effort to speak. Closed his eyes again. Turning, she saw a black backpack by the far wall. Jumping over his erg, she ran to it, ripped the zipper open, and emptied the contents onto the floor. Thermal top, water bottle, muesli bars, and then the hollow sound of a circular medicine container, then another. She grabbed them both, along with the water bottle, and scrambled back.

"Which one?" She tried to read the labels, but they blurred in front of her eyes.

"OxyContin. The green one." Oh boy. She was no doctor, but she knew from her days as a fill-in sports reporter that was only prescribed for serious pain.

She opened the first container; the round green pills were inside. Pulling one out, she held it between her fingertips. "Open your mouth."

His mouth cracked open enough for her to poke

it through his lips. "Water coming." She angled the water bottle carefully to control the flow. Last thing the guy needed right now was her drowning him. He lifted his head up a little to gulp the water, then dropped it back to the mat.

The whole time his eyes didn't crack open. "Thanks."

She stepped back over the erg and put all his stuff back in his backpack, carrying it over to him in case he needed anything else.

"I'm fine. Just give me a few minutes."

Typical English stiff upper lip. "Don't be stupid." She assessed the way he was holding his upper arm against the side of his chest. "Dislocated shoulder or rotator cuff?"

He opened his eyes and stared at her. "Rotator."

Oh boy. That was bad. Not that it took a genius to figure that out when he was in the fetal position and the color of ash.

"Do you have a car here?" He couldn't drive, that was for sure. But he needed to be home. Resting.

"Yup. I'll be fine. Honestly." All of a sudden, Emelia remembered Allie. Sitting in the car. No doubt wondering what the heck had happened to her.

Right on cue, she heard someone approaching. "Emelia?" her roommate called out. "Everything okay?"

Emelia stood just as Allie rounded the corner.

"I'm fine." She gestured to the man at her feet. "He is not."

At that, Peter somehow managed to roll himself into a sitting position, face contorted in pain. "I'll be fine. I just need a few minutes for the Oxy to kick in."

Allie skirted around the machines as Peter stumbled to his feet, his right hand now supporting his left elbow.

Allie stopped in front of him, her neck craning so she could look up at his face. "What have you done? You said you were going easy on it." She sounded like a bossy older sister.

"I was."

Emelia bit the inside of her cheek as she observed the way Peter avoided Allie's gaze. Whatever it was that she had seen, "going easy" wasn't it.

From the expression on her face, Allie didn't believe him either. She let out a sigh and ran a hand through her copper hair as she shook her head.

Emelia stepped forward. "You have a lecture. You should go. I'll make sure he gets home okay."

Allie glanced between the two of them, obviously torn.

"She's right, Allie. You need to go. I'll call you later." Peter's sweaty T-shirt stuck to him like plastic wrap outlining his muscular physique.

Emelia forced her gaze away and onto her roommate, who still looked a little uncertain. There wasn't even any decision to be made. This wasn't community college. You didn't just not show up for a lecture at Oxford.

"Can you walk okay?" Emelia directed the question to Peter. "I'll take your backpack, but I'm just going to need to grab my stuff out of Allie's car."

Peter nodded, managing something that was more shuffle than walk, but at least it was forward movement.

"I'll go get your stuff. You come with him." Allie finally accepted that she was going to have to leave this to Emelia.

A few minutes later, Emelia was holding her gear and watching Allie drive away. It was only as the ashen-faced guy leaned against the passenger door of his car that she realized her rescue plan had one significant flaw.

She had never driven on the wrong side of the road before.

Nineteen

Peter tried to bite back a groan, but one escaped anyway as he settled himself into the passenger seat and gritted his teeth against the feeling of someone taking an ice pick to his shoulder.

His arm lay useless against his side like a broken wing. Any attempt to move it sent shards of pain through his shoulder.

The last time it had felt this bad, he'd been on a bar floor in Verona, not knowing what had happened but knowing it was bad. His next clear memory was of the white ceiling of the local hospital, the buzz of serious pain meds, and the grim face of the head coach. No words were necessary to tell him the dream was over before it had really begun.

"Can you pass me your seat belt or do you need me to get it?" Emelia's voice broke through his ramble down bad-memory lane. Peter slowly moved his right hand from where it was supporting his left elbow and reached up until his fingers hooked around the belt and pulled it forward.

He squashed down a yelp as even the small movement sent fire down his side.

"I've got it." Emelia took it, and he heard a whir as she pulled it around his body. Then a click as it tightened across his torso.

He anchored his hand back under his elbow and forced himself to breathe against the fireworks display taking place on the back of his eyelids. He'd lost track of how much time had passed since the shredding pain had sent him off the erg and onto the floor, but it couldn't be long before the Oxy kicked in.

Kevin was going to kill him. Peter had promised his physio he was taking it slow and steady. That was the condition that had gotten him the okay to get back on the water. A pace that would have had a disabled pensioner passing him. And he had been. But after weeks of good easy rows out on the water and only the occasional twinge from his shoulder, he'd thought it was time to push it a little.

How could he have been so stupid? He had years until Tokyo. Enough time to rebuild his strength and fitness to be a contender in all the lead-up races that mattered. But no, he'd had to go and be the big man. And now he'd put himself back what, months?

It was the email that had caused Peter to be reckless. The weekly newsfeed from America that helped him keep tabs on the journalist who'd been responsible for Anita's death. He should quit it. Just the sight of her byline was enough to have him seeing red. This week she'd been stalking some poor celebrity who had checked into rehab. Degrading them. Smearing their character with allegations and insinuations that could never be undone. That was what he'd been thinking of as he'd pulled on the handle of the erg so hard the numbers on the display could hardly keep up.

He registered that the engine had started, but the car wasn't moving. Cracking open his eyelids, he turned his head slightly to see what was going on. Emelia sat in the driver's seat, staring out the windshield, fingers grasping the steering wheel.

"You okay?" Then he realized she was missing a key piece of information. "Sorry. You don't even know where I live."

Emelia shook her head. "Allie told me where you live. It's . . ." He watched something flicker across her profile. For a second, he didn't think she was going to tell him whatever it was. "So, I've never driven in England before."

It took him a second to work out what the problem was. "You'll be fine. Just make sure you stay left." He tried to smile, lighten up the mood. "I'll just keep my eyes shut." At least that way he wouldn't have to see if she turned him in front of oncoming traffic or something. Though even that didn't sound too bad.

Right now, death would almost have been preferable to reality.

Emelia spent the fifteen-minute drive to Peter's place hunched over the steering wheel, peering out the windshield like an old lady, and going an average of maybe ten miles an hour. Just trying to translate the speedometer from kilometers an hour stressed her out, so she just didn't look at it. The drive was a lesson in what was required to break the renowned English reserve, as drivers behind her honked and passed her, offering gestures that didn't exactly say "Welcome to England."

She didn't care. Every corner felt like it would be her last, every oncoming vehicle had her sucking in air through her pursed lips like she was breathing through a straw.

Peter offered directions but his eyes stayed shut for the journey. The meds must have been kicking in though, because he was starting to look more white-gray than the gray-gray of the gym floor.

She directed compliments to the speed junkies under her breath as yet another driver tailgated her and sat on his horn.

"I'm pretty sure I've run this route faster." Peter didn't open his eyes but did turn his head slightly to make the helpful observation.

"I am not going that slowly." She looked in the rearview mirror. Thank goodness the guy couldn't turn around to see she was being abused by a man who had to be at least seventy.

"My grandmother drives faster than you and she's blind."

She finally relaxed her death grip on the steering wheel when she knew they had to be getting close.

She chanced a glance over at him. Even when he was in excruciating pain, there was some-thing about his presence that made her feel safe. The way she'd always imagined Peter Pevensie would. "You okay?"

"I'll be fine." His pinched voice said the opposite.

Emelia knew the voice. Knew the words. They were the same ones she'd used the day she'd lost out on her dream job as reporter for the *Boston Globe* to a congressman's daughter who couldn't have told an adverb from an adjective if her vapid existence depended on it. Apparently none of that mattered when you had a daddy with a Rolodex full of prestigious contacts you could go simpering to when you needed a story.

She knew what broken dreams looked like, so she wasn't about to offer perky motivational lines that weren't worth the air they traveled on.

She turned the wipers on instead of the blinker, and then made a left into a small, narrow street. Then realized Peter had said to take the next right.

"Um, Peter? I just turned left instead of right."

Peter opened his eyes and peered out the windshield. "So you did. Know what else?"

"What?"

A smile flickered on his lips. "This is a one-way street and it's not this way."

Emelia stomped on the brakes, leaving Peter sucking in a sharp breath as his shoulder tilted forward.

"Sorry. Sorry!" She managed to reverse the car into a tiny driveway and turn it around.

"Girls aren't very good at keeping maps in their brains." Peter uttered Edmund's well-known line with a twisted smile.

"That's because we've got something in them." Emelia threw Lucy's responding line back as she turned onto the original road. Driving a little farther down, she took the next right. "Did you say you're number thirty-six?"

She looked sideways when Peter didn't answer to find him staring at her. "What? Did I get that wrong too?"

"You quoted right back. The line. You didn't even have to think about it. Who can do that?"

She came to a stop at the curb. "Someone who's read Narnia more than a few times." Avoiding the intent look in his gaze that made her feel like he was peering into her soul, she reached over, released Peter's seat belt, and watched as it traveled over his torso. His sweat-soaked T-shirt stuck to his chest, leaving little to the imagination.

Reaching across to open his door, Peter got out of the car, slamming it shut behind him. Scrambling after him, Emelia grabbed his backpack from the backseat and followed him up the path. What had just happened? One second it felt like they were having some kind of moment, the next he was stomping away like an adolescent boy losing Xbox privileges.

He turned around at the front door. His face was still contorted, but every step didn't make him look like he might be about to keel over. At least that was something. "Thanks for bringing me home. I've got it."

She raised an eyebrow at him. "You've got what, exactly?"

"I'm good."

Emelia suddenly realized she hadn't thought past this point. How was she going to get home from here? It wasn't like she could drive his car. It was a miracle someone hadn't reported her to the cops on the way here.

She returned her attention to the stubborn guy in front of her. "Tell you what. I'll make you a deal. If you can open your front door, then I'll leave you alone." There must be a bus route or something nearby. She dropped his backpack near his feet.

Leaning over, he picked it up, wedged it between his knees, and used the hand on his uninjured arm to lever the zipper open enough for him to get his hand through. It reappeared with a bunch of keys dangling off his fingers.

Giving her a smug look, Peter inserted a gold key into the lock and twisted it. A small click rewarded him. He turned the knob and went to open the door, but it didn't move. Still held fast by the dead bolt located just above.

Muttering something under his breath, he pulled the key out, flipped the ring around, and picked out a silver one. He shoved it into the dead bolt, twisted that one, and then looked at the lower doorknob as if willing it to move with the power of his mind.

He moved closer to the door and reached for the lower handle with his injured arm. But even that small movement made him wince and clench his jaw.

Short of being strung out on enough opiates to take down a horse, there was no way it was going to happen. Emelia wasn't going to stand here all day watching him try.

Without warning, he pulled the key from the dead bolt and threw the set to the ground with such force they bounced.

Emelia stepped forward and swiped the keys off the ground. "Easy. I know it hasn't been a good day but—"

"A good day?" Peter turned toward her, pain etched across his face. "I probably just tore my rotator cuff again. It was meant to be better. After eleven months—*eleven*. 'Not a good day' doesn't even come close to it."

"I'm sorry. I'm sure it's just a minor setback." And there she went, offering up a pointless platitude when she knew nothing of the sort. Exactly the kind of words that she'd hated. The ones she'd wanted to throw back in people's faces when she lost out on serious journalism jobs to people who had better connections, or had rich daddies to pave their career path, or were better looking. Never mind that the only way they could have found a story was if it was handed to them on a diamond-encrusted spoon. An apology formed on her lips but didn't make it out before Peter rounded on her, clutching his shoulder, green eyes flashing.

"You have no idea what you're talking about. You know where I'm meant to be right now? Training. With my team. I trained for ten years to get there. Ten years. Of early mornings. Hundreds of thousands of kilometers of rowing. Half the year in sleet, until my hands bled and I could taste the blood in my mouth. What would you know about that? What would you know about having a crazy, audacious dream and then getting it ripped away from you when it was finally within reach? You're just a glorified admin assistant."

Emelia stepped back as if she'd been slapped. "Excuse me?" He had not just gone there. Peter's mouth opened but she didn't even give him a chance to get out a syllable. "You have *no* idea what you're talking about. You don't know anything about me. Not really. Oh, you probably think you do. Maybe you think it's funny that I hide in wardrobes. Whatever. You probably think it's cute that I can quote Narnia off the top of my head. None of that means you know anything that matters about me." She shoved the key in the dead bolt, twisted it, turned the door handle below, and threw the door open with such force it slammed against the wall.

"Sabine is welcome to you."

Twenty

The following Thursday, Peter approached Emelia's office doorway like it framed gallows. In his hand he held a box of Cadbury chocolates. After his appalling behavior, he was hoping they'd buy him enough time to explain himself before she threw him out.

The last time he'd put his foot in his mouth so badly he'd ended up doing a similar walk to penance. Thankfully, this time Elizabeth wasn't around to give him the third degree. Her eagle eyes missed nothing.

He paused, peering around the side of the door. Emelia sat at her decrepit desk, intent on some documents. Her wavy hair was in a ponytail, a few loose strands spilling over her bare shoulders, the dark purple sleeveless, filmy top she was wearing skimming her curves in all the right ways.

As she jotted something down on the paper in front of her, a small smile lifted at one end of her lips. She turned to her keyboard and typed out a few words, then tugged a piece of hair behind her ear.

Peter could have watched her all day, except any second now she would look up and find him peering at her like some kind of Peeping Tom. And that would go down so well after everything else.

He tapped on the doorframe, holding the box of chocolates up to his chest like a shield. Maybe she'd take pity on a guy with a sling.

Her gaze landed on him. "Hi." Her face was a study in neutrality.

"Hi." He walked in. "Chocolates?"

Emelia tilted her head. "As in, do I like them? Would I like one? Or you've come armed with a large box as an attempt at a truce?"

"All of the above?" He still lurked awkwardly in her doorway, not sure whether he should enter.

"Yes, but only because I'm a sucker for Cadbury." She stood up, walked around the desk, and plucked the box from his hand. "Come in. We need to talk."

Peter braced himself for her to tell him that she'd talked to Elizabeth and told her that they couldn't work together anymore.

He had to see this through. For Anita. "All the other board members would be pants at this!" The words fell out of his mouth as Emelia was using her scissors to slice open the cellophane wrapping.

She stopped and looked at him like he was talking gibberish. "I'm sorry. Did you just say something about the board members' pants?"

He'd forgotten Americans didn't use the saying. "Pants. Rubbish. No good. I know that I've been a total jerk but replacing me with one of the other board members . . . none of them would be any good." The truth was that, from what he'd seen, Emelia didn't need a board member at all. She could get all the guidance that she needed off Elizabeth. But he was hardly going to point that out. Since the Boat Race was over and his stupid rush of blood to the head after the row-off had put his shoulder back months in rehabilitation—this, helping save Anita's charity, was the only thing that gave his life meaning.

He tried to ignore the fact that working with Emelia was also a distinct bonus.

"Chocolate?" Emelia offered him the box and he grabbed a caramel one. Dropping the box on the desk, she walked back around it and sat down. She offered him that same half smile as he stood there awkwardly. He wasn't sure if her offering of chocolate was Emelia's version of an olive branch. "You can sit." Reaching over, she picked out a circular one and popped it into her mouth.

Peter chomped his chocolate as he lowered himself into the same chair he'd groveled from last time, careful not to jar his shoulder. "I'm sorry I was such a plonker to you."

"What happened to your shoulder?" It didn't pass his notice that, once again, she didn't explicitly accept his apology. "The first time." Emelia leaned forward in her chair, grabbed another chocolate. It made a nice change from Sabine, who had pedantically tracked every calorie that passed her lips, determined to hover just on the minimum weight allowed for coxes.

Peter's body stiffened. He hated talking about that night. But she was right, he owed her an explanation. "Bar brawl."

"Wow. I wouldn't have guessed that."

He blew out a breath. Him neither. "We were at the world champs in Verona. We'd won a big race that day. So the team decided to go out for drinks to celebrate." As usual, he'd only had one beer, left the real celebratory drinking up to a few of the other guys. "We decided to go to a club. Not my thing but we had some younger guys on the squad who could get a bit cocky once they had a few drinks in them and I wanted to make sure they kept their noses clean.

"Anyway, one of them ended up hitting on some guy's girlfriend. He took exception to it and the next thing I knew fists were swinging. I waded in to try and break it up. One of the guy's friends cracked me with a bottle across the back of my head and the next thing I really remember is waking up in hospital. Tore my rotator cuff up pretty bad." That was an understatement. "The worst I've ever operated on" were the words the surgeon had used.

According to his teammates who'd seen it, he'd gone down like a tree, arm outstretched like a branch. To this day he couldn't work out how he'd fallen like that.

"I'm sorry." Emelia leaned over and picked

186

another chocolate. "I know I'm only a glorified admin assistant now, but I know what it's like to have big dreams that don't come true."

He flinched at the words he'd used to describe her. "Emelia, I was mad at myself for being so stupid. You're far more than that." He stopped himself before he could say anything else. Things that he didn't even really understand himself and would just make things awkward for both of them. "What was your crazy dream?"

She studied him for a moment, as if deciding whether he was worthy of being trusted with it. More than anything else he wanted to be, even though he knew he had a track record with her of the absolute opposite.

"I wanted to be a journalist. A real one. Like Christiane Amanpour. Reporting from war zones, natural disasters, the world's hot spots."

"What happened?"

She shrugged. "Didn't have the right connections, I guess." From the look in her eyes, he could see there was far more to it than that. For a second it looked like she might say more, but then a guard sprang up and she turned her attention to the papers on her desk. "Anyway, we should talk about the row-off. It did better than we expected. I'm just finalizing the report to the board for you to review. And we also need to talk about this cricket match and the mystery ball venue you have up your sleeve."

He didn't care about the board, or some report to review, or even, in that second, about saving Anita's legacy. All he cared about was knowing the story of the girl sitting in front of him.

Twenty-One

"How can you even be asking that of me?" The words hit Emelia as she closed the front door. Jackson sounded frustrated and hurt. The golden couple having a disagreement. That was a first. When Emelia had left to run a few errands they'd been snuggled up on the couch, so cozy you would've struggled to fit a paper clip between them.

Allie responded, but Emelia couldn't quite make out the words.

Sliding her bag off her shoulder, she dropped it to the floor so she could take off her light-weight trench coat and hang it up.

Her stomach let out a low rumble, and she pressed her hand against it. Her dinner, leftovers waiting in the fridge, was going to have to wait. There was no way she wanted to walk in on whatever was going down in the living area. At least she still had half a box of Peter's chocolates up in her room.

Grabbing her bag, she placed a foot on the stairs, only to jump when the door to the living area suddenly flew open and Jackson marched out, face set. "I need some air."

Emelia wasn't sure if his words were directed at Allie, himself, or her. He yanked his coat off one of the hooks and didn't even take the time to shrug it on before he wrenched open the front door and marched into the night.

Emelia stood frozen on the step. What was she supposed to do? She'd never been good at the whole girl-talk thing. And, as much as she liked Allie, they'd only known each other a few months. Would it be better or worse for her to know Emelia was home?

A sob made up her mind for her. She couldn't leave Allie alone. Not after everything she'd done for her. Padding down the hall, Emelia paused in the doorway. Allie sat on one of the couches, leaning forward, her head in her hands and her fingers pressed into her auburn hair.

On the coffee table in front of her sat a set of papers. Official-looking ones on letterhead.

"Is everything okay?" Emelia flinched at the stupidity of her question. Everything clearly wasn't.

Allie raised her head, eyes red rimmed. "Hey. Did you just get home?"

"Yeah. Just as Jackson was, um, leaving." No point pretending she hadn't heard or seen anything.

"How angry did he look?"

"Not angry. More . . ." Emelia shrugged, grimacing a little. "Frustrated? Ticked off?"

Allie heaved out a sigh. "I don't blame him."

Emelia inched into the room, uncertain what she was meant to do or say.

Allie poked at the pile of papers in front of her. "My parents want him to sign a prenup."

"Ah." Emelia sat down on the armchair, perching on the edge. "Why? I mean . . . sorry . . . it's really none of my business."

"It's okay." Allie swiped her hands across her cheeks, wiping away the remains of tears. "It's a long story. Let's just say my family has money and some of my relationship choices in the past haven't exactly been stellar. They're just trying to protect me the way they think is best."

"And Jackson doesn't see it that way?"

Allie grimaced. "It's hardly a good sign, is it? Planning to get married while drawing up contracts for who gets what if it doesn't work out."

Emelia didn't know how to respond. She could hardly say a prenup epitomized certainty that their love would last forever.

"Jackson thinks it means I don't trust him. The truth is I don't care. It hadn't even crossed my mind before these papers from my dad's lawyer showed up, but my family dynamics are challenging, to say the least. Jackson signing them would make things a bit easier on that end."

"Did you explain that to him?"

"I tried. Didn't do a good job of it."

"I'm sure he'll be back in the morning. He probably just needs a bit of time to calm down. To process it rationally." For reasons Emelia hadn't been able to work out, Jackson never stayed over when he was in town for the weekend. Instead, he seemed to rotate around the couches and spare rooms of various friends.

"You think?" Hope glowed from Allie's large green eyes.

Emelia had no idea. She hadn't had anything approaching a serious relationship in years, and she'd certainly never had anything close to what Jackson and Allie had. "He may be a little mad at the moment, but he's even madder about you."

"I should text him. Tell him it doesn't matter." Allie reached for her phone.

"Would it be true?"

"What?"

"That it doesn't matter."

Allie bit her bottom lip for a second. "Yes . . . no . . . I don't know."

Emelia had never seen her roommate look so uncertain. "Well then, what are the pros and cons of him signing?"

"It would make my parents happy."

"And?"

"And . . ." Allie hesitated. There was clearly some-thing there, but she didn't want to verbalize it.

"Does part of you worry Jackson is attracted to your money?"

"No!" The word erupted out of Allie. The maiden doth protest too much. Allie's shoulders slumped. "The last guy I married was after my money. I guess I still carry more baggage about that than I realized. I know Jackson isn't after me for that . . . but then I guess a small part of me reminds me that at one time I would've sworn the same thing about Derek too."

Yep, Emelia could see how that would play mind games with a girl. "Did he clean you out when you got divorced? Is that why your parents are worried?"

Allie shook her head. "We didn't get divorced. The marriage was annulled. He got nothing. Well, nothing more."

Emelia's journalistic radar was practically in cardiac arrest. She'd have bet everything she had that there was one mighty big story crammed into those four short sentences. But now wasn't the time. "Jackson knows all about Derek though?"

"Jackson knows everything." Allie wrung her hands. "We've never fought like this."

Jealousy snuck up on Emelia. Did Allie know how lucky she was that she could say that? No one knew everything about her. There was no one she'd ever been able to imagine trusting with her messy, mistake-ridden life.

An image of Peter slipped into her mind. The

only person she'd ever met who made her want to indulge in the fantasy of what it would be like to have someone truly know you. She shook it loose. That was crazy thinking. She barely knew the guy, and, as she'd so emphatically told him, he definitely didn't know the first thing about her.

"Not that I'm exactly one to be giving relationship advice, but if I were you, I wouldn't worry about the prenup."

"Why's that?" Allie looked up from staring at the papers.

"That guy is head-over-heels insane about you. He would sooner lose a limb than ever leave you. If you guys can't make it, no one can."

Peter leaned back in his La-Z-Boy, his one piece of decent furniture; settled his family-sized bag of crisps on his lap; cracked open his one Saturday-night beer; and flicked on some sports highlights. His finger was poised on the remote to change channels if there was any sign of rowing coverage. Almost a year on, it still hurt too much to see his old teammates living his dream to be able to watch without something fierce and ugly twisting up his gut. So it was better that he didn't.

He heard, then felt, the front door slam. He checked his watch. Not even eight. His flatmate, Tony, was on an evening shift at the hospital. And when Jackson was staying with them, he was

193

never back before eleven. Occasionally he'd sneak in after midnight with a slightly sheepish look on his face, like he had a curfew or something.

But Peter's couch guest stormed into the room, pulling up short when he saw Peter sitting there, staring at him.

"Sorry, didn't think you'd be home."

From the guy who was constantly giving him stick about his lack of a social life.

Jackson stomped to the fridge, reached in, and pulled out a bottle of beer. "Mind?" He was already twisting it open as he asked.

"Be my guest."

"Thanks." Jackson stomped back over, slumped onto the couch, placed his shoe-clad feet on the coffee table, and took a slug. Clearly not the right moment to remind him of the "no shoes on the furniture" rule.

"Highlights, huh?"

"Yup." Peter aimed for nonchalant.

"Anything on the rowing?"

Peter didn't bother to answer, just picked up the remote and turned the commentary on the diving down a couple of notches. "So, what's up in paradise?"

"What do you mean?" Jackson did nonchalant badly.

"It's not even eight."

Jackson shrugged, faked being glued to some

whippet-sized Chinese girl performing a double pike. "Maybe I just felt like an early night."

Peter snorted. In all the months that Jackson had been spending weekends on his couch, Jackson and Allie had only separated themselves to get the bare minimum hours of functional sleep. The pair didn't know what an "early night" was when they were in the same place. "Is this your first barney?" He'd have put money on it. He'd never seen the two of them really disagree. Which was odd, considering they were two quite strong personalities.

"First what?"

"Big fight."

Jackson didn't say anything. Just toed one shoe off and then another, leaving them to lie where they fell on the floor. Peter forced himself to take a casual sip of his beer, like it didn't bother him. The guy may have come with model looks, but he certainly hadn't come with model house-keeping habits.

They sat in silence for a few seconds, watching an Australian girl cram in a lot of somersaults between leaving the diving board and hitting the water.

Peter held out his bowl of crisps, shoulder twinging, and offered them to Jackson. He waved them away.

"She wants me to sign a prenup." Jackson's eyes didn't leave the screen.

"Allie?"

"No, my other fiancée. Yes, Allie."

"Huh." Peter snagged a couple of crisps and palmed them into his mouth. Thought while he chewed. "And you don't want to."

"Would you?"

Peter shrugged. "Can't say I've ever thought about it. I don't think there's a blanket right or wrong answer; I think it depends on the situation. I can imagine Mum and Dad would want Victor to if the estate wasn't already in an ironclad trust." Not that there was any chance of his brother making a commitment to any woman for longer than a night.

"You don't see anything wrong with signing some contract before you get married about how you're going to divvy up your assets if you split up?"

"Well, I can't say it's the most romantic thing I've ever heard of."

"It doesn't feel right. It's like having a Plan B. Like 'Oh well, hopefully this works out but if not we already know what everyone's getting out of it.' "

Peter grabbed a handful of crisps and chomped down on them as Jackson continued.

"It's insulting. It's humiliating. Like they'd better cover the bases in case I'm after her for her money."

"Who's they?"

"Her family. Her family has money. The prenup came from her father's lawyer."

"So it wasn't Allie's idea."

Jackson shook his head. "The papers just showed up today."

"So, let me get this straight. It wasn't Allie's idea, it was her father's. Her family has a lot of money. Plus, they barely know you. It's not like the two of you spent the last five years dating so you can convince them you're the guy for her. Given all that, I'd be stunned if they didn't want one."

"Guess I didn't think of it like that."

"Do you care about her money? Their money?" Peter took another sip of his beer.

"Of course not!" One of Jackson's hands curled into a fist.

"Then what does it even matter? Just sign the thing if it makes her parents happy. It's never going to be needed. Anyone who has to spend more than thirty seconds witnessing how nauseatingly perfect you guys are for each other knows that."

Jackson groaned. "I was such a jerk."

Peter didn't say anything. If he'd had any girl look at him the way Allie looked at Jackson, he would've signed the thing with his own blood if she'd asked it.

Jackson got to his feet. "I need to fix this."

Peter turned back to the TV screen just in time

to see the camera panning over a lake and a lineup of boats. He didn't even wait to see who was racing before his finger hit the off button on the remote. "Want a ride?"

Twenty-Two

Emelia and Allie made hot chocolates and settled into the comfy chairs to watch *Notting Hill*. There were some situations that just needed a floppy-haired Hugh Grant from the nineties.

Emelia was immersed in Hugh interviewing Julia when the door flew open. They both jumped and turned as Jackson strode back into the room.

Emelia looked at her watch. An hour and forty minutes since he'd left. That was fast. She'd cooked meals that took longer than this fight.

Without even glancing Emelia's way, he strode up to Allie, who'd risen from her chair. "Hi."

"Hi." Allie looked a little wary. Not that Emelia could blame her, given how he'd stormed out, but it was a different guy who was back.

Wrapping his arms around her, Jackson tugged Allie to him. "I'm sorry."

Allie's lip wobbled. "I'm sorry too. You're right. I never should have asked it of you."

"No. You should've. It's okay. Your family hardly knows me. I don't blame them for being wary. And I don't care. I don't care about any of it. I will sign whatever you want me to. Your father can have all of my stuff too if he wants it. All I care about is marrying you."

Allie reached up and fisted her hands around his sweater, tugging him down to her. "And all I care about is marrying you. I don't want a prenup. I'm so sorry that between Derek and my family I'm making this all so hard. Way harder than it should be."

Emelia really needed to get out of here before it got awkward. Allie had clearly forgotten that she was in there, and she wasn't sure if Jackson had even noticed.

She backed out of the room at a quiet shuffle, eyes to the ground. She moved the door enough for her to slip through, and she got out and breathed a sigh of relief in the hallway.

She sent a silent prayer of thanks up for their old-fashioned no-sleepovers thing. At least she wouldn't have to deal with loud make-up sex on top of everything else.

"What's the everything else?"

Pure reflexes kicked in and she spun around, her leg lashing out and sweeping the person behind her off their feet.

They went down with an oomph. A streak of orange streamed across her vision, confirming the voice she'd identified a split second after she'd kicked him. Peter hit the recycling bin Emelia had put down earlier, halfway through taking it outside. Cans and bottles rolled everywhere.

"Are you an actual ninja?" Peter offered up his question from where he lay splayed on the wooden floor.

"Oh my gosh." Emelia put her palm to her thundering chest and sucked in a couple of gulps of air. "Do you want to give me a heart attack?" Oh, wow. This was not good. "Your shoulder! Did you land on it? Is it okay?"

She was going to be the girl who'd destroyed whatever big comeback dreams he still had. She had to remember Oxford wasn't LA. And she was just a charity fund-raiser. Not a tabloid reporter who regularly received death threats.

"It's fine." He sucked in a breath as he rotated it. "Well, no worse than it was before you floored me anyway."

Well, at least there was that. To buy herself a few seconds, Emelia crouched down. Righting the bin, she picked up a couple of cans and bottles, tossing them back in.

"I'm sorry." He at least had the decency to look sheepish. He pushed his torso up off the floor, then levered himself onto his feet so he was crouching. "Jackson left his wallet in my car. I was going to just put it on the table and text him, but then you came out . . . well, more like backed out . . . and I didn't want you to turn around and just find me standing here."

"Yeah, because that would've been so much less terrifying than what you did." She reached for a bottle just as he did, both of their hands grasping it. She let go, her gaze moving up his broad chest.

"Sorry." His mouth quirked, like he was struggling to contain laughter, which made her review the last few minutes.

She felt the burn starting at the end of her feet and working up her body. "I said my last thought aloud, didn't I?" She must've. Because she distinctly recalled his asking what the everything else was.

The quirk broke into a grin as he stood. "You did."

Wow. That wasn't embarrassing at all. And now they were both staring at each other thinking about make-up sex. Awkward.

"So . . ." She cleared her throat. She tried to work out where to go from here. Then busied herself trying to pick up the nearest pieces of trash.

"What happened?" Emelia glanced over her shoulder to see that the commotion had even jolted the lovebirds out of their canoodling.

Peter stood. "I made the mistake of giving Emelia a fright. Didn't realize she was a ninja."

Emelia put her hands up. "Just a few self-defense classes." She preferred to keep her martial arts abilities to herself.

Jackson let out a low whistle as Allie picked up

the last couple of bottles by her feet and added them to the bin. "Those must've been some classes."

Peter held out Jackson's wallet. "Don't say I've never put my body on the line for you. You forgot this."

Jackson took it and stuffed it in his jeans pocket. "Thanks. We were just going to head out and grab something to eat. We'll see you guys later." The front door opened, then shut, and they were gone, leaving her and Peter alone.

Emelia went for the first thing she thought of to fill the silence. "Would you like coffee? Or tea?" She had no idea what it was with the British and their tea. Almost everyone she'd met drank so much of the stuff, it might as well have been in an IV line.

Then she blinked, realizing she'd just asked a guy she was crazy attracted to to stay. Late at night. With no one else there. She never would have done that back home. Not in a second. "So, um, how about we talk about the cricket?"

One second he'd been mesmerized by the sight of Emelia backing out of the living area muttering under her breath. The next he'd been on his back, winded. Thank goodness he'd managed to instinctively twist himself to cushion his shoulder from the worst of the blow. He'd only just liberated it from the sling.

Put on his butt by a girl. Not that he necessarily had an issue with that. Rowing, he'd met a lot of girls who could beat most guys arm wrestling just using their pinkies. But it was like she hadn't even tried. The words were barely out of his mouth before he'd been staring at the ceiling. And he wasn't a small guy.

He watched the ninja out of the corner of his eye as she put something in the microwave, then turned and poured tea into one cup and hot water into a second. Self-defense classes. Huh. There was no chance she'd learned that move from a course at the Y.

There was more to this girl than met the eye. And his eyes already liked what they saw. A lot. Peter blew out a puff of air. What was he thinking?

"Milk?" From the way Emelia said it, it wasn't the first time she'd asked.

"Um, yes, thanks. Just a little."

"Sugar?"

Did he take sugar? With her staring expectantly at him like that, he couldn't remember. "No. Thanks."

She doctored his cup and then carried them over. "Sorry if it's no good. I know how seriously your country takes your tea." She placed her cup on the coffee table, leaned over and put his in front of him, then stepped back and settled into the other end of the couch. If he reached out and moved over slightly, he could run his fingers through her gorgeous wavy hair. It was loose, spilling over her shoulders. The last few times he'd seen her, it had been in a ponytail. He liked it this way a whole lot more.

He reined himself in, kept his hands busy picking up his cup and taking a sip. It was bad. Too weak. How long had she steeped it for, like thirty seconds? And not enough milk.

"Okay?" Emelia was watching him over the rim of her cup.

"Great. Thanks." He put the cup down. Hoped he could avoid having to drink all of it. "So, how would next Sunday work for you to go and look at this potential ball venue? We could go around lunchtime. I've got church in the morning." He watched her closely to see what her reaction was to his use of the C-word again. A small foolish part of him hoped that she might want to join him.

"Okay. Sounds good. What time does church finish?" There wasn't any interest, but it also wasn't the allergic reaction he'd gotten the first time, so he'd take it.

"About eleven. I'll pick you up at twelve." He lifted his tea up again, gave it another try. Still horrid.

"Why doesn't Jackson stay over?" Emelia took a tentative sip of her drink.

Tea sloshed over the rim of his cup, searing the top side of his finger. He'd expected the question about as much as he'd anticipated her sweeping kick. "Um, I think they're waiting until they're married."

"To . . . ?"

Was she really going to make him say it?

Then it connected. "Oh. Wow. Really? That's, um, different." Her mouth said "different." Her face said "weird." "Crazy." "Unbelievable." "But they're so . . . so . . ."

"All over each other."

She grinned. "Understatement of the year." He watched thoughts shift her expression as she pondered it. "But they're so . . . he's so . . . okay, sorry, this is a weird conversation. I just didn't realize people like them existed. Especially . . ."

He could practically see what she was thinking. People who were smart. Normal. Ridiculously good-looking. In her world, the only people who saved themselves for marriage were probably losers who didn't have any other choice.

"Are you like them too?" Her hand flew to her mouth. "Sorry. Don't answer that. Right. I'm going to stop talking now." She leaned over and took a huge gulp of her drink.

Peter started laughing. He couldn't help it. The girl looked like a paleontologist who'd just stumbled over a living dinosaur. Then the scent of singed air made him pause. Something was burning. He put his drink down and stood up. "What's that smell?"

"Smell?" Emelia looked around, then wrinkled

her nose as well. Her hand flew to her mouth. "The popcorn!"

Slamming her cup onto the coffee table, she jumped off the couch and sprinted toward the kitchen. Peter strode after her, almost colliding into her when she stopped in front of the microwave. "Fire!"

Sure enough, inside the microwave a fireball rotated, the flames devouring what had once been a popcorn bag. Wow. The little boy inside who had once aspired to work in pyrotechnics was momentarily entranced.

The black smoke coming out the side was a bit concerning though.

The next thing he knew, Emelia had thrown the back door open, ripped the microwave's cord out of the socket, and picked it up off the counter.

"Wait . . . no—" But he was too late, she was already running with it out the back door. He ran after her, just in time to see her somehow launch the white box so it flew through the air before landing with a loud crack on the cobblestones outside, flipping over once and coming to rest on its back.

They both just stood there, watching the remaining flames flicker behind the now-cracked door.

Emelia peeked up at him from under long lashes, a nearby streetlight casting a dim halo over her. "So, um, maybe a little overdramatic?"

Peter couldn't help but grin back. "Well, I was just going to turn it off so the fan stopped feeding the fire, but that worked too. How long did you put it on for, Smoky?"

Emelia wrinkled her nose. "I meant to set it for three minutes but I must've set it for thirty by mistake. Guess I'm going to have to go buy Allie a new microwave."

In the sad, rectangular box, the last of the flames had dimmed to embers. Even outside in the almost dark, it was clear there was no resuscitating it. The smell of smoke still lingered in the air. "At least it went out in style. Not many microwaves can claim an ending like that." He walked toward it and started to pick it up, but the moment he attempted to lift it off the ground, his shoulder told him to think again.

"What's the prognosis?"

Emelia spoke from behind him as he let it go and stood back up.

"Unclear. No more rowing for a while, that's for sure." When he'd been forced to confess to Kevin what he'd done he'd thought his physio was going to clock him. And he didn't blame him. Months of rehab work out the window. He wanted to clock himself.

"Well, for what it's worth, the few seconds I did see of you on that erg were pretty impressive." Emelia stepped around him and scooped the appliance off the ground. Turning around, she carried it a few feet and set it against the side of the house next to the rubbish bin. He felt so useless not being able to even perform a simple task like that.

He blew out a breath. Not wanting to remember how, for a few minutes, it had felt like somehow the miraculous had happened. Maybe his shoulder had completely healed. A blissful few hundred seconds of feeling the burn again in his legs, lungs, and arms.

"Sabine mentioned you want to make a come-back." It wasn't a question.

Peter started at the unexpected mention of his ex. "Yes."

"Is it possible? With your shoulder?" The question was tentative, as if she knew how much just hearing the words hurt.

"It has to be." He rubbed his hand along the bristles that covered his jawline. His shoulder couldn't even manage a decent shave at the moment. "I need to do it for my cousin. She was my biggest cheerleader. Even on the worst day, she never stopped believing that I would be able to row again at an elite level."

"What happened to her?" Emelia dusted her hands off as she approached him. Somehow she'd gotten a smudge of dirt across her cheekbone.

"What do you mean?" Peter shuffled on his feet.

"You said 'never stopped.' Past tense."

Nothing got past this girl. "She died. Last year."

"I'm sorry."

Peter tried to shove the guilt down. He hadn't been there for Anita, but maybe he could be there for this feisty, independent girl with professional deflection skills. Something in his gut told him she'd spent a lot of her life having to fend for herself. "What about you? What brought you to Oxford?"

Emelia shrugged and wrapped her arms around herself. "I'm not nearly as interesting as you. No Olympic aspirations for me." She gestured to the door. "It's cold out here. We should go back inside."

Peter reached out, catching her elbow as she started to move past him. "Any girl who can put me on my backside when I don't even see it coming is pretty much the most interesting one I've ever met. Besides, you were right. I don't know much about you that matters. And I would really like to." Even in the darkness, he could see the wariness in her eyes. "Please."

She studied him for a second, as if weighing something. "Starting over."

What? "Sorry?"

"That's what brought me to Oxford. I made a huge mistake. I came here to try to start over. But then that's never really possible, is it? Because wherever you go, you're still there. You can never escape yourself."

Her voice was tinged with resignation and hurt.

She looked at him as if hoping he would be able to tell her she was wrong, but knowing he couldn't. Especially not when that pretty much captured how he'd felt ever since Anita died.

Some days it took everything he had not to just knock back another Oxy to try to escape the condemnation ringing in his own head. And that was while clinging to the knowledge that God still had a plan. Even if he couldn't see any of it. Emelia didn't even have that to hang on to.

He didn't know what to say, but he had to say something. He could already see her expression starting to close, as if she'd realized she'd said too much. "Em—"

"What's the worst-case scenario?" She cut him off. Changed the subject.

"For what?"

"So best-case scenario is you make a blazing comeback and win gold in Tokyo. What's the worst case? If you put yourself back into training and it happens all over again?"

"That I do permanent irreversible damage."

"Which means?"

"Lifelong weakness. Pain." Or as his consultant so bluntly put it, not being able to ever lift his arm again. The next fifty years on hard-core opiates.

"And which is more likely? The best or the worst?"

"The worst." By a long mile.

"And it's still worth it to you? The minute

210

chance of winning an Olympic medal versus the very real chance that you could become permanently disabled?"

He'd never really had to have this conversation before. Sabine got it. His teammates got it. His parents didn't but trusted him to make his own decision. How did you explain the drive to beat all the odds? No matter what the risk? To be the best? To stand on a podium and hear your country's national anthem playing? "Yes."

She shook her head. "That's crazy."

He bristled. "Aren't you the girl who once wanted to be the next Christiane Amanpour? To be a war correspondent? Do you have any idea how many journalists and photographers come back in body bags? Or without limbs? Or, at the least, with post-traumatic stress disorder? My dream doesn't involve the real risk of me dying."

"Seventy-one." She said the words as she walked past him toward the door.

"Sorry?"

Emelia looked right at him. "Seventy-one journalists were killed last year."

"Want to know how many Olympic rowers were shot? Or executed? Or thrown in prison? None." He wasn't even sure what the point was that he was trying to make.

"But at least they were doing something worth—" She cut her own words off but not before he knew exactly what she was about to say.

"Worthwhile? Worthy? Whereas my dream is just, what? Selfish? All about my ego? Pride? Ambition?"

Emelia didn't say anything.

He blew out a breath. Well, that was a great kick of reality. Nothing quite like finding out the girl you have a crush on thinks your biggest dream is self-absorbed stupidity.

"What are you guys doing out here?" Allie saved Emelia from being forced to confirm that was exactly what she thought. She stood in the doorway, a brown paper bag in her hand, the local burger place's branding on the side. Allie didn't even wait for an answer before she launched into her next thing. "Guess what? Jackson and I have talked and we're going to have an engagement party." She looked at them with expectation. What did she want? A medal? They'd been engaged for like eight months already.

"Great. Took you long enough."

"Congratulations."

Peter and Emelia spoke over each other.

Allie scrunched her nose. "Why does it smell like smoke?"

Twenty-Three

Emelia watched the English countryside pass by the car window. All lush and green with flowers poking up their bright heads. There were cobbled stone fences and pastures filled with cattle. Quaint villages with looming church spires reaching toward the heavens. The scenery was outstanding, but everything else about the drive to visit Peter's potential venue had been very mysterious so far. When she'd tried to dig, all she'd managed to get out of him was that there was a "family connection." Words that made her realize she knew pretty much nothing about his family.

She still had no idea how that had morphed into her coming with him to his parents' house for lunch, except that it seemed to make sense at the time. Something about its being near the potential location. And she needed to apologize for basically saying his dream was stupid.

"You okay?" Peter flicked on the blinker and turned a corner.

"Fine." Emelia returned her gaze to the road. Her pulse increased for a second as she instinctively reacted to being on the wrong side. "Just a bit nervous, I guess."

The silence from his side wasn't exactly comforting.

Suck it up, Emelia. Just say sorry. "I'm sorry about last weekend. About your shoulder. My opinion doesn't matter. But permanent damage to a rotator is bad. You want a medal so much you'd be willing to live a life of excruciating pain? Risk never being able to throw a ball with your kids?" She stopped herself from saying any more. She'd already said more than enough.

"You're wrong."

Maybe she was. She was dredging her memory of what she knew about sports players who had suffered a similar injury.

"Your opinion does matter." He looked over at her and captured her with his gaze.

Oh. She forced herself to break the connection. "Can you tell me about your family?" She didn't care that she'd changed the subject with all the subtlety of a Miley Cyrus music video. Staring into eyes like that as he told her that she mattered was just asking for trouble.

"What would you like to know?"

She turned her face toward him. "Um, their names?"

He looked directly across at her. "I haven't even told you their names?"

"No."

"Sorry." His fingers tightened around the steering wheel. He cast a half smile her way. "I guess I'm a bit nervous too. It's been a long time since I brought a girl home."

214

Brought a girl home. The words twisted inside her. Both terrifying and exciting, the emotions fighting for dominance. She'd never been the girl anyone brought home. Not ever.

"My father is William. Bill. My mother is Margaret; everyone calls her Maggie. My brother is Victor."

She winced at his brother's name. Even though she was sure Peter's brother was nothing like her nemesis.

"What are they like?"

His fingers relaxed slightly. "My dad is tall, big. Played rugby. Almost made the English team when he was young. Apparently was pretty much a steamroller on the field. He has the kind of booming laugh that you can hear for miles. He works hard. He doesn't really care about what we do, all that matters to him is who we are. My mum is the sweetest woman you'll ever meet. The glue that holds our family together. She was diagnosed with multiple sclerosis a couple of years ago but you'd never know it. Never complains, always looking for opportunities to help everyone else. You'll love her . . . she'll love you." He added the last sentence almost as an afterthought. She didn't know if it was to make her feel better or if his mom was just the type to love everyone.

"What about your brother?"

Something twinged in his jaw as he stared at

215

the road, face set, seeming to ponder her question. Finally, he lifted one hand and pushed it through his hair. "Look, I wish that I could say that we're best mates but the truth is we have a . . ." He paused, searching for the right word. "Challenging relationship. He's older by three years but we've never been close. He wasn't too crazy about me from the day I arrived."

"I'm sorry."

"How about your family?"

"My dad remarried a few years ago, someone closer to my age than his. I've got two half brothers and a half sister. He's pretty busy with them. Though my stepmother was excited about me coming here. She has high hopes of me snagging Harry. Or at least a member of the aristocracy with a large estate so she can come and play *Downton*." Maybe if she distracted him with tales of her social climbing stepmother he wouldn't ask about her mother.

Peter suddenly started coughing. "Excuse me. How old are your siblings? Half siblings? Sorry. I'm not sure of the terminology."

"It's okay." She wasn't sure how to refer to them most of the time herself. They were young enough to be her nieces and nephews. "Um . . ." She had to pause for a second to calculate. "Charles is six, George is three, and Katherine-Elizabeth is almost two."

He couldn't hold back his grin. "Wow. You

weren't kidding about your stepmother being a royal fan."

"Unfortunately not."

He glanced across at her. Opened his mouth as if to ask another question, but then closed it without saying anything.

Time to steer things onto a more neutral topic. "So who will be at lunch?"

"Probably just be the four of us. Victor doesn't often show up for family lunches." He turned off the main road onto a smaller side road with tall hedges lining both sides. "So there's something I need to tell you." Peter stared straight ahead as he said it.

Emelia's stomach clenched at something foreboding in his tone. "What?"

"So, um, our house isn't so much a house. And when I said my parents lived near the potential location, it would have been more accurate to say they are the location."

"I don't understand."

"Well, it's more of an estate."

She still wasn't getting what he was saying. "Are you trying to tell me your parents are rich?"

He laughed. "Definitely not with money, but there is quite a bit of land."

"How much land?"

They'd turned onto a smaller road again, one lined with picturesque stone walls and lush fields on either side. He gestured around them. "We're almost there. This is some of it."

Shadows covered the car as it passed through a stand of trees and across a small bridge. They came around a bend, and in front of them, in the distance, loomed a huge house. A mansion. And not just any mansion. One that twisted knots of dread in her stomach until she thought she might choke.

She stared at it, trying to process what her eyes were telling her. Finally words started forming in her head. "Highbridge Manor is your house?" Too late she realized her slip. Why would an average American know the name of this estate?

He grimaced. "It is."

"Stop!" She hadn't meant to shout, the outburst filling the small space.

Peter hit the brakes. Hard. The car slammed to a stop in the middle of the road. Her seat belt cut across her as it held her in her seat. Her head bounced back against the headrest. She was going to be feeling the effects of that at some point but the realization flooding her mind had nothing on the impact her body had just taken.

She turned her entire body sideways as much as she could and asked the question she already knew the horrible answer to. "Who exactly are you?"

Peter had no idea what to make of the expression on her face. It could have been anything from horror to excitement. Oh, he hoped she wasn't one of those liberal anti-aristocracy types. Probably should've thought to subtly check for that before he brought her home.

"I'm Peter Carlisle." He refused to be defined by his father's title. Especially when they'd only come into it by a combination of tragedy and rotten luck.

"Don't be obtuse."

"I'm not." It was his turn to get a bit short, which wasn't entirely fair. He probably should've given her some warning of all this. "You asked who I was. I told you."

Emelia gave a half roll of her eyes. "Fine. Who is your father?"

"William Carlisle. Also known as Viscount Downley."

With a click, she'd undone her seat belt and had her head between her knees. Of all the reactions he'd anticipated, this was not one of them.

"You okay?" His shoulder ached from the abrupt stop.

"Give me a minute." Her words were muffled, directed at the passenger's footwell.

A horn sounded behind them, and he realized the car had stalled when they'd slammed to a stop.

He restarted the engine and pulled the car over to the side of the road. Fortunately, no one he knew was behind the steering wheel. Emelia's head remained wedged between her knees, the back of it almost clipping the glove box as he bumped over the grass verge.

Finally, he couldn't take the silence anymore. "Do you hate the peerage, is that it?"

At that Emelia levered herself up and leaned back against her seat. "No. I don't hate the peerage. What is a viscount, anyway?"

"It sits between a baron and an earl. Small potatoes in the hierarchy."

Emelia made a show of looking all around them, finishing with the house. "Call this what you will. But it is not small potatoes."

"Touché."

She pressed fingers to both temples. "Sorry for my reaction. I just . . . I was nervous enough meeting everyone. Then you suddenly spring this on me. It's a bit overwhelming. Why didn't you tell me?"

Peter shrugged. Why hadn't he? It wasn't that he was ashamed of his lineage. Quite the opposite. But he just liked being an ordinary guy. When people found out his background, it always changed how they saw him. As per Exhibit A, sitting right beside him. "We weren't born into this. It was never meant to be ours. It landed on us through a combination of early deaths and title-holders without children. Dad inherited the title from his cousin when I was ten."

Emelia heaved out a breath, gathered her hair in a pile behind her head, and then let it fall. "So, what do I call your parents? Am I supposed to curtsy?" A panicked look crossed her face. "I don't even know how to curtsy. You could've at least given me a warning to learn!"

He laughed. "No, definitely no curtsies. If it makes you feel better, feel free to call them Viscount and Viscountess when you meet them, but they'll tell you to call them Bill and Maggie. They're even less into titles than I am." Unlike his brother, who threw "the Honorable" around like it was cheap currency. "If it's really that over-whelming, we can turn around and I'll take you home." He meant it as a lame joke, but she seemed to actually consider it for a few seconds. His heart thumped against his ribs. What if she said yes?

What was he even hoping for? Emelia didn't share his faith. He'd always told himself that was one line he wouldn't cross. He'd watched the reality of how that played out his whole life. His parents had a good marriage. But there was no missing the wistfulness in his mother's eyes when she left for church on Sundays, leaving his father behind. Or her hopefulness every Easter and Christmas when he deigned to attend. Or her attempt to conceal her hurt when his father made it clear saying grace was an impediment to be suffered through to get to his meal. And those were only the things he saw.

He wanted more than that. But he wanted the girl sitting beside him too. And for the first time in his life, he understood how what looked black and white could be so easily blurred into gray.

"Peter?" She was staring at him quizzically. She'd obviously answered his question while he'd been lost in what-ifs.

"Sorry, what?"

"I said I'm good. Let's go."

Twenty-Four

The minute Peter had said "Viscount Downley" out loud, Emelia had thought she was going to have a stroke. It wasn't possible. Except it was. Of all the guys she had to meet. The only time she'd ever been taken home to meet the family, it had to be this one.

This guy, who made her feel like maybe an ordinary, boring life could be possible, was also intimately linked to the web of her past. A past that managed to still reach out with its sticky threads and wrap them around her in a different country, a different life.

Stupid peerages, with their differing names and titles. If Peter's last name had been Downley, she would've broken her stupid vow and been researching him in a second. Would've made the connection in two. Would've known to never set foot in his life ever again.

But nooooo, she had to go and put herself on a

Google fast to kill her old reporter's habit of prying into other people's lives.

Peter started driving again, the wheels crunching over the stones on the narrow road. The huge redbrick house loomed closer and closer.

Before they got there, she needed to confirm one final nail in the coffin of their non-relationship. She couldn't believe she hadn't worked it out when he'd talked about his cousin who had died last year. Yet again, another flamingly obvious answer staring her right in the face that she didn't see. She cleared her throat. "So is your brother a rower too?"

If Peter thought it was a strange question, he didn't show it. "Yes. He was in the Oxford Blue Boat crew."

A tingling feeling started between her eyes. How had she not seen him in the line-up of rowers in the boat? How had she missed his face all over TV screens?

Act normal, Emelia. Your only chance of getting through this is to pretend Victor is a stranger to you, if he's there, and to hope he plays along.

"He goes to Oxford?" Was his title just as handy for charming his way into one of the world's most prestigious universities as into the beds of LA party girls?

"He's in his first year of a PhD in philosophy."

Peter couldn't have shocked her more if he'd said Victor was studying midwifery. Emelia barely managed to keep her jaw from unhinging. She forced herself to focus on the imposing house. "Wow."

She forced herself to breathe. What was she going to do? She'd come to Oxford because she couldn't stay in LA after Anita's death. Couldn't live with the person she'd become. Oxford was meant to be a fresh start and the Fates had sent her headlong into the girl's cousin.

The whole situation was so insane she had to squash the hysterical laughter rising up inside as Peter drove around the circular drive in front of the house and parked near the front door.

And the poor guy next to her thought she was overwhelmed because his father had a title and owned some land.

"Well, here we are. You'll be great." Peter sent her the kind of smile that ordinarily would've raised her pulse. The car shifted as he got out and strode around to open her door.

Peter was right about one thing though: he and his brother were nothing alike.

Her door opened, and Peter held out his hand. Like she hadn't been getting out of a car by herself for the best part of three decades. It was horribly old-fashioned. It was totally adorable. And, for one second, it distracted her from the mission at hand.

"Thanks." She stepped out, her wedges sinking into the gravel. *Game face, Emelia.* It wasn't like she hadn't spent years perfecting a poker face facade as Mia. But when she'd left the US, she'd planned to leave that behind.

But plans changed.

"Peter!" The front door opened, and a petite blonde came half tumbling down the steps. "You're late! I was beginning to worry."

Peter laughed. "We're not late. I said one-ish and it's like twenty past."

His mother reached him. He dwarfed her. Emelia dwarfed her. Mother and son looked nothing alike. She had blond hair and the same gray-blue eyes as her eldest son, which meant Peter had to have gotten his looks from . . . yep, the man who appeared at the top of the stairs. Same ginger hair, same towering height, same honest-looking face.

"Mother, this is Emelia."

Oh, drat, what was she supposed to do again? "It's lovely to meet you, Viscountess." She bobbed into something that was a peculiar mix of curtsy, bow, and poppet-on-a-string.

She looked up to see Peter smothering a grin. Oh, right. No curtsy.

His mother appeared startled. "Please, just call me Maggie. Whenever someone says 'Viscountess,' I have no idea who on earth they're talking to. Surely Peter told you we're purely accidental blue bloods."

Peter's father came off the bottom step with a

broad smile and twinkling green eyes. She liked him already. "And I'm Bill." He shook her hand. A good, strong handshake. "Lovely to meet you, Emelia. Welcome to Highbridge Manor."

Emelia's response was cut off by crunching footsteps behind them. "Bunny, you made it."

Emelia flinched. Out of the corner of her eye, she observed Peter doing the same. Interesting. And *Bunny?*

She shaped her face into an expression of polite interest.

Remember, Emelia, you have never met this man before in your life. He's merely the brother of the guy you're not dating. He was drinking at the ball. Maybe he doesn't even remember you were there.

"Bunny?" She murmured the question under her breath at Peter. A pathetic attempt at delaying the inevitable.

He glanced down at her. "Don't ask." His voice was all resignation, no humor.

Peter turned around, forcing Emelia to follow.

"Of course I made it. I was hardly going to miss Mum's cooking, was I?" Was she the only one who caught the forced cheer in his voice?

Victor stopped still at the sight of her, a strange look across his face. Her heart stopped too. Was this it? The moment that her whole crazy plan blew up in her face?

"Well." He dropped an expletive. "Bunny brought a girl home. Who would've thought?"

"Victor!" It was impressive how much censure Maggie could fit into six letters.

Emelia waited for an apology, even a token "Sorry, Mother." But none was forthcoming. Awkward silence reigned, accented only by the sound of birds chirping and tree branches bending in the wind.

Victor was the same in broad daylight as he had been in the shadows. Same blond mop, flinty gray-blue eyes, strong jaw, and sardonic smile. None of which could distract from the angry red scar that wound its way up one cheek.

Finally, Peter cleared his throat. "Victor, this is Emelia. Emelia, my brother, Victor." His voice was strained.

"Hi." She nodded. She certainly wasn't going to shake his hand.

He gave her a nod back. His gaze piercing, a smirk playing on his lips. He knew exactly who she was. "Emelia. Interesting name. Had it for long?"

She forced a clueless smile. "Just my whole life."

"Right. So, let's go inside. Get a cup of tea, shall we?" Bill's words softened the tension, but nothing could soften the dark looks the brothers were giving each other.

This was going to be an interesting afternoon. The perfect family Emelia had conjured up was not so perfect. At all.

· · ·

The only reason Peter hadn't bundled Emelia right back into the car and driven away was because of the hurt it would have caused his mum.

It was like being sucker punched twice in quick succession. First with the mocking childhood nickname he'd always hated. Then with the caustic reminder of what a failure he was when it came to relationships. Like it hadn't been obvious their entire lives that he was neither as smart nor as good-looking as his brother.

Fortunately Victor, having achieved his goal of total humiliation, had lost interest and taken off in his car, promising he'd be back for lunch. Watching him career down the drive even made the air smell sweeter.

"Peter tells me the two of you are hoping to plan a charity ball? To help SpringBoard?" His mother addressed her question to Emelia as they entered the house's main door.

"We are. It will be our one big event of the year."

"We haven't been having much luck with venues." Peter draped his arm around his mother's shoulder. "Any chance the house is free the first Saturday in December?"

"I'll have a look at the booking schedule, but I can't think of anything off the top of my head."

"On that note, want a tour?" He turned to Emelia, who looked remarkably composed considering what he'd landed on her in the last half hour.

"Sure." Emelia looked around the atrium they'd entered, her gaze trailing over the many doors and large staircase leading up to the next level.

"Do you want to come?" He directed the question at his parents. Out of courtesy, not desire, though it was fifty-fifty whether they'd pick up on that.

His mother shook her head. "Oh no. I'll go check the calendar, and I need to finish the pudding."

"I can—" His father got cut off by an obvious elbow to the torso from his mum. "I just need to do a few things and, um, stuff."

"So, we'll leave you two to it." His mother smiled sweetly.

"Okay then. We won't be too long."

His father disappeared back out the front door while his mother headed toward the kitchen with a rustle of trousers, in a cloud of floral perfume. Peter touched Emelia's elbow to steer her into the front parlor.

"How long have you lived here?"

"Not long, in the grand scheme of things. Like I said, we never dreamt in a million years Dad would inherit the title, but as life would have it, his uncle died without having any children, so it passed to his brother, then Dad's cousin inherited it. He was the only son and only had daughters.

So when he died in a car accident when I was ten, the title came to Dad. He was an army man. In fact, when he inherited, he was serving in Iraq. So things were a bit crazy until he finished his tour and got discharged."

Emelia spun around, taking in the bookcase-lined wall, the large oriental rugs covering hardwood floors, and the gleaming windows overlooking part of the garden. "I can't believe you had us checking out all those venues when you had the perfect thing right here."

"I wouldn't call it perfect. It's a decent drive from Oxford and we still don't know it's available." And if it hadn't been for her heartbreak over Rhodes House, he never would have said anything about it. Not having to wonder if someone was his friend because of his sporting accomplishments or his aristocratic connections was liberating. "We should go look at the ballroom." He steered her out of the parlor and across the main hall toward the double doors.

"Still, you owe me."

"What?"

"Hmmmm." She pursed her lips, pretending to ponder, but she didn't even need to think about it. "I want the story behind Bunny."

He groaned. "Seriously? How about something else?" Anything else.

She grinned. "Nope. Bunny."

"It's actually not very exciting." Far from being

exciting, it laid bare the animosity that had existed between his brother and him since before he'd even been born. She was a smart girl. She'd be able to read between the lines of even the most concise version.

He sighed. "Victor was two when they found out they were having me. He wasn't thrilled at the idea of having a sibling, so, as a way to placate him, they told him he could help name me." Clearly his normally conservative, predictable parents had been drunk or something that day. They still couldn't explain what had possessed them to offer up naming the baby to their two-year-old as some kind of sibling consolation prize.

"Peter Rabbit was his favorite story at the time, so he decided to name me Peter. But from the day I was born, he called me Bunny."

They would never know if the nickname had started as one of endearment, but for as long as Peter could remember, it had only been used to mock and torment him. And mockery had turned to outright disdain on the day that had changed everything.

Emelia studied him for a second, probably seeing on his face everything he hadn't put into words.

"This is the ballroom through here." Turning the cool brass handle, he opened the door and stepped back so Emelia could enter first.

"Wrrrreeeeooooow." The sound registered as something flew through the air and landed on Emelia's head. She screamed. Her hands flapped in the air as she reached up to her head, only to jerk away when an angry hiss resounded.

Oh, dear. He'd completely forgotten about Reepicheep.

Twenty-Five

One second Peter was explaining how he'd come to be named after a rabbit and the next second something sharp had landed on top of her head and latched there.

Emelia spun in a circle, screaming and trying to dislodge whatever type of creature it was while it gripped her hair and hissed.

"Stop moving!" Peter's authoritative tone cut through her hysteria, and she stopped midspin.

"Is it a rat?" *Please don't let it be a rat.* If there was a rat in her hair, she'd probably puke.

"It's okay, Reep." Peter's voice was soft and soothing. And it wasn't directed at her. He stepped closer and reached out toward her head. "Come to me." Her head got lighter, but the feeling of her hair being pulled with it caused her to cry out.

"Shhhhh."

He had so better not be directing that at her.

She could feel him trying to untangle her hair

from something. He was so close, she could smell his woodsy cologne.

"There we go. Good boy." The weight lifted from her head as Peter stepped back, taking the thing with him. "Emelia, meet Reepicheep."

In his hands was the ugliest runt of a cat she had seen in her entire life. "Cat" was almost too kind a description. His fur was calico. Where one ear should have been was a half-jagged edge. He was fat, but with stumpy little limbs. If there was ever a contest for the world's ugliest cat, he would be a sure winner.

He glared at her with evil little cat eyes. He clearly rated her about as highly as she rated him.

"Reepicheep after the mouse in *Prince Caspian*?" He couldn't be serious. This insult to cats around the world couldn't be named after one of Lewis's best creations.

"Do you know of another?" Peter flipped the cat around so he faced him. "The most valiant cat in the land, aren't we, boy?"

If he kissed him, she was gone. "Try psychotic."

"You just gave him a fright."

"I just walked into the room!"

"He likes to sleep on top of the table sometimes." He gestured to a table near the door. Presumably the launchpad for his stealth attack. "He's usually very friendly. Here, give him a pat." He held up the evil spawn toward her.

"You have got to be joking. He tried to scalp

me." Emelia put a hand up to her head, which was still throbbing. She had never been a cat person, and this little ball of spite only confirmed her perception of the species. "Why did you name him Reepicheep?" She may have hated the bearer of the name, but she was curious about the rationale.

Peter rubbed a hand down the cat's back. "He was abandoned in a ditch down the road. I found him a couple of years ago. In a sack. There were other kittens in it too. They had all drowned, but somehow he'd managed to get out of the sack and crawl up the side away from the water. When I found him he was half-dead. The vet said he wasn't going to make it, but he fought hard and pulled through. He's been mine ever since. The name just seemed to fit."

The connection between a feisty talking mouse with a sword and a psycho cat was clear only to Peter.

"And he's yours?"

"Usually he lives with me, but I brought him up here in the lead-up to the Boat Race since I was away so much. He prefers the country life. But I'll bring him home with us."

In the same car as her? They'd be building snowmen in the Bahamas before that happened.

Peter ran his hand over the cat and the little sociopath purred under his fingers while giving Emelia dagger eyes. "See? You two will be friends in no time."

She'd known Peter was too perfect. She'd just never guessed his biggest flaw was going to come in the form of a feline terrorist. While hers was that she'd killed his cousin.

The gravel crunched under Emelia's feet as they said farewell to Peter's parents and started walking back to his car.

She'd survived lunch. Survived Victor sitting there, staring at her, throwing in verbal jabs every now and then that only she understood. Survived touring the house and gardens with Maggie. Forced herself to concentrate on why they were there. The ball.

Tried desperately to come up with something, anything, that would mean they couldn't have it there. But there was nothing. Especially not when Maggie had returned with the information that the first Saturday in December was free and she and Bill would donate the use of the house for the event.

She was tied firmly in a noose of her own making.

She let her glance move sideways. Striding next to her, Peter appeared equally deep in thought. Hands shoved in his jeans pockets, gaze downward.

"Peter!" The call came from behind them. His father. "You forgot your cat." From the tone of his voice he couldn't wait to see the back of the thing.

Gah. She'd forgotten about the rabid feline. From the surprised look on his face, so had Peter. "You go get him. I'll just wait out here." She wasn't going near that cat again as long as she could help it. Named after a Narnia character or not.

"Okay, I'll just be a couple of minutes." He pulled the car keys out of his pocket and clicked open the trunk. Pulling a cat carrier out, he slammed it shut, tossed her the keys, and strode back to the house. Emelia shook her head at this optimism. There was about as much chance of it only taking a couple of minutes to get that cat contained as there was that she was going to be the next president.

Leaning against the car, she sucked in a lungful of early summer air and looked over the house. For all the hideous personal complications it posed to her, it was the perfect venue. The stately home of a viscount. Her mind churned with the possibilities. She wondered if it had been in any movies or TV shows. Country manors might have been a dime a dozen to the English but if she could get an in with the—

"So, which is it? Emelia Mason or Mia Caldwell? Or something else altogether?" Victor's sarcastic query cut through her thoughts.

He'd snuck up on her, coming from who knew where. Now he walked around the back of the car, coming to lean casually against the roof a couple of feet from her.

The one good thing about years spent as a tabloid journalist was her well-honed ability to bluff. Emelia took her time, letting her gaze sweep Victor from head to toe. "What does it matter to you?"

Victor shrugged. "It doesn't. But it certainly will to my brother."

It took all her skills not to flinch. "I thought we had a deal."

"We did. To stay out of each other's way. I don't think showing up at my parents' house with my brother could exactly be considered you keeping your side of it."

Touché.

"Look. I had no idea Peter was your brother or this was your parents' place." She tried to assume a nonchalant air. "As far as I'm concerned this doesn't need to change anything." She kept an eye on the front door. The last thing she could afford was Peter overhearing this.

Victor barked out a laugh. "You cannot be serious. The same tabloid hack who is responsible for my cousin's death is now working for her charity trying to save it? Under another name? I'd say that changes everything."

It did. And they both knew it. Her palm itched to wipe the gloating look off Victor's face but instead she reached for the only weapon she had left in her arsenal. "Look." The word came out icy. "Expose me if you want. Go right ahead. But we both know what happens if you do. I'm not the only one with a lot to lose here."

"Careful not to overplay your hand, Miss Caldwell. I'm not sure if you've noticed, but I'm the black sheep of this particular family." His voice held a lot of bravado but something flickered in his face that told her she'd gained a foothold.

"Well, I guess that remains to be seen." Movement drew her attention back to the house, where Peter had just emerged out of the front door with a squalling cat in a carrier.

When he saw Victor standing next to her, his speed increased across the gravel. "Everything okay here?" His gaze jumped between the two of them. Emelia almost couldn't hear his words for the sound of her heart trying to break out of her rib cage.

This was it. Thirty seconds from now it might all be over. She didn't have any words. Had never planned what she was going to say if her secret was revealed without any warning. Which was stupid on her part. As soon as she'd seen Victor at that ball she should've prepared for exactly this kind of thing.

Victor casually pushed himself off the roof. "Simmer down, Bunny. We were just talking about the cricket game. I'm looking forward to it."

Peter looked confused. "You said you weren't going to play."

"Well, Emelia here has helped me see the error of my ways. It is for Anita, after all."

"Okay." Peter looked like he didn't buy a word of it. "If you want in now you need to talk to Max. He's captaining."

"Consider it done, Captain Bunny." Victor gave him a mock salute.

"Great." Peter unlocked the doors and gave his brother a pointed look. "Do you mind? I need to put Reep in the car."

Victor stepped out of the way. "You're way too wound up, little brother. You need to get laid more often."

Emelia almost choked. The guy's jerkdom really knew no bounds. Peter just ignored him as he put the carrier in the backseat and slammed the door shut.

Victor threw her a wink. "So nice to meet you, Emelia. Look forward to seeing you around. Peter's very lucky to have someone with your experience on this."

He may not have given up her secret but she was under no illusions; his silence would be coming with a high price tag. The only question was whether it would be one she'd be prepared to pay.

Twenty-Six

"I still don't understand why we couldn't just get a DJ." Since they now had a date and a venue, apparently the entertainment was the next big thing on the spreadsheet. Which was proving to be more of a challenge than he'd anticipated, given their meager budget. Most of which Emelia had already allocated to a string quartet for the first half of the evening.

"Because this is a high-class fund-raising ball, not a school disco. Because a live band is so much cooler. Besides, that DJ you came up with, remind me again, he wasn't available on our day because of . . . ?" Emelia cocked an eyebrow at him.

Peter mumbled the answer under his breath. She was never going to let him live it down.

"Say again?"

"He's due to have his hip replaced."

"So I say no to the octogenarian DJ."

"You hate all my ideas." He tried to get a smile out of Emelia. Since the trip home, she'd been guarded. Excruciatingly polite, but the easy camaraderie and chemistry had disappeared like it never existed.

She crossed off something in her notebook, all business. "No, I only hate the really bad ones.

Unfortunately your track record so far has pretty much only been bad ones."

"Edible table arrangements are going to be the next big thing. It's not my fault if I'm a visionary ahead of the trend." He finally got the hint of a smile playing at the side of her mouth. He'd take it. "So, who are we seeing tonight?"

Emelia checked her list. "They're called the Groovestars."

Peter smirked. This could be entertaining.

"What? They had a flyer up at Tesco's and they have a Facebook page."

"You'll have to excuse me if I'm not brimming with excitement about seeing a band who advertise by the fruit and veg aisle."

"Oh, don't be such a spoilsport."

"And this is where they're playing tonight?" They were standing outside a run-down pub. Flakes of paint peeled off the outside. Peter thought he knew Oxford rather well. Lord knew he'd hauled his brother out of almost every pub in town. But not even Victor had stooped to this one.

Emelia double-checked the address and nodded. "Don't judge a book by its cover. They're probably young. Just starting out. Playing whatever gigs they can get. And, most importantly, we can afford them."

They stepped inside. The dim room smelled like the carpet hadn't been cleaned since the Beatles were big. Along one side ran a bar, behind it rows of the cheapest, nastiest liquor you'd find anywhere in the country. A few peeling signs displayed advertising that had to be pre-millennium. There wasn't a bartender to be seen.

Four very senior citizens sat around one square Formica table. In the corner sat a tattooed couple hunched over beers.

Emelia looked around, not even bothering to hide her dismay.

One of the old men stood up. "You right, luv?"

"We're, um, here to see the Groovestars. They were supposed to be playing here tonight?"

The old man's face brightened. "That's us!"

Peter tried to restrain the smile he felt taking over his face but failed miserably. So miserably you could probably have seen it from space.

"Boys. Look! We have gropies!"

A guy who had to be going on ninety and was wearing a gray cardigan spoke up. "I think, George, you'll find the word is 'groupies.' "

George ignored the guy. "I told you having a page on that face thingy would work!"

"I'm going to take a wild guess that someone's great-grandchild is responsible for these young startups being on the face thingy." Peter murmured the words to Emelia, who looked like she wasn't sure whether to punch him or laugh.

George turned back to them. "Sorry, we're a bit delayed. Harold needs to take his medication and he can't have it on an empty stomach, so we're just waiting for him to finish his snack." George gestured to where an old man with an impressive white mullet was eating a bag of crisps. On the table in front of him sat a pair of drumsticks, and lined up along them was a row of pills of varying sizes and colors.

Peter couldn't see. The tears of laughter he was trying to restrain had blurred his sight. His chest hurt from trying to contain it.

"We're looking for a band for a fund-raising ball."

"There's going to be a squall? Why would that be? Winter's long finished," Harold barked from the table as he popped two pills in his mouth and took a slug of water.

Peter's shoulders jumped up and down like a demented grasshopper with the effort of trying to contain his mirth.

"Don't worry. We're better than we look. Not that that's saying much. I'm Norm, by the way." It was the guy with the cardigan who spoke, eyes twinkling.

Peter scanned the room and realized he had previously missed a drum kit the size of a postage stamp, a lone bass plugged into a small amp, and a microphone.

"Help yourself to a drink." George gestured toward the bar. "We operate on an honor system while the band is playing. Just leave what you think is right on the bar."

"Thanks." Peter managed to get the word out before he walked toward the bar, Emelia trailing after him.

"Would you like something?"

Emelia cast her gaze to a brown stain on the ceiling. "Only if it comes in a sealed container."

Peter ducked behind the bar and grabbed two cans of Coke from the fridge, setting a handful of change on the bar as the twang of a guitar came over the amp. He took the drinks back to Emelia and made a show of snapping hers open in front of her. Handing it over, he did the same with his and took a long sip.

Next came the sound of something hitting the drums followed by the squeal of . . . no, surely not. But there was no mistaking the distinctive sound. Bagpipes.

"Hello, everyone." It was Norm at the microphone. "Welcome to our gig tonight. We're the Groovestars." The couple in the corner didn't even make any sign they'd heard him. The band launched into "Walking on Sunshine." Every single band member had a hearing aid. Probably turned off, going by the bumpy first few lines.

It was unlike any music Peter had ever heard before. Norm half crooning, half barking like an aged Elvis. George powering it along on the bagpipes. Harold tapping away on the drums, and the guy they hadn't been introduced to barely managing to keep up with the rest of them on the bass.

"Would you like to dance?" He turned to Emelia.

"What?"

"You heard the man. We're his gropies, Smoky. We can't let him down."

"Try groping anything and you'll lose your hand. Just remember that." The quiver of Emelia's lips finally gave her away.

"Oh, c'mon. I'd be making my move chaperoned by four octogenarians. It doesn't get any better than that. It would be the most excitement they've had at one of their gigs since Harold's last heart attack."

Emelia looked at the band, shook her head, and smiled. Ha! Got her. "Why not?"

Taking her Coke and putting it down on a table with his, Peter grabbed her hand and tugged her between the two tables separating them from the band. He put his hand on Emelia's waist and started spinning her across the 1970s-era brown and orange carpet until she was breathless and smiling.

It was no ball, but for some reason, it was even more fun.

As he turned her around on the nonexistent dance floor, he saw George's eyes twinkling at them, and the old man gave him a wink.

He lowered Emelia into a dip with his good arm, and she clasped her hands around his neck, grinning up at him. Their gazes caught and something in her expression softened. For a second, the final note of the bagpipes, the worn carpet, and the dingy pub all faded away and there was only her. Wavy hair falling out behind her, the ends touching the floor, her eyes sparkling, her smile carefree.

Friends, just friends. She thought he was crazy for wanting to make a comeback. He forced the thoughts through his brain before he did something stupid. Were there any more torturous words in the English language?

She should never have said yes to dancing with Peter. Emelia's heart started pounding again under the intensity of his gaze. Not knowing what to do or say, she tucked her chin into his shoulder as he pulled her back to her feet.

He let her go into one final spin as the song ended, and she immediately missed the feeling of being cradled against his chest.

Her gaze lingered on him for a second at the other end of his outstretched arm, then she let go of his hand and turned toward the band, clapping.

The four old men grinned and offered little bows.

Shoot. She so wanted to hire them for the ball. High society or not. What they lacked in talent, they more than made up for with chutzpah.

"Let's slow it down, gentlemen."

The opening notes of "It Had to Be You" drifted out and Peter held out his hand.

Emelia studied it for a second, then moved toward him, captivated by some weird magic. Tucking her against his chest, Peter waltzed her across the floor, the top of her head against his chin, the feel of his breath wafting down the side of her face, tormenting all her senses.

I wandered around, and finally found . . . The words drifted across the room.

The heat of his hand warmed through the back of her top, and she gasped as he lowered her into another graceful dip, his hold strong and steady underneath her. "Don't worry. I'm not going to drop you."

"I know." She looked into his face and suddenly wasn't sure if they were talking about dancing anymore. Time to change the subject. Fast. "What are your plans until Boat Race training for next year starts? Besides babysitting me, of course." She tried to keep her tone light, teasing.

He pulled her back onto her feet. "Summer is busy for beginners' courses and I've still got a couple of coaching jobs."

"How's your shoulder?" Emelia focused on keeping some distance between them, despite the almost overwhelming urge to tuck her head into the curve of his neck and rest against his chest.

"Not horrible. Not great. I'm due to have some

more scans soon. That will tell us more about when I can get back into training."

She noted his use of "when." But she kept her mouth closed. The guy was an elite athlete. He had to have some of the best sports doctors in the country giving him advice. He didn't need to hear any more of hers.

"Enough about me. Let's talk about you, Miss Mason. Starting with, what were you called back home?"

"Sorry?" She was thrown by the sudden change in topic.

"Emelia. It's beautiful, but at four syllables, I can't believe it didn't get shortened."

She drew a deep breath. "Mia. Most of the time I was called Mia."

He studied her, but nothing in his gaze made her think he was connecting the dots. "You don't like it?"

The urge came over her to pour out her entire gritty past right there in a decrepit pub in Oxford, but she tamped it down. She'd tell him one day, but not tonight. After the ball. She wasn't going to ruin this.

"I never felt like Mia." That was as close as she could get to telling him the truth. And it was true. There was a reason she'd picked Mia Caldwell as her byline. Because then, in some way, she could separate herself from her alter ego.

"What about Emmy?"

She actually jolted that time. It would have been easier to dodge the question, but she was tired of doing that. She wanted to give him something. A piece of her that was true. That mattered. Emelia sucked in a breath. "My mom used to call me Emmy. I haven't let anyone else call me that since she . . ." She choked up, unable to get the final word out. Emmy had died the day her mom did. She hadn't let anyone call her it since. "My mom died when I was six."

Peter's hand tightened around her waist, and she found herself cradled between his arm and his chest. He didn't say anything, his breath whispering across her cheek.

Slowly, she relaxed into the music, his strength, and their steady steps across the worn carpet. After a few more seconds, she lifted her head to find his green eyes focused on her. "Thank you."

"For what?"

"For not trying to make it okay."

"Thank you for telling me."

Whatever her response was going to be, it faded as she realized that at some point in the last few minutes her fingers had slid up his shoulders and were tracing the nape of his neck.

"I concede defeat. You win." Peter leaned down and whispered the words in Emelia's ear. She leaned back, tilting her head and peering up at him from under her lashes.

"I win what?"

"The band. We should hire them. We'll just have to make sure we get everyone's donations first." He gave her a grin.

For a second disappointment flooded through her but she masked it. She looked at the four pensioners, a smile coming to her lips.

"You're probably right. It is a ball about second chances, after all."

"Is that what you're in Oxford looking for? A second chance?" Peter gazed at her like he could see all her secrets and didn't hate her. Which was how she knew it was just a fantasy.

Emelia shook her head. "I don't believe in looking for something I don't deserve." She pushed off from his chest and stepped away. "We should go. We've got what we came here for."

Twenty-Seven

Cricket. Possibly the most boring game in the world. Peter hadn't mentioned that at any point. As far as Emelia could work out, a guy ran up and threw a ball, and a guy at the other end hit the ball. Other players in the field tried to catch it or pick it up and throw it at some sticks that were behind the batter. And so it went on. For hours. Occasionally punctuated by players throwing their hands up in the air and yelling something indecipherable.

Emelia stifled a yawn as she surveyed the grounds at Oxford's historic University Parks. She could now add this game to her list of things that only the English understood. They'd sold out of tickets weeks ago, even though the setting meant that people could just wander up and watch for free if they so desired. Apparently the appetite in this town for anything that featured the historical Oxford–Cambridge rivalry was pretty much insatiable.

She breathed in the warm summer air. Somehow, every member of both squads had committed to play. Along with a few of the coaching staff to make up numbers. Even though some of the guys had already finished their exams and had left their respective universities for summer, they'd come back for this.

As much as Emelia hated to admit it, it was all thanks to Sabine again. The two of them had given each other a wide berth but she'd seen her talking to Peter a few times. They'd certainly looked more friendly than most exes she knew.

"You look like you'd rather be watching paint dry."

She looked up to see Peter walking toward her. His blue fitted T-shirt highlighted his muscular physique, the strapping tape poking out from underneath one of the sleeves displaying the reason he wasn't on the field for Oxford.

He lowered himself down beside her on the

grass. After doing her last set of rounds to check on refreshments for the teams, she'd found herself a spot at the far end of the field, where spectators were sparse.

"Do you wish you were out there?" She nodded toward the pitch.

Peter shook his head. "Nah. Cricket's not really my thing."

"Oh, thank goodness." The words burst out of her. "I don't think I've seen such a boring game in all my life."

Peter let out a snort of laughter. "I wouldn't go saying that too loudly. We English are quite protective of our national sport." He grinned at her and the air crackled between them. They hadn't really seen each other since the evening at the pub. Emelia had been busy with final details for the match—thank goodness that had required zero knowledge of the game—and Peter had, well, apart from the rowing beginners' courses he'd mentioned teaching, she actually had no clue what he did with most of his time now that the Boat Race was over.

Not that it mattered. Not that he could matter. Knowing he was Anita's cousin. Knowing that at any second Victor could decide to renege on their deal. That day had been a game changer. Any foolish fantasies she might have harbored that there could ever be something between them were well and truly destroyed. The dancing at the pub had been a mistake. She'd let herself get carried away and now was taunted by the memory of being in his arms when it couldn't be allowed to ever happen again.

She searched for something neutral to say. "Oh. I finally finished the book about the brothers who rowed in the Boat Race."

If he was surprised by her abrupt change in topic, he didn't show it. "What did you think?" Peter leaned back on his good arm.

What did she think? She thought it was the craziest thing she'd ever read. Ever heard of. "In the first bit. That guy. Seb. Is that true? Did he really pass out?"

"He did indeed. Cost Cambridge the race."

"He was unconscious!" Emelia was offended on the guy's behalf. Even if it had been over a decade ago. She'd reread the first chapter over and over, trying to understand what it was that would make someone not even stop rowing when they were passing out.

"That's how it works. You leave everything on the water." Peter looked back to the field at the cracking sound of the bat hitting the ball.

"Is that how you felt on the water? When you were rowing?" After finishing *Blood over Water* Emelia felt like she had a small understanding of what might drive him to risk everything to get to the top again. But she wanted to hear it from him.

"Yeah." He looked back to her, his face

contemplative. "Those guys, they were closer to me than my own brother. You'd do anything not to let the team down. All of us would. When I came to in hospital that night in Italy, one of my first thoughts was, *At least it didn't happen in the boat*. If I had to get injured, at least I didn't fail the team."

"How old were you when you started?" This was safe territory. She could talk to Peter about rowing all day without worrying about her secrets trying to escape.

"Fourteen." He laughed. "Poor Mum. If she'd had a clue how bad I was going to get the bug, she never would have promised to be there to cheer me on at every race."

"Your mom was at every race?" But if he'd become an elite athlete, surely that must have been . . . hundreds?

"Every one in England. Rain, sleet, or sun. I let her off the hook for the overseas ones. Though my parents did manage to make it to a couple of world champs." He shook his head. "I can still see her like it was yesterday. Every race. There she was with her blanket and thermos of tea."

"That's so—" Without warning, Emelia found herself choking up. She coughed and tried to finish her sentence like a normal human being but found herself unable to speak past the boulder in her throat.

She didn't even get why this mattered so much.

She'd been fine without a mom. Sort of fine. Managed to pave her own way in the world. Then suddenly she'd gotten exposed to a stupid ordinary Peter story about his mother and all she wanted to do was curl up and cry for years.

"Are you okay?" He leaned a little closer but not enough to touch. She wasn't sure whether to be relieved or disappointed.

"I'm fine. I'm sorry. I feel like such a dork." Emelia swiped at her cheeks, mortified to find them damp. The poor guy must have been wondering what kind of drama queen she was.

"There's nothing to be sorry for."

"It's so stupid. That story about your mom. I guess I just suddenly really missed mine." She picked up a couple of blades of grass and rolled them together between her fingers. "Most of the time I don't even think about it. And then sometimes, like today, it just kind of sneaks up on me that I don't have one. I just wonder what she would have been like."

"Can you tell me about her?"

Emelia sneaked a glance sideways to find him looking right at her. She didn't know what to say. Most of the time when people found out she was motherless, they hurried to change the subject, move the conversation along, as if somehow her bad familial luck might rub off on them. No one, not ever, had asked about her.

And now that someone had, it was like a balloon

had blown up in her chest, ready to burst if she tried to squash it. "She was very beautiful. But then I guess all six-year-old girls think their mom is the most beautiful woman they've ever seen. She loved Narnia more than anything in the world." More than the world itself, in the end.

Emelia drew in a breath. "I used to come home from school and we'd play our favorite parts in the books. We would pretend that the dining room table was the *Dawn Treader* and we were sailing for the Eastern Islands. Or that our garden was the woods in between and we'd jump in the puddles and move between the worlds." Where play ended and the mental illness began, Emelia would never know. She hadn't even realized until she was a teenager that most kids didn't have mothers who forgot about things like dinner and homework because they were too busy living in a land of make-believe.

"So you got your love of Narnia from her."

"I did." She cracked a smile. "She's also to blame for why I can't even microwave popcorn. She was a terrible cook. Couldn't even boil an egg. But for some weird reason, she could make the best waffles in the world. That was it. We probably would have lived on waffles if it wasn't for cereal and takeout. And she had a heart as big as the Atlantic. She hated to see anyone in need."

"She sounds like a great woman."

Peter was close enough that she could smell his musky scent. It was an act of will not to reach up and run her hand along his jaw, which hadn't seen a razor in a few days. She forced her gaze to go over his shoulder. "She wasn't perfect, but she was mine."

"What about your father?"

The perfect topic to ruin the moment. Emelia huffed out a breath of air as she tore up some more grass. "He might as well be dead."

He might as well be dead. A gust of wind caught Emelia's caustic words and threw them back in her face. It wasn't true. A live, but uninterested, parent was definitely better than two dead ones.

"I'm sorry, that's a horrible thing to say." Emelia dropped her decimated blades of grass onto the ground between her feet and kept her focus there, not wanting to see the judgment that she was sure had to be written across his face. "I'm sure he did his best."

"But it wasn't enough?"

She chanced a look up. Searched his gaze for condemnation but found only concern. Emelia shrugged her shoulders. "We'd been close. At least I feel like we had. Then, when my mom died, it was like he couldn't be around me. I look a lot like her. Maybe I reminded him of too much. So, I became the ward of after-school programs and summer camps. The occasional trips to see his parents, who had no idea what to do with me either. They'd had children quite late, and so they were already older by the time I was born. My aunt did her best to help but she had her own family and didn't live close."

"What about your mother's family?"

She tucked a piece of wayward hair behind her ear and looked anywhere except at him. "My mom was an only child. My grandfather died of a heart attack when I was a baby and then my grandmother died not long after my mom from cancer." She laughed mirthlessly. "Great set of genes I've got."

Peter didn't say anything for a few seconds, no rushing to fill the void with pointless platitudes. It made her like him even more.

She forced her gaze away again. Focused on his gray flip-flops, which showcased feet so white today had to be the first time they'd been let out in public this summer. His second toes were longer than his big toes. She'd finally discovered a part of him that wasn't attractive. If she could hold every conversation looking at those for the next few months she'd be fine.

The silence stretched until eventually she couldn't stand it anymore. "What are you thinking?"

He sighed. "I was thinking about how I felt like I'd been robbed when I had to give up my dream of rowing at Rio. But that doesn't even come close to being robbed of a parent. Feeling like you've lost two. Then I was thinking what a terrible human being I was that I could even compare rowing to what you've been through."

"You're not a horrible human being. Far from it." She should know. She'd crossed paths with more than a few of them. Become one herself.

Peter's fingers brushed against hers and she sucked in a breath. Let herself look up and be captured by his intent gaze. "I'm sorry your father doesn't realize what an amazing daughter he's missing out on."

How could he know that her fear was her father knew exactly what he was missing out on? Emelia swallowed. "Thanks." She just managed to get the word out. Time to get this conversation back onto neutral ground.

Peter nodded toward the field, like he knew what she was thinking. "So, this looks like it's all going pretty much perfectly. Hopefully we'll make a decent chunk of change off it."

The university had kindly donated the use of the grounds, so SpringBoard's biggest expenses were in printing tickets, advertising, and hosting a reception after the event. That had been her idea after seeing at the ball how some girls totally lost their heads around Boat Race rowers. Host a reception for both teams and charge a hundred quid a head for a select number of groupies to get to be in the same room as their idols. Though she was going to hazard a guess, from the perfect hair, sultry gazes, and skimpy sundresses she'd seen around, that most of them would be gunning for far more than that.

Emelia stretched out her legs in front of her. "Well, I guess that's the upside of it being the most boring game in the world. The opportunities for it all to go badly are very limited. If all goes well we should make almost twenty thousand pounds off this."

Not even close to what they needed to save the charity, but it was still something. And since the row-off there had also been a slight uptick in potential donor interest, reversing the trend of the last six months.

"You're doing a great job."

"Thanks. I couldn't do it without you." Emelia smiled up at him, the late-afternoon summer sun setting a halo behind his hair. The green of his eyes seemed to darken as his gaze held hers. Emelia caught her bottom lip in her teeth. You couldn't deny the chemistry between them any more than you could deny gravity.

"So—"

"I—"

Whatever they were both about to say was cut short by shouts from the field. Jerking her head toward the commotion, Emelia gasped as she registered what she was seeing. On the field the teams looked to be slugging it out, while spectators wearing the two universities' blues were streaming onto the pitch, some fists already flying.

A brawl. She was pretty sure this would count as going very badly.

Twenty-Eight

Emelia shrank back into the comfort of darkness. All the better to not see the papers she held in her hands, resting between her torso and wedged-up legs.

She pushed some clothes away from her face, the hangers scratching along the rail, and breathed in the smell of laundry detergent and her own fear.

Peter was right. She never should have taken this job. Because of her, SpringBoard was worse off than it had been six months ago. Not only wasn't she going to save it, she was going to be the final nail in the coffin.

A tear meandered down her cheek and she swiped it away. She deserved no one's pity. Not even her own.

Voices echoed from outside on the landing. Allie's New Zealand accent came first, then a deeper one. English. Her pulse kicked up a notch. She hadn't seen Peter since he'd bolted into the fray of the brawl. Hadn't responded to any of the messages he'd left in the ten days since.

It had all been over ten minutes later, the

appearance of the police enough to calm even the most rabid of spectators down. But ten minutes was all it took to destroy everything she was trying to save.

"I don't think she's home from the office yet." Allie's voice. A knock at her door.

"I've tried the office. She's not there."

The click of her door opening. Them peering into her empty room with its perfectly made bed. "Well, she's not here either."

"I have an idea. Just give me a second."

Sure enough, a few moments later there came a tapping on the wardrobe door. Why couldn't he just leave her alone? Hadn't she already done enough damage? And that was just the stuff he knew about.

She shrank back into her corner, pressed her lips together, hoped he would just go away.

No such luck. The door creaked open and Peter, crouching down, stared right at her.

"Leave me alone." Her words whispered out. "Please. Just go away."

"I don't think so." He peered inside. "I'd ask if I could join you in there but I'm pretty sure there isn't enough room."

The thought of Peter trying to fold his huge frame into her small wardrobe was enough to cause one side of her mouth to lift.

"That's better." He stood, holding out his hand to help her out, and she pushed her way through her clothes to standing, the papers clutched tightly in her hands. Behind him Allie stood in the doorway.

Great. Now her roommate knew she was a weirdo who hid in wardrobes. She opened her mouth, trying to find some words to explain her particular brand of crazy.

Allie held a hand up to stop her and smiled. "You don't need to explain. Everyone needs a hiding place. I've got some engagement-party planning to do so I'll leave you guys to it." She disappeared, leaving Peter looking at her with concerned eyes.

"You didn't go to work today. Elizabeth is worried."

"Actually I did." Long enough to open what sent her scrambling for her hiding place. "I just had to leave. I left Elizabeth a message."

"This is not your fault, Emelia. This is not on you. No one blames you for the brawl."

The rational part of her knew that. In all the discussions about risk and contingencies not once had anyone raised the possibility of a bunch of tree-sized rowers turning the so-called gentlemen's game into a fistfight. The worst-case scenario had been the match getting rained out.

"Do you know who threw the first punch?"
She didn't know. She didn't even care. "Who?"
"Victor."
Of course he did. "Why?"

"Well, neither him nor the other guy are saying but best anyone can work out the Cambridge guy made some slur about Anita."

The whole debacle had been on the front page of the paper for the first three days. The reception had been canceled. All the tickets had to be refunded but all the associated bills still had to be paid.

She had failed. The only reason she was here was to save Anita's charity and after two events they were back to square one. She should just walk away now. Walk away from SpringBoard. Walk away from Peter. Walk away from all of it. Except she had nowhere else to go. All her eggs were in this one messed-up basket.

"This came today." She held out the sheaf of papers to Peter.

"What is it?"

"Estimated costs to repair the damage. Because the university didn't charge us to use the grounds, their insurer is saying the damage isn't covered by their rental insurance policy."

Peter scanned the document, turning the pages until he got to the figure on the final page. Then he let out a low whistle. "Eighteen thousand pounds?"

"Once we refund the reception tickets and pay all the costs, that's pretty much everything we've made from the row-off and the cricket match." Emelia felt tears building in the back of her eyes and blinked them away, but she didn't prevent one from spilling over.

Peter looked at her, pulled a pressed white handkerchief out of his pocket, and handed it to her. Only the English. "Why does this matter so much? I mean, I'm personally invested because Anita was my cousin. But this feels like this is much more than a job to you."

This was it. This was the moment when she should just tell him the truth, the whole sordid truth, and let the chips fall as they might. But the fear of the unknown clogged the words in her throat. "I just need to do something right."

Peter studied her, as if wanting to ask more. More than she was able to give. "Okay. Well then, I guess we're just going to have to put on the best charity ball that Oxfordshire has ever seen."

She had to give him points for sheer optimism but she just couldn't see it. "How are we ever going to put on a ball that will make a million pounds? With pretty much no money? Let's be honest. It's no more likely to happen than me getting to Narnia through my wardrobe."

Peter just looked at her, jaw sagging. "That's it!"

"What's it?"

"Narnia!"

"You've lost me."

"SpringBoard is a literature charity. It's December. Winter. Highbridge is a manor in the country.

Just like in the book. I can't believe we haven't thought of this before. It'll be perfect."

"What?"

The next thing she knew Peter had picked her up and was spinning her around. Her heels skied across the side of her bed, through the air, then along the wall. "Narnia. We make it a Narnia-themed ball."

He dropped her to the floor, leaving her breathless and giddy. Images of Highbridge's ballroom decked out with tables of Turkish delight, a huge lantern post in the middle of it, custom-made wardrobe doors as the entry, spinning through her mind like whirling snow-flakes.

"What do you think?" For a second he looked like he was doubting himself.

"I think . . ." Emelia said the words slowly, drawing them out. Then she grinned. "I think it is the craziest, most amazing idea I have ever heard."

They both stared at each other for a second, breathless with the sheer audacity of what they were going to try to pull off.

And suddenly it didn't seem so crazy when Peter leaned down and kissed her.

Twenty-Nine

Emelia walked tentatively into Peter's average-sized living area. "Hello?" No answer.

Such a bachelor pad. A couple of rowing posters and another poster for the games of the 2015 Rugby World Cup were the only wall decorations. One of the two mismatched couches had been inherited from the seventies. The money saved had apparently been invested in the huge TV that sat on the main wall. It was tidy though, which was more than she'd expected.

It had been four days since Peter's Narnia ball idea tipped Emelia over the brink of recklessness. They'd been saved from themselves only by Allie's coming to ask for opinions on something to do with the engagement party, the two of them both springing apart at her voice like a pair of teenagers busted by a parent. Emelia had spent the time telling herself it was better that way, that a little bit of distance was all it would take to get over this foolish infatuation that had somehow managed to sneak under her guard. The way her heart hammered at the sound of him on her voice mail called that out for the lie that it was.

He'd sounded stressed. Said he had to go out of town unexpectedly and asked if she could top up Reepicheep's water in the morning. Told her where to find the spare key.

In one corner sat a scratching post, and cat bowls of water and food sat on a piece of newspaper. No sign of the world's ugliest cat.

Retrieving the water bowl, she made quick work of washing it out and refilling it. In the hour since she'd picked up his voice mail her mind had spun trying to think of one good reason he would need to leave so suddenly yet still remember to make sure his cat got fresh water. She'd come up with none.

She placed the bowl back on the newspaper, then turned to leave. She'd send Peter a text back in the car. Let him know his cat's hydration needs were met.

She froze midturn. The guy hadn't been joking. On the far side of the room, by the door, sat a glass case on the bookshelf.

She walked toward it, crouching down slightly to look at the model straight on. "Wow." The *Dawn Treader* sat inside. A beautiful model, meticulously assembled, maybe fifteen inches long by ten inches high. Even from behind the glass, she could see the tiny detailing and intricate construction of Lewis's famous boat.

On one side of it sat copies of all the books in *The Chronicles of Narnia*. On the other side sat a collection of Lewis's works. *The Great Divorce. Mere Christianity*, *The Screwtape Letters*, and others. She picked up *Mere Christianity* and flipped through its pages. She'd never read it. Never really been interested in what Clive had to say about religion, no matter how much she liked him. Not when his team included people who had never met her mother but took some kind of wacked-out pleasure in insisting she was burning in hell.

But she'd promised herself when she came to Oxford that she'd try to build this new self with an open mind. If Allie, Jackson, and Peter all thought there was something to be found here, maybe she should at least hear them out. Hear Clive out. He had, after all, even called himself the most dejected and reluctant convert in all of England.

Picking up a book titled *The Weight of Glory*, she flipped through the pages.

It would seem that Our Lord finds our desires not too strong, but too weak. We are half-hearted creatures, fooling about with drink and sex and ambition when infinite joy is offered us, like an ignorant child who wants to go on making mud pies in a slum because he cannot imagine what is meant by the offer of a holiday at the sea. We are far too easily pleased.

His words struck something deep inside her. Infinite joy. What would that even look like?

Her pondering was interrupted by the sound of retching. Spinning around, Emelia saw Reep had not only appeared but was violently hacking on the carpet, his little head arching forward and back.

He was choking. Badly. Peter was going to return to a feline corpse. No matter what she thought of the squat furball, that wasn't an option.

Moving across the room, she picked him up under his rib cage, feeling the strength of his efforts as his abdomen sucked in and shuddered out. She'd never had a cat. She had no idea what to do. Smack him on the back like you did a person? She had no better idea. Lifting her hand, she tapped him on the back. He kept choking. Another whack. Firmer. This time his sound changed, like something had been dislodged.

Another cough and a hairball flew out and landed on the back of the couch. Ew.

"You all good, little guy?" Emelia held him up and rotated him to face her. He gave her squinty eyes. Then proceeded to latch both of his paws onto her bare arm and shred it like a piece of paper.

For a second, Emelia just stared into his triumphant face before softly dropping a word that should never be used in polite company.

Then her hands flew apart, and Reep fell to the ground before bounding up the back of the couch and out of her range of vision.

Her left forearm and hand featured thin red ribbons. She took a deep breath before she could give in to her desire to commit caticide, and then Emelia turned around to try to see where he'd gone.

Her spine stiffened. Where the Narnia books had been, Reep now sat. With one paw batting at the *Dawn Treader* case. She let out her breath as she saw it wasn't moving. Of course it wouldn't. He was just a little cat.

Staring straight at her, Reepicheep pushed his face between the back of the case and the wall. Slowly, the corner of the case shifted forward until it edged off the shelf. As he forced himself even farther forward, the corner moved another inch or so off.

"Here, Reep." Emelia stepped backward to his food bowl and picked it up. She tiptoed toward the bookshelf and shook the bowl, the dry cat food clinking against the metal sides. "Look, Reep. Are you hungry? Yummy food?" It smelled disgusting. Like fish and bones.

As if to tell her what he thought of her offer, Reep pushed the case so that almost a quarter of it was being held up by nothing but air.

Okay, enough was enough. She put the food down and reached out. If he scraped both arms up, so be it. The *Dawn Treader* was not going down on her watch. She grabbed the ends of the case, picked it up, and pulled it toward her.

Reepicheep leapt off the bookshelf, landed on top of the case, and gave her what could only be described as a "die, girl, die" glare before opening his mouth and sneezing in her face.

Emelia's eyes clamped shut, and she stumbled back, trying to get away from the evil spawn. Her foot went right into the food bowl and slipped, sending her sideways.

The next thing she knew, something struck her across the back, sending her flying forward. The case flew out of her hands and hit the window with a crack. A line appeared in the glass, but the case stayed intact. She held out a smidgeon of hope until it flipped and flipped again as it dove to the floor and landed upside down.

Crawling across the ugly carpet, she reached the case and tipped it over. Inside where the boat had once been sat a collection of matchsticks, string, and material.

Then, behind her, came the sound of spawn cat purring.

Peter stood in the doorway, bewildered by the scene spread out before him. Books on the floor, cat food strewn all over the place, and in the middle of it all, Emelia crouched over pieces of wood and glass. He blinked. Maybe he was hallucinating from no sleep.

Something rubbed against his leg, and he looked down to find Reepicheep. "Hey, little guy." He scooped him up and gave him a pat as he walked across the living room.

"Are you—" His words clogged his throat as he saw what it was that had gone flying from her grasp and hit the window. What she now held cradled in her arms. The case with his beloved model. The one thing he had left from his grandfather. Inside, the *Dawn Treader* lay in pieces. Not even pieces, more like shrapnel.

"What happened?" He breathed the words and blinked back unexpected moisture rising in his eyes.

It's just a boat, Peter. It's just a boat.

That didn't stop the lump in his throat.

Emelia's eyes were huge. "I'm so sorry."

Red lines ran down one of her arms. "What happened?" He repeated the question.

"I tripped and—"

"No, not to the boat. To you." He reached out and lightly touched her arm above one of the scratches.

She looked down at it as if it were the first time she'd seen it. "Let's just say it's been confirmed your cat isn't exactly an ardent fan of mine."

His pet purred and looked up at him innocently. But the lines down Emelia's arm were clearly from little claws.

What could he do? It wasn't like you could put a cat in time-out. "Stay right there, I'm going to find something for it."

Striding to the kitchen, he rummaged in the top cupboard until he found the box of assorted items that passed as his medical supplies and pulled out an almost empty tube of antiseptic cream. Better than nothing.

He took a couple of deep breaths, squashing down the well-worn memories of building the boat with his grandfather. If he dwelled on the fact that it was now in tiny pieces, he wouldn't be able to hide how gutted he was.

Returning to her side, he squeezed out a little cream and dabbed it on her arm, trying to gently spread it up and down the scratch. Emelia winced. "Sorry."

"Do I need a rabies shot?"

Good grief, he hoped not.

"I'm so sorry about the *Treader*."

"It's okay. It was just an accident. Mostly my fault. It was me opening the door that sent you flying." He kept his gaze on her wounds, refusing to look at her face.

"Reep was up there and I thought he was going to push it off, so I'd picked it up to put it somewhere safer and then—" She shrugged.

"Bad timing."

"I wish I could have seen it better. It looked beautiful. It must have taken you ages."

"Months." But it wasn't as beautiful as she was. He didn't know where the thought came from. All he knew was that after a late night drive to

274

London, then spending the small hours trying to negotiate the release of his unapologetic brother out of the latest jail cell, there was nothing he would have rather found when he came home than her. Even if she was holding the remains of his most beloved possession.

"If I tell you something, can you try not to hate me?" She blinked up at him with long, damp eyelashes.

"I'll try."

She scrunched up her nose. "I don't really like cats. And I really, really don't like yours."

He ran his hand across her jawline, then slid it into her hair, running his fingers over its wavy edges. "Can't say I blame you after what he's done to you."

She looked at him. Properly. Her eyes traveled his face, no doubt taking in his rumpled clothes and haggard face. "Is everything okay?"

He ran a hand through his hair. Tried to remember what he'd said in the message he'd left on her voice mail. "It was a long night." He was going to stop there, but something compelled him to go on. "Victor got into a bit of trouble in London."

"Ah." Her expression revealed no surprise at his words. But then, why would she after her first meeting with him? "What kind of trouble was he in?"

"Got arrested for drunk-and-disorderly."

275

"So, you went to rescue him?" He couldn't tell from her tone if she disapproved or not.

Peter shrugged. "It's what brothers do." Though in this brotherhood it was very much a one-way street. Always had been. He ran his fingers across the cracked case. "To be honest, I'm surprised he didn't break this long ago. He was always jealous of how close Pop and I were."

"When you left the party and that time you ran out of my office. Were they both Victor too?"

For once he didn't mind talking about his brother. It was a good distraction. "Yes."

"So, you rescue him pretty often?"

"I guess." Peter tried to sort through his tired thoughts. "He's always had a bit of a thing for drinking and girls. But it's gotten out of control. This last year, I've spent more time getting him out of pubs, or parties, or police cells, absolutely wasted, than I care to think about. But then a few hours later, he's on the erg pulling the kind of times that some guys train years toward and never achieve." He shook his head. "Anyway, looks like his luck is about to run out. It's looking pretty certain he's going to get charged this time."

Emelia tucked back a piece of hair that had fallen across her face. "Maybe it will be good for him. It's not your job to save him from himself."

The angry scar down the side of his brother's face insisted otherwise. And he was done talking about Victor. At least he didn't have to worry about his getting kicked off the squad anymore.

Emelia's finger traced the crack along the glass. "I'm so sorry. I'll find a way to fix it."

"No." His thumb ran across her cheek, wiping another tear away. "It's okay. It's just a boat." This time he meant it.

She tilted her head and gave him the kind of smile that made him ignore all the warning sirens going off in his head insisting that if he didn't pull back, he would cross a point of no return. "It wasn't just a boat." Her finger now traced a line down his arm.

He was a goner. Lack of sleep and wanting to forget everything to do with Victor overrode all rational thought. Resting his forehead against hers, he closed his eyes for a second, breathing in the heady scent of jasmine. "I'm just glad you're here."

He felt her relax as she leaned into his hand, her breath wafting over his lips. "I'm glad I'm here too."

Opening his eyes, Peter pulled back for a second, allowing his gaze to drink her in—her big eyes, brown hair, and naturally rosy lips that made her look like Snow White in the cartoons he'd watched as a child. They could get him into big trouble if he let them. They already had. Just being around Emelia sent every logical reason he'd ever had about not falling for someone who didn't share his faith clear out of his head.

She smiled at him, tilting her face up. Peter may have been out of the game for a while, but even he could work out that if he went in for a kiss, she wasn't going to turn him down.

He had never been so tempted. He'd split up with Sabine because even though she shared his faith and what they had was good, he knew that somewhere out there was great. That a girl was out there who would make him feel all the crazy all-consuming things he was feeling right now.

Peter sucked in a tortured breath and summoned all his self-control. Removing his hand from her cheek, he pulled back slightly.

They had to talk. He never should have kissed her in her room. It had been a moment he'd replayed in his mind over and over in the few days since. It had felt so right, yet it had been wrong.

He couldn't have great with Emelia. No matter how much she made him feel like maybe life would be okay without rowing. No matter how much he wanted something more with her. He couldn't. And right now he was being dishonorable, flirting and enjoying the feeling of her in his arms when he couldn't give her what she deserved. He needed to tell her why. He needed to tell her now.

"I have to talk to you about something."

Something he couldn't interpret flickered across

Emelia's face at his words. Whatever it was, it changed the air between them. Her expression tightened for a second, and she shifted away, as if she already knew what he was going to say.

Thirty

I have to talk to you about something. Every female over the age of fourteen could tell you the something that followed was never good. The only question was how bad it would be. It didn't matter if you were in a restaurant or a car, or sitting on a living room floor staring at a shattered model ship.

People didn't preface good news. It just burst out.

I love you. We're pregnant. I got the job. The tests are clear.

Then there were the things that needed framing.

It's not you, it's me. I've met someone else. I cheated on you. We're letting you go. The test results are back.

The iterations were endless, but the lead-ins were limited.

We need to talk. I need to tell you something. There's something I have to say.

"I don't understand." After Peter's pronouncement, she'd stood up, moved to the couch. He'd followed. Situated himself a safe distance away.

Then he had haltingly, awkwardly, told her that he liked her *a lot* but that there couldn't be anything more than friendship between them because he believed in God and she, well, didn't. At least, not like he did.

This from the guy who, only a few minutes ago, had been inches away from kissing her. Again. He couldn't deny it. She wasn't going to ask him to.

Emelia focused on a spot just over his shoulder. "I don't understand." Had she said that already? Well, she didn't. She truly didn't. What was the big deal? She'd known plenty of people who had married across religious boundaries. It had never seemed like much of an issue to them. As far as she could see, they both agreed to respect each other's beliefs, or lack thereof, and all was well.

"I'm not a guy who just goes to church on Sunday because it's a thing to do. Like . . ." He shrugged. "I don't know, grocery shopping."

"Okay." She still was no closer to getting it, but she took a shot at filling in the gaps. "So, you try to live your life with all of those kind of values?" She was mentally trying to catalog what that might include. Sex was out. She hadn't been in a relationship for years and she wasn't a casual sex kind of girl, so it wasn't like she was having any right now anyway. She'd seen him have a beer, so he wasn't a teetotaler. She had no clue where he stood on gambling, but she didn't care.

Dancing? She'd no sooner have gone back into another nightclub than she would have drunk gasoline, so whatever.

"I do."

"Okay. I can respect that." What was she doing? This was the barrier she'd been hoping for, the one that would force her to get a grip on her growing feelings. She couldn't date a guy when she was responsible for the death of someone he loved. And this was the perfect excuse. God. If she'd believed in Him, she would've offered up a prayer of thanks. Or whatever it was one did.

But despite all her attempts to tell herself the million reasons why this was a good thing, her heart wasn't buying it.

Peter mumbled something that she couldn't quite make out.

"What was that?"

He sucked in a big enough breath to fill three people and looked her straight in the eye. "That's not enough."

She couldn't have been more taken aback if he'd slapped her. It wasn't enough? What more did he want? "Why?" The three letters leaked out of her. Small. Hurt.

She wasn't enough. Even though that wasn't what he'd said, that was what he meant.

He seemed to have read her thoughts because the next thing she knew, her hands were captured in his. "Emelia, look at me."

She tilted her chin a little, but not quite enough to be able to see into his eyes. That would be her undoing.

"I really like you. I would have asked you on a date weeks ago if it wasn't for this."

Well, that was a nice consolation prize.

"I know how this goes. My mum, she believes. My dad doesn't. My whole life I've watched what it looks like when two people love each other but don't agree on something that infiltrates your whole life. I would love nothing more than to throw caution to the wind and explore whatever this is between us. Hope that along the way you'll come to believe what I do. But that wouldn't be fair. I can't do that to you. I can't do that to me."

"You didn't think it might have been a good idea to mention all of this before you kissed me?" She couldn't keep the bitterness out of her voice. Why did she even have to go there? Bring it up?

"I'm so sorry." He did look genuinely stricken. "I acted dishonorably. It should never have happened. I just . . ." He sighed. "Sometimes when I'm with you everything feels so right. And the truth is there's not much that's right about my life right now. But that doesn't excuse what I did."

"Couldn't we just . . ." The words died on her lips before she could even say it. Peter wasn't that guy. He wasn't the guy who dated for some casual fun. He was the guy who went all in. He was the guy every mother wanted for her daughter because he was honorable. He wouldn't play around and carelessly break someone's heart.

And she couldn't deny that he was right. In the haze of blazing attraction, she might like to think that she could be all understanding and tolerant of his beliefs, but she knew that when it really mattered, she wouldn't. She'd get annoyed. She'd get frustrated. Resentful. Eventually it would poison everything.

And that was before the guilt got to be too much and she would be forced to look him in the eye and tell him that she used to be Mia Caldwell. That she was the reporter responsible for his cousin's death. And then he wouldn't just leave her. He would hate her for the rest of his life.

Outside of her friendship with Allie, knowing Peter was one of the best things about her life in Oxford. It was too important to sacrifice trying to pursue something that might feel good in the short term but ultimately would end in heartache.

"Couldn't we just . . . ?" He was waiting for her to finish her question. Thankfully, he seemed to have no idea what she was going to say next.

"Stay friends?" Emelia said.

There was nothing she wanted less. There was nothing she wanted more.

"Stay friends."

For the first time, Peter understood what Dickens

meant when he penned the line *It was the best of times, it was the worst of times.*

He could no more imagine his life without Emelia than he could imagine it without rowing. But the reality—that what he desperately wanted with her would never happen—was brutal. He was going to need some space. Despite all his lofty words, the truth was that when he was around her, most of his reasons flew out of his mind.

The fact that he'd managed to utter them coherently, that she'd seemed to understand what he was trying to say, was pretty much a miracle.

Emelia bit her bottom lip. "Just so we're clear. If I were . . . If I believed like you do . . ."

Peter's fingers curled around the edge of the couch cushion. "If there's one thing I've learned in my life, it's that no one can find God for someone else. They can only find Him for themselves. My biggest hope is that you do find Him. But you have to do it for you. Not for me. Not for anything we might have."

That was optimistic. There was such a lack of single Christian girls in this town that the minute Emelia came through the doors of any church, she'd find herself swarmed by guys.

A horrible, selfish part of him hoped it never happened for exactly that reason. If they ever shared the same faith, she'd soon discover her new dating pool held options far superior to a failed wannabe rower whose current best claim to greatness was *almost* being an Olympian. It would only be a matter of time before he lost her.

He felt like the world's biggest heel that the thought had even entered his consciousness. But there it was. A tiny part of him wanted things to stay the way they were because at least then he'd still have her in his life, even if it wasn't how he wanted. Because a voice inside him told him that the minute she found God, she'd also realize she was way out of his league.

Thirty-One

"Hi, Emelia speaking." Emelia wedged her phone against her ear as she mouthed *just a sec* to Allie, who had just entered her office. Clicking her mouse, she set her computer to shut down.

"Oh, thank goodness. I was beginning to think I was never going to get you!" Lacey's breathy tones came down the line, the words tumbling over each other. Her cousin spoke at the same speed she lived her life in general.

"Sorry. Have you been trying to get ahold of me?" Emelia glanced at the unfamiliar number on her screen before realizing that it wasn't going to show any missed calls while she had a call open. Knowing her luck, if she tried to play with the screen to see, she'd hang up on Lacey.

"Have I been trying to get ahold of you? Only for like the last week."

"Oh, was that you?" She'd had a few missed calls from a blocked number, but since no one had bothered to leave a message, she'd assumed it was a telemarketer or someone equally exciting. "Why didn't you leave a message?"

Her cousin blew out a blast of air. "You know I hate voice mail. So, what are you up to this weekend?"

"Not much. More ball stuff." She and Peter needed to take a trip out to his parents' to measure the entrance to the ballroom for the wardrobe. Their first decent amount of time together since the excruciating conversation in his living room.

"Fancy some company?"

"Um, what?" Something started dawning. "Hold on. Where are you?"

"Right now? London. I'm over for the week for work. But tonight I'm going to catch the train and come to Oxford for the weekend. Surprise! I've already looked at the timetable, and I can catch a six fifty from Paddington and get into Oxford at seven fifty."

"Oh, wow." Which were not the words going through her mind, but it was all irrelevant. Her date with destiny was coming for her.

"So, can you pick me up or should I catch a cab somewhere?"

"Um . . ." Emelia was left fumbling. "I'll have

to check and get back to you. Is this the number you're using?"

"Yup. Okay, see you tonight! I'm *so* excited."

"Me too!" Emelia tried to imbue her voice with some enthusiasm. Her cousin knew she hated surprises. That was partly why Lacey loved springing them on her. She closed the call and dropped her phone into her bag.

"Is everything okay? You look a bit stunned."

Emelia startled. For a second she'd forgotten Allie was there.

"My cousin Lacey is in London. She's coming to stay for the weekend." Oh, heck. She hadn't even checked with Allie. "I mean, she doesn't need to stay with us. She can get a hotel or something."

"Don't be silly!" Allie tucked a stray piece of auburn hair behind her ear. "If she doesn't mind taking the couch tonight, she can have my bed tomorrow while I'm in Cambridge."

"Thanks. That would be great." As much as Emelia loved her cousin, she wasn't offering to share her bed. She needed her personal space while she slept.

"What's she doing in London?" Allie asked the question as they exited the offices, Emelia locking the door behind her as the last staff member leaving for the weekend.

"No idea. She's a publicist. Mainly books and movies. Does a lot of jet-setting." She should warn Allie what was coming at her. "She looks like Malibu Barbie and she plays on it, but she's one of the smartest people that I know. Any chance I can borrow your car to pick her up?"

Allie's face fell. "Oh, I'm sorry. It's in getting some work done. We were going to pick it up in the morning before dropping me at the station."

"Of course. Sorry, slipped my mind. I'll call Lacey and give her an address and she can just catch a cab."

"Well, if she's related to you, I'm sure I'll love her. I'm looking forward to learning all sorts of things about Emelia before Oxford."

Allie said the words lightheartedly, but they had the force of a brick. Lacey knew all about Mia, and she had no idea of the lengths to which Emelia had gone to cover her tracks in Oxford. All it would take was one wrong sentence over the next two days and everything she had worked so hard to leave behind would be undone.

She had to get to her before Allie did.

By the time seven thirty rolled around, Emelia was almost hyperventilating. She was sure she'd also developed a nervous twitch, not that Allie appeared to have noticed.

"I think I might grab a cab and go meet Lacey at the station. Just to make sure she doesn't get lost or anything."

Lacey would have laughed in her face if she'd

overheard. For a start, someone mute and blind could still manage to find a cab at the train station and hand over Allie's address. Secondly, her cousin had once driven in Italy without a map and knowing no Italian and successfully navigated to find their destination. But it was the best Emelia could come up with since Allie's car was out of commission.

"Okay. By the time you're back, the brownie will be done." Allie didn't look remotely suspicious of Emelia's transparent ruse, which took some tension out of her shoulders. Her roommate added a handful of chocolate chunks to the mix, gave it a stir, and then started transferring the dark brown batter to a tin.

"Okay, great. I'll just give them a call now and get them to pick me up—" Emelia was interrupted by the sound of knocking on the door.

Emelia jammed her phone into her pocket, marched through the hall to the front door, prepared to tell whoever was selling or proselytizing on the other side she wasn't interested.

Unlocking the door, she pulled it open and promptly felt all the air leak from her lungs. There stood her cousin in all her blond, long-legged, trendy glory.

"Surprise!" Lacey flung her hands up in the air. "I caught an earlier train."

Emelia just stared at her, openmouthed, no sound coming out.

"Are you going to let me in?" Lacey pushed the door open wider with a perfectly manicured finger as she spoke and hefted a small travel case behind her. Her slender legs were encased in black leather boots up to her knees. Emelia could tell with one glance they probably cost more than she earned in a week. She closed the door behind Lacey with a thump.

"Is that your cousin?" Allie's voice came from the kitchen.

"Um, yes. She took an early train." Emelia tried to force her voice to come out normally, but she obviously didn't manage entirely because Lacey quirked an inquiring eyebrow at her.

Her palms were damp. She wiped them down the front of her jeans. All it would take was one sentence from her cousin and the life she'd built here would be over. She swallowed, her mouth dry.

"Lace, that's Allie, my roommate." She dropped her voice to a whisper. "She doesn't know anything about Mia."

Her cousin's brow wrinkled. "What are you talking about?"

"I'm Emelia here. They don't know about what I used to do. Who I used to be. Any of it."

Lacey's eyes boggled. "Are you telling me that you are working at Anita's charity and they have no idea who you are? Oh my gosh."

She had like five seconds before Allie came looking for them. "I'll fill you in later."

"What do they know?" Lacey whispered back.

"Um . . ." For a second, Emelia couldn't think of a single thing. "That I love Narnia." It was the first thing that came to mind. Her cousin gave her an incredulous look.

"Hi!" Allie's voice came from behind them. "I'm Allie. Emelia's flatmate." She approached the two of them, wiping her hands on a dish towel.

Lacey immediately pulled out her most charming smile. "Lacey, Emelia's cousin. So sorry to drop in on you unannounced like this. I was in London for work and tomorrow's engagement was canceled so I couldn't miss the opportunity to come and see M— Emelia."

Allie offered a friendly smile. "No worries. I'm afraid it will be the couch tonight, but I'm away tomorrow night so you're welcome to take my room. Come in, come in. I've just put a brownie in the oven."

"Yes, come in." Emelia realized that in her panic she was being rude. "Just leave your bag by the stairs if you want." She watched as Lacey parked her travel case and then led her to the living area. She gestured toward the couch. "Grab a seat. Do you want something to drink?"

"I'm good. I've got some water." Lacey grabbed a large bottle out of her purse, then leaned back and unzipped her boots. "Oh, that's so much better. Those shoes were not made for walking."

"So, you're a publicist?" Allie finished setting the timer on the oven and came over to the couches with a mug.

"Yes. I'm just over pitching some follow-up stories from London Fashion Week for a couple of clients." Lacey levered the boots off her feet using her toes.

"And which side are you cousins on? I'm very jealous. I only have male cousins and we're not particularly close. It wouldn't cross their mind to look me up if they were in the city, let alone the same country."

Lacey's eyes widened toward Emelia.

Emelia jumped in. "Lacey's mom is my father's sister."

She was saved from any further explanation by Allie's phone ringing. Allie glanced at the screen and her face softened. Jackson, apparently. "Excuse me for a few minutes. If the timer goes off, can you get the brownie out?"

Emelia almost sagged from relief. "Of course." The brownie had at least another twenty minutes, so Allie was going to be away for a while. Enough time for Emelia to bring Lacey up to speed.

Allie was already halfway out of the room, phone to her ear. The door closed behind her.

"So, you're Emelia Mason and you love Narnia." Lacey took a slug from her water bottle.

"What? I am and I do."

Her cousin's gaze flicked over her jeans and

cheap sweater. "And why are you dressed like a hobo?"

Emelia checked out her outfit. So it wasn't exactly the designer fare she used to wear, but it wasn't that bad. "I gave most of it away."

Her cousin gagged, a trickle of water dribbling out of her mouth. "You did not."

"I did."

"Louis? Jimmy? Valentino? You kept some, right?" Her cousin said their names like they were orphaned children. Not handbags and shoes and gowns.

"Nope." They were the second thing to go. After her job. After she'd quit—or been fired, depending on who was telling the story—and cleared out her desk, the next stop had been clearing out her wardrobe.

"Not the Birkin." Her cousin's tone was almost begging.

"Yup." That one had been the first to go. The beloved Birkin handbag had been her reward for a year where she'd broken scandals at a ridiculous pace. It was her loudest accuser when the pile of cards she'd constructed her life with came tumbling down.

"You sold them, right? At least made some decent money."

"I didn't. But hopefully Goodwill did." Or not. She didn't actually care. Sometimes she liked to think they had no idea what she'd left on their doorstep in four huge trash bags. It made her smile to imagine a single mom struggling to make ends meet wandering around Walmart with a Birkin worth ten grand that she'd bought for five bucks.

Her cousin let out a strangled cry, then spent a few seconds breathing deeply, blond head in her hands. No doubt trying to find her Zen, or center her chakras, or whatever was the latest fad in such things.

Eventually Lacey lifted her head. "So, you're dressed like you shop at Target and your new friends know nothing about Mia Caldwell. Nothing about your life before you got here. That's how you got the charity job. By hiding your entire past."

Emelia let the first part of her comment slide. "No. And only little bits and pieces."

"I get wanting distance from everything that happened, Meels." Her cousin switched to her childhood nickname. "But divorcing yourself completely? That seems a bit unnecessary. And, dare I say, unhealthy. Not to mention it has the potential to blow back on you so bad if someone discovers the truth."

She had to make her cousin understand. Get through how critical it was that Lacey didn't blow this for her. "It was totally necessary. They wouldn't have hired me if they knew. And I need to do this, I need to try and make something right. It's only for a few more months. I'm not Mia anymore. I don't want to be related to her. If I could wipe my brain of her existence entirely, I would. She's finished. Over." She didn't even try to keep the desperation out of her voice.

Her cousin contemplated her with a troubled gaze. "You can't just delete years of your life."

"Maybe not. But I sure can try."

Thirty-Two

Peter stared at his phone as he pulled up in front of Allie and Emelia's house. The text had just arrived a few seconds earlier.

Surprise visit from cousin. She's coming with. Try not to ogle.

What on earth was that supposed to mean?

Jogging up the front path, he rapped on the door. Within a few seconds, he heard footsteps and the door was thrown open.

He held up his phone. "Wh—" The words froze in his mouth as he realized it wasn't Emelia standing in front of him but a tall, willowy blonde. A very attractive one.

She peered at his screen. "'Try not to ogle.' Oh, isn't she classy." She thrust out a hand. "You must be Peter. I'm Lacey. Said cousin and gate-crasher. I would say I've heard all about you, but I'll be honest, all I know is that you and she are involved in planning this high-society ball."

Peter managed to find his voice. "Peter Carlisle. And that pretty much covers all the basics."

Lacey studied him. "I feel like I know you from somewhere."

"I used to do some rowing." Just saying it felt like something jammed in his throat.

"Hmmmm." She appeared unconvinced. "Maybe."

Well, she certainly couldn't be mistaking him for Victor and his paparazzi-attention-seeking ways. One of the many benefits of looking nothing like his brother.

"I wish I could say I know more about you too, but, honestly . . ." He pocketed the incriminating screen. "That message is all I've got." It reinforced how little he knew about Emelia's background. Had she ever mentioned a cousin before?

"So, what's the plan for the day?" Lacey asked just as Emelia appeared at the top of the stairs.

"We're heading to my family's estate to take some measurements for some of the fit-out for the ball. We're planning to hold it there."

Lacey raised an eyebrow. "Gosh, that sounds very fancy. Are you like a duke or something?"

Might as well tell her. It would be obvious as soon as they got to the house anyway. "I'm not. But my—"

"Okay, we're good. Let's go." His sentence was cut off by Emelia, who was almost tripping down the stairs in her haste to get to the bottom. Tension radiated off her whole body, a sharp contrast to Lacey's relaxed demeanor. Odd. And he wasn't the only one who noticed. Lacey gave Emelia a scrutinizing look as she picked up a bottle of water from the hall table.

Emelia didn't seem to notice as she picked her bag up off the floor and pulled some keys out. They all stepped outside as Emelia closed the door.

Lacey turned to him. "Did you say your surname is Carlisle?"

"I did." Was it his imagination or did Emelia freeze for a second mid–key turn?

"Not related to Victor Carlisle at all?"

Peter tensed. "He's my brother."

Something crossed Lacey's face. Like pieces of a jigsaw were falling into place. *Don't tell me she somehow had the misfortune to meet Victor when he was in the States last year.*

"Do you know him?" If she was another of Victor's conquests, what could he do? Take her back to the estate? Introduce her to the parents of the guy who'd no doubt gotten whatever he wanted and then tossed her aside like a toy?

Lacey fiddled with the lid of her water bottle before raising her chin. "Not personally, no. So, Anita Van Rees was your cousin?"

Anita's name appearing out of nowhere took him by as much surprise as if she'd suddenly punched him. Maybe more. "She was."

Sympathy shadowed Lacey's eyes. "I'm so sorry for your loss. Anita had great potential."

"Did you know her?" It felt like his feet were glued to the porch. He couldn't have moved if he tried.

"I'm a publicist. Our paths crossed a few times back in the US. Charity events, things like that." Lacey looked at Emelia. "You never mentioned you were working with Anita's cousin on this ball."

"Didn't I?" Emelia's words were nonchalant, but not her big round eyes. Her face was ashen. Weirdly, Lacey's resembled a rolling thunderstorm. Something told him he was chauffeuring an impending storm. He just didn't know why.

"Have you lost your mind!" Lacey added an expletive at the end of her sentence. Then a couple more in case Emelia had missed the first one. Her cousin had her hands on her hips and was unafraid to get in her face. She was so close, she was almost on Emelia's toes.

Emelia had spent a car ride, a tour of the estate, and a couple of hours working through ball details with Peter's mom trying to pretend her cousin wasn't lasering her with her eyes. But her luck had run out when Lacey had sweetly asked if there was somewhere they could freshen up before lunch and practically frog-marched Emelia to the fancy bathroom they'd been directed to.

Emelia leaned back against the porcelain sink to try to regain some personal space. She wrapped her fingers around the cool rim. "I didn't know who Peter was. I only found out when he brought me here when we were location hunting."

Her cousin huffed a breath of incredulity in her face. "C'mon, Meels. You're smarter than that. You used to be a freaking award-winning reporter. It never crossed your mind to think that Peter Carlisle might be related to the Honorable Victor Carlisle?"

"No. Because I never thought of Victor by his last name. I thought of him as Victor, heir to the Viscount Downley. That's the title he threw around all over town."

Lacey ran her hands through her hair, leaving it all tousled, and not in a trendy, sexy way. "I cannot believe this. I cannot believe *you*."

"You were fine with me leaving Mia behind last night. You got it!"

"That was before I knew you were having some kind of *thing* with Anita's cousin under your new nom de plume!"

"We're not having a *thing*."

"Oh, c'mon. The national grid is about to call and ask for its electricity back. Are you seriously trying to tell me you two haven't even kissed?" Emelia's silence had her cousin just staring at her. "Seriously?"

"Just once! And it was a mistake. And we've

talked about it and it won't happen again. There's no thing and there won't be a thing. That's all been well established."

"Why not?" Her cousin finally took a step back, giving Emelia a little room to breathe.

"Because he's religious."

Lacey scrunched up her face. "So what? I've dated a few religious types. Remember Aaron? He was Jewish. Then Brad. He was a Scientologist. That was a bad move though. Don't ever date a guy who believes in a drug-free, silent birth."

"It's more than just a set of rules for him. Like, it's a real thing. He won't date someone who doesn't believe the same as he does."

"And you don't think that's something you might want to consider?" This from a girl who considered a new Prada bag a spiritual experience.

"Lacey. I'm not getting religion for a guy." Emelia had done some underhanded things in her life, but she certainly wasn't going to add faking a belief in God to it. Though she had a sense that even if she tried, Peter would see right through it. It would have to be real or not at all. And, even if she'd wanted to believe, real wasn't an option. If God even existed, it was for people like Allie and Jackson and Peter. Not people like her.

"I didn't suggest you do. I'm just saying that, you know, there might be something in it worth considering if it's that important to him. He's a great guy. Which brings me back full circle to, have you lost your mind?"

"What do you want me to say to him, Lace? 'Oh, hey, Peter. Remember that cousin of yours who died? I'm the reporter who drove her to kill herself.' "

Lacey paced the small room from one floral wall to the other. "He will find out one day. Karma kind of bites you like that."

"He's it, Lace. He and Allie and Jackson are the best friends I have here. They're the best friends I've had in years. If I tell them that, I've got nothing. I won't even have a house to live in." Even Allie, the nicest person on earth, wouldn't want anything to do with her if the truth came out.

"What about Victor? Surely you'll run into him sooner or later. Doesn't he live around here? He's Peter's *brother*. I need a Xanax or something." Lacey started digging through her purse.

"I already have."

Her cousin froze mid-dig. "And?"

"He recognized me but we've come to an agreement." Only because they both held weapons of mutually assured destruction.

Lacey let out a breath with a whoosh. "I've seen you play with fire, but this isn't that. This is a nuclear power plant. How can you do it? How can you be planning all this fund-raising together, with that chemistry the two of you have, and not feel sick keeping this from him?" She pulled a tube of mints from her purse, unraveled it, and shoved one in her mouth.

"It's not like I made her drink. It's not like I put the cocaine up her nose. She did all of those things herself. She made her choices, I just exposed them." It was a line Emelia had used many times to justify her work, and it still rang as hollow as all the others.

Her cousin's steely face told her she wasn't buying it either. The crack as she chomped down hard on her mint said all she needed to.

Emelia pushed herself off the basin. "Of course I hate it. I feel horrible about it. Sometimes it swells up inside me until I feel like I might just vomit it out all over him. But I can't. If I do, he will walk away. Just like everyone else. And then I'm left with nothing. Just like I always am."

Lacey's eyes widened as the ugly, honest words hit the air.

Turning around, Emelia twisted the cold tap on full blast. Putting her hands under the water, she splashed some up on her face, trying to gain herself a few seconds.

Pull it together, Emelia.

She leaned against the sink and watched the water swirl down the drain. Grabbing the hand towel, she pressed it against her face.

"What if he's different?" Lacey's voice was soft and tentative.

Emelia dropped the towel back on the counter

and turned around. "You know how I met him, Lacc?"

"How?"

"I fell out of a wardrobe in an antiques shop and he caught me. Then he asked me if I was a Susan or a Lucy. How am I supposed to tell that guy I'm the person he probably hates most in the world?" She could already see the loathing in his eyes if she told him.

"I don't know. But you have to. Because if you don't, then someway, somehow, he will find out. And there's no coming back from that."

"Is that a Dr. Donna thing?" Dr. Donna was a relationship expert and one of Lacey's most famous clients. Her cousin was a walking record of the woman's sound bites.

Something flickered in her cousin's eyes. "No. It's a Lacey O'Connor thing." Lacey closed the two-step gap between them and took Emelia's shoulders, forcing her to look her in the eye. "I may not be into the whole God thing, but even I know the truth always comes out eventually. And that guy out there, he deserves to know the truth. From you."

Thirty-Three

She was responsible for Anita's death. And saving her charity was the closest thing she could think of to atonement. If it weren't for those two facts, Emelia would have been out. Done. Gone.

Emelia stabbed a piece of cake with her fork. Mashed it between the prongs. She'd tried to convince herself it didn't matter. That her life as Mia Caldwell was behind her. That Emelia Mason was all that mattered. And Emelia Mason hadn't done anything wrong. But there wasn't a single cell in her body that was letting her believe it. Especially since Lacey had called her out.

It was good they had the religion thing between them. She could hide behind that without any difficulty. Her gaze lingered on Peter's broad back as he stood at the counter of the boutique bakery, ordering another dessert.

His Olympic dreams and decency and faith were far too good for her. She'd been foolish to ever hope there might be a possibility of anything different. But now she'd had a cold dose of reality.

Not even Peter would be able to forgive her for what she'd done. What she'd cost him. His family. There was no God big enough to conquer that.

Every time she saw him, a loud, insistent voice nagged at her, telling her she needed to tell him the truth. No matter how much she tried to muffle it, it refused to stay silent. It felt like she had a tumor inside her, growing and growing.

She just had to get through the next four months of planning this ball, and then it would be over. Her job would be done. She'd resign. Probably leave Oxford.

"So, are you going to tell me what's going on?" Peter returned to their table as she stabbed the cake again.

Emelia dragged her attention back to what they were supposed to be doing: choosing the two desserts for the sit-down dinner. They should have done it weeks ago, but somehow it had fallen off her color-coded, cross-referenced spreadsheet. "What? Nothing's going on."

"Sure. And you and Reepicheep are best friends."

"Ha. Very funny."

"Is it the cake?" Peter pointed his fork to the sample of black forest layer cake that sat practically untouched on her plate.

"It's a bit dry." Emelia poked at it with her fork and a few crumbs toppled off. She tried to focus on the task at hand. The sooner they got through it, the sooner she could go home, get in her pajamas, and read some Narnia. Maybe *The Voyage of the Dawn Treader*. Right now she could do with sailing off to the ends of the earth.

Speaking of which, hopefully she'd get home to find Jackson had accomplished his mission of finding and retrieving his broken model from wherever Peter had stashed it. She'd found someone who thought they might be able to fix it for her. She just needed to get the thing without Peter's knowing. Just in case it couldn't be done.

She made a show of dipping her fork into a piece of chocolate torte. "This one is better." And it was chocolate. Who wouldn't want a chocolate torte at a ball? In the background the refrigerated cabinets hummed.

She flipped through the folder that sat on the table in front of her. It held pages of all the different desserts the bakery did. The torte and crème brûlée both looked fine. And right now fine was good enough. "I think we go with these two." She pushed the folder toward Peter.

He didn't even look at it. "Have I done something?" The guy wouldn't let it go. Clearly she wasn't as good at pretending as she'd given herself credit for.

"We should split the rest of the list." The words fell out of her mouth. "There's not much left. Divide and conquer and all that." The only things left were confirming arrangements already made and getting Elizabeth to approve the deposits on anything that wouldn't accept credit cards. They didn't need to see each other to work on promotional details.

"No." Peter's voice was firm.

"Excuse me?"

"No. I'm not splitting the list unless you tell me what I've done. I must have done something." He leaned forward on his elbows, pale blue T-shirt stretching across his chest.

"You haven't done anything. It's me, okay? I'm the one who's done everything." The words burst out of her.

"What are you talking about?"

"I'm never going to believe like you do."

"What?" Peter looked at her like he didn't know what the drama was. He forked another piece of torte and popped it in his mouth, not looking the least bit perturbed.

"You keep looking at me with these hopeful eyes, like maybe one day I'm going to wake up miraculously converted, and it's just not going to happen. I'm so glad it works for you, but it's just never going to be my thing. I have too much stuff to believe in a good God. I can get a disinterested one. A vengeful one. An ambivalent one. But not a good one. So what's the point?" She gestured like an insane woman with her fork, not even caring that a piece of cake got flung across the room.

"Of?"

"Of this." Emelia gestured to the two of them. "Of just being 'friends.' " She stuck up her fingers to do the air quotes and almost stabbed herself in the side of the head. "We can't pretend we don't have chemistry. Well, maybe you can, but I can't.

I like you and it is *killing* me. I'm planning a ball with the one guy I want and can't have. But at the same time I think he is *insane* for wanting a piece of metal so bad he's willing to spend the rest of his life disabled for a shot at it. If there is a God, I've got to give Him points for the irony of it all."

Peter just stared at her, fork halfway to his mouth.

"You don't know me. If you knew the things I'd done, you'd want nothing to do with me." Emelia's fork smashed into a piece of pastry, grinding it into the plate.

Peter had put his fork down, but his mouth still hung half open.

"What?"

"You're right. There is a lot I don't know about you. And a lot you don't know about me. I wish you trusted me enough to tell me. But there is nothing that you could have done that would make me want to have nothing to do with you." His eyes shone with certainty and conviction.

"You have no idea what you're talking about." Emelia pushed out her chair and fled.

The chaotic scene played back in Peter's mind as he drove and tried to work out where it had gone so horribly wrong. Emelia had been off since he'd picked her up. Wooden. Stilted. Going through the motions. The dying world of Charn in *The Magician's Nephew* had more life.

It didn't take a psychologist to see the hurt that she was hiding. And he'd stupidly decided to push it, instead of just leaving her be. What she'd said had sliced through him. It didn't matter. It didn't matter how much they liked each other or what chemistry they had. She was right. If she never had a faith of her own it was all for naught.

He forced out a breath and reminded himself of everything. Emelia falling out of the wardrobe. The teacup. All the ways their paths had been forced to cross.

He didn't believe in coincidence. Not at this level. Coincidence was finding a free parking spot. Not this. This was God making a move. Even if Emelia didn't see it that way.

The question was, what was he meant to do? Was he meant to step back and let it all go? Or was he meant to help show her the God who never gives up?

He parked the car and half jogged up the steps to Highbridge. Opening the front door, he strode down the hallways toward the kitchen. He pushed the door open to see his mum standing with her back to him, spooning flour into a rotating bowl. It dusted the air as the beaters caught it and threw some back up.

She jumped at the sound of his entering the room. "Peter. You gave me a fright. Did I forget you were coming today?"

"Would you do it again?"

His mother turned the beaters off. "Would I do what again?"

"Marry Dad."

"That's like asking me to wish my life away. If I hadn't married your father I wouldn't have you. Or Victor." Not exactly an emphatic statement that she wouldn't change anything.

"But what if you could go back in time. What if there was no me or Victor? Would you marry him again?"

She studied him, her gray eyes processing whatever it was she was reading in his face. "No." The two letters hit him like a pipe bomb. "And the truth is he wouldn't marry me either."

Peter sank into one of the chairs at the small table in the corner of the kitchen.

His mother wiped her hands on a towel, then walked over and pulled out the chair beside him. "Emelia?"

"Yeah." There was no point in pretending.

"Do you love her?"

"I don't know. She just has so much stuff. And she won't let me in to . . ." His words trailed off. To what? To help? To make it better somehow when he didn't even know what it was?

"It's not your job to fix her." His mother's soft words interrupted Peter's train of thought.

"I know that."

"Do you? You have a habit of shouldering the

burden of things that aren't yours to carry. Victor's face. My health. Anita's addictions. Whatever it is that is going on in Emelia's life. Don't get me wrong. I really like her, but you can't fix whatever the wounds are that she bears. There's only one who can do that. And she has to want to let Him."

Peter rubbed his forehead. "I keep trying to distance myself, I do. I know we can't be anything more than friends unless she's a Christian. But, I don't know, it doesn't make sense. I just feel like God has me in her life for a reason."

"I'm sure He does. The question is, are you okay if it's not the reason that you want it to be? Then what?"

"I don't know." He hadn't let himself go there.

"It is the toughest thing in the world to spend your whole life battling with the person you love most on the one thing neither of you can compromise on. I wouldn't wish it on anyone."

"Is it really that bad?" Maybe he'd been kidding himself that his parents had a good marriage.

His mother sighed. "Your father is a good man. And he loves me the best he can. Of course it's not that bad. It's just not as great as it could be. And, for you, I want so much more than what we have. I want the girl you can share your whole life with, not just compartments of it." She gave him a wobbly smile. "Plus, I'm your mum. I don't want to see you get hurt. And Emelia has the potential to break your heart. I've known that since the first day you brought her here."

"And Sabine didn't?" Sabine was the smart choice. She was great. She loved God. She would be the first person to cheer on his comeback. It wouldn't be feckless or selfish to her. Maybe he should just give what they had another chance instead of getting tangled up in something that all the signs suggested had the hallmarks of a disaster.

Emelia didn't believe in God and thought his Olympic desires were crazy. There was no chemistry or fierce hoping in the world that could paper over those canyon-sized cracks.

His mother stared out the window to where, just a couple of weeks before, Emelia had paced out steps to work out how many outdoor lights they would need for the ball. "You never looked at Sabine the way you look at Emelia."

Over his mother's shoulder, he could see the large family sideboard. Inside the glass-fronted top cupboard sat her collection of Aynsley teacups. The latest addition sat front and center.

He felt the desperate need to grab on to something, anything. "The teacup was in the wardrobe."

"Pardon?" His mother's brow wrinkled.

"The teacup I gave you. The one that completed your set. I looked for it for ten years. It was in the same wardrobe that Emelia fell out of when we met. The day before your birthday. Surely that means something."

"I suspect it means that God is pursuing her." She fixed him with a long look. "Make sure you don't get in the way."

Thirty-Four

Going to church with Peter and his mom, followed by lunch with his parents. So much for keeping her distance. All she'd wanted was to cross a few final things off her list that could only be done on location.

"Emelia?" Peter spoke from across the lunch table. "Can you pass the butter?" He gave her a questioning look. It obviously wasn't the first time he'd asked.

"Sorry. In my own world." She picked up the cream ceramic tray beside her plate and handed it to him, holding it at the end so there was no chance of their fingers touching.

Pushing her chair back, she took her and Maggie's plates to the sink. On the way back she paused at the cupboard, looking at the teacups lined up inside it. The one at the front was familiar. "Those are beautiful teacups."

"Peter gave that front one to me for my birthday. He'd been looking for it for years."

"Years?"

Maggie came over from where she'd been serving dessert at the counter and opened the cupboard, pointing to the familiar one with pink roses. "It was the last one I needed to complete my collection. He looked for it for years, then finally found it in an antiques shop the night before my birthday."

Suddenly Emelia remembered where she had seen it. It looked just like the teacup that had been in the wardrobe. She'd forgotten all about it. He'd been looking for it for years? What was going on? She turned to see Peter studying her. "Is that the—"

Somewhere behind her there was a huge thump, followed by a crash.

She glanced around the table, but no one else seemed to have noticed. Then a man yelled, "Over there! No, not there, there."

"Um, do you have guests staying?"

Peter's mother had returned to serving up dessert. Another thump and yell pulled her attention toward the doorway leading to the main parts of the house. "Oh, sorry. We're so used to them, these days we hardly really notice."

Them?

Peter paused buttering his last piece of bread. The guy must have packed away almost half a loaf. "Film crews. Quite a few use the house as a location for period dramas."

Huh. Now it made sense that Highbridge had

seemed familiar back when she'd done some cursory research on Victor. She'd probably seen it on TV once.

Maggie scooped a huge spoonful of pudding into a bowl. "A very handy income stream to have. God bless *Downton Abbey*, and not just for being one of the best shows ever. Since that screened, we've had more business than we could accommodate."

"What's filming today?" Even though she'd spent a decent chunk of her career reporting on movie stars and their scandals, she'd never been on a set. She'd tried to sneak into a few but never quite managed to make it.

Peter's mom thought for a second, her brow rumpling. "Honestly, I couldn't tell you. I'll have it in the booking schedule somewhere. I can go find it if you—"

"Oh, no." Emelia returned to her seat. "Don't go to any trouble."

"Why don't we go have a look after lunch?" Peter suggested.

"Can we?" The two little words somehow managed to betray her excitement.

He shrugged. "Sure. It's our house."

"Thanks, darling," Bill said as Maggie put a huge bowl of apple pudding in front of him. Emelia had completely forgotten he was beside her.

Then an equally huge bowl landed in front of her. The scent of cinnamon and mixed spices warming the air. Oh, wow. She wouldn't need to eat for a week after this.

"Cream." Peter's mom placed an enormous bowl of whipped cream in front of her, the slight tremor of her hand the only sign of the degenerative disease infiltrating her nervous system. Emelia ladled a spoonful into her bowl and waited for Maggie to rejoin the table with her own dish and Peter's.

"Eat while it's hot." Peter gestured to her bowl.

She didn't need to be told twice. Within a second her mouth was filled with sweetness and spice, warmth and cool cream. It was so good she closed her eyes for a second in bliss. "This is possibly the best thing I've ever tasted in my whole life."

"So I see."

She opened her eyes to find Peter staring at her like she was dessert. His expression threatened her resolve to keep her emotional distance.

"Think I might go eat this while I watch the cricket." His father suddenly pushed back his chair and reached his spoon across her, scooping up some cream and dumping it over his pudding in one smooth motion.

"I'll join you." Maggie hadn't even put Peter's bowl on the table yet but followed her husband out of the room, carrying her own.

She had never seen two middle-aged people move so fast. Was it something she'd said?

Peter pushed back his chair and went to claim his dessert as if nothing out of the ordinary had just happened. "Would you like anything else to drink while I'm up?" He asked the question while helping himself to a few more generous spoonfuls from the serving dish.

"No. Thanks."

Peter put his bowl down opposite her and sat back down. It was piled so high, she was sure anything he added would slide down the slopes and onto the table.

"What did you think of the service today?" He asked the question cautiously, as if half expecting to find himself on another emotional landmine.

She moved her spoon through her bowl. She'd only gone because every time she saw him she felt so riddled with guilt that suffering through a church service seemed like a small penance to pay. "It was different from what I expected."

"How so?"

"Quieter. More . . . peaceful." She'd been braced for some kind of long thundering sermon that made her feel even more condemned than she already did. Instead, a soft-spoken woman with blond hair had talked for all of fifteen minutes about the Good Samaritan. She still felt off balance from the experience. Church not being what she'd expected, braced herself for, created more questions than answers.

She'd sat next to Peter's mother and spent half

the service wondering what Maggie would do if she had any idea she was sitting next to the girl who had a role in the death of her niece. A sermon featuring a vengeful God would have been welcome. That was what she deserved. She knew what box to put Him in.

"Julianne is a great vicar. Maybe I should go to her for advice on handling career change since she's managed it so well." Peter poured himself some orange juice.

"What did she used to be?"

"A trader in the city. Hedge funds. Crazy money stuff I don't even understand. Really good at it too, from what I hear. One of their biggest earners. Then one day she resigned to go to seminary."

Emelia almost choked on her first mouthful of pudding. "No way."

"Yes way. This is her first vicarage posting."

"How do you go from being a London trader to a vicar? How does that even happen?"

"God." He said the word easily. Like it was a simple explanation. Rather than the three most complicated letters in the universe.

Emelia had been as prickly as a hedgehog when they'd gone to church. Like she was expecting to be set upon at any moment from all directions. But as the service had continued, she'd seemed to relax. Unless it was optimism clouding his perception.

Peter cobbled together a mangled prayer as he loaded the dishwasher, not sure how to phrase what he wanted to say. He knew Emelia couldn't find God to make him happy. People had to do it for themselves. He could point her in the right direction, light the path with flashing runway lights, but he couldn't walk the path for her, no matter how much he wanted to.

Make sure you don't get in the way.

His mother's words rang in his ears. If only he knew what they meant. This was why he was good at rowing. You made a plan. You executed the plan. He wasn't good without a plan.

"Okay, I'm good." Emelia came back into the kitchen. She'd gone to wash her face after practically licking her pudding bowl clean. The woman could inhale food at both a quantity and a speed that would make her fit in perfectly with any rowing team.

"Great. I'm almost done." He rinsed the last remaining plates under warm water and added them to the appliance. Tried to relax. Which was impossible around her. "Did I tell you I ordered the chocolate torte and crème brûlée?"

"Good choice."

"Yup." He closed the dishwasher and turned the wash cycle on. "Okay." He grabbed a tea towel and wiped his hands. "Shall we go and see what the interlopers are up to?"

Emelia laughed. "Interlopers?"

He shrugged. "Having your home as a set loses its appeal after the first few times. Especially when they're filming at all hours of the day and night."

Peter opened the door to the hall leading to the main wing and ushered her through.

"Such a hard life you lead." She grinned up at him, and he longed to run his fingers through her hair. He settled instead for a playful tug on the end of her ponytail, like he was twelve.

Opening the door at the end of the hall, they stepped into a world of bustle. Cameras and lights were being moved all over the place. People traversed the space with purpose. A few director chairs lay scattered around. Peter took a quick glance. From the look of things, they were preparing to film in the main entryway and the parlor. In both rooms, people were busily arranging furniture, setting out props, and taking light readings.

There were no actors to be seen—they were still in makeup or costuming—meaning Peter and Emelia had a little time to look around before they'd be in the way.

They stood for a few seconds watching the swarm.

"What do you think they're filming?" Emelia's gaze followed a middle-aged woman cutting through the room holding a stack of papers.

"Looks like something set in the twenties." He

gestured at a set of fringed flapper dresses being wheeled past.

"Do you think we might be able to watch some filming?"

"Maybe. If we stay out of their way." He almost added "and if it's soon" because he wanted to get home at a decent time, but one look at her shining eyes sealed his mouth. He'd be here all afternoon if being able to watch a few minutes of filming would keep the excitement on her face.

"Let's go see what's happening in the parlor." Grabbing her hand, he weaved them between people into the other room. It was more set up in here—cameras and screens placed, the space where they were all focused immaculate.

Someone rushed past them, bumping Emelia, so that she was thrown against his chest. He grabbed her under her elbows to steady her. "You okay?"

"Fine, thanks." But she kept standing there, gazing up at him.

Peter couldn't stop himself. His fingers ran lightly down her arms. When they reached her hands, her fingers curled around his.

He tried to drag in a breath, find a rational thought, but everything dimmed in comparison to the girl standing in front of him staring at him like he was her whole world.

Something flickered in her eyes as he reached a hand up and ran his thumb across her cheek.

"So, we should, um . . ." She stepped back and

started to turn away. He felt himself sag with disappointment.

The next thing he knew, she'd spun back again, wrapped her arms around his neck, and pulled him down, leaning against him as her lips found his.

For a split second he didn't move, then his arms slid around her waist, his hands running up and down her back as he leaned into the kiss. All reason fled his brain. All that remained was the feeling of Emelia cradled against his chest.

"Wow." After a few seconds, she pulled back, both of them breathless.

He didn't say anything. Just stood there.

Emelia peered over her shoulder. He looked too. In all the hustle of the room, no one seemed to have noticed them.

She grabbed his hand. "Let's go."

He blinked. "You don't want to stay and watch some filming?"

"Nah. I'm good." She shot him the kind of smile that almost had him pulling her into his arms for an encore performance. But she tugged at his hand and started striding toward the door that would take them back into the hallway.

He tried to catch his breath as he followed her. He knew he should be sorry. Except he wasn't. Not at all.

What had she done? Emelia tried to keep the thought at bay as she dragged Peter back through the main foyer, past the safety of the door they'd entered from.

Once again, her need to poke her nose into things had screwed up everything. She and Peter had managed to find their way to some kind of even keel and she'd gone and ruined it all again.

The whole morning she'd held herself together, managed to resist the pull of his appeal. She had been turning around to walk away.

And then it had all collapsed like a sandcastle hit by a rogue wave.

Her stomach still felt curdled from the moment she'd turned around and seen Jude using his trademark smile on a simpering production assistant.

In that second, she'd forgotten that she wasn't Mia. That she didn't look anything like her. That Jude wouldn't even glance her way for a moment because he was all about blondes, and he'd never in a million years have had any reason to think his most-hated reporter would be here. Especially when she was a wavy-haired brunette in the middle of the English countryside on his movie set.

But in that moment when she thought Jude would see her, and destroy everything, she'd done the only thing she could think of. She'd turned around and laid one on Peter like she meant it. Which she did. Every single part of her.

And now she was in the world's stupidest mess,

all because she hadn't kept her wits about her. She'd lost her ability to keep her cool under pressure, something she'd been known for in LA.

"Emelia." She barely heard Peter as she kept barreling down the hall, not wanting to stop or deal with what had just happened. "Emelia!"

"What?" She dared to look up at him.

Peter smiled and it almost undid her. "Is there a fire somewhere I should know about?"

Emelia sucked in a breath, forcing herself to slow down. "No. Sorry."

"Was it that bad?"

"What?"

"Was the kiss so bad that you need to flee?"

"No." The kiss was . . . perfect. But it wasn't like she could exactly tell him why it had happened. That she'd seen a movie star who'd had a target on her head ever since she'd flirted with him in a nightclub and gotten him on record propositioning her while his wife was two blocks away in the hospital with their one-day-old daughter.

She wasn't one bit sorry his marriage had subsequently broken up and his ex-wife had taken him to the cleaners in the divorce. The guy was a grade-A creep.

"Thanks. Your fulsome denial was very reassuring."

"It was fine."

"Fine." Peter's eyebrows ratcheted up a notch.

"You've got real skills in making a guy feel good. Has anyone ever told you that?" He stepped closer, a dangerous glint in his eye. "It was much better than fine and you know it."

Emelia stepped back, bumping against the wall at the end of the hallway. Trapped between the wall and the guy she had a huge crush on, who was advancing on her with intent written all over his face. In any other situation it would have been the best thing ever.

"Now you've got two choices." Peter leaned his arms on the wall, a hand on either side of her head.

"Yes?" She hated that her voice was all breathy, like some damsel in a soap opera.

"You can either admit that it was more than fine, or . . ."

"Or?"

"I can refresh your memory."

Oh.

"Which will it be?" He moved one hand down to loop a strand of her hair around his finger, twirling it like he had all the time in the world.

She couldn't breathe. His green eyes drilled into hers. Her knees felt like they were melting. She was a cliché, every female stereotype she'd ever mocked.

You're never going to be good enough for him. Even if he never finds out the truth, one day he will still leave you. Just like everyone else.

The thought ripped through her head with the power of a nuclear bomb.

Before she could rethink it, give in to what she really wanted to do, she planted both hands on his chest and shoved. Hard.

Peter stumbled back, almost falling.

"What do you think you're doing?" Emelia pushed herself off the wall.

"I . . ." He stared at her, speechless.

"Is this some kind of game to you?"

"No." He grabbed a breath. "Of course not."

She summoned up her death stare. "You've told me that I'm not good enough for you. That I never will be as long as I don't believe in the big guy in the sky. You know how I feel about you. You know that every time I'm around you it's torture. So, what are you doing? Do you like messing with me? Get some kind of kick out of taunting me with what I can't have?" She ignored that she had kissed him first. That had been by accident. Sort of. But this, his tormenting her with what she couldn't have, was on purpose.

His face had whitened, the freckles standing out. He reached out toward her arm, then stopped. "I'm so sorry. I never . . . I would never . . . You're right. That wasn't right. You deserve better. Will you forgive me?"

He deserved better. He just had no idea how much. "We're done here. Take me home."

Thirty-Five

What had gotten into him, pulling a stunt like that? Frustration bubbled up inside him as he stormed down the hall of his flat. And Emelia had called him on it. Rightly so. Peter felt sick remembering the stricken look on her face as she'd pushed him away.

The drive back to Oxford had been an hour of strained silence.

He checked the time. A couple of hours left of daylight. Maybe enough time to get out for a row if he moved fast. After this afternoon, he needed some punishment in the boat—body screaming, lungs burning, hands bleeding. It didn't matter whether his shoulder could take it or not. There was no time to ponder all the ways your life was stuffed when you were trying to suck in enough air to stay conscious.

He pushed open the living-area door with enough force that it hit the wall with a crack.

"Nice to see you too." Jackson sat on one of the couches, a plate of food in his lap and sports blaring on TV.

"Sorry. Didn't think you'd be here."

Jackson shrugged. "Allie had a baby shower for a girl from church." He shoveled some crisps into his mouth and kept speaking around them.

The guy had the physique of a professional athlete and the eating habits of a three-hundred-pounder. "Missed you at the service this morning."

Peter headed for the kitchen and pulled a bottle of water out of the fridge. "Went home for lunch. I went to church with Mum."

"And Emelia." It was a statement, not a question.

"We had some ball stuff to do."

Jackson nodded. "So, how's that working out?"

"What?"

Jackson picked up the remote and turned down the volume. "Playing with fire."

"It's not. We're not. She's not . . ." Peter stopped talking. He didn't even know what he was trying to say.

"Not what? Attracted to each other? Because you'd have to be as thick as the Great Wall to expect anyone to believe that."

"It's complicated."

"It always is." Jackson shoveled some crisps into his mouth.

"What's that supposed to mean?"

"Just tread carefully, buddy. I don't want to see either of you getting hurt."

It was a bit late for that. The pain in Emelia's face as she'd shoved him away was etched in his mind.

"Sometimes you have to do the hard thing to do the right thing. If it's meant to be, God will work it out. Remember, I walked away from Allie. Then I let her walk away from me. Almost killed me both times."

"I'm going for a row." He knew that Jackson was right, but he didn't want to hear it. He'd already been forced to let go of one dream in the last year. Surely that was enough.

Peter strode down the hall, grabbing his already prepared kit bag off the floor. Pulling open the door, he halted, not entirely sure he should believe what he was seeing. Emelia stood on his front porch, a purple cardigan pulled around her and hair blowing in the wind.

"Hi." It had been three hours since they'd kissed.

"Hi." She shifted on her feet. "Have you got a minute?"

"Um, sure." He dropped his kit bag back on the floor, gestured toward the porch. "Want to sit?" After their conversation he didn't particularly want Jackson to hear this. He stepped out, closed the door behind him.

"Sure."

They both lowered themselves down onto the top step, leaving a good couple of feet between them.

"I'm really sorry about today."

"It's okay." She turned toward him; a sad smile crossed her face as she wrapped her arms around her torso. "It's my fault. I was the one who kissed you."

Like that was going to make him feel better about being such a cad. "It's killing me too. But the other way? It would just kill both of us slowly."

"I know." Emelia said the words with quiet resignation as she craned her neck up at him. "I never asked you how your latest scans went."

Peter ran his fingers along the banister beside him. "My shoulder's healing, but not as fast as we'd hoped."

"What does that mean for you?"

"A return to competitive rowing is possible, but it will be a long road." He tried to push the specialist's other warning out of his head. That if he tore his shoulder up again, it wouldn't be a question of rowing, it would be a question of whether he would just have normal function.

"Guess it's a good thing you're the type of guy who believes in miracles, then."

Did he? He didn't know anymore. His miracle was supposed to be a podium finish. It had been his goal since he was a teenager. Instead, he was a barely employed coach. Sean didn't really need him for the Boat Race next year. He'd call any day now to confirm it.

Everything in him had been focused on the Olympics . . . yet he couldn't see his way clear to try again. The early mornings, the soul-destroying agony, not knowing if this time it would be enough. Or if he'd fail, again. Just like he'd failed

Anita. "What if I'm not good enough? Or I totally ruin my shoulder like you said?"

"But what if you are? I know that I haven't exactly been falling over myself with enthusiasm for you trying to make a comeback, but you love rowing. I see it in your eyes whenever you talk about it."

"I do love rowing. But to get to the Olympics, it has to be more than love. It has to be an obsession. I know plenty of rowers with more talent, more ability, more everything than I've ever had. The only thing they lacked was the overwhelming desire."

"What do you mean?"

Peter studied the blue, cloudless sky, the warm, late July air seeping into his skin. "When it's five in the morning and you're rowing in the sleet and your hands are bleeding and blue, that's the only thing that matters. How much you want it. Whether your hunger is deep enough and strong enough to push you past everything else. I don't know if I still have that. What if it's more about wanting to try and do right by Anita?" Which was crazy. The same way that he knew Emelia couldn't find God for him, he knew he couldn't risk destroying his shoulder to attempt to keep a promise to his dead cousin.

"What do you mean?" Emelia's voice cracked a little as she wrapped her arms around her knees. How could she be cold? It was a perfect summer's day.

"She was my biggest supporter. She could've been an amazing rower. She *was* an amazing rower. But then she fell in with the wrong crowd at university. Started drinking. Doing drugs. As much as she tried, she couldn't seem to dig herself out. Not that you'd ever have known if you'd met her. She always said that I would win the gold for both of us." That was the last thing she had ever said to him. That she knew he could still do it.

"I'm sorry."

He stared across the street. A blue Nissan was pulling out of the driveway opposite. Somewhere a child laughed. "The night she died, she called. But I didn't pick up. I was feeling sorry for myself. I'd had a couple of scans that week and the results weren't good. And it seemed like she had finally gotten it together. Found a great guy. Gotten clean. Started SpringBoard. I didn't want to play along with her positivity about me making some great comeback. So I just let it go to voice mail. I was going to call her back in the morning. But by then it was too late."

Emelia had tears in her eyes. "Peter, it's not your fault. You are not responsible for what happened to her."

Easy for her to say. He might have been able to save his cousin and he didn't. No one was ever going to convince him otherwise.

• • •

Emelia had to tell him. She'd felt guilty enough as it was but now, knowing he blamed himself? She couldn't walk away from this without saying anything.

Maybe he'd understand. He obviously knew what it felt like to live under the cloud of self-condemnation. The slump of his shoulders and the strain on his face said more than words ever could.

He'd still be angry, upset, need some time to calm down. But for the first time she felt a glimmer of hope that maybe, once the initial shock wore off, he might not hate her. He understood what it was to live under the blame for something horrible.

So maybe somehow, when the dust had settled, he'd find a way to forgive her. Or maybe he'd hate her even more. Maybe he'd take all the condemnation he'd been carrying around and heap it on her. Maybe tomorrow she'd be without a job, a place to live, and some of the best people who had ever happened to her.

"Peter, there's something I need to tell you." She curled her fingers around the rim of the step, pressed her palms into the wood of the porch. *You can do this, Emelia. He has to know the truth.*

Peter looked into the distance, didn't give any sign that he'd even heard her.

Memories overcame her. The strength of his

arms when she fell out of the wardrobe. Dancing with him in the pub. Kissing him. Spinning around with his crazy cat attached to her head.

In a few seconds none of those things would be what he thought of when he thought of her. Emelia would be gone.

"Peter?"

He turned to her with a fierce expression. "How do those people live with themselves?"

"Who?"

"The bottom-feeding lowlifes who call themselves reporters. I'm the first to admit that Anita wasn't perfect, that she'd made some mistakes, but destroying her life? Just for a scoop? Who does that?"

Emelia opened her mouth. But nothing came out. Instead tears formed behind her eyes. She did. She had.

"She was only twenty-four." Peter's jaw clenched. "Lost. What is wrong with people that we take such pleasure in witnessing other people's downfalls? That entire industries exist to exploit someone else's pain and publicly humiliate them?"

"I'm sure the reporter had no idea what Anita would do. I'm sure she would give anything she had for it all to be different."

"No she doesn't." He said the words with complete certainty.

"How do you know that?"

Peter ran his hand through his hair. "Because she's still there. Still bar-crawling. Still preying on people. Still breaking the same sleazy stories."

Emelia just stared at him, mouth hanging open. *She was what?*

Thirty-Six

Emelia pulled her coat around her as she walked out of the Eagle and Child. Peter's revelation on his porch had been the thing that had finally broken her nine-month Google fast.

All it had taken was a few seconds to work out what he was talking about. She was no longer reporting, but Mia Caldwell still was. Her ex-boss was still using her byline. There was a different photo, but it was of a blond girl who looked similar enough that the average person probably wouldn't notice any difference.

Though discovering the truth had taken only a few clicks, finding the courage for her second attempt at telling him had taken weeks. Finally, she'd told Peter they needed to go over some final ball details. And as she was the pedantic spreadsheet queen, he hadn't questioned it.

The smart move would be to wait. Tell him after the ball. After she'd handed in her notice. But that was months away, and since the moment on the porch where he'd confessed the weight of blame he'd been carrying around and she had failed to give him the honesty he deserved, she hadn't been able to live with herself.

So she'd sat, in the Eagle and Child for two hours, waiting for him to show up. Checked her phone obsessively. Called him, only for it to go to voice mail. One vodka and soda for courage had turned into two as she'd tried to ignore the pitying gaze of the waitress.

And now she was a little tipsy and vacillating between angry and worried as she paid her bill and stepped outside. She closed the door to the pub behind her and leaned against the stone wall, sucking in a couple breaths of late-summer air. She should've stayed home and helped Allie with the final details of the engagement party that was only a couple of weeks away.

Squaring her shoulders, she pulled out her phone to call a cab. All the anxiety and fear she'd brought into the evening still rolled around inside her with nowhere to go. She began dialing, then turned her phone off and started down the street. It was a nice night. Home was only fifteen minutes away, and it wouldn't get really dark for another half hour or so. Even after a couple of drinks, she could still easily take down anyone stupid enough to try accosting her.

She'd thought the worst that could happen would be if Peter heard what she had to say and said he never wanted to see her again. It had never occurred to her he might not even come.

Emelia walked down the cobbled streets, the warm evening air swirling around her. Up ahead a couple sauntered, arms wrapped around each other, heads close together. They stopped and the woman wrapped her arms around the man's neck.

Emelia crossed the street. She was not in the mood for navigating around a couple making out in the middle of the sidewalk. When she looked up, she realized her feet had taken her to Turl Street, landing her right outside the antiques shop where they'd first met. She leaned against the glass of the second large window, pressing her palms against the cool surface as she peered into the adjacent room. Her wardrobe still stood majestic in the far corner.

Would she have crawled into it if she'd known everything that would follow that one impulsive decision?

Are you a Susan or a Lucy?

His first words to her rang in her ears. She'd flicked the piercing question off with a quick retort. From the first time she'd met him, she'd been deflecting the truth. She was a Susan. She'd always known it, and life had only confirmed it. She would end up alone. Just like Susan had.

"Emelia!" Her head jerked up as Peter's voice cut through the dusk. He was running up the street to her left. What was he doing here? He almost slammed into her as he came to a stop.

"Please tell me you didn't wait for me the whole time." His hair stuck up at all angles off his head. His eyes red rimmed. His navy T-shirt wrinkled. If she hadn't known better she'd have thought he'd been on a bender.

"Of course I did." She huffed out a breath. Waited for his excuse. *Please let it be a good one.*

Peter closed his eyes. "I'm sorry."

"Where were you?" Now that he was clearly okay, anger was gaining dominance over the worry.

"Victor—"

He didn't even get the rest of his words out because she put her hand up and shoved him in the chest.

"On second thought, I don't even want to hear it. I could not be less interested in your compulsive need to rescue your drunken lout of a brother."

"He totaled his car. Wrapped it around a tree. This afternoon."

That paused her for a second. "Did he hurt anyone else?"

"No. Not even himself, really. He was so blotto they reckon he was saved by the fact he was probably floppy at impact." Peter's expression was half of relief, half of consternation.

"Good to know I rank so highly I didn't even warrant a call or a text. Despite the fact that I left you so many it's humiliating." She heard her whiny voice, her self-centered words, and immediately wanted to shove them all back inside her mouth.

Peter pulled his phone out of his pocket and swiped down the screen. Even from where she stood, she could see her name appearing multiple times. "I'm so sorry. I've been so busy trying to work out what to tell Mum and Dad."

Whaaaat? His brother had wrapped his car around a tree and Peter was concerned with doing parental damage control? "What does he have on you?"

"What do you mean?" The streetlights around them started to flicker on, showing the stress written across his face in better detail.

"I get sibling loyalty. I do. But from everything I've ever seen, he treats you like his little lap-dog. And you just take it." In the distance a siren wailed.

He shoved his phone back into his pocket. "It's all my fault, okay!"

"All what is your fault?"

"His face."

"Are you talking about his scar?" Anita's death was his fault. His brother's face was his fault. His shoulder was his fault. Was anything not his fault?

"Yes, his scar. The angry, jagged welt that disfigures one side of his face." His legs gave way, and Peter sagged against the window next to her. "We got into a fight when I was thirteen. A heated one. He came at me. I grabbed the poker from beside the fire. I only meant to fend him off with it, but at the last moment, he dived and it slashed his cheek. It needed thirty-two stitches. Then it got infected. He's hated me for it ever since."

"And turned you into his servant as a result."

"Something like that. It would break my parents' hearts to find out what he was really up to. He's the heir. The future Viscount Downley."

As far as Emelia was concerned, Victor was old enough to look after himself. "You aren't responsible for him. Or his choices. And you always rescuing him just makes it worse. He never has to face up to his consequences. What if one day he plows into someone? Hurts them? Kills them?" She half yelled the last two questions, just as a middle-aged woman was coming down the sidewalk toward them. She quickly crossed the street to avoid them.

"I don't know how to let it go, Em. Don't know how not to show up. Then he'll really hate me."

"I hate to say it, Peter, but after all this time, I'm not sure whether your showing up or not is going to make any difference."

He ran a hand through his hair, leaving another tuft sticking up from his head. "You're probably right. I guess I just thought if I showed up enough, was always there, one day he might forgive me. That we might find a way to get past the enmity that has always been there. But you're right. It just keeps getting worse. Now he'll have a drunk-driving charge to add to the others." His shoulders slumped in the shadows.

Emelia blinked back the tears that were forming. This guy who carried the weight of the world on his shoulders. She knew too well what that felt like. She pressed her lips together for a second. Could she do it? Tell him what she'd never told anyone? Her fingers tapped the window beside them. "Why do you think I hide in wardrobes?"

He glanced around, as if only just realizing where they were. "Because you're trying to find Narnia?"

"My mom loved Narnia."

"I remember."

Emelia sucked in a deep breath. "What I didn't tell you is that my mom wasn't well. She . . ." Her voice trailed off.

"You don't have to tell me, if you don't want to."

She forced herself to look him in the eyes. Sometime soon she'd tell him the whole truth. He'd hate her. But at least tonight she could give him this. "No. I want to. I want to explain that I know what it's like to carry the weight of responsibility for something horrible.

"My mom loved Narnia, it's true. While other moms cleaned houses and made dinners, mine made up complicated stories of us in Narnia. She was Queen Isabelle. I was Princess Emelia. When you're six, it's a pretty blurry line between a fun mom and one who doesn't operate in reality. You don't know that a person you see as someone who builds the most exciting and complicated fantasy worlds isn't a great storyteller but someone who suffers from psychosis."

Peter's hand found Emelia's, and he wrapped his fingers around hers. She held on to them as if they were a lifeline.

With a deep breath, she forced herself to focus on what she needed to tell him. "But what I was slowly realizing was that we were different. I didn't get invited to other girls' houses on playdates. The other moms came to help at school. But mine didn't. My mom didn't like having other kids over to play. She said that I saw them all day at school and that she wanted me for herself after. One day, there was a new girl at school. She lived a few doors down from us. I got invited to her house to play and Mom said no. Sulked. She said that I didn't need any other friends as long as I had her. I got mad. Told her I was tired of her stupid Narnia games. That I didn't want to play them anymore."

She could still see her mom's face as she spat out her defiant, childish words, wanting to hurt her. Not realizing how much power her words had.

"I ran to Claire's house and told her mom that it was okay. That I was allowed to play. I had the best afternoon in the world. Until the sirens started. They got closer and closer. And I knew, I just knew that something had happened to her. And that it was my fault."

Tears dripped down her cheeks. "There were police and paramedics everywhere. Claire's mom held me as I kicked and screamed and scratched and tried to get to her. She'd taken a huge overdose. She left a note that said she had to find Narnia and this was the only way."

Emelia didn't even know until years later that the police were there hunting for her. That when her dad had found her mom and hadn't been able to find Emelia, he thought she'd done something to her as well.

"You want to know why I hide in wardrobes? The truth is I don't know. She always told me that if I was ever afraid, the wardrobe would keep me safe. That one day we would find Narnia. And she's right. Every time I crawl into one of those wooden boxes, even as my fingers scrape the back and I know there's no Narnia today, for a few seconds I still feel peaceful. I feel like I'm home. And I'm so scared but I can't stop. Peter, what if I'm just as crazy as she was?"

Peter sucked in a breath. Prayed for the right words. Fast. "Emelia, you are not crazy. You are

about the least crazy person that I've ever met."
She looked up at him. Even in the fading light
he could see her eyes were riddled with fear.
If only he could reach in and pull it out. "You're
not crazy." The words came out as a whisper but
seemed to have more impact than his adamant
ones.

She peered up, cute freckles smattered over
her tanned face. "You really think so?"

"I know so. You are the most beautiful,
smartest, most organized ninja I've ever met. But
you are definitely not crazy." He cleared his
throat. He was a guy. An English one at that.
He was not good at this kind of stuff. "C'mon.
Let me walk you home."

She wobbled a smile. "That would be nice.
Thanks."

They walked in silence for a little while. Both
deep in their own thoughts. Emelia's hand tucked
into his elbow.

"At least now you know the answer to your
original question." She spoke softly.

His original question?

Emelia tugged at the edge of her long-sleeved
top and studied the ground. "About whether I'm
a Susan or a Lucy."

Why was she saying it like it was a bad thing?
Lucy was great. She never stopped believing.
She had the potion that healed people. She could
be fierce and compassionate. Just like Emelia.

Susan was great too. She had the magic horn and was an awesome archer. She was brave and resilient. Just like Emelia. Neither option was bad.

"Oh, wow." Emelia was staring at him like she'd just had a revelation. "You haven't read it, have you?"

Peter attempted to laugh. "What are you talking about?"

Emelia stepped closer, studying him. "It's why you never know what I'm talking about when I refer to Susan. You don't know."

Peter swallowed.

Emelia's eyes had narrowed. He could practically see the cogs turning in her head. "You've read some of *The Last Battle* though, haven't you? Or have you just heard about it?"

"I've read some of it." The words seeped out of him. They'd just turned into Emelia's street. Were closing in on her house.

"How far have you read?"

"If Aslan gave me my choice I would choose no other life than the life I have had and no other death than the one we go to." Peter quoted the words of Jewel the unicorn in chapter nine. They were burned into his mind as surely as if they'd been inked into his flesh. The sentence he could never get past.

"The great meeting on Stable Hill." Emelia said the words quietly, as if to herself. Then she directed a piercing gaze at him. "What happened?"

"What happened?"

"What happened?" She repeated the words again, softly. "You are the only person I've ever met who knows Narnia like I do. That's why none of this made sense. Why I couldn't reconcile you asking me if I was a Susan or a Lucy when we first met. It didn't make any sense. Except now it does. Something happened and you don't know how it all ended."

Peter ran his hand through his hair. "My grandfather died."

"When?"

"When I was nine. Dad was in the army and posted in the Middle East. So my grandparents moved in to help Mum. Every night, he would read me a chapter of Narnia before I went to sleep. That night he stopped on that sentence. Said he needed to get a glass of water. A few minutes later, he had a heart attack. He died on the way to the hospital. I've never been able to read past it."

"I'm sorry." Emelia nibbled her bottom lip.

"I know it's crazy. It's just a book. He would have wanted me to keep going. I can't even tell you how many times I've tried. Sat there and tried to force myself to read the next sentence, to keep going. But I just . . ." He shrugged his shoulders. How could he explain that his eyes just refused to read any farther when even he didn't understand it?

Emelia was silent as they walked up the path leading to her front door. No doubt thinking it was one of the stupidest things she'd ever heard. Almost twenty years had gone under the bridge and still he couldn't get past it.

"Do you think he knew?"

"Who?"

"Your grandfather."

"I don't know."

"I think he knew. How else would he have left you at such a perfect place? A sentence on either side would have meant little. It's like a message for you."

"I'd never thought of it like that."

"There aren't many people who can say that. *I would choose no other life than the life I have had.*"

"Can you?"

Emelia shook her head. "Most of the time I feel like I would choose any other life than this one. You?"

"If I had any other life but this one, I wouldn't have met you." The words kind of fell out of his mouth before he'd had a chance to think them through.

"Peter, we—" Whatever Emelia was about to say, she cut herself off. "It's been a big day. For both of us. I should go."

Thirty-Seven

"Morning." Emelia opened her eyes to find Allie perched on the end of her bed, a steaming mug in her hand. She was still in her pajamas, her hair mussed from sleeping.

"Hi." What time was it? What day was it? Emelia's eyes felt puffy, her throat scratchy. After she'd revealed her twisted past on a street corner, Peter had held her, told her she wasn't crazy, walked her home, and handed her over to Allie. Who had taken one look at her face and given Peter a fierce glare that would have frozen lava. Poor guy. Emelia had tried to explain her state wasn't his fault. Well, not in the way Allie clearly thought it was. Then she'd taken herself to bed and given in to exhaustion. She'd probably have stayed in it all day if not for her roommate perched at her feet like a bird.

"Want to come to church?" It was the first time Allie had straight-out asked her.

Emelia pulled herself up to sitting and rubbed her eyes. "I don't do church."

"Can I ask why not?" Allie sounded more curious than judgy.

Emelia sighed. Since she was apparently on an honesty streak, she might as well keep going. "The last time I voluntarily went to church, I was

348

sixteen. A friend took me. I thought I'd give it a shot. Why not? It wasn't like I had anything to lose. Then the preacher got up and thundered about how people who commit suicide go straight to hell. I've avoided them as much as possible ever since."

Allie peered at her across the top of her cup. Her eyes were troubled, full of questions.

"My mom killed herself when I was six." It had been years since Emelia had said it out loud. Now she'd said it twice in twelve hours.

Allie closed her eyes for a second and drew in a deep breath. "I'm sorry."

"Me too."

Allie didn't say anything. Emelia grew disconcerted. Shouldn't she have been jumping in with some kind of theological discourse? But then, that wasn't Allie's style.

Up until six months ago, Emelia had thought she needed religion about as much as she needed to ride a three-legged camel through the Sahara. It had been easy to jam Christians into the fundamentalist, judgmental box and close the lid.

Then she'd met Allie, Jackson, and Peter. And they'd refused to fit into her nice box of stereotypes. Now a tiny part of her wondered if she might be missing out on something real. If maybe there was a God who could transcend everything the worst of His believers made you think of Him. And then she wondered if maybe

349

she was just grasping at straws because of how she felt about Peter.

"Where do you think my mom is?"

Allie lifted one shoulder. "I don't know."

Emelia blinked. She hadn't been expecting that. Wasn't the point of being religious that you had all the answers? And then you painted them on placards and marched around DC waving them?

"That man had no idea what he was talking about. The only one who knows what happens when someone dies is God. He knows every single one of us. Everything we've done, everything we haven't. Every good and bad decision we've made. What happened in our last moments. He makes the call. Not some guy in a flashy suit."

"You really believe that? That He cares about you? Me?"

"I know it."

"How?"

Allie took a sip of her drink, traced a pattern with her finger on Emelia's comforter, actually looked like she was thinking about the question. It made Emelia feel she could trust whatever she was about to say more than if she'd just launched into a prepared spiel. "Do you remember the day you asked me about my spare room?"

"Sure."

"Did you notice that I looked a little startled

when I walked into the office and you had that card in your hand?"

"Sort of." Emelia remembered thinking something at the time, but it obviously hadn't made a huge impression.

Allie pulled her knees up to her chest and wrapped her arms around them. "I never put that card up on the notice board."

"I don't understand." Emelia blinked at her, trying to process what she was saying. "But it's in your handwriting."

"I made the card. A couple of them. I had meant to put one up there. But I never got 'round to it. To be honest, I was a bit uncertain if I wanted a flatmate, so I'd procrastinated. Left them in my bag."

Emelia's eyes felt like they were about to pop out of her head. "But if you didn't put it up, how did it get there?"

Allie shrugged. "No idea. Maybe it fell out of my bag and someone saw it and put it up? All I know is that to me you can't explain it away as coincidence. It has to be more. It has to be bigger."

Emelia sucked in a breath. Well, she could see that. But then, if there was a God, of course He'd be interested in Allie. She was sweet, and kind, and funny. A much better person than she was.

"It wasn't about me."

Emelia didn't know if she'd spoken her thoughts out loud or if Allie had read her mind.

"It wasn't about me." Allie leaned forward as she repeated herself. "It was about you."

Emelia shook her head. Her fingers twisted around themselves as she tried to process what Allie was saying. Claiming. It sounded too much like a fairy tale, from a land where the story started with "Once upon a time" . . . That had never been her story.

"That first time we met? Over the photocopier? Didn't that ever strike you as strange? That someone you'd never met would invite you to a house party?"

It had. A little. But she'd been so desperate to get out of the horrid B and B, she hadn't wanted to question it too much. "I just thought you were one of those super-friendly people who invites everyone you meet to things like that."

Allie laughed and fished a half-dissolved marshmallow out of her mug, popping it in her mouth. "I wasn't even meant to be in that morning but my first lecture got canceled because of the weather. And I was only photo-copying because my first set had landed in a puddle. And I really don't randomly invite strangers 'round. But for some reason I invited you.

"You know, the truth is that sometimes when people ask how you *know* that God exists, it's hard to come up with one compelling reason. It's often such a conglomeration of so many things that, put together, create the proof that you need. But watching all the things He's put in play the last few months around you, that's all the proof I need."

Emelia shook her head, trying to absorb it all. It was all too big. Too crazy. Too overwhelming. To even consider for a second there might be an omniscient being who had made so many things happen for her. Because of her.

And if it was true, why now? Why didn't He step in and save her mom? Or Anita? Had she finally had enough bad stuff happen to her to get His attention?

"Know what else?" Allie grinned at her.

"What?" Emelia wasn't sure she could take any more.

"You need to ask Peter about the teacup."

Emelia just looked at Allie. "The one he got his mom for her birthday?"

"You say it like it's so ordinary. Have you ever sat down and really thought about what the odds are of you and the teacup that Peter has been looking for for years being in the same wardrobe? The same night he just happens to be at that exact antiques shop and find both of you?"

No. She hadn't. If she started thinking too deeply about that, then everything might change.

Thirty-Eight

Where on earth had Allie disappeared to? One minute she'd been the life of the engagement party, the next she seemed to have disappeared. And it wasn't on some lovers' escapade, since Emelia had just seen Jackson talking to a group of people.

"Emelia." She turned around, trying to spot who had called her name while she restacked the mountain of presents into something that didn't look like it might topple at any second. Judging by the large pile, she'd been the only one who hadn't ignored the "absolutely no presents" instructions on the invitation.

Kat, Allie's best friend, who had flown in the night before, was crossing the small lobby. Her entire appearance screamed exactly what she was: a hair-and-makeup guru in hot demand for movies all over the world. Just being within a few meters of Kat made Emelia feel frumpy. And this was the best she'd looked in months. "Hey. Have you seen Allie?"

"Yup. I'm just doing some touch-ups upstairs before the formalities start. Can you give us a hand with something?"

"Sure." She turned and followed Kat up the grand staircase of what once had been a country manor house for one of the aristocracy before it had been converted into a small boutique hotel.

Kat didn't waste any time and was soon tapping on a door.

"Come in," Allie called from inside.

Kat opened the door and gestured Emelia in ahead of her. Emelia's heels sank into the carpet as she walked into an opulent bedroom. The door clicked behind them.

Allie stood in front of her, like something out of a Botticelli painting. Gone was the jade cocktail dress she'd been wearing half an hour ago. In its place was a long, figure-fitting but classy cream-colored dress, V-neck, flared out at her knees. Her auburn hair was caught in an elegant knot that sat at the nape of her neck. Tall sparkly shoes completed the ensemble. "Surprise!" Allie grinned at her. Radiant.

No. They hadn't. They weren't. Oh, they were. Emelia opened her mouth, but no words came out. "Wow." A couple of seconds later it kind of croaked out. "Holy moly." Then she started laughing as she shook her head, undone by the crazy, giddy girl standing in front of her.

Allie laughed so hard the neckline had a hard time containing her cleavage. "I take it that's a good thing?"

"You look . . ." Emelia's voice trailed off. "Beautiful" didn't cut it. Nor did almost any other adjective she could conjure up. "Wow. Just wow."

"Good. That's what Kat was apparently going for. She brought it. Saved me from scary dress shopping." Allie did a slow spin. The gown hugged her in all the right places. Closely. Jackson would probably swallow his tongue.

"Jackson knows, right?" How had she lived with Allie for over six months and had no idea she was planning a surprise wedding?

Allie laughed. "That he's getting married today? Yes, he definitely knows. We decided to do it that night we had the fight about the prenup."

"Hold it right there." Allie paused midturn at Kat's command, facing the floor-length mirror set against the opposite wall. On the table beside Allie was an extensive assortment of hair and makeup tools that Kat had turned her attention to.

"Hold still." Kat stood back and peered at Allie, then picked up the world's smallest makeup brush from her kit and started doing precise strokes along Allie's jawline like an artist painting a canvas.

"How do you feel?" Emelia sagged down into an upholstered chair by the door. Jackson and Allie were getting married. Today. She'd somehow found herself in the middle of a surprise wedding. Of all the crazy things.

"Happy." Allie paused. She scrunched her nose at herself in the mirror, then looked at Emelia in the reflection. "A little weird."

"About?"

"Getting married again. I kind of expected to be scared or something after it went so badly wrong last time."

"And you're not?"

Allie grinned radiantly as Kat stepped back again and put the brush down. "Not even a little. I want to kick myself for planning an evening wedding. What was I thinking? I could have been married by now!"

"Easy, tiger, you'll be Mrs. Gregory soon enough." Kat shook her head as she dabbed something across Allie's forehead. She stepped back and studied her charge. "And we're done. Now it's your turn." Kat turned her gaze on Emelia.

"Me?" What was she talking about? Her makeup was done. Her hair wasn't perfect, but it was passable.

"Look, no offense, because you're really quite good for a makeup Muggle, but I just can't let you go to the wedding like that. It's against my moral code."

"But, I'm not anyone."

"Quite the opposite. Plus it's really your public duty."

"Huh?"

"We still have twenty minutes, and look at her." Kat gestured at Allie, who was spinning around in her dress. Bubbly as a bottle of champagne and as giddy as if she'd drunk one

357

when, as far as Emelia knew, all she'd had to drink was some sparkling water. "If you don't give us a reason to stay here, then she'll be the first bride in history to be standing at the altar before the groom or the guests."

"Are you going to do her up?" Allie had just clicked into the conversation. "Oh, you have to. Peter will be taken out at the knees when he sees you." Allie grimaced at her words. "Sorry, I know it's complicated. Not helping, am I?"

Well, she wasn't exactly going to turn down being made up by the magician in front of her. And if Peter got taken out at the knees . . . Emelia clamped down on a smile, but not before Kat saw it and let out a low whistle. "I'm always happy to give a fledgling romance a shove. Just ask Allie."

"We're just friends."

Kat grinned. "Well, that's a bonus. Jackson and Allie couldn't stand each other when they met." She pulled out a cloth and poured something from a large bottle onto it. "Sit down." She gestured to the end of the bed. "Let me work my magic."

Fifteen minutes later, Emelia stared at herself in the mirror Kat held up to her face with a flourish.

"Wow." She could barely get the word out; she was too entranced with the girl staring back at her with big eyes, pouty lips, and a flawless complexion. It was like an airbrushed version of herself.

Her hair had been pinned loosely up and tendrils

floated around her face. Her natural waves, which never took instruction or direction, had somehow been tamed into something elegant yet sexy. Her eyes and lips combined to look classy but alluring.

At least she would get to enjoy today at her best. Peter had promised her a dance and she intended to savor every last moment in his arms. She was going to remember every look, every word, every moment of magic. No regrets. She'd probably kiss him again if she got the opportunity. Call her crazy. Or stupid. Or naïve. Or foolish. But soon enough she'd have to tell Peter the truth about who she was, and it would all be over.

She was on death row. It was just that no one else knew.

"Emelia?" From the way Allie said it, it wasn't the first time she'd said her name. "I've just realized we've left the bouquets downstairs. In the kitchen. Can you grab them and bring them up? You can take the back stairs at the end of the hall down to the kitchen."

"Okay." Following Allie's instructions, Emelia made short work of navigating down what must have been the old servants' stairs to the main kitchen. Dodging caterers bustling around with trays, she made her way to a sideboard where two bouquets of peonies sat. She nestled the two bunches in the crook of her arm and inhaled in their light floral scent.

Making it back to the second floor, she breathed a sigh of relief as she started down the hallway toward Allie's room.

"Please tell me I'm wrong about what I fear I'm seeing." The haughty voice came from a small alcove to the right.

Emelia flinched, then turned. Allie's mother. How could she have missed seeing the sparkles? She'd only met her at the beginning of the party and it had taken all of thirty seconds to work out what Allie meant when she said her family situation was complicated. The woman had all the warmth of an iceberg. "Mrs. Shire? Are you looking for something?"

"I prefer some privacy when I go to the bathroom, so I came up to our suite." Veronica took a step toward Emelia, her eyes narrow. Her silver dress glittered as she moved. All that Emelia could think was that somewhere a nightclub needed its disco ball back. "Don't try to change the subject."

"I'm afraid I don't know what you're talking about."

"I think you do." Veronica stepped forward and rested a perfectly manicured nail on the blooms. "Let's start with the fact that peonies are Allison's favorite flowers. Add in that they are predominantly a spring and early summer flower and we are into autumn. Factor in that those look extraordinarily like the kind of bouquets a person might carry at, say . . . a wedding?" Veronica tapped her elongated nail against her perfectly painted lip. "But I'm being very foolish, aren't I? Because there is absolutely no way my daughter is getting married today. Not before her latest fiancé has signed the prenup. I assume you've heard of Allison's propensity to fall in love with gold diggers."

Jackson? A gold digger? Emelia would have laughed aloud at the ridiculousness of it all if it wasn't for the fact that the woman's face told her that Jackson and Allie's almost perfectly executed plan was about to go up in smoke.

Peter rounded the top of the stairs, his mind still reeling from the news Jackson had just landed on him. A surprise wedding. He had to hand it to them. It was going to be a surprise all right. At least it was a much better one than seeing his brother here, the plus-one to a brunette who looked at him with adoring eyes. The girl had to be a friend of Allie's, but Peter didn't know her from Eve.

Emelia and Allie's mother stood in the hallway. Emelia held two large bunches of flowers and her face suggested she was trying not to panic. Emelia was in on this too? He couldn't see Veronica's face but from the ramrod set of her back and the pointed finger she was waving around, he guessed they weren't talking about the nice autumn weather.

361

"Is everything okay, ladies?"

Emelia gave him a look of relief that almost melted him. "Mrs. Shire is, um . . ."

"Going to put a stop to this nonsense."

Peter tried not to squint. The woman's blinged-out dress could have made a blind man see. "I'm sorry?"

"Don't play dumb with me, young man. I know you're in cahoots on this travesty too."

Peter felt his protective instincts rise. "If by 'travesty' you mean a beautiful wedding where two of my friends get to pledge their lives to each other, then yes, proudly so."

"I demand to be taken to my daughter." The woman spat out the words like nails.

Peter glanced at Emelia, who mouthed the words "no way" at him. He thought quickly. He knew the house well. Before it had been sold and converted it belonged to the parents of an old school friend.

One possible solution came to mind. If he had the nerve to do it. He let his shoulders slump, as if defeated. "Of course. I'll take you to her right now."

Emelia just gaped for a second, which Veronica seemed to take as a sign of victory.

He gestured. "After you."

Veronica started stalking down the hall. Peter followed close behind, scanning the doors to the right for the one he was looking for. It had been a coat closet that led to a large windowless linen cupboard back in the day. He couldn't imagine the hotel would have found another use for the space. He searched his memory for whether there was a lock on it but came up blank. If not, well, he'd have to stand there and hold it shut. Jackson and Allie had not spent months planning a surprise wedding for it all to be ruined now. Not on his watch.

He found the door and almost gaped in disbelief at a gold key glinting from the lock. "In here. There's a short hallway first." He gave a quick knock, then turned the knob and pushed open the door.

Veronica stepped through the doorway. "Allison Marie Shire." Her voice was sharp enough to cut glass. As soon as she stepped past the door, Peter slammed it back into the doorframe and turned the key.

Peter pocketed the key as Veronica Shire thumped on the door from the other side. Yelling words that were thankfully muffled by the thick oak door.

Emelia stared up at him, eyeballs goggling like something out of a cartoon. "Did you just . . just . . . lock the mother of the bride in a closet?"

"Of course not!" He patted his pocket just to double-check the key was still in there. "It's a bit larger than that. She'll be perfectly comfortable for the next fifteen minutes or so until the ceremony."

Laughter burst out of Emelia. Her face was transformed by her grin as her shoulders jumped up and down with the force of her mirth, bouquets bouncing along with them. "Oh, I love you."

The words dropped between them. Peter froze as Emelia blushed. "I mean, I love that you did that."

"I think I liked the first one better." His voice was husky, his heart feeling like it was about to break out of the jail his ribs were holding it in.

They stared at each other, the air between them charged. He wouldn't have been surprised if he'd lifted his hand and received an electric shock.

He'd done it. He'd gone and fallen in love with the one girl he shouldn't. Every direction from here just held hurt. But when she stood in front of him and looked at him like that, he wanted to ignore everything and be one of those crazy fools who hoped their fundamental differences would just magically sort themselves out.

"I just . . ."

"I thought . . ."

"We should . . ."

Their words clashed together, neither of them quite able to get out anything coherent.

"There you are, Emelia." A voice came from beyond them. Kat stopped a few feet away, and her head turned from one of them to the other. "Oops, sorry. I've clearly interrupted a moment.

That's kind of my specialty. Just ask Allie."
Striding up, she grabbed Emelia's wrist and
tugged. "Don't worry. I'm sure you two will be able
to pick it up again later. This is a wedding after
all. Can you go let Jackson know we're ready?
He's in room two oh eight." Kat looked at Peter.

"Um, sure." The words were barely out of
Peter's mouth before the girls had disappeared
into a room just a few doors down.

Peter shook his head as he turned to find
Jackson's room. At least two people would be
getting their happy ending today. Emelia's "I love
you" changed everything. Except the one thing
that really mattered.

Thirty-Nine

"Ladies and gentlemen, please welcome Mr.
and Mrs. Gregory for their first dance."

Peter forced his eyes up from his dessert plate
and onto the married couple. He had to at least
pretend to be interested, even though the thought
of watching Jackson and Allie all wrapped
around each other in their little love cocoon was
more than he could stand.

Jackson led his bride onto the floor, unable to
keep his eyes off her as the band opened with a
Michael Bublé song.

Peter pinched the bridge of his nose as Jackson

took Allie in his arms. He'd had it all under control. Had managed to force all his feelings for Emelia into a box. Then she'd said she loved him. Followed by Jackson's springing a reading on him; he'd found himself standing in front of two hundred people reading the Song of Solomon, staring right at her.

Place me like a seal over your heart, like a seal on your arm, for love is as strong as death, its jealousy unyielding as the grave. It burns like blazing fire, like a mighty flame. Many waters cannot quench love; rivers cannot sweep it away.

The verses were branded in his mind. Emelia had been shanghaied into a reading too. A haunting poem by Tolkien. They had been allocated seats next to each other for the ceremony. The whole time his hand itching with his wanting to take hers.

Not fair, God.

The only good thing about their sitting next to each other was that it had prevented him from spending the entire time ogling her like a thirteen-year-old boy at his first mixed dance.

He'd managed to avoid her for the rest of the evening. During the mingling after the service, the canapés and cocktails, he was aware of where she was at every moment.

Like right now. She was standing on the other

side of the room, talking to an elegant blonde. He couldn't have stopped himself from noticing the way Emelia's red gown hugged her curves in all the right places if his life depended on it.

His avoidance was all well and good, but he owed her a dance. Had claimed one earlier in the day. And he might have been many things, but someone who went back on his word wasn't one of them. The only way he was going to manage a dance without his defenses crumbling would be major divine intervention.

"Seriously, go talk to her already."

"Excuse me?" He turned toward the voice and saw Kat dropping into the chair beside him. Her full skirt billowed around her like she'd parachuted in.

Kat pointed a well-manicured nail across the room. "Emelia. For the sake of all of us in this room, stop looking at her like a bereft puppy and go talk to her."

"That bad, huh?"

Kat rolled her eyes. "Dude, you read the Song of Solomon to her. The entire congregation would have had to be blind not to have noticed. So, yeah, that bad."

"It's . . . complicated."

"Why? Are you already married?"

"What? No."

"Excellent. I'm pretty sure she isn't, which makes you streets ahead of where Allie and

Jackson started. Don't make me tip you out of your chair."

"Anyone ever told you you're bossy?"

She smiled serenely. "All the time."

Peter ran his hand through his hair. What was he even nervous about? This was Emelia. The girl who had fallen out of a wardrobe on him. Who'd snotted all over his favorite T-shirt. Who'd curtsied to his mother. Whom he'd drawn very clear lines with. Though that line kept getting more than a little blurred. And he was to blame.

He forced himself out of his chair. Wiping his palms on his trousers, he checked around for something, anything that he could use as an excuse to talk to her. Except the dance. That required music that was upbeat and partyish. Definitely not the slow and sultry stuff that was currently crooning out of the speakers.

Emelia didn't have a drink. Grabbing a couple of flutes off a passing tray, he headed in her direction. He had to go now, before his courage failed him.

Emelia caught his eye when he was just a few feet away and gave him the kind of smile that almost made him drop the glassware.

"Hi. Um, you looked like you could use a refill." He held out one of the glasses.

"Thanks." She took it and gestured to the woman next to her. It had to be Allie's sister. Blond, perfectly coiffed. She was the younger version of Veronica. Except she actually looked happy to be here. Unlike her mother, who had spent the entire ceremony with the face of the funeral goer.

"Peter, this is Allie's sister, Susannah."

"Pleasure to meet you."

"You too." Susannah's gaze flickered between the two of them, and she gave a knowing smile. "Sorry to be rude, but I need to go and track down my children."

Apparently Kat was right. His mooning over Emelia from a distance had all the subtlety of a bathing suit at a black-tie ball.

Emelia looked around the room at people laughing and dancing. "I can't believe they pulled it off."

"I'm sorry I haven't spoken to you since the ceremony. I just . . . you look so beautiful, I wasn't sure I'd be able to string a sentence together."

So much for playing it cool.

"Thanks." Emelia tilted her head, a wavy lock of hair dangling across her collarbone. "I think."

She smelled good too. Like citrus and flowers and fresh sheets. He slammed the door shut in his mind before it could go there.

"So—" They both spoke at once.

"You go." Both of them again.

A moment of silence followed. Her all big eyes and open face. "It was for you."

"What was?"

369

"I wanted to look beautiful for you. Which is crazy, because there can't be anything between us, but . . . wow, I can't believe I said that. I feel so stupid."

He had never wanted to kiss someone so badly in his entire life. But all that would do was make everything worse. She loved him. You didn't kiss girls who loved you when you couldn't love them back. "Well, it worked."

She looked around them. "You know, sometimes, on nights like tonight, I think it might even be true."

"What?"

"The whole God thing." She gestured to where Jackson and Allie were wrapped around each other on the dance floor. "When you think about their story. Could it really just be coincidence? It all just feels too perfect, too impossible, for there not to be someone bigger behind it all."

"I know they believe that."

"But then I can't believe in a God. Because if there's a God, then He also made my mom sick and let her die. What kind of God leaves a six-year-old girl without her mother? Leaves any children without their mothers?"

Clearly not the moment to launch into a treatise on the original sin and fallen creation.

"I want to believe it all. I really do. But I don't know if I can. And I can't fake it for you."

Without his permission, his hand reached out

and tucked a strand of hair behind her ear, lingering on her face. "I know. Come with me for a minute . . ."

Without allowing himself to think through what he was doing, he grabbed her hand and started walking toward the ballroom exit. He had the overwhelming urge to show her the stars, to ask her if she thought they stood there as the result of a cosmic accident.

He whisked her out a set of French doors, and they found themselves on a side patio. The still night was broken by the sound of her heels clattering across the cobblestones beside him.

"Peter, can you slo— Oh!" A sudden jerk pulled at his arm, and he reached out instinctively as Emelia stumbled. Grabbing her around the waist, he managed to take a step to anchor himself and stop her from hitting the ground.

Her fingers grasped his upper arms. Anyone watching from inside would've thought he was doing some kind of extra-low dip.

She blinked up at him, hair dislodged and tumbling behind her. "Sorry."

"You're welcome." You're welcome? This girl was causing him to lose his grasp on his faculties. There was no recovering. He couldn't even try.

Straightening, he pulled her back to her feet. "You okay?"

"Fine. Just embarrassed. I'm really not a klutz." She peeked up from where she had ended up cradled against his chest. The stilettos that had been responsible for her fall now placed her at the perfect kissable height.

The electricity between them could have lit up Times Square. He groaned and burrowed his fingers in her wavy hair. "Em—"

"Sorry for interrupting, little brother." From out of the shadows, Victor stumbled. Peter hadn't seen him since the ceremony. Had forgotten he was even there. Emelia stepped back and turned toward the intruder. "Hi, Mia." Victor had his drunken gaze on Emelia.

The hairs on the back of Peter's neck prickled. "Her name's Emelia."

Victor shook his head in the slow, deliberate way that drunks did when they were trying to pretend they were sober. "Maybe to you, Bunny. Not to the rest of the world." Beside Peter, Emelia's whole body tensed, as if waiting for a blow. "You going to tell him, Mia, or should I?"

"I—"

Victor cut her off with a smirk. "She's Mia Caldwell, little bro. You've been duped."

His brother really was drunk. The photo Peter had seen of the tabloid reporter looked nothing like Emelia. Mia Caldwell was blond, with a know-it-all smirk.

"You're out of your mind." Just like any other Saturday night. Not even the raft of charges he had pending against him had curbed his drinking.

He turned to Emelia to apologize. But the expression on her face stopped him cold. It wasn't confusion. Or pity. Or even repulsion. But one of someone who had been cornered. Found out. Her gaze locked on his.

"I'm so sorry." The words whispered from her lips. The same ones that just a few seconds before he'd been considering kissing.

"No." He shook his head. "You can't be. It's not possible."

He must have misunderstood. She was apologizing for something else. He waited for her denial, for her to say she had no idea what Victor was talking about.

"I-I . . . ," Emelia sputtered, her beautiful eyes glowing with tears that betrayed the truth. She straightened her shoulders and looked at him unblinking. "He's right. But you have to know that I—"

"That you're a tabloid fop." Victor slurred his accusation with a drunken grin, as if the whole scenario were funny.

"But Mia Caldwell is in LA. Still working for that paper. I get the newsfeeds." His stilted sentences splintered in the cool evening air.

Emelia closed her eyes for a second. "It's a different reporter using my old byline. Has been since I left. I had no idea until that day on your porch."

Peter stepped away from her. From Victor. The

cold truth set like a block of ice in his stomach.

"You killed Anita. She's dead because of you."

She flinched but didn't deny it. "I'm sorry."

That was it. Two lone words. No explanation. No real apology. "How dare you." Repulsion surged through him, wiping away whatever he'd felt a few seconds before. "Is anything about you true? Or is it all just a cover? What do you want? Get close to Anita's grieving family? Do some kind of exposé on them?" Had all of it been a lie? Had he spent the last seven months being played for a fool?

"No." Her face was panicked. Her hands gripped the front of her dress, scrunching it in between her fingers. "I'm not a reporter. I quit right after her death. I swear someone else has been using my byline. Just look at the photos. It's not me."

Peter stepped back. Put even more distance between them. "Like I'm going to believe anything you say. You make me sick."

"I'm so, so sorry." A sheen slicked her eyes. No doubt that was fake too.

" 'Sorry' doesn't raise someone from the dead. 'Sorry' doesn't give my aunt and uncle their daughter back." He said the last few words so violently, they flew out and splattered across her face. She flinched.

"Sorry" didn't take away the guilt he'd been carrying for the last ten months.

"Steady on." A hand clamped over his shoulder.

He saw Jackson out of the corner of his eye. Allie stood just behind him, her eyes wide. At some point in the last few minutes, they'd gained an audience.

"She killed Anita."

"Anita killed herself." Allie's words were soft and did nothing to pierce through his fury.

"Because of her." Peter stabbed a finger at Emelia, Mia, whatever her name was, before storming away into the darkness.

Three strikes and she was out. Three seconds to go from possibility to devastation.

"You okay?" Allie stood beside her but didn't touch her. As if knowing that if she did, Emelia might shatter like a crystal vase hitting a concrete floor. Of all the places, it had to happen here. Lacey was right. Karma finally got her.

"I ruined your wedding. I'm so sorry."

"Don't be crazy. Here. Sit." Allie gestured to a nearby set of patio furniture that Emelia hadn't even noticed. She'd been too busy being wrapped up in Peter's arms. Now hers were cold, bare, exposed. Just like her.

Allie pulled out a chair with a scrape and tugged Emelia's elbow until she sat down.

They were the only ones left on the patio. Victor had disappeared back into the shadows. Where he belonged. Jackson had obviously had the good sense to make himself scarce.

Emelia's back collapsed into the chair's canvas covering.

She was so stupid. Stupid to think that, even here, her mistakes wouldn't find her. Stupid to hope she'd be able to escape her past. But, most of all, stupid, stupid, stupid to let herself wish for one second for what she could never have with Peter. Like a fool, she'd even said she loved him.

Her hands plucked at her red dress, bunching it up between her fingers, the fabric running like blood when she let it go. Deep scarlet, like a wound. How appropriate.

Her hair had come loose at some point, and now the wind flung it around her face as if trying to hide her shame for her. She grabbed a handful with one hand and used the other to feel for some bobby pins in the mess to pin it back. Her fingers grasped at a couple, and she pinned enough hair off her face that she could see.

Allie sat across from her, but where she expected to see judgment and condemnation reflected in her green eyes, Emelia only saw concern.

"I'm so sorry about your wedding."

Allie batted her words away with one hand. "What are you even talking about? We're married. The reception is almost finished. The only thing you ruined was the inappropriate-in-front-of-children kiss Jackson was spiriting me outside for. And there will be plenty of those in his future."

The girl was either the most serene bride Emelia had ever met, or she was seriously hopped up on the love drug, sitting with the girl accused of killing her friend's cousin like they were talking about the weather.

"So are you Mia or Emelia?"

Emelia let out a wry smile. "Both. Emelia is my name. Mia was what I wrote under as a reporter."

"Caldwell?"

"My mother's maiden name."

"Huh." Allie didn't say anything more. Just sat there, staring at the stars as if she had all the time in the world. Or was a Michelangelo statue. The only thing that gave her away was a slight shiver in the moonlight.

"Want to tell me what just happened?" Allie's tone was casual. Anyone else would have been burning up with curiosity, already pumping her for all the details.

"How do you do that? Make it sound like you really don't care one way or the other?"

"Oh, I care. I also know what it's like to have a hurt so deep that just talking about it feels like ripping open the wound again. When Victor called you Mia, I could see on your face that you do too."

"I never, ever meant to hurt her. If I'd had any idea . . ." Emelia's voice trailed off. It wasn't entirely true. She may not have meant to hurt Anita, but no one could become the kind of reporter she'd been without knowing the impact they could have on people's lives.

"Anita had been unwell for a long time." Allie shifted in her seat.

"Did you know her?"

"I met her once when she was back here visiting. In passing. I'd just arrived in England. It was a month or so before she died." Allie drummed her fingers on the table for a few seconds, thinking. "She came to a quiz night at the pub. She'd had too much to drink. One second she was flying high, the next crying her heart out. Peter mentioned later on she'd had addiction issues since she was a teenager. Had been in and out of rehab for years, but the family had managed to keep it quiet. Protected her wholesome image. I remember thinking that you could have all the beauty, brains, and money in the world, but it really didn't matter if you were hooked on booze, or drugs, or whatever your vice might be."

"I wasn't even there that night because of her. It was just pure chance that she was there. I'd heard a rumor that CeCe McCall might be there." But the A-list starlet was nowhere to be seen when Emelia had arrived.

She took a deep breath. "Anita was in the VIP room."

The scene she would never forget. She could still close her eyes and hear the thump of the bass in the song that was playing, the darkness splintered by the strobe light, the crush of bodies, alcohol on people's breath, guys getting closer to her than required as they squeezed past. And then there Anita was, snorting up a line of cocaine that was being cut for her by Victor. No different from half the room. Almost everyone snorted, swallowed, or shot something in those rich partycircles.

"It wouldn't have been a story if she was anyone else. But when you're engaged to an heir to billions who's a famous antidrug campaigner and you've been sold as his straitlaced fiancée who's committed to clean living and yoga? That's a story." Especially when you were in possession of a high-tech camera that could take a photo in the dreariest of nightclubs and turn it as clear as day.

"Two days later, the front page of the *Star Tribune* was my photo of her snorting cocaine through a hundred-dollar bill. The day after that, Logan announced the end of their engagement, and the morning after that she was dead." The girl had enough booze and pills in her system to take out an NFL linebacker. The speed at which everything had unfolded still, almost a year later, left Emelia dizzy.

"No one knew whether to call it a tragic accident or suicide. I didn't go in to work for three days. When I returned, there was an email from Anita from hours before she died. All it said was,

'This should make you happy. See you on the other side.' "

Against her boss's wishes, Emelia had turned it over to the police. Then she'd quit. Then she'd decided to come here, figuring she might as well use the one thing her mother had left her— British citizenship—to run away, to try reinventing her-self.

"So. There you have it. She's dead because of me."

Allie propped her elbows on the table between them and leaned forward. "No. She's dead because she had a lot of issues. She's dead because she decided to make some poor decisions. You can't take her choices onto you. Sure, your story didn't help, but she was heading for disaster when I met her. If it wasn't your story, it would've been something else."

"Or it might not have been. She might've gotten some help. Sorted herself out. She was only twenty-four. Plenty of people make bad decisions in their twenties and turn out to be fine."

"Or she might've walked out of another night-club one night smashed out of her mind, gotten into her car, and plowed into an innocent family. Ever think about that? Ever wonder who might be alive right now because you did expose her?"

Emelia stared at Allie, struck dumb. The thought had never crossed her mind, the idea that the horrible events that had led to Anita's taking her life might have preempted something even worse. It bounced around her brain, trying to find a place to settle, but it was too crazy.

Allie ran a hand through her hair, grimacing as she hit a bobby pin. "Here's the thing. You'll never know which it would've been. Probably neither. Probably something completely different. But you can't carry Anita around with you for the rest of your life. You have to forgive yourself for your part. As brutal as it sounds, she is dead. But you are not. If you carry this around with you your whole life, this takes out two people, not one."

"How did you get so wise?"

Allie smiled wryly. "By making some really, really bad choices. But here's the thing, Em. God can find a way to redeem even the worst of choices, if you let Him. If I hadn't made mine, I never would have met Jackson. If Jackson hadn't made his, he never would have met me."

"You really think God cares about you that much?"

"I know He does."

Emelia turned the concept over in her mind, trying to reconcile this idea of a God who could take the worst things in your life and use them to lead you to something good. But she couldn't. It clashed so deeply with the God she thought existed. If there was one at all. The one who'd left her abandoned as a little girl. Who'd let her get cheated out of her dream career. Who'd never done anything for her. Everything she had was something she'd achieved for herself. "Peter hates me."

"He sure might think he does right now. But he doesn't. He will be deeply hurt. Anita was like the little sister he never had. He was distraught when she died. It hasn't even been a year."

"I don't know how to fix it."

"You probably can't."

Truer words were never stated. Emelia glanced to her right and saw Jackson standing just inside the patio doors, waiting for his bride. She tilted her head in his direction. "You need to go."

Allie looked over her shoulder, and her face lit up even as she said, "It's okay, he can wait."

"No! Go!"

Allie gave her a long look. "You going to be okay? Call me if you need anything. Anything."

Emelia managed a half-convincing laugh. "I'll be fine. I am not going to call you on your honeymoon!"

Allie got to her feet, silk rustling around her. "I love my husband, but three weeks of talking to just each other will drive us both batty. I give us three days before one of us is annoyed about the other squeezing the toothpaste wrong." She leaned down to give Emelia a brief hug as she passed by. "I'll see you when I get back. Hang in there. You never know what might happen." And then she was gone in a whirl of cream and a hint of floral perfume.

You never know what might happen. Well, it would take a miracle to make things right with Peter. And miracles never happened. Especially not for her.

Forty

Emelia walked into the office, everything aching from a sleepless night. In her purse sat her resignation letter. Neatly typed and dated. It was over.

Entering her office for the last time, she strode around her desk and put her bag down. She hadn't even bothered to bring a box. For the most part the room was as bare and impersonal as it had been the day she arrived. Opening the bottom desk drawer, she fished out a spare pair of heels and pantyhose she'd kept there for emergencies. Moving to the middle drawer, she grabbed a couple cans of tuna. Finally the top drawer. Two packs of gum and a couple of her own pens.

That was it. All she had to show for the entirety of the seven months she'd worked at Spring-Board. Reaching into her purse, she pulled out a fat folder that she'd spent all of Sunday working on. Inside it, sheets of A4 detailed everything anyone would need to know about the ball.

The hard stuff was done. Anyone with half a

brain could follow her checklist over the next two months for the tasks that remained.

It would probably be Peter. Flipping open the cover, she uncapped a black pen, poised it over the page, and paused. Sighing. She put the cap back on. There was nothing she could say that would change anything. Everything she needed to know had been written across his face on Saturday night.

"Write a novel over the weekend?" Elizabeth leaned against the doorway.

One look at her steady, knowing eyes was all the confirmation she required. "I need to give you this." Emelia plucked the envelope out of her purse and walked around the desk, holding it in front of her.

Elizabeth looked at it but didn't take it. "Why don't we talk first. In my office." It wasn't a suggestion.

Emelia followed her heels as they clicked down the corridor. Walking into Elizabeth's office, she saw they weren't alone. John Simons, the chair of the board, sat in a second chair that had been brought in.

The door closed behind Elizabeth like a jail cell.

"So." The older man leaned back in his chair, hands folded over his stomach. "Would you prefer to be called Mia or Emelia?"

"Emelia, sir."

She looked to where Elizabeth had settled

herself behind her desk. Emelia still held the envelope in her hand. She offered it to Mr. Simons.

He also just looked at it. "What's that?"

"My resignation, sir. Effective immediately."

"We don't want it."

He could not have shocked Emelia more if he'd taken a cattle prod to her. "You don't?"

"We don't," Elizabeth confirmed.

"But I lied and I . . ." She trailed off.

"Did you actually lie? Or did you just not tell us the whole truth?"

"I didn't tell you the whole truth. I knew you wouldn't hire me if I did."

John nodded. "And you're right." He leaned forward, his chair creaking. "Peter called me yesterday morning. I'll be honest, when I heard what he had to say, my first instinct was to sack you on the spot. But Elizabeth and I had a long conversation last night and there was one question that we kept coming back to."

"Yes?"

"Why are you here?"

"I read that SpringBoard was hemorrhaging donors. I just . . . I had to help."

"And we decided we want you to finish what you started."

"I can't."

"Emelia." Elizabeth spoke the words softly. "Anita would want you to do it."

Emelia looked at her kind eyes. "Really?"

385

"She, more than anyone else, believed in second chances. She had her struggles but she was kind and generous. She would want you to have your second chance."

A tear tripped over Emelia's cheek.

"But you need to know something. Even if the ball is a huge success, even if you achieve what you came here to do, I don't think you're going to find the atonement you're looking for here."

Forty-One

Emelia fingered the ship in her hands, holding it carefully as she examined it from all angles. It seemed perfect. Apart from the hairline crack running around the middle of the boat that couldn't be completely hidden, you'd never have known it was the same one that had shattered on Peter's floor.

She nestled it back into the padded box that sat on the passenger seat of Allie's car and drew in a deep breath. This wasn't a big deal. She was just going to leave it on Peter's doorstep. She'd checked the schedule, and he would still be at the rowing club for a couple of hours teaching. There was no chance he'd be home. She'd never met his roommate, so if he happened to be there, she could just give him the box and run.

She climbed out of the car and crossed to the

passenger side. Reaching in, she picked up the box and closed the door with a swing of her hip.

Up the path, put it down, and get back to the car. The whole thing should take less than thirty seconds. She strode up the path, climbed the six steps to the front door, and paused.

She'd decided not to leave a note with it because, really, what was there left to say?

She rested her head for a second on the front door, only for it to swing open at her touch. "Argh!" She stumbled forward over the stoop, the box crushed to her chest.

Hands grabbed her elbows, steadying her.

Please let it be anyone but him. Please let it be anyone but him.

The fingers released her arms like they were hot coals. "What are you doing here?"

Of course it was. She chanced a glance up. "You look horrible." It was true. He was even whiter than usual, never good for a redhead, with glazed eyes and a sheen across his forehead. "Are you okay?"

"Thanks." Even though he'd let go of her arms, the box was still wedged between them. "I have the flu. I heard footsteps and thought you were my Panadol and Gatorade delivery.

"What are you—" His words ended as he saw into the box. "Is that my . . ." He trailed off as he studied the boat, then leaned down to look more closely.

"I didn't think you'd be home. I was just planning to leave it on your doorstep." She pushed the box toward his torso so he was forced to take it, then stepped back.

"I . . . don't know what to say." Placing the box on the hallway table beside them, he carefully lifted out the model and studied it. "How did you do this?"

"I didn't. But I found someone who could. It was precious to you, so I . . ." She trailed off too, unable to find words to bridge the distance her deceit had created.

"Thank you." His gaze softened for a second. "Um, I should probably put it back. My hands aren't too steady at the moment." He placed the boat back into its packaging before turning to face her again.

"I'm sorry I ruined everything. I'm sorry I lied. I'm sorry about Anita. More sorry than you could know." The words tumbled out of her.

He didn't say anything.

"I should go." She took a backward step toward the threshold.

Feet pounded behind her. "Sorry I took so long. I ran into Brett in town—" An expletive. "What are you doing here?"

Emelia closed her eyes for a moment. Seriously? Could she not catch a break? Not even when she was trying to do a good thing?

Victor shouldered past her, pushing her into the

door. Turning, he stood between her and Peter. "You've got some nerve coming here after what you did."

She was not taking this. She would silently take whatever Peter dished out, but she was not taking anything from Victor.

"After what *I* did? That's a bit rich coming from you, of all people."

Victor flinched and turned a lighter shade. "You wrote the story. That's what drove her to the edge."

"I didn't know she had addiction issues. No clue about her being in and out of rehab. Unlike you. Great *cousin* you are." She spat the word into his face.

Over his shoulder she saw Peter's face. Confused. Bewildered.

Oh. Understanding hit. "He doesn't know, does he?" She nodded her head at Peter.

"What is she talking about?"

"Nothing. You know you can't trust a word Mia says." Victor threw her name in with a sneer, but it was impossible to miss the desperation in his eyes.

"It's Emelia." She said the words through gritted teeth.

"What. Is. She. Talking. About." Peter's words came out staccato. Individual verbal bullets aimed at his brother.

Emelia turned toward him. Poor guy. But since

she had nothing to lose, she might as well tell him the whole ugly truth. "You want to hold me responsible for Anita's death, I don't blame you. I blame myself. But you might want to ask your brother who she was with that night. Who's the owner of the hand in the photo that cut her line?"

Who's the owner of the hand in the photo that cut her line? Emelia's words shot through Peter's ears and into his heart like a laser.

Worse. For everything she hadn't told the truth about, he could tell by the look on her face that on this one thing—this one, life-changing thing—this was worse.

Which meant . . . He grabbed Victor by his shoulder and swung him around. "You. Were. There." He could barely get the words out through his clenched jaw.

All the holes he had dug his brother out of. All the times he had taken the blame for him to try to keep his name in the clear. The lifetime's worth of guilt Victor had heaped on him and he'd accepted, for the accident that had marred his brother's face forever.

"Hey." Victor held his hands up in an attempted gesture of innocence. "Look, all I did was slice it up for her. She already had it when I got there. If I didn't, someone else would've."

Peter stared at his brother. Of everything he'd thought Victor capable of, something like this had never crossed his mind. He'd believed him without question when he'd said he wasn't even there that evening. That the last he'd seen of her had been a couple of days before and she'd been fine.

"She'd been out of rehab for five days. Five!"

His brother rolled his eyes. "I hate to break it to you, Bunny, but Neets wasn't our cute little cousin in pigtails anymore. She was a big girl." There was something about Victor's words that made Peter think he was trying to convince himself as much as anyone else. Maybe it would have been okay if Victor had stopped there, but he had to keep talking. "I wasn't her chaperone, or her conscience. At least I got her out of there before she landed herself in a stranger's bed. She got around, did our—*oof!*"

Peter's first punch was a direct hit to his brother's torso. As Victor instinctively doubled over, Peter brought his fist up into his nose. Blood spurted, drops hitting the wooden floor and splattering like violent starbursts.

"Stop it!" Emelia's scream reached his ears about the same time his brother barreled into him. They both went down, Peter's head cracking the floor, his vision shattering for a second. Which was all it took for Victor to take his second strike, a well-aimed knee to the groin. This time it was like the entire galaxy exploded in his head.

"About time, little bro. Not the good guy

anymore, are we?" Victor's grunted words cut through the haze as Peter grabbed him by the front of his T-shirt and threw him backward. The hall table flipped over and landed with a crash by the door.

"Stop it! *Stop it!*" Emelia's screaming was loud enough to wake a coma patient.

In the seconds it took for the two brothers to get back to their feet, puffing, Victor swearing a blue streak, she had managed to dart between the two of them.

"Get out of the way, Em."

There was no way they could get at each other in the narrow hallway without involving her. He certainly didn't trust his brother to let that stop him. Not after what the last few minutes had revealed.

"Why? So you two can beat each other to death? Not a chance." She shook her head with the determination that had drawn him to her in the first place.

"Em, get out of the way. Please." Desperation tinged his words.

"I'd listen to what Bunny says. You really don't want to be in the middle of this."

Emelia didn't even look at Victor. Her eyes stayed fixed on Peter. Bad move. Because of the two of them, only one played dirty. He saw Victor's foot start moving, aimed at her ankles.

"E—" He didn't even manage to get a single

syllable out of his mouth before she had spun around, grabbed his brother by one arm, and flipped him over her back. A guy at least twice her weight and almost totally muscle. Victor landed on the floor with a smack, opening his eyes to find her heel poised above his groin.

"Try that again, clever guy, and you will never have children. Not that that would be such a great loss to the world."

Victor was silent, staring at her with a vicious glare. But he didn't move so much as a finger.

"No? I didn't think so." She took a couple of steps back toward Peter. "Now get out."

Victor clambered to his feet. For a split second, Peter caught something that might have been remorse or regret flashing across his face. But it was gone in an instant, replaced with his usual haughty expression. He didn't say a word as he backed across the threshold, slamming the door behind him.

"That's going to need some ice." Emelia put a light finger to his cheek. Peter just stared at her, still dazed. "How many fingers can you see?" She held up three fingers and moved them from left to right.

"What . . . how did you do that?" It was like something from a movie. Except in his hallway. Was any of this real? Or had he just fallen asleep on his couch and this was all a dream?

She gave a sad smile. "Occupational hazard.

Martial arts training comes in handy when you have a job that makes you enemies by the week. How many fingers?" She did the same again. This time with four.

"Four."

"Any double vision?"

"No, I'm fine." The truth was the feeling of a thousand knives slicing through his groin was making him want to curl up in the fetal position and weep like a little boy, but he was hardly going to tell her that.

He looked at the ground and saw it was covered with splinters of wood. The hall table he'd flipped was intact, so what was . . . oh. He slid down the wall until he sat on the floor amid the ruins of the *Dawn Treader*. He picked up two tiny pieces of mast. For some crazy reason, he tried to piece them together, like the rest of the ship hadn't been blown to smithereens all over the floor.

They didn't fit. So he tried again, stabbing the two tiny segments together like he could make them connect through sheer force of will.

What had he done? What had Victor done?

"They won't fit." His words echoed in the hall.

Emelia's fingers wrapped around his as she knelt in front of him. She took the two pieces from his hands, studied them for a second, then folded them into her fist. "I guess some things are just meant to be broken."

Forty-Two

Well, that went well. She'd caused a brawl between brothers and the *Treader* was back in a million pieces. No one could say she did things by halves.

Emelia's phone rang as she drove up to her house. She pulled up at the curb and answered the call. "Aren't you supposed to be on your honeymoon?"

"I am." Allie laughed. "Italy. I've sent Jackson to go find some sports to watch. Told you we'd only last three days before we got sick of each other."

"It's been over two weeks."

"Has it?" Allie sounded genuinely surprised.

Emelia leaned her head against the headrest. The two weeks may have felt like two minutes to Allie but they had felt like two years to her.

"I guess we'll see you soon then."

"I've started packing." If worst came to worst she could just go stay at a backpackers' hostel until the ball was over. She didn't have much.

"Why?"

"I just . . . assumed you and Jackson would want the house to yourselves when you get back." Allie's contract at Oxford had been extended for another year and she definitely

395

wouldn't want to be sharing four walls with the besotted newly-weds.

"Don't be silly. We're going to base ourselves out of Cambridge while we work out what Jackson is going to do with himself. We've got his apartment there and I'll just commute for the first term. Stay a few nights a week at our house when it doesn't make sense to go home."

Allie's blithe tone made it sound like it was no big deal when it was. Emelia couldn't have been more wrong about one thing. Allie hadn't abandoned her when she found out the truth. "Why would you do that for me?"

"Because you deserve good things. No matter how much you struggle to believe it."

"Peter doesn't want anything to do with me." Emelia's voice betrayed her with a wobble.

"Peter needs a bullet." At least that was what it sounded like Allie muttered under her breath.

"Sorry?"

"Nothing. Just an expression from home."

"I just took the *Treader* over to his house. I never should have gone. He and Victor got in a fight. It got smashed again. Everything I touch goes bad."

"That's not true. That fight has been waiting to happen for years. Just give him time. He has a lot to get his head around."

Emelia sighed. "Not that it matters anyway. Even if he could somehow get beyond all of that,

I still don't believe the same as he does. That's the dealbreaker. I've gotta be honest, Al. Between you and Jackson and Peter I was beginning to wonder if there might be something there. I know it's not fair but if Peter can't forgive me, then it's kind of impossible to believe in the God he says does. At this point, I'm going to need an unmistakable sign. I'm talking like writing-on-the-wall, booming-voice kind of stuff."

Allie sighed. "Don't equate Peter with God. Believing in God doesn't make a person perfect. We're still just as prone to messing up and doing the wrong thing as everyone else."

"It doesn't really matter anyway. Lacey called this morning. She thinks she can get me some freelancing work with her firm. After the ball."

"Are you going to take it?"

"I don't know. It's not like I have anything keeping me here once the ball is over." That was what she'd come for. She'd never actually thought about what would happen after.

She asked a question that had been bugging her. She wasn't going to get an answer from the one person she really wanted to hear it from. "That teacup. In his mom's collection. Was it really the same one that was in the wardrobe that night?"

"What do you think?"

What did she think? The truth was she'd been trying not to think about it. Because if she thought too much, connected the wardrobe with the teacup, with Peter's being there, with the mysterious notice that Allie never put up, it all started pointing to a rather uncomfortable reality. "I've gotta go, Al. I'll see you when you get back."

Getting out of the car, she set the alarm and headed up the path. "You heard that, right? Writing on the wall, big booming voice, something really unmissable." She directed her words to the sky. Nothing came back except the sounds of birds and the cool fall wind rustling leaves.

Well, that was that, then.

Sitting on the porch was a square cardboard box.

Getting closer, she saw that her name was on it, written in cursive script. No address. No postage. It had obviously been hand-delivered.

Sitting on the porch, Emelia picked it up and turned it around. No return address. No sign of who or where it had come from.

She put it down, then reached her fingers inside the gap and released the tape. Lifting the lid, she peered inside to see a small, rectangular card with bunches of cream-colored tissue paper underneath.

She picked up the envelope, slid her finger under the seal, and tried not to hold her breath as she pulled the card out. She didn't even know what she was hoping for, but she prepared herself for disappointment.

The same cursive writing was inside the card. *Emelia, This will probably sound really strange to you, but God told me this was meant to be yours, not mine. Love, Maggie.*

Lifting the tissue paper, Emelia peered inside the box, already knowing what she would find. And there it sat. The pink rose teacup.

The one that had been in the wardrobe the night she met Peter. The one that he'd been trying to find for years for his mom. The one that said more than any booming voice from the sky or writing on the wall.

"Okay." She breathed out the words. "You're real. Now what?"

Forty-Three

"You're a hypocrite." The morning's wake-up phone call from Allie echoed in Peter's mind as the rising sun bounced off Highbridge.

"Have you ever thought that maybe she was exactly who she said she was? Maybe you were one of the few people she let in to see the real her? She is Emelia Mason, Peter. There's a reason that she wrote as Mia Caldwell. There's a reason she came here."

The more he let Allie's words sink in, the more he knew she was right. He had been left a trail of clues. Emelia had told him she had been called Mia back home. That she'd wanted to be an investigative journalist. Had told him multiple times she had a past he would hold against her. But, like a fool, he'd just bowled on through her assertions.

"Why on earth would she believe in a God who forgives her when you won't?"

It was Allie's final words that had propelled him out of bed and out onto the water. She was right. About all of it. Peter was a hypocrite. Anita had been playing fast and loose with life long before Emelia, Mia, whoever she was, had written that article.

His oars had cut through the water with power. About the only good thing he had going was that his rowing was the best it had been since the accident. His shoulder felt smooth and stable when he went for a big reach. But not even a good row had managed to wipe away the storm whirling inside him. So he'd gotten in the car and started driving. Found himself almost home before he even realized that was where he was going.

His feet crunched on the gravel as he let himself into the back entrance. A pot of coffee sat, still hot, on the counter, so he poured himself a large mug and took it with him on the trek to the library. His mother would be there, reading the Saturday paper, as was her habit. He could only hope she had the words he needed to help bring clarity to this whole mess. He was certainly getting nowhere on his own.

He walked down the hall, averting his eyes from the spot where he'd trapped Emelia against the wall, almost kissed her. Even his parents' house wasn't safe.

As much as Allie's telling-off from Italy had knocked the air out of him, he still didn't know how to forgive Emelia. Didn't know even where to start. She hadn't told him. That was what burned deepest of all. All their time together and she'd let him think the biggest thing between them was faith, when there'd been another canyon equally wide. And then she'd sat there and just listened as he'd told her how he blamed himself.

She'd let herself get outed by Victor, of all people. He supposed he should be grateful to his brother for shattering the moment before Peter had done something that would have had him wallowing in even more regret, but he couldn't. Especially not now that he knew Victor had been there that night.

He was almost to the door to the parlor when footsteps came from his right, along with a dragging sound. He turned and sucked in his breath.

Emelia. The ball was still weeks away. It hadn't occurred to him for a split second she might be here.

She wore an old T-shirt and yoga pants. Hair pulled back in a haphazard bun with a pencil stuck through the center. A long roll of shimmery silver material was tucked under one arm and dragging beside her. Her attention was focused on that. She had no idea he was standing only a few meters away.

He gripped his mug so tightly, he wouldn't have been surprised if it shattered. There was nowhere to run, nowhere to hide. In a few seconds she'd be right on top of him. "Hi." It was brusque. He didn't know how else to do this.

Emelia started and dropped the roll of material. It unraveled across the wooden floor, spilling a shimmery silver lake in its wake. They both just looked at it until the wooden tube came to a stop.

Emelia spoke. "It's going to be puddles. For between the worlds."

"I'm sorry?"

Emelia gestured at the material. "We're going to put Astroturf down in the entranceway. Then this will be big puddles over the top."

From *The Magician's Nephew*. The woods and pools that transported people between Earth and Lewis's magical worlds. Narnia nerds would love it. "It's a great idea."

He looked up to see she'd come a couple of steps closer. Was looking straight at him. She looked tired. She looked beautiful.

He searched for something neutral to say. If she kept standing there just looking at him like that his heart might crack open. "Is everything going okay? With the planning?"

She looked at him, big blue eyes filled with questions. "Do you hate me?"

He flinched. "I don't hate you. And I owe you an apology." He tried to loosen his grip on the poor mug he was strangling. "I told you there was nothing you could have done that would make me walk away and then I did. I spent months lecturing you about God, and then when it really mattered, I didn't even live what I said I believed."

"I believe now." Something like surprise flitted across Emelia's face. Like she hadn't meant to say it.

Peter stared at her. "Believe what?"

"*'Yes,' said Queen Lucy. 'In our world too, a stable once had something inside it that was bigger than our whole world.'*"

It was a Narnia quote she had spoken, no doubt, but he didn't know it. Which meant it had to be from *The Last Battle*. The part he hadn't gotten to.

Emelia seemed to realize it too. "He sent me a teacup. God."

"What?" Was this a really weird dream? He bit the inside of his cheek, the pain confirming it was reality.

"Via your mom. The one in the wardrobe. When we met. She left it on my porch. You didn't know?" She sounded surprised.

He shook his head. Not that it surprised him.

403

His mother was frequently carrying out mysterious errands of kindness that she didn't want anyone else to know about.

"Why did you never tell me the full story? That the teacup in the wardrobe that night was the same one you'd been looking for for years."

"I didn't know if you'd even seen it. And if you had it just sounded too . . ." Something caught in his voice.

"Crazy?"

He gave up a half smile. "Wouldn't you have thought so? We don't exactly live in a world where magical teacups spring up by the dozen."

She shrugged. "True. I don't pretend to even begin to understand any of it now. Least of all why God went to so much effort to get through to a girl like me. But I'm glad He did."

"Me too." He meant it.

"Are you ever going to forgive me?"

His sigh was ragged as he poked at the shimmery ocean with his toe. "I'm trying. You have no idea how much I wish that I could get past this. I just don't know how. Even when I forgive I don't know how to move from there."

Emelia gave him a quivering smile. "It's okay. I get it." She dropped to her knees, started rolling up the material. "I need to get on with this. I'll see you at the ball. Maybe both of us will manage to get at least one thing we're hoping for."

He wanted to be the bigger man. To crouch

down beside her and help her cut out magical puddles or whatever it was she was about to do. But there was no wishing on make-believe magic in the world that could fix this. So he turned and walked away.

Forty-Four

By any measure, the ball was a success. The huge wardrobe doors providing the entryway into the ballroom. The garlands hanging from the ceiling. The statues positioned around the perimeters of rooms and in unexpected corners. The huge lamp-post that oversaw everything from the center of the dance floor.

Outside, pairs of horses took people on sleigh rides around the estate, complete with cups of hot chocolate and boxes of Turkish delight. A dusting of snow had fallen during the day, giving the countryside a newly whitewashed look.

Since she'd been given the chance to finish what she'd come to England to do, Emelia had spent the last two months eating, sleeping, and breathing the ball. Hadn't given herself any time or energy to think about anything else.

The result? A sellout event featuring some of London's wealthiest Americans. Emelia had never been more right about anything in her life than about targeting the moneyed American wives living in London and pricing the tickets at an amount that screamed "exclusive." Once Lacey had used a few of her London contacts to plant the seed that it was the winter event to be seen at, there was a virtual stampede for tickets.

She had achieved exactly what she had come to Oxford for. She'd saved Anita's charity. And yet it felt meaningless. Flat.

Emelia didn't know what she'd expected when the money was tallied and the outcome known. Relief? A small sense of satisfaction? But all she felt was hollow. Deep down she'd always known this ball was never going to give her the absolution she was looking for. But working out how to forgive herself . . . she didn't even know where to start with that.

There was nothing to keep her in Oxford now. No matter how much she wanted there to be. It wasn't like she'd expected God to sprinkle some magical fairy dust and conjure up a happy ending. Except that was exactly what she had hoped for. If He could land a teacup on her porch, surely He could fix things between her and Peter. Instead all there had been since the day they ran into each other at the house was silence.

Then he'd walked in tonight with Sabine on his arm and Emelia had let go of her final hope. The one that had held out that maybe, maybe, if he knew that she believed what he did, they could still find a way through. But she'd been kidding herself. She'd hurt him too deeply, betrayed him too fully, for that to be enough to glue their relationship back together. She'd tried to summon up a glimmer of gladness for them that they'd worked things out. Sabine was nice. They had history. She'd be the best aspiring Olympian's girlfriend in the world.

Allie was right. Believing in God didn't mean she didn't have to own her stuff and the fallout of her own decisions. Which included losing the best guy she'd ever known.

Focus, Emelia. She almost tripped as a couple pushed past her on their way to the Turkish delight bar. The man offered her a quick "Are you okay?" and at her nod, kept moving. Everyone had places to be, people to be with, except her.

What next, God? Lacey had called that morning, needing an answer on whether Emelia was going to accept the work for her firm. Emelia had managed to hedge a few more days instead of answering. She didn't even know why she was hesitating. It was just freelancing. Hardly a lifetime commitment.

In the corner of the ballroom a string quartet played. Two of the four sat in the thrones that had been created to look like the ones from Cair Paravel in Narnia. The other ground-floor rooms had been equally transformed. The library had turned into Uncle Andrew's study from *The Magician's Nephew*. The entranceway was the wooded area between the worlds. The parlor, the underground land from *The Silver Chair*. Even if you weren't a Narnia fan it was still pretty spectacular.

Speeches were half an hour away. She should do one final circuit of everything. There was no room for complacency just because everything seemed to be going perfectly. Cutting through the crowd, she took the hallway to the kitchen. The same hallway where only a few months ago Peter had threatened to kiss her and she'd thrown it in his face. Her stride was constrained by her red gown. The last time she'd worn it had been the second-worst night of her life. But she couldn't afford a new one.

"Emelia! Just the girl I was hoping to see. The caterers were asking about whether you want the petit fours right at midnight or a little after."

Emelia massaged her temples. There was a run sheet. Why could no one check her beautiful color-coded run sheet?

Breathe in through the nose, out through the mouth, Emelia.

She certainly wasn't going to be rude to Peter's mom, who had given up her house and had insisted on taking charge of running the catering for the evening so that Emelia could focus on everything else.

"Right at midnight is fine." Honestly? She had lost the care factor.

"Got it."

Emelia fished into the folder she was carrying. "Here's an extra run sheet. It should have everything on it." The thing was eighteen pages long. Every detail was covered.

Maggie took it. "Thanks."

"Why are you so nice to me?" The question slipped out before Emelia could even think about it. But she wasn't sorry that she'd asked. In all the time she'd spent at the house in the lead-up to tonight, Maggie hadn't said a single negative word or given her the slightest scathing look, even though she had to know the reason her son had suddenly quit having anything to do with the ball. "Your niece would still be alive if it wasn't for me."

"You know, a lot of people seem to be taking responsibility for that." Maggie made the observation as she arranged some chocolate truffles in a large crystal bowl.

Emelia looked at her.

"Peter blames himself. You blame yourself. Victor blames himself. You're all very determined to condemn yourselves and yet not one of you was there in her last moments. Anita was the one who made the choice that she did. None of you made it for her."

"But I took the photo. I wrote the article."

"And if it wasn't that, it may have been something else."

But it wasn't.

Maggie placed the last truffle on the pyramid she'd constructed. "What the three of you are all looking for isn't going to be found in saving a charity, or winning an Olympic medal, or in the bottom of a whiskey bottle." She quirked up a sad smile. "Emelia, even if you wanted to, you and Peter can't fix each other. Only God can do that."

Peter thought he'd known heartbreak after his rotator cuff had been shredded and he'd lost his shot at Olympic gold. But it didn't come close to comparing with the last two and a bit months.

Sabine looked gorgeous. Blond hair piled in some sort of fancy updo. Shimmering fitted gown. Any guy in the room would have been lucky to have her.

He felt sick. She probably thought there was a chance of their reconciling, but every second with her was proving to him that it didn't matter that she ticked all the boxes; she didn't tick the only one that really mattered.

She wasn't Emelia.

"You don't need to tell me, I already know."

"What?" He looked down to see Sabine surveying him with knowing eyes.

"You were trying to work out a way to tell me that it's not going to be me. But I've known that for months. You've never looked at me the way you look at her." She cast a glance across the room; he followed it to see Emelia weaving her way through the crowd in the same red dress she'd worn to Jackson and Allie's wedding. His breath caught just looking at her.

He turned back to his ex. "I'm sorry, Bine. I wish it was you. I really do."

She shrugged. "Me too. But it's okay. I'm okay."

He didn't know what he'd done to deserve such graciousness.

"I heard about her connection with Anita." He couldn't quite see her eyes at the angle her head was tilted, but he didn't detect any satisfaction in her voice.

Peter couldn't find anything to say. He just stared at the dance floor traveling by under their feet.

"I'm sorry."

"Me too."

"Is it true that Victor checked himself into rehab?"

"That's what my mum said." He hadn't spoken to his brother since the fight but he could only guess it had shaken Victor up as much as it had Peter. What had happened to him? He wasn't a guy who swung fists, no matter how good the reason.

"What happened to us, Seven?" Her change in conversation should have caught him by surprise, but not much did these days. "I know it's all in the past but I still need to know. I feel like one second we had this great relationship, then the next it was over. And I've been telling myself that it was because you were hurting and it was just too hard to see me still living your dream. But that's not it. Well, it's not all of it."

Peter let his gaze travel down to her set jaw. She tipped her head up and her eyes blinked rapidly, a sure sign that she was trying to hold back tears. He'd seen it many times. After disappointing races, when she'd missed out on something she'd had her heart set on.

He didn't want to hurt Sabine anymore. But he couldn't give her what she wanted. "Bine, do you remember our last six months? We weren't good."

"But . . ." Sabine opened her mouth, then closed it. She knew it was true as much as he did.

"I know we had crazy training schedules, but we used that as an excuse not to deal with us. I knew it before I got hurt, but I realized how much we weren't working after. It wasn't because I couldn't deal with you still living the dream. Without rowing we had little to say to each other." They'd tried to fill the gap with watching TV shows and seeing friends. But it didn't change the fact that when the TV was off and the friends had left, there was just awkward silence. "I didn't even know your dad had had a cancer scare."

"I said I was sorry."

"It's not about being sorry. I love you. I will always love you. That means I want you to be happy. I want you to be with a guy who is the first person you want to tell when you have big news. The good, the bad, and the scary. I haven't been that guy in a long time. We just didn't want to see it. Maybe we bought too much into the whole rowing-golden-couple thing. Neither of us likes to let people down."

That was what it came to. When he was with Emelia, she had made him feel like there was more to him than rowing. That there was a life for him beyond it. Now that he'd met Emelia, there was no going back. Even if there was no going forward with her.

Sabine blew out a long breath, the resignation on her face revealing she knew it was true. "So, are the two of you going to get together?"

Peter bit back a bark of laughter. "Not hardly."

Sabine stared across the room for a long few moments, thinking so hard he could practically see the wheels turning in her head. Finally, she spoke again. "I want you to be happy too. I know how much you loved Anita, but you can't hold what happened against Emelia. She was just doing her job."

"I told her about Anita, Bine. About how I blamed myself. And she just sat there. Didn't say a word."

"What did you want her to say, Peter? 'Oh, by the way, that reporter was me'? I don't know any-one who would have been brave enough to do that. Especially if she feels about you the way you do about her."

Peter rubbed his hand across his brow. "Even if we manage to find a way past all that, I don't think she's okay with me wanting to make a comeback." That was one thing he'd learned in the last couple of months. The rowing bug was still in his blood. He couldn't give the dream up without one more try.

Sabine stepped toward him so another couple could pass behind her. "But that can be worked through. You talk about it. Work it out. Like every couple does when someone has been injured. You take too much responsibility for things that don't belong on your shoulders. Always have. Your responsibility is to forgive her. Tell her. You don't just give up on the person who might be the love of your life. The rest is in God's hands."

"You make it sound so simple."

"It is. Doesn't mean it's not hard, but it isn't complicated. And, Peter? If it's not me and it's not Emelia, there will be somebody else. And she'll be even better for you than either of us."

"You don't know that." He wasn't sure where the words came from, but they struck even him. They sounded bitter. Resentful.

"Except I do. You're a catch, Peter Carlisle. Even if you don't know it." She got up on her tiptoes and dropped a kiss on his cheek. "Now I'm going to go find myself someone to dance with, because it's not a whole lot of fun dancing with someone who wishes I was someone else."

And with that she let go of his hand and stepped away.

"Bine?"

She paused.

"Thanks."

She tilted her head. "You can thank me by winning gold in Tokyo."

Forty-Five

" 'Yes,' " said Queen Lucy. " 'In our world too, a stable once had something inside it that was bigger than our whole world.' " Emelia's words had come back to Peter as he watched Sabine walk away. They'd tormented him as he'd tried to play the role of board member. He couldn't remember a single conversation he'd had in the last hour of the event. Hadn't even asked how much money they'd raised. Whether they'd achieved their goal.

He hadn't even stopped to get himself out of his tux when he'd gotten home. He immediately went to a book that had sat in his bedside drawer for over a decade, with a bookmark that had never moved from the last time his grandfather had placed it there.

Peter rested his head against his headboard,

closed *The Last Battle,* and placed it beside him on the bed cover. Everything had clicked into place. He had been such a fool. If only he'd read it sooner, realized earlier, things might have been different.

"A true Narnia fan would never ask a girl if they were a Susan or a Lucy." Emelia's words from the first time they'd met circled around his head.

I'm a Susan. And he hadn't understood what she was saying. How she viewed herself. Until now. Emelia saw herself through a distorted looking glass, condemning herself for who she thought she was.

He picked up the book again. Flicking back through its pages to the crucial scene, he read the critical line again.

" 'My sister Susan,' " answered Peter gravely, " 'is no longer a friend of Narnia.' "

Susan had grown up and called Narnia just a silly game from their childhood. Ultimately, the rest of her family had been summoned back to Narnia and she'd ended up alone.

A six-year-old Emelia had told her mother she didn't want to play her silly Narnia games anymore and her mother had died. Emelia's father had abdicated responsibility and she'd ended up alone. That's why she believed she was a Susan.

He might not have been able to change everything that had happened, but maybe he could change that, figure out a way to show her the truth.

There were now only two things on his to-do list. Win Emelia back. And row his way to Tokyo in 2020. One was hopeful. One was nonnegotiable.

He picked up his phone, selected the required name on his contacts, and let it ring. "Allie, it's Peter. I need your help."

Forty-Six

"This is the place." Of course it was. Of all the places in Oxford, Allie had to want to buy her chair from this one. Two days before she and Jackson flew to Iowa for Christmas. What was she planning to do? Take it back on the train? Did they not have decent antiques shops in Cambridge?

She'd never told Allie which shop she'd met Peter in.

They opened the door. The grizzled proprietor was sitting in the exact same position as the first time Emelia had come into the store. She was pretty sure he was even wearing the same shirt and knitted vest. If not for the absence of cobwebs, she might have suspected he hadn't moved in the last ten months.

Allie pointed toward the archway. "It was in this next room."

Why was she not surprised? Emelia stepped under the archway, preparing herself for whatever it was she might feel when she saw it again. Everything had changed since then.

She stopped. Turning around, she found that Allie had disappeared, the sound of the bell tinkling giving away her rapid exit.

Spinning back around, Emelia tried to take in what was there. The room had been totally cleared out. The hodgepodge of furniture was all gone. In the middle of the room sat a lamppost—a large wrought-iron one, its head grazing the ceiling as it leaned toward her, beckoning. The one she'd commissioned for the ball. The wardrobe was where it had always been, except it had been moved so it sat against the corner at an angle.

She laughed. A row of mismatched artificial Christmas trees fanned out from either side of the wardrobe. Some looked like the evergreens they were pretending to be, others were outrageously loud versions in silver and gold, like they'd been dragged back from the eighties for the occasion.

Fairy lights crisscrossed the ceiling, their tiny bulbs flashing and dancing to something unheard and magical.

From nowhere, snow started falling. In an antiques shop in Oxford. Wisps of fake snow settled on her nose. Her hair. What in the world? She walked in farther.

On the other wall, a life-sized picture of a fireplace was taped. In front of it sat two armchairs and a small table set with plates and food. Emelia tiptoed forward and peered down. Boiled eggs, sardines on toast, cakes. Just like Mr. Tumnus the fawn had laid out for Lucy when they had afternoon tea.

Something in the room changed. She knew without even turning around that Peter had entered.

She turned slowly, biting back a nervous giggle. Peter was wearing the same ugly sweater that he had at Allie's party. "Hi."

"Hi."

"Hi." Again. She didn't know what else to say.

He smiled. "I think you already said that."

"Then it must be your line. No one gave me the script."

"I need to clear something up first. Actually a few things."

"What?" Emelia batted some fake snow away from her face so she could see Peter more clearly. Whatever this was, she didn't want to miss a moment of it.

"I'm not with Sabine. I forgive you and I'm sorry."

"You're not? You do?" The words came out all breathy. She struggled to hold in the ridiculous grin that was threatening to take over her face;

the invisible weight that had been on her had disappeared the moment he said it.

He crossed the room in two strides. "No. Yes. And you are not a Susan."

"You read it?" Fake snow wafted onto Peter's hair and her fingers itched to brush it away.

"For you, I would do almost anything."

She blinked, completely unprepared for the knowledge that he'd finally finished Narnia. For her. Something warm settled in her chest and flowed out into her limbs.

"But I am a Susan. Don't you see? I let myself get distracted and I lost everything. Just like Susan did. Everyone left me." Including him. Or so she'd thought until right this minute.

"You're a Lucy." His words were definite, no doubt in them.

She shook her head, unable to find the words of rebuttal in the face of his insistence.

"Lucy never stopped looking for Narnia. Yearning for Narnia. I met you right here, in this wardrobe, when you fell on top of me. And what were you doing in there?"

"Looking for Narnia." Her words were soft, tentative.

"And then, in Allie's wardrobe, you were . . . ?"

"Looking for Narnia." This time her words were a little more certain, matching the growing hope in her chest.

"And what is the one thing that you can't stop

yourself from doing, no matter how hard you try?"

"Climbing into wardrobes and looking for Narnia." Maybe, just maybe, what she'd thought of as the crazy gene inherited from her mom was actually something more.

Peter reached out and grabbed one of her hands, entwining his fingers around hers. "Susan never looks for Narnia. She follows Lucy there through the wardrobe. She gets summoned there by her own horn. Then she grows up and says it was all just a childish game. Susan is cautious and content with positions of ease and comfort. You're one of the bravest people I've ever met."

"I . . ." She wasn't brave. That was the last thing she thought she was.

Peter reached for her other hand and tugged her closer to him. She peered up into his deep green eyes. "Remember the dwarves, in the end, when they're in the true Narnia, but they think they're still in the stable? No matter how much Lucy and Tirian and the others try to tell them the truth. Not even Aslan can convince them otherwise."

Emelia nodded. Not quite able to find words.

"Like the dwarves, you've so convinced yourself as to who you think you are, what you think your life is destined to be, that you can't see the truth even when it's standing right in front of you."

"And what's that?" She could barely force the words out. Terror and anticipation warred inside her.

"That you're a Lucy, who always hopes, always seeks, who never stops believing, no matter who tells her that she's wrong. That you're an Edmund who made some bad decisions but doesn't let that define you. That you're a Peter who stands up for what is right and just. That, of all the Pevensies, the one that you aren't is Susan. And you're not alone."

It sure didn't feel that way. "Who do I have? My mother is dead, my father is one in name only, I have no real brothers or sisters."

"Me. If you'll have me."

She stared at him. "What are you saying?"

He drew in a shaky breath. "I don't know what I'm saying. I kind of hoped these words would show up and now I'm left with white space."

Wow. That wasn't an anticlimax at all.

Then he reached forward and pulled her to him, tipping her chin up with the pad of his finger. Fake snow flurried around them. Out of the corner of her eye, a garish silver Christmas tree glittered.

"I'm saying that I'm crazy about you, Em. I'm saying that I started falling in love with you the day you fell out of that wardrobe, I've been falling ever since, and I never want to stop. I'm saying that I don't know what this could be, but I will regret it the rest of my life if I don't give it everything I have to find out. And it seems to me that God has gone to some pretty crazy lengths to bring us together, so we should at least try to see what this could be. Oh, and I should tell you I've decided I want to try to make a comeback. A proper one. To get to Tokyo. For me. Not for Anita. I know it isn't exactly—"

Emelia stood on her tiptoes, bunched his sweater between her fingers, and pulled him down until their noses touched. "Peter. Seriously. Just kiss me."

He gave her the kind of languid smile that stripped away her breath. "With pleasure."

As he buried his hands in her hair, she wrapped her arms around his neck and let her eyes drift closed. For the first time in her life, she allowed herself to begin to believe that maybe she was a Lucy after all.

Author's Note

As a reader living in New Zealand, there is nothing that annoys me more than a character in a book who is supposedly in New Zealand or who is supposedly from New Zealand, and they just *aren't*.

And so it was with much trepidation that I wrote a book set in Oxford (where I've never been) with a hero whose sport is rowing (which I knew nothing about, beyond screaming myself hoarse at the TV every four years during the Olympics). Since, alas, I'm not in the echelon of authors with bank balances that facilitate gallivanting to the other side of the world to research their books, I've had to work with the next best things. But, let's be honest, there's only so much that the combined powers of Google Street View, YouTube, books, and the knowledge of those who actually know what you don't can do before you inevitably get something wrong.

So to those of you (odds are you're either English, a real rower, or in my worst nightmares both) who have caught some kind of error that has made you want to throw the book across the room, my apologies.

First up, thanks to Cambridge for going and winning the Boat Race in March 2016 when I turned this book in in January. The underdog-cheering part of me was thrilled for you. Not so much the author part of me that had Oxford winning. But good news! It's a novel and, like it says on the copyright page, "any references to historical events, real people, or real places are used fictitiously." Which is great when you forecast an event that will be a historical one by the time your book comes out and get it wrong.

Second up, an ode to the British government for forbidding reading from sacred religious texts during a civil wedding ceremony (that is, a ceremony not held in a church). So, no, in real life Peter couldn't have done a reading from the Song of Solomon at Jackson and Allie's wedding because it would have been illegal. But since I was writing a romance novel, not a how-to guide on getting married in England, I chose cute over bureaucratic correctness.

Thirdly, my apologies to those advisers in the many aspects of this story that I knew nothing about who provided their experience and knowledge, and yet I still managed to get something wrong. I give you the gift of anonymity so you are not tainted with my mistakes.

Finally, my eternal gratitude to YouTube for the many wasted hours when I started off watching rowing tutorials and somehow found myself following that evil sidebar and ending up in some weird corner of the Internet, watching dancing rabbits set to Japanese pop songs.

Acknowledgments

If *Close to You* is the dream-comes-true story, *Can't Help Falling* is the dream-gets-real story. Every book requires a village, but this one felt like it required an entire tri-state area. As always, there are no words that are adequate enough to describe how grateful I am to the team that makes this author life possible.

Jesus: I still can't believe I get to live this writing dream. Thank you for showing your faithfulness in this story. For showing up in all the moments when I was out of my depth and somehow weaving it together when I had no idea how all the pieces fit.

To my husband, Josh: Thank you for being my biggest supporter and my superhero when I had to abandon our Christmas holiday to hibernate in the library for a week and rewrite this book. This living the writing dream wouldn't be possible if it weren't for you.

To the Buddy, the Buzz, and the (ever-growing) Bump: You're still too young to really understand this whole crazy book thing, but I hope one day it inspires you to chase whatever your crazy dreams are (unless they involve risking life and limb, such as being a professional base jumper or rodeo rider, in which case I encourage you watch as many videos on YouTube of said dream as you like and find great fulfillment in pottery or origami).

My amazing SisterChucks: Laurie Tomlinson, Halee Matthews, Jaime Jo Wright, Sarah Varland, and Anne Love. This book would not exist if not for the five of you. Thank you for the brainstorming, the not laughing when I confessed I had 80,000 words but no real plot, assuring me it wasn't as bad as I thought it was (even though it really was), for putting your own writing to the side to read terrible drafts and slightly better rewrites on crazy timelines, and for believing that I had it in me to get it done in the times when it was just a really tough write. But most of all, thank you for your incredible friendship.

My editor extraordinaire: Beth Adams. There had to be moments that you were holding your head in your hands wondering how on earth this story was ever going to come together, but you never showed it. Instead, you made me believe that I had what it took to turn it into something great. You could probably have a lucrative second career as a poker player, if you so desired.

Katie Sandell, Ami McConnell, Bruce Gore, and the rest of the team at Howard Books: for believing in my writing, yet another gorgeous cover, and all the hard work that you do to connect my stories with the right readers. I am so grateful that I get to be on your team.

To my family and family-in-love: Thank you for being so excited about this adventure and for doing your part to help the sales numbers. I'm pretty sure there are people all over the world who have received *Close to You* and who didn't even know we were related!

Elizabeth Norman: for not only agreeing to make sure Peter could pass as an Englishman but for the stream-of-consciousness messages that you sent as you were reading. You loving this story was when I first started believing that maybe, just maybe, it might not be terrible.

Ann-Maree Beard, Olivia Williams, Fiona Conway, Anna Holmes, Bec Bonnevie, Tina Robilliard, Jen Gibbs, Ally Davey, Steph Mowat, Myra Russell, Nikki Parlane, Elise Teves, and so many other friends who have prayed for this story and stepped into the gap for my family when I have been on deadline and completely overwhelmed with all the balls I'm trying to keep in the air. Thank you.

To Team Harper and Team Benson: for the best dinner parties in the world, where religion, politics, and money are not only perfectly acceptable topics of fierce debate but are actually encouraged. The world would be a better place if everyone had friends like you.

To those wonderful readers out there who loved *Close to You* and took the time to somehow let me know how much you enjoyed it: In the moments when this writing gig has felt beyond me, it's hearing from people like you that makes the hours wrestling to get words on the page worth it. Thank you.

Center Point Large Print
600 Brooks Road / PO Box 1
Thorndike, ME 04986-0001 USA

(207) 568-3717

US & Canada:
1 800 929-9108
www.centerpointlargeprint.com